HALF
MOON

K.L.VIDAL

HALF
K.L. VIDAL
MOON

JESPERSON PUBLISHING

JESPERSON PUBLISHING

100 Water Street • P.O. Box 2188
St. John's • NL • Canada • A1C 6E6
www.jespersonpublishing.ca

Library and Archives Canada Cataloguing in Publication

Vidal, K. L.
    Half moon / K.L. Vidal.

ISBN 1-894377-19-2

    I. Title.

PS3622.I343H34 2006   813'.6   C2006-903978-X

Cover design: T. Eppridge
        © K.L. Vidal
Cover art: Christoffer Wilhelm Eckersberg. Woman before a mirror. 1837?
        Oil on canvas. 33,5 x 26 cm.
        © The Hirschsprung Collection. Copenhagen
Copyright material:
        #8 (11 lines) & #107 (13 lines) from THE POEMS OF CATULLUS
        translated with an introduction by Peter Whigham (Penguin Classics, 1966).
        Copyright © Penguin Books Ltd, 1966.

Editor: Tamara Reynish

The Canada Council | Le Conseil des Arts
for the Arts | du Canada

We acknowledge the financial support of The Canada
Council for the Arts for our publishing activities.

We acknowledge the support of the Department of Tourism, Culture and
Recreation for our publishing activities.

Printed in Canada

FOR JACK LEVY

PRELUDE

"There's a strong wind," warned the steward. "And the staircase is steep, Madame. Please be careful."

"Yes. Thank you," murmured the last passenger to emerge onto the frail metal landing pulled up against the aircraft that had just arrived from New York. She paused for a moment, gripping the railing to steady herself, for it was dark still. Dawn was just breaking over the rooftops of Paris and the hot, sultry wind shook the steps as she descended. It was odd to feel such heat so early in the summer, barely a pale streak of gold in the gunmetal sky.

Warmer still was the hall where a long line was advancing toward the row of officials inside their glass booths. In spite of the fans, the air was already close, fetid almost in the seemingly endless heat wave that had taken France by surprise. Most of the tourists had come prepared – women in sundresses, husbands in shirtsleeves, children in sandals and shorts and large wide-brimmed hats. Most of the businessmen, no choice remaining, loosened their ties, unfastened their collars, finally slung their jackets over their shoulders as the line snaked through the hall.

All the more remarkable, therefore, was the outfit worn by the last passenger to reach the customs booth: long-sleeved black turtleneck, long black flowing skirt. The woman was elegant, tall, though it may have been the high-wedged espadrilles crossed twice around her legs that gave the illusion of height.

There was also the sensation of vivid hues when she appeared – a curious anomaly given the dark heavy sweater until one looked up when she spoke and saw her eyes, colour of Tyrian dye, very large and intense. Her complexion was fair, pale to the point of extraordinary iridescence. Her long thick hair was black, gathered in a shell comb at her neck, although a few wisps, which she kept trying to gather unsuccessfully, had escaped to frame her cheekbones, high and flushed in the heat. Her mouth was small yet pronounced, slightly ironic in its curve, like a Fragonard nymph, betraying melancholy beneath its congenital surface amusement.

She was perhaps thirty-five, thought the official as she approached his booth. *Thirty-five*, he remarked to himself smugly, opening the passport she presented.

"You are, Madame Devereux, an American citizen?"

"Naturalized. Yes."

"And you plan to stay..."

"A month," she said vaguely.

"Ah."

"Longer perhaps. I cannot say. Six weeks at the most."

"Holiday?"

"No."

"Business perhaps?"

The fans in his booth drowned out her response.

"Reason for coming to France?" he repeated.

"Funeral services."

The uniformed officer stamped her passport, waving her baggage past.

"My condolences," he said gravely, repeating his sympathies in French as though the unfortunate situation required more appropriate expression.

The pianist laughed, shook his head, closed his book, and stood as if to go. The harpist insisted, took his sleeve, offered what seemed to be her own score and prevailed. After a moment or two there was one final set beginning with Gershwin's *Embraceable You*.

Caroline sipped her wine; fans and the waiters made their rounds; chandeliers dimmed above the palms, and then abruptly, toward the end of *Someone to Watch Over Me*, conversation subsided in the silk and fringed room.

It was the pianist, Caroline realized. He was playing alone – an impromptu reprise – looking away from his score, hands barely touching the keys. Yet in the understated, direct, almost erotic caress of the keys, he had conveyed the bedrock loneliness at the core of the song, hope and despair intertwined.

There wasn't a sound in the room when the final note faded. The artist himself seemed surprised, and then he smiled and acknowledged his colleague and stood again and once more sat back down, for the applause was sustained, and the guests would not be denied. There was another brief conference, another score shared, and then no longer Gershwin but a French farewell, *La Vie en Rose*, rendered sweetly by the harp, with disillusion by the piano.

Caroline let her shawl drop, superfluous in that June's trial by fire, stunned by the piano still, moved to the depths of her soul by what it was unable to hide.

When the waiter approached, much later it seemed, she took the menu he offered and stole a glance at her watch. Quarter to nine. She ordered a second glass, wanting to keep her seat. The musicians, meanwhile, had retired to their table beside the grand arch.

In her flowing black dress and red undisciplined hair, the harpist seemed to embody the sunset just passed. Large-boned and vivid, she was perhaps still in her twenties, poised and confident beyond her years among the patrons who approached her as she had been secure in the enfilade of harp strings beneath her hands.

The pianist was older. He was a powerful man, broad-shouldered and lean, in his mid-fifties perhaps – at home too with his song and the crowd, and, Caroline saw, the experienced lines in his wide, weathered brow. His eyes were light, his chin pronounced, his mouth quick to smile, his smile a compress in the heat. Only his fingers had betrayed a need beneath the surface of his savoir-faire.

The vivid harpist clearly adored him as did the guests at his table, the waiters around him, the maitre d'hôtel, the night concierge – *was it already the night concierge?* Caroline checked her watch again. Nine twenty-five. She decided to leave, asked for the cheque, dawdled, delayed, and then – for some reason rooted to her own solitude by the garden – she slipped an additional hundred francs into the leather folder beneath her cheque.

"For *La Vie en Rose* again," she said to the waiter, surprising herself most of all by the spontaneous extravagance.

Ever so slightly he bowed.

"Only if there is time," she added, colouring. "And if he is willing."

"I shall pass on your request."

"I am indebted."

By the time the song began, Lucien Barthes had arrived. Slim, debonair, apologetic and irresistible in his navy blazer, navy eyes, maroon tie and black moustache, he had hurried to his cousin's table, ordered a fine Courvoisier, decried the endless negotiations that had delayed him at a board meeting, and had at last begun to relax.

"Again, please forgive me – ah, *La Vie en Rose*," he remarked, interrupting himself, raising a finger toward the chandelier, cocking his groomed handsome head, hearing the solo behind him.

"Yes. Yes it is."

"The tourists adore it."

"Understandably."

"The rest of us, though – well perhaps we hear it too much. This version, though" – he turned around to the piano – "quite lovely, really – unexpectedly so."

The harpist too had impressed Lucien by the time she returned to her place.

"Another cognac, Monsieur?" the waiter asked as he passed.

"I think not. Unless of course Madame..."

Caroline shook her head.

"In that case the cheque, please."

"Very good."

"And your musicians are exceptional. Have they a card?"

"One, Monsieur. The harpist. The pianist is a guest."

Caroline was stupefied.

"Though we see him here often. From time to time he tries his hand. We are fortunate."

Caroline felt anything but fortunate at that moment. She who was always reserved – some would say distant – somehow she had abandoned caution to pay a stranger as though he had pleased her, as a tourist might tip the organ grinder in Montmartre for his song. The thought of it made her face burn. She looked away from the musicians.

"Are you all right, Caroline?"

"A little hungry, perhaps."

But Not for Me began softly, harp and piano together again as at last the leather billfold with the cheque inside was brought their way.

"Monsieur Jude was most happy to honour your request, Madame," the waiter said. "Not as well as he would have wanted..."

"Caroline," warned Lucien.

"His words not mine," the waiter managed to add, before Lucien continued, determined, having opened the billfold to find her franc note tucked very carefully still beneath the cheque.

"None of your tricks while we're here. No advance payment. Not for the drinks. Not for the meal. Is our table ready?" he asked abruptly, for he was sure that his splendid, improvident cousin had attempted to manage the dining room too.

"It is, Monsieur."

"Then this is yours," he instructed the waiter, placing the quickly signed cheque in his hands. "And this," he went on, turning to Caroline with the billfold, "belongs to the lady. Shall we go in now?"

When they passed the pianist, Caroline stopped. The guest nodded. She wanted to acknowledge his gift somehow, but merely stared at him as the refrain of *Love Walked In* soared above.

Not a word was exchanged. Unbeknownst to her though, she had accomplished her objective. He had been acknowledged. He was after all Jude McCallister, portrait painter *par excellence*. It was his business to notice colour, seek out shape, find the one remarkable face that could elicit a masterpiece from his hands. The hyacinths in her eyes would haunt him hereafter. The loneliness in his hands would never again give her peace.

☾

Rebecca Chase covered her harp and took Jude's arm as they left the Crillon.

"You were subdued tonight, Jude. Are you well?"

"Was the music not right?"

"The music was exceptional."

"Then I suppose I am well."

"You know what I mean."

After a pause, "Weary perhaps," he replied, "nothing more."

"Come with me then."

"Where?"

"Jockey Club."

"Now?"

"Private party for a friend of mine."

"Don't you ever get weary?"

"Not when I'm with you I don't."

"I'm flattered."

"Then you'll come?"

Jude reflected as they crossed the plaza.

"I can't. I am teaching tomorrow."

"That again," she said flatly.

"That again," he said gently.

"Why do you do it? A whole afternoon each week – light wasted, time squandered…"

"Perversity, my dear Rebecca," he said hailing a cab. "Nothing more."

He smiled, kissed her cheek lightly, placed her into the taxi and walked down toward Pont Alexandre. He could have crossed as usual at Pont de la Concorde but filled with ennui, he sought relief in the intricate beauty of the Belle Époque arch – its matching twin columns, gleaming gold statues, ornate candelabras, nymphs from the Neva sporting with those from the Seine.

Relief did not come. He thought of the Tsar and his wife, received in splendour for the dedication of the bridge; he thought of their grandchildren, shot in the concealment of Russia's outlying woods.

Vanitas vanitatis, he said to himself, repeating the stanzas of Juvenal as he approached Les Invalides. Dwarfing the double cupola, an immense solstice moon rose above the dome. Leaves in the night wind swirled like ambition around his feet. Only the ashes of empire remained in the Bonaparte crypt.

And yet the sight of that church had always thrilled him. Beauty in all of its forms was his life, the air that he breathed. He couldn't remember when it wasn't so. Thinking back to his earliest days as he walked, trying to see a boy, a youth, a student, a lover, there was only a painter to be glimpsed in his recollection – a man obsessed with colour, light, harmony and the truths hidden therein. He'd taken up sculpting to master dimension; architecture for exactitude, music for composition and to worship the grace notes beyond anyone's grasp. And success had come soon. Too soon had said his rivals, when a stunning portrait of his first wife, Hope, took the Paris art world by storm.

Thirty years ago this June, he mused, incredulous, for it seemed like yesterday when he'd entered Hope's portrait in the Academy's exhibition.

"Ill-advised," one of his teachers had warned him. "Far too hasty," said another, noting how keen the competition would be in an exhibit planned to promote new artists in France.

He had discounted their suggestions, as he had done often enough since his arrival from Tucson five years before that.

Now, pausing for a moment to gaze at the perfection of the main pavilion of Les Invalides straight ahead, he was amazed at his audacity.

"It's only a lark," he had insisted. "I'm putting this portrait in on a bet."

"Do as you please then," had been his mentor's reply, knowing Jude McCallister would do just that. Since the young painter's arrival – brash, barely nineteen, as full of life and vast dreams as the endless horizons of his native state – he'd seen him paint with an almost demonic commitment to his own way, taking instruction when it inspired him, rejecting advice when it did not.

"How can you work with him?" was the question most often asked of his teachers. The reply, toned in a mixture of exasperation and awe, was consistent. "Touched by the gods somehow," they'd confess, though whether Roman, Aztec, Celtic, or Greek, nobody knew for sure. Most likely a combination. Divinity's spectrum seemed to preside in the vivid colours, strength and almost mythic simplicity of Jude's work.

Certainly they were there in the painting he'd entered in the grand French competition, cavalierly, without the slightest perceived interest in any results. Only his model knew the truth. For weeks he had denied himself rest, food, sleep, any semblance of peace while he had worked on that portrait. When it was done he had said simply, "Done," and Hope knew, without even stealing a glance, that it would be unique.

The judges were mystified. They decided against first prize for him – the rendering was too fine for that – and created a new rubric, *Prix d'Honneur*, hoping thereby to indicate their unabashedly frank approval. Grand Prize. Never before awarded. Jude McCallister. Never again out of work.

Vanitas vanitatis, he said again to himself, walking in the eerie brightness of the silver-grey moon. He neared the white building that was once Rodin's home, passing the sculptor's fine garden. How well he knew those stone walls! How familiar the trees, the gravel pathways, the silent eternal statues unaware of his footsteps as he walked on.

Just to be close to that house he'd made his own home in the building facing the park behind Les Invalides. The unique top-floor apartment was grand – eight light-filled rooms, sunniest of all, his studio.

Nearly three decades ago, Jude reflected, stepping from the antique cage elevator into the polished hallway that led to his door. It was the only home he'd ever owned, bought in the first flush of his sudden success, house and his triumphs and yesterday's rain somehow interchangeable.

He put the key into the lock and stepped into his hall. It was wide, filled with bookshelves that reached the ceiling and rare engravings on the walls. To his right was the living room, beyond that his study, beyond the study his office which doubled as a dressing room during sittings, and at the end of the hallway through the last arch, filled with pots, paints, paintings, an easel – his studio. Like the other three rooms on this right side of the apartment, French doors in the studio led to a terrace facing the park. The rooms on the left – kitchen, dining room, two bedrooms, two baths – faced a small inner court.

Even when he had bought the place, the immense apartment had been expensive – an extravagance, he remembered, that he had been happy to commit although he was alone at the time, not needing half those rooms, divorced by the woman whose painting had launched him, divorce in progress from his second wife.

Bittersweet beauty, he mused, thinking of life then, not love, as he entered his study, again feeling the weight of an almost crushing ennui. He took a book down from its shelf and began to prepare for his class the next day.

After an hour he'd written three lines. He stood, stretched and walked to the window. The breeze had cooled a bit – benediction on the sleeping streets. When he returned to his work, Rebecca's question was on his mind. He'd begged it shamefully with his flip response. Teaching mattered to him, enormously. Only in the classroom did he give and not take, share with disinterest, surrender without conditions what he was, what he knew.

The rest of his life was the obverse of this. Friendship, love, sex, even happiness, when it had come to him – all of it was in the service of his passion to paint, all of it, ironically, turned to ash when the painting was done.

"A self-absorption that will ruin you," Hope had predicted as she left him, though in the beginning she had enjoyed the challenge of presenting a new artist to Arizona's elite. And she was good at it – he'd always confessed it. In her cool moneyed ways she was as sleek as she was efficient. Even in Paris, in the first years, she had devoted herself with a socialite's keen sense of timing and skill to the cause.

Answered prayers, Jude thought with a sigh. Each new commission had brought more work; more work had enshrined her rival.

"My mistress awaits," he would say to her with a kiss, running at daybreak to his atelier, afraid to lose light, strength, or – worse still – ideas that had come to him in his feverish nights, thoughts that had forced him to pace in their room, murmuring as though the form taking shape in his head could respond.

The pacing disturbed her. The smell of paint became too strong. He moved his studio to Montmartre, where the models could come at dawn and stay 'til dusk and one stayed longer once, and then others did, and for some odd reason Hope minded them less than that damnable light he would run to – the only mistress who mattered.

Everyone else was there to be used, stolen from, sacrificed, cannibalized. That was exactly how his wife had put it in their final conversation – presciently, as it happened, for that in fact had turned out to be Jude's fate.

His second wife, Annelise, had stayed just under three years. She had worshiped him as his model. As his spouse she could not compete with the light that dawned every day, trailing behind gifts of fortune and fame and repeated commissions to ensure both.

In spite of those gifts, he'd never married again, though he was often seen with his models and, on the Riviera, with Nathalie Berne, wealthy patron, occasional model, mistress too for six years.

"It will end," he'd answered frankly, lying naked in the bedroom of her elegant home on avenue Foch.

"We could marry," had been her suggestion.

Her tone had been languorous. She'd lit a cigarette in the dark after that. By the time she had finished, their affair too was an ember, nothing more, and yet he had sketched her beautifully that after-noon, and, for the last time, an even finer face on the following day.

And so it had gone. The years had flown by. He would have loved to have loved; he'd had to settle for desire.

Survival of the fittest, he reflected that June night, putting his pen down, finding it hard still to focus. *Keeping whole. Bottom line. No subjugation to another's will.*

And who could argue with the results? Erotic passion, at least, had never consumed him. Desire had never kept him from seeing possibilities, from seeing people – the thought was vaguely unpleasant – from seeing people as subject matter: their clothes, their smile, the tint of their flesh, the way they shrugged. Without that there would have been nothing. No art at least. In his case then, nothing.

The breeze continued to cool. He tried to concentrate but drifted still. In the distance he heard an accordion reprising the song the stranger had liked – and then he closed his book and walked again to the terrace and watched the lights on the dome across from his garden go out. At last, in the dark, the Esplanade rested.

He returned to his desk. As dawn broke over the city there were three lines on his pad still – nothing more – except for a face drawn, repeatedly.

☽

Caroline Contini Devereux was sleeping still, not even a hint of the tentative day in her dreams, for she had unfastened the thick floral drapes from their red silken cords the evening before. Then she had turned out the lights in her room one by one, and had walked back through the hallway, which she had also darkened completely. She had loosened her hair, slipped off her shoes, filled up the tub and then, turning out the chandelier in the dressing room, she had walked slowly into the bathroom, closing the door behind her. Only then had she unzipped her long skirt, letting it fall to the floor. She'd had no panties on – the skirt alone had made her legs sweat unendurably in that day's heat – nor had she worn a bra under the heavy sweater that had covered her torso completely. Turning away from the full-length mirror on the back of the door she'd just closed, she'd slipped her arms from the sleeves and pulled the turtleneck over her head and shook her head in the sudden freedom and coolness at last against her skin. Directly, in the low light of the tiny wall sconce she'd left on beside the sink, she had stepped into the tub, gathered her hair up again and sunk into the bubbles that had formed. Only then had she relaxed, surrendering to the water, the cool porcelain, the stark white tiles, the gold-toned swan fixtures watching her in the darkness, making no judgment.

Thirty minutes later, when she'd stepped out onto the mat alongside her tub, Caroline was already wrapped in an immense soft white towel – dripping, refreshed, bubbles just brushing her knees still, swans still observing in silence.

It was only later, after she'd turned out the wall sconce and made her way to the canopied bed by the window that Caroline had again let her hair fall, stretching her naked body, relieved, across the crisp cotton sheets. She traced the scar tissue on her torso – the intricate tendrils like vines in the courtyard tumbling down onto her collarbone; the crossed swords on her hips, or so it had always seemed to her since the fire; the abstract brushwork on her rib cage; the matching abstraction on her inner thighs; and finally – only mark to be found on her right side – the raised and perfect half moon along the outside of her breast. She knew every millimetre of each scar. Although only in darkness, she touched them all often, neither with love nor disgust but with the disinterest of a wrangler checking the brands on a wandering calf.

And yet she could not look at them. Not since she was eleven had she tolerated light or a mirror unless she had dressed for the day, head to toe, leaving only her arms bare on occasion, temperatures notwithstanding. Thus her remarkable scars – all the more astonishing because of the splendid body they adorned, or disfigured, depending upon one's tolerance for the exceptional – had remained the unique and mysterious province of her fingertips, nothing more.

⌒☾⌒

"And this," said Jude McCallister, concluding his lecture that afternoon, "is, without doubt, among all of the works of Goya, my favourite."

On a screen in a darkened classroom at the Delacroix Museum's studio, he flashed an image of the *Bordeaux Milkmaid*, surprising his students with his unexpected selection, for he had spent the two previous lectures extolling the realism of Goya's etchings, the ghastly monsters of *Proverbs*, the brutal panorama of *War's Disasters*. With eloquence he had insisted on the magnificence of the former, the refinement of the latter, stressing the sensitivity of the masterly techniques employed.

Now in the final minutes of the third class, a different Goya had appeared, almost the obverse of the first one – nostalgic, reflective, revelling in the tenderness of an exquisite palette. The students stared.

"Nicole, you look puzzled. Have I disappointed you?"

"No," said the student reflectively. "The face is beautiful, but unreal somehow, a fantasy. People don't look like that."

"They don't look like *Proverbs'* monsters either."

"That's different. The painter was making a statement. He was indicting injustice. There was a purpose to the phantoms."

"Realism, you mean."

"Yes. I thought you preferred it to some romantic ideal."

Jude thought for a moment.

"They are one and the same," he said. "At least I have found that to be true in my own work – in my own life as well," he added candidly, for he was completely at ease with his students, trusting their instincts as they did his wisdom.

"What is most real," he went on, "not necessarily palpable but enduring, year after year, fortifying the frail amalgam of body and soul that each day assaults, is what we yearn for. Sometimes, if the gods smile, and after much discipline and many attempts, it is vouchsafed to an artist to express that ideal."

Jude's voice had grown fervent. "There is nothing more real on this earth if he succeeds, as Goya did with his milkmaid, for there we see his whole life, everything he ever dreamed of, longed for, loved, and, by implication, despised."

The students listened, rapt with attention. Jude thrust his hands into the pockets of his cardigan – oversized, unbuttoned, taupe like the abstract designs on his navy silk tie.

"Conversely," he said slowly, pacing between the podium and the screen, "think of the romance in reality, the arresting uniqueness in each day. Anything can happen. Consider the people around you as you walk to your houses tonight – each face astounding; not one body without its allure. Not one," he repeated, as though to respond to the scepticism he sensed he'd raised. "Why do you think you stared so at the phantoms in *Proverbs*? Because they repelled you? Turned you off? No. Quite the opposite. In their outrageous excesses they intrigued you. Their arresting expression of one man's soul thrilled you. So did the horrors of war.

Yes, even that. Violence and brutality have their allure; they always will, like a cockfight in the plaza or Torquemada by his rack. Even death has its allure" – here he smiled, incongruous coda – "and yet what, may I ask you, is at the end of the day more quotidian than the death that awaits us?"

A bell in the hallway rang. Not one of the students moved.

"As banal as my question was, the answer is poignant, no? And with poignancy we have romance – *voilà* – and dream fugues and visions and the ultimate fantasy" – he had stopped pacing by this time – "life lived to the brim, come what may."

In the ensuing silence he looked at the faces – young faces searching his own – and then he looked at his watch – he had not heard the bell ring – and then, somewhat chagrined, more for having kept his class than for having confessed to them, he offered a simple vale: "'Til next Wednesday."

On the next Wednesday he spoke of Picasso, gave a studio class, reviewed the portfolios of his advanced group and finally left just past eight. Only then did he allow himself to feel fatigue, for the day had begun at his own easel toward sunrise. Now again there was beguiling light in the sky – greys, blacks, splashes of peach and mauve above the roofs. He turned into the courtyard of Place Fürstenberg and sat on a bench in the little circle facing the archway beyond. With the heat wave just broken, the fresh air felt like a blessing on his hands and face as he relaxed. He let his eyes close for a moment, resting his head against the back of the bench, hearing the rustle of leaves in the elm trees, the closing of shutters in a townhouse, the rumble of a cart on the cobblestones beyond the arch. He may even have dozed – he wasn't sure – but when he opened his eyes again the globes on the candelabra of the square pedestal were lit. He looked at his watch – five after nine – and hurried out through the arch back toward the bustle of life (fantasy, he would have insisted) along the boulevard St-Germain.

There was a group already waiting for him at Le Petit Zinc restaurant, for it was Jude's custom to dine there on Wednesdays, sometimes with students, sometimes with the models who had posed for them during class. On this night there were both, Jude saw, as he made his way through the crowds – two students, two models, and in between them Irena Malivert, Executive Director of the Delacroix. Across from her, next to her brother, principal cellist at the Opéra Garnier, was Rebecca Chase, just arrived.

The fact that Rebecca adored him was not lost on Jude. They had performed together often enough for him to see it. Her longing was like a descant above their duets.

"It will end," he'd told himself the first time they'd kissed on Pont de la Concorde. He had enjoyed it – her soft tongue was insistent – yet for that very reason their first encounter was their last. For his sake as well as hers he'd held back after that, wanting to spare himself the disruption, Rebecca the disillusion.

Here she was though, every Wednesday, meeting him with his protégés under the globes and intricate grillwork that adorned Le Petit Zinc's façade.

This particular Wednesday, with the breeze like a longed-for parole come at last, all of Paris seemed to be strolling the glistening streets. Friends of the artist passed by; colleagues of the harpist stopped; scholars from the past and present students lingered a while. Even Irena Malivert, who never, categorically on hallowed principle stayed beyond ten o'clock, found a reason to remain at the table.

The reason was Malachy Chapman – chronicler, photographer, witty and perennial fixture in and about the Sorbonne. For at least fifty years – two world wars so far, he'd say – he'd taken the pulse of those streets with his unerring eye and a camera that never failed him. Most of the time he'd sold his portraits to the subjects who'd posed for him, or whom he'd caught unaware – both groups only too willing to return home with his dramatic prints.

The lady he'd photographed that afternoon, though, he explained, drawing a chair up at street side between Jude McCallister and Irena, had simply refused to take the print home.

"Not that she didn't pay me. She gave me double – said it was lovely, but that she had no need, no room, no inclination – I can't remember exactly – just that I should dispose of it, sooner rather than later, any way I saw fit. Can you imagine?" He fumbled inside the compartments of his faded portfolio. "Not wanting this in your house?"

Rebecca Chase knew at once why Chapman had joined them. A double sale was in the offing. Whoever the recalcitrant subject might be, she'd paid the photographer handsomely and Jude McCallister would no doubt do the same. He was always buying faces – postcards from bouquinistes, publicity from the theatres – anything that would present to him an arresting image to reinvent.

This image, Rebecca noted, seemed to have captured his imagination. Jude couldn't take his eyes off it as the white-aproned waiter appeared to refill their decanter.

"Malachy, where did you take this?"

"Where else?" replied Malachy with a smile. "Tourists always find the Panthéon on a fine day like this."

No tourist, thought Jude, staring at the iris-eyes and matching turtleneck and amethyst pendant outdone by the gaze.

"A thousand francs," he said suddenly.

The whole table stared.

"More if you need it."

"No. No more, Jude. Not even that much. I *couldn't*. She didn't even want it."

"I do, though"

"Yes but still..."

"Deal or no deal?"

"Are you crazy?"

"Incurably."

The waiter brought the menus.

"I don't know, Jude. I mean, if it means that much to you..."

"It does."

"You sure?"

"Christ..."

"Sold then. But the next two are free, the next three..."

"Whatever you say," Jude replied, slipping the photograph into the left pocket of his oversized cardigan.

Nobody dared asked to see it then, though they all stayed on 'til the moon was high and the crowds thinned, just past one.

By half past one Jude was back in his house. He opened the terrace doors, passed through to his study and sat down at his desk. Only the silent stone figures in Rodin's garden were out still, for the night had turned cloudy and a light rain had begun to dampen the sidewalks below him.

He had left only one light in the living room on. Although it reached him in the study, spilling expansively onto the polished floor, he turned on his desk lamp to study the face Malachy'd sold him. After a moment, impatiently, he tossed the photograph onto his blotter.

Wrong, he fiercely said to himself. *Hopelessly maladroit, absolutely incorrect.*

He turned around to the dome, which was by long experience impartial, then looked out at the city, by nature even more detached, and then he returned to his print.

No question about it. He had painted her falsely from memory. Repeatedly. Every morning for over a week. Her mouth was fuller, her brows not so arched. Above all it was the expression that had somehow escaped him, bemused and wistful both it seemed – courtesan and ingénue, sorrow and hope intertwined.

How had he missed the contrast? No, not the contrast. The coalescence. Well it had only been a moment. And yet – again he was forced to concede the point – hadn't that been the main theme of his class all these weeks? Life only offered its moments. Therein the romance, the fable in each dawning day.

Again he tossed the photo down. Again the thought of her rejecting it consumed him. It was magnificent. So was she. Why refuse such an homage which could not in any case be denied?

Caroline had refused it because, like the glass in her mirror, it was simply not to be endured.

And yet the photographer had been so winsome, so persistent, the cobalt sky above the Panthéon's dome had been so striking, she simply hadn't had the strength to disappoint.

"A quick one," she'd said, not even chasing the black wisps of hair on her neck, and Malachy Chapman had complied, focusing his practiced eye on her improbable ones.

And then she had paid him, and tipped him, and walked down the steps toward the Law School on her right, its four columns imposing, its elegant pediment incontrovertible – like its graduates, she'd thought with a smile, among whom were her father, Allessandro di Contini, buried back home over a decade ago, and his twin brother, Raphael, buried in Paris the week she'd arrived.

All that remained now was her uncle's apartment. Fortunately, she would have the help of Lucien Barthes, nephew to Raphael's wife. Lucien and Caroline had been entrusted to arrange for an auction of the home's contents, revenue to go to Anne-Sophie, Raphael's mistress of twenty years – love affair that had been confined to Raphael's lecture assignments in France, secret shared only by the worldly Lucien and the discreet, some would say distant, Caroline Devereux.

Tomorrow I will go, she had promised herself as she walked down from the Law School toward the left bank of the Seine. Until the memorial the preceding day, she had been unable to enter the apartment. Now, with little over a month left before her return to Connecticut, she could no longer delay.

Tomorrow, she had repeated, suddenly weary as she paused at the boulevard St-Germain. Tired as she was though, she was reluctant to return to her rooms on the rue Séguier. She decided on late-night supper in a deserted street side café.

And so it was indeed her face Jude had glimpsed that night – not on the print in his sweater pocket, but reflected in the window of an antiques shop on the rue du Bac. He had been walking with his two students still, along with Rebecca Chase, about to part from them all at the Solférino Métro. Something in the shop window over his shoulder made him turn. Twice he'd looked; twice he had been distracted by the conversation of his friends. It was a distraction he'd welcomed. He had to guard against obsession – what Goya would have called, while fully respecting fantasy, unguarded reason. And the stranger from the Crillon threatened obsession. Why else would he see her face every which way he turned?

Caroline had a box seat at the Comédie-Française later that week, compliments of Lucien Barthes, who arrived just before curtain – harried, apologetic, slipping his paisley scarf off with a sigh of relief as he slipped his thin perfect form into the armchair that dwarfed him.

Discreetly, as lights in the chandeliers under the dome began to fade, a noiseless usher closed their door. Globes in the balcony dimmed. After a moment or two, only a few stubborn shadows remained in the grand, hallowed hall.

"Roxane herself," Lucien whispered, having managed in those few moments to notice how lovely his cousin looked – long full taffeta skirt, long-sleeved ribbed turtleneck, garnets in her pendant matching the dark wine of the clothes.

She smiled, touching his arm. The curtain rose. As though on cue they both straightened, for it had been years since the company had presented Rostand. Not a line of the play was unknown to Caroline or Lucien, or Jude McCallister in the orchestra, two rows behind them.

He had not seen them before the lights dimmed, having also arrived, breathless, just as the curtain was rising. Nor did he see them during the first intermission, approached as he'd been by a colleague who had designed *Cyrano*'s sets. When he finally looked around, midway through the second break, focusing as he always did on the elaborate ornamentation on the multiple balconies, Lucien's box was empty, although there was a wrap on the red velvet chair by the railing.

Jude studied his program. He heard the lobby bell ring, the closing of doors in the boxes, the murmur of conversation subside. In the ensuing hush he looked up as the seemingly thousands of lights dimmed again, imperceptibly, until only embers remained deep in the long, tapered bulbs. And then again darkness, total absence of sound except for the plush undulation of the curtain as it rose, and in the stillness he sat motionless, disbelieving, having in that one instant before illusion's void seen her profile, her arm on the railing and then Roxane walked onstage, smitten by a man she did not know.

"Brilliant," proclaimed Lucien as the immense folds of the curtain fell to the floor at play's end like the confident fabric of a dowager's ball gown. After sustained applause the crowd dispersed slowly.

"Shall we?" he finally asked, reaching behind for Caroline's shawl. "It may be raining still. I'll take you home."

"Lucien, you needn't. Rain or no rain, I'd rather walk."

"Your skirt will get soaked."

"Nevertheless…"

He looked at her. Though she had brushed her eyes quickly, the splendid irony of the final couplets – destiny fulfilled in the last breath of life – was in her face still.

He touched her cheek. She too stood. A knock on the door interrupted their exit.

"This was left for Madame," the usher explained.

"A mistake…" began Caroline.

"In box eleven."

"This is box eleven," said Lucien.

Caroline held the large envelope in her hands. She untied the string clasp and carefully removed the contents. The wafer-thin paper had no words on it, only an illustration, though in the glow of the small crystal wall sconce she did not at first know the subject.

"You, Caroline," said Lucien, astounded.

She nodded.

"Amazing," he repeated, for sketched there, sublimely, was her head, her hair, pendant and ear clips and comb at her neck and oversized eyes that matched the garnets, exactly.

She thrust her hand into the envelope, twice, but found no note, no explanation, so that all she was left with was the artist's signature, Jude McCallister, in the lower left-hand corner of the drawing.

And so again she was stunned when she walked out into the corridor and made her way toward the grand staircase and saw, beside the bust of Molière, the pianist from the Crillon on the top step, observing her.

"That one you did not request," he said with a smile as she approached him.

"No, but it is beautiful."

"So you will keep it."

She looked puzzled.

"You have been known to return portraits, I've heard."

Who was this man who always surprised her, who seemed to know her so well, who held back so little and seemed to regret even less?

"Hello there," called Lucien, disengaging himself from some colleagues who had approached him in the hallway. "How are you? I so enjoyed your music at the Crillon when we were there."

Jude took the hand Lucien offered. Was he a friend of hers? A lover? Her husband perhaps?

"Lucien Barthes," he heard then. "You may remember my cousin. She was at my table the night you played."

Crowds streaming past them muffled the rest of the introduction.

"Caroline," repeated Lucien. "Caroline Contini Devereux."

She too offered her hand. There was a moment.

"Still at the Crillon?" Lucien asked directly, trading a robust politeness for the evening of Gershwin he had enjoyed.

"No. No I'm not. I never stay at the Crillon. I live here in Paris."

"Where can we hear your music then?"

"Lucien..." murmured Caroline.

"I mean as long as my cousin is here still – and not for too much longer," he added, less buoyantly, as though the inevitable fact of her departure had suddenly dawned on him. "Only a month remains, am I not correct, Caroline?"

She nodded.

"So you are both then at the Crillon?" managed Jude.

"Just me," pronounced Lucien, responding for his younger cousin from habit and outdated protocol, mixed.

Jude studied Caroline, as though he were sketching her again.

"I'm on the rue Séguier," she heard herself say then. She could have added the place, the address, the name of the small hotel, but did not. *If it matters to him he will find me,* she thought, and then she drew back, thoughts swirling around in her head, not the least of which was the strange fact that it mattered to her.

"Lucien, we must go."

"Still determined to walk?"

"I am."

"It is raining still," Jude interjected.

"I hope so," was her response.

She gave Jude her hand, thanked him once more, and then, clutching the portrait he'd done, swept down the staircase on the arm of Lucien Barthes.

When she arrived in her rooms at l'Hôtel du Dauphin, there was no message at the front desk.

"Are you certain, Rémi?"

"Well, I have only been here since midnight."

"Yes, of course."

"I could go ask Jean-Ives."

"No. Please. It is not urgent."

Rémi nodded, all discretion. Caroline took her key, turned and walked through the arch toward the rear garden wing. *Better this way, far better,* she said to herself, making her way down the narrow corridor to her rooms, regretting her unprecedented boldness at the Comédie-Française. Twice for some reason she'd let her guard down with that man. A stranger. An artist. Lover of people and the light, it would seem, and her own comfort the dark, solitude her confidant.

She pushed open her door and saw a note slipped underneath.

"There was a call for you, Madame, just past eleven. No message left."

At twelve-thirty exactly – Caroline had already bathed and had slipped, naked at last, onto the coolness of her cotton sheets – her telephone rang.

She let it ring a second time, and then a third and then she reached for the receiver, knowing somehow that her life would never again be the same.

"I was going to tell you you'd left an earring behind," she heard a man say – no other greeting, no identification – "but you'd have known at once it was a lie."

"Yes," she replied, nothing more, knowing Jude's voice in the dark.

"Fact of the matter is," he went on, "I haven't been able to sleep for two weeks."

"I am sorry."

"Make it up to me then."

She didn't answer.

"A cup of coffee will do."

Still she didn't answer.

"That much at least I've a claim to, Madame Devereux. – Is it Madame Devereux?"

"It is."

"Ah."

Her heart ached.

"I thought so."

"Because I've such a settled air?"

"Because harmony so often eludes."

She recalled the short-lived incandescence of the chandelier bulbs that night, the flickering wall sconces in the bathroom, the light that Roxane was vouchsafed in the end, only to have to relinquish it, after so long in the dark.

"Not that I care, mind you. I just thought if I could see you, if I could paint you…"

"With a coffee cup?"

"However you say," he said with a laugh. "I'd just like to get some sleep."

"You have already done my portrait."

"That is yours."

"And I am not, as a rule, fond of my image."

"I do not, as a rule, do things by the rule."

They agreed to meet at Place des Vosges, west side of the arcade, after sunset the following day, because he had a mistress, he confessed.

"No wonder you don't sleep," she said, knowing instinctively he meant the light.

☾

"Hard to predict exactly," said Jude, leaning back in his chair, his shoulders almost touching the base of the arch curving above. "Five days, perhaps more."

"That long?"

"Just for the sittings. After that I refine alone, although sometimes, if it is not yet done – I mean to my liking – more sittings."

"But if the client was satisfied?"

"The client is pleased when I am, Madame Devereux."

It was said with pride, not arrogance, as a clockmaker might of the precision in his timepiece. Nevertheless, Caroline smiled.

"What if the opposite should occur?"

Jude seemed puzzled.

"If the client is *not* pleased at that point."

Jude considered a moment, ate another black olive, dabbed his mouth carefully with the corners of his linen napkin.

"In that case," he replied finally, "I fix the objection."

Her soft laughter echoed, as though from a party remembered, under the vaulted stone roof of the outdoor arcade.

"Of course," added Jude after a moment, "not all my subjects are clients. They can be models, or students, or bowls of fruit beside a shawl."

Unfolding her own napkin in her lap, Caroline said, "Each in its way must be pleased though, I expect – the fruit and the shawl above all. The fruit and the shawl trust you the most."

Jude stared at her.

"How did you know that?"

"I have studied some."

"Painting?"

"Poetry."

"Well, yes, but language…"

"Not pigments, admittedly. Not applied with a brush. Yet like your medium unforgiving, a palette of infinite possibilities – syllables, notes, chords, emotions…" she stopped. Her face coloured – a shade that resembled the coral pavilions around them.

"Go on," he said, softly.

"You didn't come to hear a lecture."

"I came to plan a painting. It helps to know the subject – what the subject knows, doesn't know, what she feels…"

"There's a lot I don't know."

Jude discounted the disclaimer. Although they had spoken, all told, including the phone call to her hotel and the exchange after Rostand, a total of forty minutes, he was aware that she knew much of his craft – his duty, as he preferred to phrase it – for she had defined, whether instinctively or not he could not yet hazard, its ultimate challenge: the innocent, unassailable domination of the fruit bowl. She'd grasped the tyranny of its reticence, obdurate and hermetic, concluding rightly in the end that in spite of that silence – or because of it, rather – he was obliged to render faithfully, without misstep, the porcelain essence offered so frankly, like the faith of a child in his hands.

The sun cleared the spires of St-Paul church to the west, splashing a wash of crimson on the brickwork around them.

"Ancient Rome, ancient Greece, a bit of Morocco thrown in," remarked Caroline, chin in her palm as she surveyed the day's end.

"The symmetrical arches around us?"

"My senior thesis at Yale."

Jude smiled.

"I didn't mean to entrap you."

"I am happy to be ensnared. Or at the very least instructed. What was the topic?" he asked genially, taking a sip of his wine.

Attican Sources in the Epicureanism of Lucretius.

Jude nodded.

"Cutting edge at the time. Somewhat outdated by now. The one and only copy's still in New Haven."

Jude continued to nod.

"Students, of course, have used microfilm."

"I once spent a weekend there," he managed.

"Not even long enough for the preface," she said. Then they both laughed this time, although for some reason the echo resembled one voice above them.

In days to come he would be haunted by that vague bell-like sound, try to hear it again, even a syllable, faintly, but for the moment he just surrendered to the approaching evening, as though an eternity of such evenings, like silver aircraft on a runway, were stacked up behind it to replace its vanishing possibilities.

The sun in the meantime seemed to have doubled in size, hovering on the horizon, causing the slate in the sharply pitched roofs to resemble hot coals, the windows below them to blaze.

Caroline turned away from the intensifying incandescence. She seemed uncomfortable, took a sip from her wine glass, then a second sip and then by sheer force of its weight perhaps, the sun all of a sudden surrendered and left the plaza in shadows.

A waiter appeared with matches to light the candle on their table.

"No," Caroline said abruptly.

Jude turned to her.

"We do not need that light."

"For the menus, perhaps…" Jude began.

"There is enough light," she cried, raising her hand to block the waiter's hand – a superfluous gesture, as it happened, for the waiter had already retreated in silence.

Jude too was silent, not from shock – nothing shocked him – but in an attempt to decode the bizarre subtext in her refusal. It wasn't the light, he concluded. She had withstood light all afternoon. That left only the heat – perhaps just the flame – both intertwined, he surmised, in an occult kiln of her own she routinely repressed.

"Forgive me," she stammered.

"For what?"

"I – that is…" She clasped her hands; unclasped them. "Perhaps we should go now…"

"We haven't eaten yet."

"It will be dark soon."

"Can you not eat in the dark?"

Crickets beside the fountain began to chirp in the dusk.

"I can do everything in the dark."

"Lucky you, then."

"You think so?"

"Mostly in the dark I'm only sleepless, Madame Devereux."

One by one, efficiently, the waiter lit candles on the other tables under the arch.

"Caroline," she murmured, at a loss still, avoiding his gaze.

"Jude then," he answered, at a loss still, searching her face.

The brick pavilions turned brown in the retreat of the sun. The slate roofs turned black. A mist shrouded the trees, the fountains, even the bronze stolid figure of Louis XIII.

Yet even at that moment, Jude could still see her eyes, mauve like the sky over Place Fürstenberg. The fact that her mouth trembled still he could not see. The fact that fear had gripped her heart he could.

Before this week's passed, he vowed to himself, *I will know why.* He deluded himself into thinking his interest was but the broad-based curiosity most of his portrait friends felt. He thought it quite healthy, in fact professional. He was not prepared yet to acknowledge a much darker need.

"Menus?" asked the waiter, moving back to their table as patrons began to fill the café.

"No," Jude decided. "Thank you." Night would fall quickly, he knew, and in the dark they would be useless. "Today is Sunday, is it not? I know the specials. Carrot soup and a salad and the lamb, I think – if the lady has no objections."

Caroline shook her head.

"Done then," he said, turning his attention to the square once again. "And not a moment too soon. The divisions in the rooftops are not yet lost in the sky. We can still make each house out."

Thirty-six of them, she mused. *At first glance identical. And yet each has its own soul, its individual markings.*

"Have you a favourite?" he asked briskly, as though they'd gone shopping in the plaza and nothing untoward had occurred.

"Yes," she said.

"Let me guess."

"If you like."

"Six. Right in the corner. Victor Hugo's house."

"No."

"No?"

"Close, though."

"Be honest now."

"I will always be honest with you, Jude. That has been there from the start."

It was a statement of fact – neither reprimand nor invitation – as one might observe that the tides had gone out, or a flock of wild geese had just passed.

And yet, Jude was aware, in their layered simplicity, tissue-like, the words had presented beneath their promise a gift. She would in time reveal herself – a matter of trust in his hands – letting him glimpse the essence existence had forged, like that fruit bowl on his sideboard. When and where this would occur he could not say, nor could he calculate what it would cost her – no doubt a great deal, for he sensed that the very concept of disclosure, and the concomitant candour it would require, were both, from force of habit perhaps more than nature, foreign to her. He also sensed he too would pay dearly for the privilege of participation in the exposition that lay ahead, as though a tax would be levied on his own soul for having trespassed on grounds the gods had marked No Entry.

Nevertheless it had to be done, or rather experienced, for he began to see clearly, as the space between them continued to dim, that it was the *experience* of Madame Devereux – some temporal, visceral, yet boundless connection, more detached than possession, far more intimate than art, which he had craved from the start.

"Number One," she announced, having decided at that point that he just could not guess.

"Madame de Sévigné's house?"

"Are you surprised?"

"Not surprised. Intrigued. She didn't live there long."

"She never lived far. Always next door to the place she was born. Or in the house two doors down, or in the one across the square. I envy that."

"I gather you've travelled."

"Some," she replied.

"Some," he concluded, was a code word – among others she favoured – all of them diversionary whenever she meant the opposite.

Again she faced the square – lost in the recollection of the itineraries she hadn't shared. Jude noticed the way her breasts, outlined beneath the pale ribbed silk sweater, resembled ripe apples in the yard beyond his front porch in Tucson. He saw too how her hair chafed beneath the clip at her neck.

"Your soup, Madame," said the waiter, bringing her back from the reverie Jude was content to observe.

They spoke of many things as they ate, forgetting the Marquise de Sévigné, the court of Louis XIV she adorned, the incomparable correspondence penned to the daughter she longed for.

But Jude did not forget that Madame Devereux had wandered. He had also begun to place her speech somewhere, and by extension her background, for in her English he heard other lands, barely audible, and in her French another time. He would return to it, he determined, first opportunity. Already he needed to paint what she felt compelled to omit.

Later, as a group of tourists passed their table, the chance presented itself.

"More people visit Place des Vosges than Versailles," he observed languidly. "Do you believe it?"

"I do. Time can be limited on a trip."

"*Your* trips," he continued, taking a slice of bread from the basket between them. "All that travel, I mean…"

She stiffened.

"Was it before or after you got to the States?"

"How did you know I'm not American?"

"I don't know."

"You do know. You're a musician."

"Would-be musician."

"Enough to hear what you need."

"I have heard only…" He stopped. Like a lingering coda, her voice was clear in his head. "Someplace warm," he decided. "And distant… as you are – and vivid," he added. "And not too far from the sea."

Caroline smiled, in spite of herself.

"Venezuela," he ventured.

She shook her head.

"Uruguay."

"Still too far."

"Where then?"

"Argentina."

"Ah."

"Paris for high school."

"That's what misled me."

"Rome before college. Amsterdam after that."

Jude could not tell, as she smiled again, quickly, if in her expression he'd seen weariness or a deeper nostalgia.

"Father was a diplomat, born in Florence; Mother a diplomat's wife, born outside Bonn. She died in childbirth – mine, I was told." Again she paused. The nostalgia was clear this time. "After Yale I stayed in New England. Father too until he died. And that," she concluded, "is the extent of the long version. None too soon, I might add. Here is our supper."

Jude looked down for his fork. She did not seem to need her eyes, absolutely at home in the dark.

Maddening skill, he thought after an hour, watching her sip her coffee as he at last found his spoon.

The night wind by then had turned brisk in the arcade, making the tablecloths flutter like courtiers' ghosts. Lamps came on in the plaza. Music drifted down from an open window above them. Jude listened intently a moment. Then he surprised them both by asking, as he refilled their glasses, "And your husband?"

"Plastic surgeon."

Her tone – like an old house moments after the movers have emptied it – was absolutely devoid of content.

"Yale Medical Center, Critical Care. At least that's where he was when I met him."

He heard the crinkling of fine paper as she unwrapped the chocolate on her saucer.

"Private practice in New Salem now."

"That's near New York, is it not?"

"Connecticut."

"Ah."

"Just across the state line."

He nodded, carefully replacing the top of the decanter. The music continued.

"Children?" he asked.

"None," she replied, "though not by choice. No doubt that's why I love La Sévigné," she went on, breezily almost, at home with pain as she was in the dark. "After all, lots of people live near home. She managed to send that home back intact, more so

K . L . V I D A L

perhaps than it was in real life – whatever that is – over and over again, hundreds of letters. Have you read them?"

"Several times."

"Have you married?"

"Several times."

As she unwrapped another chocolate she said, "You must have children…"

"None."

She looked at him.

"Too many weddings," he went on, blithely almost, matching the tone she had sustained. "Too much work in between. And then of course the light each day…"

"Unforgiving and impatient girl."

"Just so. I was not, after all, Victor Hugo there in Number Six. Bloody convoy at the border when *that* man was expelled. His own carriage. His children's. His wife's ahead. The mistress and her sons behind. I am not that complex."

"Perhaps," she said, thoughtfully, "just more self-contained."

He bowed slightly. There was silence again.

"Are you married now?" he heard in the dark.

"That, Madame Devereux, is where we are different. I am, at the present moment, free to do as I please. You are…" he paused.

"Still without an answer."

The waiter appeared and placed their cheque by his plate. Jude glanced at it, could read nothing, calculated roughly, slipped more than was needed into the billfold.

Meanwhile a tentative moon had appeared, causing the rooftops to glisten like mother-of-pearl.

"No," she heard as they stood, "No, I am not married now."

Not until they reached the Seine, heading for the walkway along the Pont St-Michel, did he discuss – as a physician would with his patient – the procedure she should prepare for on the following day.

"I could come sooner," she said.

"Nine's fine. That will give you time to change."

"Change to what?"

"Well I envision – I mean it would seem to me appropriate, given the formal portrait I'd like" – he fumbled, uncharacteristically. "Have you brought something formal to France?"

"No."

"Cocktail skirt?"

She shook her head.

"Little black dress in your bag?"

"What's wrong with this," she asked, stopping halfway across the bridge.

He looked at her. The long sheer pale skirt, caressing her legs in the breeze, seemed almost diaphanous in the lamplight. The turtleneck revealed her torso, very long, and her body, very lean. Still, there was no flesh to paint, nothing of her texture – save for her face, her hands, her naked ankles tied to the ropes of her shoes.

I could perhaps just do her face, he thought.

"What's wrong with this," she repeated.

The Seine, diaphanous too in the light, was in no hurry to pass through the experienced arches beneath them.

"I mean am I a client or a model?"

"Something in between, I'd say."

"Fruit bowl?" she persisted.

"Fruit bowl," he conceded.

"This should be fine then."

"If you were porcelain."

"Does the material count so much?"

"Insofar as it is a conduit."

"Let us compromise then."

The immense lamps on the bridge, like gems around a socialite's neck, lit their way as they walked on.

"I will bring jewels. Something to go with the sweater, and the sunlight; something – I don't know, more formal, Jude, if that's what you need. Should I fall short, though, you can send me home."

His answer was muffled by the laughter of students passing by.

"Send you home?" Jude repeated. "After what it took me to reserve you?"

"Only should appearance fail..."

"Appearance is all," he insisted.

"Sometimes."

"Always."

Loose strands from her hair, pried by the wind from her neck, brushed across her eyes like a transparent veil. In vain she reached up repeatedly to catch them.

"Wear whatever you want," he said abruptly, fiercely almost, for he had decided as they stood there and the blue-black of the Seine matched the iridescence underneath that veil that he would paint her however she came, just as long as she came.

"Well that's settled," she murmured, as they turned south onto the quay that bordered the left bank of the Seine.

They stopped at the top of a sinuous and narrow street, passage to a labyrinth of others just like it, all leading to truth, time-tested shibboleth of the Sorbonne.

"This will be fine."

"I can take you to your door."

"No," she insisted, and then she turned and walked away and then retraced her steps and found him there still.

"Yours or mine, Jude?" she asked.

"What, Mrs. Devereux?"

"The painting. Whose is it?"

"Shared I suppose."

"Shared?"

He nodded.

"How?"

"To be arranged."

"Will you want me seated or standing?"

"Dressed."

"Well of course dressed, Jude..."

"Unless at some point, somehow, should my mistress demand it..."

Caroline had begun to disappear once again, into the warren of byways that led away from the Seine, southward, toward the certitude of the university and her reserved rooms in its shade.

Orpheus in the Underworld, Caroline said to herself, pondering the selection as music drifted in from a record player in Jude's study. She was alone in the living room, enjoying the breeze that billowed the curtains beyond the open French terrace doors.

"I won't be long," Jude had promised, vanishing across the hallway into his kitchen beyond.

After some time, hearing her step in the hall, he had turned to find her standing in the doorway behind him.

"Is breakfast always included?"

"No," he said, checking his pastries in the oven.

"Can I help anyway?"

"There is nothing to do. I will join you where I left you."

She had returned then to his sofa. Offenbach had continued. Slowly she'd grown accustomed to the penetrating smell of paint. It seemed to be everywhere in the immense apartment, part of the very fabric of the house, like signature perfume on a woman's clothes. Indeed, Caroline reflected, the decidedly chemical smell was somehow sensual, not unlike perfume. Everything in the house seemed to be first and foremost – and unexpectedly – sensual. The flower-filled terrace resembled splashes of primary colours; stretching beyond was an even richer palette: the black and gold of Les Invalides, the malachite of its Esplanade, the verdigris of Alexander's bridge, the deeper teal of the Seine, sweeping on to the sea, like some heavily beaded train on a Belle Époque gown.

A gown that would suit this room, she mused, noting how textures within vied with the splendour beyond – tapestries on the walls, Persian rugs on the floors, hundreds of books behind bevelled glass shelves, smooth abstract sculptures on richly carved stands.

Beyond an arched open door she could see more books in the study. Some volumes seemed new; others old – no doubt rare – with faded gold letters on cracked dark brown spines. These, she decided, invited a closer investigation, but as she stood to approach the archway she heard Jude call out.

"Ready at last," he announced, appearing with a tray of fruit, pastry, coffee and cheese. "You'll wonder what took me."

"I know exactly what took you. I smelled your cinnamon baking."

"Most people smell paint here."

"That too."

He watched her closely as she ate – the way she bit into the thickest part of the fruit tart, far too ambitiously, she discovered, trying to rescue the crumbs as they fell to her plate. In vain. Sugar stayed on her mouth. He was tempted to remove it, but let it remain where it lay, in the centre of her lower lip; for it was then that he fixed exactly the shape of her mouth.

She passed her tongue over the sweetness, unknowingly, and the distinguishing mark disappeared. Jude had no need of it then. It was only her eyes he had not yet found.

"I warn you I do this once, Caroline. First time a client comes."

"Half a client," she reminded him.

As he collected her tray he said, "Half the breakfast is all I gave you."

Offenbach's first waltz began.

"Besides," Jude called out from the kitchen, "we're already acquainted. I'll leave the rest to unfold."

"What?"

"I said sometimes surprises make the grace notes."

He finished clearing, rinsed the dishes, walked back into the living room, and found that she'd put her jewels on.

They were not what he had expected. He had thought perhaps of a pendant such as the ones she'd worn before. This was an intricate chain, looped in triplicate under the folds of her turtleneck. Its remarkable gems seemed to dance like the song that was playing – lapis, citrines, amethysts, aquamarines – all the same size, all perfectly spaced along the long thick gold ropes. Her earrings were amethysts. Her bracelet, matching the necklace, encircled her wrist several times.

"I thought these might enliven things. I mean me," she went on unevenly, noting that he had continued to stare. "I…you had wanted a gown…"

"I remember."

"You may find these don't suit."

"Let them be."

"I have brought pearls, Jude," she managed, reaching up to unclasp the ropes. "A double strand… priceless –"

"Don't," he said sharply.

"The effect may be simpler though –"

"No," he repeated, moving at last in her direction. "Some other brush can paint those things. What I want now," he went on, his voice growing eager, matching the slate in his eyes, "what we need here, that is…" he plucked an iris from the vase on the table as he crossed. "Can you turn your head a bit? No, that's too much. Permit me." He put his hand under her chin and moved her face to him, obliquely. "There," he pronounced, standing back. "Perfect."

She raised her hand to the bud affixed to the comb at her neck. Its rich velvet texture felt inexperienced.

"I'll take your word for it," she conceded.

"Always a good beginning," he replied.

She was seated still, a wash of not so primary colours, hyacinth dominant, though he had not yet subdued her eyes, and therefore could not paint them yet.

It will all come to me, he told himself, meaning the essence to be captured, and in the process dismantled – not yet aware of the fact that this one time in his life it would be life that would triumph, mastering even art, and that in the process, all would be altered.

As Jude prepared his materials, Caroline walked around the studio. It was different from the rest of the house – spare, last in the enfilade of rooms to the right, monastically single-minded.

Directly ahead the French doors were open. To her left, unlike other rooms on this side, there were two more French doors facing south, so that light from the whole of the Left Bank poured in, privilege of a corner flat on the old building's top floor.

Between these south doors was a fireplace, its stone mantel simple. Jude had positioned only one object on this mantel: a vase filled with cuttings from the terrace beyond.

Meissen, decided Caroline, running her fingers along the smooth bell-shaped form. Its floral pattern was vivid: deep greens and pinks and intense navy hues catching the light from the morning. On the opposite wall there was an ornately framed mirror, beneath the mirror a loveseat covered in tapestry that echoed the bell jar's dark hues. Two small tables flanked this sofa: one with a white rose-filled bowl, the other with books and an ebony clock.

Everything else belonged to the artist and his craft. Left of the entrance was an easel; next to the easel a cart; next to the cart a cabinet; on the floor alongside a landscape in progress.

Jude moved to his cabinet, still selecting his materials, thinking of the portrait he was about to begin. Most of his clients posed easily by his mantel. They'd stand in comfort beside it, lean in silence against it, seat themselves grandly in the midnight-blue chair alongside. Light was best in that place. The easel welcomed its charm.

But Mrs. Devereux? Jude pondered the setting. It would not do, he suspected – not in her crisscrossed rope sandals and long raw-silk skirt.

Far too formal, he had to admit, despite the other remarkable bejewelled ropes at her neck. Even the navy chair – well perhaps with a shawl, a basket beside it – he turned – she was seated on the sofa, legs tucked beneath her, one hand at her side, the other stroking her necklace, her face toward the terrace, unaware of his gaze. The exceptional comb and the iris he'd placed there – both, for the moment having managed to hold her defiant hair – could be seen in detail in the mirror behind her. Her profile was also reflected, as was the Meissen vase, the mantel, the terrace garden beyond.

Artlessly, thus, she had posed twice for him. He could paint her full face, angled as it was in its three-quarter turn. He could capture the ropes, the clothes, the lithe and perfect body seated so comfortably, languidly almost – a strikingly sensual pose on the richly hued loveseat.

And he could also depict what the mirror had caught – long neck, black mass of hair, wisp or two by her temple, terrace and mantel and flowers that had entranced her.

It was all of a piece – a wash of pale pinks and blues, deep rose and citrine – the woman and her necklace a metaphor for the morning, and the space where he worked, and the bell jar he'd kept by his side all these years, to remind him of perfection.

"No," he cried out, for she had begun to move then. "Just like that. Just as you are." His voice had grown eager again. "We have only 'til noon. Sunlight will hit the mirror then and at that point I'll have to stop."

He swivelled the easel as he spoke. She was too startled to respond. He reached for his palette, rolled the cart toward him, found the jars that he wanted, the brushes – all done in a moment, with a kind of perfervid precision, almost a fierceness – something she'd never seen in his body before, though she had heard it once in his voice, on the bridge.

"Jude…" she stammered.

"Talk to me later. Just as soon as I'm set here. I don't mind if you talk while I paint. Sometimes it helps. Sometimes I talk. But not now."

And then she was still – silent, unmoving, new to posing, not yet grasping his mandate, knowing only that like the fruit bowl she had to trust what he'd seen.

At half past twelve he put his tools down.

"I will refine after lunch."

They had said nothing, as it happened, in the intervening long morning.

She felt stiff as she stood, disconnected. Jude did not seem to notice. He was in another place still, wiping his brushes, closing his paint tubes, deconstructing the day's achievement – with precision still, though no longer perfervid.

"Are you hungry?" he asked vaguely, looking up, as though she had suddenly, like Galatea, come to life in his room.

"I – yes, a little bit, but I will eat at my uncle's." She called it that still, stubbornly. "Lucien's meeting me."

"Ah."

She walked toward the easel and glanced at the morning's achievement. There, on a cream-toned cloth slightly lighter than her sweater, was a sketch of his room, his view, the Left Bank, a languid woman on his sofa. A bit of colour had been added: upholstery, jonquils, the black of the ebony clock alongside. Her full mouth had been suggested; her hair was still brush strokes; the eyes were hollow, unsettling, as Jude's too seemed when she turned to him.

"That's your last look," he said. "I like to keep a work in progress to myself 'til it's done."

"You should rest now," she murmured.

"I will."

"I mean before you refine."

"If there's time."

There was a moment. She raised her arms to unclasp the necklace.

"Shall I leave these here, Jude?"

"If you like." He smiled, rubbing the tip of his long, tapered brush with a cloth. "I am insured, Madame Devereux."

"I hope that includes my painting."

"You have decided it will be yours?"

"I have decided I know where you're heading," she said, slipping her earrings off, then her bracelet, staring still at the canvas, barely sketched, full of grace.

"Here." She placed the jewels in his hand. "Keep these with those other gems."

"What other gems?"

"The other half of the breakfast."

He laughed then, as she did, both feeling relief from the strain of that first day.

"Let me at least give you coffee."

"No,"

"Sherry."

"I have to run."

"Is it so far?"

"I could not say."

He looked at her.

"Like you," she said thoughtfully, "I have been in some other place here."

He wanted to touch her all of a sudden – not merely paint her – and then it unnerved him that he'd thought of painting as *mere* and decided it best after all that she run, the sooner the better, this woman who threatened a lifetime's devotion.

She'd turned to go. He finished wiping his brush.

"Nine tomorrow?" she asked from the door.

"Have dinner with me."

"I...no. I couldn't," she said, lingering still at the door. "There's Lucien."

"He'll manage."

"And my uncle's apartment."

"You'll have to stop sometime."

"And then there's tomorrow, here – bright and early." She stopped. "What do you do if it rains?"

"If it rains I can't paint."

"I see," she said, glancing back at the easel behind him, the form barely shaped, the concept emerging. It would cost him much to have to pause. The thought greatly disturbed her, for she recalled how fiercely he had worked, as though light, volatile beloved, might turn on him and take revenge and leave him bereft of his chance.

When she turned back Jude had approached her.

"Do you plan to wear that iris while you work, Caroline?"

She darted a hand to her neck.

"Leave it there. I have others. It would not last in any case."

The petal, still soft to her touch, felt not so much inexperienced as frail now, capricious – violet metaphor for inspiration.

"It will last some."

"Give it back to me at dinner then."

"If that is what you need, Jude."

"That is what I'd like."

Long after she left he savoured the scent of her, already mixed with his paint.

$\sim$ ☾ $\sim$

"Did you wait long for me?" asked Jude awkwardly, standing beside Caroline's chair at Chez Marianne. He would have liked to have inclined his head and kissed her, taken her hands – with anyone else it would have been second nature – but he had worked on the portrait all afternoon, his head full of her as he'd retouched, improved, shaded, adjusted. He was startled now when he saw her, not because he'd worked badly – on the contrary, the developing canvas was excellent – but because he preferred her that moment, intense and vibrant before him, and he feared this surging ascendancy of evanescence over art.

"Not too long, Jude, no."

"Did you work hard today?"

"Yes."

"Have you at least had some wine? Some bread? Have they given you menus?"

"No," she said laughing. "And if you don't sit down they never will."

She looked around as he ordered and saw that theirs was the only table without a centrepiece of candles. She also saw that Jude looked haggard.

"You did not rest," she said.

"I will."

"Is it always like that?"

"When I begin it is. That charcoal sketch you saw can sometimes just tease – not even close to what I really need. That's when I have to decide what it is I need, maybe start all over, should it come to that."

"And has it?"

"Not this time. I changed very little – erased not at all – except a bit on the height of the rose bowl beside you. The figure was fine. I began shading in fact. I shadowed you all – from the comb at your neck to the ropes at your feet."

"Then what?"

"Then it got dark."

"Ah."

"Just a moment too soon."

"The days *are* growing shorter."

"Yes, but I'd mixed up more paints. The temptation to wash in a bit of your clothes – enhance the value of your hair – well, it was all just too strong. I made some mistakes. They had to go before things dried."

"But the sketch is still there," she said cautiously.

"Yes."

"As I am," she added, regretting the phrase the moment she said it.

In the ensuing silence they studied their menus.

"You've changed your clothes," Jude remarked suddenly, unaware until then of the absence of textures he had been shading all afternoon.

"Yes, well I can't live in them for a week, Jude."

"Where did you dress?"

"In my hotel."

"I have a changing room, you know."

"So you've explained."

The next pause resembled the moment before a gold leaf falls from a tree.

"Why didn't you use it?"

"Well after all..." she began.

"You left your jewels with me."

"That was different."

"I don't understand."

"I was in a hurry."

"So you traipsed up and down the Left Bank?"

"No. I mean yes. Yes, my hotel has a service – an arrangement with some cleaners nearby."

Jude watched as she stirred her coffee, her eyes fixed intently on the little spoon as it repeatedly circled the tiny cup.

"In by three, back by six," she went on, stirring still. "Guaranteed. Never failed. Since I've been going there as a matter of fact."

He reached over and touched her then, finally, laying a hand on her hand to stop the spiralling of the spoon.

"You needn't clean your clothes each day."

"I am fastidious."

"They will be fine."

"Nevertheless..."

"In fact the process might change the colour."

"Jude..."

"Not to you perhaps, but to me. And that would be worse than rain. My palette would be off. It is needless."

She made no answer.

"So use the changing room – settled? You'll be quite fine in there. There's a vanity, triple mirror, another mirror behind the door. And," he then laughed, for he sensed she was shrinking from him as he spoke, although her face never left his, "there is a lock. You'll be as safe as your clothes. All my models know that and not one of them, once...," he stopped. Her eyes were large pools, eddying depths of mauve, occulting even the pupils, it seemed.

"Plum wine?" asked the waiter, presenting two cut-crystal goblets, bell-shaped, compliments of Chez Marianne.

"Thank you," Caroline managed, glad for the opportunity to deflect the topic, her answer, Jude's unforgiving gaze.

"Settled?" he repeated.

Not in twenty years had she undressed anywhere but under the absolute cover of darkness.

"It will give us more time," he insisted. "Make things easier. You'll see. The work will be better, finer." Again he laughed. "At least not worse."

"*Voilà*, Madame."

The waiter poured carefully from a rose-toned decanter. The thick wine seeped slowly, almost by force of will it appeared, through the fine and constricting passage of glass.

Like Jude, she observed to herself, and then she could not turn back to him – not because of the clothing, or the room where she changed, but because she was shaken by the improbable likeness she had perceived. He was a vessel, nothing more, although a fine one, for his passion gave him no quarter and the ideal he envisioned would always refuse to pour freely. It was the first time in a lifetime she could imagine longing greater than hers.

The silver tray was placed between them.

"To your work, Jude," she said.

"To you in that case. At the moment they are one and the same."

She raised the goblet to her lips. The thick, near-black juice swayed with impatience inside the glass. It seemed imprisoned, though not resigned; powerful, though without guile. She took another sip, looking down still, unaware of the fact that he was smiling then, deeply relieved. He'd fixed her eyes in that liqueur – the colour at least, the shape, their reluctantly sensual, barely audible song.

꧁ ☾ ꧂

Jude prepared his palette in advance the next day, repositioned his easel, refilled the rose bowl and vase, paced back and forth through the hall. As the clock on his living room mantel struck nine, he heard the elevator door open, then close, and then there was silence again.

The old cage descended. For a moment or two he paused by his own door, dismayed by the absence of footsteps approaching. Then he walked back into his studio. Not much time had elapsed after all. Someone else may have been in the cage. In a few minutes she would arrive.

In a few minutes he walked again to his door, for the elevator had not returned. He looked at his watch, turned back down his hall, stopped, retraced his steps, opened the door and saw Caroline in the hallway, still beside the iron grillwork of the elevator's enclosure.

"Hello," was all she could think of to say as he stared.

"Good morning."

"I'm sorry I'm late. I – there was traffic."

"No matter."

Still she did not move from her spot by the grille.

"I suppose I could paint you out here, Caroline."

The remark was made gently, as he moved toward her, for already he was accustomed to her inexplicable hesitations.

"Not enough light, though," he went on. "Not nearly enough. And I've already set my things up."

He was standing close to her in the shadows. She was in the same black skirt and sweater she'd worn at the airport. Over her shoulder she carried the same large black bag. Her face was pale – an almost unearthly translucence – framed by the black mass of hair and black folds of the turtleneck. Hot weather had returned to Paris, and yet she had tied a fringed silk floral shawl around her waist. He saw as he stood there that the effect of translucence was due in part to the beads of sweat that had formed around her eyes. Even in the dark their plum wine was remarkable.

"Come inside, Mrs. Devereux. It is cooler there."

"Yes. Thank you," she murmured – nothing more – and then she walked behind him into his apartment.

She stood in his hallway, blindingly white in contrast to the corridor, and yet the colours, the textures, above all the smell of his paints were already familiar. Strangely, the odour was soothing. Even more than the flowers he'd cut – and they were everywhere – it was redolent of his work, and therefore absolutely pure. It drew her into the space. The world outside faded. She slipped the black bag from her shoulders and smiled, quickly, though she left the knotted shawl where it was.

"Those are your clothes, I presume," he said, pointing to the leather bag on the floor.

She nodded.

"Would you like coffee?"

"Is there time?"

"If you don't mind getting it while I mix more paint."

After a while he heard her place a tray on the hall console outside his studio door.

"I didn't think you'd want these near your work, Jude."

"No," he said from the doorway. "I don't eat in here. Not since the time I got distracted and stopped painting a model – who was expensive – and began sketching a pyramid of sweet rolls in a basket."

She smiled but made no answer.

"No place to sit, though. I'm sorry. I'm always afraid if I sit I'll find it hard then to stand."

"It's fine out here. Really."

The hallway was warm. The coffee was steaming. It always amazed her that Jude could drink hot things quickly, as though impervious to extremes.

"If you like, though," he went on, sipping his coffee, "you can take your cup into my office. The models all do when they change there."

She placed her cup gingerly onto its saucer. "Thank you, Jude. I'm finished."

In the renewed stillness he noticed she'd taken no more than one sip after all.

"Well," he said brightly. "Come directly into the studio when you're dressed, Caroline. There's a door that connects them. I'll show you."

She shook her head. "No. I'll find it. Thank you, though," she repeated, and then she turned and walked down the hallway and entered the room next to his studio.

Jude remained by the console, eyes on the heavy door she had so carefully closed. Something about the way she'd slung the bag over her shoulders, the way she had turned from him, as though they had shaken hands one last time, made him suspect she planned to leave, slip back into his hall while he was mixing his paints and then out of his house and down the wrought-iron cage to the street, like a chestnut leaf on the Esplanade.

The heavy door did not open. Jude saw though that the lights in his office went out, temporarily, allowing only the palest illumination to slip reluctantly under the door.

That was the sunlight Caroline could not shroud. Though one switch on the wall had controlled both the desk lamps, and though she had closed the French doors that led out onto the terrace, morning still filtered into the room through the glass curtains on the bevelled panes.

She listened, waiting to hear Jude's footsteps as he walked back into his studio. Instead, from the hallway, she could hear only the sounds of Jude pouring more coffee.

Her black bag was by her feet. She was facing the window. The mirrors were all behind her – five of them: three on the vanity to the left of the entrance, an oval on the bookcase opposite, an oversized full-length on the door she'd just closed.

Jude began to pace a bit. The changing room quickly grew hotter, sealed as it was then, with the sun forcing its way inside. Caroline undid her shawl and let it drop to the floor. She slipped off her sweater, then her skirt, and then they too fell to the floor.

But for her high wedged rope sandals she was naked, for she could endure nothing under her heavy clothing in the humidity that had returned. She reached for her shawl, still without turning, planning to wrap it around her as she dressed.

The silk felt cool to the touch, sensuous – though in a vaguely disturbing way. She passed the long black fringe through her fingers. Jude moved at last from the hall. She raised the shawl to her face and stared at the deep greens and rose and navy hues on the cloth.

The heat in the room intensified. The floral pattern on her shawl took on the shape of Jude's bell jar. The paint smell grew stronger – no doubt he was mixing again – and then in the stifling air something sharper mixed with the paint.

Turpentine? she wondered. *Linseed oil,* she decided, feeling increasingly unsteady. *Or the perfume on my shawl, hydrangeas perhaps, that strong coffee again...*

She closed her eyes, trying to find a focal point in the dark, which never deceived her, and even at that the room started to spin, slowly, in a clockwise direction. The fringe in her hands no longer felt soft, but soaked, for she had broken into a sweat.

"Air," somebody whispered, very near to her, in her own voice.

She opened her eyes to reach for a table, a chair, anything to lean against. The nearest thing was Jude's desk by the window. The stool and vanity were closer, but she did not seem to remember them.

She let her shawl drop and moved toward the desk. Its smooth top felt sturdy, so that she worked her way round it, grasping its edges, until she reached the latched windows and threw them wide open, leaning backward against the desk, letting the cool air – or so it seemed to her in comparison to the heat of the office – blow against her face, her hair, down across her body as she stood there motionless, eyes closed once again.

The room ceased to spin. She opened her eyes. The chair beside her, the lamp, the doors had resumed their normal shape, as had the rooftops, the dome, the Seine beyond Les Invalides. All that was different was the fact that she was standing there – no, stretching there – facing Jude's garden, in the broad light of his morning, with only her sandals on.

"Caroline?" she heard. "Caroline, are you all right?"

She did not answer, trying to reconstruct the dimensions of the present.

"I...yes," she stammered.

"Are you sure?"

From the other side of the door, his voice seemed louder now, more distinct.

"Yes. I'll be right in. I am sorry I have delayed you."

"Don't be," he answered. "It can take time to adjust to a new place."

He moved away from the door. She moved away from the desk, pausing to experience one last breeze against her skin. It was then that she realized she no longer had the shawl in hand. She moved back to the spot where it lay, damp still, crumpled on the carpet beside her black bag.

Jude began humming Gershwin's *But Not for Me* – another tune she knew well. It was a habit of his, she realized, humming whenever he prepared his paints, or cooked, or cleaned his brushes, or cut from the garden outside. Only while he was painting was he silent. It was as though he were hearing another song then.

She reached down for the shawl. Jude hummed the refrain one more time. Inside her head were the lyrics – bittersweet recollection of time passing by, love passing on, solitude managed in the absence of alternatives.

All she heard after that were sounds of his paint cart as he positioned it by the easel and the lilting last bars of the tune. Then, as though another hand had let the shawl drop, as though other legs had kept on walking, she found herself by the vanity next to the hall door surrounded by mirrors – five silent servants seeing everything, proffering no opinion.

She too saw everything, surprised first by how tall she was, how long her legs were – even allowing for the high-heeled wedged sandals roped several times around her calves. Her body was very lean, her waist long and thin, which made the globes of her breasts, full and round, also surprising. So too was the thick black mass between her legs, matching the other mass held with a comb at her neck. Hard to tell where the tendrils that had escaped that comb became the tracery that followed her neck, she thought then. But for the fact of colour, they were one and the same – intricate and untamed and somehow intriguing, vines on a stalk that had no beginning, no end – some very black, some a kind of burnt umber, the last disappearing into the curve of her collarbone, which was pronounced, as were her high cheeks, wide hips and the crossed swords on her hip – lighter in tone than the vines on her neck, shimmering almost, a dark mother-of-pearl – weapons displayed on a pale armoury wall.

She moved her leg to one side but could not find what she looked for. She could have reached with her hand – infallible guide over the years – but it was the sight of the brushwork on her inner thighs she needed then, if only just once, and so she spread her legs wide and then merely stared, once more surprised, at the mystery of the calligraphy so near to her vagina – ancient inscription, it seemed, alongside a portal, both occulted. She merely glanced at the other mark, the abstract brushwork on her ribcage. Her hands had told her since she was a girl that they resembled the one on her thigh.

Which left only the half moon.

It was dark – the colour of her nipple – and like her nipple raised, textured, stark against the contrast of the white skin beneath. It was also precise, as though an artist had set out to make this *demi-lune* indelible, so that all the baths and all the showers and all the rainstorms of a lifetime could not erase its perfect curve.

How long she stood there she could not say. She no longer smelled paint, or felt heat, aware as she was at that moment first and foremost of colour – ivory black in her hair, permalba white in her skin, a palette of browns superimposed – taupe, terra cotta, Italian ochre, Havana bronze – and finally twice, toward the top of the canvas, unlikely splashes of magenta, repeated wherever she turned, as a roomful of mirrors returned her deep stare.

Little by little, in spite of the window left open, she once again smelled Jude's paint. In spite of the door closed between them, she again heard that tune, a jar or two opened, another jar closed and then a knock on the door.

"Caroline, stop fussing. That new place to change can't be new anymore. Just leave your things in a heap and we'll clean it up later."

As he spoke she pulled her pale skirt on.

"And leave your hair alone," he said as she thrust her arms into the sweater, "before this orchid wilts or my mistress walks out; either one disastrous."

Finally he heard her voice from the open doorway behind him.

"Forgive me. I remembered I'd left my necklace last time. After I dressed I tried to find it without disturbing you."

"I have it with me," he responded, brush and paints by his side, ready to go into that other place where shape and colour pushed the world to one side and even yearning dissolved, though it often left behind something enduring, like notes on a sonata score.

Caroline took her seat, affixed the flower to her comb, placed her right hand on her shoes, her left on the ropes at her neck.

"Gaze again at the terrace," Jude said after a moment. "Try to see what you saw yesterday."

She turned her head as instructed, fixing her eyes on a basket of jonquils, but all she could see was what she had recently seen – nothing more – even more vivid in her recollection than in the triple mirrors of his office.

Nevertheless, unmoving, she stared out over the city, forcing herself to keep the position of the previous day, exactly.

Jude, on the contrary, was far more restless than on the previous day. He moved back and forth, grasping the palette in his hand, filling in brushstrokes up close, combining colours far away. He shaped her hair, washed in the pallor of her skin, indicated shadows and a bit of the sun's glow on her face. All the while he was silent, except when he'd murmur some new instructions as the light in the studio shifted a bit. She too said nothing, hoping he wouldn't notice she wasn't really looking at the scene ahead.

As it happened, he had noticed at once. Something had changed – not in the pose, which she had maintained with exceptional discipline, down to the tilt of her head and the turn of her shoe, but in her expression. Her eyes seemed deeper, and yet the colour and shape he'd fixed at Chez Marianne were the same.

Her mouth perplexed him still more. Though slightly upturned still, as though the scene beyond pleased her, there was something new on her lips – neither pleasure nor amusement, but a more fulfilling resonance whose melody eluded him.

And yet he needed to score it. He had to define it, for this woman was different, essentially, from the person he'd sketched on the previous day, as identical twins stand apart. Until he succeeded, Jude knew his portrait would be a picture, nothing more – mere reproduction of a woman who'd come to visit him once and never returned.

Two more days passed; two more sittings. As he had never done better it seemed, Jude had captured even the most difficult textures with his brush – the velvet tapestry on the sofa, the difficult softness of the buds beside, the sheen of the mirror, the glaze of the bell jar reflected across from that sheen.

More striking perhaps were the colours he'd managed: a rich blend of jewel tones surpassed only by the precision of detail in the scene, summoned twice (one could almost say conjured) – once directly ahead, once inside the mirror's gaze.

Mrs. Devereux, though, had eluded him. Although her features were technically faultless – a perfect likeness in fact, absolutely correct within the proportions of her pallid face – they did not speak of her, or rather they spoke of another woman, someone who resembled her as the person at Place des Vosges did: exactly, and yet not at all.

Bedevilled, he would retouch after she'd go, rethink before she'd arrive, take extra time with each tone as she would sit for him, motionless. Her black hair alone had taken almost a sitting, for he had painted it slowly, as if he were running his fingers through it, loosened, though he had never seen it unclasped.

It was no use. Toward the end of the fifth day, he knew he was stymied. He was tempted to cancel the last session they'd scheduled, but as she changed out of her clothes in his office – for some reason always a lengthy procedure – he stared at the canvas and wondered if the fault lay, of all things, in the absence of sound. For a week he had worked in silence – an atypical procedure for him – but one which had occurred because of his increasing concentration, his increasing frustration and Mrs. Devereux's clear reluctance to break the stillness in the room.

True, Jude reflected, every night she'd talk freely as they savoured their pleasant suppers at Chez Marianne. She would speak of her travels, books that she'd read, others she'd translated during her brief stay in Holland. She would describe her father, her uncle, her uncle's apartment, her cousin Lucien. Yet of herself she had said little. The few times he'd asked, she had deflected the intrusion with a related query of her own, as deft as it was courteous, about his own life, his own career, his aspirations – public and private.

Thus he knew next to nothing of her home in Connecticut – just that it was large, an old farm, with many acres – a place that she loved. Still less did he know of her husband, for she had referred to him only once, in the dark arcade of Place des Vosges, afterwards avoiding any mention of his practice, his person, the Critical Care Center where they met. And yet, Jude surmised, with the perception not uncommon to an artist with his eyesight, therein lay the key – one of them anyway – the one that would open the vault, deep in her head, where the portrait he wanted was stored for safekeeping.

Had he the right, though, for a canvas, to force entrance there? She'd taken great pains to exclude him. She was entitled to her reasons. She was entitled to remain inviolate. She was taking an awfully long time to reappear from his office.

He looked up from his easel. Not a sound could be heard. Whatever it was that would be on her mouth when she did emerge – and she would emerge in good time – looking radiant, refreshed, her lips somehow fuller, the smile more enigmatic – whatever it was she wouldn't share, he decided, carefully wiping his brushes, she could keep to herself. He had other commissions waiting. Two years' worth of work. For that matter – he scraped his palette clean – it would not be the first time a soul had escaped him. Indeed, one or two of his works had disappointed him in this regard. And yet they had been applauded. They'd fetched astronomical sums. No one had ever suspected what he had known. They were shells, nothing more, done with a mastery all the more poignant in the absence of spirit eluding capture.

"Again I have detained you," he heard. "I am sorry."

She was standing at the entrance of the changing room, hand on the doorknob still, smiling. Her sweater – he had come to expect one – was a brilliant, arresting cerulean blue, her long floral skirt tones of black, sand and blue. She walked to him, slowly, with that same, barely perceptible swaying step – poplar-like – he had first noticed at the Crillon.

And yet it was not the same. This step was surer, the strides longer, the sway of the hips ever so slightly more pronounced – all of it contained, nothing overtly sexual, the whole movement full of allure nonetheless, like a slow tango in Montmartre, or the lush controlled strokes of a painter who can see at last.

"You could let me help you with your brushes, Jude. Just this once. Unless" – again she smiled – "like that canvas you won't show me yet, they belong to some hallowed ground traversed only by the anointed."

He stared at her.

"Please don't deny me."

Still he said nothing.

"Lucien won't mind waiting. He's grown to like Raphael's place – more so now than before – now there's a stillness that seems to include him."

Knowledge, Jude said to himself.

She took the brush from his hand. "There. You look exhausted."

How could I have missed it? he wondered.

"I promise. I will not look at the picture. Not 'til you tell me I can, Jude."

Knowledge, he said again in his head.

He glanced one more time at her face, then again at the painting, then back again at the face, just to be sure.

He was right. There it was. When he had met her it was absent, or banished, or unimagined – he could not yet say. There was experience now in her violet eyes, worldliness on her mouth, so that her smile – still enigmatic – was no longer wistful, but knowing.

Hence the change in her expression. Like Eve, she had trespassed, and very recently, tasting a rare and proscribed and very powerful fruit, something that had made her wise – no, not wise, not even informed – that she had been before – but hungry.

In the process – now it was clear to him – her vague and ethereal beauty was gone. In its place – this too was now clear, despite the pallor and slender proportions and supple grace she still managed, there was a more profane appeal – unassailable, ripening, fruit of the fruit that had been kept from her, stringently, because of the hold it would forever have.

She was wiping the brush in her hand, unaware of the fact that he was searching her, searching himself, wondering how he could have been so blind. Then, as she returned the brush to him and asked for another and began stroking the bristles, calmly – in spite of the sun that had moved and was now in her eyes and the fumes from the turpentine jar he'd just opened – he understood. She had willed his confusion. Expertly, with a self-mastery that was habitual and an abhorrence of revelation that had made deception second nature, she had withheld from him, daily, what he most needed to know. For almost a week she had succeeded. But for that moment in his doorway, when he had somehow remembered a sunset dance step in Pigalle, she would have succeeded. They would have parted in a day or so – a soon-forgotten friendship – her sampled fruit a secret still, his painting forever failed.

Failure now, Jude decided, was out of the question. In fact, he determined, as he surrendered yet another brush, arranging the ones she returned to him in meticulous order beside his paint jars, he would now accept only the painting he'd dreamed of. Nothing other than a triumph. She had attempted to deceive him, or at the very least hold back from him – they were one and the same between model and painter – and his scruples no longer obtained. His reluctance to intrude was gone. Only the portrait ruled now, its demands, like a descant, soaring above the mere needs of this girl.

"Chez Marianne again?" he asked. "Nine o'clock thereabouts?"

She seemed uncertain.

"We could make it later."

She placed the rope with her jewels on his cart filled with paints.

"You needn't feel each night, Jude – I mean because there are no fees involved – whatever models charge that is…"

"They charge what we settle on. We agreed on the pleasure of your company, for a week's worth of sittings – a day or two more if the portrait took longer. I have perhaps been greedy in wanting to extend each day. Certainly presumptuous."

Coaxing the bracelet from her wrist she replied, "You make my time here sound like penance."

"It can be difficult."

"It has been wonderful."

"At the very least a challenge," he allowed with a laugh. "You'll remember that much for sure."

As he closed the last of his paint jars, he felt the pressure of her hand on his arm.

"I will remember it all, Jude," she said. "I will remember your garden, your sculptures, your office, the way that you work here…" She faltered, then withdrew her hand, as though surprised by where it rested. "I will remember it all," she repeated, and then she was silent, looking down at her hands again.

With effort, he forced himself to say nothing, remain motionless, giving her time to look his way again. Somehow, he sensed, without intrusion on his part, she was about to reveal what he had determined to pry from her.

He was mistaken. If anything, as she left that afternoon, she had become even more of an enigma, for all she had confessed in the renewed stillness by his paint cart was that she was capable of understanding things he had never expressed.

"I do know how you work, you know," she had said, looking up finally from her hands. "I have recorded every detail, though you have posed me looking elsewhere. I've heard you fret, and pace, and sketch, and mix; I've heard the scrape of your knife when you've applied too much paint; I know each brush that you use." She'd cocked her head slightly, as if straining to hear the echo of things remembered.

"The square brush makes a bolder sound – that's when you're sure of yourself – too sure sometimes," she'd rightly guessed, "and then I hear that rag you use, and I lament, though I'm looking away, as it rubs up and down against the obstinate cloth and makes the day's work disappear."

It had taken him years to know this. He had not yet confessed it to his students.

"The narrow one scratches," she went on. "You almost never paint with it. It has occurred to me that it may be too flimsy, not like Saturday's child – I mean that thick saucy brush – the one you call on when you're in a matching mood, which isn't often, but when it is and you stop pacing and let your hands work as they're meant to do – that's the one that loves you back, no questions asked."

Abruptly she'd stopped then. And then again quickly, as though the words were a parcel recovered, "I am glad I got to clean that brush. I have loved it, Jude, by proxy."

Preparing for their supper at Chez Marianne later that night, Jude pondered the irony. He had revealed himself, saying nothing, day after day for almost a week. She had continued to elude him, speaking freely. Over supper, he promised himself, he would rectify the disproportion.

☽☾

Over supper, as it happened, the disproportion increased. Jude queried; Caroline demurred; Jude responded; Caroline parried. Thus they had each sparkled like fireworks over the Tuileries, providing nothing more than amusement as a near half moon rose over the Seine.

A chess game, Jude concluded, walking along the Left Bank toward his home behind Les Invalides. She had never let him accompany her to her rooms near the Sorbonne. Instead they would linger each night on the deserted corner beside the café, hearing the heavy doors lock behind them, watching the bistro lights fade inside, talking of many things still – always of many things, never of Mrs. Devereux – and then they would part, she toward the shadows of the Latin Quarter to the west, he to the grand boulevards in the opposite direction.

Tomorrow, thought Jude, entering his darkened house, *I will not paint in silence.*

He turned the lights on in his studio, removed the sheet from his canvas, stared at his failure, tried to imagine her caught off guard by the change.

She'd keep her pose to be sure, but it would be a strain in the heat, and he had determined with a single-mindedness that masked a cruelty he preferred not to investigate that there would be heat, not even a breeze, for he would close the river doors this one time – there remained this one time, nothing more, and without its critical revelations his portrait would forever fail.

She would of course show no fatigue. He would not once appear tired. And yet at some point – he was sure of it – whatever she wouldn't share would collide with the means employed to conceal it, like mismatched plates in the earth.

He would know it at once. He'd see a shrug perhaps, a smile, a blush – faults in the surface of the smoothness of her demeanour, things he'd been trained as a boy to observe – and yet he'd press on, work 'til the sun set, and she would never object, never resist, surrendering more hints in her exhaustion – suggestions, a recollection or two and then hopefully truth – a confidence shared at the end of the day, in the heat of the day.

At the end of the day she was exhausted, as he'd predicted, from the strain and the heat and the endless conversation.

His portrait, however, had forever failed. She had disclosed nothing.

Jude walked out onto his terrace that night, sank into a chaise longue beside the railing, lit up a cigarette and sipped a martini in the stillness. He had invited Mrs. Devereux to dine at Chez Marianne after they'd worked, but she had declined.

"I need a bath," she had said, "and then a long walk to stretch my legs. It isn't often they're tucked beneath me for the better part of a summer's day."

It was said brightly, without the slightest annoyance – not even a hint of the resentment another model might have expressed.

"Tomorrow night then?"

"Tomorrow?" She had considered, carefully folding her clothes. "I can't. Lucien's box at the theatre. I thought for sure you'd be there, Jude."

"No. I'll want to touch up some tomorrow. No telling how long I'll be at it."

The necklace and bracelet were already in her shoulder bag. As yet she had not been invited to look at the portrait.

"Well you must call me when it's finished, Jude – when you're happy, I mean. I haven't forgotten your first lecture."

And then she had paused before repeating, "The client is pleased when I am, Mrs. Devereux."

"I did say that."

"Do you remember my answer?"

"It was a question."

"Yes," she'd said, surprised that he hadn't forgotten. And then she had laughed – not at him, she'd explained, but at the absurdity of her *not* being pleased with something he'd worked on.

He'd heard the firm zip of the black bag as it closed.

"Which is why I've been so patient, Jude. I don't mean sitting here. I mean not looking yet. When it is ready you will let me know. I may even know before you announce it. There will be something in the air."

The clock in his hallway had chimed then. Six-thirty.

"Time for us both now to rest," she'd said simply. "You above all, I think."

Jude remembered those chimes, counting them in his head as he lay on the terrace, lighting his third cigarette, while a gossamer cloud shrouded that slender half-circle trying to light up the side of the Seine he loved best.

He poured himself a second drink. Songs from the Esplanade reached his veranda. As he listened he heard that old prophesy, resurrected.

"A self-absorption that will ruin you, Jude."

Well at least this time, he thought grimly, the fault was not his. She had wanted him blind. With self-absorption greater than his, she had succeeded.

And yet, he had to admit, as he watched that cloud stubbornly cling and the night remain dark, he was impressed by her endurance. She had withstood him, serenely. Model, assistant, devil and muse, Caroline was, above all, a worthy opponent.

He was about to doze off. He may have slept a bit – he was not sure – but something startled him after a moment. He sat up quickly. Wisps of clouds only remained, trailing northwards. In its place was the half moon, seemingly perfect, needing no other fullness.

Of all things light, he thought, *nearing midnight.*

He looked around one more time. The railing was yellow, the roses off-white, the whole terrace transformed in a pale citron glow – not enough to paint by, more than enough to think things through.

After a while he stood, walked into the living room and rang up the little hotel by the Sorbonne.

"Can you come back?" he asked.

"To see the painting?"

"To pose one more time."

The silence that followed seemed endless, infernal.

"If that is what you need, Jude…"

"That is what I need."

"I could do it on Monday."

"Tomorrow."

"Tomorrow?"

It was a feeble sound, uncertain, like the cicadas in Tucson after the frost in September.

"First thing," he insisted. "You'll have to bring your clothes again, your jewels. Better still wear them all – we haven't time for preparation."

He could almost feel her exhaustion.

"I said a week to you, I remember that. But I also recall that I said *more or less*. In this case I have decided — after time spent again with the work…"

"No need to explain, Jude. I'm only sorry you have had to work tonight. Please get some sleep now. I'll be there in the morning."

As he walked out again onto his terrace, he was irritated, almost unnerved. Could the woman truly be so naive? Did she not resent in the least his bad behaviour that afternoon? Or was she instead – as he increasingly suspected – supremely, uncommonly, magnificently arrogant?

He hoped in his heart it was the latter, for he had determined on a tactic that could not possibly fail him. On a trusting soul, he well knew, the manoeuvre would be unforgivable. On a worthy opponent it was brilliant. He decided to assume she was the latter – absolutely – because of her endurance, the rhythmic way in which her skirt moved and the fact that his art demanded he distort life, come what may.

⟡

It was as Jude had suspected. After two hours the next day, despite Caroline's cheerful willingness to maintain her pose perfectly, as long as might be required, the painting remained a failure. He put his brush down, wiped his hands with his rag, laid his palette on the cart and called for a break.

"Are you sure, Jude?"

"No one is ever sure."

"Then let's go on for a bit…"

"No. Yesterday's session left me exhausted. I shouldn't have worked then but I did. I've got to pace myself now."

Doing as he instructed, she answered mildly – and it was part of his plan, this politeness she relied upon – "If you like."

He opened the terrace doors that faced west onto the Seine. She stood, stretched and smoothed her skirt out a bit. Not since their first sitting had she glanced at the portrait. Now for some reason, having seen how stubbornly he had pushed himself, she felt an overwhelming temptation to see the image that had bedevilled him.

She looked behind her. Jude had moved from the door. There was a chance now, she told herself as she began moving toward the easel. Halfway across the room she stopped. Jude was nowhere in sight. Yet she remained where she was, motionless, not out of scruples, or reticence, but because he would know. He would return from his break, take up his paints, see that his work had been invaded, know that the intruder had been his model.

How could she say to him then, "I was curious, Jude," or "I was impatient," or "It was time, Jude, after all?"

It was not time as yet, and she knew it, and so she turned and followed Jude through the open doors to the veranda.

He was on his chaise, next to a wrought-iron table, a pack of cigarettes in his right hand, a box of matches in his left.

"I didn't know you smoked, Jude."

"When I want to relax I do."

"Not once, though, during all of our suppers…"

"I didn't need to relax then."

Nodding, she slipped into the seat beside him.

"Join me?"

"I don't smoke."

"Never tried it?"

"No. Not that I can remember. No, I never have," she repeated, clearly agitated by the question, which he had guessed would be the case.

"You don't mind if I do…"

"Please," she said, assenting with a slight, barely perceptible wave of her hand.

The match burst into flame, then failed abruptly.

"There's always a breeze in this spot," Jude remarked, "even on the hottest days."

"Lovely, though," she responded, yet she had not raised her face to it, nor to the view stretching beyond, but was instead looking fixedly at the small box of long sticks.

He struck a second match, holding his hand over the box, and that too failed in the wind.

The third time, turning his back to the wind, he struck the match slowly, then raised it carefully into the space between them. He saw her eyes widen, the colour drain from her face, her right hand rise ever so slightly while he held the match there, as though to shield it from the wind. It was a needless gesture, as it happened, for the flame was burning vigorously, with an almost demonic defiance.

And then – astonished – he watched her place her palm over the heat, not to shield the match but extinguish it, slowly, letting the flame burn her flesh until the increasing weight of her hand put the match out beneath it. As she did so – and it seemed to Jude to have taken forever – she'd raised her eyes to his. It was a look he would never forget: neither rebellion nor supplication, but a calm reflection of her decision to confront whatever demons still lay within. To have stirred up those demons had been Jude's intention, to have sparked a reaction – the only one he felt assured of – and in so doing to have shattered the shell that kept her from him. Now, watching the shell burn – the outer casing at least – he would have given anything – his heart, his eyes, even his hands – to have annulled what he had done. For a moment or two he just stared at her, speechless, the view of Paris behind her a mere flame-coloured blur.

"Caroline," he murmured, as she began to move her hand away. "Forgive me…"

"It was not your fault…"

He grabbed her wrist, holding her hand in the air. "Yes, yes it was…"

"There are things you don't know."

"That's just it. It *was* my fault. My God, look at this," he cried, staring at the ugly blue-black stain on her hand.

And then he was on his knees holding her wrist still as though to examine it more closely, in reality to beg for the forgiveness he did not merit.

"Jude," she said, trying to wrench her hand free, for she had suddenly sensed the beginning of pain in her palm.

"Come," he replied standing, pulling her up with him in the process, for the sensation of pain seemed to have passed into his own hand and he was focused no more on the deed but on its result.

She was quiet, almost impassive, as he dressed her hand in his bathroom. He too said little, concentrating on the delicate task of cleansing the wound before he could anesthetise it, slightly, with a cooling sweet-smelling unguent that made her head spin.

"Just a little more," he said, pulling another jar from his shelf. "This will ward off infection, for the moment at least, until I can get you to a hospital."

"No…"

"They can perhaps do something more…"

"*No*, Jude," she repeated.

"I am not a doctor," he insisted.

"You've dressed my hand like one."

"Nevertheless…"

"It has amazed me, in fact."

"I work alone here," he explained. "With chemicals. From time to time, there has been need."

She noticed the way his artist's hands wrapped the long bandage in a pattern.

"Until today," he went on, his voice as subdued as his fingers were firm, "I've been the only one to get treatment."

"Well there you are," she said, forcing a buoyant tone. "Look at *your* hands."

"No," he replied, "Look at yours. I did that, Mrs. Devereux. You must allow me now to be certain you have at least had proper care."

He took a box from the shelf and searched in its contents for a clamp. Meanwhile, very carefully, as though she had not heard his last words, she picked up the scissors he'd placed alongside her.

"There," she said, snipping the long strip of gauze that dangled down below her wrist. "Nothing more to be done. I'll just put this clamp on..."

"And then we'll go," he said.

He heard the scissors drop, saw her pale face in his mirror, felt her well hand on his arm – much like the pressure he'd felt when she'd described his work to him, two days earlier, although that heartfelt confession now seemed light-years away.

"We will go nowhere, Jude."

"Caroline..."

"Nowhere, do you understand me?"

He did not recognize that sound. More than resolute, it was unsparing, unconditional – as far from the lilt he'd first heard at the Cyrano play as Rostand's hero that night was from the shy man he was hiding.

"You must," he began.

"No," she cried. "*Never!* No one will touch me! Not a particle will be scraped from me! Not one knife – no black thread – none of that gauze that they use that keeps the air from one's mouth. *I will not go, Jude, do you hear me?* What you have done for me will do."

She stopped, suddenly showing the strain. He turned away from her, only to be confronted by her image in the mirror. After a moment it spoke to him also, though in a steadier tone, one that he recognized now as merely surface self-possession, something akin to a delicate skin graft, precarious defence against the raw wounds of life.

"I am immensely grateful to you for your efforts," the voice went on. "We can still work in fact. I am assuming you will not need this hand for what is left to be done."

He was unable to answer.

"Just let me just wash up here – I won't be a moment – and then I'll join you and we'll work again."

She took the clamp from his hand and affixed it clumsily to her bandage. "I won't be a moment," she repeated before he turned, closed the door and crossed the hall into his studio.

Caroline found a washcloth and rinsed her face with her free hand. With the same hand she smoothed her hair back, tucking as many strands as she could into her comb. Then she too stepped into the hallway – only to stop again and listen – for there was something about the silence that unsettled her, as the stillness in a cypress grove under livid clouds always did.

Jude was on the south veranda when Caroline opened his studio door.

"I'll just take my place," she said, uncertainly.

He did not turn.

"Though we may need another iris, perhaps not – this one might do, Jude, what do you think?

Still he did not answer.

"Jude?" she asked slowly.

He was leaning against the railing, looking southeast over the fortress of l'École Militaire, its inscrutable, immense façade casting a shadow across the park alongside.

She noticed he still held the scissors she'd dropped. Then she recalled that the silence had not been a true peace – there'd been a tearing sound – twice, she recalled, irreversible, like the rending of illusion's cloth.

She remained on the sofa, reluctant to join him on the terrace – for that would have meant skirting the portrait, off limits still, although nothing at that point seemed to resemble what it had recently been.

"The light will fail soon," she ventured.

"Yes. Yes it will," he replied, staring out at the view still.

"Jude," she said after a moment. "Please, let us begin now – something at least – you may yet find what you need today."

He turned to her and shook his head. Still she did not understand. Not until he entered the room and stood beside the easel, silently, scissors in his hand still, did she begin to sense what had occurred.

It cannot be, she told herself.

"We cannot work," she heard him say.

Carefully, Caroline stood.

"Forgive me," he added.

She moved to the easel. He did not try to stop her. Facing the painting still, after what seemed a long time to him she spoke – or rather whispered, as if her fingernails had scratched the words.

"You had no right, Jude."

"I had no choice."

"We both owned this work."

"Yes and no."

"Yes and no?" she repeated, looking at last into his face.

The stillness in the room resembled the Seine before dawn.

"Well of course there was no contract. I never signed papers, forms – not even a napkin over dinner. Nevertheless," she continued, although it was clear to them both she would not manage. "Nevertheless," she repeated, and then she stumbled, irretrievably. In the presence of her defaced portrait her self-mastery failed. She felt humbled – no, something far more public, worse, something she'd spent a lifetime avoiding: humiliation.

In its wake – and the force of it stunned her – came a great surge of anger, checked for decades, now a dam burst, destroying her final, carefully crafted, unassailable line of defence. For the first time since her childhood, Mrs. Devereux was without grace.

"What made you think," she asked hoarsely, "that you could destroy me?"

"I did not cut you."

"You slashed it all."

"All but you."

"It was all one, Jude!" she cried. "You said so when you posed me! The bell jar, the flower, the mirror, my hair, *me*."

"Yes. Then it was."

"And now what?"

"Now it is finished," he replied, his tone devoid of expression, although his eyes remained – almost tenderly – fixed on his canvas. "Although you are there still."

After an appalling silence she took the scissors with her free hand.

"Caroline," he said warily.

She seemed not to hear him.

"Caroline, *don't...*"

She studied the painting a moment. Pointing the tip of the shears at the longest gash that he'd made, left to right across the mirror, she observed, "I really don't see, Jude, why you stopped here."

"Please give me those."

With the same tip she touched the comb – painted beautifully, although reversed, because it was reflected – and then she touched the iris, also backward, left to right, and then she cut them both.

"As to this other gash,"

"*Caroline...*"

"Why is it also too short?"

"Enough," he begged.

"Enough for what?"

"Enough to remind me of what I have done."

"Nonsense," she answered, cutting the loops in her necklace

He took a step toward her. She cut the sandals next.

"No more," she heard.

"Half of it mine, Jude. I've a ways to go still."

He saw the sweater go, then the diaphanous skirt. Then, as she dragged the shears upward, she heard again, although in a voice no longer pleading, "No more!"

"One more."

"Not your face," he warned.

"That's all that's left."

"That will remain!" and then she felt his grip on her wrist.

For a moment they struggled.

"Have you no feelings?" she gasped.

"Not your face," he repeated. Still she resisted, clutching the scissors like a lifeline.

She had more strength than he'd imagined. He was compelled to apply more pressure, slowly, although it hurt him to do so, but in the end he had his way. With a splintering sound the scissors fell to the tiles.

The noise recalled them to the room – verifiable rectangle – quotidian dimensions indifferent to desperation.

And then there was quiet, save for the rustle of a lemon tree on the veranda, as they both simply stared at the shears on the floor. When they looked up again, finally, they were across a great precipice, in some foreign land, wordless.

Jude broke the silence. "I am sorry," he murmured, "I have done nothing but hurt you."

"You have hurt only your work."

"That no longer matters."

He looked at the canvas. Strips of torn cloth hung down; other cuts seemed to be biding their time, as though they preferred to fall later, under cover of darkness.

Perhaps to allow this, very slowly, Jude unfolded a drape and covered his portrait, adjusting the sheet as a coroner would, with professional precision.

Caroline watched in silence, stroking the wrist he had grasped with the one he had bandaged. Both hands for some reason had become one source of pain.

Jude guessed this when he faced her. He was about to speak and then he stopped, deciding he hadn't the strength to hurt her once more. *She needn't know after all*, he told himself. *It will be better this way*.

He was wrong. As he untied his paint-stained smock, she said, "If I only knew *why*. To the end of my days I shall want to know why, nothing more."

She tugged the iris from her comb. It resisted her and then gave way.

"I will always wonder why you hated my image so, Jude."

He took the flower she gave him. Its texture was docile, alluring, yet for once he felt no need to reproduce that sensation onto a cloth. There was only one pressing thing now and it had to be spoken after all.

He was glad he had removed that smock, covered his canvas, placed the scissors he had retrieved back into his toolbox, for nothing lingered then of the artist, and so he was able to say, without avoiding her eyes, "It was not an accident on the veranda."

She failed to process his words.

"Which means..." he went on.

"Jude, what are you saying?"

"I am saying..." he continued, and then faltered, and then he reminded himself that the truth would hurt less than the misconception she would harbour when she left him that day – and she would leave him that day, he was sure of it – never knowing that he had defaced *himself*, the painter – not her, the woman who had consumed him.

"I am saying," he repeated, "that it was planned out there, every moment of our break today, though by the third match I thought I'd failed and then the wind held off, and I succeeded."

She still seemed perplexed by the invasion of syllables.

"If you could tell me again..."

"Christ..."

"I don't understand."

"What else could I do?" he burst out, "facing a failure of such proportion? As a model you failed me!"

No sooner uttered, the words repulsed him. He had intended to blame himself. He had stripped himself, draped his portrait, locked away his tools and yet in the end the artist had lurked nearby, forcing the words from his mouth.

"I never moved," she stammered.

"Yet you were here only once, that first time. And still I looked for you, Caroline, day after day, as I have never searched before," he went on clumsily, condemned to shape his longing with language, a hard tool, inexpressive – not like his courteous, pliable paints.

She glanced at the sheet he had draped.

"Not there," he cried, "*There*, where you sat for me, not moving a muscle."

She turned where he pointed. There was neither the loveseat, nor the rose bowl, nor the ebony clock alongside. She saw only herself once again in the mirror above them and Jude moving toward her, until the precipice disappeared.

"I'd've done anything to paint you," she heard him say close behind her. "*Anything, do you understand me?*"

"Madness," she whispered.

"Madness, yes. An obsession I've known before, many times, each time I've held a brush in my hand. But nothing like this."

He reached out for her hair. She could have moved from him then – she told herself she should move, and quickly – but she just stood there, watching him touch her in the gilt-edged frame straight ahead. He traced the curve of her neck, her shoulders, her forearm, the fingers he'd bandaged with care.

"Until you offered this hand," he said, stroking it lightly, "nothing had ever mattered to me but a cloth stretched over a frame. And yet there it was, outstretched like a child's – first to extinguish the flame, then to have me dress its wounds – both with a kind of trust only a porcelain bowl has ever shown."

She let him caress the charred hand.

"You should have known better, Caroline. I had already chosen art over the flesh you had offered."

"You can't mean that," she managed.

"Every word of it."

"*You wanted to burn me?*"

"I wanted to see you."

She kept her eyes on the mirror, so as to decode the sounds with her sight, which she had just learned to use.

"Dredging that fear up," he continued, "the one that made your eyes wild at Place des Vosges Sunday night. I didn't know why then – I still don't know why – except for the fact that a flame would expose you. That was all I had to go by. It was enough. For a canvas, now covered, I was willing to make you afraid once again."

She thought she saw a bitter smile, quickly, play on the face still reflected.

"To no end, as it happened. I never did see the hidden you. Only the man I have kept from myself all these years. It is a soul more in need of repair than any canvas I may have destroyed." He let his hand drop as he said again, "I am sorry."

Caroline did leave him that day, as he knew she would do, with absolute understanding. It was what he wanted – no illusions about his motives, no false assumptions about her allure. Because the latter had been so unsettling, the former had been so cruel.

And yet he could not help wondering, as he watched her gather her things, how prudent his candid confession had been. To release her from self-hatred, he had made sure she would loathe him. There was no comfort in the gesture.

At the doorway she turned one last time. "We should have been satisfied with *la vie en rose*, Jude. It is always a mistake to try and see things distinctly."

Her footsteps resounded down the long, polished hall. His heavy front door closed. Off in the distance it seemed, like the bizarre denouement of a violent dream, the frail metal cage slowly returned her to the street.

For the next four days it rained. Caroline didn't mind. Just after sunrise each morning, as the old courtyard gate of the Hôtel du Dauphin closed behind her, she would set out for Raphael's house on the Île St-Louis. Not once had she noticed the sheets of rain assaulting the Seine. Even her steps on the stones as she advanced seemed to belong to someone else moving east, away from the cold and impassive façade of the Mint, past the empty Pont-Neuf, the battered boats underneath, everything gunmetal grey in the mist.

She had walked that route west the first day she'd arrived – could it have been just three weeks ago? – strolling languidly along the river on her way to the Crillon. The wind had been hot and fierce against her body that day. Now it was wet and cold, blowing against the awnings that shielded the bistros south of the quay, banging the shutters above them, the painted signs alongside, the metal locks on the bookstalls, the recollections inside her head.

And yet she would continue, determined, a solitary figure beneath the lamps casting their glow in the rain. She'd pass St-Julien church, St-Séverin just behind, the deserted maze of alleys twisting south toward the Sorbonne. Off in the distance a bell would toll Matins. She would be halfway across Pont de l'Archevêché by that time, heading north toward the tip of the Île St-Louis. There, above the misty towpaths along the prow-shaped tip of the Quai de Bourbon, was Raphael's apartment – empty like everything else.

It was not a large place – living room beyond the entrance hall, bedroom beyond that – both with beamed ceilings, white walls, French windows facing the river across a wrought-iron railing, black and gold against the stone.

And so it all ends, Caroline mused at Raphael's desk on this fourth day. *Everything to be catalogued and prepared for auction, proceeds bequeathed discreetly to a Mademoiselle Anne-Sophie d'Alembert.*

She had never met Anne-Sophie. Still, from Raphael's conversations, she felt she knew much of her life – how they had met in the bookstore she owned beside Place de l'Odéon, how they had fallen in love in spite of his obligations, his wife, his children, the impossibility of a marriage between them. Twice she had given him up. Twice she had returned to him. All throughout she'd kept her house in the Marais, her shop, the ordered life she'd always lived – for Raphael's stays in France were never extended, and even in Paris his writer's commitments could surface.

Nevertheless, she had existed for him and him alone from the first moment they'd met. He had asked for a volume of Keats from her doorway. She had said "English or French?" and he'd said "Italian."

"That may take me a day, perhaps two," she had managed, avoiding the navy eyes that matched his suit, the slate-grey tie just like his hair.

"I am not in a hurry, Mademoiselle."

"In that case, please return."

He did return; his Keats was there; they'd gone out for some tea; she'd never again failed to appear whenever his circumstances had allowed.

Nearly two decades later, arriving at nine as arranged on the first warm night in March, it was she who had called an ambulance, finding Raphael sprawled on the brick-toned kitchen tiles.

"Heart attack cause of death," she was told – simple as that, for she seemed to them all but an acquaintance, a neighbour perhaps – certainly not a wife to whom condolences would have been offered.

Caroline tried to picture Anne-Sophie as she worked, venturing upon the letters marked *Private Correspondence* in the last drawer.

Dark-haired no doubt, slim as a reed and dressed mostly in black, she surmised, for there were no pictures of her in the photograph file, no letters from her in the bulky folder of faded notes. It was as though she had never existed, except in Raphael's recollection. At the memorial service, where friends and family of the poet had all gathered together, she had made no appearance.

Or had she? Who would have known if she had sat in the draughty last row at St-Germain-des-Prés that day, mourning the love of her life, knowing she could never speak of it?

Caroline tried to remember the service in detail. She opened the guest book, scanned the signatures scrawled on the ivory sheets, searched for a name, initials – some trace of the woman whose existence made her own life seem real.

There was nothing.

Faithful to the end, it seemed, Anne-Sophie had discreetly disappeared.

Bitter destiny, Caroline thought, carefully closing the signature book. *To have loved for almost half a lifetime. To have been denied any avowal.*

Angelus was announced from the nearby church of St-Louis-en-l'Île. An eternity seemed to have passed since Caroline had heard *Matins* crossing Pont de l'Archevêché, and yet it was only one day, fourth in the week since she was no longer Jude's model, and the rain was still heavy upon the river beside the quay.

She put the folders aside, turned the lamps out on her desk, stood in the shadows and heard a step on the stairs.

"Lucien?" she called out.

The apartment door opened slowly.

"Lucien, is that you?"

"No," she heard a woman's voice respond. "No it is I, Caroline. Anne-Sophie d'Alembert."

Caroline reflected later, as they talked over coffee, how little Anne-Sophie resembled the image she had formed of her. She was plump, very fair, with light brown hair, a round face, a small heart-shaped mouth and dark merry eyes. Her hands were graceful – also plump – with beautiful nails painted pale pink. They showed to advantage the lovely diamond ring she wore, not on her left hand but her right, and the one single gold bracelet with its locket charm on her wrist.

"Caroline," she had repeated then, sensing she was being studied. "I should have called before I came. I just never imagined…"

She fumbled, folding and unfolding her expressive hands.

"I came to return the keys, pick up a few things, clothes mostly, some letters – I did not want strangers…"

"I would not have read them."

"I do not count you a stranger."

Said so simply, the words fell like rain on them both.

"Anne-Sophie," Caroline said after a moment. "They are not here. I have been through the files."

"They are here."

"Perhaps in a vault…"

"They are here," she repeated.

Caroline made no answer. Anne-Sophie rose, crossed to the fireplace, took down a fine painted box and returned to her seat.

"Your uncle once said his only treasures were in this box. In all these years I never looked. And yet I am confident…" She looked up searchingly as she spoke so that it was quite clear to Caroline she was not certain at all.

"We needn't look now, Anne-Sophie."

"There is no other time."

"I will be here several days."

"There have already been many days. I…The sooner I know the better," she said abruptly. "And I need to know, Caroline. I need to know this one thing. I was only a part of his life, never enough you will think, but like a first love unbidden, never forgotten, it was in its own way more enduring than any sanctified bond."

She leaned forward a bit, like a penitent in the dark at St-Séverin's church. "He said as much to me – many times – but now, tonight, when his voice can no longer answer and no other witness remains…" Again she broke off. Through the raindrops streaking the windows the arc of the street lamps became distorted.

"I need to know," she repeated, smoothing her skirt out. "That is all."

Caroline opened the box.

"There are two envelopes here. The first," she said reaching inside, "is marked *Family Photos*. The second is tied with a pale yellow ribbon."

There was a moment.

"They are your letters."

Anne-Sophie sat back. "I knew you would find them," she breathed.

"Yes."

"He felt just as I did – I was sure of it – although it was hard for him to say things, which is surprising," she reflected, taking the packet Caroline offered, "as he was a poet."

"It is not craft which bedevils an artist. It is life," Caroline heard herself say.

"For that very reason, I guess, it was often not easy. He could be difficult. He had a temper. Sometimes in fact…" she stopped.

"Forgive me. He was your uncle."

"And therefore difficult," replied Caroline, "like my father, his twin."

Their eyes met.

"Though as a diplomat my father was forced, over time, to substitute protocol for his passions."

"Raphael couldn't risk it. He was like a man possessed. It almost drove me to despair – that fierceness he had – the way he'd get angry, intemperate, desperate for the sounds denied to more timid souls. Ah, but when he'd find it – and he would, Caroline, in a piece of music, in a book, often right there," she avowed, gesturing to the window and the intensifying constellations of city lights in the night. "He would gaze out at the river and then return to his desk and I could tell from the sound of his pen on the page – swift, no hesitations, a sound that would last until dawn when it occurred – that he had won that night's round. Whatever glimpse the gods had vouchsafed had been recorded, etched for all time in blank verse, or a series of couplets – sonnets perhaps, so that the timid souls would see and understand your uncle's need."

The delicate box on Caroline's lap seemed suddenly heavy in the dark.

"In fact, Caroline, I will confess to you, since you have been so kind..." Anne-Sophie paused one last time as she stood, "It was enough for me then, lying at noon in his arms, to have been a part of his triumph."

Shortly past seven, as Caroline locked the apartment, she recalled having seen signs for a concert at St-Sulpice church that same night.

"I can make it," she decided, not yet willing to face her rooms on the rue Séguier.

⸺☾⸺

All throughout Bach's *Goldberg Variations*, Caroline found herself staring at the Delacroix mural on the wall above her. She had slipped into one of the extra chairs that had been placed beside the side chapel. Behind, soaring like gates around some celestial space, were the immense pipes of the organ of St-Sulpice church. Ahead were the curves in the double staircase to the pulpit. Like everything else it seemed unreal that night, a pillar of fire suspended in shadows.

But it was the mural that held her attention. She was transfixed by it for some reason, unsettled by the image of Jacob wrestling with the angel, his powerful body straining, every muscle pushed to the limits of human endurance. His head was down but not bowed; his left arm gripped the angel's waist, his right hand pushed in vain against the angel's left hand. Pale tones across the background seemed to herald night's end, and therefore the end of the contest, and for that very reason, perhaps, Jacob's left leg was raised, bent at the knee, all the strength he could summon pushing that knee into the angel's thigh – last crucial chance to pin his enormous opponent.

Sensing this possibility – unthinkable until that moment – the angel fought back. His right hand gripped Jacob's thigh. His head too seemed to bend until it engaged Jacob's brow.

And then the music intruded. The concert's end was approaching, its penultimate *Variation* recalling Caroline from that strife on the banks of the River Jabbok.

Yet she had not been called back. It was all of a piece. She listened intently in that vast room consecrated to immortal things, and heard in the *29th Variation* the contest played out on the canvas above her – a standoff, a struggle, a draw declared, and then one more clash in the dark – no quarter given, none required, a last test of wills before the finale poets liked to call dawn.

How else to describe the rugged opening of the *Variation*? Or perhaps it was just Bach's resilience – harpsichord pushed to the very limits of its endurance, or those rose streaks on the canvas, or Anne-Sophie's anguish as Raphael struggled, or that other man, self-contained, needing only his paints.

Caroline closed her eyes, besieged, like the angel above her.

Without so much as a half-rest, the last *Variation* followed into her space. She listened, then glanced again at the mural, half expecting to see the figures regrouped. They had not moved. The contest, however, was no longer in doubt.

It was not just the wings running the length of the huge angel's back, nor the fact that the contestants seemed to be fighting on the angel's home ground. It was the composition. The painter had chosen to show only the angel's face – undisturbed and serene, privileged in his access to perfection as he was, and therefore unassailable.

And yet he had been impressed. More than impressed. Challenged, assaulted, nearly bested twice that night, he had managed to win in the end – an almost foregone conclusion, because he could not die as mortals must, unless they had glimpsed what he had seen, and then they might become like him.

"Israel," she could swear she heard the angel say then, as the pale streaks of paint seemed to intensify on the cloth.

"Jacob," managed his enemy, overcome.

"No longer Jacob," replied the angel, renaming his enemy. "Israel," he repeated – "father of many, and therefore creator, and therefore we will meet again."

The words were right there, in the painting, Caroline was sure of it – as they were in the *Variation*'s grand resolution – metaphor for the pulpit and the organ pipes and Raphael's vigils; all of them variants of art's violent nights.

Israel, Caroline said to herself once again, as she walked down the steps into the shadows of Place St-Sulpice. A pale moon was shining upon the chestnut trees, no longer in bloom, fitting adornment nevertheless for the orators' statues in the centre of the square.

She passed the tall and austere and ecclesiastical figure of Bossuet, cast in stone, as were his words.

⌒ ☾ ⌒

Caroline missed the rain, which by the following day had moved on. In its place warmth had returned – brightness that seemed out of place, almost rude in Raphael's sepulchral house.

Far more obliging were the mists of the week just gone by, the empty streets and damp quays. Now, she reflected looking out over the Seine, there would be lovers on the towpath, pleasure boats at the point where right and left banks joined beneath her, that mistress of his, welcomed, outside his studio door.

She looked down at her hand. The blue-black mark was still there, though somewhat reduced and no longer raw. From time to time it would throb, unexpectedly, so that already twice that day she had stood and thrown open the windows and scanned the afternoon sky for some hint of a storm, a shower perhaps, any promise of triumph over the developing light.

Not even the wisp of a cloud pierced the cobalt above her.

Twice therefore she returned to the desk, forcing herself to sift through papers and photos and to catalogue documents in the heat.

At the sound of *Angelus* she locked the apartment, crossed the footbridge toward the cathedral, and made her way to her rooms on the rue Séguier. But under the chestnut tree in the courtyard she paused. Beyond the French windows overlooking her garden, she knew the sky would be fair still and very blue. She sighed, paused again, and suddenly said at the desk, "Jean-Yves, since it's still early, not much past seven, I thought I might find a museum still open."

"You could go to Rodin's house, Madame, just beside Les Invalides."

Mme Devereux considered, running her fingers along the edge of the desk.

"Then again there is Cluny," he offered. "Plenty of time for an unhurried stroll up toward the museum, Madame."

"That is more practical, Jean-Ives."

She retraced her route of the previous evening, making her way through the crowded streets around l'Odéon, then turning east towards the Sorbonne. Hence she never saw Jude McCallister, never even guessed that he was about to join Rebecca Chase at Le Petit Zinc – usual table under the awning, several blocks from Cluny Thermes.

Having just finished a class, he had forgone his usual rest on the small bench in Place Fürstenberg. Instead he had searched for a phone booth along the narrow streets around the Seine. Halfway down rue Christine he'd dialled the number he knew by heart. For the fifth time that week, Mme Devereux was not to be found.

But for the fact that he'd been facing west, toward a deepening sky that seemed like a glaze on some canvas, he might have seen her as she passed behind him, walking away from the river toward the boulevard St. Germain.

~ ❨ ~

Caroline's steps resounded in the seemingly empty museum. Not even a guard was in view as she made her way across the mezzanine. She paused outside the tapestry room, then took her seat in the silence. Before her, arranged like a half moon, were five of the tapestries. The sixth was directly behind.

The sixth had always been her favourite – luxuriance of navy and gold against a wine-toned profusion of flowers and flags and mysterious icons. Centred among these icons there was a stately and clearly safe tent, or so Caroline had always thought – home of the life of the mind. At the tent's door there was a lady, also in wine tones and gold, unicorn safely at a distance. Somewhat wistfully, she was placing her treasures in a box to be carried away.

Strangely that evening, all alone in the dimness, Caroline never glanced at the tapestry behind her. Instead she fixed her gaze on the five textiles ahead.

There, recalling scenes on some mysterious stage, was the inescapable and evanescent allure of the flesh. There was *Taste*, number one, a woman in persimmon reaching for the finest fruits; *Smell* – roses held up to a demure woman's breast; *Touch*, always disturbing – a fine woman fondling the rare beast's one horn; *Sound*, perhaps the loveliest – a serene lady featured, midnight blue sleeves draping discreetly over her hips as she inclined her slim form, ever so slightly, toward the keyboard beneath her hands.

And then there was the centrepiece – *Sight* – never appealing to Mme Devereux. Its composition baffled her. Its meaning escaped her analysis, always so well-informed.

Yet again for some reason, seemingly still alone in that room, she stared at the treasure called *Sight* straight ahead – unicorn undone at last, captured by his attraction to a maiden in the forest, gazing with love into her face, climbing eagerly onto her lap.

She does not seem to mind, Caroline thought, *although the weight of him up against her has pushed aside her brocade skirt.*

A closing bell sounded in the dark hallway beyond. Caroline kept on staring at the tapestry called *Sight*. The unicorn was elegant, out of time – creature doomed by his singularity, though in his yearning universal.

The lady seemed to know this. With her left hand she caressed him; with her sad face she tried to grasp the expectation in his eyes. And yet the title of the tapestry came not from these gestures, but from the mirror the lady held, gilt-edged oval tilted at an angle that revealed the longing in that encounter.

Odd, Caroline said to herself, as though she had never before studied that cloth. Only the face of the beast was in that glass. The lady's eyes were on him, half in guilt, half in love, watching him search in vain for the woman who had eluded him, seeing only himself, nothing more, knowing only too well that he would no longer be free.

Lights dimmed overhead. A second bell sounded. Guards now stood at the door as she passed through to the court.

Night had already fallen on the Left Bank as she emerged.

Jude had already left his table at Le Petit Zinc off the boulevard St-Germain. With Rebecca Chase he had gone to the heights of Montmartre, to her small apartment beside the basilica overlooking the city spread out like a fan.

"We have to rehearse," Rebecca had told him. "Weekend's approaching, after all. They want us back at the Crillon."

"You mean they want *you* back."

"Perhaps. But your piano makes my harp sound so much more…chic. Only an hour, Jude, I promise – one run-through only, and then I'll fix you a martini and off you'll go into the night."

Gallantly, and because he could not bear to phone those rooms once more, he'd pushed his chair back and stood and said, "If you say so, Rebecca."

After all, he'd told himself as they'd stepped into a taxi, *how can I perform in public without appropriate preparation?*

Caroline was at that moment crossing the place St-Michel. She had heard neither the students, far too loud and carefree, nor the tourists, even louder, nor even the taxis heading north just over the bridge to her right.

Only Jude's words, remembered exactly, seemed to be clear as she approached the quay.

I never did see you, Caroline, insisted the voice in her head as she advanced. *I saw only myself this afternoon.*

"Have the taxi stop here, Jude."

They had reached rue des Saules, just above Montmartre Vineyards.

"It's a bit of a climb still to my apartment," Rebecca confessed, "but after these past days of rain, tonight's a gift, don't you think?"

"That it is."

"Besides," she went on, taking the hand he extended as they emerged from the taxi, "the view alone is worth the climb."

They stopped on a hillside next to a sloping walkway that led to the old Inn Franquette.

"Truth is," continued Rebecca, holding onto his arm still, "I always think of you on this corner. Not just the lights," she went on, allowing a wistful note to colour her tone, "but there, inside the inn. I imagine those suppers long gone."

She paused by the window, bathed in the glow from the many candles within.

"Zola exhausted…Pissarro inspired. I try to picture you among them."

"Also exhausted," replied Jude, laughing at last.

"Come. Not too much farther."

At the top of the hill they turned to the right, then to the left, then climbed even higher until Sacré-Coeur rose behind them and the bejewelled streets spread out below.

For a while they leaned against the railing overlooking the park. Jude seemed lost in the colours filling the night sky's horizon. *Like that necklace*, he thought, recalling gashes through fine citrines, until he heard, "Jude, we still have to rehearse."

"Yes. Yes lead on, Rebecca. It can't be much higher."

She took his arm once again. They crossed in front of the church. At the very summit of the hill she said, "There," pointing to an elegant building that followed the sinuous curves of rue Lamarck to the north.

"Well, you were right about the view," he remarked. "Well worth the climb. Even from here I can imagine what you can see from within."

"No more stairs, Jude," she laughed. "When you arrive with a harp, you take the ground-floor apartment."

The living room seemed suspended, like the prow of a ship, moored at a courteous distance beyond a spectacular bay. Facing the windows, placed at an angle, was an antique grand piano. Facing the piano in a corner was Rebecca's harp, also antique.

Jude paused at the threshold. The simplicity within pleased him. The extravagance beyond took his breath away. As he removed his scarf he observed, "Your harp is turned from the window."

"Too much distraction out there."

"So you let the pianist lose his way."

"That's up to him," she said, taking his scarf.

For a moment, their eyes met. Then he turned and walked to the window and gazed at the city below.

"I'll fix you that drink, Jude."

"Thanks."

She disappeared through an archway to the left of the salon.

"You can come in," she called out. "It is only a dining room, or a study, or a place where I store chairs when I give concerts up here. It's also the bar, and a bedroom," she said with another quick laugh, sensing him standing behind her.

"A room for all seasons, is that it?"

"One has to make do at this height."

"Ah."

"I wanted the view so I sacrificed space."

"Well here's to your view then."

"Cheers, Jude."

They rehearsed for an hour – mostly Gershwin again, for they knew it would be Gershwin the Crillon audience would expect of them.

"Shall we end with *The Man I Love*, Jude?"

"If you like."

"Do you know it?"

"If you play it."

Rebecca leaned into her harp and played the beautiful ballad with extraordinary tenderness. Her red hair caught the light from behind. Her elegant fingers reminded Jude of the hand he had burned.

"Got it?" she asked, in the long silence that followed after she'd finished her song.

"Yes. Yes I think so."

"Try it; I'll follow."

They played together again, spontaneous counterpoint, for as musicians they were finely attuned.

"Perfect," she said.

"I've got time for one or two more. Anything other than requests I'll just sit out."

"Nonsense, Jude. Whatever happens, just wing it."

"That would embarrass you."

"You did it with *La Vie en Rose* last time."

"Barely," he replied, feeling something akin to a slap at the recollection, so that he turned and busied himself searching among the sheets of music beside him.

Rebecca stood, crossed to the piano and sat on the bench next to him.

"What are you searching for, Jude?"

"An old tune, nothing more."

"An old story, you mean."

"They are often the same."

"Yes they are."

There was a fresh herbal scent in her hair, always damp, he recalled, as though it had been washed recently.

He took her hand and kissed her palm and then again she felt him distant.

"I should go," he said.

"Kiss me once more first."

"Rebecca…"

"Not on the hand this time."

He leaned down to her and kissed her mouth, lightly at first, and then as her arms encircled him, he kissed her harder, with great hunger, although the yearning was not for her – not for this woman who was pressed against him so that his hand found her breast and her tongue found his mouth and he knew it meant all the world to her and that therefore he should stop himself, what with *La Vie en Rose* still in his head – but as he tried to pull back he smelled her hair and thought that perhaps he could lose himself, then and there, and forget just for one night.

There was no forgetting. He took her face in his hands and saw the one he had painted and his gaze became thoughtful, tinged with remorse or maybe just sadness, so that in the end it was she who drew back, knowing his body craved another.

"Rebecca," he murmured, not a caveat this time, more like an apology.

She shook her head.

"I don't want to hurt you…I never should have come tonight."

She fixed her green eyes on him. "Where else could we work, Jude? I can't take my harp to your house, can I?"

"I suppose not."

"Well there you have it."

"After tomorrow though – it might be best – I mean perhaps we should cancel…"

She touched his lips with her fingers. "Don't even say that. Don't ever say that. There are people who like to hear us play together. We owe them that, pure and simple."

"I owe *you* a lot more."

"You owe me nothing."

She stood abruptly. "Forgive me. I take that back. You owe me a song or two from time to time, and the pleasure of your company."

Her tone had softened, for she knew she had wounded. "And one more drink, Jude, if you will fix it for me before you go."

When he came back with her glass she was standing beside the window, staring at city lights and monuments, brilliance in every direction.

"None for you?"

"I can't. There's not a cloud in that sky. The day will dawn clear, and very soon, and with the light comes my work."

She nodded, took a few sips of her drink, and said, "Let me call you a cab."

"I'll find one down the hill somewhere. I'd rather walk a bit now."

He lingered a moment, awkwardly.

"Thank you anyway, Rebecca."

From her place by the window, she could see him moving below her – solitary figure heading south from the heights.

He had lied to her about his work. He hadn't painted since Mrs. Devereux left.

⏾☾⏞

Caroline did not return to her uncle's apartment the next day. She had slept fitfully, dreams stalked by a succession of strange and wonderful beasts – some pale and kind, others clearly malignant, all seeking relief in a mirrored woodland where she too was lost.

Well before dawn she had awakened, suddenly feeling trapped in the canopied bed that resembled a web. With a glance at the ormolu clock by her bed – five-fifteen – she'd thrown her sheets off, reached for her robe, unlocked the French doors and stepped into the yard. The sky was still black, the air quiescent, the stone bench by the elm not even discernible in the dark. Nevertheless she found that seat, dismissing its dampness, not minding its cold, seeking a place there with a view of the last stubborn stars.

Seven left, she had counted as the dark space steadily lightened.

One by one these last stars had diminished. She'd heard the baker arrive, not too long after six; the housemaids arrive, not too long after eight; and then Jean-Yves at his desk, taking calls after nine. The sky by that time had turned a resolute blue and the air had turned warm. On her bench she had decided, bare feet in the jonquils, not to return that afternoon to Raphael's apartment.

Last day before they close Rodin's house for repairs, she had remembered. *I should go after all although it is west, beyond Les Invalides, and the day will be warm, and perhaps I should sleep before that long walk.*

Not until three did she leave her room, heading out along the Seine, following the same route she had taken the night she had walked to the Crillon. This time, however, she passed the bridge and turned left, moving along the Esplanade toward the Hôtel de Biron, once the home of Rodin.

She entered, passed through an archway and walked toward the rotunda – her favourite space – where the statue of Eve was displayed behind dark red silk cords.

She was surprised, though, when she reached the rotunda. The cords and stanchions had all been removed. Indeed – and this was more of a puzzle – it seemed as if the group who had preceded her had been invited to approach *Eve*, even to touch her body.

After a moment she realized that this was exactly the case. It was a tour for the blind. Eleven students from the university, none of them sighted, had been invited to tour the collection. Their guide was lecturing quietly as Mme Devereux approached.

"Sculpted in 1881," he explained, "she is of course a companion to *Adam*, rapidly modeled that same year, though she took far longer to create – a far greater challenge.

"Vianne," he continued, addressing an intense, dark-haired woman standing beside him, "take your time and walk up and let us know what you think."

The woman approached *Eve*, very slowly, with the help of her guide. She passed her hands over the legs, the thighs, the torso – bulging slightly – then seemed perplexed by the strong arms crossed over Eve's breasts, one hand protecting her head, which was lowered, as though to ward off a blow, the other clutching her ribs.

One more time Vianne passed her hands over the bronze, and then she turned back and said, "It is not finished, René. It is too rough."

Her guide beamed with pride.

"Others I've touched here are smoother," she insisted.

"You are correct, Vianne. Absolutely correct. The sculptor left this work aside, bedevilled as he was by the model he'd paid."

Caroline had remained motionless, her eyes fixed on the exchange between Vianne and this defeated Eve.

"She never told him she was pregnant," continued René. "She kept that secret to herself. Yet every day she would grow, ever so slightly – so that Rodin would be lost, although there'd be light, for she had changed somehow, essentially."

"So that is why it is unfinished?" asked a student behind Vianne.

"No, Paul. Rodin was told in the end. It made him pleased to know the truth. It led him straight to Eve's soul, to her sin, or so he once claimed, but too much time had elapsed. His model had left by then, finding his studio cold."

Paul too felt the bronze.

"There is shame here," he said, running his hands along the arms of the powerful Eve. "Was it a blow from the sculptor she was expecting, do you think?"

René thought for a moment.

"Well he was driven to distraction, almost to madness by his dilemma. She may have sensed this. It may have helped her to pose."

His students turned to him, expectantly.

"But no," he went on. "No I do not think there were blows. The wrath was God's wrath, revenge of the Lord…"

"For what?" asked Vianne.

"For wanting too much, chère Vianne," said a fellow student with a laugh.

There was a moment.

"You are wrong, Charles-Antoine," replied Vianne softly. "You need to touch her again. She is a creature made for pleasure and knowing, and thus could never want too much."

"Unless a spiteful God made her," Paul interjected.

"We are not speaking of myth," flashed Vianne. "Only the shape we have touched. The shape we have touched belongs to the artist. It is he who is angry, because what he needed she kept hidden so that he could not work, or live – it was the same for him, no, René?"

"I expect you are right," said her guide.

"That is why her head is bent, her arms have shame. She has sinned gravely, against the creator," Vianne concluded, and then fell silent.

One by one her fellow students approached the statue and felt the woman.

"You may be right, Vianne," conceded Paul, who had remained standing beside the guide. "And yet it worked well for Rodin. It was, after all, shame and guilt he was paid to portray. In this model he found it, whatever the cause."

René considered a moment before answering, somewhat sadly, "Not every artist is so lucky," and then the students moved on to Room Four, left of the Rotunda, and Mrs. Devereux remained standing there, stupefied, staring at *Eve* all alone.

When she rejoined René's group they had moved on to Room Six.

Once again the cords and stanchions had been completely removed. Once again the students approached the sculptures, lingering on the figures entwined ecstatically in *The Kiss*.

"Their lips barely touch," murmured Paul, running his hands along the woman's face, lifted to meet her lover's mouth. He felt her elegant arm, embracing her lover's neck, her breast leaning in to him, his hand on her hips, pulling her close to him, her unashamed legs about to spread.

"Is it a chaste form or an erotic one?" asked René as he explored the forms.

"Both, somehow," Paul replied, hands lingering on the man's back – taut and muscular, erect, yet about to incline somehow.

"You see I was right, Charles-Antoine," persisted Vianne, although she did not turn to him, for she could not see where he was standing. She too had passed her hands over the ecstasy chiselled beneath them.

"No one who modelled that kiss could have made Eve ashamed of her needs."

As the class turned to leave, René told them to pause. One by one they approached a pair of stone hands – devout, absolute – forming their own knowing shape below a tall window beyond.

"It is entitled *Cathedral*," René told Vianne, who lingered a long time exploring the delicate wrists, the intertwined arms, the palms never touching, destined forever to yearn, the remarkable ogee arch formed by the space in between.

"Does it remind you of a church?"

"No," she said pensively, running her own hands again over the stone ones by the window. "No," she repeated. "Something more sacred."

Nobody asked her what she meant as they filed out carefully toward the exit. But Caroline knew, left alone again in the room. She had seen hands like that – proud and tender at once, longing to touch, condemned to create.

Jude, meanwhile, was once again at the piano, just across the river, playing "*Who Cares?*" with an abandon he'd never displayed before that night.

Although the museum closed at eight, Rodin's garden remained open 'til nine-thirty that night. Caroline found a table at the end of a long gravel path, its single chair next to a row of poplars that lined the garden's west wall. There were no sculptures around her, no other visitors so near to closing time, and yet she did not move from the isolation that intensified as night fell. She could not move. She was reeling from the impressions of the past tumultuous week: the rain-soaked walks, her throbbing hand, Anne-Sophie's singular fidelity. She heard the *Variations* in her head again, saw Jacob defeated, felt the rare beast's confusion when only his own face was returned to him in the midst of that tapestry's wealth.

And then, like a blow, Eve's guilt smote her heart. The lovers' kiss made her eyes burn. The hands that had made them both, called of all things *Cathedral*, filled her own hands with a longing that swept aside everything but Vianne's words – Vianne, who could see nothing but who had perceived what had occurred. The artist had been seduced; the creator sinned against, for he had in good faith sought eternal things, had been lured toward them, was deceived in his quest and made to lose faith, and curse the task, and in the end surrender his gift.

Absolute silence surrounded her table beside the wall. The museum was empty, but Eve was still in there, all alone in the rotunda, still warding off the creator's resentment, her figure modeled on a woman who had bedevilled him with her secret.

Caroline looked around. There was no one in the garden. One by one, high over the poplars, stars that had vanished at daybreak reappeared in the dusk.

Jude, she heard herself say as she watched them take their shape again, *Jude I am sorry*. The only response was the rustle of leaves overhead.

Jude, she repeated, folding her arms across the table and leaning her head on her hands, hoping to muffle the sobs that had broken at last, no longer to be contained.

It was all she could do now, cry like a child recalled from an old sepia print, for like that child she could never reverse the damage her fierce pride had caused.

Mrs. Devereux cried for a long time in the dark, not looking up until she was startled by the sensation of something odd beneath the trees, some imperturbable invader, something akin to brilliance overwhelming the garden.

She was confused for a moment, absolutely at a loss. In the next instant she saw that the burnished dome above Les Invalides had been illuminated for the evening.

Its light had spread over the gravel, over the sculptures, over the semicircular building – half moon beside her – with its sensual rooms on the uppermost floor.

She could see them all from her chair. She could see his veranda, where he had nourished his own yard. She could see his French doors, every one of them dark, save for a low lamp which she remembered was on the large desk in the changing room. Every detail of that room was forever fixed in her mind – the mirrors, the paint smell, the heat, the revelations. Every detail of the studio was also ingrained – the bell jar, the scissors, the rose bowl, her offence.

And then, on the gravel beside her, she had heard footsteps approaching.

"*Désolé, Madame,*" whispered a guard by her chair. "At the moment, the garden is closed. We will reopen tomorrow, ten-thirty a.m."

"I am so sorry…"

"Please," he responded, waving his left arm in a gesture that was half apologetic, half munificent.

"The gates behind you are open. I shall escort you. It is quite late after all," said the guard as she stood, wondering what could have kept such a lady tucked into the shadows so close to the wall.

Fortunately, Mme Devereux remembered the code numbers on the keypad. Jude had insisted she learn them during their first sitting in his studio. Thus she was able to use them, last resort in the dark, for there'd been no response to the buzzer she'd pressed at the entrance beside the park.

No doubt he is still in his study, she decided, as the heavy oak door opened discreetly before her.

Straight ahead was a second door, two long frosted panes with elegant nymphs etched into the glass.

This door opened too, as did the frail wrought-iron grate beside the old cage in the hall.

When she emerged on the top floor, everything seemed familiar – the long narrow tables, the four crystal sconces, the wine-coloured wallpaper, the black Persian rugs.

She turned to the left and walked to Jude's apartment. After a moment or two she knocked softly and waited.

Jude did not answer.

She knocked a second time, then a third and then she looked at her watch, barely discernible in the half light.

Ten twenty-five.

She walked back to the cage and pressed the buzzer to descend. At the first floor lobby she lingered. It was early after all. Beckoning night in July. He was perhaps taking a walk or returning home from a friend's. She would wait until eleven and then return to her own rooms on the rue Séguier.

Just past midnight, Jude had another request – Gershwin again – a duet with Rebecca that they had never rehearsed.

He smiled and shook his head and stood up to leave the floor to her, but she struck her harp strings and whispered, "Improvise, darling," and so he complied, and, as it happened, they played with a synchronized yearning that made *They Can't Take That Away From Me* breathtakingly fine.

Two more requests followed, and then an encore, and then, just past one, Jude finished his drink and kissed Rebecca goodbye and left their table and walked home.

He followed his usual route across Pont Alexandre, down through the Esplanade, past Rodin's garden, around the park to his house.

He opened the outer door, the frosted door, the grate to the cage on the top floor of his building. The hall was empty of course, utterly still at one-thirty, and yet as he took his keys out in front of his door a familiar fragrance, like a dream half-remembered, made him turn toward the stairwell just to the left of the cage.

There was something fragile in her voice when Mrs. Devereux said, "Hello."

She was seated on the second step, hardly visible in the darkness, and yet he knew her sound, her form, the smell of her and he simply stared in disbelief.

"I should have called first," she managed, rising with some hesitation, like a schoolgirl.

He moved toward her.

"Am I too late?"

"That depends," he said tenderly, standing beside her in the shadows. "I can't make music out here, or cook – or paint out here."

"Can you paint inside?"

"After sunrise."

"I shall come back then, after sunrise."

He had taken her hand by then, the one he had burned, and raised it up to his mouth and kissed it. She had stroked the side of his face.

"Come whenever you want. Wear whatever you like," he had murmured, longing to kiss her mouth – afraid, though, to pull her against him, for fear she might vanish.

"Sunrise," she repeated, drawing away from him and stepping down. "We can't waste the light, Jude."

"No, Caroline, we will waste nothing."

And with that she was gone, and he was inside his own hall, and neither believed they had touched one another again.

Jude was up early, restless and fretful, convinced that Caroline would change her mind. Just past sunrise though, he heard the cage in the hall descend, then again reach the top floor and when he opened the door she was standing there. He was surprised to see her all in black – turtleneck, long skirt, no jewellery of any kind. She had a small purse in her left hand, high-roped sandals on her feet. Not until she was in his hallway did he notice the silver shell comb holding her hair back. He also saw then she'd brought no shoulder bag.

"Nothing has changed," she observed, a little awkwardly still, looking around the corridor.

"Everything has changed," he said.

When their eyes met she saw a hint of the impasse that had stymied his work for seven days.

"Except for my breakfast," he added quickly. "I have prepared you some breakfast. I mean I decided, given the length of time and all..." He faltered, then straightened himself. "I decided to consider you a new client, Mrs. Devereux, which meant of course breakfast."

"Half a breakfast?" she asked with a shy smile.

"Well yes...yes, that's what I thought we might do. That is if we're sharing again – I assume we are sharing again."

"No," she said after a moment.

"No?"

Caroline shook her head.

"You mean somebody has commissioned?" – He stopped, horrified at the thought that a third party would be involved.

"I mean this portrait is yours, Jude. To keep, never to sell. To keep here, in fact, where you live – not on exhibit though."

Again he was vaguely aware that she had brought no shoulder bag.

"Therefore," she said, in what she hoped seemed like a steady tone, "I'll be wanting a whole breakfast. That's only fair after all, since I have surrendered all rights. I mean if you agree to my terms."

There was silence.

"We needn't sign anything. I shall rely on your word. Never to be displayed. Always in your possession."

He stared into her eyes – those remarkable goblets filled with plum wine that had undone him with their knowledge. For a week he had not slept, had not worked, seeing them everywhere, wanting to drink from them.

"Jude?" he heard her say somewhere close to him. "Are we agreed, Jude?"

"Yes," he murmured.

She seemed dissatisfied, as though something else – some more formal statement were in order.

"I shall keep what I paint here," he promised her, touching her hair. "It will be mine, only mine – a secret, just like its subject."

While he finished preparing their breakfast she noticed that something had changed in his house – something essential – although it was not the furniture, nor the art work, nor even the fragrance from the cuttings he had brought in from the terrace.

An absence, she mused, *not a presence*, and then she realized, despite the aroma from the kitchen and the white lilies beside her, that the odour of paint was greatly reduced. It was there still, but in the background like a memory, so that the artist's vocation seemed somehow diminished.

"Here we are," he announced, walking in with his tray.

He has not painted, she understood.

"One full breakfast, as ordered."

Not every artist is lucky, the guide had said to his students. As she took the pastry Jude offered, Caroline pondered those words. She thought of them over and over as they sipped from the delicate cups.

Jude could tell she was distracted, though he could not know she had decided, in the stairwell the previous evening, to reveal herself, unlike Rodin's Eve, and let the destined work take its shape.

⁓ ☾ ⁓

"Well I shall get ready, now," she announced, carefully placing her cup down.

"Yes."

She seemed hesitant for some reason and did not stand.

"Take your time," he said kindly. "I need to prepare things."

"Now is fine, Jude."

They both stood then. He returned the tray to his kitchen as she turned and walked down the hall. At the narrow console she stopped. The studio was clearly visible through the last door on her right, first light of day streaming in through the French doors west and south.

It is as I suspected, she said to herself – the cart pushed to one side, the brushes pristine, the cloths in a neat pile, the easel propped up on the fireplace wall.

Everything else was the same – the bell jar, the mirror, the cut-crystal rose bowl, the clock.

No flowers, though, she reflected, as she heard his footsteps approaching.

"As I said, Caroline, take your time. I'll be a while setting up."

"I will, Jude."

"In through there," he said after a moment, pointing to the changing room directly behind them.

"I remember."

She was about to turn when he said at last, "Will you be in black for this portrait? The reason I ask," he went on, fumbling, "is that I shall have to decide on the background, canvas tone, even the setting, if need be. None of it very complicated," he added hastily, since she did not answer.

"I will not be in black."

"I do not see your bag."

"I do not need my bag," she replied.

He thought he detected an oddly resigned note in her voice, and then as she looked at him he understood. For whatever reason – and it would all come to light that day, he was certain of that now – she had come to him to be painted stripped of all illusions, clothes and jewellery included.

"Take this, then," he said steadily, handing her a sheet from a pile just inside his door.

⌐☾⌐

To give him time she took her time – although she was anxious at that point to have it over with, or begun at least, and so she slipped off her sweater and stepped out of her skirt and stared again into the five mirrors which reflected her uniqueness.

Vaguely, wrapping the sheet around her body, she was aware of newness in the rooms – again an absence, not a presence – a lack of sound this time, not smell. Jude was not humming as he prepared his easel and his paints. There was only the twisting of jars being opened, the prying open of boxes, the dragging of an easel to its old position across the floor.

Those sounds too diminished at last, and then there was silence. Then Caroline walked to the door and glanced at the pile of carefully folded black clothes and readjusted the sheet around her scarred skin. She had fitted it on tightly, like a toga, so that only the merest hint of a tendril forced its rude way onto her neck.

She put her hand on the doorknob and saw for the first time she'd left her sandals on – ropes still crossed around her ankles, high wedges silent on the floor.

"Yes, Caroline, I am ready," she heard, for Jude had felt her presence there and he too was anxious to face the demons that had crowded around his easel all week.

He looked up at her as she opened the door. Her right hand was on the doorknob still; her left hand reached across her breast toward her right shoulder, so as to keep the drape in place.

"Where do you want me, Jude?"

He took a step toward her, for he could see she was trembling.

"Where?" she repeated, and then he sensed that he should go no further, that it was costing her all her strength to remain there, hand on the doorknob, and that he needed to remain detached, almost nonchalant, as though she were a model who had worked for him many times or else she would shrink from him and from whatever she had come there to do.

And so he too stayed where he was and merely looked at her – at her arms, bare for the first time before him – her neck unadorned, also for once, the arc of her collarbone fine and pronounced and exposed on her left, covered still on her right, although he imagined he perceived something like a shadow there, escaping the drape.

Confusion passed over his face, a compulsion to paint mixed with another need, but he forced himself to say as he picked up a brush and began wiping it, absently, "I have been thinking about that. I am not sure. I don't believe the couch will do."

"Won't it?" she asked, barely a whisper.

Beneath the whisper there was disappointment. It would be harder for her standing, Jude knew, yet he wanted nothing to remind him of his earlier failure.

"You were there before, after all..."

"I understand."

"And I should like this to be different."

Caroline nodded.

"Perhaps the mantelpiece," Jude continued, turning his easel a bit and looking at the light beyond. "You might stand by that bell jar."

As she lingered still by the doorway he added, in a low voice, "We could try, Caroline."

"If you think it would work, Jude."

She was glad at that point she'd left her roped sandals on, for there was no sound as she crossed, turned and faced him mixing his colours on the palette he hadn't touched for a week.

"Move to the right a bit. Good," he said, striving above all for efficiency, for both their sakes. "I think I might want that jar to be seen, just beyond your left shoulder – and perhaps your right hand on the mantelpiece...Excellent. As for your left hand – well I don't know – we'll have to take that as it goes – for the present though, you can remove it from your shoulder...Excellent," he repeated, a hint of the old fervour beginning to colour his tone, for a portrait was emerging inside his head somewhere, or inside his hands – he never knew which – only that when it happened, if he stayed focused, yet humbled, if he controlled things yet at the same time surrendered all of his needs to some higher force, he could put onto the canvas what the canvas required.

It was for this that she had returned – to give him his gift back – and she could see it occurring and so she was able to do as he asked and move her left arm from her shoulder, although she did it slowly and was glad when the drape stayed in place – a moment's delay, she knew, nothing more, but a welcome one. She left her right hand on the mantel, according to his instructions.

"Don't mind the cat," he said.

"Cat?"

"Nero. Behind you. Black stray I picked up seven years ago along the Seine."

Only then did Caroline notice the magnificent cat curled on the mantel.

"I may even include him in this – who knows," Jude went on. "It just might balance the vase well. In fact..." He broke off abruptly. The cat, intrigued by the figure beside him, had unwound himself and stood.

"Caroline," Jude said warily, "Ignore him. Simply remain where you are."

Again she complied, holding her pose, although it was clear to him that the cat's movements, so unexpected, had shaken the frail composure she had struggled mightily to sustain.

"We needn't use Nero," he continued, reassuringly. "Just keep looking at me until he settles himself. Caroline, look at me," he repeated.

The cat arched its back.

"He will not harm you."

"No. No, of course not," she managed.

"He is simply unaccustomed – I always keep him in the bedroom...Nero," Jude cried, as Nero leapt onto the floor, barely missing the model, brushing against the bell jar so that it tilted somewhat, then tilted more and then the model, wanting of all things to keep the bell jar intact, turned with a start and steadied the piece and then turned back and was aghast, for her white drape was on the floor.

She stared at the rumpled fabric around her sandals for a moment and then she looked up at Jude, wide-eyed and astonished, but also resigned – for it had all happened so quickly – the moment she had dreaded had come and gone – and there was no turning back.

He too gazed, intently, not at the drape but at her standing there.

The surprise in her face turned to wonder. Not twenty feet from her was this man – unimagined until she'd heard his song – staring intently at her body. She herself had only done so for the first time days before. Oddly enough she felt no shame, only this awe, with just a hint of relief that played on her mouth and parted her lips ever so slightly.

Nevertheless she coloured deeply, not out of shame, but because he continued to stare, for he had also been stunned, first by the cat, then by the vase, then by the drape, finally by her face and magnificent shape and the uniqueness of her flesh.

So intense was his gaze that she began to draw back.

"No, don't. *Don't*," he commanded.

She froze, like a naughty child trespassing, with no alternative but to surrender, although with absolutely no remorse.

"Please," he begged. "Just like that. Please don't move. Whatever thoughts you've just had, please do not lose them. And keep your eyes on me. I'm going to move toward you, Caroline."

A shadow of fear passed at last over her eyes.

"I have to. I need to move your hands where I want them, your head, and more than that I need to see closer –" he searched for the words, "I need to see closer what I have to paint."

Her heart pounded as he approached her.

He took her right hand and placed it again on the mantel.

"Turn to me," he murmured.

She did as he asked her.

"Spread your legs a bit – left foot forward – as if you'd been startled, as you were before. More. A little more. *I need more, Caroline.*"

Because she had begun to tremble, she was unable to comply this time.

Undeterred, Jude placed his hands on her hips and moved her torso in his direction.

"No, not your head. Your head stays where it was, looking at where I was before. And your left arm –" he reached for it, "that too goes where it was, outstretched a bit, expectant, as though attempting to catch what will always elude…Yes. Yes, that is good. Can you stay like this? Can you remember what you felt before?"

Only her eyes spoke in answer, but he saw there the fact that what she had felt before, and what she was feeling still, could not in a lifetime be forgotten.

He studied her beautiful neck – vines across it like a necklace – then looked down at her rib cage, also marked in sienna.

She tried to withdraw one more time, but he put his left hand on her waist so as to steady her where she was. Then he moved his right hand, very gently, until he could feel the crossed swords on her hip.

Beads of sweat appeared over her mouth, and a tremble returned to the arm he had placed, and yet still he kept his left hand on her waist and moved his right one much lower until he could find the mirrored markings on the inside of her thigh.

Were it not for the fact that there'd been no paint smell when she'd entered, no music as she'd undressed, not one rose in the bowl on that small table beside the sofa, she would have pushed aside the fingers that were at last tracing her half moon.

He felt the arc, the fullness beneath, and then in a careful tone spoke to her. "I am almost ready, Mrs. Devereux."

For all the world she could not imagine what could be left still for him to learn.

He removed the comb from her neck. The black mass fell to her shoulders.

"There," he said. "Yes, that is what was left to do."

There was absolute silence.

He took a handkerchief from his pocket and dabbed her remarkable mouth and moved back to his paint cart and the easel beside it.

"Please don't move, Mrs. Devereux," Jude remarked as he started to paint.

⏾

After about an hour of silence, Caroline heard the sounds of the brush he loved best. Sounds of the rag followed then, and then another brush, and then the rag again, erasing.

This time perfection, she thought. *That is the only thing he will settle for.*

She held her pose steadily. The slightest movement would distract him. As she did so she began to think of that violent struggle in the darkness on the high wall in St-Sulpice.

Reenacted this morning, she reflected, and so after another hour – because he was fighting so, and with full disclosure he might triumph, and without it she would not – she said, "It was a fire."

Cloth in his hand still, Jude looked at her.

"First Communion day. I was eight. We had come back from the cathedral to a grand lunch at our ranch, about an hour's ride from Buenos Aires. I..." she stopped. It was all still so clear, yet she had never spoken of it and so the words seemed badly shaped now, like jagged glass on a beach.

"Go on," Jude said from what appeared to be a great distance.

"I was made to stay in my dress," she said, "which displeased me, because it was long, and I couldn't skip well in it, and because the organdie lace scratched my neck." Her voice grew dim. "Besides, the day was hot."

Jude was no longer painting. He was standing rock-still, eyes fixed on her, listening.

"This is perhaps a disturbance," she stammered.

"This is everything," he responded, barely audible. He wiped his hands silently and put his rag down. "For us both, I suspect."

She thought for a moment.

He waited.

"As I said it was hot. The formal luncheon was long. I could hear the fountain in the courtyard splashing over the stones alongside. I longed to be out in the sunlight, on my young mare, with Jesús, the head wrangler, who had promised me a ride that day. Three became four...and then five...and then at last I was allowed to go – not to ride, just into the air, for there were guests still in the library – my uncle Raphael, my cousins, and a photographer was expected. Hence I could not take my dress off."

A substantial pause followed.

"'Mind you don't play near that fountain,' my father warned as I bolted, for he could see in my eyes what he called the mischief that lived there, and he was a proud man, and very stern, and had had to raise me without my mother, and did not want my dress wrong in the photo, after all the trouble I'd already caused, by which he meant my mother's death – even then I knew – though Raphael said with kindness, 'Come, come, Allessandro, the milk she spilled was only a drop.'"

When Caroline paused one more time, although still he said nothing, Jude reached again for his brush.

"In any case – this too I knew – my father's guests were all waiting, and the library windows did not face the courtyard, and as the organdie collar was scratching still, worse than death it seemed, I slowed my steps demurely, while he could see me still, and then I slipped into the hallway and waited until there was silence and then I ran to the fountain."

Again a pause followed.

"I am hearing you, Caroline," Jude said finally, for she had stopped again at the sound of his favourite tool on the cloth – "every word, every note – the only way I know how."

It was as though immense floodgates had opened, seeing him work as she recollected, hearing him paint as she conjured scenes that needed imaging, that day or never.

"The fountain was tiled, Jude, and very slippery, and my favourite trick was to climb onto the ledge that bordered the wall close to the top. Sometimes I'd dance there – sometimes just sit and think, very close to the edge, secure in the thought that the spray would land below me, well below my sandals, below the bricks and the begonias, so that no one but the wranglers would know where I'd been all afternoon.

"That afternoon, Communion day – in spite of the milk I had spilt – I felt especially charmed. I did my usual dance, then sat and thought for a while, then stood up for some reason – daring the fates, I suppose, for I was a naughty child, with what my father called devilry instead of eyes, and so I hopped on one foot in my organdie dress atop the porcelain ridge of the uppermost ledge.

"My white shoes were new. My white dress was long. I lost my footing and fell, not toward the stones but into the pool."

Jude McCallister kept on painting.

"'For this,' said my father, when they had fished me out and brought me in, 'you will not go to the party this evening, where there will be music and sweetmeats, and a full moon overhead.'"

"'Allessandro,' Raphael had interrupted, 'she is but a child.'"

"'You will stay here, in your room, and wash out your dress, and ask the Lord to forgive you. I have heard He is indulgent on the day of Communion.'"

"So there I was, Jude, with the violas downstairs, and my soaked veil over the sink, and then I heard another song – an old *ranchera* from the barracks behind our large kitchen downstairs.

"Jesús was playing to me – he had heard of my disaster and could do nothing but offer his song, as he had offered his hand to steady my horses since I was too small for any saddle.

"Down the back stairs I crept. I was surrendering any credit I might have had still with the Creator – I was aware of that, I believe – but there was that moon in the sky, and those guitars by the veranda, and I followed them all across the yard and up the old staircase into the barn.

"Jesús played every song I liked – songs of conquest, songs of love, songs of an empire destroyed, songs of passion surviving.

"I wanted to laugh, to clap, to encourage him – but did not dare. And yet I knew he could see me as I was sitting straight up by the octagonal window at the top of the barn, watching his comrades smoke and join in and drink beer and sing along – not seeing, however, the cigarette tossed into the straw, close to my spot in the dark, so that when the flames engulfed me, like the Lord's absolution, I was simply too lost to understand."

The sun had shifted by then, to Jude's windows facing west.

When she spoke again, Caroline's voice had changed, as though an adult had abruptly replaced a small girl in his room.

"I am, Jude, in medical parlance – a miracle, nothing less. There was bliss first, and then pain it would seem only a child could withstand, because a child believes what is told to her, and I was told I would live.

"I did not want to live. My skin and nightdress had merged, melded together in the heat, so that to undress me involved a flailing, which of course could not be accomplished all in one sitting, you understand."

Painting still, Jude nodded.

"There were weeks in between, years it seemed to me then, and yet I was assured it was weeks, and as I could not hear well or see at all, I must assume it was weeks.

"Jesús came, I know – I know he came every day to that hospital room – I remember his smell, and I remember another smell, another man by my side whose hands wouldn't dare touch me – through the layers of gauze I could not abide any touch – yet who sat beside me nevertheless.

"It was not my father's smell."

Jude continued, with precision, to fill out his canvas.

"I never again smelled my father. He never once came to that room. He was broken when that barn burned down, convinced he was to blame somehow, as I had been to blame for the death of his beloved, so that only curses had configured our fragile days from the beginning. He wanted to be alone after then.

"It was Raphael's smell inside my room."

Jude had painted that before she'd said it.

"I had been entrusted to his care before the last graft was completed. He took me back with him to Rome, to more surgeons, more long 'vacations' from each school I attended, more reconstructions paid for by my father, who had surrendered his post in the consulate by then. Wanting to leave Latin America, not wanting to return to Europe, he'd bought a large farm in New Salem – I believe we have discussed this, Jude – which he rechristened *Todd's Farm*, after my mother, Catherine Todd, and which is there to this day, on the Connecticut border close to New York.

"I saw its beauty for the first time the day after he died. He is buried in a plot nearby. All forty acres were left to his daughter, 'sole and deserving issue' – that was the term – along with some jewels from my mother and the house – exceedingly grand.

"The place had allure, I confess. I was eighteen, college age and reconstructed; much to be done still, but no longer unattractive.

"Besides…" here Caroline faltered, "there was also" – again she was stymied.

"Raphael," supplied Jude, with an almost clinical dispassion as he strengthened the finishing touches on the portrait he was born to paint.

"Raphael," repeated his model. "He made love to me for the first time the day I turned twelve. I was ugly still – I thought so at least, although he kept assuring me I was lovely, and after what we'd been through – after all, Jude – I had to assume he was right, although what he did to me gave no delight, none for me, that is to say; an enormous amount for him I have to conclude, since he came back to me every night, to my little room above his, where his wife, my aunt, was asleep next to the room where my three cousins slept, also protected."

It was with effort that Jude then concluded his portrait.

"Yale New Haven seemed exciting. Or at the very least, a way out. I accepted their offer – full tuition, room and board, world-class reconstruction at the university hospital down the street from my dorm. Their chief physician, Elliot Devereux, took a special interest in my case.

"'Final frontier,' was how I heard later he'd described me. 'If there were ever Galatea, this girl is it.'"

"Perhaps that was not his phrase. Perhaps the words were kinder, I do not remember. I only recall that I married him, out of gratitude, because he all but erased that night in the barn, and my wilfulness on Communion day, and because I had money, which he needed, and a house, which was splendid, and because I had nowhere else to go."

Jude was wiping his favourite brushes by that time, his portrait completed.

"Whatever he did to me on my wedding night reminded me of Raphael. Every other time did as well, until I miscarried our first child, and then a second one, and then I was glad when I heard he had taken a mistress – there are no secrets in New Salem – because at last I was free of his hands, although Todd's Farm was still our home. It would forever be our home. I had no place to go after all, longing notwithstanding."

There was absolute silence, Jude having completed his task.

Like an experienced model, compensated in proportion, Caroline reached for her drape and began to cover herself, sensing the portrait was done.

"Please don't do that yet."

"There's no more light, Jude."

"I know that."

"I need to go then."

"There's still the glow of day's end."

It was said so simply, that at first she thought she had misjudged things; that the work was not done, after all.

When their eyes met, however, she knew there was still something he wanted.

For some reason – and this would haunt her in the months to follow – as he placed the brush he loved best into the cart by his easel, she complied one more time and let the drape fall.

"Your portrait is finished," he said.

"So I have assumed."

"Would you like to see it?"

"I do not need to."

"I have not exaggerated your…difficulties."

"It would have been in bad taste."

"Nevertheless, they are there."

Catching her hair in her comb she replied, "To have omitted them would have been a lie."

His gaze again caught hers.

"Come have a look, Mrs. Devereux."

She felt exposed walking in his direction, wearing only high-wedged rope sandals, although she had not felt that way while he was painting her.

"Are you pleased with it?"

She merely stared and said nothing, so that he too felt exposed.

Indeed, it seemed to Jude, no vernissage, no retrospective, no gallery showing of his work had ever caused him such anguish as did the silent scrutiny of this woman – who had already, he remembered, sold his masterpiece back to him – and yet who continued to gaze, betraying no emotion, giving no hint of any reaction to the fact that he had retold her tale, exactly.

"I believe, Jude," she said finally, "that you have exaggerated the markings."

"That is how they are, Caroline."

"You have only seen them once."

"Have you seen them much longer?"

A last revelation remained, she knew then, to bring their long day full circle.

"No, Jude," she whispered, "I saw them for the first time in your changing room, twelve days ago, and I found them attractive although I did not tell you so. Thus you tried to find me in your last work and I escaped you."

"You have not escaped me now."

She looked again at her image, and saw that he had said the truth, with comely pride, and that her own pride no longer obtained, for it was all there, all on his canvas – pain, defiance, abandonment, violation, long legs, small waist, full breasts, violet eyes.

There was also surprise at the fact that that she had survived, like the bell jar, uniquely – monochromatic recapitulation of the Byzantine scrolls on the vase.

She could also see yearning, Galatea reaching out for what would always elude, a fierce quest, forged in the literal kiln of her past, subject of the finest portrait Jude had ever created in his life.

Nero wandered in and chose a new spot, on the sofa.

The artist closed his paint tubes.

The model kept on staring, no longer aware of the absence of clothing, indeed despising the accumulation of fabric that seemed, after all that had been said, somewhat constricting, like a bandage.

Not until he was on his knees, untying her sandals, did she turn away from his work.

"Jude, what are you doing?"

"You don't need these..."

"I have to leave now."

"Please don't leave now."

He slipped one foot from the ropes, and then another, and then he remained on his knees so as to kiss the mirrored grillwork on her inner thigh, and then he kissed the place above it, much darker, spreading her legs with his hands called of all things *Cathedral*.

To the best of her recollection, not even her uncle had put his tongue there. No one had ever done to her what Jude McCallister seemed to want.

Far more astounding, she thought, as he parted her legs one more time, no one had ever made her want it.

And so when she was in his bed – somehow his clothes were gone – she raised her arms to him to pull him down to her.

He was a powerful man and when he entered her he was afraid that the ghosts of the others might be hurting her.

"Move with me," he murmured, "so that I can love you as it must be."

Although she did not know what he meant, she did not draw back.

"Good," he said.

She arched her back.

"Good, Caroline," he repeated as she wrapped her legs around him and continued to move.

"Jesus, that's good."

It was no longer praise, she knew, but pleasure in his husky voice, and the concept excited her – she had never before been aroused – so that she found his mouth and put her tongue in it and kissed him deeply as he began to thrust.

She caressed his back with her hands, then his hips, then his thighs, at last his buttocks, pulling them slightly apart – and again this was new, a rough primordial caress, a fearless celebration of his body in hers.

Sweat poured over them both. Her hair was drenched as he grabbed the black mass by her neck and pulled her head back so as to lick the markings on her neck as he continued to move.

His other hand stroked the half moon.

"Jude..." she managed.

"Tell me."

"Don't leave anything."

"Of course not," he answered. "I want it all, Caroline," and then he moved to the side and pulled her over him and thrust from beneath her, caressing her own back with his hands, parting her own buttocks now so when she climaxed he had his hand there, the other still on the half moon, which he adored.

Her cry of pleasure stunned them both. It seemed to have come from the depths of someone else's throat. The release in it, both an end and a beginning, made Jude want her all the more, and so he kept on loving her until she again called his name out, with that same astounding surrender, making him say words that resembled "This is who you are, Caroline," and then he too climaxed, fiercely, for he had wanted her desperately since they'd met, and it was only because the painting had to be done, and her story had to be told, and because he was capable of an almost abusive self-discipline – fruit of the years he had spent in solitude, with only his paints and their needs – that he was able to endure the nearness of her and render it on the cloth before he touched her.

For a long time, with the smell of paint mixing with her smell, they lay in each other's arms. She knew he was caressing her, very lightly, and he sensed her arm across his chest and her hand in his hair, but in all this time they did not speak. Nor did they sleep, although the room was utterly still. The sun had long set; the sky had gone from grey to mauve; those same stars she had counted the night before had appeared, and then at last he said simply, "I plan to paint you forever."

She raised herself up on her elbow and looked at him.

"As you were today," he went on, "or as I have seen you other days. I will perhaps just paint your hands some days, some days your head, or your figure from a distance in some field or in a park or down by the river."

It was then – she saw this clearly in the darkness – that she was obliged to say something that sounded like *Jude, there are only two weeks left*, but she said nothing. She remained very still. She knew that he knew, and merely wished to forget, and so it surprised her when he continued, "Even when I paint other things – landscapes, for example, or still lifes, or the face of some client – I will be painting you. And you will know it of course."

She put her hand on his mouth and with her eyes tried to tell him to stop, but he pulled her hand away, roughly.

"I will ask you to show me where you are in my works – all of them – and you will point to the place on the cloth where I have painted you, although the face might be some other face, and the field only heather."

If she had only then replied, *Forever has not been vouchsafed to us, Jude*, they would have parted that night, next morning the latest, with an ache in their hearts, a swelling thing to be sure, but something which would have receded in time, leaving room in the end for other things, maybe.

Like that other phrase, however, these words too remained unsaid. To have shaped them would have made time real, the word become flesh – her other life, her husband, the farm handed down to her, sole and deserving issue, acreage that resembled family, precious assemblage in an orphan's collection.

Jude's private world too would have appeared in detail – cabaret nights and gallery shows, models, his mistress, above all his mistress, who would in time take her place – she herself would never thwart it, devoted as she was to the perfection that bedevilled him – and thus, though it had taken her a lifetime to find love, she did not say to him, *I must leave next week, Jude,* but instead remained silent, keeping hard, real things at bay.

Over the terrace, insistent, a handful of stars became hundreds. She watched them intensify – Jude's caress too had become insistent again – and so she was reminded of what he had done to her beside his palette, the way he had kissed her, and in that same place those same feelings surged so that she was pleased when he did it again and therefore decided – without shyness this time, before he entered her again – to put her mouth on his mouth, then on his shoulders, then his hips, then on the place below that, spreading his legs as he had done, for she assumed it would give him pleasure, as his tongue on her dark place had done.

When she slept at last in his arms, nearing dawn, she had learned how to pleasure him in many ways, reflecting his own needs as she perceived them within her, for it was not until he expressed them that she understood them for her own. Nothing he had done to her had offended her, or frightened her, although he had explored her body deeply, every way that he could. She trusted his passion and accepted its fierceness. In response he fell in love for the first and only time in his life.

There was simply no point then, when she awakened, to return to the words that remained to be said. Each time he had loved her they were there of course, web-like things in her head to be brushed aside by his hands, only to surface again in the silence, still unspoken, increasingly preposterous given the fact that this force which had joined her to Jude – not just his portrait, or her story, but a fearless physicality for which all harmony was a metaphor – this thing could not be dissolved, although forever had not been vouchsafed to them, and she planned to leave in two weeks, and what's more she knew in her heart that he knew it in his.

They never spoke, then, of the end. It was both inconceivable and inevitable. By some mutual understanding, unarticulated, they simply allowed each day to pass. He painted her often those days; she showed him her hotel at last; they'd walk in the evening by the Seine or return to Place des Vosges, or stroll the Pont St-Michel, or dine at Chez Marianne, where he had first fixed the colour of her eyes in his head.

How long ago that moment seemed to Jude, for there was nothing about Mrs. Devereux he couldn't portray at this point – no gesture, no expression, no thought, no uninhibited desires.

These he had come to know in the darkness of his room each night. They were superbly matched as lovers. After the first time there was no hesitation, no fear on his part that she would recoil from him, remembering other things, no fear on hers that she might be found wanting. There was only a passion that he had somehow unlocked, and for which he had searched all his life, and although they made love mostly in silence, she was so feral, yet at the same time so tender, so fierce yet so frail still, that repeatedly he was astonished, for he was exactly the same.

Perhaps he had sensed this from the beginning, when she had paused by his piano and fixed her improbable face on his, just for a moment, so that he would know it was she who had paid for *La Vie en Rose*, excessively, because hyperbole was in her nature, though few could see it in her slender ways, covered totally as she was, head to toe, except for the tango in her careless walk.

Yes, Jude reflected, undoing her hair that last night, for it pleasured him to undress her slowly, like a schoolboy, leaving the tangled black mass for the end, for the moment she would come to him. *Yes, it was there from the start.*

This was not the start though, and somehow he guessed it. In fact it had become clear to him, nearing midnight, as a full moon rose above them that she would be leaving France the next day.

How he had learned this he was not sure. He only remembered that it had occurred to him in the dark, as he lay above her, no longer thrusting but still wanting, and she too was utterly still, no longer moving but still yearning, and that then they had climaxed, motionless but together, a thing of the head more than a thrill in the loins, or perhaps it had come from the heart, encompassing both.

In any case it was an elegy.

Thus he asked later, as lights dimmed around Les Invalides beyond his sheer curtains, "It is today, is it not?"

"It is today."

"I thought so," Jude replied, as though by assenting he could understand. "Your cousin did say, at the beginning, you had only a month left."

"You have counted exactly."

"Yes, well I've a slight interest in the case," he said with a false laugh.

"Jude, don't…"

"I really can't see, though," he heard himself add, or perhaps it was another voice, speaking on his behalf, "why it is you do not stay."

"I cannot stay."

"After all," he went on, "I have loved you as no other."

"And I you."

"And yet you are leaving."

She made no answer. In the silence he felt splintered and so he moved away from her and reached for the cigarettes by his bed. Since her return to him he had often smoked, although he'd always asked her if she minded, and each time she had told him she did not mind – not anymore.

"May I?"

"Of course, Jude."

He lay beside her again. She watched the end of his cigarette brighten, then diminish, then brighten again in the stillness. She heard the sound of it crushed into the ashtray when he finished – a violent noise she thought as she lay there, somehow recalling the day he'd defaced her, and for which she was to blame, she remembered, and so she managed, barely audible, "There is the farm, Jude."

"Named after your mother."

"I have been there over ten years."

"So you have said."

"The day I arrived there was no life. The orchard was overrun, the flower beds memories, the stone walls mere sinuous mounds, secretive, abused from neglect. As for the river..."

She stopped. It was clear to him she liked the river best.

"Well it was there to be sure, coursing through aspens and willows, oaks and elms all tangled up – quite lost as well, like the mill and the footbridge."

She turned her head on the pillow. Her black mass of hair, damp still from their passion, streamed out beneath her – *like those woodlands*, Jude thought.

"You may wonder," she said then, "what I found appealing in that wasteland. It was the wasteland. My father was dead, buried in a churchyard nearby – buried nevertheless – along with all the trouble I'd caused. I had brought nothing but pain to those whom I'd cared for, and I had cared for him, Jude, before he left me, and for my mother, whose picture alone remained, and for Raphael – even for Raphael – although his wife, when she had thought I had gone upstairs, would say to her husband *sfortunata* – 'unlucky one' – never dreaming her husband would follow me once it got dark and she was asleep and my cousins were also asleep in their rooms.

"The wasteland was a chance for luck. In that dirt mass were acres that hadn't yet learned to judge. I could make life there perhaps, even beauty in the orchards – and Jude..." here she paused, "Jude, my beloved, if you could just see them now."

Her intensity struck like a blow, although the force should not have surprised him, for it was a subset of the passion he had come to know well.

"The house too has been restored. Very beautiful. Most authentic…I prefer the orchard."

He reached down to remove a stray curl from the strands that were permanent on her neck. In that brief gesture her need to leave him, she thought, seemed based on sand for some reason.

"There is also Elliot," she stammered.

"Pygmalion," he muttered unkindly.

"The name no longer applies. I have long ceased to feel indebted to the Chairman of the Department of Reconstructive Surgery for his contribution. I merely mention him because," here she stumbled, "like the woods, things between us are tangled."

A night wind over the river billowed the curtains beside Jude's veranda.

"He is a man of great pride," she went on, "obsessed with his place in the town, and his reputation as a physician, and both, as it happens, are now gravely at risk."

She paused, momentarily weary it seemed.

"He lost a patient last year. He had been drinking heavily the night before and should not have been operating. There is a lawsuit now pending. Malpractice – possibly worse. Nevertheless he lives well – he always did – better now than before, I should say, as though to prove to himself, and to his colleagues, that things will work out in the end. He goes to his office, spends time with his lawyer, his brokers – mostly his brokers I believe, I am not sure. I have never been sure. When we married, he – I was so young, so grateful – he made me sign things."

"He owns the farm you mean."

"No. The farm is mine. Everything else though, my inheritance, my investments – all in both names, managed by him over the years, as I was busy…" – the explanation seemed ridiculous on the eve of her departure – "I was busy repairing the footbridge."

"Not an unworthy endeavour," was Jude's reply.

"Well no, but now…"

"Now there is only this."

"Now he controls things," she said with insistence, "all but the farm, whose life depends on me, and for which I am grateful. Yes there I am grateful. Not even embryos could live in my flesh before that. I believe I explained this to you, Jude."

There was no longer bitterness in her tone – only weariness, resignation, and one additional thing beneath her resolution which baffled Jude as she lay there, bathed in a glow more blue than gold as the moon climbed.

"Yes, Caroline, you did mention that."

The clock beside him, like a metronome, kept time with his thoughts as he relived the explanation she'd taken such pains to craft well – the farm, where she had made beauty, the marriage which had ravaged her – and yet something remained still.

He reached for another cigarette. The moon above cleared the courtyard and bathed them both in frank amber. So that he might have the ghost of a chance of enduring her departure, he pressed her.

"It isn't the farm, Caroline."

"It is immense," she replied.

"Nor is it Elliot."

"He is a powerful man."

"That does not matter to you."

"The battle could strip me!" she cried, striving for conviction.

"Stripped I have always found you irresistible, Mrs. Devereux."

Had he not said that phrase – spoken from the heart, not as a ploy, though he knew from her weakening tone that that thing he had sensed, the motive withheld, was like a splinter nearing the surface – he might never had known the truth.

As it was, when again she did not answer, he turned from her, desire and anger mixed in equal parts, and finished his cigarette. Thus he was not aware that her immense eyes had filled with tears, never saw them spill onto her cheeks and down over her mouth, never guessed that with those last words he'd made her see, like Vianne, the one thing that mattered, in spite of the lies she was telling them both in the dark.

She forced herself to stifle a sob, for the thought of Vianne made her remember Rodin's garden, her vigil there, where for the first time in decades she had cried like a child.

Now again she was nearing the precipice.

She strove again for conviction, which refused to be summoned.

It isn't the farm, she said to herself. *The farm will always be cared for. There will always be life there, as one's children have life, and I would never be far. I would return when I could.*

Jude looked away still, now staring fixedly at the clock as one would an opponent, for it had become to him a hateful face.

Nor is it Elliot, she realized. *I have faced battles before, longer ones – uglier, and he is welcome to his victories. The farm is mine. The rest is nothing – nothing. Jude does not need it.*

Jude had faced her by then. He had counted five, perhaps six hours remaining, and the pitiful number had tipped the balance within in favour of anger, and so he had turned, and was about to respond, and was surprised when he looked down to see Caroline's face all wet, glistening like something pearlescent in the glow of the moonlight no longer blue.

In spite of everything – the pain they had each inflicted, the passion, the revelations – he had never before seen her cry.

"Don't, Caroline," he said at a loss. "If I have hurt you again like that first time, I am sorry. *Please* don't," he begged, for the tears had continued to fall and when at last the sob broke, and he too was undone, he wiped her face with his hands, a rough gesture, nothing at all artistic, feeling her hair damp again, this time from sadness.

"It is your mistress," she confessed when he bent down to her.

"What?"

"Not the one I have met. The one I have met I would always befriend, whatever the cost. It is the fact that I know – I *know*, Jude – that in the befriending, I would have to accept the others, because you would remain who you are and would always seek what you need."

He said her name out loud.

"It would not be easy," she insisted, as though he had said some other thing. "I have lived just such a life and it is an immolation.

"Yet for you Jude – for your work – to have had a part of it no one else could claim – I would try, but I would fail again, for I could not bear…" She broke off abruptly.

Replacement was not the word. Caroline knew in her heart that for Jude she could bear replacement.

"I could not bear to be a burden – a coda, an afterthought," she said at last to them both, in a calmer voice, lower, for his hands were all over her body, as though he were sculpting her.

"It would be unendurable," she murmured, beginning to move in response to his hands, although she thought that was finished.

"It has happened before to me, several times – as I believe I have explained before, but from you, Jude" – he had buried his head in her hair by that time. "From you it would take whatever was left still to give."

Their five hours had become three by the time passion was spent once again.

"Go," he said as dawn broke. "I know now why you must. Spend six weeks away from me. You will have learned by then, having endured a span of time that mirrors exactly the days spent nearby – you will have learned the most essential thing" – he was stroking her still – "that you will never be a coda, always a prelude, song most precious to a man with only an easel at his disposal."

Light in his room intensified as a determined morning replaced dawn.

"On that very day I will write to you – September tenth, Caroline, one week to the day when my show opens at Beaux-Arts – a significant retrospective, though the very concept makes my brush feel old."

She merely smiled, leaving her arms around his neck.

"I will ask you to marry me in that letter, and by then you will understand why it is you must agree."

"Yes, Jude," she whispered.

"I shall expect an answer, Mrs. Devereux."

"As well you should," she acknowledged, drawing him down to her, fearing nothing at all but the days in between.

Caroline was due at the airport no later than ten that same day.

It was already hot, not quite as warm as the dawn she'd arrived in, six weeks before to the day, but the gold on the Seine below the rue Séguier reminded her of that day as she turned back by the quay and smiled for the last time at the porter who kept on waving as she stepped into her cab.

Last to arrive at the counter, she reached the gate just in time, then proceeded to the tarmac and the plane waiting in the distance. She was no longer covered, as there was no longer a need. Instead of a turtleneck, she had on a tank top, scoop-necked and sleeveless, so that the breeze might refresh the vines that could not grow on her neck.

And yet still she was stared at, more than ever it seemed, not for the vines, or her height or the mass of hair caught at her neck, but for the allure in her walk – a tango she had learned to dance to.

ANDANTE

It was no longer surprise Dr. Devereux felt on the night his wife had arrived from Paris. Surprise he had felt when she had stepped out of the limousine earlier, wearing of all things a tank top which sculpted her breasts, revealing their fullness, and her long torso and the narrow waist and sepia tendrils he himself, as her surgeon, had been unable to eradicate. Not once in their married life had she exposed anything but her face and hands. New too was her smile, no longer shy – and her eyes, no longer veiled – and something he could not identify. It would come to him before long, to be sure. It was his business to study faces, as if he were a painter, although he worked with a scalpel on his subjects.

And yet he was still mystified during the dinner he'd planned to welcome his wife home. She had descended the staircase wearing a new gown, colour of plum wine, sleeveless and low-necked, displaying as if they were jewels on her neck his rare but occasional failures as a physician.

Irritated, he had watched her welcome their guests. He studied her as she circulated – no, not circulate, but rather undulate, a slow sway in her step that had always disturbed him, all the more so on this night with her neck and a bit of her breasts bare, and that long skirt cut on the bias swaying whenever she moved.

Even Walter Reston, Elliot's attorney, could not take his eyes from Mrs. Devereux, although it was not her markings he was looking at – these he seemed not to notice.

"My dear, you must be exhausted," remarked Dolly Reston, watching her husband watching their hostess. She was a large woman, not yet old enough to be considered handsome. Her navy dress, like her hair, was well cut and plain.

"Such an arduous journey," she continued, taking three sweet rolls from the silver basket Mme Devereux passed her way.

Caroline nodded.

"Paris in the summer, I mean – tourists, students, so many good restaurants closed."

"One manages."

"Barely, I should think," interjected Bunny Overton, arching her brows as she too stared at Mrs. Devereux. Bunny was tall, very thin, with luminous skin and blue eyes the colour of marbles. Her clothing always conveyed some sort of equestrian motif, on the off chance nobody mentioned she owned the largest horse farm in New Salem. Her brooch was larger than Mrs. Reston's, reflecting a slightly lower social standing. Her husband Barry had been Elliot's partner for over a decade before he'd retired.

"Yes, well, Caroline is, if nothing else, clever," went on Mrs. Reston, breaking her roll into minuscule pieces, hoping to neutralize its effects.

"That she is," said Dr. Devereux, handing the basket to Susan Foreman, New Salem's premier realtor, Chair of the League of Women Voters, Vice-President of the Garden Club and Elliot's mistress.

Susan was always tanned, winter or summer, with full golden hair brushed to perfection around her shoulders, large deep green eyes, elegant legs, fingernails painted coral.

"None for me, Elliot, thank you," she said with a marvellous smile, offering the basket to her escort, Tony Briscoe – debonair, newly divorced, or, as he preferred to put it, newly downsized.

"One perhaps, Susan."

Again Susan smiled. Then, as Bunny Overton was describing her horse farm, Susan stole another glance at her hostess. She had already noticed something remarkable about Mrs. Devereux that evening. *Not just the gown,* she had decided, *although it is exquisite.*

Dolly Reston unwrapped a chocolate.

It is what the gown represents.

She had, of course, heard from Elliot about his wife's body, her passivity. And yet on this night, for some reason, the former had been displayed, the latter seemed nonexistent. Warmth hovered about her, languor like midsummer's wind. As a matter of fact, Susan remembered afterwards, as Barry Overton slept in a lounge chair on the terrace, Mrs. Devereux had risen twice during the dinner, beads of sweat on her brow, throwing open the hall doors so as to admit August's breeze.

"We could extinguish the candles," Walter had said then, solicitous.

"Ah, but then there would be darkness," Caroline had responded, "and my dessert on its way."

And so the candles had remained there, flickering in the hall draft and Susan had pondered the curious fact that Mrs. Devereux had never allowed candles in her home before.

She continued to ponder while Tony Briscoe drove her home that night. In fact, as his Porsche slowed to a stop by her door, she allowed him to kiss her, long and deeply, having decided that Caroline, for whatever reason, had become a worthy opponent.

꙳ ☾ ꙳

"I thought for sure you would go for your usual walk tonight," Elliot said to his wife, after the last of their guests had departed. They were alone on the veranda.

"No, it has been a long day. I should like to sleep now."

"Very wise."

"And you?"

"I can't sleep yet. Walter's returning tonight."

"At this hour?"

"Just to go over some papers."

"They might be clearer first thing in the morning."

"Yes, well, they're due first thing in the morning."

"Ah," said Mrs. Devereux.

"This malpractice thing – well, it just never ends," he muttered bitterly.

"It will end when it's time," was her answer.

Her husband made no reply. After a while Caroline stood, walked to the railing and gazed at the fireflies dancing above the back lawn. A light breeze moved her hair back. She lifted her face to it, then to the tentative moon.

In that hesitant light, Elliot noticed, his wife seemed even more exposed than among the candles when his guests could not avoid observing her, above all when the flames had gone out and she had asked for some matches and had re-lit the tapers herself with only one match, which seemed to have reached her fingers long before she shook it, and then she had smiled and taken her seat.

It was, Elliot had to admit, a ravishing smile, so much so that nobody seemed to notice her most indecorous gown.

"Well," he heard in the stillness. "For now then, good night. As I said, I am tired."

They both knew he would be leaving after Walter left.

"Sleep well," he said.

"And you."

He watched her carefully as she turned.

"Caroline?" he called, as she reached the doorway.

"Elliot?"

"That dress of yours is new, is it not?"

"Yes."

"French, I suppose."

"Purchased in Paris."

"I do not think it flatters you," he said after a moment.

"I did not think you would," she replied.

Caroline's bedroom overlooked the back lawn. Elliot's room was also on the right, overlooking the front lawn. In between these was a dressing room – Elliot's office away from his office, although he rarely went in there, preferring the library below his bedroom.

Now, as he waited for Walter, he remembered how Caroline had reconfigured that space for a nursery. Its walls, in fact, had remained a pale yellow; a colour he did not care for. Twice he had told his wife to change those walls, but twice, for some reason, she had not done so.

Two large guest rooms on the left side matched the twin bedrooms on the right. Mostly their doors remained shut, as overnight guests at Todd's Farm were infrequent. Like Mrs. Devereux, Elliot had no siblings. His parents too were both gone. His world was his work, his women, fine wines, finer cars.

And yet there had been a time, recollected Elliot, when he'd been in love with his wife. He pictured it all precisely as he heard her moving about upstairs, turning of all things a light on, which she had never before done in the evening, not even on their wedding night.

Over a decade ago, he remembered. He was at the time her physician, a fact that had surprised his associates, for he was in demand then as a surgeon, and had repeatedly refused to take on new patients.

"Yes, but this girl is different," he had insisted.

Sipping his brandy, he could almost smell Yale University hospital's cafeteria, always a strange blend of cleanser and gravy. Over the sound of the crickets he could hear the squeak of the surgeons' soles on its black and white plastic tiles.

"I tell you," he had repeated eagerly then, "we're talking final frontier here."

"There has been work done already," a resident to his right had remarked.

"Lots of it," another colleague had added.

"Nothing compared to what I am determined to do," he'd replied.

Suddenly she had walked past them all – not in the cafeteria, but through the arcade alongside that led directly into the quad. Still, it was impossible not to stare at the odd languor in her walk, the mass of black hair, those improbable eyes that looked directly ahead, fixedly, as though she were watching events no one else could decipher.

Even then, barely into her early twenties, her figure had a ripe yet distinctly disturbing allure, though she seemed unaware of this fact, covered as she was that warm March day in a turtleneck, ankle-length skirt and high boots.

"If there were ever Galatea," Dr. Devereux had murmured as she disappeared, "that girl is it."

"Galatea indeed," the young resident had agreed, sceptical tone tempered in part by envy of the opportunity that had presented itself to Dr. Devereux. The other part had been a darker thing, for always somehow, unwittingly, even draped and at a distance, Miss Contini managed to stir fierce and unwanted intentions.

She'd stirred those same things in him, Elliot remembered. As he remade her he'd fallen in love with her, or with his creation, he was never sure which in those days – just that the sight of her called up strong things in his heart: pride in his achievement, which had been spectacular, lust for her body, which he knew better than his own form, fear of her courage, displayed repeatedly during the pain he had had to inflict, and one last undisclosed thing, unworthy of the Chairman of Reconstructive Surgery, Yale University Hospital. In her unabashed gratitude he saw submission, even adoration, and it aroused him to think he would own her from henceforth, as one would own a fine slave, controlling her flesh – his flesh, technically speaking – in his bedroom, whenever, as he had done in his office, although now it would be for his pleasure.

Graduation day he had proposed. Within a week she had accepted. He was proud of her elegance, her intelligence, the fact that they would be living comfortably in the large farm she had inherited.

Of that darker thing he wasn't proud. There it remained, though, drumbeat growing insistent as their wedding drew nearer – his erotic obsession for an almost incestuous domination of the woman who was, in a real sense, the child of his genius.

Within a year, the obsession had vanished. Indeed, within months Dr. Devereux had tired of the passive woman beside him. She was not a virgin – that he had known on their first night – although in her childlike inexperience, she seemed more virginal than a newborn. At first it had charmed him, then intrigued him, then bored him. In the end, it had left him enraged.

Yet he was at a loss to understand why. She had never refused him, whenever he asked her, whatever he asked for. She'd simply failed to respond, or was incapable of responding, and while he had intended to dominate, and did so often, viciously on occasion, there was in the end no Eros, no play, not even sport, he realized grimly, in the submission of a creature more like a doll than a passionate slave.

Partly in disappointment, partly to spite her, he'd had an affair before the year was out. A second one followed after she'd lost their first child. By the time she had lost the second, there had been countless women; some lasting longer than others, most of them known to her, for Dr. Devereux felt no need to occult things she would never challenge. Though she in time moved into the bedroom that looked back toward the river, and though she refused to repaint the nursery – for she was more wilful than damaged – she had no place else to go.

The light upstairs went out at last. How it had rankled him – that glow spilling over the stones! How it reminded him of her unpredictable ways, above all that one last unexpected rejection: she had refused more operations. One, two at the most, and he could have made her whole again – he was certain of it, and the concept had obsessed him long after her flesh had ceased to excite.

No, no that wasn't it, he saw in the clarity of the August moon. Her flesh had excited him still. It had never ceased to excite him – not as a lover, but as a doctor – and it was there that the doll had struggled, and denied him, and refused his entreaties, and had won her revenge.

⌐☾⌐

Free of her clothing at last, Caroline let the breeze blow through her hair.

Could it have been this morning? she wondered, hands vaguely redolent still of Jude McCallister's bed.

The moment seemed distant, yet at the same time about to happen – yearning which only deepened as the first week dragged on.

Five more still, she told herself firmly, then counting four…three, marking the calendar every evening, staring at the roadway each morning, finally counting one day remaining. By then her mind was made up. She would return to Paris by Christmas, New Year's the latest, finding new tenants for the main house, setting Elliot free once and for all.

Outright sale of the farm was out of the question. It was the only dirt that claimed her. She would come back to it often, whenever Jude could, for there was a guest house which would remain for them. This, she had determined, would be settled with her new tenants before her departure. So too would a civilized, swift, long-overdue divorce – finality which she was certain her husband would welcome.

Not for a moment did Mrs. Devereux think she might have misjudged things. At some point, perhaps, had she not been focused on the weeks that were passing so slowly, Caroline might have seen some intimation of trouble in the late-night meetings with Walter Reston, an indication of strain in Elliot's frequent and increasingly violent outbursts of impatience.

But she perceived nothing – only the calendar and the moonlight, ever changing, and the shiny black mailbox at the end of the driveway. Even passing languidly by that box each day, she seemed suspended somehow, oddly out of touch with the reality it represented, or could represent. For not once, not even fleetingly, did the thought occur to her, lost as she was in her dreams and such a fierce love, that the promised letter might not come. She simply waited, carefully planning as she'd go through each hour's obligations, planning again as she'd take her long evening walks through the farm, passing the guest house to the right of her driveway, the orchard across on her left, moving on down the back lawn which sloped to the woodlands, the footbridge, the river and mill house beyond. Here she would linger – here, where the wilful stream widened, then dropped abruptly beside an immense wheel which turned slowly, like time, alongside the old building.

He will paint this again and again, she reflected as the days waned – thoughts that the roar of the falls never diminished, certainly not toward the end of those seemingly endless six weeks, when just one more night had to pass before her life would change forever, and she would lie beside him, sometimes in the guest house, sometimes in the mill house, mostly in the studio overlooking Les Invalides.

One more night did pass, and then another night, and then a week went by and Caroline's life did change, completely, for no letter from Paris arrived.

In the first days it was as though some essential organ had failed her and yet the inconvenience of living remained.

Toward the end of the fourth day relief in the guise of self-deception appeared.

Six weeks from today I will write to you, he had said – she remembered it suddenly – not *Six weeks from today you will have word of me, my beloved.*

Of course there was no way for his communication to have arrived. Several more days remained to be endured still – five, six perhaps, seven more at the most.

Seven more days did come and go. They brought no word, though, from Jude McCallister.

Jude, began Caroline, in the letter she finally wrote.

I arrived safely, and all is well here, and the farm is lovely in autumn. So, I imagine, is the terrace garden outside your studio doors. I hope you are painting, long into the sunset, and finely.

The pickers have come to the orchard and were all finished by nightfall. Heavy rains fell thereafter, nearly a week as I remember, so that the river rose over the footbridge and I could not get to my mill.

I have been to the guest house, though – every day on my walks through the north fields, no longer in bloom.

In fact I've spent most of my time during these storms in that house, for I have books there I treasure, and cider and jam from the trees to put up, and the view of the ridge to the west is unobstructed.

By now, 17 September, your retrospective is due to open. I know it will be a success for you, both in a personal way, and, of course, in terms of your profession. All my good wishes for a stunning review go with this letter.

Caroline.

P.S. The letter you sent me somehow got lost on the way.

P.P.S. I hasten to add, then, since I know you must be wondering, that what you explained to me in your apartment on our last night was true, every word of it, for no sooner did I leave you than life elsewhere lost all meaning, and even this dirt I adore is foreign sand to me without you, so that home to me now is where you are painting – as you insisted it would be, which is my answer to the question that somehow got lost on the way.

Rains were heavy again the next the morning as Caroline took her letter out to the mailbox. Carefully she secured the small latch, raising the tiny red flag alongside so that the mailman could see from the ridge there was correspondence to be retrieved.

Another fortnight at most, she judged, turning back toward the main house. It would take no longer, she knew, for the note to reach Jude and his response to return.

Skies were clear two weeks later, the weather uncommonly warm, leaves in the orchard beginning to turn, bills and circulars still all she had found in the mailbox.

These she would from henceforth remember, as she would recall the fine weather, the breeze, the way the light played upon the orchard stone walls that afternoon – the same afternoon, as it happened, that she sat on a bench in the garden, clutching her daily packet of correspondence, unseen by the men whose voices drifted down from the library above.

"Elliot, you must have salvaged something."

"Christ, Walter!"

"I mean, I know there was need…"

"Need!"

"What with this lawsuit, your lifestyle…"

"My lifestyle, as you call it, has nothing to do with this thing."

Caroline missed Walter's response.

"Doctors lose patients," her husband replied then.

"Of course doctors lose patients. I've represented the best in my time. But they were sober when it happened."

"So was I."

"Not according to the blood tests."

"One drop of gin."

"More like a litre."

"Who's the client here?" exploded Elliot.

A flock of starlings flew out of the pines facing the library then, causing a ruckus with their cries and the seemingly aimless flapping of wings, so that for a while Mrs. Devereux merely sat on her stone bench, hearing nothing at all but confusion, until at last, after the birds had vanished, her husband's voice once again: "So there you have it."

"Yes, well, still…"

"Nothing, Walter, do you hear me?"

Caroline stared straight ahead, wide-eyed, as though sight had slowly but surely been restored to her. Outlines of things she had missed until then began to take shape as the men spoke: Elliot's fits of temper, the bills she would place on his desk every morning, the letter she'd never placed onto her own desk in the evening – everything unperceived, denied, misinterpreted day after day until this day, when in bright sunlight illusion, like morning's dew on the grass, evanesced.

And yet…

Yet Jude had surely been real. Surely, if for some time at least, he had felt passion, inspiration – these she had not imagined. No doubt he had planned to write, call for her once again and begin life anew as they'd planned.

And then his old life had intervened – fame, inspiration, commission, models and music his once again after a doubtlessly splendid retrospective, summertime's brief intermezzo no more than that come the fall.

How blind she had been, autumn days notwithstanding! How deluded until this refulgence, seated rock-still in the sun's glare, hearing her husband outline in detail their unavoidable ruin directly above her.

Indeed, there in the cloudless blue afternoon, Caroline did more than hear. She took a strange comfort in the unfolding. Why this was so she did not care to examine. It was enough for her simply to experience the substitution, more than blissful transfer, sudden absence of a far greater hurt as Elliot's voice drowned out sounds that resembled Jude's promise, and a forgetting appeared where Jude's image had taken hold, and, as the sun slowly shifted, the plans they had carefully made in some far-distant time seemed no more substantial than the ruckus of those starlings in flight.

"How, Elliot, how – that's all I want to know?" she heard Walter ask.

"The way these things always occur. There is need. One makes investments. One's decisions turn out to have been less than enlightened."

"Elliot, be specific."

Caroline listened, nothing now interrupting her focus.

"Even before the malpractice suit, Walter, I'd made investments with Caroline's money. It was a joint account, as you know. All but the farm here. That was separate – something to do with being sole and deserving issue…Well, since the thing wasn't liquid, but merely land here, and rather run-down at the time I might add, I never gave it a thought. You know how she is, Walter."

"Yes. Yes I do."

"Of course it's not run-down now. I give her credit for that. It may have taken ten years, but you can see what she's done here.

Not that it wasn't costly. She had the money, though, and my practice was thriving...It continued to grow –" Elliot paused, "though my way of life, too, became somewhat expensive."

"Elliot, did she never look at the books?"

"No."

"Demand an accounting?"

"No."

"She has never seemed to me to be stupid."

"Of course she's not stupid! She's just not smart, Walter, that's all, with her head all filled up with Ovid and whatnot, and this thing she has for the fruit trees, and the footbridge, and I don't have to tell you" – he lowered his voice, not because he suspected his wife was seated below them, but because this part of his story demanded discretion – "at one time she was damaged..."

"You needn't explain this."

"I have to explain this! She's been a child all these years, planting and reading and leaving the practicalities to me."

He must have moved closer to the window at that point, for Caroline heard every word clearly, like that bell tolling *Matins* outside Raphael's house.

"As I said, like a child, trusting me with her money as a child would her father."

"Well, yes, yes I see that, but that still does not tell me..."

"How I could have possibly run through it all?"

Caroline imagined Walter nodding then, in the stillness.

"It didn't happen at once. I rode a rise in the market, took a fall when it dropped and then I switched brokers. Somebody more aggressive. Another fall followed, though..."

"And Caroline kept on restoring."

"No, that was over, thank God. The major part anyway. It was just that my own life – my other lives," he corrected himself, "It all took time, a great deal of money, a lot of my attention...Even so, Walter; even so..."

Walter waited.

"I did not lose that patient because I was drunk. I lost him because…because my luck ran out, simple as that, as it had done in the market after I'd switched one more time and began taking tips from a colleague who was living well and seemed to know things. Well, he wasn't exactly a colleague."

"Nor did he seem to know things."

"Technically I could still operate. I still can, pending the hearing, but all this talk of malpractice…"

"Possibly manslaughter."

"Possibly manslaughter," repeated Elliot, with an exaggerated correctness. "It's a small town after all. Many patients have left me. Few have replaced them. I needed one last big tip." He almost faltered, despite his bravado. "It was the last one, all right. Caroline's fortune is gone. There are only my debts, overhead for my staff and the immense and stupid expenses involved in running this farm."

Had he not said those last words, uttered with such savage force, Caroline might have experienced something akin to compassion. As it was, hearing the desperation in his tone, she managed, just for a moment, to feel its poor surrogate, pity. But then in a clear voice above her, he felt compelled to add, "She'll have to sell, of course."

"All of it?"

"Christ almighty, who needs it? Who needs a main house, and a guest house, and a broken-down mill she wanders to in the rain as though she were mad?"

"She could work, perhaps…"

"Caroline?"

"You said before she wasn't stupid."

"I said before she wasn't smart. Besides, as I also said, she's been like a child all these years. Not so much now, not since this last trip, yet still there is damage…Surely you've seen it, you and Dolly both over the years."

After a moment: "No. No we have not. Dolly's merely noted, over the years, that she is very beautiful, and also distant, which is not coldness – more like disinterest – as though she were often in some other place, and that she dresses oddly, but with some flair."

"Picture it," pursued Elliot. "Odd, distant, inexperienced, doctorate in lieu of skills. In *Classical Antiquity*," he specified, as if it were soured milk.

Walter made no reply.

"Todd's Farm's up for sale, Walter. There is just no other way."

"Elliot, you don't own it."

"I know that."

"You can't sell it, then."

"No, but she will."

"I doubt it. She knows, after all, about – how did you put it? – your several lives? Once she learns these new facts…"

"She'll have no choice."

"She could keep the house and divorce you – did you ever think of that?"

Elliot whispered his answer, although for some reason Caroline heard it as though he were standing next to her, shouting. "No she won't, Walter. She's got no place else to go."

Long after dinner had been cleared that night, Elliot sat alone in his library, pondering. His wife had not appeared all afternoon. She had not joined him for dinner – no word sent, no note – a fact he'd found strange, given her confounded correctness.

Nearing nine he'd gone out to look in the guest house. Its usual low lamps were on, but she was not to be found.

No doubt still in that damned mill house, he had decided, returning to his thoughts and his brandy and the solitude of his library. For a while he'd relished this unlooked-for quiet, for he had much still to consider – decisions he hadn't even yet shared with Walter, let alone Caroline, planning as he himself was to sue for divorce.

Hard to believe, he reflected, almost incredulous still, and yet it had happened. He had fallen in love with his mistress – unforeseen entanglement he had always sworn he would never permit. Still, he had to be patient, wait 'til the hearing was over, sell the large farm in the meantime. Then and only then, with access to at least half of the handsome proceeds from the house sale, could he leave his wife and marry Susan. Divorcing any sooner would most assuredly cause a scandal – last thing he could afford awaiting a verdict concerning his probity.

The clock in the library hall tolled ten, then half-past, and then, hearing eleven chimes, Elliot stood and looked out over the porch to the driveway. All was in darkness – the guest house by now, the orchard, the wide lawn leading around to the back fields and woodlands. With a mixture of irritation and foreboding, hearing again half-past the hour tolled, he took out a flashlight, then heard the front door slam abruptly, followed by a knock on the library door.

"I saw lights on still, Elliot..."

"Where the hell have you been?"

"And so I thought I could interrupt now."

"Have you any idea what time it is?"

He stopped and looked at his wife, wearing that tank top again and a long skirt and boots that were scuffed now, clutching a yellow slicker in her left hand, her right hand still on the doorknob.

"No – no, I couldn't say, exactly."

"Nearing midnight."

Mrs. Devereux nodded.

"I haven't seen you since..."

"Sunrise," supplied his wife.

"Christ," he began, and then he broke off, enraged instead of relieved. He had planned to tell her that day that he had somehow lost her fortune, which she had entrusted to him like a child, but the time was not right now, and besides, Susan would be waiting.

"Well, you had better eat something," he managed.

"There is no need."

He broke his pencil in two, at his wit's end. "Milk and cookies at least!"

"When I am hungry, I'll eat," she replied, letting her slicker fall on the rug as she moved with that step he disliked towards his desk. Then, slipping into the red leather chair facing his desk, she said, "Elliot, I know it all."

Confused more than stunned, he made no reply.

"Everything you have kept from me all these years I now know."

Was she speaking of Susan? The countless affairs before Susan? Did she know how drunk he'd still been on that day in the surgical wing?

"I am referring," she said, as though reading his mind, "to the reckless investments, unorthodox advisement and irresponsible lifestyle which in the end robbed me of the inheritance I had a right to expect."

Now he was stunned. Still, though, he remained silent, his mind racing forward, backward – wondering how she had gained access to the darkest secrets of his financial morass. No explanation occurred. In a whisper at last he managed, "How did you learn?"

"I was in the garden this morning. The windows above me were open – your windows, Elliot, while you were speaking with Walter. I should have moved, of course – I confess I was most impolite – but as the subject concerned me, I was rude and unmannered and stayed right where I was."

He stared hard at her for a moment, conflicting emotions surging deep in his heart: anger at his own imprudence, mortification that she had heard his assessment of her and finally, washing over him like a great wave – relief. Their precarious situation was known to them both at long last.

"Caroline," he began. The next words should have been "Forgive me," but apology came hard to Dr. Devereux and, after all, he had not deliberately set out to sabotage her resources. Others too had lost fortunes in the downturns of the market, just as other doctors had lost patients, and she'd been so damnably passive.

"Caroline," he managed again, and then he straightened himself and said, "I am at least glad you have learned all there was to impart. We can move on from here, swiftly."

There was an appalling silence.

"We can address ourselves – not tonight, of course, when you must be exhausted – but in day or so, after you've had time to get over what must have been a terrible shock – we can address ourselves," he repeated, "to the practicalities of selling this farm."

"Todd's Farm will never be sold."

"You cannot possibly mean…"

"While there is life in me, Elliot, one breath remaining, this dirt will be mine, sole and deserving issue, along with the houses, the fruit trees, the mill and the river."

"But this is madness…"

"No doubt."

"Suicide…"

"My decision, though, and it is final."

Once again hardness washed over his face. She seemed not to notice.

"And just how, Mme Devereux, do you propose to survive here?"

"My plan is to rent the main house. The market is high right now, above all for large homes. That much at least you must have learned from Susan," she added pointedly. "She will also confirm that I can get five thousand a month for my house, which will more than cover the maintenance of Todd's Farm every year."

Not even the merest hint of dwindling conviction coloured her tone as she went on, "You and I, in the meantime, will move into the guest house – ample enough, I can assure you, though not quite the grandeur you've grown accustomed to, Elliot. Supplementally, I will work."

"*Supplementally?*"

"Oh, I know I am – how did you put it? – distant, inexperienced, odd and overqualified. Nevertheless, this dirt is mine."

At that point she sat back as though the discussion were concluded, and for a moment they merely looked at each other across what seemed a huge canyon.

Finally, in a conciliatory tone, because it had occurred to him that she might have concocted this scheme in order to spite his description of her, he said, "Caroline, be reasonable…"

"I have been."

"You cannot possibly make enough for us to live on…"

"There will be surplus from the main house."

"Still, there are debts and my practice has suffered, and the hearing could go badly…"

"Then you, too, I suspect, will have to look for a job."

He fell back in his chair, as though he had been struck by her.

"After five years," she continued, taking no notice of his reaction, "if we economize, those debts can be paid. With luck your practice or whatever other position you will have taken by then will have expanded."

She rose, picked up her slicker and crossed to the doorway. "I hope I have addressed your concerns tonight, Elliot."

Only her perfume remained as the door closed behind her.

The clock in the hallway struck midnight, then one, then two a.m. exactly.

His wife would calm down, he had decided.

How little he knew her.

Madame Devereux could be stubborn, that much he did know, but of this darker determination, the bedrock wilfulness she had somehow called forth – of this he knew nothing, for he had never seen her in that other life, as the head wrangler had seen her, when she'd race bareback at daybreak on wayward horses that were forbidden. Her father had seen it when she would dance on the fountain, also forbidden. Raphael too had had a glimpse, when she would struggle against him in her tiny bed above his wife's larger one.

And that other man, the one she had loved blindly – he too had been witness, for she had burned herself on his veranda and with her bandaged hand had slashed his work.

It was because of him in fact, because he had not written, because he would never write, she had decided – because of this she would never, while there was life in her still, lose the only thing that remained.

Elliot was mistaken, thus, on two accounts. He felt sure she would submit in time. She would not. And he believed himself to be the cause of the enormous anger he had perceived. It never occurred to him – indeed how could he know? – that it was another betrayal which had dealt the fierce blow, with a pain that recalled Communion day, and that another man had made her determined to defy anyone who tried to break her again.

In one respect, though, Dr. Devereux was not mistaken. September became October, the days became shorter, and his accomplished wife could not find a job.

"I am beginning a new life here," she had repeatedly written in her ornate old-world script, carefully fitting the phrase into the small space marked *Reasons for Application* at the bottom of the paper attached to each clipboard.

Above this line, next to *Pertinent Special Interests*, she had listed, in ascending order, "Classical Archaeology, Mediterranean History, Brahms, Pre-Colombian artifacts and state-of-the-art equipment in trauma centres, worldwide." Next to *Additional Information*, she had listed her seven languages, although there was barely room for the last one, Catalan, which she managed to squeeze into the margin. Alongside *Clerical Skills* she had written nothing, nor had she entered information in the box provided for *Typing Speed, Most Recent Test Scores*.

These glaring omissions, along with the catalogue of qualifications she somehow considered important, unfailingly managed to make potential employers squint. Stillness would follow – lengthy, it seemed to Caroline, filled with dwindling promise, and so she would hastily interject that she was in need of no vacations, could work overtime, anytime, and was available to start immediately, next day the latest.

At that point, her (no longer) potential employers would nod, extend a weak hand instead of an offer and promise to communicate, absolutely, should circumstances change in the future.

They would stare when she'd stand, as they had stared when she'd entered – at her shape, and her height, and the mass of black hair seemingly soaked with the humidity in the blistering Indian summer that had assaulted Manhattan.

Thus, towards October's end, the thought of her only remaining interview filled Mrs. Devereux with dread. It was, after all, the end of the day, end of the week, no end in sight to the heat.

Best to cancel while there's time, she decided, causing two taxis to veer as she stopped absently in the traffic. She fumbled in vain for a dime. The fruit man beside his pushcart had no change. The bars along Eighth Avenue, where she might have found a phone, were still closed.

No choice but to continue. She made her way toward the Hudson, skirting vacant stoops and garbage cans until she reached a row of red buildings partially hidden by peeling identical posters.

She re-checked the address in her small Moroccan notebook, then checked her watch, hoping she'd arrived too late, then realized this was indeed the place and that she was exactly on time.

A pair of brown dogs, one muzzled, one barking, both chained to a hydrant beside the entryway, caused her to check again, then slip gingerly between them into a narrow hallway beyond.

Over a hand-scrawled *Out of Order* sign beside the elevator, a bare, feeble bulb burned. An arrow next to the sign pointed to the emergency stairs. Caroline walked up, counting three landings in the darkness, emerging directly in front of the entrance to Suite 304, double-locked, peephole secured, *Anatole Kramer and Associates, Employment*, affixed to it in black individual letters that slanted downward.

Associates turned out to be a young boy, eighteen or so, with aquamarine eyes that stared through the peephole before a bolt within was withdrawn and Mrs. Devereux was told to enter.

"Won't be a moment," he mumbled, pointing to a black vinyl sofa beside a tall plastic palm.

She sank down onto the sofa, grateful for a seat by any palm tree at that moment. The whir of the desk fan was also most welcome, for it drowned out the recurring fear that had made her exhausting days fruitless since her confrontation with Elliot, three weeks before.

And then she let her eyes close – *just for an instant*, she promised herself – although she heard nothing ten minutes later when a second door opened.

She felt a touch on her shoulder, then a second one and then she looked up to see *Associates* pointing behind him toward a second man, framed in the open doorway.

"Mr. Kramer," whispered *Associates*.

"Come in," said Mr. Kramer, who had declined to advance.

Caroline stood, dropped her Moroccan notebook, picked it up quickly and followed Mr. Kramer into the office behind him.

"I am beginning a new life here," she started, for she had seen no clipboard, and had been given no application, and then abruptly, as she was about to tell him of her special interests, her availability, and her general education, she stopped.

"Is something wrong, Mrs. Devereux?"

"Wrong?"

"May I get you some water?'

"No, no I'm fine," she replied, transfixed it appeared, for he had turned and lifted his window shades so that suddenly, directly beneath them it seemed, the Hudson River had appeared – languorous and silent, its mixture of black, gold and purple reflecting sunsets over the Seine she had tried so hard to forget.

Anatole Kramer stared – not as the others had done, for the woman seemed out of time to him then, certainly out of place so near to the river – and yet oddly, with her colours reflecting the water – jet black hair and violet eyes and that strange pallor of hers slightly bronzed with the heat – she seemed at the same time to partake of it.

A steamer horn sounded. Caroline listened as the sound was repeated. *No more chances after this last one*, she seemed to hear in its mournful farewell.

"Mrs. Devereux?"

"Forgive me," she murmured. "I – it's just that the view from here…," she checked herself. It would not do to reminisce. She had to stress her potential in this final meeting, admitting her deficiencies before Mr. Kramer could ask her, for that was the Hudson below her, Palisades in the distance and Jude McCallister's footsteps would not be heard on those banks.

"I have not had, Mr. Kramer, a lot of experience," she began – haltingly, despite her resolve. "Recent experience, that is to say, in the general clerical arena."

She straightened herself in his brown leather side chair, which was cracked on the armrests, where most of the brass nails were missing.

"And of course I am out of school a bit," she continued, smoothing out her skirt, making no mention of her doctorate, her travels, her lifetime of scholarship.

Mr. Kramer merely nodded, for he had already assumed she was in her mid-thirties, recently divorced, had never worked a day in her life and was unemployable. "Nevertheless" – here there was silence, for the ship had moved on, leaving behind just the shimmering river, its waters now charcoal, like the woods by her mill at day's end – "nevertheless," she tried again, "I can translate, Mr. Kramer."

"You can do what?"

"Into English, out of English, via many languages in between."

"Yes, well, that is all very good…"

"And I have no other commitments."

"However…"

"And I am reliable, prompt, discreet, good with details and…and my penmanship is excellent, as your associate, who has my card still, can attest to."

Mrs. Devereux did not add then, though she felt in conscience she should say it, as it was the most important thing – that she was absolutely alone, and desperate.

She did not need to.

When she raised her face to him then, concluding her catalogue of possibilities with a mixture of triumph and pain in her fine, humbled eyes, Mr. Kramer unexpectedly saw another face, indistinct for decades until that moment in his office.

John Jacob Kramer, Ph.D., the old man's cards had once read. For some reason, Anatole remembered then, his father had kept those few cards. There had never been need. He had not learned English in Moscow. When he had fled with his family during a World War I pogrom, a teaching position in Physics was therefore out of the question in New York. Still, as head custodian in a high school, he had managed to tutor some, correcting equations outside the utility room.

Caroline assumed in the absolute stillness that her qualifications, presented so forcefully, had fallen short once again.

"I can begin immediately," she said hastily, and was about to decline vacations, when he waved her silent, thought for a moment, then reached for a grey metal box on the right side of his desk.

She watched intently as he took a stack of index cards from this box.

No, he said to himself, shuffling and reshuffling and shaking his head from time to time. *No. No, that won't do. This one's not it.*

He pressed his intercom buzzer and called *Associates* into his office.

"Justin," he asked, "has our contract with Mr. d'Olivier expired at this point?"

"Yes and no, sir."

"Yes and no?"

"Well, he was not pleased with the lady you sent him and was hoping you would find him another and therefore he said he would wait some before deciding."

"So what's the problem?

"The contract ended today."

A substantial pause followed.

"I'm sure he'll take the lady we sent him, sir, as there's been no other candidate, and besides, at this point, if we send him another, sir, technically…"

"That will be all Justin, thank you."

The boy made his exit.

Caroline waited.

Anatole Kramer stared at the river. He had earned his commission. Monsieur would take the girl sent – he had admitted as much – and if he now presented this woman, what would the agency make? There'd been expenses – phone calls, listings, and while Maximilian d'Olivier would reimburse him for these, he was certainly not a man to forget dates on a contract.

Technically speaking, Anatole Kramer and Associates could not demand a commission.

Bad luck, he said to himself, turning back in the swivel chair that always groaned whenever he moved. *Business is business, after all. This place is hardly non-profit.*

And yet there she was still. She had not moved. In fact at that point she leaned in to him, laid a hand on his arm and raised that face of hers that resembled Dr. John Jacob Kramer's expectations, never to be fulfilled.

"Is it a position I might be qualified for?" she whispered.

Anatole was at a loss. He had earned his commission. It was late. He was hungry.

"Yes," he said after a moment. "Yes it is," and then he looked away, ashamed of himself for forgoing money earned, although his fees were never large ones, and the pogroms were not his doing.

"Take this," he said, almost roughly. "There's a name and address there. I will phone and alert the housekeeper to expect you tomorrow, five p.m. sharp."

"Housekeeper?" repeated Caroline, faintly.

"Well you cannot expect Monsieur d'Olivier to answer the door himself now, can you? He is not young – somewhat infirm, I've been told. You will be taken to him directly. He will interview you in his home."

"But what does he do?" she blurted out, suddenly seized with a terror that like the first candidate she too would fall short.

"He reminisces."

"He what?"

"Just what I said. Recollections. He's writing his memoirs."

"I see," said Mrs. Devereux, although she didn't.

"As I understand it, his publisher's American and the book must be in English, although Monsieur's memories are in other tongues. He is Austrian, raised in France, led the Resistance during this last war. Well he will explain all that, no doubt. Main thing for you to know now is that he wants to speak as the thoughts occur to him, in the language they occur to him, although he wants the results to be English, simultaneously, as it were."

It was now Caroline who stared, wide-eyed, for the position seemed at once daunting and perfect, and yet it all seemed so improbable.

"Your *penmanship*" – Anatole stressed the incongruous word – "will come in handy. It is all to be done on the spot, as it were, on location, with his own pen in some special notebooks."

She nodded.

"Can you be there tomorrow?" he asked abruptly.

"Yes. Yes, I can."

"He despises tardiness."

"With good reason," said Mrs. Devereux, who for the first time that afternoon had smiled wondrously at Mr. Kramer, who in turn no longer – not for a moment – regretted his decision, for she was astoundingly beautiful, as his parents had been.

Among the pedestrians enjoying the end of the heat wave at last, only Caroline seemed concerned as she hurried down 86th Street. At five p.m. exactly she was standing outside an immense beige stone building, its twin archways leading directly to a courtyard within.

With consummate indifference, a doorman surveyed her.

"I have an appointment," she managed, producing Mr. Kramer's frayed card. "Five o'clock this evening. Maximilian d'Olivier."

"Monsieur d'Olivier receives no visitors."

Caroline turned to a street sign, which was too far away to decipher. The doorman also turned, bowing deeply to an elderly woman just emerged from the archway, gloves on, hat in place, neck wrapped in mink skins with little paws that tapped her shoulders as she disappeared into the twilight, leaving behind the oddest mix of *L'Air du Temps* and camphor balls.

"If you would ring, please," suggested Caroline.

"As I explained, Madame…"

"I can't be late tonight," she insisted, so that a second doorman appeared under the dark, ornate arch.

"Trouble, Matthias?"

"It's nothing, Eugene…"

At that moment the phone rang. Eugene disappeared into a small octagonal office carved into the stone of the arch.

"Yes," Caroline heard. "No, I was not informed. I shall tell her at once, Mrs. Varig."

Eugene emerged. He bowed slightly. "Apartment eleven," he said. "Do go right in."

Caroline hurried through the archway, then stopped abruptly in the courtyard. *But which entrance?* she wondered, for there was a door at each corner under identical awnings, each approached by identical pathways.

Both doormen re-entered the archway, catching a glimpse of Mrs. Devereux. The setting sun vanished, so that colours inside the courtyard went from deep amber to mauve.

"He'll take this one," Eugene judged.

"You think so?"

"Wouldn't you?"

Matthias made no response, but merely watched for a moment as Caroline shaded her eyes and stared at the doorways ahead. Her suit, violet tweed that matched her shawl, was fringed in a darker hue – half charcoal, half black, like the evening. For all of her efforts – and it was clear she had made them – stubborn wisps of her hair had escaped the comb at her neck.

"Yes. Yes, I would," was all he could think of to say then, before a frail child on a tricycle appeared in a doorway, picked up speed on the pathway, circled around the fountain and bumped headlong into Mrs. Devereux, almost sending her into the water.

Matthias by then had reached the courtyard's fountain.

"Please – which door?" Caroline pleaded, still shaken, for it was now five-fifteen, and the tricycle had brought to mind another fountain, another fall.

"On your left there," gestured Matthias. "Southwest corner of the building."

Caroline walked away quickly, wrapping the tweed shawl around her as she approached the doorway that led to the apartment of Maximilian d'Olivier.

It was on the first floor, to the right of the entrance.

Caroline stood in the shadows, reading his name below the knocker, aware of a silent, almost monastical coolness in the hall. There were no other apartments – only a warren of mailboxes on the left, elevators beyond that and then the hallway forked, curving right toward a staircase, left to another hallway, the division marked by a polished table on which a classical urn filled with white roses had been placed.

She knocked, eyes adjusting to the darkness. The door opened slowly, revealing an even deeper obscurity. And then Elsa Varig appeared – grey-haired, correct, uncommonly inaccessible.

"I am Mrs. Devereux."

The door opened wider.

"Monsieur is expecting you."

Caroline followed through an oak-paneled vestibule. Beyond, hard to make out in the ever-increasing dimness, was the living room.

They stood in silence there a moment, Elsa Varig watching the candidate, squinting her colourless eyes.

"The heat wave has broken, I understand."

"Yes."

"Will you take coffee?"

"No, thank you."

"A cool drink perhaps."

"I'm fine."

"Please have a seat while you wait then."

Caroline chose the nearest possibility – a tapestried armchair by the vestibule. Elsa turned and went up the curving staircase left of the entrance behind them. Her shoes struck unevenly as she climbed, for she had a perceptible limp, and the gleaming staircase was bare. The second floor must have been carpeted, for suddenly all human sound ceased. Then, as though only palpable in the silence, outlines of the living room began to take shape.

It was a long room also paneled in oak, with tall matching windows facing the courtyard beyond. Everything inside was overscaled – the massive armoire, the velvet bergères, the antique chandelier, the Aubusson rug. Largest of all was the handsome stone mantel on the opposite wall. To its left was an archway that led to a dining room in the distance. To its right there was a second arch, a magnificent shell in the wall where a set of porcelain was displayed.

Caroline felt buoyed by a grandeur that seemed lovingly cared for. For a while she just sat there, motionless in the half-light, and then a clock struck upstairs. It struck again a second time, and then a third, and by then she had risen, transfixed by that set in the arch.

Service for twenty, she mused, running a finger along the rim of a soup plate on the middle shelf. It was richly hued, with a trio of navy, maroon and gold initials in the centre. *What stories these old plates could tell.* She smiled, in spite of the heat in the room, wishing they could tell her something about the man who was now – she checked her watch – forty-six minutes late. Discreet and solid, though, fine servants all, the plates said nothing, and so she turned and suddenly noticed another space – a library left of the living room, even darker than the living room, for it was in the interior of the apartment.

Peering inside the door, she could see book-lined walls, maps, a large desk at the far end, a door alongside leading to yet another space, even deeper within.

No doubt he works here, Caroline said to herself, feeling a soupçon of uneasiness – first she'd had since she'd arrived – at the prospect of sharing these hidden catacombs with her employer.

She pushed the door open some more, as though the library might reveal what the plates would not say, but her reverie was interrupted by Elsa Varig behind her.

"Monsieur will see you now," announced Elsa, having clearly returned from some rear staircase beyond.

Caroline was mortified, as though she'd been caught reading somebody's mail. She turned, ready to enter the dining room, but Elsa Varig had crossed toward the staircase.

"This way, Mrs. Devereux."

Caroline paused.

"Mind the first step here. It is uneven."

The interview, it appeared, was to be held on the second floor.

Suddenly everything seemed bizarre. The whole assignment seemed odd. Who even knew she was in that house then? Well, Mr. Kramer knew to be sure, although the thought of him at that moment was hardly reassuring.

She looked up and saw Elsa waiting, her impenetrable froideur no longer correctness but something darker, like the absence of light in the rooms.

To her left, Caroline knew, was the small vestibule which led to the corridor and then to the courtyard and beyond that the street. She could walk out through that door. There were no chains, no extra locks, only a direct route to the corridor, the awning, the fountain – that desperation in the streets again and the memories submerged in them.

"Thank you," Caroline murmured, following Elsa Varig up the steps.

The second floor hallway was, as she'd surmised, carpeted. They passed a closed door on their right, then a small dining room, also on their right, uncharacteristically bright, overlooking the courtyard. Across the hall from this room was a small interior study. Finally, at the end of the corridor, above the larger dining room she imagined, there was another closed door. Elsa Varig knocked, waited and then a voice from within responded – from a distance it seemed – "Come in Elsa. I am waiting."

It was indeed a distance. The room was huge, as dark as the salon below, darker perhaps – Caroline wasn't sure – for Elsa Varig was introducing her then and a man was approaching them both in the dimness.

"Caroline Contini Devereux," Elsa announced, mispronouncing it, disdaining to read from the card she'd been given. "About the translator's position."

"Thank you, Elsa," responded the voice, clearer as it got closer, and then Caroline saw him – medium height, powerful build, white hair brushed away from a wide, knowing forehead. His light eyes were intense, his lips firm, his steps unsteady as he leaned on a transparent cane, slowly approaching.

"Thank you for your patience," he said, extending a hand to her in the shadows. "It was kind of you. I am grateful."

"The room was beautiful. I am indebted."

There was a moment.

"That will be all, Elsa," he added, then the door closed and the shadows increased, and Caroline barely made out the man's crisp white shirt, dark paisley ascot, midnight blue jacket, carefully belted.

Instinctively – for until recently she was the chatelaine, never the supplicant – Caroline slipped off her glove and took the hand he had offered.

"I am happy to meet you," she said sincerely. The waiting was over at last, and, like the furnishings, the fact had buoyed her. "How do you do?"

"Well enough this evening, thank you," he answered, in German.

He studied her in that pause that followed.

"Weather is warm still?" he continued.

"Joyfully no," she responded, her German refined. "Autumn arrived last night – like a tardy schoolgirl, very pretty, so of course nobody minded."

He smiled, then glanced again at her card. No address. No telephone number.

"And the trip in from – where again was it?"

"New Salem."

"Ah."

"Just over the border."

They both nodded.

"Not too arduous, I hope," he remarked then in French.

"Not in the least," she answered in kind, removing the other glove, at home in his bedroom for some reason, as she'd been earlier, alone, reviewing the tri-coloured service for twenty ensconced in his shell.

"Two hours and then some…"

"Plus a third one downstairs. Again, I am sorry. I was indisposed, Mrs. Devereux. Or is it Miss. Or Ms. Or none of the above," he went on, clutching the vague card in his left hand, the sturdy cane in his right.

"All of the above."

He looked again at the card, rereading only "Caroline Contini Devereux."

"So it is I who must be tested," Maximilian responded archly.

Caroline made no answer. Her head was swimming all of a sudden, what with the heat in his room – twice that, it seemed, of the salon directly below him – and the extraordinary uniqueness of the moments passing between them.

"I suppose I shall say then 'Miss Caroline,'" he decided. "That is an option down South, I've heard. I have yet to visit those states. I shall have to trust the rumour."

They were still speaking in French – his like a beach in Provence, throaty and low, hers balanced and crisp, like a Parisian hotel. Nevertheless, because of this music they shared – sounds that predated the Romans, similarities that resembled relatives – they could banter, perhaps with a smile here and there, taking liberties that would be thought license in a more cautious Saxon exchange.

"Please sit down," he said abruptly, pointing with his transparent cane to a writing desk left of the doorway.

He took his own chair with effort, having first helped Mrs. Devereux into the applicant's chair, facing his own. Then, awkwardly, reverting to English again, he said, "Mr. Kramer sent no résumé –"

"I don't believe there was time."

"Do you type?"

"I do not."

"Shorthand?"

"I am sorry."

"Speedwriting, perhaps…"

Mrs. Devereux shook her head.

"Yes, well, some people rely on Dictaphones," murmured Maximilian.

"I suppose they do," replied Mrs. Devereux.

The clock in the hallway struck six-thirty.

"Will you have tea?" Max asked all of a sudden.

"No, thank you."

"Sherry then," he insisted, reaching for a decanter on the table behind him. The elixir was sweet and welcome, in spite of the heat, and neither spoke for a moment as they sipped from their small crystal globes.

"Miss Caroline," Max said all of a sudden, "do you cry openly on occasion?"

Taken aback by the question, she replied simply, "Yes."

"Do you laugh as much?"

"More so."

"Remember things well?"

"The remarkable ones."

"And when you translate?"

"I do not translate," was her answer.

"I don't understand."

"It is more like creating."

"But the position here..."

"Not from whole cloth, to be sure."

He put his glass down.

"Forgive me. The word was ill-chosen. I render, Monsieur – recreate, reshape thoughts anew so that the sound fits them exactly."

She too put her glass down, no longer ashamed of her inexperience, just angry that he had made her admit it, over and over again, when it was clear he had wanted someone more technically suitable. Well, that someone skilled could have the job. Before she left, though – because this last chance too seemed doomed – she felt compelled somehow to explain herself, at least the allure words had for her when the sound fit them exactly, which was perhaps self-definition.

"And the sound must fit exactly," she said abruptly at that point, as though Max had followed her thinking. "If there is to be music, I mean, something beyond a series of marks on the page or shapes in the mouth, something that resembles what the lark does by instinct."

He refilled his glass slowly. She declined any more.

"Harmony, then..."

"Yes," she replied. "A most complex union. A perfect marriage," she concluded, and then she leaned back a bit, resignation in the gesture.

Maximilian d'Olivier said nothing for a moment. He too leaned back, looked away and then as though from a distance she heard, "Regrettably..."

"I understand, Monsieur."

She rose.

He put his hand on her arm.

"Sit down please," he said, in a tone somehow both vulnerable and commanding.

"I am ill. And therefore under a deadline. A nightly one, I must add, as I can allow nothing of mine to be published unless I have seen it first, and borrowed time goes the fastest."

He drained his glass.

"I must work quickly," he continued, "signing off every day on the words for that day. Only then will sleep come, in the wake of a bit of peace perhaps, followed by the chance to work the next day, if I am fortunate. Do you understand me?"

Caroline nodded.

"Because I understand you, the way that you work, I mean, the desperation, and while the perfection implied in your translations" – he corrected himself – "renderings, I'm not so sure I can afford them. All that emotion recollected in tranquility. It just might take too long."

For a few moments the room, the courtyard, the whole city was silent. He was rejecting her, that was clear, yet his hand was on her arm still. It was a firm grip – powerful still – transmitting his own desperation and more than a hint of his passions, stronger than ever perhaps.

"Wordsworth was referring to focus, Monsieur. Inspiration can happen on the wings of a dove."

She raised her eyes to his. He drew his arm away, having seen clearly, for the first time, their intense and incredible hyacinth hue.

"This can be done, then, is that what you're saying?"

"This can be attempted..."

"But can it be done?" he insisted.

The words were English still, though the gravel in his voice had returned, like high tide at Nice.

"Mind you, I need precision here – no adaptations, no half-truths. You must see what I see, simple as that, rendering the view exactly" – he paused – "with splendour, though, absolutely. Since you have dangled the prospect of both to me this evening, I shall accept nothing less."

He sat back in his chair. It was more a challenge than an offer. Was she to think on it? Accept at once? Should she mention the pay scale, the hours, the labyrinth of benefits that always seemed to be her downfall?

"You will render in English," he continued. "It is Americans who have asked for this life – the war years mostly, the Resistance, a free

France in the end. I will speak as I remember things – now German, now French, on occasion a bit of Spanish. Is Spanish a problem?" he queried, as if an extra language were an afterthought.

She shook her head.

"We'll work in here." He motioned to a table and small chair next to a daybed beneath the windows. "You will think that chair too close perhaps, but I must see your face well, how you react from time to time, even if only fleetingly. If I have said something incorrectly, I'll know it at once. It is the only way I'll have of gauging things."

Her head was swimming again. She began to feel faint. For the second time since she had entered, she was aware of the extraordinary heat in the room.

"Miss Caroline?"

"Monsieur?"

"Call me Max."

"Then I am Caroline."

"Which means you'll take it?" he asked bluntly.

She did not answer – nonplussed, not undecided, although he feared the latter. Nevertheless he pressed on, lest he himself lose his nerve.

"I don't rise early. We cannot begin before eleven. I shall have Elsa Varig bring us coffee at twelve-thirty each day. Lunch will be served at two. I believe you passed the small dining room on your way in here before."

Caroline turned toward the hallway, grateful to have been grounded – even for an instant – in time and space and his corridor, recognizable dimensions.

"Yes, that's it. Facing the courtyard. Have I tired you?"

"No."

"Good. I myself do tire. I wish I did not," he confessed. "So after lunch I must rest. You may too if you like. At four we begin again – a review, no more renderings – a chance to correct what you said I said before lunch. Tea at five-thirty. Music at seven. Yes – a long day," he agreed, for although she had said nothing, her eyes had widened, if wider were possible. "The music is overtime. Still, it is required. A coda to our efforts. A preparation for the next day's work." He smiled, beginning to hope that her silence meant acquiescence. "I have a light supper at nine. You're free go before that, of course, back to..." he couldn't remember.

"New Salem," she said gently.

"Forgive me. You brought no résumé, though Mr. Kramer did mention credentials. Yale University, *summa cum laude*. Classical Civilization. Emphasis Greece, I believe."

"Yes."

"Fifteen years ago."

"Fourteen."

"Nevertheless I must ask you..."

"Why have I have done nothing with them?"

"On the contrary. You seem to have done much with them. You've made the Greek way your own – outwardly, at least. One presumes inwardly." He'd switched to French again. "Why now, that is all. A job now..." He broke off.

"I need the money."

She spoke in English still – narrow conduit to her motives that made it clear that's all he'd see.

"Of course."

French was abandoned.

"Forgive the intrusion. As I said, I am pleased."

She smiled. He remained perplexed. Did she have a habit? Was she ill? A gambler perhaps? It all seemed unlikely. Mr. Devereux had found another, no doubt. Yet that too seemed odd, given her effortless allure.

"How much do you need?"

"As much as possible."

There was a knock on the door.

"The musicians, Monsieur."

"Is it seven already, Elsa?"

"Ten minutes before."

"I'll go right in."

Elsa retreated. Max opened a drawer and took an envelope

out. "I pay by the week. In advance. One thousand dollars in cash. Cheques take too much time."

He placed the envelope in her hands, to spare her having to reach for it. "There will be raises of course. Bonuses. Overtime, if we can't stop – above and beyond the music of course. Which is live, by the way." He smiled, amused by his thorough presentation. "And it is required."

She too smiled again, thinking him like his furniture, oversized and somehow right.

"Will you listen tonight?"

Caroline had said she'd be returning by nine. The next connection was not until ten. "I'd like that, Max."

"Berlioz," he informed her, taking her arm as they passed through a doorway behind him.

Directly ahead was the small room she'd seen from the hallway before.

"Your study, Max?"

"Once."

The cellists were tuning their instruments.

"Now it is a music room."

Making his way with some effort, Max took his score from a table, offered Caroline another one, then sat on a sofa facing the musicians. She took the armchair beside him, at right angles to both.

Later, over supper in the little dining room, Caroline realized she'd missed the ten o'clock too. But Max had been lost, out of time, transfixed by the yearning transcribed into the Berlioz piece.

"Can you imagine," he asked abruptly, refilling her wine glass, "loving a person so much, stalking her every move, filling her world with music until she'd no choice but to surrender to the harmony in your soul?"

"Yes. Yes I can."

"Would you have done it?"

"Stalked or surrendered?"

"Both, I suppose."

With a candour that surprised the two of them she replied, "I have done both in my time."

Max looked at her then, intently, noticing for the first time that her mouth was more sensual than sad in its enigmatic nostalgia.

After that they ate in silence by the light of the candles until a knock at the door interrupted their coffee.

"Antonin has arrived," announced Elsa from the hallway.

"Ah. Right on time. Have you a wrap with you, Caroline?"

"I – yes. I left a shawl downstairs."

"Well, you mustn't leave it behind. It will be cold in New Salem, though I will remind Antonin he is to leave you right at your door."

"There is really no need, Max…"

"There will be need every day – snow here, rain there, delays on your train for no reason at all. I cannot have delays. Nor will I have you finding your way late at night. Car fare goes with the position."

Elsa returned with the shawl.

"Or more precisely the car," he went on. "You will like Antonin – will she not, Elsa Varig?"

"Everyone is fond of Antonin," Elsa responded, picking a tray up.

Again the door closed behind her.

"Well," said Max, leaving his cane by his feet as he stood, "'til tomorrow then, Caroline."

"'Til tomorrow, Max," she replied, and then she turned slightly, for he had extended the shawl intending to drape it around her, deluding himself into thinking the gesture was out of politeness.

"Thank you," she murmured. "For everything," she added quickly, turning to face him again.

"We will work long and hard," was his answer.

She nodded. He heard his door close behind her, the sound of her high heels on the staircase, a pause and then as though from a distance his front door vaguely closing.

Caroline stopped under the awning.

"Antonin?" she called softly, seeing a solitary figure beside the fountain.

"I am Antonin, yes. Good evening Miss."

The figure began to move to her. He was a huge man, powerful, dark hair framing a wide face, dark eyes that stared when he reached her, then lowered quickly again. His mouth was full; his cheekbones high; his skin toughened by exposure more to life, it seemed, than cold. His jacket, a short navy pea coat, frayed a bit, was unbuttoned, though he had turned his collar up against the chill. He wore no gloves.

"I am sorry to have kept you waiting. I am Caroline."

"I did not mind the wait, Miss."

A harvest moon cleared the roofline leaving the white night air pure, almost ethereal, like the fountain's murmur behind them.

"I've left the sedan in the west arch. It is ready to take you now."

"Thank you, Antonin."

"Mind the cobblestones, Miss."

They did not speak for a while as he guided the car into the street and proceeded west toward the river.

She leaned her head back and closed her eyes and sleep came to her until the bridge span, brighter than ever in the moonlight, awakened her. They climbed the Heights and left Manhattan behind them. Ahead was the parkway and an hour's drive to Todd's Farm.

She noticed his neck then, for he had tucked his collar down. It was thick and strong, like his hands, and no doubt weathered, like his face, Caroline thought, although it was too dark to ascertain that.

"You won't be home 'til late, Antonin," she observed finally, in the darkness.

"Rarely am, Miss."

"You mean you drive others at this hour?"

"Only you, Miss," he responded.

After about an hour, she saw a row of pine trees along the top ridge that outlined the county where she lived.

"Not too far from here, Antonin."

"I know that, Miss."

"How do you know that?" she asked, leaning forward, absolutely confounded by his combination of diffidence and authority.

"Max gave me instructions."

The first name, fluidly uttered, spoke of an intimacy that surprised her.

"Did he tell you it was over there – beyond that second ridge – a curving road around the watershed that leads right down to my house?"

"He did not, Miss."

"Well we should get off here."

The car, like the service for twenty, did exactly as was expected.

"Tomorrow, then?" Antonin asked standing beside the rear door he had opened below the columned porch that led into her home.

"Tomorrow – yes. If you could manage nine or so. I would not want to be late."

"You won't, Miss," he answered, and with that he was off, guiding the immense black sedan back down the long gravel drive.

⌣ ☾ ⌢

At eight forty-five on the following morning, the car was again parked beside the porch steps.

"Antonin, did you find your way?"

"I find my way, Miss, most often."

"Yes, but things can be tricky when there's fog out on the ridge."

"Nevertheless, I find my way."

She slipped into her seat.

He adjusted his mirror.

The old black sedan climbed up to the ridge, turned south on the parkway, crossed the state line by the watershed, merged adroitly into the traffic of the wider lanes up ahead. And then Caroline cried abruptly, "Notebooks!"

"Miss?"

"I forgot to bring notebooks!"

"He'll have them."

"But he specifically told me. 'Fill in the left pages only; leave the right pages blank for corrections.'"

"He will have notebooks," repeated Antonin.

Caroline sat back in the immense leather seat. Max was known to this man – not as employer, but in some deeper way.

The car reached the river. She pondered. It would be rude to press Antonin. It would be more foolish still not to understand her employer.

"Antonin?"

"Miss?"

"How do you know Max?"

"He and my father were friends before the last war."

Caroline nodded, knowing he was watching her in his mirror.

"Max is Belgian on his mother's side, Austrian on his father's, a native of Nice, as you know."

"I do know."

"They had a large home near the sea there, at least before Paris fell. Max was young at the time. This part, too, you know."

"Some of it. Yes. The Resistance. He played a part..."

"Max was the Resistance. Some even say – but that is nonsense. It would have happened anyway. We would have opposed them, even without him, although we may not have known how, in the beginning. Max knew how, though. He spoke German, like a native..."

"How was that?"

"His nanny taught him. Austrian lady. It was the speech he liked best as a child, though he rarely spoke it in public, and few remembered that he could. He'll tell you. Yes – when you get to that part in the book, he'll remember."

"You tell me, Antonin," Caroline said quietly.

The car slowed to a stop, Antonin paid the toll and then there was silence as they descended the Heights.

"Dumb stupid Frenchman," she suddenly heard him say from the front. "That's what they'd call him, shouting orders his way, talking, making plans even. And he was taking it in, every word of it, and passing it on."

"To your father, is that it?"

"Among other friends."

"And they never caught him?"

"Oh, they caught him. They – I was a boy still. I don't remember well."

Silence followed again. Their exit appeared in the distance. He looked into his mirror and saw her eyes fixed on his.

"A stupid mistake," he went on, for in her gaze he had seen that they both knew he remembered. "One little slip – a filthy remark about a woman they'd seen on a magazine cover then. Some English society ball."

Caroline waited.

"She'd been his wife once. He let on somehow, not in words – Max was too smart to do that – but with his eyes, where his hatred for them welled up, just for an instant, long enough for them to figure out he could understand what they were saying. They took him in that night."

The car turned off the highway.

"You will most likely not see the cigarette burns on his chest, Miss, and that is good, because they're awful still. You probably did see though…"

"I did see."

"The left eye."

"It is glass," she said.

"Yes."

"The leg," she murmured.

"That they didn't do."

"No?"

"Since you asked me, Miss…"

The car lurched, having struck a pothole in the road.

"I did that."

"But you were a child…"

"Yes. Seven or so. Max was taking me out of France, as he

promised he would." He coughed, as though he were clearing his head of some recurring obstruction. "My father'd had word that they were onto him too, that they planned to take him in that night. They wanted Max, of course."

"But they'd had Max."

"Not what he knew. Max had said nothing. Through it all he had said nothing. 'I am different, though,' Father warned him. 'They'll make me talk, Max.' 'No,' he said. 'Yes. Not tonight perhaps. But soon.' Father stared at Max then. His eyes were like mine, I am told."

Caroline searched the mirror, but Antonin's gaze remained fixed ahead.

"'Take the boy,' Father begged. 'Tonight. They'll get him too if you don't and you'll have no way to stop it. They will have killed you by then, after the secrets I'll have imparted. Watch out for him, Max.'"

Antonin paused, lowered the window, spat on the asphalt, guided the car toward the fortress.

"Max left after dark. He carried me on his back, by the side of the railroad tracks, then again the next night and the night after that. During the daytime, he'd hide me."

"Where?"

"Between the railroad ties."

"Ah," Caroline whispered.

"One train was too heavy. Destination Dachau. Stalled for the afternoon east of Marseilles, with Max underneath, and me below that, feeling his hand on my mouth."

There was that cough again.

"'Not a sound,' he said into my ear. He said it many times, so I remember. 'And then there'll be ice cream at the border and a toy boat if you're good.'"

"In Santander, where he had friends at the clinic, his leg was lost, crushed by a cattle train, unbeknownst to the authorities."

Unbeknownst to Caroline, the old black sedan had stopped at the gates, northwest stone archway, where it had left the night before.

"So you see," Antonin said, suddenly awkward again. "I know Max quite well."

"I do see," Caroline murmured, closing her eyes once again, hoping to find relief thereby, only to see it all more distinctly.

⸜ ☾ ⸝

"On time exactly," said Max, as the clock in his hallway began chiming.

"Antonin's very particular," Caroline answered, hurriedly slipping off her shawl.

"He made that clock, did he tell you?"

"He didn't."

"He will someday."

One last chime rang out.

"Coffee at twelve-thirty, Elsa. Thank you."

Max turned to the windows. Caroline watched him – left hand clutching the cane by his side, right hand tapping his own thigh, distractedly, as though waiting for some cue to start.

"Shall we begin now?" he asked abruptly.

"I believe I am ready."

She followed him to the daybed, just below the windows, catching sight of the leather-bound notebooks on the table beside him. The chair had been angled to face him. Two pens, initialled like the plates below, had been placed by the books.

"These will bring us good luck," he remarked, "unless you've your own pens."

"I do," she responded, "although I much prefer your lucky ones."

They were addressing each other in German, as they had since Elsa had left and then, without warning, like a sleeper train leaving the station, he switched from present time into past tense, and they had begun.

Five minutes later, her sense of displacement, if anything, had intensified, for he had begun not with his youth – not even with his school days – but with his start as an architect, brash, hopeful, haunting the streets of Paris for inspiration and work.

Both had come to him quickly, as did his recollections. He spoke rapidly, the subject pleasing him as though he were seated beside a dinner companion whom he had known in those days.

Caroline fought to keep up. The steam in his room hissed; the temperature soared; Max noticed neither, increasingly drawn into the canvas depicted, like a painter who places his own face in a crowd scene.

"A townhouse in the Marais," he murmured. "My first big commission – client who never let me forget she was a descendant of Voltaire...I didn't forget. I built her a splendid home, worthy of her provenance." In return, Caroline heard, she had presented him to the cognoscenti, who adored her and her home. Within a year they were competing for her protégé's abilities. Within six years, he had built summer homes, reconfigured apartments, restored a grand old hotel to a splendour undreamed of.

"Did you get that, Caroline?"

The steam hissed again.

"I think I did, Max."

"Yes or no?"

"I – yes, Max, I believe so."

She stole a glance at her book, line after line filled, page after page. Then she saw blurs on the last page.

Sweat, she realized, horrified, watching another drop fall on the next line to be filled.

"'Rumours,' some clients believed," Max said after an hour, in German still. "Others weren't so sure."

Caroline followed quickly, water stains notwithstanding.

"I was sure though," he went on. "The cease-fire in my childhood had been no more than that – dream-song, intermezzo."

She stopped and looked at him.

"Write," he exhorted, more in fear of losing his own way than in doubt she'd lose hers.

She bent her head down and continued. He spoke of the last days of peace, then of the fall of Holland, Belgium, Luxembourg – then of the fearful French crowds who knew their capital wasn't prepared.

"It was the army who wasn't prepared," he avowed, switching abruptly to French, continuing another hour, never hearing Elsa's knock, astonished to find her there, and, by extension, present time.

"On the writing desk, Elsa," he managed, and then he turned back and saw that Caroline was writing still, hurriedly, turning yet another page, catching the last halting phrases he'd said with such effort, crossing a line out, then a second one, for it seemed to her they weren't right – not true enough, or not beautiful – all the same thing to her – so she rewrote in the silence, some sentences watermarked, some crystalline, like his recollections.

He noticed too for the first time – how had he missed it? – the unendurable heat in the room, reflected in her damp hair and wet face.

"Caroline,"

She kept writing still.

"Time for our break now…"

"In a minute Max."

She kept on writing; he kept on watching, long after Elsa had left the coffee and scones on his desk.

"There," she said triumphantly and then she turned, for the aroma of the coffee had surprised her. "I – were you waiting for me?"

He was holding his handkerchief out to her. "Forgive me. I'm always terribly cold. Circulation, they tell me. I should have noticed though."

"Thank you," she murmured, wiping her forehead, letting her shawl drop, pushing away the tendrils that had escaped from her comb only to curl in the dampness and stick to her neck.

He struggled to stand. She thought it best not to help. He looked for his cane, motioned for her to pass, then followed behind her, noticing for the first time how she swayed as she walked. Taking his own seat, he checked his watch and was pleased, for they were on time so far and the careful plan had gone well.

To his surprise, therefore, they ate awkwardly in the beginning. He'd said, "Cream"; she poured too much. She took her scones plain; he'd put jam on them both. Things – palpable objects – even the smallest ones – were oddly cumbersome between them. Theirs was to be another harmony, briefly perceived that first day.

"This house of yours," he asked, helping himself to more jam, "describe it."

"Old, large, some would say rambling." She reflected a moment. "So's the land. Forty acres and then some, although I've help to maintain it."

Never a plural pronoun, he thought.

"It is very dear to me," she felt compelled to add, then took a sip of her coffee.

"So it would seem," he responded, answering not her words but the nostalgia on her mouth.

The rest of their day, full and arduous, went according to plan. They worked again until two, then moved to the dining room alongside. At three, after lunch, Max retired for his rest.

"You may perhaps wish to stroll now," he said. "We won't be revising 'til five."

"I'd like to rest myself," she replied, for she was drained – spent by his story, only just started, already full of his passions. "Besides, I may lose the thread if I stray."

He laughed.

"I mean it, Max. Balzac felt that way. He ate his meals at his desk, standing up, afraid of the very same thing."

"Well you needn't stand here. I've a small room – a perfect space – behind the library downstairs. Sanctuary, I called it when I moved in years ago. I put a desk in there, a daybed, hoping to write near my books. The stairs proved too much."

He pressed the buzzer beside him.

"I shall tell Elsa to call you at five. We'll start again after that."

Aptly named space, Caroline thought, standing in the little room at the end of the library. A small recessed bed, built into the north wall, was protected by red velvet drapes, drawn back and secured with a gold silk rope tassel. A fringed lamp on a table cast a quiet glow next to the bed. On the opposite wall there was a matching lamp by some books on a low walnut desk.

Caroline sank onto the daybed; hair unclipped, boots off, surrendering to the silence. She tried to picture Max above her, sleep no doubt eluding him, for he too – like Balzac – would never risk straying far.

Neither must I, she murmured, *not now at least, not 'til this day is done...and I won't,* she affirmed, until Elsa Varig's knock awakened her and she hurried to join Max for the next session of work.

He was astounded hearing the pages she'd filled, for she had captured the start of his tale as he had lived it, on the wing as she had said it must be, with an accuracy that had sacrificed not even a quarter-note of his song.

He made revisions, of course. "That is not quite what I meant," he would say, or "Perhaps we need another word," or, more often, "Let me rephrase that more exactly."

She did as he asked her each time, happily. This part of her work – meticulous, as an artisan might embroider – was always a relief to her after invention's dark strife.

The musicians too brought relief, arriving again before seven. Caroline chose what was by now her usual seat, though only an evening had passed since she'd first found that chair. Max took his score, gave her another, sat on the sofa and nodded politely to the pianist.

On the stroke of nine she was in the car, Antonin at the wheel, the splendid bridge span ahead. As on the previous day, she opened her eyes as they passed it, drawn as if by destiny to the iridescence overhead.

"How did it go today, Miss?"

"It was difficult."

"It will get easier, Miss."

"You think so, Antonin?"

"Like the air that you breathe; soon, you'll see."

Ninety minutes away, Dr. Devereux lay on his huge, rumpled bed, clothes tossed on the floor, arm curved under his head, eyes fixed on the curves of the chandelier overhead. A breeze from the open French windows billowed his curtain from time to time. A half-empty bottle of wine stood on the night table beside him.

Susan Foreman lay beside him, her naked leg across his, her hand stroking his body ever so lightly in the stillness. She raised herself up after a moment and looked at him.

"Elliot, what is it? You've been somewhere else all night."

"I've been with you."

"Far away just the same," she murmured as another light breeze filled the room, blowing her hair from her neck, bringing a ripe harvest scent from the fields into their bed. She lifted her face and enjoyed the sensation. Her perfume mixed with October as Elliot traced her form with his hands. Like the night, she had a frankly sensual appeal – full breasts, wide hips, long legs always tanned. He let his gaze linger, then pulled her down to him and kissed her, feeling her hair on his face. She spread her legs so that he could stroke her insistently before he entered her. He climaxed slowly, murmuring obscenities.

Later on, in the stillness, he refilled their glasses.

"It's Caroline," he said abruptly.

She knew he would tell her, once relieved of his anger, part of it, and his lust, for the moment, and wanting a confidante in the interim.

"She's got a job now – some scheme to save the farm and get us through this mess, put things right, so to speak."

"What kind of a job?" Susan asked without expression.

"Translating."

"Oh."

"That's what I thought at first."

"Did you."

"This one pays. Nothing to live on, though she's got the whole thing worked out – rent the main house, move to the cottage for guests, build up my practice again after the hearing's done." He reflected a moment. "She's convinced I'll be cleared."

Susan made no response.

"Of course it's all built on sand – rentals, overtime, a legal judgment down the road that is in no way assured. I've told her so, repeatedly, but she is determined. I've never seen her like this."

Something in Elliot's voice caught Susan's attention. It was not irritation, not even impatience, but a new thing, unsettling: the beginnings of admiration. His wife's tenacity had impressed him. Her defiance, perhaps, had even intrigued.

Her own tone remained languid, however, when she offered, "Caroline's sudden vigour must have been heartening, though, in its way. Not that she didn't always have her own interests at heart. We've all seen that over the years. Still, the plan's certainly bold."

"You think so?"

"Risky things often are."

Elliot made no reply.

"Some tenants don't pay when they should," she went on, arching her back as she stretched once again so that her breasts caught the glow of the chandelier overhead. Then, still in an offhanded way: "Dribs and drabs when they come – if they come. Rarely enough to cover expenses. Well your wife must have factored that in. Always the first thing a savvy owner perceives."

Again there was silence.

"Any more wine?" Susan asked, holding the rare crystal glass up to the light.

Antonin was right. Caroline did find the second day easier. She was ready, at least, for Maximilian's way of remembering – headlong sometimes, halting others, both like the river that ran through Todd's Farm. She had also taken care to dress for the heat in his room, wearing her black tank top again, long black skirt, high silver sandals; nothing around her neck. The rope sandals she'd worn all summer she had discarded.

"Won't you be cold like that?" Elliot had asked.

"I'm taking a wrap," she'd replied, grabbing her shawl and a purse from the table as the sedan slowly moved toward the steps.

Elliot had watched the car disappear.

A thousand a week...Well all to the good after all. She'll keep the place up. The sale will net top dollar then, he'd reflected. Hearing the phone ring, he'd turned back to the house to learn that the appraiser Susan had contacted on his behalf would be at the farm by eleven.

By eleven, on 86th Street, Max and Caroline were just beginning. He'd been relieved to see that she'd dressed for the heat he wouldn't feel. Her arms were bare, no jacket, just that colourful shawl loosely draped.

"You won't even need that," he said, taking his seat on the chaise.

"Probably not."

"Leave it beside you, then."

There was a moment's hesitation.

"You'll forget later, Caroline."

"All right," she said, placing his pen on the table. Watching his face as she did so, she undid the knot on her shoulder and let the shawl fall.

Max registered nothing.

"You are ready, then, Caroline?"

"I am ready, yes."

They began at once, taking up where he'd left off the day before, though it was only with effort that he had forced himself to do so.

Fingerprints, he had assumed, or welts of some kind – he could not tell in the dimness, for the curtain had been only slightly drawn, enough to shed light on her book, and he would not allow himself to stare.

All he could do was return to his story, which he told swiftly so as to banish the other thoughts – images of Mrs. Devereux abused perhaps, possibly often, maybe even a willing victim. After all, he knew so little about her. She'd been so reluctant to speak of herself. He determined to ask Elsa to open the curtains during their break.

"Of course, Monsieur," complied Elsa, although the sun by then was high and the room already sweltering.

"Coffee now, Caroline."

"Just give me a minute, Max, to fix these last words."

It was what he had wanted – a chance to look closer, while she was writing.

The first thing he noticed was that in spite of her summer clothing she was sweating again – no doubt from the steam, perhaps too from the fact that he had pushed her hard that day.

The second thing he noticed was that like him she'd been burned. Once there was light on her flesh, he knew the marks that were on his own. It was tissue he'd lived with since his interrogation in Nice.

"Done!" she exclaimed – again with that schoolgirl's satisfaction she had displayed on the previous day – and then she reached for her handkerchief, carefully placed on the table when she'd arrived. She wiped her forehead, her temples again and then her cheeks, mouth and neck.

"Caroline," he managed.

"Max?"

How did it happen? was what he wanted to say.

"Let us eat now," was what he said.

☽

Someone who knows, Max thought as he lay on his daybed that afternoon. *I have been sent one who knows – not just the words that I know, not even those words made flesh, clothed in metre and rhyme – but flesh itself understood.*

When it is time he will tell me, she said to herself, on the little daybed fit into the north wall in the red velvet room beside all the books. *For now it is enough that we have both been tried, in the same way, and have not been found wanting.*

⌒ ☾ ⌒

"Tonight's Debussy will have to linger awhile in your head," Max announced later that day when the musicians arrived. "There's to be no music tomorrow."

"Why not?"

"Elsa's day off."

"Why should that mean we can't work?"

He was surprised by her directness.

"Because," he said emphatically, "I do not go down stairs."

"Antonin can let me in."

"Antonin doesn't cook."

"I can."

"I didn't employ you to cook."

"Nevertheless…"

"Besides," he went on, "your wages have been calculated on a five-day work week. No Thursdays. No Sundays. Simple as that."

"I see."

"Good."

The musicians were tuning their instruments.

"You could give me a raise, Max."

He said nothing for a moment, nonplussed, as he had been when he met her, by the energy she could muster when she wanted her way.

"Do you need money that badly?"

"I do."

"Caroline…"

"Antonin could open up. I could fix lunch; we could forget about the music – that might cost too much. I could provide a substitute."

"You play an instrument?"

"That other harmony, as Dryden called it..."

"Dryden was referring to prose. I couldn't take more prose then."

"In that case some poems. In the music room, as we do other days – I could read aloud to you – sonnets perhaps, an ode or two. The choice would be mine." She smiled. "And it would be required."

"May I tell you this evening?"

"You'll have to then, won't you? I mean if you want me to come tomorrow, or stay away, Max, you'll have to tell me before I go."

Before she left Max sat by his desk and took an envelope out.

"I have refigured your wages. Two extra days weekly, plus the talent, and that other harmony you promised, and the terrible annoyance it would be to replace you."

She took the envelope but did not open it, as he knew she would not.

"Here is the key to my home. Let yourself in and join me, just before eleven, so we can start things on time. I'll have our food sent in. It is my understanding you will provide music – minus the instruments."

"That is the arrangement," she confirmed.

Nearing midnight, in the quiet of her room at Todd's Farm, Caroline opened the envelope and found a second thousand, note attached.

"Mostly for the talent," she read.

Among her favourite books she chose a volume of Rilke. *Sonnets to Orpheus*, she decided, would be just the right thing.

It was indeed the right thing.

Max sat back on the sofa, after a long day's recollection, surrendering to the symmetry delivered in kind.

Caroline too lost herself – relieved to be reading another soul's words, not her own approximations, nothing she had had to submit for corrections, something already judged fine, 'til time and the earth should both dissolve.

Toward the end of the hour, though, she faltered, not from exhaustion, but from love of the piece.

It was Max they both heard then. He had learned those lines once – perhaps in the drawing room of Voltaire's descendant, perhaps by the rock beach in Nice – and he pronounced them all clearly, not needing the book she'd let fall.

The words were in German, also remembered clearly, despite the fall of his Paris.

"'Til tomorrow then, Caroline."

She picked up the volume she had let fall on her lap.

"'Til tomorrow, Max," she responded, knowing Antonin would be waiting.

Susan Foreman had gone to London for her sister's wedding that weekend. When she returned she found a box of flowers left on her porch.

Welcome home, read Dr. Devereux's card. *I have missed you*.

She called to thank him at once. There was no answer. She tried again just after supper, but there was still no reply. She dared not call a third time, not knowing exactly when it was that Caroline would be returning.

Thus Susan waited, until shortly past midnight, when at last the phone rang and she heard Elliot's voice.

"Did you like the flowers?"

"They're beautiful. Right here in my hallway. Are you all right?"

"Yes, I'm all right."

He sounded weary. "I tried calling you twice."

"I had a phone call from Emergency. Car crash out on the ridge. Young boy at the wheel," he explained. "Nearly severed right hand."

Susan was silent, dreading to ask what he would have to tell her in any case.

"I saved the hand," he went on. "The boy should be fine in good time."

"Congratulations," she breathed.

"Can I see you tomorrow?"

"Of course."

"First thing?"

"Whenever you like."

"She'll be gone by nine-thirty."

"Why don't you come here then? We could have breakfast in the garden. It's supposed to be quite warm again. The change of scene will do you good."

Somehow – it seemed a miracle – Elliot no longer felt overwhelmed. "I'd like that, Susan. Our own Indian summer."

Susan made sure she was waiting, and the day was indeed just like spring. *California interlude,* she reflected, recalling what seemed now-distant days spent on the West Coast. She'd gone to school in San Diego, married a graduate student from Berkeley, spent the first years of her marriage in Santa Barbara, not far from the sea. Her husband was clever, ambitious, restless by nature, political by force of will. He'd made his way nimbly through the corridors of corporations, finding himself promoted, protected, advanced in his turn, transferred out of town.

Susan had seen to the details each time. Chicago, Milwaukee, Milan, the West Coast once again. At last it was Manhattan – company headquarters – chief financial officer, bonus larger than God.

New Salem, he had decided, having sought a town that might be worthy. Impressed by its beauty, he'd bought a large clapboard house on a prestigious side street near the Lutheran church. It was purchased, gutted, enlarged and done up, including the tassels on the window drapes, within half a year. Susan herself had directed the operation, in absentia, from the seventh home they'd lived in, second time around in Santa Barbara.

The eighth home they'd lived in turned out to be their last. Stefan turned fifty, two years after he bought it. Susan gave him a party – filling his opulent rooms with envious colleagues, the finest champagne, a jazz quartet that played Top 40, conversation that never varied. Nothing varied that night. Out by the pool, in by the bar, everywhere in between there were women in black, men who wanted his job, couples shifting position as their social timers went off, glass after glass raised in celebration of hyperbole.

He'd made his way through it all with his customary elegance, yet when the last guest had gone, and Susan was in the kitchen directing the caterers as they cleaned, Stefan went up to his marble bathroom and vomited. It was not overindulgence – he'd had but two glasses of wine – but overwhelming ennui. He staggered out of the bath, heard the bustle in the kitchen still and went out into the garden.

The monolith that was his home loomed even larger in the darkness.

Perhaps, he thought then, watching the predictable constellations, *if there had been children to fill those rooms*, but they had postponed that too long and he had refused to raise another's child.

Through the windows he could see his wife – more stunning at forty than at twenty when he'd married her, after she'd dropped out of college – having been chosen prom queen, class president and girl most likely to succeed.

Well that part came true, he told himself grimly. She was still giving orders, firmly, in a kitchen easily larger than the first home they'd bought. He suddenly longed for that home – a little ranch near the beach. He longed for his youth, long since lost, and his candour, gone before that; and then, quite without warning, as the garden turned cold and the earth unfamiliar, he longed for faith once again – not belief in himself, not even belief in others, but religious faith, bedrock and simple, such as he'd known as a boy.

He saw the light in the kitchen go out. He heard the caterer's truck drive away. Then other lights faded – living room; dining room; library; bedroom suite; bathroom where all he had wanted 'til then had repelled him. The next morning, he had decided, he would go to the white church by the hill. He would sing at least, if he found he couldn't pray, for he had sung in the choir as a boy of eleven, then again in prep school, and that much, he knew, he could remember from those early days.

He did remember; every note. Within a month he was asked to join the choir, if he could manage it – rehearsals on Thursday evenings, services Sunday mornings.

Stefan managed both.

Susan attended neither.

She was irreligious, not from conviction, but because her spirit was fully nourished by her position as wife in his prominent world. Therefore she never saw it. Though her husband was gone more and more, devoting weekends to his church, hours to their outreach, she never even suspected he'd fallen in love again, deeply, with a woman he'd met singing hymns in the choir.

Nan was tall, fine-featured, with curly blonde hair that framed a face which liked to smile. Above and beyond that, Stefan observed, though it was difficult to discount her perky and athletic charm, she somehow found time to give of herself, over and over again, with remarkable generosity.

She cooked for the Men's Picnic, helped work the Men's Summer Fair, took food to the housebound with the Men's Task Force for the Elderly. *How does she do it?* he wondered, for Nan was divorced, worked as a paralegal in town, had two teenage sons to raise and studied piano.

She also lingered late after rehearsals, putting the music away, while the Men's Bible Group met in the adjoining salon. Stefan hadn't joined this group – he hadn't the time – but he too found himself staying later each Thursday, filing cantatas, oratorios, any responsibilities he may have accrued in his two decades of marriage.

Susan was staggered when he left her. He moved in with Nan 'til the divorce became final; a week after that he married again, then bought a small house in the woods on the outskirts of town where the boys, as he called them, would have enough room to romp. Then he retired, well ahead of his time, figuring he had enough to live on, for the rest of his life, singing psalms and doing good.

The monolith on Chapel Street was sold of course – just under market, hotly contested, all cash up front. Susan took her fair share, also hotly contested, and bought a co-op in town; she invested her settlement, lived on the money her lawyer had wrested from Stefan's pension, spent eleven months in therapy, and took up real estate.

At that point, uncannily, her college prediction came true. Susan was born to succeed. She had mythic energy, undeniable ambition and a total absence of scruples, all reinforced by years of practiced sociability – all underscored recently by the trauma of rejection.

Within a year she'd redone her co-op; two years later she owned a second. A year after that she'd sold them both and bought her own house, heavily mortgaged, a pale yellow ranch on the west side of town, where the sunsets were finest, above all on the reservoir that lapped the road across from her lawn.

Pure New England, that scene from her porch steps. California interlude everywhere else, for Susan's home, like her career, harked back to her youth. There was nothing within to remind her of the hiatus – two decades and then some – of marriage and mahogany and the English preferences of another. It was open, airy, with a terra cotta entrance foyer that led to a living room two steps below. Left of the living room was a dining room, also spare and white. Both had Mission furniture that matched the oak beams overhead. Both had French doors that led to a garden – walled and secluded, with lush plants and white chairs surrounding a brightly tiled pool.

Susan's room too had a wall of glass overlooking the garden. One of three bedrooms originally – all off to the right of the entrance hall – Susan had reconfigured the space, against her own realtor's instincts, making the three rooms into two. *This is my world*, bedroom and study announced – *customized, elegant, no apologies, no empty beds*.

Indeed, the statement would have been cogent but for the passage of time, for within a few years – five since the divorce – her phone had begun to ring less and less, and her listings had dropped. Friends were moving from town, simple as that – some of them transferred, as she'd often been; others off to their second homes in retirement bliss. Those who remained extended fewer invitations. When they did call, more often than not on the eve of a party, it was to fill out a table, suddenly widowed, because of a relative who'd taken ill.

More often than not, Susan accepted. Her nights were long; the hours lonely. Generic cards came her way in the weeks of December, form letters, typed, with news of grandchildren, cruises, anniversary celebrations. She herself tried a cruise – twice – and twice had endured the walkers who'd made their way to her table for conversation, sex and her diminishing income, in that order.

Never again, she had vowed, returning home in January the year of Caroline's trip to France. *People know where to find me if they need me.*

Still, there were monthly payments on the Mercedes, her mortgage, endless furniture bills. She joined a church after all, the Rotary Club, the League of Women Voters, networking with renewed vigour. Yet the phone rang even less. Younger women had moved into town, prepared to make friends with newer residents, also younger, with their husbands in tow still. Then, around March of that year, she'd picked a colleague up after surgery – eyelids contoured, outpatient, elegant offices overlooking the water in neighbouring Stamford, twenty minutes away.

White-coated still, mask at his neck, Elliot Devereux had emerged with a sheet of instructions, assurances and last-minute details as to payment.

He'd emerged again a week later, not from surgery then, but from the liquor store in New Salem. And then he'd turned, walked to his car, fumbled for his keys and noticed Susan watching him.

"I've the same one," she observed, pointing languidly to another car, identical, parked right next to his.

"You like it?"

"You like yours?"

"I might if you ride with me."

And that's how it started.

He had intended a fling – nothing more – a couple of months at the most. That's all there ever was to these things, he made sure of it, taking pride in what he liked to call his integrity in the matter. There would be caveats from the outset, well-timed signals presented. He would mention his wife, refer to his home, insist over dinner he wanted nobody to get hurt.

And he meant it.

Above all he meant he wanted his own heart untouched, and therefore his worlds – the well-run splendour of Todd's Farm and that other splendour, brief and chaotic, of uncommitted, unaccountable, uninhibited sex – also without violation.

It was his wife, ironically, who made the delicate, eternally shifting equipoise of his double life possible. *She does not mind*, he would say to himself, easing whatever pinpricks of conscience remained.

She can't really object, was the more probable reality. Either way, until he ran into Susan Foreman, he'd managed his distinct worlds with remarkable agility.

And then, quite without warning, he failed. He managed neither well. His wife, for some reason, had become ungovernable. And the fling, programmed to wane within the predictable ninety days, was raging out of control. How had he let this happen?

Susan knew. Her sexual repertoire was comprehensive. Stefan had been demanding. Susan had learned to like it. Toward the end of their marriage, as his ardour had cooled, she'd missed the pleasures she'd learned to love giving, as well as the ones she had come to expect.

Once divorced, she had found neither had reappeared. She'd had affairs, short ones and shorter, but mostly the men were timid, if they were married – afraid, she suspected, that their darker side, more than their dalliance, would come to light by the dawn. Those who were single were singularly predictable. At best they were perfunctory, relief their obvious goal, her own needs – her darker side – never even glimpsed before dawn.

Elliot was different. He was married, unavailable, yet unafraid of exposure. He was also addicted, without apology, to the sensations she couldn't forget. Matched superbly as lovers, they were also soul mates on a deeper plane, for both were desperate, fragile, increasingly lost in their gyrating, parallel, free-falling worlds.

Susan thought about this while she waited, setting their breakfast out in the garden, springtime surpassed as the mercury climbed.

By the time he arrived it was the warmest day on record for that late autumn morning.

They kissed in the sun by the side of the pool.

"I promised you springtime," she whispered.

"And you've outdone yourself..."

"For your sake."

He unbuttoned her sundress, then stood back and surveyed her naked body a moment, burnished like the morning, her breasts a vivid contrast to the rest of her tan. Between her legs she had shaved – that place too was stark white – and as he moved to her he felt he was nearing sanctuary – female and exclusive – where he could enter with his yearning, fearing no reprisal, finding instead renewal and his pride restored, his body refreshed, both resurrected in pleasure, mixed perhaps with some pain, the two freely exchanged and supremely enjoyed.

He kissed her mouth again.

"We could swim today," she murmured.

"With crimson leaves in the pool?"

"They're not all red."

He knelt.

"Some are green still."

He put his face against her.

"You go then," he responded, kissing the place she had shaved.

And with that she was gone, slipping out of his arms and into the water, reappearing at the shallow end, hair slicked back, sun glinting on her shoulders like the caress of a naughty god. She swam back to him and splashed him and gripped the ladder rungs and emerged, dripping, laughing at his soaked shirt, slicking her hair back again.

He took off his shirt and walked to her, towel in hand.

"Don't you dare," she said.

"What a bad girl you've been, Susan."

"I couldn't help myself."

"Come here."

She did not move.

"You know you can trust me," Dr. Devereux said.

She crossed to him, dripping still, and stood motionless while he dabbed her face and dried her breasts and worked the towel in and around her legs.

"I shall have to be punished, I suppose."

"Rules are rules, love," he responded, kneeling again and taking each foot in his hand as he continued to dry her, most carefully. Then he stood, draped the damp towel around his neck, took her hand and said, "Come."

He spanked her hard when they got to her room. When he was done he kissed the marks he had left, and then he entered the place he had kissed and then they climaxed together, neither saying a word.

Then they slept.

She awoke first, cradled still in his arms. It would be wintertime soon, she reflected – nights long, days longer, passion and sun both the weaker perhaps, like indistinct forms in an old sepia print.

If he should lose this lawsuit, she said to herself, *his only recourse will be that house. And the sale could take months, if his wife comes around. It will break him*, she concluded, *and he will leave me then, thinking he can give me nothing.*

Forty minutes passed. She slipped out of his arms and into her bath. The thought of rejection again – the spiralling lies and stammered cancellations and heartfelt talks which had no heart – filled her with dread.

She'd have to be clever this time or time would outwit her. And that meant, she saw, as Elliot stirred once again, he'd need some assets to fall back upon – no fortune yet, just a hedge against humiliation. In time he would remake himself, of that she was sure. But in the interim, in the fragile weeks fraught with peril for the two of them – it never occurred to her to count beyond that – she'd have to keep both her wits and his interests in hand.

"I've never seen you in that," she heard Elliot say from the bed, watching her as she brushed her hair, reflected in a mirror, wearing exquisite lace panties and a matching brassiere.

"Stefan gave them to me," she said. "I had the presence of mind to take them, along with every other gift he'd bought, the moment my lawyer informed me that everything would be contested."

Elliot made no response.

"Smartest thing I ever did back then. He'd've thought he had a right to it all. What had been mine from the start, he might have been willing to part with – but *his* gifts? Jewels he still had receipts for? He'd been a generous man – I don't deny it – but things got so ugly. Always do. He'd've reclaimed the whole lot – almost succeeded when my back was turned – and I'd've spent a good fortune getting a piece of it back."

Elliot listened, still mesmerized.

"I must admit," Susan continued, hooking her hose onto her garter belt, "there'd've been some logic to his position. I mean, he did buy them all…"

"Technically…"

"Cash, darling, nothing technical about it." She slipped into her high sandals and walked back toward the bed. "As I said, I got there first. Squatter's rights and all that." She smiled, looking down at him. "Hungry yet?"

"Yes," he admitted, reaching again.

⁓ ☾ ⁓

Soon after Elliot left, Susan returned to her bed, not to sleep, but to think.

Things had gone well, after all. She had planted the seed; he had listened; she had aroused him; he had planted his seed.

From that moment on, there would be nothing left to chance – not even one, single, apparently meaningless detail, so that with luck and the vigilance she'd lacked previously, she would emerge this time the victor. No more clumsy advances in hotels and airports and seminars and her church. No more approaches, furtive instead of fervent, discreetly managed after cocktails by the new husbands of old friends.

She longed to be free of it all, exempt from the predatory imperative, irresistible when authentic, laughable when replicated – the former a devastation; the latter insulting.

That man on the plane back from London, for example. He would be devastating, without question. She had seen him first at the ticket counter, before they had boarded the plane.

"Window seat, if you've got one," he had said to the attendant, moments after flashing a most remarkable smile.

"I'll do my best." She too smiled then, flustered by his intensity, and then typed away.

"No, that's in smoking. Do you smoke?"

"I do not."

"Mind the last row?"

"That depends."

"I've a window seat there." She stopped. "On what?"

"On the crew. I'd rather an aisle if you're working this flight."

She returned to her keyboard.

"Last row. Last window. 49 C," she said efficiently, producing his ticket.

"I'm disappointed."

"Don't be," replied the attendant, raising her eyes to him, briefly. "I'm helping out on this flight."

Oddly enough, Susan thought, watching the ceiling fan as she lay on her bed still, he had managed it all with absolute sincerity.

Partly it was his charm, boyish and free, though he was no longer a boy and no doubt rarely free.

Partly it was his style. Tall, very lean, with unruly blonde hair and gunmetal eyes, he was expensively dressed in an offhanded way so that the care he'd expended – and it was clear he had done so – appeared carelessly reassuring.

After their trays had been cleared, standing in the bathroom line beside row 49, Susan had observed him more closely.

He was attentive, almost tender, to the elderly lady beside him, pouring her wine and chatting, and nodding with brightness whenever she spoke. To the businessman on the aisle he was affable, though more distant, giving his newspaper up when the purser passed with just one. Later, when Susan again walked about, she saw the attendant from the counter offering pillows and a blanket. He chose to accept neither. Instead, as the cabin lights dimmed, he'd strolled to her station behind. Not too long after that he was perched on the arm of her chair where she sat, talking, it seemed, of compelling things, smiling from time to time, enjoying the quiet laughter of other attendants around him.

Born to seduce, Susan had said to herself as she'd slipped back into her own seat, row 26 on the aisle.

Unexpectedly, she'd had one final glimpse of him moving toward the taxi stand – his walk confident, his brightness if anything refreshed by the flight. She noticed his luggage, well travelled, as he was, though with the monogrammed letters clearly visible still. *MMD*, they proclaimed, an almost offhanded reference, like his insouciant clothes.

She smiled then, in spite of herself.

Off to break another heart, she thought.

For once Susan Foreman was wrong.

Mikhail Matson d'Olivier was on his way to greet his father. Even at that late hour, ten o'clock, he couldn't arrive at his hotel without stopping first, out of respect, at the grand house on 86th Street.

He didn't stay long. He was exhausted, though no one could tell. His father too was very tired – something about his memoirs – having worked hard since eleven.

"I'll come tomorrow," Mikhail said as he rose.

"Tomorrow?"

Max thought for a moment.

"As a matter of fact," he too rose, making an effort, "that might not be so good. You'll need to rest a bit. And have some excellent food. Tomorrow is Elsa's day off, so I suggest you sleep long and late – there'll be only simple fare here – and come 'round the day after. Lunch would be good."

"Lunchtime it is, Max, day after tomorrow."

Mikhail grabbed his jacket and stole down the steep curving steps, not wanting to bother Elsa, who'd make a huge fuss and even give up her day off.

Elsa Varig, as it happened, would have heard little that night. She had had red wine with supper, some claret to follow and had gone to bed early before her free day.

Her employer, on the other hand, found that he could not sleep, no matter what he drank. The sudden appearance of his son had somehow disturbed him; and for the first time since Nice and the ordeal of his youth, he felt fear and resentment and a need to hide what was his.

After her Sunday break, as expected, Elsa returned to Maximilian's house.

Mrs. Devereux, though, was absent.

It was November, after all. Indian summer had vanished, and two days of rain had become wet, heavy snow.

108th Street was silent. Garbage cans by the stairs resembled boys in white sheets on Halloween. Antonin's front stoop looked like a slide.

He pulled his boots on and walked to the river, hoping the roads had been cleared. There wasn't a car to be seen.

"I could try, Max," he ventured, calling from a phone booth on the corner.

"Later perhaps," said Max with a glance toward the courtyard. "Far too risky now, Antonin."

With that he moved to his desk, did a bit of research, had a bit of breakfast, watched the snow taper off and saw it begin again, fiercer.

Six weeks to the day she had arrived with no résumé. Not once had she failed to appear at eleven a.m. exactly. This time, as the clock in the hallway struck two p.m. precisely, Mikhail arrived for lunch.

"How are you feeling today?" Mikhail said heartily, entering the little dining room where his father was waiting. He had expected three places set, yet only two were in view.

"I'm fine, Misha, fine…"

"Aren't you working today?"

"The storm has delayed things a bit."

Mikhail waited until his father had resumed his seat, then took a chair opposite. Then, as though to an old neighbour: "It's good to see you again, Max."

He never said "Father," only "Max," and his affection, though deep, stopped just short of love. They had not known each other in his childhood. Max had sold all that he owned to get that ticket – only one left, he'd been told as every parent was told, and like every parent he knew otherwise and paid anyway for a seat with Kindertransport connections – worth any price asked. Max didn't argue, guarding his ticket with his life until the boy was lifted out of his arms into the sleeper car, seat 39 B. Minutes before that he had whispered, "Yes…yes Misha, my love, my child, yes I will send for you, when it is over here – when it is safe again." He had said it a second time when the boy's face leaned from the window, steam from the train masking the tears on the man's mouth.

Nobody understood why Max had done such a thing. Why part with the child? He had nothing to fear. Max was cooperative, respected, head of one of the oldest, most reliable families in Nice. "Absolutely beyond suspicion," the police had said as they fruitlessly tracked the director of the seemingly protean Resistance. Only a handful knew the real Max. Those who did also knew that his luck would run out, as theirs would, sooner or later. Thus, like Jean-Luc Onegin, who feared for Mikhail's playmate Antonin, Max had been forced to make plans.

Misha's train, as it happened, was the penultimate one of its kind to leave Provence. Max followed the route through his contacts in each place: overland to Biarritz, ship then to Belfast, private boat to Liverpool. "Safe," he'd whispered finally, relief washing over him, when his last source confirmed that the boy's name had been called. A couple from Winchester had taken him home. Mikhail's life had started over again.

Soon, it was the only life he would remember. The Kirklands grew fond of the boy – who could resist him? – with his array of disarming disavowals, his tousled blonde head, tourmaline eyes and low, gravel-like voice, which made him seem wise beyond his years.

He would inquire about his father in the earlier months, always receiving the same measured responses: "Max is doing great things," or "Max has sent word that he loves you dearly."

How they'd discovered this, the child never knew. He never received a letter. For the sake of the boy as well as his work, Max never risked one. The Kirklands knew only vaguely that the boy's father was in France still, devoting himself to the war effort, heroically. From time to time they would get a phone call – never the same voice – to say that Maximilian was fine; that he was grateful; that he would repay them as soon as he could. After a while, the calls became infrequent. After another year, they stopped. Mikhail entered school. His grades were fair, barely that, but nobody minded; his chores, more often than not, completed a day or two late. By the time he turned six, Papá was just Max. By the time he was seven, the image of Max had disappeared, not even a memory in his head, just a shadowy figure the Kirklands would rather not conjure. Only they knew by then that the unspeakable had happened – that Papá had been discovered, chastised, left to die in agony as the strongest of them always were. They told the boy, finally, the year he turned eight.

"Max is dead," they said simply, for want of any other words, their measured tones graver than any other time they'd mentioned him.

It meant nothing. By then Max was a myth, nothing more, to the boy with the winning ways and throaty voice and an eye for perfection should it perchance come his way.

Max in the end did come his way, walking deliberately, trying not to lean hard on the cane in his hand, his gait remarkably firm given the loss of one leg. Jean-Luc had warned him, it seemed. He'd gotten out – no one knew how – along with that dark and silent boy who was still by his side, so out of place in the sunlight of Winchester's Green. From Gibraltar they'd gone to Mexico, then to the Florida Keys, then to New York and a job, beginner's salary designing, enough to return and reclaim the boy – the second boy, it seemed then to Misha, though to Max it was all he had lived for since he had promised he would be back.

Mikhail chose not to go. He was English now, his manners like his schoolmates, his speech like Anthony Kirkland, who had remained tactfully in his study while Max and the dark boy met with Mikhail in the garden.

Max understood. With Antonin he returned to New York, to his hard life again, then more work, investments, prestigious commissions, fame and fortune once more.

Antonin Onegin saw neither. Brooding, adrift, he skipped school, skipped work, found false haven in drugs and a wrong crowd. Max was there for him through it all – one vow that wouldn't crumble – from prison to rehab to a car, a flat on 108th Street and a life by his side to the end of his days.

"So, Misha," Max asked, as he deftly served the meringue, "what brings you now to New York?"

"Yacht sale, nothing more."

"Nothing more?"

"Well you of course, Max."

Elsa entered with the coffee.

"Any calls for me, Elsa?"

"None, Monsieur."

"You've asked her that twice, Max. Is everything all right?"

"Everything's fine." He took a bit more dessert. "It's just this storm. Things get delayed a bit – deliveries – will you take brandy?"

"I don't think so. The snow's letting up. You should rest perhaps now. I have tired you."

"I will rest, Misha. Though it's the years that have taken their toll, I'm afraid, not the storm."

Max returned to his room, Mikhail to the darkening streets. Snow crunched under his feet as he turned right onto Broadway and into the crowds.

⸺ ☾ ⸻

Snow was also crunching under the feet of Elliot Devereux then. He had crossed to the gates, seen that the roads had been cleared, then followed a path toward the woods just as the sun broke through the clouds. Todd's Farm was never lovelier. It was utterly still – tentative and iridescent, matching the undecided sky above.

Elliot saw neither. He felt only debt's burden wherever he looked – the blanched lawns, the buried hemlocks, the footbridge that seemed to be spanning a moat.

Appropriate, he thought grimly, turning back toward the main house, *for a castle only fools would keep.*

As he traversed the south lawn he looked up at his wife's room. He stopped for a moment, suddenly puzzled. It had remained dark all day long, no sign of life beyond the double doors to her terrace. She couldn't have left the farm – not at the height of the storm, nor was it like her to have remained in her room, buried and still like the stone walls she adored, in heavy snows above all, when she would tramp along beside them – hearing, she would often avow, tales of their hidden past.

He paused again in the hallway before he knocked. On the window seat, Caroline stirred. Her right arm was stiff; the room around her was dark; the vista beyond a mixture of lead and pearl grey.

"Caroline?"

There was no answer.

"Caroline," he called more firmly.

"Yes, I'm all right."

He opened the door but chose not to go in, seeing her hurriedly tying her robe as she crossed.

"What time is it?"

"Nearly five."

"I must have dozed…"

"You did more than that. You slept the day away."

Neither an accusation nor a display of concern, it was merely a statement, as one might observe how long a chess game had lasted.

"You must be hungry."

"I'll be right down."

"No need to rush. Worst of the storm's over by now. Most of the roads have been cleared. I'll be eating in town."

Elliot turned. Caroline closed her door, turned on the light by her bed, called information and was given a number for d'Olivier on 86th Street. Odd that they had never exchanged numbers, she thought, as though from the start they had never imagined any disturbance in their almost secretive life.

"Just what I needed," said Mikhail grandly, sipping the coffee Elsa Varig had made him. He had come in from his walk, all the brighter it seemed for the cold on his face, and was perched on a stool in the kitchen while his father rested upstairs. As Elsa passed, he reached out for her hands and stood away a bit, wondering how it was she never changed.

"Hard work," she replied, straightening herself, although she offered to make him another coffee – exactly the way he liked it – as soon as she came back down.

And then a strained silence ensued, for Antonin Onegin was also in the kitchen, preparing his afternoon tea.

"Cake, Mikhail?"

"Kind of you, Antonin. I'll wait 'til supper though."

Supper, both knew, would be taken with Max after the music. Antonin never dined with Max – both men knew that too – so that in Misha's demurral more was said than expressed.

Thus it had always been between them – primordial resentment beneath a vermeil of good form, for Mikhail only remembered that it was he who had been dispensed with, tag on his shirt reserving the last car, never to be embraced beneath another car, fiercely, and Antonin only knew that he was never to be the blood son, flesh of the hero's flesh, and time had underscored the irony. Ursine, marginal, one boy had become the lodestone of a great life somehow; the other – the lithe one – a predator in the savannah stalking daily out of despair.

Antonin turned with his tea, sliced up his cake and sat on a stool facing Mikhail. The telephone rang.

"Elsa will get it," announced Antonin importantly.

"It will disturb my father," Misha corrected, dealing a blow with the pronoun which he would have disdained to give with his hand.

"Hello?" he said firmly.

"Monsieur d'Olivier?"

"Oui?"

"I – *Je me'excuse* – *C'est moi. Caroline.*"

Mikhail's mind raced ahead. Sometimes he forgot a name – rarely – but it had happened. Never the name of a woman he'd loved. And this was a woman he'd loved, at least pursued – that was clear from her voice – intimate in spite of its absolute correctness, and that she felt she could still use her first name.

"Caroline?" he repeated, as though it were a French name, as she had said it.

Caroline was puzzled. Was he not well?

She repeated her name, and said that the snow had kept her away, and that she was worried lest he'd been worried, or ill, or worse – all in French still, a little breathless but a song still – and then it dawned on Mikhail, while she explained herself so intriguingly, that it was his father she was looking for.

"Je m'excuse," he interrupted, still in French, partly to match hers, partly because Antonin's had been forgotten. *"Je suis Misha – Mikhail Alexander. Le fils du Maximilian."* He smiled as though she were in the room. *"Aussi Monsieur d'Olivier."* Then, as his father had done, to probe deeper, and because he was at a loss still, he switched to English – Cambridge and Eton and a bit of Winchester's Green. "Therein the confusion. My apologies. Father is resting still. May I give him a message?"

Caroline was astounded. Max had never mentioned a son. He had begun with his work, as though there'd been no life before that, nothing before the fall of Paris, the only love of his life or so it had seemed to her before that, despite Antonin's revelations.

"When he awakens," – she spoke in English now too – "though he may not have slept; he may only have rested; please don't disturb him sooner in any case – not until four at least, and then tell him I'm well and that I too have rested, and that I would have called sooner, but, well – this is going to sound ridiculous – I overslept. All day long. Please tell him also – no, that is enough." It was Misha's turn to be astonished. *A woman in a snowstorm – French was she? American? Calling to excuse herself for having slept the whole day?*

"I'll explain everything when I see him," she said. "Tomorrow. Regular time. The ridge should be clear by then, which will make Antonin Onegin glad. Can you get word to him too somehow? Forgive the long list of a stranger's requests so late," she concluded with a barely audible laugh, so that he wondered on what ridge, in which land, they were playing that song.

"I shall be happy to tell them both," he said.

"Thank you."

"Until tomorrow then."

"You will be there still?"

"I plan to spend Christmas in Manhattan."

"Ah," she murmured. "Your father will like that."

"Yes."

There was a pause.

"*Au revoir*," was all she could think of to say in that pause.

"Until tomorrow," he repeated placing the receiver down, pondering the hint of another place in her English – South American, to be sure – if only in the rhythms, wondering even more about her own place in his father's house.

Mikhail never felt lonelier than when he left that house later, just as the musicians arrived. He paused in the courtyard, lights from his father's windows spilling onto the snow, sounds of a grand piano filtering down. *Brahms*, *Hungarian Dances*, he said to himself, thinking the choice out of character for Maximilian. Then he walked out to the street and turned west to his hotel. It was small, very quiet – fine elegant suites that reminded him of his London flat, each with a view of Riverside Park and the Hudson beyond.

That November evening though, for reasons he could not explain as he walked toward the lobby, Mikhail wanted neither his rooms nor their view. He put his keys back into his pocket and turned toward Broadway. It was Friday night after all – end of the work week, end of a snowstorm, holidays around the corner, holiday mood in the air.

Crowds had begun to gather at a trendy bar two blocks south. Misha stopped as he passed the window, surprised by the reflection of his own image there – wavy, somewhat distorted – clearly visible though in a mirror behind the bottles arranged on a shelf.

Music reached him again – Jerome Kern now, not Brahms – as the couple behind him opened the door and went inside. Mikhail too waded into the throng. Men and women both looked as he advanced, for it was impossible not to notice him, even among the thickening rows at the bar. He ordered a brandy, saw that the seat beside him was vacant and decided to remain standing – whether chivalrous gesture or stratagem, time and the evening would decide.

He sipped his drink slowly, *A Fine Romance* in the background, memories slowly receding.

"Sorry," he heard, as a woman's purse brushed his shoulders.

"No problem," she heard, as he admired her, mostly looking away.

She was auburn-haired, fair, very confident; strikingly beautiful. And yet she was alone.

He smelled the perfume on her neck, 24, *Faubourg*, and the faint odour of suede from her skirt, and then he noticed her sweater, form-fitting, finely ribbed.

White, Misha thought, until he looked once again and saw that it was, like her eyes, a fragile shade of pale blue.

A second seat became available.

"If you're waiting for someone..." he said politely.

She glanced at the lobby. No one appeared in the doorway. Mikhail asked for brandy again, two this time, and Claire Tierney did not object.

He never did know whether anyone else had been expected that night, although she glanced again through the crowds and the smoke as they talked, once more as they left, both times with a practiced, insouciant air, both times in vain.

They talked long over supper at a bistro he favoured. She'd studied art history, sculpted some in Rome, was at the time employed as a buyer for the prestigious gallery La Ronde, Inc. Mikhail spoke of the yachts that he loved, the one he hoped to sell that month, the one he had vowed once he would never part with.

"And did you?" she asked.

"Yes," he said after a pause.

"Why?"

"Long story," was his reply.

She smiled. That winter's tale, she sensed, was for another night, another woman.

It was almost midnight when they reached his elegant rooms at the Riverside Suites. He undressed her slowly, befitting the practiced air she'd maintained, and made love to her quickly, befitting his need and the hour. And yet even then, as he lay on his bed and she gathered her things, aware of the gift her splendid body had been, Claire Tierney was distant – force of habit – and disillusioned, price exacted by time.

"I'll take you home, Claire."

"No..."

"I'd like to."

"Mikhail, there is no need."

"A taxi then..." He too had begun to dress. "Let me at least get you a cab."

She touched his cheek.

"If you must."

For a moment he held her before he opened the door. He could not tell if she smiled. She could not tell if he'd call. All she was sure of was that she'd failed him that night – not physically – they had both needed the evening, but in a deeper way, in some secret place where his heart was locked up, so that she'd left him lonelier than when he'd found her, and bereft somehow, though she had offered him all she had.

She kissed him briefly as she entered the cab. At the corner she turned and looked back. He was still standing there. She managed a wave before the taxi turned left and then she was gone and Mikhail felt a sadness mixed with relief as he walked back to his rooms overlooking the river. Claire's intuition had been correct. Misha was drawn to beauty like a moth to a flame. No sooner found, though, than it escaped him – illusory vision that tempted his days and disturbed his long nights.

And yet on he pursued. His predator's heart had no choice. Indeed, the quest empowered him, in direct proportion to its torment, refining his raffish eagerness into a visceral intensity that clients, as well as women, found impossible to ignore.

Hence his eventual business success. Misha had already grown wealthy. The beauty of the yachts he sold electrified his instincts for the art of the deal, so that charming a buyer became loving a woman, and vice versa, both fleeting variants of the perfect erotic transaction, both leaving him bankrupt, with millions, and restless, with two apartments, and searching, in spite of himself, for a mind to match his in a vessel too fine to part with.

Dr. Le Brun's white coat billowed as he ran back across the courtyard of the old Hôtel-Dieu.

Dawn was just breaking that September morning in Paris. He'd been on night duty – a quiet six hours, unusual for the large hospital beside Notre-Dame. Hence he had left the surgical wing a few moments early to check for messages before signing out.

The immense inner garden had been utterly still as he'd crossed. Its boxwood-lined pathways were barely visible as night receded. Shadowed too were the dogwoods, tinged with autumn already, although it was warm still in Paris, and the new day seemed like June. Somewhere – the sound had startled him in the stillness – a lark deep inside one of those trees had sung out.

He had paused to glance up then – not just at the trees and the fountain, but at the two-storied arcade surrounding the court. Its succession of arches had seemed to him then romantic, mysterious – anything but medicinal. And for an instant, as the sun rose and the paths turned pink, all thoughts of patients fighting for life inside vanished.

Again the lark sang.

An aubade, he had said to himself, moving on toward his office, glad that his night watch was over, or almost over – ten minutes to go before he could leave the hospital to join his wife at their small country house to the north of Limoges.

As it happened, Dr. Le Brun was not to leave Paris. When he'd approached the door to his office, he'd heard his name called twice, urgently, over the loudspeaker in the corridor. Beyond the window he could see lights flashing over the archway that admitted vehicles into Emergency, west side of the court.

"Le Brun here," he'd answered, grabbing a house phone in the hallway.

"Code Ten," the voice had announced. "On its way up now from the ambulance."

Code Ten was shorthand for the most critical, extreme, life-and-death surgical situations.

Thus it was that Le Brun re-crossed the courtyard that morning, white coat billowing behind him, bursting through the double doors on the east side of the garden.

Code Ten preparations were underway. Staff and nurses moved with speed. The patient was wheeled in by the ambulance crew –

standard procedures, all handled deftly, and yet in spite of his seventeen years as Chief, Surgical Department, Hôtel-Dieu, Paris, Théobald Le Brun had never seen anything resembling the body awaiting his hands that day in autumn.

"Mugging," said his assistant, suited up already, waiting.

The victim lay unconscious, skull crashed in, face grey and formless, blood seeping still from his ears and his nose.

Within minutes Le Brun was also suited, also masked, peeling on his transparent, form-fitting gloves.

"Left hand's broken."

"Yes," said Le Brun, glancing at the x-rays presented.

"Both legs too."

"So I see."

"As for the chest…"

"Get him ready."

Not until later, leaning over the table with a tray of instruments by his side – after the caked blood had been cleaned from what had once been the victim's face, did Théobald Le Brun recognize his good friend, Jude McCallister.

"Jude," murmured Le Brun, inaudibly.

Over their surgical masks, the eyes of his colleagues glanced at the chief physician.

"Jude," he repeated, still barely a whisper.

His assistants and nurses were ready.

"Anaesthesia," he said abruptly, forcing himself to push the anguish away, bending slowly over the shattered man, preparing to make a miracle if it were his fate to survive.

The operation took most of the day. Throughout – and nobody noticed this until it was over – a curious silence had prevailed. To be sure, there had been words exchanged. Le Brun had spoken frequently during the eight hours and then some, calling for instruments, procedures, even suggestions from time to time. Two other doctors had assisted; the head nurse had directed a staff of nine in that room; and twice, when the patient's heart had simply stopped, there had been the usual controlled frenzy as death itself was twice postponed.

Nevertheless, there had been none of the banter so often relied upon to relieve anxiety in such cases that warm day. Le Brun's manner had set the tone as the sun had followed its own course outside.

Similarly doubtful, just past four that afternoon, he announced simply, "I have done all I can do."

The patient soon after was wheeled into recovery. Like those who had worked on him, only his eyes could be seen, although they were closed, and though it was not a mask, but intricate bandaging that covered his face.

Bandages too wrapped the rest of Jude's body – absolutely immobile, as though he were one of his sculptures, for by the time he had reached recovery, he had slipped into a coma and his vital signs were unstable.

Le Brun by then had slumped into a side chair beside the washroom in the staff lounge. His plastic cap was in place still; his mask had slipped down to his neck; his scrubs were no longer green but spattered with blood from his chest to his hips.

Then, in lieu of premature congratulations, his first assistant pressed his hand on the chief surgeon's shoulder.

"Thank you, Étienne," said Le Brun, looking up at last, "and you, Olga, and your nurses, and everyone" – and then he was silent.

He was sitting there still, when everyone but Étienne had washed up and gone home.

"Théobald," Étienne said, avoiding at all costs a sentimental tone. "Théobald, you must leave. We will go together."

"There is no need."

"I will wait for you, Théobald."

Le Brun was aware, all of sudden, of an overwhelming exhaustion.

"That is kind of you," he replied. "I won't be a moment."

When he emerged from the washroom, he seemed even more haggard. Étienne pretended not to notice. In fact he was all-business when he reported, "Théobald, I've seen his chart just now."

There was a moment.

"Not much worse, at least."

"It will get worse," his friend said, and then, as they turned toward the exit doors, Théobald stopped abruptly.

"Can you tell me how this happened?"

"I know very little. Just what the crew on the ambulance knows."

"Tell me what the crew on the ambulance knows."

They sat on a bench beneath the dogwoods.

"He was discovered by a janitor, shortly past daybreak, deep inside the gardens off the Champs-Élysées. The path was deserted then, of course, although the old Pavillon des Ambassadeurs was directly behind. Normally, so early, there would have been no one on that pathway, but a fashion show had been scheduled for nine-thirty at the Pavillon. The models were due before eight, the photographers even earlier; the janitor was washing the walkways before unlocking the place."

"So it was the janitor who called the hospital."

"No. The janitor called the police – no need for a doctor judging by that pool of blood – but when the police arrived, within minutes I heard, seems there was, after all, urgent need of a doctor. His wallet, of course, was missing – there was life in him still, some final moments at least."

Le Brun made no answer.

"The rest you know. Herculean effort. Outcome uncertain – although we much hope for the best."

A hoot owl called down, having replaced dawn's first lark.

"Yes," Le Brun replied, and then they both walked toward the door and out to the plaza beside Notre-Dame.

Jude alone could ever have filled in the details, such as he would have remembered them, until he had fallen, unconscious, outside the Pavillon.

He had left the Orangerie, close by the Seine on the Right Bank, where a current exhibit including some of his own work had opened. Then he had walked to the Madeleine, heard a Beethoven concert, stopped for supper at a favourite bistro facing the Madeleine.

There, sipping red wine, he had read and reread the letter he was to have posted the next day, as promised, asking Mrs. Devereux to be his wife. He had written it so many times, had revised it so many times, that at last, he concluded, breaking the bread they had brought with his wine, he had done all he could do. He could not live without her, he had said simply, and so he would await her answer.

Along with his wallet, and the life he had led up 'til then, and the plans he had made for the future, the letter had vanished.

Of course he could not have known what was in store for him that evening. Indeed, as he left his small sidewalk table and strolled toward the river past the boutiques on the rue Royale, Jude had felt restored – almost buoyant – having endured to the date the six weeks he had promised.

At Place de la Concorde, as was his custom, he turned to the right, preferring to cross the river on Pont Alexandre. As he did so, however – and this he had never done before then – he decided against the walkway that bordered the traffic-filled Champs-Élysées. Instead – perhaps because he considered the occasion romantic, perhaps because the evening was fine still – Jude McCallister chose to walk through the park on his way home that night, preferring the maze of inner pathways to the outer street crowds and the noise.

Now and again, making his way in the seclusion, he passed couples, lovers, solitary wanderers with seemingly no destination.

Then, for a long stretch, he passed no one. He reached the Pavillon des Ambassadeurs, an almost dreamlike apparition deep in the trees and hidden gardens. He paused there, savouring the ethereal calm of the semicircular approach. He even sat for a moment on one of the curving stone benches, facing away from the Pavillon, almost reluctant to continue on toward the bustle and busyness of the street. It would be loud still, he knew, though it was well past eleven.

Much better, he reflected, to sit for a moment and take in the evening. The park was perfectly safe. He had often walked there before with his friends, absolutely secure.

Thus when Jude heard what sounded like footsteps behind him, he paid absolutely no attention. Nor did he even turn after a moment, although they seemed to be heading in his direction – more than one person it seemed, perhaps even three. Not until two of the three, young men in their twenties, stopped in front of his bench, and a third stopped behind him, did he look up and suddenly sense that the serenity of the pathway had been an illusion. Instinctively, he stood. The two men closed ranks. Jude moved to the right in order to pass them only to encounter the third man blocking his way. Only then did he realize they were out to rob him – possibly worse.

Had he not struggled, had he not fought with a fierceness all the more tragic in view of the odds against him, he may have perhaps not enraged his attackers to the point where the beating went on long after the wallet was gone. With his arms pinned behind him, his ribs were broken, then his jawbone, then both of his arms, for he struggled still – he was a powerful man, violent in his emotions, as he was in his passions, his art, his love, minding the loss of the letter more than his life it seemed then.

When he lost consciousness they kicked him, having thrown him down on the pavement, face up, so that his skull shattered. Then, in one last random act of rage and blood lust, fever pitch at that point, one man crushed Jude's hand with his boot, breaking that too before they fled.

It was the artist's left hand. The right one – the one he painted with – was the only part of his body seemingly whole there in the darkness.

At the plaza in front of the hospital Dr. Le Brun stopped again. In the setting sun, Notre-Dame's west façade seemed to be hot to the touch. Charlemagne's statue was also aglow straight ahead, as were the benches beside it, the stones, the elegant elm leaves, drifting downward with dignity.

"Théobald," said Étienne, "let me get you a taxi."

"You go," said Théobald. "I've a last detail to attend to."

Étienne looked at him – out of place there in his suit, as he always seemed to be without his mask and a challenge before him, yet at the same time determined, full of passion, for it was all in his nature, and thus, he well knew, it would be fruitless to contradict him.

"We'll speak tomorrow then."

"First thing," promised Le Brun.

His friend sped away.

Le Brun walked back up toward the surgical wing of the old Hôtel-Dieu.

"No change as yet," said Sœur Eugénie, head night nurse, just come on duty.

"I did not expect change, Sœur Eugénie."

She raised her calm eyes to his.

"I came to request a room for my patient."

"Room?"

"He'll be needing a room," replied Théobald brusquely.

"Well, yes…"

"When the anaesthesia's worn off."

The head night nurse nodded.

"Is there a space in the tower?"

She had no words to tell the chief surgeon his patient would most likely never need a room, much less one in the tower, overlooking the west façade of the cathedral, and so she glanced down at her chart. Then, apologetically, she said, "There is one, Docteur Le Brun, but as the Minister's wife is in labour tonight…"

Théobald gestured impatiently.

"And as it has always been her favourite…"

"I want it."

"*Mon Docteur?*"

"Whenever my patient can be transferred."

There was a moment.

"I have studied it from the plaza. It is most perfectly placed. There are rooms below it of course, but the windows on that floor do not clear the elm trees, and hence the façade of the church will be lost. Of course the elm leaves are falling…perhaps in winter then, a partial view…" Le Brun considered. "No, no that will not do. My patient will need a full view, Sœur Eugénie, unobstructed, if he is to survive."

Still Sœur Eugénie stared.

"Please be so good as to inform Recovery. My patient is to be placed in the tower, facing south, with a full view of the cathedral as well as the rooftops and the balconies and the Left Bank bookstores on the Quai St-Michel."

He turned, then stopped abruptly. "Sooner rather than later," he added.

Only then did his head night nurse manage, barely above a whisper, "The victim is in a deep coma still, Dr. Le Brun."

"All the more reason," was the doctor's response, and then again he pushed through the double doors and walked down toward the plaza.

The ineffable alone will save Jude, he reflected, Notre-Dame now deeply shadowed, *if his fate is to be salvation.*

Sœur Eugénie was at that moment contacting the offices of the First Minister.

"Identical," she insisted. "Larger, in fact, Monsieur, with the same view, of course – close by the elm trees outside, and the Virgin's window to the left."

Monsieur le Ministre seemed satisfied. Sœur Eugénie alerted Recovery. Only Le Brun remembered that the cathedral's west rose window, with its magnificent reds and impossible blues, was never visible, completely, until the elm leaves had fallen – mid-October the latest. Jude would be awake by then. He retrieved the rumpled card found in the victim's torn pocket.

"Frères Durand, Inc." the card announced. "14, rue du Bac."

Le Brun was familiar with the gallery. He would contact the owners first thing in the morning, for Jude was as passionate about his privacy as he was about everything else that moved his heart, and his agents, known for their discretion, were most assuredly aware of this.

A taxi pulled up.

"14, rue du Bac," said Le Brun suddenly, having decided he might still find the gallery open.

He was correct. Indeed, on only one count that evening had Dr. Le Brun failed in his calculations. Not until early November would his patient even open his eyes.

⤙ ☾ ⤚

Mikhail was disappointed. He arrived, as he had promised, in time for lunch with his father, surprised again to see only two places set.

"Aren't you working today, Max?"

"Mrs. Devereux was detained. Impossible roads still up north." He unfolded his napkin with exaggerated precision. "I am sorry you have missed her one more time, Mikhail."

"Next week perhaps. I should be back by Monday."

"God willing."

"Opera tickets this evening, or else I'd stay and keep you company."

Max passed him a basket filled with sweet rolls and bread.

"Supper afterwards," Misha continued. "Then bags to be packed, papers to be reviewed, car coming to take me to the night flight tonight. I could of course leave tomorrow – meetings don't start 'til day after – but I prefer to be rested before negotiations like these."

"Wisely done, son…wisely done," Max replied, busying himself with choosing a muffin.

Mikhail left his father's house just after four. His evening engagement was not 'til six-thirty.

More than enough time for a long twilight stroll, he thought.

In spite of the snow and the frail sun receding, the pathways throughout Central Park were still crowded. Joggers, shoppers, tourists, lovers, now and again a dreamer alone – as he was – passed under the wrought-iron lamps.

A waltz from the skating rink drifted over the hill. Holiday carols rang from the clock at the zoo. Mikhail stopped near the clock, watching the children stare as the mechanical creatures endlessly circled. Then he turned back through the park toward the opposite side.

Passing his father's building he saw both gates wide open – the one which controlled access to the pedestrian arch, and the one further down, customarily closed, which allowed vehicles into the court. There was something about the large, polished car under this arch which made Mikhail pause. It was elegant, though not a late model – all the more intriguing for being somehow out of time.

Could be a painting almost, he said to himself, *an Edward Hopper perhaps, or maybe even*…He stopped. Antonin Onegin had emerged from the car – dark, huge silent form, like the opaque sky overhead. He closed his door gently, opened the passenger's door, and then a gloved hand took his. Mikhail stared as this second figure emerged, vaguely old-world like the car, wrapped in a grey fur-trimmed coat, clearly visible in the lamplight. She smiled then it seemed, and then gave him a bag – a small suitcase it appeared – and then took his arm and they both walked into the courtyard and disappeared into the night.

A moment, nothing more, dreamlike in its fragility, stark in its contrast of bright lights and shadowy forms. Yet Mikhail had been mesmerized. There, visible for an instant, confident as he had imagined ideal form would have to be – a rare face to match the voice that had unsettled him, only yesterday. She hadn't seen him. He had stood motionless, five feet away perhaps, unobserved in the darkness, lost in the crowds passing by. He knew only one thing by the time he did walk away, a few moments later, to dress for dinner and the gala opening of *Rosenkavalier*. He would change his plans after all, taking a flight on the following day.

⟨ ❨ ⟩

Songs Without Words, Caroline mused not long after she'd arrived, hearing the opening bars of the piece from her usual seat next to Max. It seemed fitting somehow, like her life at that point, music still in her heart, text somehow gone.

Appropriate, Max reflected, vaguely discomfited at the thought of his silence during lunch with his son that afternoon. Well it had not been deliberate after all. No intent to deceive. The topic had just not come up – simple as that. Besides, why would Misha care if his father had convinced his assistant to come at the end of that day, when the ridge would be cleared at last?

"Time is my opponent," he had reminded Caroline when they had spoken.

"Yes. Yes, I know, Max."

"Along with this weather – so unexpected – and that confounded distance two times every day."

The implication had unnerved her. Now that the cold months were upon them, did he prefer to replace her?

"Just say you'll come," he had insisted. "Not to write today. There'll be no time. To be ready for tomorrow's work."

Relieved to be still employed, Mrs. Devereux had agreed. Antonin had managed the ridge just past dark. They had arrived in Manhattan on time.

Mendelssohn, thought Maximilian, focusing once more on the present, never sounded lovelier.

⟨ ❨ ⟩

Dr. Devereux never felt luckier. His wife had gone out for the night – something about the storm and an assignment that couldn't wait – and so he'd had time and the house to himself.

Utterly providential, he decided. Caroline rarely locked her closets. Her wardrobe was always unlatched. He could search at his leisure, tying and untying the little silk pouches she kept here and there, judging the pieces he himself had provided, carefully choosing the right ones – and they had to be right, for God alone knew when a similar chance might come his way.

After twenty minutes or so, he was no longer in need of a similar chance, for under the shawls toward the back of her wardrobe was a box he remembered at once. There would be two velvet purses inside, he knew – one containing rare black pearl earrings, the other a matching necklace. They'd been his gift to her when she'd miscarried – first or second time, he couldn't remember. She'd never worn them, not even on Christmas. Yet over the years, like the barren peach tree at the back end of the orchard, they had become part of the earth that was the soil of her heart. She would no more have sold them than the river beyond it, silent and still in the wake of the storm.

"No," Susan agreed, hearing the story at midnight. "She'd never sell one of her things. She'd rather *translate*," – the concept baffled her – "placing you and the pearls and that whole orchard at risk."

He stroked her hip as she spoke, glad, after all, that he had taken her wise advice. After a moment he heard her murmur, as though remembering: "Roger Gachet."

"What?"

"Owner and president and middleman extraordinaire."

"Owner of what, my love?"

"La Ronde on Fifth. I've used him myself several times. Pays well. Discreet. He will appreciate your treasures."

The possessive adjective soothed his conscience. Susan's passion soothed his needs. Then, for the first time in a long time, sleep – long and dreamless – came his way.

Even Claire Tierney, who repeatedly swore she couldn't possibly rest on those long flights to Paris, somehow managed to sleep well that night. She had said yes to champagne in First Class – upgrade compliments of her shrewd employer, who'd sent her off with a smile, a big raise, and her first truly impressive assignment: *carte blanche* to bid, on behalf of La Ronde, for a work she thought worthy at the Contemporary Painting Exhibition. Her favourites, he knew, would be the McCallisters on display.

⌒ ❨ ⌒

Maximilian alone had slept fitfully. By daybreak, he was already consulting the volumes of history he kept on his desk for reference.

What he was looking for was not to be found. Although the recollections he had been conjuring before the week's snowstorms had been difficult – the flight from Paris back into Provence after the fall of free France – he had remembered it all: every town, every river, every bridge and meadow and terrified face glimpsed en route. Caroline had rendered it faithfully, her precision a match for his faultless reminiscence.

Yet the story told had been incomplete, purposely, and therefore disingenuous, for he had neglected to mention a parallel tale – one the reference books would never mention. Banished by force of will and many years' effort, it had surfaced that morning as though possessed of its own will, equal to his. Perhaps it was the sight of the boy again, now a man; or the sounds of the woman stirring below, drawing her bath; or the scent of the roses the boy had brought him upon his arrival – he could not say, but as he drew triangles, absently, on the pad of paper beside his textbooks, the floodgates opened at last. Long-subdued images found their way to him, in spite of him. He pushed his books aside and crossed to his daybed. Then, as a pale and tentative day gathered strength, Max put his head back and remembered.

The first thing he saw was an old sandstone house in Nice. Its green-shuttered windows faced a wide street in front, a private garden in back. He had been born in this house, as had his father before him. Now, in his recollections, he was rushing back to it – a young man still, desperate, barely a week after Paris had fallen.

In the brief space of that week, he had managed to cross the countryside, sleeping little, eating less, always a few kilometres ahead of the huge tanks behind him, desperate to reach his home and the two people alone there – his mother Hélène, his little boy Mikhail.

His own nurse, Anna Berg, had died a year earlier. "Old age," the priest at her bedside had said. Maximilian alone knew the truth. Anna's stout heart had broken after the Anschluss uniting her native Austria to Germany. Nothing thereafter had been the same for her in Provence. She was watched closely wherever she went throughout Nice, despised for her Viennese ways. In time she had ceased to leave the old sandstone house. "I am too tired," she would say to Max whenever he'd ask her to take a stroll to the sea, or "The afternoon is too hot."

These words she *would* say in German, but only if they were alone, for it was the only language they had spoken since Max was a child. Because of Anna he felt more at home in it, on occasion, than in his own native French. Indeed, perhaps more than French, German *was* his mother tongue, for Anna Berg, far more than Hélène, had been his mother, hired on the very day Hélène had discovered she was with child.

Hélène had not relished the prospect of motherhood. Young still, and lovely, she had only recently married into one of the oldest families in Nice, but Jean-Baptiste d'Olivier had longed for a son; his pretty wife had complied; and the boy was promptly, if carefully, handed into the arms of his nurse. A German-speaking nanny, after all, would be useful. Jean-Baptiste was a musician. They were often in Leipzig for concerts.

Not that the competent Anna Berg couldn't manage in French. German, however, had remained their secret world, sealing them off from the adults and traditions and responsibilities of Provence. In the end it was all she left Max, but it was everything, for few people knew he had been given this gift. He was just Paul Maximilian d'Olivier, first-born scion of one of the most respectable families in Nice.

As it happened, there'd been no siblings. Hélène had been firm about that. Thus, when Jean-Baptiste died, Max at fourteen became sole heir to the estate. He stayed in Provence for three years, moved to Paris for university, Vienna for advanced studies, Nice again to open his architect's office, finally coming full circle to the sea of his youth.

In truth, he had never been far. Provence was in his heart. He'd spent vacations there, weekends whenever he could, for Hélène was there, proper as always and even finer as the years passed, and Anna Berg, born to love him alone, and the old sandstone house with the secret garden out back, like that Viennese waltz in his head.

He dated, of course, fell in love at the Sorbonne, once more in Vienna – but another woman in that house? Impossible, sacrilegious almost. Not 'til he was past forty – Anna Berg had turned eighty, Hélène sixty-eight – did Paul Maximilian d'Olivier take a wife. She wasn't yet twenty. It was the only rash thing he had done up 'til then, utterly reckless, totally out of character, answering deeper needs, doomed from the start.

Daughter of an English client who'd come to Provence to build a second home, Cecilia Matson, just seventeen, was already a beauty when they'd met – elegant, doted-upon, known even then for her pale golden *hauteur*.

She was also utterly without scruples. Accustomed to adulation, she had long since grown tired of the hothouse affluence that was her birthright. There'd been pranks first at ten, more serious charges at twelve, at fifteen items "borrowed" from London's premier boutiques. Yet few people could resist her – even after they saw through her, for the smouldering passion beneath her correctness enhanced an allure that was impossible to ignore.

Maximilian ignored her. Not that he failed to notice her, but he had a job to do. The commission was important, the house he'd designed complex and large. He was too professional to be distracted, too passionate an artist to be derailed from his course.

At least at first. Cecilia saw his reserve and was determined to have her way. She'd watch him work with his men, surveying the land, clearing it, creating a shell first, slowly a work of art. She adored him openly – shamelessly, wearing little diamond stud earrings, little skirts that skimmed her panties, expensive T-shirts that sculpted her round, perfect breasts.

Max felt her force more deeply the second summer – the year of actual construction – when she was eighteen, just back from England for vacation. He'd miss her when she wasn't there, when her father would come without her to inspect the site – days not unplanned by her, for like bait on a fishhook she would allow herself to be glimpsed, smelled, brushed against, yearned for. In the end Max was caught. He stumbled twice – once on a hillside overlooking the sea far below, once again at the gala party James Matson gave when the house was at last done.

Max had walked up alone to that hillside, as he often did, wanting the landscaping of the house to blend perfectly with its surroundings. He'd stood for a long time near the top, staring out at the sea, leaning against a stone wall that seemed to be sinking beneath the weight of the roses hugging its side. To the left of the wall, running seaward, was a clear narrow stream; to the right an old oak, sturdy and full, with a rope swing still firmly attached to one of the branches overhead.

"Don't you get hungry up here all day?" he heard a voice ask from behind, instantly knowing that lush and impertinent tone.

"I do, yes," he said turning, smiling in spite of himself at the sight of Cecilia, sitting in a little clearing near the swing, barefoot, wearing a pale aqua sundress that matched the Mediterranean.

"I always bring lunch when I come," she said – half to direct him, half to deride, sounding at least twice her age as she opened her basket and took out some bread, cheese, fruit and a tablecloth.

"And is that often?" Max asked approaching, still with a smile, while whitecaps danced without shame around practical sails out in the bay.

"Whenever I can," she said nonchalantly.

The empty swing behind her swayed, as did the tall grass on the hill.

"I don't blame you," said Max.

"Father does."

"For coming here?"

"For hiding here. Well, not so much now," she corrected herself, "but when I was little…"

He couldn't imagine her little.

"And he'd get cross with me…"

Max sat with her.

"I'd run up all the way up and spend the day here. Half the night too sometimes," she laughed, carelessly peeling a peach. "Well we won't talk about those nights. It's a wonder we both survived them."

"Why do you come here now, Cecilia?"

"Same reason you do, Max."

"I'm here to work," he replied, far too stiffly. "Mapping out your garden."

"Has it a hiding place?"

"Do you still need one?"

She thought for a moment, licking the peach juice that had dripped on her wrist. "You'll have to ask my father, I guess," and then they both laughed, and the breeze rustled her skirt and somehow got into her very short hair.

"Share some wine, Max?"

"Yes," he said simply, feeling of all things, for the first time, inexperienced. "If only to keep you from drinking it all."

They'd shared the cheese and bread and fruit too before long, for Cecilia had made sure she'd brought more than enough, and Maximilian was hungry. By the time they had finished, the afternoon had turned brisk. Not even the whitecaps seemed at ease in the swift windswept sea.

"We'd better be going," decided Max, scanning the skies. "You aren't dressed for this cold."

He finished repacking the basket. She lay back on her blanket, as though to defy his concern, curling one arm under her head, ignoring the skies. He couldn't help staring. She seemed more at home under that swing than in the house he was building. Honeysuckle, somewhere, surrendered its scent to the wind. He stood, shoved his hands into his pockets and gazed at the sea.

"Penny for your thoughts," he heard her say from the grass.

He did not answer.

"Monsieur Max?"

"It's getting late," he said sharply, stretching his hand down to help her stand, "and my men will be waiting."

Again that release from some honeysuckle branch.

"You're probably right, Max."

"I'll take the basket," he offered, because it was expected, more to let go of her hand. Then they turned toward the path that led down to the sea.

"Swing me, Max," she said suddenly.

"No."

"Once…"

"We haven't time."

"It isn't four yet. No, don't look at your watch! I can tell by the way the sun hits that topsail."

Max scanned the coastline.

"The one heading east."

"Just once then," Max agreed, seduced by that fine navy schooner rounding the curve of the bay.

"More!" she called to him, exactly as he knew she would, and so he pushed the flimsy swing, over and over again, sending the aqua plaid sundress soaring into the sky. "Higher, Max!"

For once he refused.

"Just to the lilacs…"

"You're high enough!" he called out, moving away to let her glide. Instead, to his alarm, she swung her legs stubbornly and started to pump.

"Cecilia, slow down!"

She pumped even harder.

"You're clearing the rose wall, Cecilia!"

He heard her laugh as she kicked her sandals off, pumping still.

"You'll break your neck!" he cried, moving in front of her now, standing between the oak and the rose wall, as if to shield her from the sea somehow. "Come down easily now…"

She leaned all the way back, holding her arms stiff and letting her skirt blow up and spreading her legs as the swing carried her, slowly descending, glad for the weight, it appeared.

"Catch me, Max!"

"Not from there…"

The wind tugged at her dress again. She coasted, legs spread apart still, and as she approached he could see she had no panties on.

"I'm jumping now…"

"Wait!"

She started pumping again, gaining speed and momentum and carving a dangerous arc in her frail airborne raft. Reaching the heights again, she let the ropes go.

"Here I come," she called out, flying into the space where he was.

Max did catch her somehow, staggering under the impact until they both fell against the wall. He sustained her, incredibly, along with the impact, refusing to collapse with his precious cargo, maintaining his feet planted firmly on the ground beneath.

"Are you all right?" he murmured – stunned, relieved, holding on to her still, afraid she would take flight again, down into the sea.

"Of course I'm all right," she said buoyantly, and he looked at her then – wild and free in his arms – and then they both laughed with relief, and he pulled her against him and put his tongue in her mouth and raised her skirt again, thinking she ought to be spanked for her wilfulness, wanting to enter her instead.

"Do it, Max," she said hoarsely, half a woman's whisper, half the caprice of a child, and in the overlapping sounds he pulled away a bit.

"Please," she insisted…

How could he take advantage?

"While there's time still…"

There was no time, he must have decided – not on that hillside, with her so young and his need so intense – for he pulled away a second time, and they walked down to the sea.

It would happen again, he knew only too well, though he hadn't expected it before September. Yet on the night of the Matson reception in August, Cecilia saw Max excuse himself to go to the wine cellar for her father.

The subterranean room was across a small courtyard to the rear of the house. Max lit the two entry lamps, then proceeded on into the silent, secluded space. At the sound of a step behind him he turned. Suddenly, magnificent even in shadows, she was standing before him, her white strapless sheath another fine column under the arch he had built.

"Cecilia…" he stammered.

"Congratulations," she said, approaching on high golden sandals that struck the old stones with disdain.

"You approve of the wine," was all he could think of to answer.

"I approve of the house."

She seemed to him years more mature than that day on the hill two months before.

"Everyone does," she said with a smile. "Even my father."

"Thank you."

She looked at the wine in his hand.

"Shall we toast to you?"

"If you like." He too smiled. "Upstairs."

"Down here."

"You'll be missed."

"I'm always missed."

"Well I'm not. I am expected." He almost laughed then, in spite of himself, at the self-importance in his clumsy defence. "At least the wine is expected…"

She took the wine from his hands.

"Cecilia…" he managed.

"There." She placed the bottle carefully on a small bench beside him. "Now they'll do without both."

When she faced him again he was amazed at her beauty. Her cropped blonde hair, bright and wayward as her smile, encircled her head like spun gold. Her eyes, colour of bronze, fixed on him fearlessly, as though daring the worst in him. Her copper-toned skin seemed to glow.

And so the kiss he gave her was long, and he let his hands lose their way, and he was stunned when he pulled her head back by those curls and realized he could have encircled her neck with one grip – worse, his longing encompassed the wish, for as she pressed herself against him and he found her mouth again, part of him wanted it, some sane part of him wanted to kill her there, last chance to save himself, her too, perhaps – a kindness, murder of mercy.

Savagely he called out, "No!"

They stood in the half-light a moment, taking their breath back, taking stock, taking the measure of each other's will.

"I'm thinking of you," he gasped.

"You're thinking of *you*..."

"*Believe* me..."

"No!" she repeated, echoing his hateful word. "No more. I've no time. I'll be missed." She was finding it hard still to breathe. "So will the wine," she flashed stepping back, grabbing the bottle and turning away, her angry gold sandals spurning the stones as she walked, and the old stones forgave, for she herself had been spurned. At the doorway she stopped, her backless white dress architectural once again.

"On second thought, Max," he heard her remark, "I may not go right in. *You'd* better take it." She turned, hurled the priceless vintage onto the floor by his feet, and walked out.

Max stood there a moment, stunned by the sound of shattering glass on the floor. He watched the liquid seep out, stunned too it seemed, running in little rivulets toward timeworn crevices that would not judge. And then he heard footsteps – people running to the doorway, a perfect arch that must have amplified the explosion's effect.

"Nothing serious," he said at the entrance. "A little mishap, that's all. House wine dropped. Very clumsy of me. I'll clean it up and rejoin you, and bring two perfect ones in exchange."

James Matson offered to help.

"Nonsense. I'm almost finished. I'll be up in a minute," Maximilian assured them all as they started back to the house.

By the time he re-entered the cellar, their voices had faded. He paused in the dimness, leaning against a cool wall, heart splintered still like the shards at his feet. Then he brought over a lantern and cleaned up the mess.

When he returned to the party, Cecilia was not to be found. She still hadn't appeared by the time he left late that night. She had gone straight to her room, unbeknownst to Maximilian, telling her father she had had far too much sun.

Yet not for a moment did she sleep. All through the night she lay in her large, dark new room, lost, having never before failed to get her way, willing to cut her heart out now to have it.

Max too lay awake, having returned to Nice, lost in his own house, lonely and forty and having gotten his way. She had been right, he heard someone say, or perhaps it was the tide going out, leaving all false things on the sand. His chivalrous stand had had nothing to do with her youth, still less her honour. It was his soul he had tried to preserve, his pride – bedrock and endangered, for he had seen the way men looked at her, the way she played with them in return, and he would not be among them. Better to cut his heart out rather than to have it trifled with.

Throughout the following week, as Max worked on the many details that had remained still on the Matson house, Cecilia did not appear. Nor did he see her the next week. Not until after a fortnight did he see her again, leaving church on the arm of James Matson, more beautiful than ever he believed, even more mature, or perhaps simply more elegant. She did not speak to him. Nor did they speak at a party in town the next week, where she was again with her father. It was not to be until the next morning, when Max was again at the Matson house, that he at last saw Cecilia alone. He had caught a glimpse of her passing through the arcade across the back of the house as he worked, but James Matson entered the study then and delayed him a bit, asking a question or two, and so she had started to climb the hill by the time Max reached the arcade.

He called out her name but she seemed not to hear. He ran up behind her but she did not turn. He reached for her arm and whirled her around and saw her eyes blazing as she tried in vain to pull away.

"What do you want, Max?"

Not to be toyed with, he thought, though he did not answer.

"Max?"

To be more than a puppet –

"Let me go, Max!"

"Marry me."

She stared at him. He loosened his grip and let her arm fall. A crow in the elm called as she took in the meaning of his words, uttered fiercely, with effort, as his violent "No!" had been once, and just as unexpected.

"You can't be serious," she protested.

"Now, tonight…"

"You're mad."

"Or in a church next month, whatever you like…"

"But my father, my schooling…"

"There are schools here. I will speak to your father; he will understand. He will say yes, Cecilia, he'll have no choice, if *you* say yes" – Max stumbled here – "if you want Nice and a fine old stone house…and – and me."

For perhaps the first time in her life, fleetingly, Cecilia was moved.

"Max," she murmured, "*sois prudent…*"

"I have been prudent since I was your age," he replied, and they both smiled.

"Give me some time then."

"Whatever you need."

As it turned out, she didn't need much. She liked the old stone house in Nice, had no objections to Anna, no real dislike of Hélène, no strong desire to go back to school. Her father, as Max had predicted, made a virtue of necessity. He gave an elegant wedding befitting the house Max had built him, and the daughter he was parting with, and sent them off with his blessings on a month's honeymoon to Sardinia. Not until October did *Monsieur et Madame d'Olivier* return to the house by the seawall in Nice.

Hitler by then had begun an expansion few had foreseen. Violent rains, seemingly in despair, had fallen constantly throughout Europe. Provence itself, uncharacteristically, had had weeks of grey dampness, and Madame d'Olivier was already with child.

She had said nothing to Max. She could barely bring herself to face it, so unacceptable was the concept, so preposterous the result of his passionate lovemaking a mere six weeks before.

Another month passed, more rain, more international fears, and still she said nothing. It seemed obscene – this thing growing inside her – making her sick when she awoke, making her clothes tight, shunting off her vitality. Only yesterday – a matter of tides, a summer at the Riviera – and she herself was a child. And now there was this new – what? – generation? Unthinkable. She would not have it. She was not ready. She was, at heart, scared.

Anna Berg knew of course. Max would soon present her with a new child to care for. That was clear from the moment Cecilia pushed her plate away, pallid and ungenerous, saying abruptly she did not care for eggs. Hélène also knew, seeing herself in the girl, growing outsized against all reason, wanting her father back.

But for the rain perhaps, some frail pact might have been made with the place. But there was no end to the dampness. Storms came in like columned soldiers, dragging in tow unpredictable winds.

"Warnings of war again," whispered the baker, Laocoön-like, as the breakwater swayed and collapsed one afternoon. His neighbours dismissed him; hailstones drowned out their voices; Chamberlain faltered; and not a single thing Cecilia owned fit.

She returned to London for the holidays. Anna, Max and Hélène had their usual Christmas in the fine stately home. He called the Matsons that day, and again New Year's Eve.

"Yes, I've booked a flight back," she assured him. "A month from today, Max, assuming Papá gets over his cold."

James Matson recovered slowly. Cecilia did not return 'til March. When she walked off the plane there was no disguising it anymore. Madame was *enceinte* – six months along – motherhood imminent, childhood a recollection.

It was the first Max had known of it. He was struck by the sight of her, feeling a surge of conflicting emotions as she approached: relief in her safe arrival, joy in her beautiful face, rage at her reticence – no, not reticence, duplicity – there was no other word for it. How else to explain the fact that she had guarded her secret so long, keeping their child, their future, badly concealed in her belly, as a little girl might hide a doll.

"Max!" She held out her hands.

There were no words.

"Max – how are you?"

"Cecilia…"

"You're looking fine," she went on.

"Welcome…" he managed.

"None the worse for the filthy weather," she said breezily, looking around, "although it seems to have let up a bit…"

"Christ, Cecilia," he burst out, taking her bag. "I'd've come for you if I had known. I'd've come sooner, stayed with you there if need be…"

"There was no need."

She said it serenely, bordering on the matter-of-fact, and in her *désinvolture* Max knew at once that Cecilia Matson would not stay.

He was right, though she could not leave soon, sick as she was again within a week, unable to travel after that given her fragile condition. Anna Berg did what she could toward the end. Hélène was as unfailingly kind. Cecilia hated them both, and their garden, and the ten rooms they presided over – no mistaking it – despite their irreproachable generosity. She would leave them all, she determined, just as soon as this business was done with – deliverance into the past again – six more weeks at the most.

Only her timing betrayed her. Cecilia did not rejoin her father until the beginning of September, three months after the birth of her son, Mikhail Alexander Matson d'Olivier. He had appeared after prolonged labour had extracted every ounce of his mother's youth. He had demanded it without mercy, and she had surrendered, grudgingly, cursing his supremacy in the most extreme agony, challenged by a little stranger whose will had been forged from her own.

Infection had followed, a grim lesson from the gods, perhaps, threatened by her defiance. The once golden face was ashen by then, though chiselled still, like a death mask in Advent. Born to seduce, Misha had taken everything.

Max saw him briefly that first day, then placed him into the hands of his own mother, Hélène, who, nearing seventy, was ready at last. Then, as the summer slipped by, Max called for him some, not out of love – there would never be that, for his child was Cecilia and he was losing her – but out of duty. He knew who he was, after all – who they all were – even this boy who had shattered his world, this Mikhail Alexander, firstborn son and heir, thriving in grandmother's arms while his little girl fought for life.

She won the fight, barely, surprising even the doctor with her primordial determination. In mid-July she broke the fever. Later on she sat up, looked around, asked for some tea, never asked for the child. Max was wild at the sight of her, wan and triumphant, death itself outmanoeuvred.

"My fine and stubborn Cecilia," he murmured, caressing her hands and kissing her face. Yet still no word of the child, not even a query – *boy or girl? Healthy or weak? Brown-eyed as she was? Fair like her father?*

Not until three days had passed did Max attempt to speak of it. He faltered, then let it go. Two days later a second attempt: "Cecilia," he began, taking her hands again, "my dearest love…"

She gazed upon him, listlessly.

"You have enriched us with a son."

"I am glad for you, Max," she responded, sincerely. "Glad in the extreme."

Then she sank back against the pillows Anna Berg had provided, and in that moment Max knew. She would never ask for the boy. It would be up to his father to present him, to introduce Misha into their world, which he did shyly, two days later. She held him gingerly, but with dignity, as a dealer would cradle a prized object for sale. Then, stretching her arms out so that his father could take him again, she said simply, "He will bring joy to this house. I am certain of it."

It was a valedictory, though she held him again after that, always with the same respect, counting the moments 'til Hélène would return as she was counting the days until she could walk. By mid-August she could manage. By the start of September she was gone – a brief holiday, three weeks, no more, she promised Max, kissing the boy he carried awkwardly, behind her. They both knew the truth. Even the boy knew – somewhere deep in his fine, perfectly formed little head. Even the boy knew Cecilia Matson would never come back.

Which is why Max had to rush when the end came, Paris taken at last, Anna Berg gone, only Hélène there with the boy.

I must keep on, he remembered repeating, and then he thought he heard knocking somewhere, somebody calling his name, and then another knock, footsteps, and as he opened his eyes he saw Mrs. Devereux beside his daybed. The sight of her startled him – no hat, no coat, not even a purse – just a slim white skirt and scooped-neck top and a sweater tossed over her shoulders as though she lived there, as though she were – what – his wife? – what was a wife? – he did not know – not the one he'd had, not this one – and yet their images blurred – the only two women who had ever disarmed him – one with her wiles and copper-toned nonchalance, one with a deep purple sadness even her smile could not hide.

"Two minutes late, Max, can you imagine? And only a staircase to climb today. Well you can blame all your books down there...Max?"

He was staring still, fixedly, as though they had never been introduced.

"Are you all right, Max?"

He made no answer, and despite the steam she felt suddenly cold.

"Quick," he said finally, "Open your notebook there – while it is fresh still."

He spoke rapidly, mostly in French. She wrote just as quickly, putting it down in English, rendering his recollections with a precision to match his passion. If the clock struck at noon, they did not notice. If the bell rang at two, lunch right on time, they neither heard it, nor cared to, for Max had by then abandoned history and political theory and his magnificent erudition to walk deep into that other world – the one he had never mentioned in the eight weeks she'd been beside him – the boy, Anna, Cecilia, Hélène, – somehow appearing today, for what reason she could not guess, knowing only that today, forged in pain, his memoirs had become memories and the heroic fighter a man.

Not until he stopped at last – almost as abruptly as he had begun – mentioning his wedding gift returned, a cameo he'd given his bride left on their dresser when she departed – did Caroline stop. She became vaguely aware of the silence first, then the dimness, then a searing soreness in the fingers, then a compelling hunger. Yet still she said nothing. The image of a young Maximilian, sturdy and whole, not yet fifty, fallible, hurt, proud and abandoned, had overwhelmed her. She stared at him as the clock struck, four times she thought, and he laid his head back and closed his eyes and was silent.

"Max?" she whispered.

There was no answer.

"Max, you should eat something. A cup of soup perhaps – a sandwich." She rose. "I'll fetch something."

He opened his eyes. "Later." It was barely audible. "If you don't mind, Caroline. Just a rest now. Then a bit of supper." He smiled at her, gamely. "Then music of course. Although it is Sunday. I asked them to come because you missed Friday." His head fell back again. "Schubert. *Death and the Maiden.* Lovely, in spite of the story."

She rose after a moment and crossed to the door. When she looked back his face was turned toward the window, as though the winter courtyard beyond would somehow supplant the secret garden long gone.

Then she let herself out, longing too for her bed and some rest – not the great antique bed at Todd's Farm, but the small velvet one beneath his.

༄ ☾ ༄

When she awoke, but for a small shaft of light spilling onto the rug, Caroline's small room was dark.

"Elsa?" she murmured, for the outline of a figure had appeared at the threshold. "You've returned early," she began, and then she broke off abruptly and sat up, feeling small and white against the velvet and utterly without recourse.

"Forgive me," said a man's voice.

She drew even further away.

"I knocked but there was no answer. The musicians have arrived. My father is also asleep."

She stared at him, wide-eyed. He smiled.

"You must be…"

"Misha," he responded. "Cupbearer to the gods."

Only then did she notice the tray in his hand.

"I've another one waiting to go up to Max," he went on, placing the tray on her little table and stepping back toward the door.

"Thank you" was all she could manage, fully visible now as the door opened completely and light from the library splashed onto the bed. She pushed her black hair from her face. "This is all so – unexpected."

He smiled again, warmly. "I'll attend to Max now. Come up when you're ready. The musicians will play as we eat; they have agreed to do that; even on Schubert alone one cannot possibly live."

The door remained open.

"In the meantime," he added, graciously still, as though the house and the building and the whole courtyard were his, "start with that sherry. A fine one. Very rich. To bring you back among the living, Caroline – if that's who you are."

The door began closing.

"I'll wait upstairs."

And then there was darkness in the sanctuary as she heard his footsteps on the staircase. She reached for the glass, took a small sip, then drank a second time, long and deeply. Then she lay back once again, collecting her thoughts as best she could. He had appeared out of nowhere, in the flesh, his father having conjured him, finally, a mere two hours earlier. Max would be stunned, she thought, or at the very least overjoyed.

He was neither, as it happened. He had assumed Misha had left. Nothing would be the same now, he felt, as Schubert's *Andante* began.

⁓ ☾ ⁓

Completing his rounds, Dr. Le Brun climbed the narrow staircase to the hospital's top-floor suites.

He could have made use of the elevator, newly installed, but he favoured the view from the landing as the steps curved one last time, for there – eye level exactly – ninety feet away at most, were the stone statues of the Kings' Gallery above the central portal of Notre-Dame. There too were the figures of the Last Judgment in the portal's tympanum and, like a goddess presiding over the kingdom of this regal western façade, in the centre the Virgin, set in the deepest possible primary colours.

It was for this that he had insisted his patient be placed in the tower, though six weeks had gone by before Jude McCallister had opened his eyes. When he did so, reported Sœur Eugénie, it was only to make a most inhuman sound, as a maimed wolf would have done, which had sent Sœur Chantal down the hall, dragging her morphine cart behind her.

Twice a day after that – sometimes more – Jude would open his eyes and feel the pain once again and call again for the bag, which would then make its appearance, like the Virgin in the west façade, unstintingly sending its benediction his way.

"On this particular day, though," Sœur Eugénie confided, inclining her head as Le Brun bent over his charts, "your patient said something else."

Le Brun looked up at her.

"Delusional, to be sure…"

"Yes, yes, of course…"

"Thinking poor Sœur Chantal some sort of painter's model, naked he seemed to believe, although of course morphine –"

"But what did he say?"

"'Not over there,' he called out. And then he cursed her and someone called Nero and insisted she move to the left and for once in her life try to stand still.

"Well there was need of the bag, that was clear, but he became angry when Sœur Chantal moved. 'I cannot paint you, damnable woman, if you come near me like that,' he cried, and then his eyes closed again, which made it possible to inject his arm at least."

Dr. Le Brun turned toward the plaza. Then, after what seemed like a long time: "I will go in now to see the patient."

When he emerged from the tower suite, 411, he returned directly to the head nurse with his chart.

"Morphine to be cancelled in 411?" she gasped.

"Not all at once," he replied. "Slowly, within the next week, after which, with his mind clear, I can make further assessments."

Sœur Eugénie merely stared. She had seen others like this patient, though not as bad as this patient. She'd heard them plead for death, sleep, the devil, their mothers – anything to bring relief once the anodyne had been removed.

"He needs to fight now," continued Théobald, as though reading her thoughts.

Still Sœur Eugénie stared.

"He wants to live, can't you see? I don't know why yet – just that the longing is fierce – for when I announced myself I took his hands, and he looked at me – he opened his eyes, Sœur Eugénie, and there I saw that nothing mattered but survival now – not in the abstract – mere existence he would have surrendered – but survival *for a purpose*, which of course I cannot guess."

The immense bells of the cathedral rang out, tolling the hour.

"It is not my task to guess. Much less is it to make things happen. It is my duty to make things *possible*."

"Well, yes, of course…"

"Yours too, I might add."

Sœur Eugénie lowered her eyes.

"We cannot begin such an effort with a man growing dependent on that which makes effort out of the question."

His voice softened; his heart too shrank from the thing.

"It will be hard for you, *Ma Sœur*. Hard for us all, hard for him above all – but it must be done. I will make plans for new daily procedures beginning a week from today."

A steady November rain began falling as he turned toward the staircase. Even the twenty-eight Kings, fruit of the tree of Jesse – sentinels keeping guard over the portals of the cathedral – seemed to retreat in the sudden darkness.

"Storm or no storm," added Le Brun at the doorway, all business again, pen still clutched in his hand, "I'll want an update tomorrow."

Try as she might to reduce the impact of that update, Sœur Eugénie had no choice but to surrender the facts, as requested, shortly before six the next morning.

Le Brun looked them over with a seeming impassivity, though when he raised his eyes once again, Sœur Eugénie saw her own anguish reflected.

"We could perhaps give some more," she suggested.

Théobald reflected, respecting her expertise as he did her compassion. But in the end he demurred. "Time, Sœur Eugénie, is our enemy here. I have been making plans to begin therapy. Yes,

I plan to rebuild him," he added at that point, for Sister Eugénie's eyes had grown wide. "If he wants life he shall have it."

And with that he was gone, down to the surgical wing, leaving the nurses in charge of a man begging for morphine or death. His doctor had somehow divined that by death he meant life. They followed his orders, though more than one of them would have sold her soul to have assuaged the man. That is what they called him: *the man*, for as to his identity the police seemed foiled, and the doctor seemed not to care; no family had appeared, nor had there been the slightest mention in any papers.

It was anonymous suffering thus in tower suite 411, all the more heartbreaking in its isolation.

⌐ ☾ ⌐

Claire Tierney walked from the Hôtel de Crillon to the École des Beaux-Arts on the opposite side of the Seine. She paused, shielding her eyes from the sun as she looked up toward the roof and the silk banners floating above. Among the offerings announced, in elegant white-and-gold script, was the one of most interest to her: *Jude McCallister, Paintings and Drawings: Silver Jubilee Celebration.*

She was aware, to be sure, that she would never – not even for a moment – have a glimpse of the painter. Though he was an icon in the art world, having earned a fortune to match his status, he was a private man – part-time musician, full-time genius – erratic and independent when it came to both his life and his work. From time to time, she had heard, he still accepted commissions, not necessarily from the well-connected. There, it seemed, he was consistent. What moved him still was what he had always sought: inspiration.

"Something without par," Roger Gachet had insisted, briefing his young assistant on the eve of her departure. "A grace note for La Ronde. A jewel. – Well, you will know it when you see it."

"Yes."

"And when you see it, Claire, I want it."

But will I see it? Claire wondered, staring fixedly at the banner still. It all seemed so daunting, mysterious – just like the painter, whom she'd heard preferred solitude to celebrity, except for an evening or two at some piano bar, unannounced.

It might be weeks after that before he'd emerge again. Sometimes he'd stay in his house near Rodin's street, painting models or patrons from sunrise to sundown. Sometimes he'd travel – no one really knew where – returning to Paris with landscapes and still lifes, abstracts and portraits – faces of strangers from strange towns he'd passed through.

The names of those towns were known to his agents alone, Frères Durand, who had represented him for fifteen years, thoroughly understanding the terms of their agreement. The agent before them, they well remembered, had been replaced for indiscretion, and neither Armand nor Auguste Durand – identical twins – had any intention of risking a similar fate. If Jude McCallister did not attend openings, if he refused to submit to publicity tours, if he had never yet agreed to meet a buyer in person – insisting he could not leave his mistress, by which he meant his art most times, but not all times – that was his prerogative. His work sold high, and consistently, and Frères Durand, Inc., which was never known to have any comment – not one, not even after the break-up of McCallister's second marriage – had remained the exclusive representative of an increasingly astonishing body of work.

Hence, when the attack by the Pavillon des Ambassadeurs had occurred, and the victim's wallet was missing, and only a card in his pocket was found containing the name and address and telephone number of Frères Durand, Inc., Armand and Auguste had been faced with a decision. Of all times now, they were certain, Jude McCallister would insist on having his privacy protected. Intrusion of any kind would be deemed loathsome, unforgivable, especially at the hands of those entrusted to preserve his anonymity. Besides, the attackers had not been caught. They could return if given the chance to silence the man who might remember.

Finally – and the logic here, admittedly distasteful, was incontrovertibly sound – should the doctors prove right and the patient not last (a matter of hours did they say?) McCallister's œuvre would double in value – quadruple, soar off the charts – for there could never be another addition to the abruptly finite collection. Though most of his paintings at the gallery had already been priced and displayed, the most recent – those representing this past summer's work – were upstairs, barely uncrated, awaiting evaluation.

Thus it was that they had agreed wholeheartedly with Dr. Le Brun on the night of the surgery.

"Providential," the doctor had said, taking his leave of the brothers Durand then. "Your card in Jude's pocket, I mean."

"Utmost discretion," confirmed Auguste, elder twin by four minutes. "At the very least, *Mon Docteur*, until the attackers are apprehended."

"Good. I will speak to the Inspector. To all intents and purposes, for the time being at least, the mystery of my patient's identity remains unresolved."

Le Brun was as good as his word. No one, not even Claire Tierney, was ever the wiser. Like all the others in the courtyard of the École des Beaux-Arts when she arrived, she was anticipating a retrospective – significant and comprehensive – of a brilliant, somewhat eccentric, oftentimes reclusive world-class genius.

She was also there to do her homework. While the paintings would not be for sale, she could study McCallister's style, his development, his uniqueness as an artist. By the end of a week, perhaps less, she could approach Frères Durand with the knowledge she needed to negotiate wisely. And wisely she must, for these agents, she knew, were sole representatives of his work, their gallery the only repository of available McCallisters, and her employer completely intolerant of anything but achievement. His expectations were already the stuff of legend. So was his gallery, La Ronde, one of the largest on Fifth Avenue. There seemed to be no end to its growth, for Roger Gachet was driven. In his own way he had a share of the genius of the artists he represented.

He knew how to find a work, how to position an artist, how to predict sudden trends, how to eschew rapid slumps. Not only in paintings, but in *arts décoratifs* and, more recently, jewellery – estate pieces, fine antiques – he had an uncanny eye for value. He also knew everyone in Manhattan: those who could buy from him, those who might have to sell, the amount the former could pay, the price the latter would have to take. His greatest talent, perhaps, was in hiding his hunger. Whether turning a phrase, a compliment, or the combination to his office safe, Roger Gachet was remarkably deft. Hence he was sought after, fought over, included at parties, invited for weekends. It was his staff, he'd confess, making an open-handed gesture almost as handsome as his cufflinks. *Without them I should be lost.*

Claire Tierney, for example.

Well-trained, well-versed, only slightly less driven than he himself was, she was the perfect envoy for this trip to Paris, Roger reflected, carefully tying his white tie en route to a private gala at the Frick. If there were a McCallister to be had in France, at the right price of course, one that would be worthy of La Ronde, Claire Tierney would find it.

"*L'Exposition McCallister – c'est par ici?*" Claire asked directly, her French as stylish as her Adolfo wool suit.

"*Oui, Madame,*" the guard answered in kind. "*Tout droit, puis à gauche.*"

As instructed, she walked ahead, then turned left at the arch into a room filled with portraits, landscapes, still lifes, immense abstract forms.

Astonishing, she said to herself, transfixed above all by the McCallister portraits, some in the grand style, some more informal – all palpable and unique figures, rendered as though they were in attendance there, gazing back at those who stared each day.

She repeated this tour on the following day, and for three days thereafter, returning each night to study the notes she had written, the catalogue taken, the volume she'd bought containing a sketch – tantalizingly brief – of McCallister's life, and an analysis – satisfyingly ample – of his work.

Finally, after a week, Claire Tierney knew the man – not as a man – that, it appeared, was a jealously guarded secret, but as creator: how he worked, where he excelled, what he enjoyed painting, what had cost him great pain. Then and only then did she contact Frères Durand, planning to bring back a worthy McCallister to La Ronde, determined to have it at an exceptional price.

Even among the fine shops and hotels around Les Invalides, the stately townhouse with the gold sign *Galeries Frères Durand* stood out.

Within, contemporary artists were exhibited with elegance, Jude McCallister among them, some on the first floor, some on the floor above. The brothers Durand had their offices, identical, on the third floor, next to space for their staff and a conference room in between. Under the gables in the fourth floor, they explained, was a workshop for framing.

"You have the whole house then," observed Claire, complimenting the renovation. She was as sleek in her small talk as she was in her appearance, so that the brothers Durand, normally wary, felt justified in allowing themselves to be charmed, just this once. Armand succumbed first. Auguste held back, certain she'd stumble, surprised she held fast. In the end it was her knowledge of the McCallisters which impressed him.

"Yes, they are for sale, Mademoiselle," said Armand.

"Those on the first floor," corrected Auguste.

"There are others?"

"An abstract," allowed Auguste.

"Along with a still life," added Armand. "Both of them now in the framing room, on four."

"I meant other portraits."

"Mademoiselle," repeated Auguste. "Every available portrait has been displayed."

Claire Tierney smiled. It was not unusual for gallery owners to hold back certain pieces, not priced as yet, most often the finest. On four, she was certain there was a portrait worth viewing.

"Perhaps, then, Messieurs, the still life. Even the abstract, if there's time."

What she saw when she reached the framing room was utterly remarkable. One work depicted a vase of hydrangeas, set on a black and gold and pale orange fringed shawl; the second, pure juxtaposition of form, was somehow its mirror image – shapes embracing, nothing more – yet the palette was identical to the still life beside it: black, orange, gold and what appeared to be Tyrian dye.

Claire studied them closely, tapping her forearm with a rolled-up brochure. The still life was magnificent; the abstract superb; yet it was the pair she found irresistible, its totality far in excess of the glorious parts.

"How much?" she inquired, catching the brothers off guard with her bluntness.

"As Mademoiselle can imagine," managed Armand, "such a fine still life…"

"I meant the pair," Claire interrupted. "I will consider both – but only both – clearly what the artist intended."

There would be no keeping one back, Auguste knew at that point. Just as well. She was willing to pay. She would even pay more if he delayed just a bit.

"May I let you know tomorrow?"

"I will be here until noon."

Auguste smiled briefly. Armand bowed slightly. The little procession moved forward among the boxes and frames all around.

As a pair they'll fetch twice the separate amount, Armand was reflecting.

Three times, his twin thought.

So preoccupied were they with their calculations that they had reached the end of the corridor before either of them realized that Miss Tierney was no longer behind them.

She had stopped to stare at a canvas in the middle of the storage room. Still on the floor, it was lying against some frames, as though about to be framed, or wrapped, or shipped. Without even crouching, she knew McCallister had painted it. Without even a step in its direction, she knew it was his finest.

"Mademoiselle?" called a voice from the door.

She simply stared still.

"Are you all right, Mademoiselle?"

A naked woman – a cat – a flower vase overturned, irises matching tendrils on the model's neck, her right breast scarred, her face somehow a replica of both the still life and the abstract – works she had just seen but no longer desired.

She bent down to read the inscription. *Half Moon* was all she could see, dated that very same year, location: Paris.

"I have the elevator, Mademoiselle," Auguste called.

There was no answer.

"Perhaps more light," suggested Armand, reappearing. "Mademoiselle's lost her way."

She was standing before the painting still, transfixed by an allure at once metaphysical and erotic.

"A McCallister," she remarked, more as a challenge than identification.

Armand nodded.

"His available portraits were all displayed, I thought."

"They are, Mademoiselle," confirmed Auguste from the doorway.

"But this is clearly…"

"His masterpiece. I agree. It is not for sale, though."

"Monsieur Durand," said Claire after a moment. "*Everything* is for sale."

"*Hélas*, would that it were," he sighed. "This work would fetch thousands – millions – but his instructions were clear: 'Never – not in my lifetime or after – to be sold, loaned, or placed on exhibit. In the event of my death, it is to be burned.'"

Claire was speechless. The thought of destroying such a thing was inconceivable, preposterous – surely another stratagem of the brothers Durand.

Her mind raced ahead; her face betrayed no emotion. With a last glance at the painting, she said merely, "My loss, then, Messieurs."

"Ours too," said Armand, wistful still, turning back to the door.

She moved with them both across the landing. Suddenly, she exclaimed "My catalogue! I've left it in the framing room."

"We have others," answered Armand.

"I've made notes in mine," Claire protested, turning back toward the storeroom.

Auguste thought to follow, then remained where he was. His brother, too, stayed behind. Poor form, they both knew, to shadow a client among priceless works.

They would have done well, this one time, to have escorted the lady. Claire let the door close behind her, crossed, took out a small camera, and quickly photographed *Half Moon*. Then, calmly, she put the camera back into her pocketbook, took her catalogue out, and rejoined the brothers Durand by their antiquated elevator.

"Mademoiselle has what she went back for?"

"I do indeed."

Everything was for sale, she well knew, and the Durands were good at their game. They had delayed on the still life, as well as the abstract. Well they could them keep both now, she decided, squeezed in between the twins as the little cage rattled downwards.

Half Moon would belong to La Ronde, whatever the price. Once Roger Gachet saw that print, he would pay.

Roger was at that moment acquiring another piece for his gallery – not a McCallister, not even a painting, but a find nevertheless. It had come to him quite unexpectedly – these things always did – during a dinner he had attended for patrons of the Metropolitan.

He had been seated between Walter Reston, a New Salem attorney, and his guest, Dr. Elliot Devereux, when the subject, or rather the absence, of Dr. Devereux's wife was brought up.

"Pity she couldn't join us," Dolly Reston said, unfurling her napkin.

"Well, with her duties," began Elliot.

"That new job, you mean…"

"Yes."

"Seems like three jobs to me."

"Translations take time," Elliot managed.

"Good ones," echoed Walter.

Dolly nodded. She had hoped to get information – it was all so mysterious – but all she received was some sauce for her chicken.

And that was all she would get that night, for Elliot was determined to keep up appearances – not a hint of his marital troubles, not a whisper of his financial morass, no insecurities about whatever was left of his practice. His blows were hidden, like those gems in his office. He could not afford, above all in New Salem, to seem disheartened, discarded, or worse by far, bankrupt. Once cleared, he could begin anew. For now though, his wife's project had to remain that: a scholarly jaunt, a spree – anything but a full-time, intense, desperate attempt to save them both.

Lester Lanin's band played *Stardust*.

Dolly Reston tapped her foot.

Hard times for the doctor, Roger Gachet decided. It was a talent of his – this scent for disaster – second only to his ability to make himself liked. Indeed, the twin skills worked in tandem. More often than not, unfortunate people sold things. La Ronde was built on acquisitions.

"What kind of medicine do you specialize in?" he asked with a smile, refilling Elliott's glass before his own.

Elliot was impressed. The verb most people used was *practice*, making the question awkward, the answer more so. After a pause he responded, quietly, discussing his training at Yale, breakthroughs in plastic surgery he had worked on, grafting techniques he had perfected. Roger was fascinated. Even Walter turned to listen. Elliot continued, much of his summary in the past tense, but Roger didn't seem to notice, Walter was paid to be supportive, and the Cabernet was superb.

Twenty minutes later, after Walter had at last agreed to dance, Roger was still engrossed, the wine was still vintage and Elliot was still remembering. It never occurred to him that Roger had already figured things out. Nobody would have sensed this. Roger's gifts lay in dismissing a man's failings, sublimely, while giving him every possible opportunity to display his virtues, if he had any, or his achievements, if he did not.

By evening's end the men had bonded. First thing the next morning Roger took Elliot Devereux's call. They agreed on a meeting late the following day.

"As you can see," Elliot said then, undoing the clasp on the black satin box, "Mother's black pearls were unique."

"Extraordinary."

"Earrings to match."

Roger caressed the triple strands.

"Mother wore them when she was young," Elliot ventured, growing more confident. "After the stroke, of course, they remained in their box. There they stayed after she died...a painful reminder –"

"One never recovers," Roger murmured. He traced the fine diamond clasp with his thumb. A discreet silence followed. Then, abruptly: "I should like to buy them from you," La Ronde's owner announced. "With affection, of course, because that is the only way you would sell them, *if* you would sell them. I am sure you've had offers. Mine will be handsome, I can assure you, as well as efficient."

He was right on both counts. Roger's appraisers were summoned that evening.

"Two hundred thousand," Elliot heard the next morning. "That was the estimate. Given the sentiment," Elliot didn't breathe, "we will pay ten thousand more."

It was Roger's policy to be generous. It was Elliot's luck that he was also discreet, competent, and only paid cash. The transaction took ten minutes, that very same afternoon. Elliot left directly. As he strode across the elegant lobby, heading straight for the safe in his office, he held the door open for an attractive young woman who was just entering La Ronde.

"Thank you," murmured Claire Tierney.

Elliot nodded, then hailed a taxi. Claire walked on directly, a few minutes early for her meeting with the Director, carrying in her briefcase a remarkable photograph of Jude McCallister's portrait of Dr. Devereux's wife.

ARABESQUE

Max worked Caroline hard during Misha's brief trip to Bermuda. He recalled swiftly, paused rarely, switched languages constantly. Far more revisions than usual were demanded. Above all, Caroline noted, his manner was different.

"Are you not well, Max?" she ventured to ask during their break once.

"I am rarely well," was his reply.

"I meant…"

"Let us now take our break. We will revise at four p.m. sharp."

Pondering Maximilian's anger as she lay without resting, Caroline could not have guessed what he himself was only vaguely aware of – the strange fear consuming him, ever-increasing with the days that would bring Mikhail back. He had concluded it was due to the immense task before him – much to be remembered still, deadlines from his publishers, health in no way guaranteed – and so he had simply pressed on.

By the 23rd of December, Caroline was exhausted. Traffic had delayed Antonin. She rushed up the stairs, hoping the clock had not yet struck twelve.

"I am ready, Max," she called from the door. "There was an accident. Overturned truck ahead." She tossed her coat on a nearby chair and took her seat before he could stir.

"Your pen is there," was his greeting.

"I see it."

"You will need to be sure it does not fail you."

Caroline looked at him.

"It has not failed me yet, Max…"

"Nevertheless," he went on, "please have another on hand."

She did not answer. He felt suddenly small in her silence, for it was not by choice that she had summoned that infuriating correctness, but because he paid her, and she knew it, and days were passing so quickly. Lost, he played to his strength once again. It brought him the obverse of relief.

"We are falling behind. No choice, with the holidays near, but to dispense with the revisions yesterday's pages still need. They were under par."

The rebuke fell like stones on them both.

After a moment she managed, "As I said earlier, Max, I am ready."

He raised his eyes to meet hers and saw not her hurt but his own. Wishing the latter away, he looked out over the courtyard, finding only the reflection of overcast, ungracious skies in the opposite windows.

And another thing slowly took shape as he stared, still not the hurt in her eyes – that would be forever veiled – but the cruelty which had inflicted it. Yes, at long last there it was. The scene he knew he would have to remember someday, and describe to her seated beside him, had appeared without warning.

"Jean-Luc Onegin did his best," Max said abruptly, in his Provençal French, turning to face his assistant again.

Caroline bent over the copy book and began to render quickly, in English, not because Max paid her, but for the look on his face.

"Record that he told me. That much he did do. And for that I am grateful. The night before it was to be his turn he found me."

"'I will not endure long,'" she heard Max repeat then, lowering his voice so as to replicate his colleague's warning. "'I am not, after all, Maximilian d'Olivier.' –You got that, I assume, Caroline."

"Yes. Yes, I did, Max."

"Because I did not. Not at that moment I mean. Not until it was my turn in the cell. Seems there were expectations – unwarranted – that I could somehow" – he shifted his weight, "due to the old sandstone house perhaps, and the name, and my love of that shore…Write this down, Mrs. Devereux! I am paying you to write this down! *There was a sentimental presumption that my flesh would not burn.*"

Caroline tried, but could not write that down.

"Mind you I revealed nothing – at least I do not think I did. I can never be sure. It has tormented me over the decades more than their cigarettes did."

His assistant by then had placed his lucky pen on the table. Max raised himself up and fixed his blue eyes on her mauve ones, as if to see clearly there, somehow, what had eluded him for a lifetime.

"I lost count in that room. I can recall only twenty. The marks number thirty." The thought occurred to him, fleetingly, to unbutton his shirt there and then, for he felt a deep need to confirm things, once and for all on that day, to this woman before him. And yet, though she'd removed her shawl for him once, with deliberation, and many times after that when it was soaked with her sweat, he chose to spare her that sight and perhaps himself too.

"Thirty," he repeated instead. "Take my word for it. Thirty reminders have remained – French ones, French cigarettes – it is important, I think, that we record that, Caroline – the fact that they were French, I mean – not their number – that would be inappropriate – for I myself do not recall…" he looked again at her, not seeking forgiveness but clarification, and, despairing of finding what had eluded him since his young years, he stared back at the courtyard, saying nothing.

"There came a moment of surrender," he finally murmured.

And then Max stopped. The scene in the window became indistinct. Try as he might, he could no longer record the thing. He became desperate, feeling the memory fade, sensing it would most likely never return to him in his lifetime.

He turned again to his assistant, about to admit to her then that he could not remember, or would not remember, when he saw her head bent down once again, her hand moving swiftly, with her ornate old-world script filling the pages of her copy book.

What on earth she was rendering he could not guess at first, for after all, he had said nothing, in what had seemed to him a long time.

Suddenly though, watching her hand move, he knew.

She was writing his own life, as she always had, this time as she'd lived it – at least the sensations that would not come to him, because of his pride, even grander than hers, and the pain, for sure somehow less.

He remained silent as she continued.

Sweat appeared on her temples.

He longed to remove her shawl when he saw the watermarks on her pages, but dared not move toward her as she remembered.

Not until she was done with that part of their lives, and had placed his monogrammed pen on the table beside her – in a grave way, without flourish – did he reach toward her, slowly, and take the book from her hands.

He placed it beside his pen on the desk. She said not a word. He reached again and removed her shawl, and traced the marks on her neck, several times, brushing against her skin like the wings of a dove, no longer seeing hurt but comprehension in her eyes, and then he said, softly, "Go now and sleep, Caroline. There will be no need for revisions."

She stood, leaving her shawl on the chair, her face without expression, and walked down to her room.

On the ride home there was silence until the lights of the bridge passed – not a painful absence of sound – just an elegant peace driver and passenger had come to expect. When it was time, Antonin knew, she would speak to him – perhaps of small things, perhaps great, and, as it would be time, he would reply.

They descended the Heights.

The lights of New York disappeared.

"Antonin," she said abruptly, "are you ready for Christmas?"

"There isn't much to prepare."

She wondered how he would spend the day, where he would eat.

"And you, Miss?" he asked.

"Yes," she said after a moment. "Yes I am ready."

"Lots of friends expected? Family?"

"Not a soul."

She laid her head back and closed her eyes and thought of the following night, Christmas Eve. Elliot had decided on a much-needed rest in Santa Fe. Understood but unspoken, he would not be alone.

Unspoken too had been Maximilian's surprise when Misha had appeared a day early, positively golden from his days in the sun.

"White Christmas tomorrow!" he had predicted. "I say we celebrate, Max. I'll prepare dinner. One of my famous London feasts. Elsa too, of course. And Antonin. And perhaps your assistant?"

Stunned, Max had made no reply. Slowly then, turning: "Yes – yes why not, Caroline? I need a day off from my work, and for sure your farm will allow you this one holiday absence…"

With that most tactful reply his voice had trailed off. Long ago he had guessed that no festivities awaited Mrs. Devereux. Twice he had thought to invite her to his house, to work in spite of the day; twice he had rethought the intrusion. And now suddenly – almost against his own will, certainly against his own judgement – it had been done: subject broached, party planned, invitations extended, invitations accepted. Caroline had had no choice, after all. Like Maximilian she had been caught off guard, and, like Max, had refused above all on this night to appear chagrined.

Reflecting upon this in the renewed stillness of Maximilian's car, she suddenly heard Antonin say, "I'll be eating with Max Christmas Eve, Miss."

Caroline opened her eyes.

"I always have. Ever since I was ten, our first winter here, with the exception" – he stumbled, then recovered, for he was increasingly finding it easy, unaccountably, to speak to this woman who had been entrusted to him, who listened every night in the dark to him, unseen and unseeing.

"There were a few years when I couldn't make it. Those were the dark years. Seven of them. Seven summers. Six autumns. Six Christmas Eves. I was in prison then."

He looked straight ahead as he spoke, having no need of his mirror. He knew she would be leaning forward then, resting her arm on the division between them.

"Other than that, though, Miss, I've been with Max. And Elsa. Just the three of us." He stared straight ahead still. "Mikhail never managed it."

"Not even in the dark years?"

"On two of his trips to Manhattan he tried. Flu came on him the first time. Second time clients appeared. Couldn't very well bring them to the jail."

His car moved ahead with a will of its own it seemed then – darkness behind, darkness ahead, a vague matching obscurity of country woodlands on either side.

"Mikhail will be with you tomorrow," Caroline said.

"No..."

"I'll be there too. I've been invited."

Ahead was the road that led to Todd's Farm.

"So we will be five this year, not three, Antonin. I hope that pleases you. I am only sorry you'll have this long drive again, first thing in the morning, when there will surely be things you will want to be doing at that time."

"I'll be here, Miss," was his response.

Mikhail had left his father's house after the concert, then ambled south toward the crowds and bright Christmas lights on the shimmering Fifth Avenue shops. Yet in spite of the gaiety, more likely because of it, he had felt an ennui that had made the whole scene almost repellent. Still he'd walked on, increasingly disinclined to return to his hotel. Suddenly, through an especially ornate window – a rare little shop devoted exclusively to evening bags – he had spotted Claire Tierney. She was not far from the door, holding two beaded purses, undecided.

"I'd take them both," Misha said as he entered. "Or at the very least the blue one. Matches your scarf, Claire," he insisted. "Even more so your eyes."

"It's a gift, Misha," she laughed, kissing him on both cheeks, "Eye colour's not an issue."

"Buy the other one then."

"You really think it's nicer?"

"No, but I'm taking this one for you."

"Mikhail…"

"Gift wrapped," he told the clerk, who found it impossible, in the face of this last-minute dual sale of two of the costliest items in his store, to maintain his habitually withering indifference.

"Thank you, Misha," she said sincerely. "It is a beautiful present."

While they were waiting for the parcels, she told him of her trip to Paris, carefully avoiding any mention of the frères Durand. These expeditions were top secret – competition was keen for fine works – and Mikhail d'Olivier knew many players in the art world. Of her own find, of course – the masterpiece in the collection – she breathed not a word. She had not even shown the photograph to Roger Gachet yet, for he had run off to a luncheon after his meeting with Elliot, and they had rescheduled their conference for the week after Christmas. Until then, she decided, she would keep the photograph in her possession, having no intention of sharing her treasure, and thereby her bonus, with any competing co-workers, anywhere.

Half Moon – rare and alluring work– thus found its way into Claire Tierney's study, a pale walnut space off the living room in her exquisite apartment on Park Avenue South.

"How elegant," exclaimed Misha, as they stepped off the elevator and walked into Claire's world. The living room, directly ahead, reminded him of the best yachts he had sold – burnished woods, low tables, spare but refined art. Left of the living room was her study, once a third bedroom, she explained, not without pride in the intimation that two were more than enough for a globe-trotting buyer with far more books than relations. To the right, with its remarkable Chinese screens, was a dining room; beyond that was a kitchen – sleek, steel and polished, like the owner.

"The small one's a guest room," Claire said matter-of-factly, waving her hand in the direction of two bedrooms left of the entrance. Again, no apologies. Her life, like her income, was hers to dispose of as she wished.

"Open your present now," Mikhail urged.

"Drinks first."

"If you like."

"And some French songs," she said with a smile. "Music to unwrap an extravagance by."

The bag was indeed splendid, shaped like a shell, pale blue and gold like a Caribbean dawn.

"More wonderful now than when you chose it," she murmured, and then she thanked him, and kissed him, and pulled away a bit.

"I have nothing for you though. I mean, had I known you were stalking me..." she laughed as she stood. "How about dinner?"

"I'll take you out."

"No. I'll fix us something. What do you like?"

"Everything," he said. "You should know that by now," and then he reached for her and pulled her down and found her mouth once again.

He had not intended, standing outside that window on 57th Street, to make love to Claire Tierney that night. Yet the blue of that bag did match her eyes, and his yearning matched hers, and he was a stranger wherever he went, except for the primordial welcome his body received whenever it merged, ever so briefly, with another's – fulfillment lasting a heartbeat, price exacted renewed exile.

"Claire," he later whispered, moving his weight off her, taking her in his arms, wishing of all things he could have said "Claire, my love," but his honour stopped just short of that, or perhaps it was only his need no longer in need.

She too said nothing, though something trite from her school days had occurred to her as she lay there, something like "Penny for your thoughts, Mikhail," but it was a long time since she'd been a schoolgirl, and even longer since she'd done trite. Instead, as he dozed, she smoked a cigarette in the dark. Then a bell chimed from a church nearby, waking him.

"Christmas Eve, Mikhail."

"Yes."

There was a pause, shorter no doubt in real time than it seemed to them both in her bed.

"Where will you be later today?"

"With my father."

"Ah."

"And you?"

She would have split her commission for the McCallister to have been able to answer, as he had, "with someone who matters."

"Long-time colleagues," she responded.

"Sounds lovely."

"Yes."

Again a long silence you could remove with a brush and a dustpan.

"Hungry?" she finally asked.

He nodded.

"I'll get things going."

"I'll go."

"Nonsense…"

"I'd like to, Claire, really," he said as he slipped from her arms. "Stay and relax here."

She thanked him and said she was sure he would find what he needed, since he had already sailed twice to Bermuda, alone.

Claire Tierney was right. Misha prepared something simple, set two places on the lacquered table, and while everything slowly warmed, wandered through the living room across to the study. For a while he watched the taillights of the taxis disappear down the street. Then, as he turned toward the desk, among the papers and notes and small books neatly piled there, he saw it. It was the only thing he saw, in fact – because of the tones, he supposed – black, orange and gold, turquoise and greens, all setting off the violet depths of those eyes he knew well, even now looking his way.

Then again it may not have been the gaze. It was the body perhaps: elegant, like a dancer's – lean, long-waisted, firm rounded breasts, confident legs. Like a dancer she had been caught in mid-air, in the arc of her movement – reaching out for a cat whose black fur somehow matched the lady's improbable hair. And it was a lady, no mistaking it. As naked as she was there, as intimate as the Paris setting – it had to be Paris, judging by the dome in the distance – she was as fine as she was unfettered.

Mikhail picked up the photograph. He studied it, deeply shaken – to think that Caroline Contini Devereux should have those markings, that she had them still – covered, to be sure, whenever he'd seen her, yet displayed once so wantonly – worshipped, it almost seemed to him, by a loving brush that knew her well.

"Ready, Misha?" he heard a voice call from the bedroom.

"I – Yes. Just about, Claire."

"I'm coming to help you."

He had on only his slacks and a T-shirt. As he heard her steps in the hallway, he slipped the photograph under his shirt, secured by his waistband. Then he walked back into the dining room, seconds before she arrived.

They sipped the wine he had poured, ate the meal he'd prepared and then the tower clock next door chimed again.

Two a.m.

"Claire," he said gently, for he sensed she would have wanted him to stay. "I've got to go, Claire."

"I should rest too," she said rising.

Another kiss, a long embrace, or so it seemed to him, and then he was gone.

She heard his measured steps down the hall, the call bell responding, the elevator taking him down. And then a last glimpse of Mikhail after she walked to the window and stared down at the street and saw his loafers disappearing on the pavement that turned at the church.

It never occurred to her that he had taken more than a small piece of her heart.

⌒☾⌐

Max had been anxious all morning, his recollections jagged, disconnected.

"Useless," he pronounced just before lunch. "Best to stop now perhaps."

He looked away. Caroline placed the book down. When he turned back after some time though, she was still seated beside him, for their gaze had met before he had turned, and in his deepened, almost navy blue eyes she seemed to have read then, *Wait. Do not go yet. There remains an epilogue to yesterday's tale – a place, more than a place, a face to be conjured today or most likely never again.*

"Germaine," he said finally, settling back on his daybed so that he could see his assistant more clearly.

"I had heard about her, of course. All of us did whenever we needed a doctor, although she was not a physician. We couldn't take chances with physicians. They were connected to the hospital, which was connected to the Gestapo, where any Frenchman with a flesh wound could find himself more incisively cut."

Max paused, inclining still more toward Mrs. Devereux. Then, switching of all things to German – that secret Austrian waltz distantly playing again perhaps – he explained, "Germaine was a nurse. She'd left her job at the clinic soon after France fell, for though it was France still, and neither the flag nor the anthem had altered, no one dared sing that song. Even so, but for that other fact, she might have believed and stayed on in the hospital outside Nice."

Fluidly Caroline rendered, not despite Maximilian's undisguised efforts here, but because of them.

"That other fact," he went on, "was her brother Émil, thirteen months younger, taken to a Vichy jail for activities deemed unseemly – buried a week later.

"She was lost," Max recalled, "living alone and adrift in a farmhouse up in the hills, out of the sight-lines of the Gestapo, numbed by her pain and a vague sense of guilt each time she awoke and found the sun rising too. Only on Sundays would she go into town, even then just for Mass, unobserved, to an old church on a side street in the gypsy square north of town. After the service sometimes she would sit in that square, watching the shoppers and vendors and families out for a stroll, under the flag of a country she no longer knew, soaring above them all, not responsible.

"Once, late in July, needing supplies from a pharmacy not due to reopen 'til five, she lingered long in the square.

"'I'll take a night bus,' she decided, emerging from the drugstore, the day still too humid for a ride across town and the long climb to her house.

"Parcels under her arm she returned to her bench, once again watching the fluid movements of the crowds in the square. Here were policemen, still in the smart navy blue of the old France for some reason; there was a band, playing French tunes in the gazebo.

"'And there,' she said to herself, seeing a few parishioners enter the church where she'd heard Mass that same day, 'is an odd group to be sure.'

"They had gone in through a side door off a cobblestone alley – singly, five or ten minutes apart. And yet there was no service, no music, merely a tentative light – votive candles perhaps – flickering in the basement. After about an hour, the same group emerged, singly again, blending into the crowds.

"Intrigued, Germaine remained in the park after Mass the next week, reading a book, waiting for dusk, wondering if the little group would reassemble. It did not. The gypsy church was in darkness, save for those candles below.

"Once more Germaine stayed, the week after that, and then she saw them again, entering singly again, through the narrow side door in the shadows.

"'Too earnest to be tourists,' she concluded. 'Not devout enough to be in prayer.' And then, as if bewitched she waited, night spreading over the square.

"'You watch keenly too,' said a man seated beside her.

"She was too startled to speak.

"'I am also aware,' he confided, inclining his head, though still staring ahead. 'You must admit they are peculiar.'

"Still she said nothing.

"'Never a priest in the group,' he observed, darkness in the statement, as lamps in the square went on abruptly lighting the fountain ahead. 'Never the sound of a hymn from inside. What do you make of it, Mademoiselle?'

"'I think, Monsieur,' – she was by then finding her wits – 'I think as you do. Absolutely. It is peculiar indeed.'

"'Ah.'

"'Although one can never be sure.'

"'What do you mean?'

"'They could be converts…or students.'

"He shook his head.

"'A death perhaps.'

"'Who dies four times?'

"'You have seen them four times?'

"'Since April alone.'

"She faced the old man. In his small close-set eyes, fixed on the cobblestones, there was part blood lust, part greed, combined equally, disguised as concern. How well she knew that look. Was it not, after all, her next door neighbour who had reported Émil?

"'One must not allow,' Germaine stopped, putting her hand to her lips. 'Best not to speak of these things.'

"'And yet by speaking' – the man also stopped. They both stared at the candles in the dim basement ahead. 'Unless one does speak, that is…'

"'It goes hard on us all,' Germaine supplied flatly.

"He turned to her. She nodded knowingly.

"'A most unsavoury and suspicious group,' she judged.

"He was satisfied.

"'Best to be watchful. – Ah here is my bus. God bless you, Monsieur.'

"'*Au revoir*, Mademoiselle.'

"Germaine rode the bus to the beach, two miles below, doubled back through the streets, bypassed the square and waited beside a garden at the back of the church. She would have preferred to know more, to be convinced, but there was no time. As it was perhaps, she was too late. The churchyard was silent and the votive lamps had gone out.

"One last bus was announced – it was past ten – and still no one emerged. Germaine let the bus go. A guitarist in the street began. Around eleven, the narrow door opened and a man walked into the alley from the darkened chapel ahead. Germaine hurried to follow. He must have sensed her, for he too quickened his steps. At the corner, as he was about to blend into the crowds, he heard a woman call, or a child perhaps – she was slender, waif-like – 'Stop. Wait please, Monsieur. There is need.'

"He turned then and saw her – indeed more girl than woman – for she was breathless and flushed and did not look her young years. She rushed up to him and pressed a note in his hand and vanished, knowing full well about these things and that it could go hard for them if they were seen. Jean-Luc Onegin was astounded. He waded into the crowds and opened the paper. *You have all been observed*, he read, *and must take care. If all else fails, I am a nurse, prepared to be of service to the only country I can remember.* Scrawled below was a signature: *G.V. du Pannier, who can be found near the same place, near the same time, in one fortnight exactly.*

"In one fortnight, exactly, we found her there," Max remembered – "little Germaine – with the hands of an angel and the heart of a king, offering up to the Resistance all she had left – the ability to heal, if healing were still an option – a soothing touch, and a capsule, on the more frequent nights when it was not.

"In my case," said Maximilian, vaguely aware of the scratch of a pen reliving his life, "healing was an option. Or so Germaine assured me, night after night when I would beg for that capsule, insisting they'd left me nothing. Turned out she was right. They had left me my life, in spite of themselves, as others before and after me learned, saved in that farmhouse by that girl."

Max was silent for a moment. Beside him, somewhere in the present time, Caroline was writing still.

"To the best of my knowledge," he concluded, "Germaine was never discovered. We would have been told. There wasn't one of us who wouldn't have surrendered to those torments again to protect her. My hope is that she lived to see a free France, and fine children, some perhaps married by now, their own families thriving."

He rested his head on the back of his chair – not spent with the effort, as he had been on the previous day, but revelling in the image, precious and precise in outline, of Germaine somehow surviving.

"Time to get ready for the feast now," he murmured. "It's Christmas Eve, after all."

Susan Foreman was dressing. She and Elliot were to dine in town – Christmas Eve supper at a Navajo restaurant just off the main square. The night air was crisp, the mountains dark in the distance, the wide Western sky filled with stars by the millions.

She opened the doors that led to a terrace beyond. Her silver necklace, set in jade, set off her hunter green eyes, as did her outfit, a costume almost, or so it would have appeared in New England, although in the foothills of the Sangre de Cristos it seemed as fitting as the night sky: black silk fringed shirt, slightly sheer, displaying a hint of her bare rounded breasts, soft short suede skirt, taupe boots to the knee. Like her hair, perfectly brushed – indeed like this whole Southwestern escape she had so carefully planned – the allure of her clothes had been predetermined: a blend of control and caprice, daring and decorum, designed to unsettle her guest, little by little, until any vestige of resistance to a full commitment had vanished.

So far, she concluded, things were progressing. Elliot had arrived, as promised, on the night of the 20th. She'd been relieved when she caught sight of him among the crowds at the airport, for not until then did she truly believe he would leave his wife home for Christmas. By the time they had reached her condo, she was convinced he would stay, for he had relaxed almost at once as Santa Fe's night lights had faded behind them. Only the woman beside him seemed real – the smell of her perfume in the car, the scent of sandalwood mixed with it, the rustle of aspens like the suede of her skirt riding up under his hands, and that breeze picking up as the foothills loomed larger.

"Elliot, there it is."

They had emerged from a cypress grove onto a splendid plateau.

A *mirage*, Elliot thought, seeing a cluster of dwellings, redolent of cypress still, approached by a long curving drive that led to a gate house beside the entrance.

"Good evening, Miss Foreman."

"Hello, Johanssen. Dr. Devereux will be my guest for the holidays."

"Welcome to *Rancho Soñado*, Dr. Devereux."

Twin gates opened slowly. Susan's convertible entered the enclave. Ahead were pathways, fountains, long sage-lined drives winding through clusters of adobe homes.

From a fireplace somewhere came the aroma of mesquite. From another patio, another scent – cottonwood he believed – like honeysuckle on the Atlantic, strongest at day's end.

The Atlantic. How far away it all seemed. How distant his bankers, and his brokers, and his wife with those eyes that hovered, like New Mexico's night sky, undecided, between charcoal and mauve.

Susan turned at the last house – off by itself it appeared, a long and low ranch commanding sweeping vistas of the scene.

And then that word again.

"Welcome," Susan said with a smile.

Ahead was a sunken living room, kiva-like, sparsely furnished.

It was all he needed it seemed, as he pulled up her skirt and tugged her panties down and pressed himself against her.

"What does it mean?" he murmured.

"What does what mean?"

"Rancho Soñado."

"Dream Ranch."

She had dropped to her knees. They were standing by the door still. He was aware of her hands undoing his belt, her mouth kissing the place she had been stroking during the long climb from the airport, glad when he climaxed fiercely, inside her welcoming mouth, calling her name out, lost to New England.

All this and more Susan remembered, reaching for the car keys as the sun set Christmas Eve.

"Ready?" she asked, standing over Elliot as he lay out on a chaise longue. He looked at her – lovely, like the landscape around him – yet also primal and exotic, like the night creatures about to appear.

"Come," she said, taking his hand.

"If I must."

"The night is young, my love," she laughed, tossing the keys to him as they walked to the car.

Elliot drove through the gates and onto the highway that led through the hills. After three days in Rancho Soñado, he always drove. He knew his way into town, out of town, up into the mountains, down into the washes that skirted the tracks. And he knew his way into Susan, to whose beauty he was addicted with a force as potent as her ambition.

"I've some mail to post," he remembered as they neared the plaza downtown.

"There's a mailbox on the corner."

"They should go certified."

"Not on Christmas Eve."

"Tomorrow then…"

"On Christmas?"

"Day after in that case."

"We're in Tesuque day after."

"No post in Tesuque?"

"A small one nearby."

"I'll take care of it near Tesuque."

As it happened, near Tesuque, Elliot never once thought of his letters. He had in fact left them behind, tucked away in his navy jacket – payments long overdue, withdrawals he preferred to postpone. After all, he was on holiday – Dream Ranch, as they called it, far from the drain on his resources, physical and financial, and the elegant farm he had once called his home.

The navy jacket had stayed in Susan's closet. It was not needed on the hiking trip they had decided to take at year's end. Thus it had occurred, irreversibly, that the utilities bill, the gardener's bill and the insurance on Todd's Farm went unpaid. It was the third lapse that quarter. Elliot had intended to mail the cheque Labour Day, absolute latest, but he had needed the money for Walter's retainer.

Next month, he had promised himself.

But Thanksgiving had come, along with the rent due on his office suite.

December, assuredly.

Yet in December came Christmas, followed by New Year's, and in any case he was in the Rockies, well past the continental divide of his life, and so he simply forgot, or not so simply forgot, and Caroline Contini's house was no longer secure.

～☾〜

As promised, Mikhail provided everything for a splendid dinner that night. As foreseen, Max had a special concert prepared, two of Haydn's *Sun Quartets*, because of the gypsy finale that sounded like Nice, he explained, as his guests took their seats in the music room after supper.

The minuet started. Lights from the tree danced in the mirror behind him. Time itself seemed to be waltzing in Maximilian's recollections, past and present embracing, changing partners, forming intricate patterns, drawing apart once again.

There was Antonin, looking far too immense for the straight-backed chair he had chosen, and Mikhail, next to his father, having easily made a home for himself on the cream-coloured sofa. There too was Elsa, seated stiffly between them, as though she might crease the fine silk. She had folded her hands when the music began, placing both sturdy shoes on the floor, yet when her foot began keeping three-quarter time on the floor, Max in his reverie was learning to waltz, Anna Berg by his side.

Antonin shifted his weight in his chair, no doubt impatient for the night streets. Mikhail leaned forward as if it were all he could do to keep from dancing, and two playmates – so different, soon parted – came and went in his head.

So too did his mother – elegant, restless Hélène – or was that his wife, headstrong Cecilia – or that pale woman beside him, intent on the music?

She has never looked lovelier, Max reflected. *Well it has never been Christmas*, he reasoned, *and I have never seen her dressed like that*.

He stole a second glance in her direction. Her long dress was simple, sleeveless – midnight blue velvet, skirt cut on the bias so that it swayed as she moved. Her sapphires too resembled the night – earrings, necklace, ring and bracelet to match – a set she wore always on Christmas, as her mother before her had done, or so she vaguely remembered Allessandro recalling each year as he wistfully stared at the only photograph in his study.

When the concert was over, she stood to thank the musicians.

"Not quite over," announced Misha.

"Is there an encore?"

"Several," he said, assuming a cryptic air before a tenor appeared to sing old German *Lieder* – mostly Schumann's – Misha's gift to Maximilian.

"Thank you, Mikhail. How beautiful."

"More to come, Max. Each of us must still sing – a tradition once, wasn't it? Lights on a tree like this, sounds of the tides, a violin case…"

"My father's," Max murmured.

"And you. I can still hear you singing." Mikhail hummed a few bars, then stopped abruptly. "Song's gone, I'm afraid."

"Yes…Yes it is."

"You try it, Max."

Everyone turned, marvelling not at the suggestion, but at the fact that Antonin had suddenly spoken.

"Perhaps," continued Antonin, omitting the fact that he too remembered those nights and that room – and in particular Maximilian's voice – "you could start us off with that song."

Max thought for a moment.

"That is music for another time."

"Nevertheless –" insisted Mikhail.

Max waved his right hand, large and powerful still, and though the gesture was graceful, and Misha was sure his father recalled the melody still, not a lyric forgotten, he was also aware that he could press him no further.

"You, Elsa," Max said politely. "Something like one of those *Ländlers* you hum by the dozen downstairs."

Elsa complied, her contralto's voice steady, and then Misha sang Welsh carols – only ones he could remember.

"Antonin?" Max suggested, and again everyone turned, for the concept of harmony, even on Christmas, shaped into notes by the silent man, was a novel one.

Antonin shook his head, seemingly in agreement with the general consensus.

"And yet you remember," said Caroline quietly – first words she had uttered since the gypsy finale.

"A few things," he admitted.

"It needn't be an old song," Max offered.

"If he doesn't want to," said Misha brightly, "then perhaps Caroline..."

"It isn't my turn."

Antonin looked at her. Her improbable face, for once not reflected in an overhead mirror, was fixed on him. A fleeting smile brushed her lips, as though he had already sung and it had pleased her.

"Do you know Borodin, *Second Quartet*, third movement?" he asked the cellist, astounding everyone, Maximilian included. "There was an old folk tale once...My father sang it to that tune. I will try."

His voice was raspy, unmelodious; all the stranger for the Russian lyrics he hadn't spoken in decades, but Max closed his eyes when he heard the refrain, moved to the very depths of his soul, recalling Jean-Luc Onegin and the old gypsy church and Russia before the war that had parted them all.

"Captivating," pronounced Mikhail, applauding broadly when it was over. "I'd no idea you could speak Russian."

"I can't. I just sing it."

Misha reached for the decanter. "To white nights in the motherland," he said with a flourish, filling Antonin's glass far too high.

Everyone drank.

Antonin drained his glass far too low.

"And now it *is* your turn," Misha insisted, turning to Caroline, again filling Antonin's glass.

"Misha," Max said softly, laying a hand on Mikhail's arm. Antonin had been prone to heavy drinking before his prison term. He had relapsed twice after that.

Mikhail chose to ignore the reminder. After all, it was Christmas.

"Shakespeare," said Caroline.

"Shakespeare?" asked Elsa Varig.

"A song from his first play."

Mikhail listened intently, as did Antonin, draining a third glass.

Elsa was surprised – not so much by the voice, haunting yet barely audible – but by the selection, set to music by Schubert, overheard in the play by a fervent, forsaken lover.

Max heard the lament and knew it for hers. He also knew it for his. It seemed fate had decreed they were to have lived but one life.

"What a fool that man was," proclaimed Mikhail, applauding broadly again. "Not to know the real thing when he saw it."

"Some men don't see well," said Antonin thickly.

"Nonsense," said Elsa.

"Others don't deserve the view."

"Coffee," Max announced, thinking it best then for Antonin. "While we open some gifts. Start with the red present, Misha. It has intrigued me all evening."

"Sorry Max, not for you."

He handed the box to Antonin, reading aloud from a small silver tag. *For Antonin, Merry Christmas, from C. Contini Devereux.*

Antonin opened a box which revealed a second box – a slipcase, containing five leather-bound volumes.

"Cooper," said Caroline, in the long pause that followed. "*Leatherstocking Tales* – the lot of them, because reading's your passion and the Hudson Valley your home, or so it has seemed to me since I've come here, dragging you up and down the shore twice each day."

Antonin fingered the lettering on the gold-trimmed spines of the books.

"I hope it has pleased you."

He looked again at the eyes he had come to know as his own.

"Have you got them already?"

"I...No. No, I don't. Thank you," he finally murmured, declining to make a longer speech, not because of the wine he'd consumed, but because he had never, in his tumultuous ragged days, ever received such a gift.

"We'll have much to discuss now," he managed to add.

"We always have."

"Time for another gift," announced Mikhail.

"Something for you," called Maximilian, as Mikhail crouched again by the pile.

For Mikhail, Misha read, choosing a large blue and white box. "Also from Caroline."

He parted what seemed to be pounds of white paper and removed a glass bottle, tinted a pale shade of green, containing an antique schooner inside.

"One ship you can't get your hands on," laughed Max. "Not without breaking it."

The boat went round for admiration, more gifts were exchanged, more sherry was poured, until at last there remained two presents only – a large box, grandest of all that night, splendidly wrapped, and a small one, covered in tissue, off in the corner beside the fireplace next to the tree.

"The little one now I think," decided Mikhail as he read from the tag. *For Caroline, from Maximilian.*

She found a smaller box inside the outer one – black velvet, frayed on the corners, hinges worn on one edge.

"From another time," Max felt compelled to explain.

Caroline unpinned the cameo from the faded silk lining. Its stark-white face was serene. A filigree border surrounded the oval, golden and thick, like a mass of fine curls.

"Max –" she began.

"Put it on," he insisted, wishing as she crossed to the mirror that he hadn't sounded so gruff.

Elsa Varig also crossed, wanting a closer look.

Even Mikhail walked to the mirror.

"Perfection, Max," he announced. "Where on earth did you find this?"

Caroline raised her eyes.

Max was observing her in the mirror.

"It's very old, is it not?" asked Mikhail.

"Yes and no," answered Max.

"Suits you," pronounced Elsa.

"Wonderfully," murmured Mikhail.

Caroline spoke at last, turning away from the mirror. "I can't, Max. Not this…"

"Yours now," he interrupted, and again his strong hand cut a firm gesture through the air, and the musicians played an intermezzo, and she resumed her seat beside him, wearing the wedding gift Cecilia had left on his bureau once, never to be reclaimed.

"One final gift here," Mikhail called, near midnight, placing a large, ornate box into Caroline's hands.

"Mystery gift," murmured Caroline, for there was no card attached. She untied the white ribbon, undid the gold wrapping, parted oceans of tissue, and then suddenly stopped, colour drained from her face.

"From me to you," Mikhail said in the stillness.

"A vase!" Elsa exclaimed, as Caroline lifted the gift from its box.

"So it is," Max confirmed, thinking the present an odd one for a man like Misha to have selected.

The beautifully painted porcelain – a replica of the vase that had tumbled behind her in Paris – was in her lap by then, perfectly balanced, more dramatic than ever on the velvet folds of her dress.

Caroline was speechless. Jude had sworn he would never sell her portrait, not even display it in exhibition, and while he may have forgotten her, had forgotten her, he was not a man to betray a promise concerning his art.

And yet here was the vase. Well not exactly the vase – close enough though, in colour, shape, and design, to be a message. Mikhail had seen the painting. He was letting her know that, Christmas Eve.

The pianist began a barcarolle.

"Very beautiful," stammered Mrs. Devereux.

"I thought so."

"Did you find this in Europe?"

"Portofino".

Caroline's heart sank. Jude was often in Italy.

"Not the town," Misha continued. "A shop here in Soho."

Max rose to study the vase. Elsa placed it on the table.

"Charming boutique. Came upon it by accident."

"Accident," she repeated.

"Just before closing," he added, omitting to say that he had set off early morning, hunting for something that would recall the photo he'd seen.

"Certainly lucky," pronounced Maximilian.

"I should say," murmured Elsa.

Caroline dared to relax. A fluke after all. A coincidence – nothing more – despite the uncanny resemblance. She even smiled. She thanked Misha twice.

"There's a card inside," he said blithely, like a refrain to that dance she'd sung.

She reached again into the box. The gift was still on display.

"Merry Christmas," said Misha softly, as she looked up at the gunmetal eyes fixed on her.

"Thank you," she murmured, recovering, though barely. She was, after all, in Maximilian's music room. Come what may, she could not falter.

"Not just for the gift, Mikhail, but for the sentiment, the card, the black cat on the card."

"Black cats on Christmas?" asked Elsa.

"Mrs. Devereux likes them," said Mikhail.

Antonin's clock in the hallway began to strike midnight.

Caroline stood abruptly.

"Max, I should go. It's Christmas Day as we speak. Much to be done still in my home. "

The spell broke in half then, as Maximilian knew it would, as in some old *Märchen* he'd heard during his childhood in Nice.

"I shall call you a car."

Antonin had no objection. He was sleeping, mouth open, head resting awkwardly against the back of his undersized chair.

"I'll take Mrs. Devereux," offered Mikhail all of a sudden.

"No…"

"I'd be happy to, Caroline."

"I can manage…"

"I can be trusted, Max, can I not, with your priceless assistant?"

Misha's question remained unanswered a moment as unease again overcame Maximilian. He would have preferred to have had Antonin at the ready, as always…He sighed. There was simply no choice. "Very kind of you. If you do not mind, Mikhail."

"It would be a pleasure," he responded, again finding the gaze Caroline tried in vain to avert.

Just as well, she thought later, standing inside the courtyard while Mikhail went for the car. *He has known all along. Somehow, no doubt in Paris, he has seen who I was. Let it be now that I hear it.*

⌐ ☾ ⌐

Bells across Paris were pealing the dawning of Christmas. Loudest of all was the tolling from the cathedral, high above the old towers, directly across the plaza from Jude McCallister's room.

Distressed by the sound, Sœur Eugénie rushed down the hall. The tolling would startle her patient – she was certain of it – causing more than the usual struggle that every morning involved. She fastened the shutters, checked to be sure that the casements were closed still, left the long heavy drapes drawn. Nevertheless, after a moment, as the muffled tolling continued, her patient stirred.

The room was not dark, though the curtains had muted December's brightness. Still, Sœur Eugénie knew, the man would need time to adjust to the light. He always awakened with caution, mornings above all, reluctant to emerge from that sweet darker place where his head did not ache and his vision was clear.

"And yet awaken he must," Dr. Le Brun had instructed his staff. "By nine every morning and then again after lunch." His nurses would comply of course, taking the most extreme care each time. They knew only too well how a sound might disrupt the frail peace taking shape inside the man's shattered head.

Thus it was that the chief nurse had tried Christmas morning to silence the bells. So intent was she on her task, in fact, that she never heard the door open behind her.

"Yes. Yes that is good," said Le Brun, observing the long heavy folds of the draperies drawn still. "Such a pealing, so early – it could have been too much."

He walked to the bed and looked into the eyes – sometimes vague, sometimes clear – of the patient before him. On this day they were clear. He took the man's pulse, studied his features, moved the right hand a bit, glanced at his chart.

"If you won't be needing me, *Mon Docteur*, I will slip into the chapel a moment. Christmas Mass has begun. "

"Fine, *Ma Sœur*, fine," murmured Le Brun. "Take more than a moment."

Soundlessly, the nurse retreated.

Bells echoed still across the Place du Parvis Notre-Dame. Out in the hallway, a large rolling cart passed. Jude tried hard to focus as his physician sat beside him.

"Merry Christmas, Jude," said Le Brun.

"Thank you, Théobald."

Le Brun smiled, stretched out his hand, felt Jude's forehead, his temples – no longer bandaged – and with something not unlike awe whispered, "Nativity miracle, these last days of yours."

Somehow Jude too managed a smile.

"Not that I ever doubted. You would survive this, I was convinced."

"Is that what you call it?"

"I have no other term."

"Well if you say so," said Jude, letting his head fall back onto the pillow he had recently learned to call home.

Le Brun fingered the rubber strands of the stethoscope around his neck.

"If anything," he went on, "I doubted myself these past weeks. I second-guessed each decision, reviewed each procedure…"

"Théobald…"

"Was there something else I could have done? Did I stop too soon? Too late? Should I have called in someone else?"

Jude waved his hand – a quick move, barely perceptible, but his physician perceived it: nothing escaped him – and in the gesture, perfect, precise, despite the debility in the arm still, Théobald saw on that morning that his doubts were unfounded. His friend would paint again, brilliantly.

"There will be breakfast soon, Jude – a special one."

Again the hand moved, this time in repulsion.

"An effort, Jude…"

"Tomorrow."

"You will need strength before tomorrow."

Wearily, Jude conceded.

Théobald understood. Food, like the morning, was a daily occurrence to be endured. His patient's sense of smell was gone. So too, as a result, was any capacity to taste.

"Lost for good perhaps," Le Brun had felt obliged to confess some days before. "Nevertheless…"

Jude had turned away.

"There have been cases…"

"I've heard."

"That's just the point," Théobald had insisted. "You *can* hear, Jude…Words. Christmas bells. Music that may come your way."

"How in the name of God you managed that," Jude had said, turning back.

"Not my doing."

"Whose then?"

Dr. Le Brun had shrugged. "Everything has its time. Yours was not finished yet, I expect."

Jude had made no reply, daunted by the prospect of seemingly endless endurance. Théobald had leaned in toward him, picturing endless possibilities.

"And Jude – need I add…I mean, for a painter – your sense of touch is intact; your sight will clear in time; the coordination between them will also return, not as it was in the past to be sure, but in terms of your work…"

"Work?"

"Which will change to be sure," Théobald had continued. "Everything finer somehow. Not necessarily on the canvas. That is mere cloth. But in another place…" He had begun to unwrap the head gauze. "Here," he had announced, his tone growing ardent, "home to inspiration – secluded – where none are invited," and then he had stopped, astounded, as a clearly proud smile had slowly played on his lips.

"I have not saved this head for nothing, *mon ami.*"

Now, less than a week later, after Christmas Mass in the chapel, Sœur Eugénie announced breakfast. Sœur Mathilde rolled the cart inside. Le Brun reached into the pocket of his long white starched coat and thumbed through a worn address book while the steel tray was being prepared.

"Therapy, Jude," he murmured, "that's the key now."

Sœur Mathilde placed the tray down.

"Daily, intensive, unforgiving routines. Head to toe. Right to left. Left to right again, though you will resist by that time, yet it is then that you must persist – above all your hand."

Jude heard the sound of metal utensils unwrapped.

"There is a nurse," continued Le Brun. "Retired now, out on the Normandy coast, where she has chosen to live since the Resistance brought triumph. Not too far from Deauville. More to the north near Honfleur, I should say."

Sœur Mathilde picked up a spoon and began to scoop up some eggs.

Le Brun laid a hand on her arm.

"I have a colleague who rents his home nearby. I could put in a call. I mean if you'd go, Jude – the sooner the better – after you eat your breakfast, of course."

Le Brun placed a fork in his hand.

"And I recommend," he went on, almost matter-of-factly, "that you do go there Jude, to Honfleur, New Year's, the latest – after you've eaten, of course – for this woman's hands have been known to have brought back the dead."

Sœur Mathilde stepped way. Théobald thumbed once again through his book. In the ensuing silence Jude made an effort – searingly painful – to pick up his fork.

The scrambled eggs fell on his chest.

"Try it again," said Le Brun, perusing his book still.

Again Jude missed his mouth.

Le Brun remained engrossed in the faded pages he was holding. On the third try Jude swallowed the cold tasteless mass. And then of all things he smiled, although a vague nausea returned.

"I won't be finished 'til supper," he said.

"I can wait," answered Le Brun.

Little by little, the mess on his plate disappeared – most of it on the sheet, some of it in his mouth, until Le Brun heard the fork fall with a clatter onto the tray.

There was a moment. "If she can bring back the dead, Théobald..."

"She can."

"I'll take Honfleur."

"I'll go today."

"But it is Christmas..."

"Therefore," said Théobald standing, "I am certain to find Germaine du Pannier. I will speak to her this afternoon. If all goes well, New Year's Day I shall arrange to have you transferred direct-ly to the south quay in Honfleur. I'll have your paints sent ahead – your cloths – whatever your agents suggest."

The patient closed his eyes again, as though to ward off some new blow.

"Is it that head pain again, Jude?"

"No. No it is nothing. Only a recollection..."

"Recollections are what we're after."

"Not this one."

"This one above all. Everything must be faced now. If it is powerful, Jude..."

"It is sublime."

Sœur Mathilde closed the door as she left.

"A portrait I did once – a woman."

Jude faltered, and yet his eyes, often so febrile these days, shone with a passion Le Brun hadn't seen there since November's awakening.

"Left with my agents, I believe. Frères Durand, rue du Bac. I should be grateful –"

"I'll take care of it, Jude."

The door closed behind him. Jude McCallister put his head back. He would see her again, if only as he had rendered her.

☽

Caroline took a few steps toward the car and paused, judging the protocol demanded. Of course she could not sit behind him. He was an escort that evening, not a driver. Her conclusions were confirmed as Mikhail came round and opened the front passenger door. She slipped in quickly. The streets were nearly deserted, as indeed the car seemed to be, neither driver nor passenger saying a word as they moved toward the Hudson.

"A little night music, Caroline?"

"If you like."

"My apologies. Not a holiday song," he said switching the radio on.

"Festive in its own way though. In fact the finale…"

"Do you need directions?"

"Later perhaps," he said genially, as though she had said something kind. "When we get closer. For now I know you live due north, and the river's still to my left, right where it should be…"

"You'll have to leave it behind after the bridge."

"I'll still have the stars though. More than enough on a clear night like this."

"Are you never lost, Mikhail?"

"Not on the sea."

"We're going inland."

"Dead reckoning anyway."

The lights of the bridge loomed overhead. "People are not like signposts, Mikhail. They are not so easily read."

"On the contrary, Mrs. Devereux. I have found, in my experience as a go-between..."

"Go-between?"

"That is my profession." She coloured. He was mocking her, surely, or worse – "Most brokers are. Yachtsmen above all. No nets. Huge risks. High return always in doubt. Not for the faint of heart, I can tell you."

"Why do it then?" she asked languidly.

"No choice."

"No other options?"

"Oh there's plenty of those. I've even tried some from time to time," Mikhail shrugged. "No allure."

"And this *matchmaking* beckons."

"Yes," he replied, again as if she'd been kind. "Yes it does. The sea, the ships, the ideal fit..."

"Your profit you mean."

"I mean the fit."

From the New World played on. Caroline glanced at the card he produced – fine white vellum, block lettering, midnight blue border.

Mikhail Alexander Matson d'Olivier, she read aloud. *Yachts of Distinction*. "No telephone?"

"I'm hard to find."

"You mean you make yourself hard to find."

"I let my clients do their homework."

The river widened beside them. The road ahead narrowed as they climbed the long curving Heights. City lamps, bridge lights, even the stars disappeared, so that the car – a refuge on most trips – seemed to Caroline unfamiliar on this night, almost ominous.

Dvořák's first movement ended, paean to discovery, and, as it happened, Mikhail's favourite piece of music.

"Sailor's chords," he murmured.

"I hear the earth in it – not the sea."

"On long voyages, when one is alone, they are one and the same, don't you think?"

Caroline made no answer, sensing that he was tacking deftly from his love of the sea to the love of her life.

And yet she was not sure. Perhaps it was just his tone, wistful and so unlike him, hint of a loneliness so unrelieved it echoed her own desperation. Either way, she decided, as they approached the thickening woodlands, she would bring up the subject that was consuming them both in the dark.

"Yes or no, Caroline? You seem distracted."

"I – not at all. It's just that I think you should turn here. There could be fog up ahead, what with the temperature rising and the inland road being higher."

He did as instructed. There was indeed a spreading ground fog, thick and damp east of the river.

"Mariner's instincts," he said with approval. "I should perhaps carry your card…"

"I have no need of a card."

"You mean the people you meet have all done their homework?"

"The ones who matter."

"Ah."

"You for example, Mikhail."

"I'm flattered."

"Don't be. Your father employs me – simple as that – and while his work is important, critical you might say, my wages are more so. Without them I should be lost. To that extent I suppose, my solitary journey resembles your pandering. No nets. Huge risks. High return always in doubt."

He was struck by her bluntness – sting of a slap unexpected. And yet the sensation was somehow familiar. In a flash he remembered his stepfather's study; poor school marks again, boxed ears for his pains. The recollection, so vivid, made him determined to wound in return.

"You are silent, Mikhail."

"I am thinking."

"I have been thinking too," she replied, suddenly warm, peeling an elbow-length glove from one hand. "We should speak frankly now, once and for all, while a bit of the night's left."

"I believe you just did."

"There remains one small thing."

"It can wait."

"It cannot."

Welcome to Connecticut was barely visible on the sign they sped past. Caroline paused, expecting an answer. Mikhail merely stared at the road straight ahead. Finally – as had been his intention – the lengthening silence unnerved her as she remembered the evening: the bell jar, his greeting, the black cat on the card. Of course he knew more than he was willing to share. For some reason though, the more they moved through the woodlands, the more he seemed determined to bury the details.

She decided to ask several times if need be – for though she had worked round the clock and had fought for her home and had exhausted herself to suppress Jude's betrayal, not for a moment had she forgotten. Day and night he was there still, filling the dark space around her.

"Mikhail," she began, far less commandingly than earlier, "I am aware that you've seen – I am at a loss to know how..." she stumbled; he seemed not to notice. "We will be reaching my home soon. You must tell me now what you know."

"As I said, it can wait."

In the renewed silence, her colossal pride crumbled. He felt her hand on his arm. She felt something like pain on the palm that had extinguished a candle once.

"Mikhail," she insisted. "We may never again have the chance. *You have to tell me what you know.*"

It was not her grasp but her voice, something akin to a wave breaking offshore, which made him realize he could wound more then with words than without them.

"I only know," he finally said, "that you were not always as you are now, dead of winter, in a fine blue velvet gown, *translating*. You were somebody else, having no need of a gown, not even a drape, caught by a hand that could express such a moment supremely." The grip on his forearm perceptibly weakened. "To see it is to yearn for what he yearned for, that too I know. And your painter yearned, if only for a moment. Had he not, his brush could not have spoken so. A magnificent rendering. It will enhance whatever setting awaits."

He had lied with those last words, for there'd been a note attached to the photograph in Claire's study: *Roger, not for sale, though I think we should try.* And yet these were the words Mrs. Devereux remembered, along with that other phrase, harsh and hateful, like a slap: *if only for a moment.* She drew away from him, dwindling, as though that same wave had found the sand and had spent itself there. What she had feared was now confirmed. She was on view somewhere – at auction perhaps, for sale in a gallery, maybe even hawked near one of the quays by the Seine.

Dvořák's symphony, fourth movement, began.

"This painting," she finally managed, "Is it framed now? Well presented? I..." She peeled off her second glove, the sensation of heat now unendurable. "I would like to buy it. What is he asking? No, no that is a fool's question. What will he take? I believe that is the way one goes about things like this. I should be grateful..." again she broke off. Only sailor's chords lingered. She heard herself say at last, "When I know the price I shall figure a way."

After a moment, she continued, "Promise to help me, Mikhail. You must find out what you can...names I might need, addresses. I will of course pay you too – whatever you ask of me, *anything*."

It was what Misha had wanted: the priceless assistant – cool, self-possessed, belonging to Max at one time, his alone now, and undone. No sooner tasted though, his victory turned to ash, for somehow he sensed that the thing was unfinished. There were words to be said still – some revelation, he feared, which would cost them both a great deal.

"You'll need to know," she went on, "I would insist on it, yes – along with your fee, Mikhail..." He heard a vague rustling sound, as though of clothing being removed. "You'll need to know why a woman like me would have posed in that way." Her shawl slowly slipped to the floor by her feet. "Before that rendering – I believe that was your term…"

"Magnificent rendering…"

"Absolute darkness was the place I called home. Not the black of those sea-storms you love, the wide skies that you scan. Mine was a night with no dawn. I had been burned once, severely."

This last fact she had added without the slightest emotion. Mikhail looked at her. She was undoing the long row of buttons on the front of her dress.

"My face alone was exposed. I had to cover the rest – body and mind and soul deep within."

The last of her buttons came undone.

"Everything has its time," she went on. "Perhaps it was Paris, or a French song somebody played – who can say? – but on a hot night last summer, with the sirocco wind out of Marseilles, I suddenly longed for that wind. I wanted it on my legs, on my hips and my breasts. In fact I wanted more than the wind, indifferent caress after all. I wanted my life back – *nothing less than my life* – and it was vouchsafed to me, Mikhail, unexpectedly, in exchange for a trinket. Well at the time it seemed a trinket – my portrait, no clothing, one condition only: Never, under any circumstances, was it to be sold, loaned, or placed on exhibit."

She reached up and turned on the light overhead. When he looked again at her he was astonished, for very carefully, but with no shame whatsoever, she had opened her dress and pulled it down from her shoulders, exposing the intertwined tendrils and perfect half moon on her breast.

"There are other marks, as I assume you have seen. Those too I will show you, sometime soon to be sure, so that when you again see this portrait – when you track it down for me – as you must, you will be sure at that point that it is absolutely authentic. Copies you will know at once. One cannot duplicate what I have lived through without having touched it."

And then she fell silent.

From the New World came to an end.

Mikhail was shaken. He'd seen those dark marks before, but only from a distance, in a photo, not displayed for him openly.

"One last thing," she said all of a sudden, with a simplicity far more poignant than her initial agitation.

"I loved the man."

"Caroline," murmured Mikhail.

"I have nothing more to report."

Misha was overcome – filled at once with remorse and a surging great passion, ashamed of his meanness, aroused by her body.

The fog around them had become opaque. He pulled to the side of the road.

In the glare of the overhead light, her face, so often pale, was flushed and yet luminous, as a lover's might be, as indeed her lover had caught her once, and though Mikhail knew it was anger and fear now, not desire that had suffused those cheeks, he was also aware that the same wellspring – passions to match his own – had been tapped. Her mouth trembled once, and threatened a second time, so that she parted her lips and moistened them with her tongue and left them parted, slightly, as though to ease them a bit, having forced them to say what had had to be said, come what may.

"I should be grateful…" she repeated.

"Hush, Caroline. No more now. Be still."

Never in his tumultuous, elegant life had he experienced such desire – partly erotic, partly a thing of the spirit – a need to protect yet possess, dominate yet hold inviolate, so that the art of the deal, its allure paltry at best, lost all fascination, leaving behind only a sailor, world-class, and the vessel of his fitful dreams.

He turned out the lights overhead. She remained utterly still. He inclined toward her, paused, then positioned the dress over her shoulders and carefully closed the long row of buttons. And then he moved away, determined, despite the conflicting emotions, to take no more advantage.

Caroline too felt a surge of conflicting emotions – fear still, confusion, something akin to desire, which his hands had made her remember.

They both remained silent, unmoving, by the side of the road.

"The portrait is now in a private collection," Mikhail finally said, unable to reveal the fact of his theft from Claire Tierney's apartment. "I have seen only a photo. Through my channels I've learned that the work is not to be sold." Carefully, he reached into his pocket. "Here. This is not mine, after all."

She took the photograph he handed her, although he noticed, after a moment, that she never looked at it.

"Do you want the light on again?"

"No," she said thoughtfully. "No, I am sure you have given me what you've described, Mikhail. There'd be no other reason to look."

He heard the faint sound of paper tearing, and then a cold blast as she lowered her window and stretched out her arm and tossed the shreds into the fog and tangled mass of the woods.

Though not for sale yet, she had concluded, she was most likely soon to be, as evidenced by the circulation of this preliminary photograph. Slowly she closed the window.

"We should move on, Mikhail."

"If you wish."

"Before the fog gets any thicker."

Later on, in the woodlands, she stole a glance in his direction.

Jason, she thought, as he followed the curves in the dark. *Seducer and sailor and golden, even in this light.*

Medea, he said to himself, *capable of destroying the only thing she holds dear.*

They reached the top of the ridge, two parallel stars in the night.

"Turn to the left," Caroline said. "Westerly Road will be off to your right. It curves like a snake but it's the only way to my home."

Mikhail nodded, slowing the car down, driving through mist that rose from the earth like steam from underground pipes.

She did not repeat her directions. There was no need of that, she knew, though all but a few feet of pavement was lost, impenetrable even to the beams of his fog lamps. He would turn when it was time. The serpentine road to her house would be traversed. He was, after all, at his best in the dark, and besides, they had already bonded in a blacker place. Trust, of all things unconditional, had mated the predator to his prey.

She was glad she had left some lights on – not so much because lights made it seem as though she were expected, but because the main house could be seen from the end of the drive. They turned through the gates, passing the guest house on their left, the orchard to the right, sounds of gravel and slush crunching under the tires. When the car at last came to a stop, she felt a surge of relief, for the night had been treacherous, though it had brought out the best in him.

"You drove expertly, Misha. Even without stars."

"I didn't need stars."

"Dead reckoning?"

"Fine navigation."

She couldn't remember who smiled first. He couldn't explain the awkward pause.

"Wait," was all he responded as she reached for the door handle.

She hadn't planned to take his arm, but the walk underfoot, like the night, was unsafe. Twice she almost slipped; twice he caught her; not once did they speak until they'd climbed the stairs to her porch.

"Home," she heard him say with relief.

"So you *were* scared."

"It wasn't the fog, Mrs. Devereux. It was those shoes you have on."

She looked down at her feet. The elegant strappy sandals looked utterly ludicrous in the snow. She laughed and almost fell again and again he caught hold of her and again there was silence. They stood for a moment under the protection of the porch. It was she now who broke the silence.

"Misha…"

"Mrs. Devereux?"

"Will you find your way back?"

"I am never lost." He was holding her arm still. "And you?"

She looked puzzled.

"Will you find your way inside?"

Antonin would have been back in the car by this time, driving away, leaving her to her loneliness, never daring to intrude.

Mikhail moved in closer, saying her name once again. His voice was intimate. It was as close as he ever got to tender. He pulled her against him and kissed her. Behind her was the empty house, filled with the falsehoods that were weighing her down and the recollections that lingered, although she had torn them, and so she let herself be kissed again, this time with his desperate need, for hers too was immense, and passion was in her nature, even if love had retreated, so with her mouth she matched his hunger, and with his hands he found ideal form.

At last he pulled back, slightly.

She rested her head on his shoulder.

"A perfect fit," he said then.

She shook her head.

"You'll see."

He kissed her hair, damp now from the air. He traced the half moon on her breast, knowing exactly where it was.

He took the key from her hand and opened the door. The elegant hallway, well-lit and empty, appeared behind her like a stage set. She stepped inside. He remained on the porch.

"Good night, Serena."

She looked at him, quizzically.

"Name of a lady I knew once. Sleek and fine, just like you. A vessel I vowed I would never part with."

"And did you?"

"That is for another night."

He smiled, reached for the handle, pulled the door shut behind him and stepped off the porch. For a moment he stood on the walk, taking in the expanse of lawn, woods and fields she called home. Then he walked to the car, glanced once again at the house and drove away slowly.

"Jude will paint well here," Dr. Le Brun decided, standing on the seaward staircase overlooking Honfleur. Even in midwinter's pale light, the narrow stone houses around the semicircular quay recalled a profusion of colours splashed on a cloth. Some façades were deep turquoise, others pale coral, others burgundy, sandstone, taupe, gold, or green. Most of the shutters were white – many closed to the wind, ten or twelve opened wide to the Atlantic beyond. Small hardy sailboats, moored near the paths by each door, rocked to the bells of a buoy offshore.

Thirty, perhaps forty, Théobald concluded, counting the elegant masts piercing the blue of the sky. *Hard to tell though*, he mused as he made his way toward the south quay, for like the rooftops and steeples, the ships' forms reappeared, over and over again, in the undulating surface of the shimmering bay.

He stopped at a narrow brick house, pulled a bell-string by the doorway, heard the latch on the ancient oak door slowly slide.

"I am sorry to disturb you," he said. "Above all on Christmas."

"No trouble at all," replied Marie-Claude. "Dr. Meurice already phoned."

"I am his colleague."

"About the winter rental?"

Théobald nodded, moving from the narrow entrance into the parlour. Off to the back, through a tiny tiled passage, he caught a glimpse of the garden. Off to the right was a kitchen. In the right rear corner, he saw, carved walnut spindles lined a steep staircase.

"And so your bedrooms are all above," Dr. Le Brun asked politely, seated between twin parlour windows that faced the harbour beyond.

"Two, Monsieur. Also a bathroom. Above that a storeroom, another toilet – and then there is my room," she added, pouring red wine from the vineyards nearby. "On a clear day you can see Étretat's cliffs from that floor."

Théobald sighed. It had all seemed ideal. And yet it was clear that his patient could not climb those stairs – not even one floor – despite the sea and the cliffs and Doctor Meurice who had promised his house while on sabbatical in Venice.

"Of course there is also the consultation room," said Marie-Claude, pointing behind the fireplace to a brick-lined archway cut into the left wall.

"Once it was part of the neighbouring house. When Doctor Meurice bought that house, he made some adjustments, needing an office here in Honfleur. Please," she directed him, seeing Le Brun so intrigued, "he would of course want you to inspect it."

Like the hearth room beside it, the smaller study looked out over the ships and the harbour and the cobblestone paths that bordered the quay. There was a couch – easily made to a bed – along with a writing desk, reading chairs, shelves lined with books, ample space for an easel and paint carts. The paints and the easel, on fine days, could be moved through the double doors leading directly from the study to the water's edge, just past the walk.

"You will find that the bathroom is small," confessed Marie-Claude. "It is new though, complete, very efficient..."

"I will take it," announced Théobald, interrupting the maid with a smile that was even broader than the wave of his hand. "Everything. Every room." He stopped. "That is to say...It is not exactly for me. I – has Doctor Meurice explained? There will be a patient..."

Marie-Claude nodded gravely.

"He will need attention."

"I will be of service."

"Also the assistance of a therapist known to me over the years. Germaine du Pannier. In her time she was a legend."

"She is known to us too, *Mon Docteur*. Who does not know Germaine?"

Théobald's eyes shone. If she would only agree. She hadn't worked in ten years. Perhaps she *could* not work.

"I must go," he said abruptly. "Villerville, is it not? Around the bay to the south?"

Marie-Claude nodded.

"Then I must hurry."

"There is no need."

Théobald looked at her, puzzled.

"Germaine attends church here, Sundays and feast days. She walks up from her farmhouse."

"Marie-Claude," said Le Brun, "that would take several hours."

"In each direction, *Mon Docteur*."

"The lady I remember must be close to seventy now."

"*C'est ça, Mon Docteur*."

Nativity bells rang again, not from Notre-Dame this time, but from the half-timbered Ste-Catherine's "basilica" built by ship's carpenters above the bay.

"Last Mass of the day," said Marie-Claude at the threshold. "*Angelus Communion*, seafarers call it. Germaine's favourite Mass."

Théobald stopped – suddenly awkward it seemed, as he often appeared without his long white starched coat.

"But how will I know her, Marie-Claude?"

"You will know her, *Mon Docteur*."

☾

Marie-Claude was correct.

Although the old church was dark, hewn from the forests nearby, Théobald did find Germaine du Pannier.

He had slipped into a seat toward the back of the church, under crossbeams traversing vaults that resembled immense upturned hulls. Behind him, like phantom mastheads on a ghost fleet, illuminated organ pipes soared toward the roofline. Beside him was a statue, also carved from the woods, vividly painted in cream, gold, turquoise and red.

Saint Ann, reflected Le Brun, *patron of seafarers*.

Nativity music poured from the organ – sounds so rich and immense they seemed like waves bearing aloft the church built to resemble the prow of a ship.

He studied the face of Saint Ann – rich golden complexion, full rounded shape, dark heavy brows, eyes glancing downward. Her cheeks were sunburned, it appeared; her small mouth was upturned, not in amusement, but in some higher contentment, as though grace and compassion had lived long on her lips.

Absolutely uncanny, decided Dr. Le Brun – for the more he looked at the statue, the more he saw Germaine's face, exactly, remembered from another time.

It was not just the features, although they were similar, nor the ruddy complexion, which was also the same. *Something more indefinable*, he thought, as the line of communicants formed in the centre aisle.

The expression, he concluded – so ambiguous, unique – portrayed a tenderness that was tough somehow, innocence that had survived it all.

He searched the faces of the parishioners as they returned from the Communion rail.

Last to walk back was an elderly woman – dark Christmas dress, white crocheted shawl, light brown hair in a knot at the nape of her neck.

The years have changed her but little, he thought in amazement, for as she slipped into her seat again, he saw a girl in her twenties – proud, ramrod-straight, remembered from a photograph recovered once among his father's things.

Le Brun's father too had been a physician – full-time surgeon at the city hospital, Nice; part-time teacher at the neighbouring clinic. After the Occupation, he had joined the Resistance. After his capture – an unforgiving interrogation – Jean-Cristophe Le Brun had died.

Among the papers his son found were Jean-Cristophe's diplomas, his license to practice medicine, a medal for distinguished service at Verdun in the Great War and a few cherished photographs – one of his nursing class, recently graduated, Germaine in the front row, seated erect as she now was.

Highest honours, his father had written, in a large ornate script beside her name.

The boy had studied that picture. Over and over again. Then he had taken a match and burned it. He could not leave a trace –

already he knew that – not even a name, a distinction, for no telling who might denounce the images rendered.

Unforgettable thus, decades long since come and gone, was the proud yet still soft face of Germaine du Pannier.

⌒☾⌒

Théobald waited beneath the steeple in the tiny square outside the church.

When she emerged at last he approached her.

"Forgive me," he stammered, for the sight of her so near to him recalled that moment with the matches. "Germaine du Pannier, am I correct?"

She was too startled to respond.

"It is appalling of me to intrude. I – Christmas Day of all days" – he put his hand out. "I have a matter of some urgency…I am Théobald."

Nativity bells once more pealed.

"Théobald Le Brun," he went on, "Surgeon, Hôtel-Dieu, Paris."

Her dark eyes seemed to deepen.

"My father, you may remember, was Jean-Cristophe Le Brun, Chief Surgeon, municipal hospital, Nice."

Crowds from the church – sailors' wives mostly – filed down the cobblestone street toward the quay.

The little plaza was suddenly still. Light shifted abruptly as the sun dipped toward the horizon. The carved wooden statue seemed to come to life by the fountain – sunburned kindness, a smile, recognition that blurred the decades.

She took his hands in her own.

"No intrusion, Théobald. Never. Above all on Christmas."

"Still," Le Brun managed, "I will only steal a moment. We can perhaps speak nearby. There is a house I plan to rent…"

"There is the house where I live," she replied, taking his arm as she turned to the south, so that the afternoon sun glinted upon the waves to their right.

It suddenly dawned on Le Brun that Germaine planned to walk. Darkness would fall long before they reached Villerville. Time and exertion seemed irrelevant still to the girl.

"I have a car, Germaine – I should like to drive you on Christmas."

High on the banks to their left were great orchards – *apple trees by the millions*, Théobald thought – and then the scene disappeared as the car turned one last time and made its way to the shore.

"Built on sand," Germaine suddenly said.

Le Brun thought at first she was referring to the orchards.

"So that is said of my house – no doubt it is true – for the tides have on occasion reached the end of my pasture."

The house indeed seemed to have grown from the sand that sustained it. Unlike the other homes along the highway, it was neither pink nor half-timbered, but rather a cream-coloured stucco with bold turquoise trim and matching blue shutters.

The sea-facing door had been painted blood red.

"You will understand," she began, and then she stopped, hoping the roar of the sea would drown out her hesitation.

"A replica of the Liberation," replied Théobald.

They never again spoke of the landings.

Instead, over plum cake and cider, he at last mentioned the matter that had brought him to Normandy.

"Théobald," she replied finally, though with the respect that was due him, "I am retired now."

"So I have been informed."

"I have not worked in ten years."

"You worked for decades before that."

Germaine lit a candle, as she had no electricity. More than ever, Le Brun thought, in the incandescent glow of that flame, the old woman's face recalled the photograph he had burned.

"I am not asking for the impossible – Only that you remake a man. You will not need to walk. I'll have a car for you, every morning, one to bring you back each night. As for your wages..."

She waved her hand.

"I'll pay you handsomely, Germaine. You'll see. You won't regret it if you work for me. Just this last time."

The tides shifted then. She paused to wait for the change.

"And why does he matter so…this Monsieur Jude?"

Théobald thought for a moment, then replied fervently, "Because he creates what does not die. So much else did in our time. Because he has fought like a beast to hold on to his life, although his life is just pain, yet there is something he wants still, something he glimpsed once – beauty, love – both, I suspect."

Germaine looked away.

"Because he is a friend, Germaine. And my father trained you. And for his sake I beg you to make a last miracle now."

It seemed a long time to Le Brun before she faced him again. "The miracle he must do himself. In his own heart. I can only make him walk, make his back strong, his hands…"

"Above all his hands…"

With a sigh she repeated, relenting, grace and compassion having lived long on her lips, "Above all his hands, Théobald – if that is what you want of me."

They agreed to meet at the brick house, south side of the quay in Honfleur, New Year's Day, just past noon.

꒰ ☾ ꒱

Slowly, so as not to disturb the patient propped up on the stretcher behind him, the driver guided his ambulance out of the hospital ramp of the old Hôtel-Dieu.

He crossed the Seine at Pont Notre-Dame, then headed west, as per instructions, planning to reach Honfleur before noon.

Jude McCallister would never remember that this was the same route they'd followed, east from the Champs-Élysées, on the morning he had been found senseless beside the Pavillon. Even now all he could grasp – and it was an effort still to make connections – was that he had just left his bed across from the west façade of the cathedral, that the façade had filled his head with primary colours he remembered mixing in some other life, that the stone statues on the portals resembled models he'd known once, also in that other life, and that one particular window was ineffable.

He struggled to avoid nausea as the ambulance followed the sinuous road through the Bois de Boulogne. Soon the woodlands thinned out, then came the flatlands, then the verdant valley of the River Seine appeared. Even in winter, its misty pastures seemed lush – citrines, Jude recalled – pale green and gold with a hint of the sunflowers soon to emerge. Immense walls of poplars resembled sentinels along the road. Dovecotes and cider mills dotted the banks of the river – a vivid cerulean blue in these fields, no longer the well-mannered grey of the Right Bank – so that the patient sat up to try and remember that tone, endlessly twisting beside him.

The need to vomit returned. Everything was so different, everything kept moving – the Seine to their right, the patch-eyed cows to their left, the barren orchards on both sides that swayed unsteadily in the wind.

"Two hours – perhaps less, Monsieur Jude," said the driver, both apologetic and efficient, cleaning his passenger by the side of the road. "It is New Year's Day, after all. There will be no other cars."

"*Merci...merci, Marcel,*" Jude replied, putting his head back, incapable of imagining any place other than the side of the road.

Nevertheless Honfleur touched him – in some deep treasured place not completely remembered, like a palette he had favoured since the time he was ten.

Still on his stretcher, he simply stared at the bay – the proud narrow houses, the prouder boats moored beside them, their profusion of colours – above all the sea. Strangely enough, although the gentle waves in the harbour gave back the scene to him, distorted, he felt no nausea. It was as though he had fixed on some more potent point of reference. What had occurred, although he could not guess this yet, was a desperate compulsion to render the scene, reflect what he saw there – as the sea did without effort, although he would have need of a brush and his paints.

Traffic was light in the town. So was the New Year's first

sun. With special access to the west quay, the driver stopped and went round to the double doors of his van.

About to slide the stretcher down, he saw the patient wave his hand slightly.

"Have you no chair?" Jude asked.

"Chair?"

"Something with wheels – but not this, so that I might arrive…less defeated."

The driver couldn't imagine anything on this earth less defeated.

"I have a chair, Monsieur Jude…"

"If it would not be an inconvenience."

"Not at all," said the driver. "Not a problem at all."

Thus it was that Jude McCallister arrived sitting upright, outside the tall red brick house on the south side of the quay, Théobald and Marie-Claude and Germaine du Pannier at the door, expecting him, water's edge just beyond.

"*Je vous ai tous dérangé*," managed Jude from his chair. "I have disturbed you all," he repeated, for though his French was superb, his native language came with less effort – though not fluidly yet – due to a thickness around his tongue still whenever he wanted to speak.

"Nonsense. We have been waiting with great excitement," said Théobald, stepping forward.

There was a moment. He took Jude's hands in his own. Words seemed to come to him too now with effort. "To think that I am seeing you here – that you have left that place…"

"The view wasn't bad," answered Jude gamely.

"You will like this one too."

Jude turned toward the sea. A bell buoy sounded as the afternoon tides began shifting. In the strong offshore wind – was that a vague taste of salt? – his fine hair blew back, thin and sparse now, although in time, Le Brun had promised, the grey fullness would return.

Seeing Jude focused so intently, Théobald said, "Later perhaps – when you have rested, Jude – I'll wheel you back out here again."

Jude faced him slowly, holding on to his hand still. "You should be home, Théobald. What are you doing here New Year's Day?"

"I was afraid you wouldn't show up."

Again that weak smile – a little stronger this time, for Jude was determined to convey a debt he could never repay.

"And now for the introductions," said Dr. Le Brun heartily, deflecting the tribute.

"May I present Marie-Claude," he began, leading the slight dark-haired housekeeper out to the chair by the quay. "She will be living here. She has lived in this house for ten years – have you not?" he inquired, turning again to the housekeeper, who seemed reluctant to advance.

"That is so, *Mon Docteur*."

"My colleague, Dr. Meurice, could not get along without her – is that also not so, Marie-Claude?" Théobald asked.

Marie-Claude turned beet red. "If Dr. Meurice has reported it," she replied.

"I shall need you more," Jude said abruptly, and then she looked at him and was filled with great pity and was no longer shy. "Too much, perhaps, Marie-Claude…"

"Never too much, Monsieur. You will find that you can count on me."

And with that she fell silent again, though she stayed close to the chair, for it was not in her nature to speak when efficiency would suffice.

Dr. Le Brun had by then returned to the doorway. "Jude," he said simply, leading an old sunburned woman out to the edge of the quay. "I should like to present to you…"

"Germaine du Pannier," Jude supplied, surprising everyone then, himself above all, for his recollections were erratic still, above all for names.

"You remember," whispered his doctor.

"More and more, I find," said Jude.

Germaine had by then crossed to the side of the chair. "I am happy to meet you, Monsieur Jude," she said.

Jude made no answer, for the sun behind them had emerged from a passing cloud, bathing the woman's face in an almost ethereal burnt-sienna tone. Jude was transfixed by the hue.

"You are," she went on, thinking perhaps that words, or rather the shaping of words, had again become hard for him, "you are, Monsieur Jude, just as Théobald said you would be. Storm-tossed a bit – yes – that is so, after a great rage at sea." She studied his face, above all his eyes. "Still intact though – that too I can see – and soon to be righted."

Her voice was like an unguent; her gaze recalled comfort; her touch had made him want to sit up straighter in his wheelchair.

"Well," said Dr. Le Brun, after the long pause that followed. "Let us go in now. The rising wind is turning cold."

Everything in the studio had been prepared: rolling carts, paint jars, standing easel, palettes. There was also something which resembled a trapeze toward the rear, next to some other equipment, equally challenging.

All that Jude saw was what seemed like a canvas on the floor, still wrapped in brown paper, shipped from Frères Durand.

"Yes, that came yesterday," said Le Brun approaching the parcel. "Shall I unwrap it while you rest there? It would fit perfectly on your easel."

"No!" Jude called out, so unexpectedly that they all turned.

"I...that is – no, thank you, Théobald. I plan to unwrap it myself when the time comes – when the day comes, I mean, when I can stand by myself, and walk by myself, and cross to that wall and remove that brown paper. It is brown, is it not? The afternoon seems to have passed."

"It is brown," answered Le Brun, in the fullest sunlight of midday.

Heavy rains had come up as Le Brun drove back toward his apartment on the boulevard St-Germain.

Winds in Honfleur harbour made the sailboats knock against the quays. The buoys rang louder offshore. Ropes on the flagpole snapped like metronomes stuck in the sand.

Yet it wasn't the storm that had interrupted Jude's sleep. Lying awake in the dark it had dawned on him. Only that parcel remained of the love affair that had remade him. She had never written. He himself could never write now – a shell of a man, shards of a shell, although Germaine had kindly called it, in the end, a hull to be righted. This he could not offer her. This above all things he would never reveal. And yet he would push himself to the limit to walk to that wall and unveil her as he had done once before, placing her back on his easel, where she belonged.

☽

Weather conditions in New York were unprecedented New Year's Eve. After a few days of warmth reminiscent of June, cold driving rains lashed the coast. By nightfall, when Mikhail called his father's house from Saint Maarten, where one of his yachts had unexpectedly sold, temperatures had plunged in the strong offshore winds.

"Misha, how are you?" Max said. "Happy New Year! Yes, we're fine here. Yes, it is bad outside."

Antonin heard the sound of sleet on the windows.

"Filthy weather, really, and getting worse," Max went on.... "No, I did not know the airports were closed. Of course I'm sorry you're stranded. It's the wind, I suppose. Hail you say? I can't see from here. I wouldn't doubt it though. We've gone from summer to winter since noontime...Yes. And the weather there? Sounds wonderful. Well enjoy it. – What?...Yes she's here. Hold on for a moment."

Max studied Caroline's face as she took the receiver.

"Hello Mikhail," was all she said, steadily. "Health and good fortune to you too. No, I am not going to stay. I know it's bad out, but Antonin feels – Antonin's fine. I'll be home before midnight."

Her colour deepened, Max saw.

"Yes I remember," she managed.

"Be safe yourself. What?" She glanced down, caught off guard. "White," she said, barely audible.

Max signalled suddenly.

"Mikhail – Wait! – Antonin Onegin wants to wish you Happy New Year."

Antonin's voice, more insistent than usual, could be heard across the hallway through the doors Max had closed. Several times he repeated there would be absolutely no problems. Twice he stressed the fact that he had driven in worse storms.

In his heart – and this she would never hear, for her safe conduct was a point of honour with him after the Christmas debacle – Antonin wasn't sure. Still, he had to take her. He could not fail a second time. He would concentrate; his car was his ally.

Thus he had reassured Max after the concert, for Max was by then also concerned.

"She will not be at risk," he had said. "The storm has passed in the main."

Maximilian chose to trust him – partly because he knew how much it meant to him, partly because he himself could not gauge much beyond the parametres of his courtyard.

Antonin's predictions, for about an hour or so, proved correct. Sleet became drizzle by the side of the river. Even after the bridge, where the temperatures dipped, there was enough holiday traffic to keep the road surface wet.

Reassured, Caroline slept, soothed by the sound of light rain on the windshield.

They reached the woodlands and she slept still and at that point, as the freezing rain started again, Antonin worried. Had he wanted to then – and the thought occurred to him, finally, that his pride had put them both at risk – he could not have turned back. The next exit was not for nine miles, where there would be no corresponding

southbound ramp. He had no choice but to continue, scanning the
road up ahead for black ice.

"Antonin?" he heard then.

"Miss?"

"Has it been sleeting long?"

"A fair bit tonight, yes."

Cellophane seemed to be wrapping the grass; icicles dripped
from the power lines along the road; hail bounced off the car's
windshield as Antonin added, "We're almost there, though. You'll
see the lights past this curve."

They rounded the bend. Well into the valley below and beyond,
there was absolute darkness.

"There's been a blackout, Miss," he said quietly after a moment.

"Yes."

"They had predicted a possible outage tonight," he went on, still
in that uncoloured tone as they followed the sinuous curves of
Westerly Road toward the farm.

"Lights, Antonin!"

"Candles," he thought.

"There!" she insisted. As they descended the ridge there were
indeed lights to be seen, scattered at first, then consistently, house to
house, despite the expanses of woods in between.

"That's it," she said. "Todd's Farm at last – is it not? Up ahead to
the right?"

The farm was indeed up ahead, the guest house at least – *that*
could be seen, its approach, spotlights on, its small courtyard beside,
but the other lights, the confusion, the trucks – they were trucks, it
appeared...

She said his name again.

He pulled to the side of the road and lowered his window. Puffs
of smoke hovered above the orchard. A large black column moved
slowly southward, toward the river, away from the pile of rubble
where the main house had once been.

"Explosion!" someone shouted nearby. "Power surge through
the downed wires by the road."

Caroline had left the car by then. She was running along the side of the road, coat open, wild-eyed.

A policeman called after her to stop.

Caroline kept on running.

A fireman blocked her way.

"Let me go!"

"You can't go! No one can! It's a tinderbox still..."

"But I live here!"

He caught her again.

"That house is mine," she insisted, pointing to a place that no longer existed.

He tightened his grasp. Antonin came up behind them. At the sight of him she somehow wrenched herself free.

"Antonin – Antonin Onegin!" she cried, reaching for him. "*Tell* them!"

Antonin put his arms around her, shielding her from the heap of debris.

"Mrs. Devereux?" a voice called.

She did not reply.

"Mrs. Devereux?" repeated the Police Chief, catching up with them in the confusion.

Still no answer.

"Devereux, yes," Antonin offered. "I don't think she can hear you."

Joe Mara looked at the stranger – and stranger he was, no question about it, for residents were known in New Salem, above all to town officials, and this huge man – rough-hewn, misbegotten – was decidedly out of place, ice storm notwithstanding.

"And you, sir..." Joe Mara queried.

"I am..." Antonin faltered. In a flash it had come back to him – police cars, confusion, the glint of handcuffs when his luck ran out.

"I am a friend," he said after a moment, shielding Mrs. Devereux still, so that the frayed sleeves of his coat were in view, as was his tattered scarf, which he had managed to wrap around her.

A volunteer van pulled up.

"Walter Reston's on his way," called the driver. "And the service reached Dr. Devereux."

Caroline looked up at last, a vague expression in her eyes.

"Elliot –" she murmured.

"Reston's to act for him 'til he can get here himself – tomorrow, day after – whenever the storm breaks. On standby at this point for a seat on the first plane."

Caroline looked at the rubble. As quickly as it had appeared, the brief flash of recognition seemed to have slipped from her eyes. She disengaged herself from Antonin and began to walk again toward the gates.

"Mrs. Devereux?" Joe Mara called. "You are to stay with the Restons. Your husband has said specifically…"

"Why should I stay with the Restons?" she asked distractedly. "I live in that house there."

Antonin caught hold of her arm once more.

Another car lurched to a stop at the gates.

"Caroline!" Walter called out. "Caroline, thank God! – You could have been in there! What a miracle!"

"…Miracle?"

"God yes!" He was almost in tears. "The rest is nothing. Shattering, yes – ghastly – but in comparison…"

She shrank from him, back into Antonin.

"Caroline, dear," Walter continued, noticing for the first time the improbable stranger sheltering Mrs. Devereux. "The police will need to speak with you – the Fire Chief – but not here. They don't want anyone inside that wall yet. Back at my house might be best. They can speak with you there."

"They can speak with me here."

"Well, yes, of course…"

"The guest house, Walter," she said, aware, all of a sudden, of names, dimensions, the conversation around her. And yet she was not aware, for the more Joe Mara insisted she could not go to the guest house, the more she explained she would wait for them there.

The paramedics arrived.

"The lady's in shock here."

All of a sudden, with uncharacteristic insistence, Antonin's voice could be heard in the confusion. *"I'll stay here, Caroline."*

"Sorry," Joe Mara said. *"Nobody goes in there."*

"I meant in my car," he said, making eye contact with Caroline, turning his back to Walter Reston, dismissing Joe Mara too with the move.

"I'll stay as close as they let me," he murmured. "You go on with the Restons – sleep some, eat some and when they tell us we can go in I will come for you."

Joe Mara looked at Walter, who looked at the paramedics.

"I will come for you," he repeated steadily, motioning to the guest house. "Then we'll drive in together, like always – same land, same car, same gates over there. Tomorrow latest, I promise. Wouldn't you say so?" he asked the astounded policeman.

Joe Mara considered. "Will you allow him to do this, Mrs. Devereux?"

Caroline looked from Joe Mara to Walter and then back into Antonin's eyes – only face she seemed to recognize.

"Please let me do this. You know I won't fail you."

The paramedics awaited their orders.

"Yes," said Mrs. Devereux, suddenly. "Yes I will wait with the Restons."

"Done then," said Walter, relieved that Elliot's wife would be in his care, as per instructions received.

She turned, headed toward Walter's sedan, stopped again.

"Ten tomorrow, Antonin. No later," she said unsteadily.

"Make it noon," said Walter.

"Noon it is," Antonin answered.

She had her hand on his arm still.

"'Til tomorrow, then," she said finally, as she had so often said to him on that road, by those gates, at the end of each day, and then she turned and entered Walter's car, and Joe Mara walked back to his men.

⁓ ☾ ⁓

The police cordoned the land off that night. For Mrs. Devereux they were prepared to make an exception the next day, having been assured by the fire crews that a second explosion was unlikely.

Hence at noon, as promised, Antonin's car was in front of the Restons'. Caroline ran to him. He got out of the car to open the rear door as usual, but she opened the front door and slipped in beside him.

It felt odd to him not to be facing her in the rear-view mirror above – odder still to be on strange empty roads, curving through woodlands at midday, not another car in sight New Year's Day. Everything seemed to have imploded in the power surge by the ridge. Though the sleet had stopped nearing dawn, the day had dawned cold and grey – a raw wind in the air, temperatures around the freezing point, ice coating the power lines, which dipped even lower with the weight.

At the farm they were stopped, then waved onto the drive.

"Mind the tray on the floor," he warned, guiding the car into the courtyard of the guest house to their left. Not until then had she noticed the large cardboard box and brown bags in the car.

They entered the guest house. Antonin spread their breakfast out beside a window that overlooked the road beyond. It had no view whatsoever of the south lawn and gardens and what had once been the main house. Indeed, there was an almost eerie normalcy as they sipped their coffee beside that window, for despite the destruction behind them, smouldering still, the guest house had lights, heat, gas for cooking – everything that its generator, independent of the main line, had continued to provide.

"I've told the insurance agent to come at once, Antonin – today, three p.m. sharp. He sounded extremely disturbed, although I've known him for years. Must have been the fact that I called him on New Year's. Anyway, he said he'd come."

Antonin nodded. They ate quietly a while longer. She was accustomed to his introversion – his few blunt, well-chosen words –

and so again she spoke, far more deliberately than usual, discussing matters of business, rebuilding costs, unaware of the fact that his silence on that day sprang not from reticence but increasing concern. He was observing her carefully – her control, tighter than usual, her odd detachment. She seemed abstracted from the catastrophe – the opposite of last night's wildness – an unsettling denial he knew only too well. Mostly, among his fellow inmates it had appeared at the start of a long incarceration. Often it led by degrees to a deeper despair.

"Caroline," he announced – he had not said "Miss" since they'd rounded the bend the night before – "I need to rest now."

"Good."

"If *you* will."

"I slept last night."

"Last night's past."

"Well then tonight."

"Tonight it is," he replied, sitting back in his chair.

She looked into his face – large and haggard and smudged with soot over one brow.

"Yes," she sighed. "Yes I will lie on that sofa. We still have some time 'til the investigator comes. I will not wake you of course."

"I will awaken."

He stood and turned to the door. She put her hand on his arm, half afraid to be left, half distraught at the thought of him out in the cold again, sleepless. "Please. You'll find a bedroom beyond the archway there, two more upstairs – lots of hot water in the bathrooms, either place."

Not until he heard her breathing calmly, rhythmically, tucked under an afghan on the sofa, did he leave his seat in the stairwell and climb to his own rest on the floor above. Within minutes he was asleep. As it happened, he stayed asleep, having misjudged his own exhaustion, and so he did not hear the knock at the door that awakened Caroline two hours later.

"Jeb Valenti," she cried, throwing her afghan off as she ran to the door.

"Hello, Caroline."

She noticed he was accompanied.

"Dennis Ballantine," Jeb explained. "District Manager, New England Life."

"You are both kind to come. On New Year's Day, I mean, in all this ice still..." She broke off.

"Caroline, I'm so sorry."

"I know, Jeb."

"My sympathies, Mrs. Devereux."

"Thank you, Mr. Ballantine."

They took their seats. Jeb looked at his hands. Dennis brushed ice from the cuff of his pants.

"Elliot's away, I hear," Jeb began again, awkwardly.

"New Mexico. Yes. Not a seat to be had on a flight this way yet."

"Couldn't land if there were," Dennis observed. "Airports are closed still."

"Have you spoken to Elliot?"

"I – no. No, I haven't, Jeb. Not today, I mean."

"Recently though, I assume."

Caroline looked at him.

"You've spoken recently," Dennis repeated.

"Well, yes, of course..." Caroline reddened. "Before he left we spoke..."

"About the state of things here..."

"Mr. Ballantine," she replied tersely, "we could hardly have discussed a catastrophe that hadn't occurred before he left."

"In that case," Dennis suggested, "it might be best to wait a bit."

"Wait for what?"

"When your husband arrives –"

"When my husband arrives," Caroline said, "which will be soon I understand, he will be only too conscious of the destruction that needs repairing. That is why I have called you. The house is gone, after all..."

"Caroline," Jeb managed softly.

"Insured through your company," she continued, waving her hand, "all of it, handsomely, for over ten years now."

Jeb repeated her name.

"I'll want a replica, Mr. Ballantine. There are plans in my study. No, that is gone. No matter. They are not gone from my head. There's not a dimension I can't recall, not an inch of that house..." She stopped. "Come to think of it now, there are some photographs with the policy. My copy's gone of course. Yours, however, Mr. Ballantine..."

"Nonexistent, Mrs. Devereux."

"New England Life's, I meant..."

"So did I."

"I don't understand."

"The policy's gone," Jeb blurted out, fiercely almost, angry that it had fallen on him to explain things. "Cancelled. Lapsed for six months now."

Antonin stirred, awakened not so much by voices as by some palpable uneasiness that stole into his rest – a common enough occurrence in his penitentiary years, when trouble stalked mostly while people slept. The foreboding increased as he started back down the stairs.

"This cannot be," he heard a woman's voice say. At first he could not place the uneven, frail sound. "There's been a mistake made."

"No mistake, Mrs. Devereux.

"I wish there *were*," offered Jeb lamely. "But Dennis is right. There simply is no insurance."

Unseen by them all, Antonin had reached the landing. He stood silently for a moment, transfixed by the sight of the little group by the sofa.

"Not on the house," Jeb went on, "not on the land. Not even on this," he said waving his hand, dismissing the guest house and gates and the stone walls beyond that. "No payments received since the 10th of July."

"Half-payment then," Dennis supplied. "Though two reminders were sent."

Caroline had reverted to absolute silence, hands crossed in her lap, gaze somewhat unfocused.

Leaning in to her, Jeb confided. "Caroline, Elliot had his troubles. He may have needed the respite...collateral – I don't know, debts..."

"Fact is," broke in Dennis, for there were company policies against conjecture, "it has been weeks since New England Life ceased to insure Todd's Farm and its land."

Antonin stepped into the room. Try as he might to avoid it, his large boots reverberated on the wide oak-plank floor.

Jeb and Dennis turned toward the sound.

Caroline raised her face to him. She had wanted to say "Did you sleep well?" or "Hello" or perhaps – above all – "Uninsured, Antonin," but no words came out.

It fell to Antonin to fill in the silence.

"The owner's just had a shock," he said. "A second one."

Jeb and Dennis nodded, almost in unison, wondering who this rudimentary apparition might be.

"So if you're done here..."

"We're done here."

"Uninsured, Antonin," Caroline finally managed, as a schoolgirl might explain an unfinished assignment.

"Is there anything to be signed?" Antonin asked Mr. Ballantine.

"There is no policy," he repeated, as if the large man had problems grasping.

Jeb by then had also stood.

"Well then," said Antonin, feet striking the floor once again as he crossed, "The policeman will open the gates by the road for you. Mind the ice on the steps."

Long-time friend of Dr. Devereux, at a loss now when it came time to parting, Jeb Valenti turned at the threshold. "Caroline..." he began.

"Thank you again," replied Antonin.

"Good afternoon, Mrs. Devereux," Dennis felt compelled to add – superfluous, as it happened, since Caroline had by then buried her face in her hands, rocking herself back and forth, not having responded since he'd stood.

Jeb and Dennis left. Antonin closed the door, turned to face Caroline and was glad he had slept.

Elliot too was glad he had slept before his plane touched down in Newark on the following day. He would have much to face once he arrived at Todd's Farm, or what was left of it: debris to be cleared, the hearing in March, his wife to be dealt with once she discovered how great the debt had become, how he had juggled what funds had remained, how the farm had ended up – he winced at the thought – at the mercy of fate.

It never occurred to him that she had already been informed – that she had spent the last eighteen hours locked away in her guest house, attended to only by her driver, her friend, whoever he was – nobody seemed to know – and that she had gotten through it somehow. She had collapsed from exhaustion and the friend had revived her. She had wept and he'd let her cry. She had slept a bit, after the brandy they'd shared, and he had covered her, dozing then too in the opposite chair, waking when she did, bringing tea, food, an eager face when she suggested at last they step outside for some air, although it was evening, and take a tour of the place. She had leaned on his arm, although she knew every inch of the way. They'd stood in silence by the rubble, then gone around it, flashlights in hand, past what had once been the terrace toward what was still the bridge down below.

"Shall we cross, Antonin?"

"If you like."

In a few moments they'd reached the south bank, heading for the river falls in the woods.

"Well?" she had asked, after they'd toured the old mill. "Will it work do you think?"

Antonin had walked round the hearth room again. She'd heard his boots on the floor of the grain room, the kitchen beyond, the wooden staircase by the hallway, the small bedroom above. When he'd returned she had opened the door and was watching the wheel turn by her deck.

"It's too cold for you there. Come back inside, Caroline."

She hadn't turned, hadn't heard him in fact, for the sound of the falls had carried his voice to the wind. Thus he had joined her, stared at the wheel for a moment, then carefully closed the door and crossed back with her toward the fireplace.

"What do you think?" she had repeated.

"I think," he said slowly, sitting on the high-backed bench facing hers, "I think it is good."

"Really?"

"More than good."

As accustomed as she was to his terseness, she had pressed him a third time, for it was the key to her plans now, and she trusted him.

"I am sure of it," he had insisted, again with that firmness she'd never seen before these last days. "My eyes can see finished things. My hands have been taught to create what I see." He omitted to add that his instructor had been a prison guard. "I will help build."

She smiled, searching his dark face. "No. You have your work with Max. He relies on you, Antonin, more than you know. Perhaps a woodworker here..."

"Still, I will help. The furniture, yes. You will see."

Again she'd smiled, bravely, as hope reappeared where desolation had been. She would not have to sell. Insured or not, she still owned Todd's Farm, minus the main house, temporarily. While she rebuilt it, she would rent out the guest house. It would bring a good fee; she would work harder than ever with Max; she would sell the few jewels she had left – the holiday sapphires left up in the guesthouse, some fine gems she had locked in a bank vault downtown. That would pay for the clearing, the preparations, the new plans for the main house – which she herself would oversee.

Easily done, to be sure, for she would be living at the mill.

⌒☾⌐

"The mill!" Elliot gasped, having at last reached the farm, still cordoned off, only to find his wife in the guest house, calculating figures, her driver asleep in one of the small rooms upstairs. "Are you mad?"

"I am desperate," she said simply, not even glancing up at him, recalling that she hadn't the courage to shape those words, a mere four months before then, in the offices of Anatole Kramer and Associates.

"Well yes, yes of course, so are we both, but that old heap of stones..."

"We will be fine there."

"That unendurable..."

"We will have to be fine."

When she looked up at him, finally, he believed he saw something dark in those depths, deeper than blame, as though that improbable mauve had turned into a bruise.

Elliot studied that bruise. It was his profession, after all, to scrutinize expression. And then, though the room had grown dim in late afternoon's light, he saw clearly at last. Hurt had become obsession not even death would erase.

"The timetable, as I see it..."

"Caroline..."

"Near as I can figure," she continued, bending back down over her books.

"You *are* mad," he whispered, as though revealing the fact to them both at one time.

"The very first thing here – one must be practical, Elliot; it is wintertime, after all – there will be need for some heat."

"I won't go down there with you, Caroline."

"Water, of course, will be plentiful, Elliot."

"Caroline, can you hear me?"

Her husband leaned in to her, so as to put the sound as close as possible to the face that had looked up again.

"Listen to me. I'm going to say this very carefully, but I am only going to say it once. I will never, not for a day, live in that old filthy ruin of yours down in the woods."

Although she made no response, she appeared to comprehend.

"You have a right to be angry," he continued, "even to want revenge, if that's what this is about…"

Once again Antonin came down the staircase.

"But I will not pay with my life for the mistakes that I've made."

"I did not think you would," his wife said.

Elliot straightened himself.

Facing away from the steps, hearing only the anger inside him, he replied, "Then you must have figured I'd leave, Caroline – now – tonight, unless you come to your senses and let me manage things."

Her glance turned arch.

"The land alone's worth a fortune…"

"My land will never be sold."

"Utterly mad," he repeated, baffled by the veil over that bruise which now dulled her gaze. "Damaged, scarred in your heart – a place I could never reach – never can reach, though God knows I've tried."

Elliot turned and looked for his coat, only to be startled by a stranger in the stairwell. "Who the hell are you?"

"Mrs. Devereux's friend."

The doorbell rang.

"Christ," muttered Elliot, flinging the door open.

"Hello, Antonin," said Joe Mara, looking behind Elliot to the dark man. Then, respectfully, although it seemed an afterthought, "Dr. Devereux. Good evening. Glad to see you're home safe."

"Come in, Mr. Mara."

"Thank you, Antonin."

"You've missed the worst of it, Doctor. It's been pretty grim for three days. Well I suppose you know that already. "

"Yes, yes I know everything. Whatever I needed to learn, Mrs. Devereux has informed me."

And with that Elliot left, storming past the Police Chief to his dark green Mercedes parked by the orchard.

Antonin closed the door behind him. Joe Mara retrieved a stack of papers from his pocket. Caroline looked at them, forcing herself to focus on the dates, times, sequence of events.

"Three days have gone by!" she said all of a sudden.

"Three and a half," Joe corrected.

"We haven't let Max know…"

"He knows," Antonin said. "I called the house right away. I've called a lot since then. He is calmer now, though at first…" Antonin stopped. "I am to bring you back as soon as possible, while the mill is fixed – whatever you need as long as you need."

She put the papers down. A sigh of relief came next.

"It's working wonderfully, isn't it Mr. Mara?"

Joe saw the immense jumble of figures in the book on her desk. The guest house still smelled of smoke.

"If you say so, Mrs. Devereux."

She nodded.

Elliot's car sped down the road.

Mikhail's car was crossing the Triborough Bridge, his plane having landed at last in New York.

"She's all right, isn't she, Max?"

"From what I can gather, Misha, yes. The shock of course – house gone, possessions, no way to replace things…"

"What will she do now?"

"Things are uncertain still. Antonin tells me, though…"

"Antonin!"

"Surely you must remember he drove her home New Year's Eve."

Mikhail put his glass down.

"Well, he couldn't just leave her there."

"No. No, of course not. Though when her husband returned – I assume he's arrived – there was surely no need of a *chauffeur* at that point."

The reference was wounding. Max chose to ignore it. "I mean the doctor himself can't be expected – the husband's a doctor, I've heard…"

"There is no longer a doctor."

"No doctor?"

"He has left her."

This was a turn of events Mikhail had not envisioned.

Max relayed what he knew – what little he knew – for Antonin had only told him that Elliot Devereux had gone, that his wife planned to rent the guest house, rebuild the main house, live someplace else on the grounds – he was not exactly sure where.

Misha's mind darted back to the one and only time he'd been there. True it had been dark and foggy, but he couldn't remember any buildings – liveable buildings – other than the main home and the guest house. The gate house was a closet, nothing more than that, once used for security, now a storage shed. The mill she had mentioned couldn't possibly feature now.

"A mill in the woods," his father remembered.

"But that can't be…"

"First things first, of course. There's the rubble to be cleared. Along with the debts. Dr. Devereux, it seems, has long been in troubled waters. He has also had options, to use Antonin's words. This particular option has taken him in. End of story. End of marriage. End of the farm as she's known it."

Antonin's clock struck five-thirty p.m.

"End of her job here?" Mikhail asked when the chimes stopped.

"On the contrary. She'll need work more than ever."

Mikhail weighed his words. His father's memoirs – precious, admittedly – could not possibly provide what was needed at this point.

"For the next three weeks," Max went on, "Mrs. Devereux will be on vacation. She has earned it. I need the rest. Six thousand dollars, to get the debris off the land. She would not take any more."

"Three weeks go fast," Mikhail ventured.

"I have told her she can stay here."

"She won't."

"Probably not. Until the new tenants arrive, she'll stay on in the guest house."

"Not alone, Max…"

"Alone, Misha, yes. She prefers things that way. As it is she feels indebted. Antonin was, after all, a huge help these past days. As for more facts…" Max stopped. "Why not call him yourself? He's only been back one full day. I told him to rest 'til the weekend, so you should find him at home."

Mikhail nodded.

When he left Max that evening though, as he turned west toward the Hudson, Mikhail had no intentions of contacting Antonin. He planned to go directly to Todd's Farm himself.

⠂☾⠄

Sifting through papers still, Caroline bent over her desk. The stark facts were more vivid, it seemed, in the gathering darkness. Whatever income she could envision was exceeded by her expenses.

She heard the guest house clock chime five p.m. She reworked the numbers twice, each time to no avail. Another hour passed, and then seven chimes, and then she reached for her coat and went outside.

The air was bitingly cold, the night deceptively calm, the stars crystal clear like those facts on her desk.

She passed the rubble pile – less and less out of place there it seemed, like the remnants of a shipwreck already at home in the sand. Then she moved down toward the river, where more and more she felt at home. On the opposite banks she turned east, not yet feeling the wind chill of three degrees and falling, for the moon had grown large, its light masquerading as the illusion of warmth.

Only after she slammed the mill door shut did Caroline start to feel cold. She sat on the bench in the hearth room and closely retied her scarf and dark hood. For a brief time her mind was clear, heightened alertness in the razor-sharp air.

All possible – doable, everything, she considered, clapping her hands to ward off the chill.

Yet as the evening advanced, the mill began to seem of all things unfriendly. Like her, after all, it was cast in a stubborn stone. Immense sums would be needed to coax that stone into life: a warm kitchen, walls that would resist the wind.

And there would be wind by the falls, there'd be no changing that. Even now there was wind – she could feel it as the moon climbed and her feet numbed and then her breath took the shape of those small opaque puffs that had drifted slowly over the farm, six days before.

No, that was smoke, she reminded herself, sensing the alertness she had felt earlier beginning to wane like her light. In its wake came a drowsiness increasingly hard to resist.

I'll just rest, she decided. *With some sleep I'll find my way again.*

She put her head back. If anything, as the water wheel turned, the chaos in her head increased.

Upstairs is better, she thought, climbing the staircase to the little bedroom under the eaves.

She let the flashlight fall by the rope bed, for it had gone out as she entered the room and would not be revived.

The loosely tied ropes creaked beneath her slight frame. She undid her scarf, wanting above all to sleep well, caring no longer for warmth, but for the absolute absence of sensation. It came quickly, more soothing than she had dared to expect.

Delicious, were the last words she remembered being able to shape.

The moon inched along, nudging its beams off the bed across to the opposite wall by the door. There they flickered a while, as the flashlight had done, growing weaker past midnight, disappearing toward three.

A voice called from the stairwell.

Had she wanted to, Caroline could not have answered – that was clear to Mikhail when he approached the rope bed in her room. She lay utterly still, her face a translucent pearl white except for the blue-black on her mouth and lids. He fumbled at once beneath her thin glove, found an attenuated pulse, scooped her up quickly and held her close to him. Her face remained without expression.

"We're going home now," he said, knowing full well she could not hear. He repeated these words as he stumbled back toward the bridge, hoping the sounds might call her back from whatever cave she had preferred to the chaos of life outside her mill.

Inside the guest house he stoked the embers in the kitchen hearth, turned on the oven, carried her back and forth as he talked without stopping – anything he could think of – his work, current events, stanzas remembered from *The Rime of the Ancient Mariner*. Sweat from his body poured over hers – partly the result of his frantic exertion, partly the sauna he had created as he moved about with her, rocking her rhythmically, talking as a fool might speak, expecting no answer.

He saw that her mouth was no longer blue. It must have been then that he sang – in years to come he would try to remember – but in that kitchen at some point he managed some Welsh tunes, long forgotten.

Perhaps it was their strangeness, perhaps his sweat in her hair, but something not unpleasant made her risk facing the light once again.

"Misha," she murmured.

He moved the damp hair from her cheek.

"Mikhail," she repeated.

"There you are," he replied, seeing her hollowed eyes, larger than ever it seemed, open at last.

She heard the hot water running, felt her clothing come off, welcomed the steam in the bath as though an old friend had returned.

By the time dawn broke at six she was fully awake, sipping the second cup of coffee Misha'd brought.

"Breakfast will be served," he announced, "in thirty minutes exactly. We shall be having," he continued, trying to keep them both alert, "corn muffins, bananas and coffee."

"Not more coffee," she said, putting her head back as she closed her eyes.

"Caroline?"

"Mmmm?"

"No sleeping yet..."

"Twenty minutes, Misha..."

"No."

"Twenty quick ones."

"Twenty questions first," he said, putting his cup down with a clatter. "I feel the need of a challenge."

"It's too early."

"Half a challenge then. Ten questions. Divided equally." He opened the drapes wide, letting the dawn in. "There must be something you want to know about me."

Pensively, after a long pause: "There is, Misha."

"Good."

"Did you call the police last night?"

He was not prepared for the question.

"Did you tell anyone?"

"That's your second question."

"Answer it anyway."

"Does it really matter?"

She nodded.

A thin shaft of light played on the wide oak-plank floor.

"That's your first question, by the way."

More than alert, he thought, and it pleased him, although she was asking a thing he had hoped to postpone. After a moment, though, he replied honestly, "No."

"Why not?"

"Because there would have been questions. Intrusions. People would have assumed perhaps..."

"That I had done it on purpose?"

He chose not to answer.

"Did *you* think so?"

Gently, begging the question nevertheless: "I know only how the night can beguile, and that you are here now, and well," and with that he bent down to her and kissed her mouth.

"Mikhail…"

"I just wanted to test your temperature."

She smiled weakly, letting her head fall back.

"No sleeping," he warned.

"I am not sleeping. Merely wondering…"

"How is it that I found you?"

"That I already know. You are never lost. No," she insisted, "I should like to know how it is that you won…I should by all rights be gone. I think I did glimpse that place you described – silent, eternal, and then there was light again, and a rushing sound, and a force pulling me back against my will it seemed, because nothing matters when that peace begins, that absence of unseemly pain – what the trees in my orchard must feel when the frost comes, as it must."

There was silence.

"Mikhail, *tell me*. Why were you not denied?"

"You should perhaps thank *Serena*," he said at last, thoughtfully. "Sleekest, most elegant girl in the world."

"The love of your life?"

"A boat I had once. Close friends had bought her…Then they left for Antigua. I agreed to sail it on over while the autumn was fine still. Crew of two to assist. Not the first time I'd done it. Routine as a matter of fact, or so it seemed to me when I left England."

He had never before remembered precisely.

"Southampton…the Azores…and then a storm came up mid-Atlantic which was anything but routine. Larger ships than mine went down that night, into waves so immense they seemed like a shoreline, so that I had to steer clear of them, ride them high if I could, hoping my boat wouldn't break while I sent up flares and radioed out and then all I had left were the flares because sheets of rain interrupted the rest."

He shifted his weight in the chair, as though burdened heavily by what remained.

"Dead reckoning, Caroline. Not once had it failed me – not heading into snows off the North Sea, not in the South Pacific, not in the Strait of Magellan, only ship in high winds."

He took in a deep breath here, tried in vain to avoid her gaze and then almost offhandedly: "It failed me in the Atlantic, south-southwest of the Azores, when *Serenita*" – the diminutive expressed a tenderness that had perhaps gone down with her – "took a wave twice her size. She couldn't right herself – that was clear in the lightning – and I was glad in a way when I felt her stop fighting.

"In the roar of the sea my men's voices diminished. I lost them. She too was soon lost – split in two when I looked, struck by another wave that recalled some sheared cliff at night.

"I was picked up at dawn, holding on to my woman, a plank from the prow that had somehow survived."

Wedges of sunlight, ever-widening, spilled across Michael's chair.

"Well!" he concluded, somehow still in that even tone which belied the sweat once again on his face. "Since you asked, Caroline…I was not about to lose you. No," he repeated firmly, "I would not be cheated a third time," and then he suddenly stopped, never dreaming she'd already transcribed the first time, seat 39 B out of France.

"Time for breakfast," he murmured, slipping away from her while he could.

She ate well. He was pleased. They both slept some then, he in his chair beside her, she on the sofa. By noon, as he watched her eat again, he felt he could make inquiry, carefully, as to her plans for the future, for the events of the past days had shown him – beyond question – that she needed assistance.

"Max heard from Antonin," he began, "that you've made plans for the next months."

"Some plans, Misha, yes."

"Please let me help you."

She thought for a moment. "Yes. Yes, there is one thing you can do."

"Anything."

"Bless the endeavour."

"What?"

"A benediction. Today. When everything's star-crossed. It would mean all the world to me to hear you say to me now, as a sailor might say – 'Godspeed.'"

"Godspeed with the mill you mean?"

She nodded.

"Even should the river freeze?"

"Yes."

"And the money run out?"

"Yes."

"And no one left to help you?"

He meant should the worst of all storms come up – a second one, without warning, from which there would be no reprieve.

"Yes, Mikhail," she said fervently, for the third time.

"I am prepared to do more."

"That in itself – "

"That in itself will not suffice."

He took his chequebook from his pocket.

"This may not either…"

She stared at the amount he'd filled in.

"But it will get heat in there, water at least…"

"*Fifty thousand dollars?*"

"*Serena* was insured for more."

"That was another time."

"And now again one plank remains. Nothing more, Caroline. You haven't a prayer of saving your land unless you rent this place quickly, and while you can rent it furnished, for a significant sum, your tenants might not have bargained on the owner thrown in."

"The owner has a plan."

"Staying with Max?"

"Another plan."

"A second job? The night shift somewhere? You're working eight days of the week as it is."

She flushed. He was pleased to see it – not because she was desperate and he knew it – but because she was well enough to turn that shade. He reached over and removed the afghan.

"I don't want you burning up on me."

The gesture had been gentle, exquisitely so, but as it was she owed him her life.

"It would be a gift," he said softly, as though reading her mind.

She shook her head.

"I would expect nothing."

"Of course you would not."

"Then we're agreed?"

"Mikhail…"

"Tell me –"

"There are some jewels left," she confided. "Not in the house – that's gone with the wind – but in a bank vault downtown. Plus the ones over there. I had them on New Year's Eve. Well, they might not ransom a king, but they'll get me started, you'll see. There's a way out of this mess."

"But in the meantime…"

She put two fingers on his mouth. "You have rescued Eurydice. That is enough."

He stood on her porch late that night, longing to kiss her again, fearful his mouth would oblige her somehow, in spite of her pride.

"Caroline," he said instead, "there's no date on that cheque I left on your desk."

"You left the cheque on my desk?"

"Should you ever have need – I mean should that raft of yours not be rescued…"

"Plank," she corrected.

"At that point will you cash it?"

She gazed at the fields which no longer seemed hostile.

"Yes," she said simply. "Yes I will, Mikhail."

⁓ ☾ ⁓

Claire Tierney was frantic. Since Christmas Eve she had searched her apartment, turning each room inside out, but the photograph of *Half Moon* was simply not to be found. In the end she concluded it had somehow slipped from her desk – she had a habit of leaving the window ajar in her study, preferring even winter's breeze to the stale solitude of her apartment – and so for sure it had fallen of all things into the trash, only to be discarded by the cleaning lady in the morning.

But what to tell Roger? How to confess to him that there was no image of the portrait she had insisted he buy?

"They simply wouldn't allow it," she explained to him, dismayed. "Well, you know how the twins are. I knew they were hoarding a masterpiece, driving the price up, whetting the appetite of every buyer in the market. Nevertheless my hands were tied."

Starchly, after a moment: "The painting is there still, I presume."

"Unless someone's bought it."

Roger leaned back in his chair, took out his Hermès silk pocket square – one of a dozen he had – and cleared his small rimless glasses. It was a habit of his, wiping his spectacles with those scarves, as though the tiny creatures depicted were also on his payroll, prepared to improve both his vision and his insight.

They did both then it appeared, for after another pause he reached for his pen, opened the slim upper drawer of his mahogany desk and reached for his chequebook.

Claire was taken aback.

No date, no amount, signed simply, *Roger Gachet*.

"*Half Moon* is mine, Claire, understood?"

"But it may have been bought by now."

"If it's been bought track it down."

"Roger, at this point…"

"Do whatever it takes. Go wherever you must," he insisted, fixing his olive-grey eyes on her. "Pay whatever I'd pay, Claire. I trust you."

It was then that Claire knew. She had triumphed. In the absence of a photo – in the eagerness of the twins to hide what was clearly the jewel in their crown – Roger's desire had turned into obsession, a transition he frowned upon when it happened to colleagues.

He made no effort to stem the tide though, lost as he was, coveting a woman he had never seen – ideal form in a frame owned by some shrewd competing collector.

"I'll leave tonight then, with your permission."

"Yes, yes go. Go at once."

"I'll call as soon as I can."

"Just bring her back with you, Claire."

"*Désolé, Mademoiselle,*" said Auguste Durand the following day. "Nothing has changed since the last time we spoke. *Demi Lune* is not for sale."

"Someone has bought it?"

"Someone still wants it."

"Then the work is in play still."

"*Hélas, non.*"

Claire glanced around the main gallery of Frères Durand, Inc.

"There's the pair you liked so," offered Armand.

"Despite the bids we have had," said Auguste.

"Pair?" asked Claire distractedly, studying the exhibition still.

"The abstract, black, gold and mauve – the matching vase and flowered shawl…"

"I do not see them displayed here."

"Still in the storeroom, Mademoiselle," said Auguste as he offered his arm.

Thus it was that Claire gained access to the storeroom again – that narrow corridor of treasures between the frail cage and the framing room.

Thus it was too that she saw a wrapped parcel, addressed to the artist, care of a Dr. Jean-Paul Meurice, Honfleur, Normandie.

⹌ ☾ ⹍

"Normandy, yes," Claire shouted over the phone that afternoon. "The artist wants it back, it seems."

"Impossible."

"His address was on the wrapping."

Static interrupted Roger's initial response.

"On the other hand," she heard him at last say, "final adjustments can sometimes be called for. Clients can be demanding. Claire, have I lost you again?"

"Not as yet."

"Claire, please speak up."

"I'm still here," she called into the phone.

"Some buyers don't pay 'til they're pleased," he went on pensively, as though she had whispered. "Some painters can't please them. The artist falls off his stride, doubts his inspiration, parts with a treasure he had once thought above trade."

Claire was then searching for her timetable westward.

"Book a train to the coast. Express to Rouen perhaps. Or Le Havre. Or whatever's the best local to –"

"I have it all here," Claire assured him.

"Call me when you have more."

Roger hung up the telephone, polished his lenses and stared at the midday Fifth Avenue crowds. Suddenly – it always startled him – the intercom buzzer beside his telephone rang.

"Your one o'clock, Monsieur."

"It's ten 'til."

"Shall I ask her to wait?"

Roger glanced at his agenda. "No," he replied, sitting straight up in his chair.

"Have her come up directly."

This was indeed an event. He'd seen the husband often enough, twice in fact since the museum gala in November, both meetings resulting in exceptional acquisitions for La Ronde – but he had never yet met the wife.

She was lovely, he'd heard. Accomplished. Somewhat elusive. She was also – but this had only recently come to his ever-vigilant attention – soon to be the former Mrs. Devereux.

He sighed, recalling his Corsican father's favourite proverb: *Castello diviso, due capanne*. Time and again it had proved only too true. *Castle divided, two huts*, he said again to himself, as he repeated the circular motion that cleared both his judgment and his eyewear. Under no circumstances was she coming to buy. Few of them did at this point. On that sad fact alone he'd built a large part of La Ronde.

"Monsieur Gachet?" he heard from the doorway.

Roger turned back in his chair.

"I am early. Forgive me."

"No, no, come in," he replied, offering his hand instead of a greeting, for it had occurred to him as he stood that he didn't know how she wished to be called.

She smiled, slipped off her gloves and placed a dark-grey suede purse on his mahogany desk.

"I may as well disappoint you directly," she said.

"I should prefer it if you took more time."

"You are gracious, Monsieur."

His fine white hand dismissed the compliment.

"Above all discreet. That too I've been told. As you can see, I've done my homework."

Roger wondered if her source was the husband who'd left her. Most likely not, he decided. Women of former means followed their own paths to La Ronde.

"I have not come to buy," she managed after a moment.

"There are many reasons to visit La Ronde."

Caroline nodded.

"How can I help you, Madame?"

She opened her purse, took out a black velvet box, unclasped the lock and lifted the lid.

Roger Gachet knew at once that the sapphires were priceless – earrings, necklace, ring and bracelet to match, all set in diamonds and white filigreed gold, all shown to advantage on thick taupe silk folds.

She inched the box toward him, silk hinges straining, midnight stones glinting in midwinter's light.

"For years they were mine," she said forthrightly. "They belong now in another life – a wedding perhaps, a debutante's ball, gift for a wife after the birth of a child."

He looked from the jewels to her face – eyes almost as fine as the gems she had offered.

"I leave the occasion to you. As well as the price," Caroline said. "In fairness though, I must warn you, I'll bargain harder on the latter."

Roger made no response.

"And they must be bought as a set."

"Any other conditions?"

"That is the only one, Monsieur."

He studied the gems for a while, then once more her features, then the exquisite cameo on the black lapel of her suit.

Finally: "I will buy them, Madame. Today. All six pieces."

"You have miscounted, Monsieur…"

"I think not…"

"There are five."

"Six, including the cameo."

She stiffened.

He smiled.

"Surely Madame could see I could not take my eyes from it."

Mrs. Devereux made no answer, a silence that in no way disconcerted Roger Gachet. Under the circumstances, he knew, some women – often the sentimental ones – came to him reluctant to part with their favourite piece. Frequently it was their finest piece.

They had little choice in the end, and he knew it. Still, pride in these things had to be salvaged – a shred of it, somehow – for who knew in what guise the lady might appear next time around? La Ronde was, after all, more a metaphor than a gallery. The circle of life could surprise.

He returned gingerly to the discussion, striking the ideal mixture of commerce and reverence. "Such perfection, Madame, is what

La Ronde has built its name upon. A global name, I might add. Your six pieces will be treasured…"

"My brooch is not for sale, Monsieur."

Roger was moved then, ever so slightly, more to commerce than reverence.

"We said the set, Madame."

"It is not part of the set."

"It matches though…"

"Coincidentally."

Something about her eyes – a sudden darkness, as though colour film had reverted to its black-and-white progenitor – made Roger Gachet forsake reverence.

"Without the cameo…" he observed.

"Without the cameo," she interrupted, "La Ronde can be the owner of five magnificent gems."

He looked again at her face. Trained over the years to recognize even the most finely veiled hunger, he could find none of it there – nothing, no expression – not even a shadow of the despair he'd learned to read like his own name.

"I've taken too much of your time," he heard her say as she stood.

The velvet box was still between them.

"Though I shall always thank you for your kindness…"

"Mrs. Devereux…"

"Along with your expertise. Most comprehensive. A reputation well-deserved, Monsieur."

She reached for the purse on his desk.

He placed a hand on her arm. "There is no need for such haste."

"On the contrary…"

The little clasps on the velvet box made a faintly perceptible click as they closed.

"Other galleries are prepared to buy the sapphires today. They are not La Ronde of course." She shrugged, placing the gems in her purse. "One cannot always have the best in this life."

Two disappointments in the space of an hour. Roger was beside himself. First *Half Moon* – so elusive – and now these fine gems about to slip through his hands.

Worse – the thought was distraction – perhaps the same buyer was after both acquisitions. That new gallery facing La Ronde – its owner unpolished, yet in his crude way successful...It would not do. He would let her hold on to the brooch, he announced.

"If you're certain," she said demurely, slipping again into her chair.

She will pay for the concession, he promised himself as he peered again into the box.

"As to the price for the set..." He took an immense magnifying glass, its long gold handle shaped like a lizard, and hovered for an eternity over each piece. "Perhaps your appraiser," she offered, breaking the silence, as he knew she must.

"Fifty thousand dollars for the sapphires," he pronounced. "For the set of five, as you have insisted."

She sat back in her chair, crossed her black-stockinged legs, met his gaze directly, and said not a word.

"My own personal cheque. Morgan's next door will cash it, no questions asked. They are accustomed to my ways, Madame."

Mistaking her silence for acquiescence, he once again took out his pen.

"For the set of five," he repeated as he opened his chequebook.

"One hundred thousand, Monsieur."

There was a moment.

"Because you have been so kind" – colour had returned to her eyes – "and because you can value what is beyond price."

He was impressed. She had discounted his capitulation. In fact, though he would never have guessed it from her insistence on the cameo, she was more clever than sentimental, for he had underpriced the gems, and she knew it, and there had been nothing gracious in his offer.

"Sixty-five thousand."

"Eighty, Monsieur, and the set of sapphires is yours."

His pen made a scratching sound as he filled in the amount.

"You have been most discerning," she said winsomely as she rose.

In spite of it all, Roger savoured that smile. Why not? She may have beat him at his game but she was elegant after all, just like her jewels. If he could have such things cheaply – but ah – such things rarely came cheap. She tucked the cheque into her purse. He escorted her down the hall. In the elevator he suggested they stop at floor two, estate jewels, where her glorious set, he insisted, would be most fittingly housed.

The vitrines themselves, Caroline saw, were works of art – Venetian glass, Chinese lacquer, fine French *Empire* woods. Within them were more treasures – emeralds, diamonds, gold that was priceless, jade impossible to replicate.

"My favourite room," Roger whispered, guiding his client toward the left so that she could see the intricate patterns on the display cases there. He moved a bit more to the left, lecturing still, allowing himself to wax erudite in the splendour, his natural habitat after all, when he suddenly noticed that Madame was no longer beside him. She had stopped in mid-room, before a Victorian case, and was staring inside at some pieces displayed there, a stunned expression on her face.

"Ah," murmured Roger as he crossed back beside her. "One of our finest acquisitions."

Her silence spoke volumes in the sparkling hush of the salon.

Castello diviso, he could not help thinking. Her mother-in-law's treasures now belonged to La Ronde. Not her own people, of course. Still…had the marriage endured…

He turned to her. There was a pallor in her cheeks that made her eyes resemble garnets.

"Are you all right, Madame? It is perhaps too warm in here. The lights sometimes…"

"Yes. Yes, I'm fine. Beauty…affects me deeply on occasion."

He was happy to hear this. The affairs of its clients were not, after all, La Ronde's affair – how many times had he stressed this to his staff? – yet some heirlooms, he knew, somehow retained a secret life of their own, haunting the hands that touched them, cursing the hands that bought. Such gems were trouble. With relief then, he chose to believe Madame's explanation.

"Say no more," he replied, linking her arm into his as they walked back toward the hall. "I nearly fainted once at Versailles, from the proportions alone. At Mont-St-Michel…" The elevator arrived; they stepped inside. "I could not speak – just like you today – mute for a day and a half from it all."

It pleased him enormously to share the recollection – a moment of intimacy with a beautiful woman, whose grace – he had to admit it – belied the stubbornness she had displayed.

Wilful gems all, he recalled, as the elevator stopped abruptly, ending his musings at the lobby floor of La Ronde.

$$\sim (\sim$$

"Where to, Miss?" asked the driver.

She couldn't answer. The stunned disbelief she had hidden from Roger erupted at last in the cab. Tears fell hot on her cheeks, over her mouth. Her hands trembled as she fumbled for a handkerchief inside her purse.

"You got a place in mind?"

The sobs she had tried to stifle made him turn back in her direction. He turned back to the road, about to pull to the curb when he heard, "I am so sorry."

"Where to?" he repeated.

She did not know. She belonged to no place.

"Central Park, please. A short ride."

He turned left toward the gates, left again onto the drive that meandered, split in two, then doubled back upon itself – a figure eight in the meadows, beautiful even now, with the earth brown and worn and lengthening shadows matching the buildings that pierced the perimetre's sky.

He turned his radio on. *Chantilly Lace* drifted back. He followed the figure eight like a skater, alone, limbering up before the fans arrived.

The more the cab circled, the more things became clear to her, sitting there, weeping no longer.

Elliot had stolen from her, long before the house burned, before his trip out West, perhaps even before the winter began. Well, it would not have been hard. She'd been away so much. But why not just ask for the gems?

They turned round the carousel, heading southward again, and in the darkening afternoon things became clearer still. He had been planning to leave her, long before he left her – planning with care; that was his way, in spite of the trial and his troubles and the money so rapidly gone.

God only knew what else was gone – what he had slowly taken, systematically – for it had all turned to ash.

"Another spin round the lake, Miss?"

"I – if you've time still."

Two joggers passed by; lovers kissed in the distance; skaters laced up on the bench to the left. The lunch box beside them seemed inviting somehow – comforting, like her safe deposit box in New Salem's main bank.

"Thank God," she thought then. "I can sell those gems at least. I can still, when the time comes, and it will soon…"

Unchained Melody began. She sat bold upright at the refrain. Elliot too had the key to the vault.

"Driver, please! I've got to go back. Can we make it to Grand Central?"

Within an hour, she was in Stamford. After another hour, she was outside her bank, main branch, New Salem.

"Mrs. Devereux," said the manager, with that skittish courtesy people who knew of her troubles used these days. "Of course the vault's open still."

Caroline signed the card, took the key, took a deep breath, opened box 57.

The documents were intact – her father's diploma, her mother's First Communion book, her medical records from the Burn Center in Buenos Aires. There too were the deed to the farm in New Salem, marriage license, rings, naturalization certificate.

And that was it. Nothing more in the box. Jewels her mother had left her – lapis set in white gold, opals, fine rubies – all of it missing.

The closing bell sounded.

As she walked out into the street she put the vault key back into her purse, deep in the zippered compartment where she had also placed Roger's cheque. It was the only one she would receive from him – that much she knew now – but it would cover her taxes, expenses, food and survival a bit, that and her work, while it lasted.

"Can I give you a lift?" asked the manager, uncertainly. No one in town knew where she was living these days, or with whom – just that her house, like her life, had gone up in smoke.

"I'd rather walk now," she insisted, heading off toward the ridge already blue-black in the moon.

The farm was eerily quiet. *Nothing to sell*, was all she could say to herself, over and over again, as the clock in the guest house hallway struck nine, and then ten, and then midnight as she sat there.

Misha's cheque was on the desk still. She hadn't looked at it since he'd left her, three nights before this one, although it seemed more like a year to her when she picked it up and studied it, objectively, as though another person were tracing the figures, written so clearly, while the moon rose even higher on the farm named for her mother.

Claire Tierney strolled the cobblestone harbour quay, glancing into restaurants, peering into studios, wondering which coloured entrance might lead to the offices of Dr. Jean-Paul Meurice, Honfleur, Normandie.

She saw no sign by the awnings, nothing on the corners, not a plaque in the archways leading to the hidden gardens beyond. Thus, nearing noon, she walked away from the quay toward the mariners' church.

Yet again Claire was baffled.

Each narrow street, steep and gracefully curved, paved with precision before the start of the Hundred Years' War, hoarded its secrets. There was not a house to be seen with a Dr. Meurice in the town.

And yet she is here, Claire was sure of it, convinced that *Half Moon* had found its way to the world-class reclusive artist's picturesque hideaway beside the sea.

While the afternoon's light was still clear, she walked again to the quay. Twice she circled it; twice she saw nothing, except for that gaunt man by his easel painting abstract shapes by the boats. His right hand was unsteady, though it moved with a curious confidence across the canvas before him. His left hand – odd, ineffectual appendage by his hips – dangled, as though by inclination, toward the cobblestones beneath him.

One more time she passed. By now the man's blanket had slipped. As she stopped to glance at his canvas – he was retouching his cloth still – she could see that his old cane-backed seat had large wheels.

The new year's uncertain first sun slowly dipped, and then its virgin sky paled, and the harbour turned cold, and Claire Tierney just stood there, rock-still by those paints.

⌒☾⌐

"L'exposition McCallister – c'est par ici?" she recalled asking, not long before that, at a November retrospective not far from the Hôtel de Crillon.

"Oui, Madame. Tout droit, puis à gauche," she'd been told, and she had followed those directions, straight ahead, then to the left, and she had seen that same hand – not in the process of creating, to be sure, as she was seeing it now, but in the works displayed.

"The sun has gone down, Monsieur," called a trim housekeeper from the doorway.

Jude McCallister kept on painting.

"Perhaps you should finish now."

"Yes. Yes, I will finish. Just as soon as I get the indigo blue of that doorway facing the quay."

Marie-Claude retreated.

Claire Tierney stayed where she was.

Jude McCallister finished his work – an astonishing, subliminal rendering of the fine huddled houses – shapes, nothing more, improbable colours, all defying the sea.

Slowly, with effort, he began cleaning his brush.

Winter's sun disappeared.

Claire Tierney approached and asked, "Why not sign that, Mr. McCallister?"

Jude merely stared at her, too startled to answer. Far too often still, his memory failed him. Names, places, events blurred in his mind, although never before this moment had he forgotten a face. Features, in his painter's head, had remained incontrovertible. For a moment he seemed lost. Confusion passed over his face. Was even that stronghold to be surrendered he wondered, despairing?

"We have never met," said Claire Tierney, seeing the sudden anguish in his eyes. "Although I know your work – more than most people do, I think – I would know it anywhere, anytime…"

"Even here?" he asked after a moment, and it touched her, for she knew he meant "even now?"

"Anywhere," she repeated.

He looked away for a moment, first at the wavy reflection of the coloured houses in the water, then at the bold brilliant strokes with which he had recovered them.

"I cannot sign," he confessed, pointing with his brush to the lower left-hand corner of the painting. "I cannot sign now, that is. The way I always have, clearly. Soon, though," he added hastily, turning back to her, and it was then that she realized that whatever had happened to him had happened recently.

Once more Marie-Claude approached the chair by the boats.

"Monsieur Jude," she said gently, "the tides have now changed; the winds will come up, and at that point..." she stopped, looking quizzically at the woman beside him, for she had been told by Dr. Le Brun that Jude's only requirement was inviolate privacy.

"Marie-Claude," Jude replied, feeling a social obligation – first such imperative he had experienced since he had awakened in November. "This is..." he fumbled a bit..."This is," he repeated, and then he too stopped abruptly. He hadn't a clue who the stranger was – only that she knew him, or rather his work, which for most of his life had been one and the same.

"I am Claire," she supplied.

"Mademoiselle Claire," Jude continued, "who was passing my chair and knew me somehow – somehow still in my work."

"More than ever," Claire murmured.

Jude glanced at the canvas. "Perhaps you are right," he replied, with a barely perceptible hint of the old pride, for though he could not write his name yet – not as he had always done – he could judge precisely what he had painted, as he had always done, knowing the failures from the successes and the ones in between. That afternoon he had succeeded.

Marie-Claude nodded in Claire's direction, her silence cool, not impolite – merely indicative of her uncertainty. For reasons she could not fathom, Jude somehow seemed pleased by the sudden intrusion. She could not possibly guess, although she had come to know his ways by then, that a bedrock loneliness had seized his soul as he had painted that afternoon – something akin to a great animal's hunger. He himself could barely define it. He only knew that it was there, an immense thing, caused perhaps by his ordeal, vivid still, or his black need to paint, or the cosmic solitude of his convalescence, or the woman who haunted his days and his nights still.

Whatever it was, bereft as he was, he surprised Marie-Claude and Claire Tierney and himself above all when he suggested abruptly, "Mademoiselle Claire, won't you join me for tea?"

"I should like that, Mr. McCallister."

"Please. I am Jude."

"Jude, then," she repeated, as she followed behind the chair Marie-Claude wheeled into the studio.

They had their tea by the round table near the large windows overlooking the sea. Jude conversed freely – the thickening around his tongue had diminished greatly in the last weeks – speaking of the attack, the operation, Dr. Le Brun and Germaine and their unstinting ministrations. He did not, however, mention the parcel, still wrapped, hidden beneath a blanket, leaning against the floor by his paints. Nor did he mention the woman caught once and for all and forever without her drape there.

It was Claire in the end who brought up the painting. She had looked around as they'd entered, seen other works here and there, some from the retrospective, some from Frères Durand, Inc., a few from this new abstract stage he was in, but of *Half Moon* – the masterpiece, the one she had come to the Normandy coast for – there was still not a trace.

Marie-Claude placed an apple tart from the fruit of the nearby orchards between them. Claire sliced their pieces, Jude's into smaller bits, for she had seen that he had managed to drink from his cup – cautiously, but very neatly, and that for sure he could eat.

She was right, though from time to time she looked away, so that he would not guess she'd sensed the effort.

"You have many paintings here, Jude," she observed, glancing around again after they'd finished their tea. "Most of them I know well."

"You have been diligent, Claire."

"Well I am not, after all, just a tourist on the beach," she laughed. "As I explained, I work for La Ronde in New York. You have perhaps met Roger Gachet."

Jude's expression became clouded. No doubt they had met, perhaps many times, but it was a name that had not yet returned to his head.

"My superior," she explained. "He has sent me often to France. I went for days to your exhibition last fall, then twice to your agents in Paris – each time in search of your best piece for La Ronde."

"Frères Durand has a large selection."

"Yes."

"You will no doubt find something."

"I want the best," Claire repeated.

"Hard to define," Jude reflected, wiping the crumbs from his chest. "Some buyers want one thing, others another; some leave without buying at all," he went on, surprised at the fluency with which he was speaking. Well, it was a subject of interest, after all. And she seemed so keen on his things.

"I will speak to the Durands – tell them you want something fine. They'll find you something," he promised.

"Jude," she said finally, placing her cup down as the sun set, "I already know what I want."

"Well then I'll tell them exactly."

"I *have* told them."

"Is it the price then?"

"It's not for sale."

Jude's face paled.

"Never, not in your lifetime. I was told that distinctly as I happened by chance upon the portrait in the storeroom of Frères Durand. Well of course, as we both know, things are always for sale. It is a stunning work, Jude – your finest, without question – a nude woman, a mirror, a bell jar, a cat – and if indeed it is available, if I've a chance for it still, Jude…" She stopped. "I will pay what you ask – it is worth what you ask…I…Jude?" she repeated, for he was staring fixedly at her, his blue eyes having turned a deep charcoal somehow.

"Jude, are you all right?"

He made no answer.

"Shall I perhaps call Marie-Claude?"

Claire Tierney stood, about to rush to the main room, when with the hand he had not moved in four months, he detained her.

"Claire, please. Sit down, Claire."

She again took her seat, slowly, for his grip was intense, astonishing the two of them. After a moment he released her, though his hand stayed on the table. His darkened eyes remained intense; his expression was clear; he appeared to be seeing something other than the space they shared. After what seemed a long time he spoke, as though to conjure the most potent of recollections precisely, relive it somehow, perhaps break its spell.

"Did you have a long look?"

Claire nodded.

"Then you know she was lovely."

"Yes."

"Hard to capture in her passions, for she would not be forth-coming, at least not at first, and so we had to fight to the death for the disclosure I needed, so that I could paint her as she truly is – unashamed now and free."

Claire watched in amazement as he shaped every syllable, perfectly, not even a hint of the beating that had made speech such a struggle.

"Feral, I'd say, Claire, with those magnificent markings that proclaimed her uniqueness. Still, in that struggle –" his hand again gripped her arm, "although I painted as I never had, never will…"

Claire shook her head.

"Victory was hers. I learned to prize something – someone – more than my work, more than my paints, my life – though I fought hard for my life, because once she had shared it…Yes, the triumph was hers. In the end I loved without measure, desperately – which is the only way, I suppose. Even now – I…Now of course she is a memory. That is all she can ever be. *Half Moon*, nothing more."

As abruptly as he had begun Jude McCallister fell silent. The room was utterly still. Never in her calculating, carefully programmed young life had Claire felt such sadness – sadness for the love lost, the art lost, the fierce struggle behind and the fiercer ones still to come – sadness of all things for herself that afternoon, for never having known what he had known, for never having lost herself, surrendering everything, even the things she most prized – thereby finding herself.

"There is always the portrait," she managed.

"Not for sale," was his simple reply.

"No. No, of course not," she responded, having heard in his confession, albeit an echo, grander harmonies than she had ever imagined. "I didn't mean to imply, Jude – I mean you should never, not in your lifetime, even consider parting with..." she fumbled. "Forgive me. I do not know the lady's name."

"*Half Moon*," he repeated.

"*Half Moon*, yes. She is yours and should remain so."

By now the sky had turned grey. Jude lit the lamp by his chair.

"Jude, I must go," she said after a moment.

He seemed to be struggling – not in his body so much but in some darker place.

So as to reassure him – for she thought perhaps he was concerned lest his secrets, and above all his portrait, become known – she swore, "I will tell no one of our conversation. Not even that I've seen you, Jude. I'll simply say – well, I suppose I'll tell Roger that the painting has indeed been sold, and that I'll find him another. Two perhaps. There are two still for sale, both of them yours, very beautiful – one a still life, one an abstract – meant to be a pair, I think."

"Yes."

"She inspired them both," murmured Claire, her statement part question.

"That," Jude replied, "you must judge for yourself."

Claire was puzzled at first, then almost frightened, for she could see that he had pushed his chair from the table as though he intended to stand.

"There is a cane by the wall, Claire, next to the easel, behind a parcel under some blankets. Perhaps – if you would be so kind..."

He *was* going to stand, she could see that now and somehow she knew he had not stood before, not since the beating, and she grew still more fearful. How to deny him? How to let him risk a fall? There might be more breakage – damage for sure that could not be repaired. She would call Marie-Claude after all.

He seemed to have read her thoughts.

"Please," he said, hoarsely, so that the whisper seemed oddly

loud, "while there is some light left, and you are still here to look –
look *again*, I should say, for you have already seen, and plan to take
back with you other versions."

He fixed his eyes on her then, and she saw monstrous passions
as well as great grief in those depths. And then, for the first time in
her life, she was totally lost.

At last, she decided. "I will bring you the parcel."

"I wish to go to it, Claire." His gaze had remained unflinching.
"This is the day it was to happen, why you came to Honfleur, why I
was restless all morning. I wanted to walk again, starting today."

Such a simple explanation. And as definitive as his work. And
Claire Tierney then, mesmerized by his intensity, or perhaps undone
by his desperation, crossed to the easel, pushed back the blanket,
stared at the parcel remembered, and returned, almost mechanically,
with the cane to Jude's chair.

"Let me help you at least."

"There is no need."

Despite his insistence, she stood by his chair while he seemed
to gather his strength – he had once been a powerful man, with
enormous reserves of intense concentration, and as he stared at the
parcel, he seemed to be mustering – if not those lost things – at least
enough of their memory to enable him to have his way.

Have his way Jude did that day. He made a blistering effort to
stand, waving Claire off as she reached, and then he walked to his
painting, and leaned on the wall as he unwrapped it and placed it
onto his easel, where it belonged.

And then he just stood there, as though unveiling it for the first
time, and she truly did think he would fall, for he swayed a bit, but
then he was still.

"Now, Mademoiselle, now you can come and stand by me, and
if you do not mind, I shall lean on your arm, and we will both look.
You've come so far, after all. I can at least give you that."

She was already beside him by then, feeling his weight or his
strength, she was not sure which, just determination on her forearm
as they both gazed in wonder.

"More beautiful than I remember," Claire breathed. "Not just the woman. She is, of course –" Claire broke off. "I mean the rendering. That awakening caught. God, Jude," she added, laying her hand on his damaged one. "No wonder you've fought so." She had wanted to say "loved so," but did not dare use those intrusive words, and besides – as he had already confessed – in his case they were one and the same.

When they parted, he was back in his chair. Marie-Claude had brought sherry, noticed the painting, thought that Claire had unveiled it, pronounced it exquisite.

On the following morning, when Germaine arrived just after nine, she was stunned to see Jude once again by his easel, cane in his hand, standing, slightly sturdier than the night before.

Claire was by then in Paris. Roger had instantly taken her call. She had had to work hard then, harder than ever it seemed, convincing him in the end that the pair – which she insisted she had not seen before – remained the true masterpieces of the collection. In any case – and this she had had to repeat several times, each version louder, until he had digested his disappointment – *Half Moon* had indeed been sold: private collector, no longer in play, never to belong to La Ronde.

"The pair, then," he finally sighed, like a cirrus cloud crossing the sea. "Bring me something back, Claire. Something grand – signed McCallister."

"Yes. Yes I will do that Roger. Guaranteed."

All she could remember as she hung up the receiver was that he could not sign his name yet, not as he always had, though what he was again painting surpassed grand.

ADAGIO

"Max, do you ever design still?" Caroline asked on the day after her trip to the bank vault in New Salem.

"I haven't designed in six years."

"But if a client were to come to you – not with a grand scheme, of course – something trivial…insignificant," she coloured. "Well of course nobody would."

"Somebody did. Four decades ago. A little boy's tree house, carved out of redwood, fitting into the leaves so discreetly that the boy's father – mayor of Nice at the time – never could find the child when it was time for his chores."

As though the boy were hidden nearby still, Max smiled.

"There was also the bird cage…"

"The boy had a bird cage?"

"Separate commission. Downtown Antibes. Little canary would never sing unless he thought he was free. I made him think he was free."

Max reflected, placing his cup down.

"A space that sets someone free. My best designs, I suppose, came down to that in the end. Mind you the bird was not charged.

Nor was the owner. I've worked for my supper sometimes, sometimes even less – nothing at all if the project fulfilled me."

Absently, Caroline stirred her coffee.

"Yes," he confirmed. "If the project fulfilled me – I would design even now, for the sheer joy of it all."

They returned to their work. She spoke no more of his designs – indeed, she would never say more – Max by then knew her pride – yet he had seen how her eyes had deepened as he had reminisced.

When she went downstairs for her rest, he took up his sketchpad and pencils, for from Antonin he had had a full description of the stone mill in the woods. He moved his hand quickly over the large sheets of paper – interior views, exterior views, hints of a river, water wheel alongside. He was still sketching, in fact, when Caroline reappeared to begin their revisions.

She walked toward the daybed, wondering at the fact that he had never glanced up as she approached. She was even more perplexed when he remained looking down, hand working swiftly, room utterly silent as the winter sun weakened, then disappeared below the rooftops.

At last he paused, letting his pencil fall as he looked up, startled it seemed to see her beside him, for he had imagined her so intensely inside the shapes he'd just made.

He studied her face for a moment, then the length of her body, so that she felt herself colour again beneath his gaze. Once more he reached for his pencil, made an adjustment, then flipped the page over and touched up the next sheet.

"Yes, yes now I am seeing," he murmured. "A place that sets someone free. One alone for each person…each lifetime."

She dared not move in her chair, let alone speak, transfixed as she was by the sight of Max the artist at work, never vouchsafed her until that afternoon.

Finally he stopped, handed over his sketchbook, and said simply, "What do you think?"

Pictured faithfully there, as though for months it had been her life not his they had rendered, were the only things left to her still – the water wheel, the veranda, the river in the foreground, suggestions of trees in the rear. Max had never once seen those stones, nor that uncertain terrain, and yet there they were, absolutely correct, as was the mill, standing as it had stood for centuries, yet at the same time renewed.

On the next page, at first glance, nothing at all had been changed, for the number of rooms and their configuration remained the same.

Magically, though, Max had altered the whole. He had designed a small hallway to shelter the entrance. He'd taken a part of the kitchen, created a bath, found a space for a smaller bath in the tiny attic above. *New study*, he'd written, where the old grain room had been. Where the old bedroom remained, he'd added only some dormers – *for solar heat, and a view of the woods*, he had noted.

Just as Antonin had described them, he had sketched in the rope bed, the mat, the blue and white pitcher on the table beside them. Somehow, he thought, the room would seem ready that way – unchanged since the days when others had lived there. That she had been found on those ropes once, he had never learned from Mikhail.

Caroline turned to the third and last page. There, figured exactly, were well-water sites, potential ducts for the heat, insulation plans, utility lines. Across the top margin were more detailed instructions. Mathematical computations crammed the side borders.

The silence seemed long to Maximilian as she pored over each page.

"It's just a draft," he began.

"Max…"

"A first one."

"Maximilian –" she repeated, and then she fumbled, for she had never once used his full name.

"Are the rooms not correct?"

All she could do then was nod.

"Then you believe it might do?"

The question was posed so artlessly, yet with such undisguised fervour, that she clearly saw other rooms, another time, a child soon expected, Max redesigning his home for a wife soon to leave.

"There would be no fee, of course..."

"Dearest Max..."

"None whatsoever."

She shook her head.

"Do you mean to say – "

"No."

"No?"

"I couldn't possibly. Not from you, Max...*not this*..."

"Caroline," he interrupted. "You and I both know there is no longer much time left." He waved his hand round the room, roughly it seemed, for he did not mean the room, nor even their work, but the precious fact of them together. "I have to make sure you are free, which means the right space. Otherwise, later, I mean...when I can no longer accompany," he felt compelled to add with a smile, "you won't sing."

She looked into his face at that moment and suddenly saw no longer an old man, but an artist of no age, timeless in talent as well as his passions. And then it was clear. From as far back as that first day, when she had taken his pen in her hand and he had said to her, simply, "Let us begin," their singular love affair had continued – uninterrupted, unexpected, indissoluble, unique. To be sure it was never a union such as the one she had forged on Jude's bed in Paris – Max had kissed her hand only once, and that time in farewell. This was a different thing, finer perhaps, for unlike an embrace it could not dissipate. That Max desired her fiercely she was not yet aware. She chose instead to see only a most extraordinary synchronicity, souls so intertwined that a corruption of that union seemed unthinkable, gross. Yet in some vague way she was afraid, as though what could not even be imagined had somehow been decreed.

He saw the shadow pass over her face.

"You will owe nothing, Caroline."

"But I will, Max," she cried. "You and I both know – forgive me, those were your words, but I am accustomed to giving them back to you – one must pay for one's freedom! You have to allow me to do that. I can't now, I admit it. Somehow though, *someday* your plans..."

"I've no claim to your *somedays*," was Maximilian's response, almost savagely said as he turned and stared at the frost clinging still to the dogwoods out in the court.

She uttered his name, but he remained facing away.

"Max," she repeated.

"Will you barter?" he suddenly asked.

"Barter?"

"Artistic exchange," he said, turning back. "Common enough in my trade."

Seeing her puzzled he leaned in, confiding: "I don't know Latin. I studied it decades ago, yes, but in a lazy and indifferent way, and the loss has been mine ever since. Above all the poets. One in particular...I've had translations, of course. Meagre ones. Certainly not what the lark does by instinct."

Wonderingly: "How did you remember that?"

"I remember it all – every proud fierce thing you said that first day. 'Sound to fit the sense exactly, Monsieur.' Lord, you were angry. I thought you were going to kill me, or leave me, and I feared only the latter because I so desperately wanted what you said you could provide."

She felt a grip on her arm not unlike the way he'd detained her that day.

"I should like it again, Caroline...Catullus. In exchange for my plans." He stopped. "Such a poet might require a castle, though..."

"You've just designed one," she smiled.

"Then we're agreed?"

Maximilian waited.

"I have coveted those poems for a lifetime, Mrs. Devereux."

"Then you shall have them, Max. Every one of them. Elegant larks to fill your tree house."

"*Your* tree house."

She nodded. Max thought he saw that strange shadow pass over her face. But in an instant she smiled again – ever so wistfully though – that too he perceived.

"Mine at long last, Maximilian. Yes."

⁔ ☾ ⌐

During lunch the next day, Mikhail sensed Caroline's unease. Max too noticed something – a hesitation in her manner as he presented his sketches.

No doubt concerned about the costs entailed, he concluded, and so he said gently to Misha, "Caroline will need a contractor. Perhaps you can provide this one kindness, Mikhail."

"I will give it some thought."

"Mind you don't suggest one of your globetrotting designers. Competent shipbuilder, that's what we're after. My plans are simple, after all."

"Yes."

Soup was served. Max was buoyant. She would remain at Todd's Farm. It could be paid for. She'd have her work still, a bonus, income from the guest house, proceeds from some sale she was planning. This last fact he had heard, in strictest confidence, from Antonin Onegin, although like Antonin, he was unclear as to the details.

"Heirlooms she is willing to part with, that's all I know, Max," he had been told. "Enough though, she is certain, for the little mill house she needs."

Of the theft from the bank vault Max hadn't the slightest suspicion. Not even Antonin had been informed. Only Mikhail knew why she had accepted his gift.

A loan, not a gift, she later said to herself, as Max and his son continued to study the sketches. *I will tell Mikhail when the chance comes. I will insist on official papers. The debt will be paid in time. Max need never know who provided the money.*

With these thoughts Caroline tried to banish the vague discomfort that had recurred. Not until Max offered port with dessert, which Misha accepted, uncharacteristically, did she begin to perceive there was nothing vague in her dread. She feared collusion, a betrayal of Max which under no circumstances could be allowed. What she did not see, or rather refused to accept, was that the opportunity to prevent it had long since come and gone.

Max returned to his room for his rest; Mikhail took his leave; Elsa by then had gone off to the market and so the house was utterly still as Caroline opened the library door, sensed a presence in the dimness and found Mikhail in the shadows seated at Maximilian's desk.

"Misha," she warned.

"You looked lovely at lunch."

"This cannot be."

"It already is."

"The money, I mean – the mill house…"

"I am prepared to give more."

"No! You have already been too kind. You must allow me now…"

The front door opened slowly. She put her hand to his lips.

"Elsa Varig," she mouthed.

The heavy boots were not Elsa's.

Antonin, heading for the kitchen, turned at the library door and saw Mikhail at Maximilian's desk. Caroline was already seated in the armchair beside him.

"Antonin?" she called as he passed. He made no answer.

"Antonin, why don't you join us? Mikhail is reviewing Maximilian's design for the mill."

"Don't figure they need much reviewing."

"Nevertheless…"

"Got my own work to do," he insisted, noting the flush in her cheeks – brazen, out of place there, like Mikhail Alexander at Maximilian's desk.

He turned from the doorway and headed straight for the kitchen. There, seated on a high stool by the counter, he carefully sharpened his carpenter's knives, using Elsa's latest equipment, as he did each Friday night. Then once again stillness, forcing Caroline to whisper.

"So will you allow me to sign a paper?"

"No."

"Gentlemen's agreement then."

"You are a lady."

She sat back in her chair. He studied the filigrees on her cameo, recalling the marks she had shown him on that Christmas Eve car ride.

"There is another solution," she heard as his eyes wandered still, almost in spite of himself, to the breast – covered now – which she had displayed on that ride. The memory of that night caused a yearning for her mouth again, for her body – so cold once when he'd found her, so full of life when they'd parted, when he had promised her he would take nothing – yet more than ever he wanted.

"A barter," she told him. "Between artists. Common enough in my trade. I've made the same arrangement with your father."

Mikhail stiffened.

"In exchange for his sketches, I have agreed on a translation."

"You have been doing that for months."

"This is different. Catullus. He's always wanted Catullus."

"Yes, well in England one studies Latin…"

"Then Baudelaire. Rilke. Whatever it is your heart desires."

"The money is yours, Caroline," he replied sharply. "And I will find you a builder. And by the spring you will have the house you have sold all your gifts for."

"It wasn't a sale," she said fiercely.

"Whatever."

"And I have offered you the same exchange…"

"I do not want the same things."

Antonin's heavy boots left the kitchen. They could be heard in the dining room, the living room, the entrance to the outer hall. Caroline stood abruptly when he passed outside the library, planning to call him in a second time, but he never glanced in her direction, although the door had been left ajar.

Hearing the outside door close she sank again into her chair. Mikhail remained motionless, having turned from her face to the wall of books on his right.

No way out, Caroline thought, for only that morning the couple who'd seen her guest house had decided to rent it, moving in April first – absolute latest. To return Misha's cheque now would leave her defenceless. Cashing it would strip her bare.

Mikhail studied the books on the wall still. Rain on the window behind him grew heavy. In the storm Caroline grasped for the one straw remaining, although her voice appeared changed, as if another woman were speaking.

"Will you not barter with me, Mikhail?" she heard herself ask one more time.

He knew her by now, and yet he dared not turn to her. She would take nothing without giving, although – and this too he well knew – she had nothing but herself left to give. That she was prepared to do this was clear in the touch of her hand on his arm, at once tentative and insistent, recalling the pressure he'd felt on that Christmas Eve ride to Todd's Farm.

She will lose all but her life for that place, he reflected, *and that too almost once.*

He shuddered at the thought of her stubborn independence, sensing that in the end it would ruin her.

He remembered his promises to protect her, his repeated assurances that she could trust him, and, deeply conflicted – lost at sea in his heart – he wished his phrases unsaid, wished her body undone, wished himself always lost, lust and wilfulness intertwined in an embrace she preferred to call barter.

No, he could not take her that way. Not as payment for a kindness she was unable to endure. Had she felt something akin to his own fire he would have recanted any promise – but it was her pride in that touch, nothing more, and the fact hurt his own pride, and so he decided to ask for another thing. He would see what her painter had seen – nothing more than that, nothing less – but it would cost her a great deal, and she would no longer be beholden, and it would cost him a great deal, and perhaps he would no longer yearn.

"You are determined, then, Caroline," he slowly said to her as he turned.

"Yes, yes I am. For everyone's sake."

"Can you not accept kindness?" he demanded hoarsely, one last time.

"In my lifetime I've had but a passing acquaintance with the term."

He sat back in his chair. It would be done then – that evening – not as she'd offered, but as he himself would insist.

Neither spoke for a moment.

"Rain's gotten heavier," he observed.

"Seems that way."

"Perhaps you shouldn't risk that ride home in this storm."

He fixed his gaze on her, steadily. She made no answer.

"You've stayed before, Caroline. On nights such as this above all."

"Well not on nights such as this…"

"Speak to Max anyway. He'll be relieved you're not riding once again in a storm."

She sat back in her own chair. Collusion between them – what she had wanted most to prevent – was now unavoidable.

Yet there was no turning back. She would give what she had. She would owe no one for her mill house – neither father nor son.

⸎ ☾ ⸎

Max was only too happy to keep Caroline from taking a long ride in the rain. Declining to share a brandy with Max and Mikhail after the concert, she bade them both goodnight by the hall.

"Sleep well," added Mikhail, as she turned away toward the stairs.

She closed but did not bolt the door that led into her room. There would be time, she well knew, and so she slowly undressed, bathed, slipped into a silk robe belonging to Max, then sat at her desk and opened Catullus' *The Lyrics*, slim red leather volume she had found in the library.

The room was utterly still, nearly dark, save for the small red fringed lamp on the desk. For reasons as yet unclear to her, she chose to begin with the eighth poem, perhaps the darkest of the lyrics, certainly the most disturbing, she decided, as rain fell with a vengeance on the ivy-covered windowsill.

Break off, fallen Catullus – time to cut losses, she wrote, translating the poet's fierce words of advice to himself. With effort she rendered his recollections of a great love – passions that had consumed him, lust that had equalled the fabled beauty of his beloved. Capriciously, she had abandoned him. Viciously he had cursed her. The last lines of the lyric – a bitter prediction of despair and loneliness for the woman – seemed on that night of all nights unendurable to Caroline. And yet she continued, rendering the poet's anger, spoken in savage farewell to his Lesbia.

You are ruined. What will your life be? Who will visit your room? Who uncover that beauty? Whom will you love? Whose girl will you be? Whom kiss? Whose lips bite? Enough. Break, Catullus, against the past.

There was a knock at her door.

"It is open."

Mikhail entered.

"You are working…"

"I am finished."

She put her paper aside, closed her volume and stood.

"What were you writing there?"

"Misha, you know that I scribble…"

"Show me your efforts," he said, tossing his coat on the antique red silk chair.

"Did you come here to look at my efforts?" she asked him.

"I came here because you insisted," he said, carefully locking the door.

He crossed, opened her notebook, read through the lyric she'd rendered, then looked at her standing beside him in the shadows a moment.

"Why did you start with the eighth, Caroline?"

"I happen to like it."

"Did you think I would break – as he did – with a woman I loved so?"

"It is a beautiful lyric," she managed. "I only wrote what was there."

He sat in her chair by the desk. She remained standing beside the doorway.

"If you remain so far from me I shall have to shout."

After a moment she approached him.

"Much better," he murmured, reaching up and drawing her closer.

For what seemed to her a long time he studied her, but did not touch her.

"As I remember," he continued, "it was she who left him."

Caroline made no answer.

"Maybe that's why you chose number eight."

"It is not," she replied, barely audible now.

"Then why such a dark thing tonight?" he asked her one more time – also barely a whisper – beginning to untie the navy blue knot in her robe.

"Because passion's a dark thing."

The paisley silk robe parted.

"Although language is lovely."

"As you are," he murmured.

She heard a rustle as the robe slipped and fell to the floor by her feet. He remained seated and pulled her closer and stared at her a moment longer, before he touched her. She did not watch as he did so. He let his hands linger long on the crossed swords marking her hips, then traced the swords that seemed to match them across her ribs just above, and then at last she felt him move her legs apart. She looked away from him still, though she was aware, after a moment, that he stroked only the place where her inner thighs remained marked. Finally then he stood, and took her face in his hands and made her look at him. He traced the intricate tendrils that fell down toward her shoulder and then he encircled her neck and she thought he would strangle her as he kissed her mouth again, as he had done in her guest house, although now with a fierceness she somehow returned, though she trembled by then, so that he steadied her as he traced the half moon, kissing her mouth still, and then he reached round and pulled the comb from her hair and felt it fall wild around her shoulders. Only then did he pull away from her, commanding her, thickly, "Stand there for me Caroline, just as you are now."

Unsteadily, leaning against the nightstand, she did as he'd asked her. She had agreed to this evening, come what may, out of pride, she had thought, for she had not yet begun to sense any more complex motivations.

He studied her standing there, making no move toward her, merely gazing as though taking notes for some future description – long legs, slim waist, firm breasts, untamed hair that matched her heart and a body marked, so uniquely.

Finally, in the shadows, she heard him pronounce at last, "The debt is paid."

Completely confounded, she was unable to answer.

"I have had what I wanted. To have seen you as he saw you, the day of the portrait."

She felt all strength sink from her.

"To know what it was he conveyed on that cloth. Not just an image – not even flesh, or magnificent form – I mean some other dark thing, utterly wanton, inches below an elegance that fails to control it."

She was holding on still to the table, her breath coming harder – he could see it in the lamplight – though from defiance or yearning, he could not be certain. Both he suspected, recalling the way she had disdained to meet his gaze while he touched her, remembering too how she had parted her mouth when he at last forced one kiss.

He could find out, to be sure, if he but touched her one more time.

That, though, was impossible, torn as he was in his heart. The debt had been paid. He had announced it already.

"I am satisfied, Caroline," he merely said after a moment.

One last time he glanced at the red velvet curtains that draped her small bed. Then he silently opened the door and made his way into the courtyard.

Anything but satisfied, Mikhail walked to his rooms at the Riverside Suites. He had mistakenly thought that if he looked at her – as an artist would have looked at her – he would have fulfilled both their needs, leaving her free to rebuild the house Maximilian was designing, leaving him free to sail off toward new horizons again.

Now, he discovered, as his steps echoed along the street that inclined slowly toward the river, he was a sailor still, not a painter. He wanted to explore, not recreate, although perhaps that was the starting point for painters too – he could not guess. He only knew he could never return – not to his father's house, where ideal form moved with ease, in his father's robes, among his father's books, rendering.

He won't miss you, he vowed. *He won't crave it*, he said, maybe even aloud – although that he would never remember. All he recalled were those lines from Catullus, a final gauntlet tossed to Lesbia – number eight, he believed – though even that was not clear.

☽

Caroline was also lost. He had excited her – something she hadn't expected. His hands had aroused her, although she had tried not to show it. Thus she was warm still, long after he'd left her, after she'd slipped on the paisley silk robe once again and opened the red leather volume of lyrics again, then closed it abruptly and placed it back on the shelf and moved through the library – restless, uncertain – surrounded by what had seemed important before then, wanting the weight of him now, wanting him – although the debt was paid, fully – he had been clear on that point.

Again the robe fell, this time with care onto her bed. She slipped under the starched and sweet-smelling sheets. The little fringed lamp was turned out.

Sleepless, long into the night, she pondered the fact that in the slow fashioning of desire was the dissolution of love.

Mikhail never came once to his father's house the next week. After the sixth day, as the musicians prepared for their concert, Caroline said, matter of factly, "Heaven only knows what tropical paradise Misha's escaped to. No doubt he has sold some fine yacht by this time."

"Mikhail is in New York."

"Is he."

"Not a moment to spare though – or so he tells me over the phone."

"Yes, well his clients," she managed.

"That and some paperwork, friends…a meeting with two designers."

Caroline nodded. The musicians continued to tune.

"He's also found us a contractor," Max whispered, delighted. "Assistant shipbuilder, really. Excellent craftsman. Very fair prices. Mikhail gave me his number this morning."

"Very kind of him…"

"I'll call tomorrow if you don't mind."

"Of course I don't mind, Max."

The *Piano Quintet* of Dvořák began. Caroline opened her score, determined to lose herself in the music. All she could hear though, above the music unfolding, was the dissonant sound of Misha's excuses. He'd stayed away for a week – not from the house or his father, but from her, with deliberation, having been *satisfied* – that was the word he had used, while she had grown only more restive with each passing day.

Max hadn't noticed this fact, absorbed as he was with the wartime chapters of his memoirs, and – perhaps even more – the little mill house he was perfecting.

Antonin, on the other hand, was keenly aware of a change. Her silences were longer on the rides home every night. On the rides back in the morning, she seemed increasingly anxious. He deluded himself into thinking that her recent disasters were taking their toll. *Perhaps not, though*, he reflected, having also noted Mikhail's absence. He would have to be watchful.

"Exonerated," said Elliot grandly to Susan at week's end.

He had driven straight to her home from the courthouse that morning, still disbelieving the turn things had taken, how quickly the jury'd decided, how many people had stopped in the corridors to congratulate him. Was it only a matter of weeks since he had walked past the heap that had once been a grand home, only to find his wife making plans for him to eke out his days in her mill? All had seemed lost at that point. There'd seemed to be nothing remaining to offer to Susan. And then a car crash, a boy's hand saved, his father Judge Dawson forever grateful – a medical practice restored.

"Half of Todd's Farm will be mine now," he swore, fumbling with the buttons of Susan's blouse as he spoke, for his hands, normally steady as steel, trembled from the enormous tension he had felt earlier that day. "The guest house, the land – still worth a fortune."

"You'll have to divorce first," she murmured.

"Yes. I can do it now. No quarter given," he added, as Susan slipped out of her panties. "It is my way, as you know."

He was as good as his word. Caroline returned home from Manhattan the next night to find Elliot's papers in the mailbox. She read them through carefully. He would fight hard now; perhaps even win now, for she had never altered an agreement that had given him vague emergency powers even over her land when they'd married. It was still valid, from what she could tell as she read.

She walked out toward the south lawn and paused where the house had once stood. The rubble pile had been cleared. Only the earth remained now, cold and hard and uneven, and yet underneath, biding its time, springtime was in attendance.

She tried to imagine what that dirt would be like in the spring. Patches of grass here and there? Weeds with their flowers having grown wild in the wind? As she gazed she thought she saw the outline of the old house taking shape. She saw the terrace, the hall, the candlelit dining room where Dolly Reston had stared at her gown. She saw the bench in her garden where she had sat two months later, bills and circulars in her hand. Directly above was Elliot's study, her bedroom beyond that, her wardrobe, priceless black pearls gone, the porch down below where Mikhail had said goodnight.

Imperceptibly the vision faded until only the image of gemstones remained – three strands of black pearls secured with a fine diamond clasp, opals, rubies, a rare lapis necklace.

If I can prove what he's done, she thought all of a sudden, pulling her thick shawl around her, *he will not have this land.*

But how to do such a thing? Despite the bank card on file, with Elliot's signature in December, she herself could have taken her jewels from the bank vault. Still – if she could find those gems quickly, trace their sale, the date, the fact that he'd sold them. But how to prove they were hers?

She ran back to the guest house, phoned Dennis Ballantine, discovered that copies of the lapsed policy were still remaining at New England Life.

"In that case I'll stop by," she said. "Tomorrow. First thing. After I've gone to the bank right next door."

By three p.m. that same day she was again at La Ronde. In her purse were two copies, more precious by far than the pearls she had lost – one of her signature card, one of her policy lapsed.

Roger was not surprised to see Mrs. Devereux again.

They all return to sell more, he reflected, and so he was taken aback when she told him serenely, "Just a small gift, Monsieur. That is all I can afford to buy. My godchild's Communion," she added, taking his arm as they returned to floor two, estate jewels.

At her leisure she strolled through the elegant room. She stopped to study a brooch, enamelled in primary tones, then an ormolu phoenix inside an antique glass case. As she passed by her pearls, still displayed to perfection, she observed with dispassion, "Pity there's not been a buyer for my husband's black pearls yet."

"Ah," replied Roger, surprised again by Mrs. Devereux, "everything has its time."

She knew the gems after all, he realized then. More to the point, he thought with a wash of relief, her *désinvolture* made it clear she felt no claim to the set.

"I would buy them myself if I could," she went on, drifting away from the case toward another display on the opposite wall. "Under the circumstances though…it's not just the money – "

"No, no of course not."

"I knew the lady well," she confessed. "She seemed to enhance those rare pearls. It was a beautiful match once, Monsieur."

"So your husband insisted."

"Well," she said demurely, drawing him out still, "somehow you'll find an equally worthy successor."

"Hard to equal a mother," Roger said gravely. "Dr. Devereux's above all. The very presence of her gems in his house grieved him still. Well, of course, this you know."

"I do know," she replied, before taking one final turn around the treasure-filled room. She went back toward the brooch. She studied the phoenix.

"I have almost decided. May I come back in a few days?"

"Madame is always welcome at La Ronde."

Caroline paused outside the store. There remained one last thing – the gems from her vault – yet not a single piece was on view in any display case at La Ronde. Already, perhaps, they had found a new owner. Perhaps they were stored still in Elliot's safe. She looked at her watch. Max would be waiting for her in an hour.

Time enough, she decided, for a brisk tour around Monte Carlo, the ultra-modern new gallery across from La Ronde.

She was shown through the paintings, the silver, then at last estate jewels. The room was bright, simple, its steel cases gleaming under the track lighting above. Caroline peered through each case, recognizing nothing.

And yet they are here, she reflected, sensing her distant past in the place named for the casino her father once loved. *Catherine Todd's gems are inside these spare rooms.*

She turned. Off to the right she saw a smaller room. "Our most recent acquisitions," whispered Franco Martelli, guiding Mrs. Devereux toward the sleek, glistening shelves. All of a sudden she stopped. For what seemed like a long time, without saying a word, she stared at the gems in the last case – opals, rubies, a lapis necklace set in white gold.

"I can open the case if you like."

"Very kind of you. I should like that."

She ran her fingers over her heirlooms, lingering over the initials on the clasp of the bracelet.

"C.T.," she murmured.

"Charlotte-Therese," explained Franco Martelli.

"Relative of the owner?"

"His mother," was the reply, made with dignity, eyes downcast.

"A woman of fine taste," was Mrs. Devereux's answer. "As yet, though…I am not quite decided. May I come back?"

With a deep bow so that his bald head shone as well under the track lights:

"Madame is always welcome at Monte Carlo."

From a booth on the corner, Caroline phoned Walter Reston.

"Can you get a message for me to Elliot?" she asked. "Yes it is urgent, Walter. I need to speak to him, in person, tonight if he can."

"You should perhaps speak through me…"

"Walter, it is an intimate matter. It will be very much to his profit. I will be waiting for him in the guest house. Can you at least tell him that much?"

"Very well, Caroline," he sighed. "Nine o'clock at the guest house."

Elliot found her at her desk once again, exactly where she'd been seated on the evening he'd left her – more serene somehow, he reflected, her steady gaze more disconcerting.

"Congratulations," she said, declining to stand as he approached. "The hearing went well, I understand."

"Absolved on all counts."

"Everything new again, finally."

"My whole life, Caroline – as I know you've been told."

"Surely you must have meant *ours*, Elliot."

Uninvited, he took a chair by her side.

"Why else would I want you – this one time."

"Walter said it was urgent," said Elliot sharply, stung by her bluntness.

"That, I suppose, you shall have to judge for yourself," she replied. "I'll take a stroll as you read. You needn't be here when I return. Simply sign at the bottom, add the date too if you will, take the second copy to Walter, or keep it wherever you lock up your secrets."

With that she dropped the papers she held onto the desk, reached for her cape and left him alone in the guest house.

Over and over in the deepening shadows he read of her trips to La Ronde, her visit to Monte Carlo, her return to the bank, signature copy attached, her stop at New England Life, policy copy also attached.

Then, again several times, he read the last page, handwritten.

I, Elliot Devereux, forfeit all claims to Todd's Farm – guest house and mill house and the river between them, pastures and orchards and the birch grove between them, stone walls around them, grass underneath them, weeds growing over the house no longer remaining – and I, Caroline Contini Devereux, forfeit disclosure of the above craven thefts, until the day of my death, and all claims to my pearls, black set of five, along with the opals, the rubies, and the fine lapis necklace set in white gold. Like my home, they are gone with the wind. The land remains mine, and any buildings still standing.

She had added her name and the date carefully, in her ornate old-world script – oversized, as befitted the occasion.

He was long gone when she returned from the bridge, though he had left the papers, signed on the line she had provided, on top of the desk by her chair. As she also requested, he had informed her, in writing, that all title and deeds to his half of Todd's Farm would be delivered to the guest house, first thing in the morning.

They were never again to meet. Neither knew it that evening.

$\smile$ ☾ $\backsim$

"Things have gone swimmingly, I understand," Max said during lunch on the following day.

Stunned, Caroline wondered how he had learned of her meeting with Elliot.

"Misha's appointments," he went on. "Seems he has sold a new yacht. Well I suppose there is nothing Mikhail can't sell. He'll be off now for the Bahamas."

"Short trip?" she asked absently.

"On the contrary. He'll be returning to London directly from Nassau."

Max reached for his cane, made an effort to stand, then thought for a moment before he crossed to his daybed.

"Always the restless one," he murmured. "Just like his mother."

Not since the day he had conjured her had he mentioned Cecilia.

"I expect he'll stop in to say goodbye this afternoon. Tomorrow the latest. He'll be gone day after that."

"Of course he'll stop in," Caroline said, walking behind Max.

Of that one thing she was sure. He would not leave New York without a proper farewell – at least to his father, Antonin, Elsa Varig, the beautiful house on 86th Street.

But would he leave without seeing her? He would have to do it in the stillness, after lunch had been cleared, when he would be certain to find his father upstairs alone on his daybed.

After lunch had been cleared she waited, lying still dressed on her bed, door to her room unbolted, listening keenly.

No footsteps passed up the steep stairs to the second floor landing.

Max too was disappointed, for he too knew that Misha would feel obliged to pay a formal call – a final farewell, and he had hoped it would happen after lunch had been served. Only then would he be alone; Elsa Varig would be summoned; she could come up the back stairs with Antonin; Caroline's sleep would remain undisturbed.

Undisturbed, he reflected again, staring out toward the court-yard, convincing himself that her rest these last days was of the utmost importance. Indeed – somehow it came into focus at this point – she had seemed oddly distracted, unsettled, paler than ever during the past two weeks' sessions. *Best not to awaken her should Misha arrive still*, he mused. She could always write to his son, in the near future sometime, thanking him for the contractor who had agreed to rebuild her mill house. Max himself was indebted to Mikhail for this favour. He reminded himself to thank him, profusely, the moment he appeared.

The afternoon's revisions passed, the concert was finished, a light supper was served, but Mikhail did not appear.

Tomorrow for sure, thought his father, although on the following day, by the time lunch had been cleared, Mikhail had not stopped by.

It was at that point that Caroline knew. He would never see her again, never touch her again, the barter between them concluded. His cheque was hers now, free and clear, as was the contractor he had recommended. That too, she suspected, had been a gift she had paid for while the rain had assaulted her windows two weeks earlier in her room.

"Mikhail has had to say goodbye to me over the telephone," Max informed Caroline on the following night. "Out of town these past days. Flight to Nassau tomorrow morning. Of course he was still hoping to come later this evening, but I told him he'd miss you by then, and Antonin, and Elsa, and…well…I myself would be exhausted. Ah – the violinist is ready. *Méditation from Thaïs.* To soothe us both after a long day."

The brief performance was crystalline, flawless. Its last note remained like perfume in the room. Max closed his eyes, as if in joyous submission to some ethereal partnership that had somehow escaped him for the greater part of his life.

Caroline too closed her eyes, not in an effort to remember, but to forget – futile endeavour – while the musicians again tuned their instruments, and Maximilian reached for additional scores, and then abruptly, just before the end of what was to be their last unsullied concert, she heard a voice that resembled her own say, "We must alert Antonin, Max – I forgot to tell you while we were revising – I will be meeting with my attorney directly after the concert."

"At such an hour, Caroline?"

"Well it's barely past eight, after all, and his office, on Broadway, is only minutes from here, and as he lives just over the ridge from Todd's Farm, he'll take me back in his own car, so that Antonin can have a rest tonight – well-deserved, to be sure, though we should alert him at once," she repeated, moving a stray and recalcitrant black strand of hair from her neck.

"Yes," said Max after a moment.

She was never to know which of her lies he was assenting to.

All Caroline would remember about her walk to the Riverside Suites was that the sound of her boots on the pavement resembled some other woman's winter shoes.

Her voice also resembled another's – she would recall that as well in days to come – as she asked at the desk for Mikhail d'Olivier.

"Left at noon for the day," she was told. "May I give him a message?"

"No – no I'll wait for a bit."

She found a chair beside a palm tree overlooking the river.

Thirty minutes, she promised herself, staring off in the distance at the lights of the grand bridge. *More than enough time to catch the next train to New Salem.*

After an hour beside the window, still telling herself she had waited to say goodbye, to thank him for the cheque that had saved her, and for saving her before that, Mikhail had not appeared.

She remained a half-hour more.

Dozens of people, most of them couples, made their way through the door that revolved slowly into the lobby. She watched them pass by her chair on the way to their rooms – some arm in arm, some holding hands, most of them unaware of her, alone and silent beside the palm tree that shaded her face from the guests.

At last, toward eleven, she could no longer avoid recalling a similar vigil – was it only last summer? – when once before she had waited well into the night for a man.

But that was Paris, she reminded herself, *another world, another life, and my reasons for waiting were different...clear, understood...my reasons for waiting* – she stopped, eyes on the water, as though the Hudson River were the Seine and the bridge ahead were the Pont St-Michel – *my reasons were one and the same*, she saw as the scene before her seemed to change, and instead of Jude's house it was her own form in the window – body no longer hidden, determined soul deep inside, and, even deeper, marking her more than her scars ever did, the thing that would not go away.

She stood, horrified, but was unable to turn from her vivid reflection. She moved even closer in fact, as though transfixed by the revelation, until she could touch the cold glass, ever so briefly, and in the touching erase the picture.

The gesture was fruitless. It only confirmed what was there – an unsparing starvation that had defined all her days – hunger of spirit, not of the body – partly her nature, partly calamitous deprivations – fused in any case now, forming near-violent longings to touch and be touched, keep nothing back, take it all in her turn, and though this hunger in France had shaped itself as expiation – gift to an artist traduced – and though tonight she had come in gratitude – response to a mariner's gifts – both times, she now saw, the same desperation had welled up in her heart, suppressed in a shattered childhood, unacknowledged in a loveless youth.

She turned in fear from the sight and hurried away through the lobby, certain she'd missed the next train, waiting for her chance to slip through the door that was once again turning, too fast to accept her, until a man from the walkway stepped into the lobby, and she found herself standing there, face to face with Mikhail.

He simply stared at her, disbelieving.

"Mikhail," she said unevenly.

A porter with baggage passed between them.

"Misha," she said a second time, but that was all she could manage, and so he moved toward her, astounded still that she had come to him – finally – which is all he had wanted in the two weeks he'd waited.

"How are you – I – you're looking fine," she began again. "I was in the neighbourhood" – she stopped. It was after eleven. Her excuse sounded absurd. "Well, I remembered I hadn't told you – I mean the last time we spoke I hadn't told you…"

He took the cape from her shoulders.

"What with both of us working so hard…"

"Yes, Caroline…"

"Our paths never crossing…"

"Why don't you tell me upstairs?" he said at last, tenderly.

She glanced behind her again, wishing she hadn't come, longing to be in his arms, lost and conflicted, hearing herself say then, without the slightest conviction, "I see a sofa there beside the window," to which he gently replied, removing her scarf, "How can I make love to you on a sofa beside the window?"

She looked up at him, finally, and at that moment it seemed to him that her eyes were pools he could drown in and her hair a web from which he would never emerge. He remembered her body as one remembers tracks in the desert sand, long after the wind has come up, and thus, though there were people moving around, and the door behind them kept revolving, he kissed her mouth then and there and said, "Here then if you want, Caroline."

"No…"

"Wherever you want."

"Upstairs, Mikhail."

It appeared to them both that the elevator took forever. Couples got on and got off at each floor, crowding Caroline up against him, so that it was not until they reached the top floor and he had guided her, finally, into the pale quiet hallway that they found themselves suddenly, absolutely alone.

Neither spoke as they turned and walked to the end of the corridor.

No words were exchanged as he double-locked the door behind them.

She placed her purse on the chair and moved toward the window, where her reflection remained on the river although by then she no longer feared it, for the inevitable cannot intimidate.

Hence she was glad when his image blended with hers, gladder still when he touched her, kissed her, removed her clothing and turned her around to face him – as she had faced him in her small room – only then she would not look at him, disdaining to acknowledge that what he was doing she wanted. Even now acquiescence came hard, so that she buried her face in his shoulder, pressing herself against him, murmuring, "Why did you wait so long, Mikhail?"

"I had sworn I would take nothing."

"And yet now…"

"Now you have found me," he said, removing the comb from her hair and laying her down on his bed.

He knelt above her in the shadows and kissed her mouth deeply, then traced with his tongue what he had touched once with his hand – the marks on her neck, her ribs, her hips, the lunar curve on her breast – analogue for his obsession, matching half of the coin, marked soul as he was from the day he'd been sent from the only safety he'd known into an alien land.

"Mikhail," she murmured, beginning to move underneath him.

"Caroline, yes," he replied, "but not yet," for there remained the crossed swords on her inner left thigh. These he kissed for a long time, pushing the unburned right thigh even farther away, so as to linger with his mouth in the dark place above them, and then at last he entered her withholding nothing at that point, for they had both known such yearning, and so it did not surprise him that she responded in kind to him, fiercely, taking an almost objective delight in his unconscious roughness, which he could no longer control, and which, in an odd way, she found exceedingly pure.

In the end it was this which was essentially different – this objectivity – for not once, though their mating was almost terrifyingly feral, did she lose herself in the intensity of Mikhail's domination. Such absolute abnegation, bordering on despair, starting and ending with a love beyond reason – that she had done in Paris. It was never again to occur. What remained on this night, and for all evenings to follow, was a nascent yet distinctive erotic sophistication – clear-sighted, unencumbered – never again to approach the submission she'd had no choice but to offer to Jude.

Vaguely, as he repeatedly consumed her, Mikhail sensed this. She was generous with her body, giving pleasure with abandon, taking it back almost with greed, and yet, though she cried out when her pleasure was near – fierce sound befitting the woman whose face had appeared in the window – she'd held something back, some precious part of her body somehow, an even finer part of her soul. Mikhail's conquest was thus more seeming than real. He had fulfilled only as much of her hunger as she would allow. Hence, for the first time in his life – and the irony did not escape him as he made love to her with a superb yet almost savage abandon – it was the predator who had surrendered. The prey had escaped him – at least the part which obsessed him, so that the corporeal union failed in its deeper dimension, and in the imperatives of the flesh there was only a brushing of souls.

And yet he believed still, as he lay spent there above her, that if she were ever awakened again – in some undiscovered constellation – she would be capable of the great love that he now felt, to desperation.

Caroline too reflected as they lay together in the darkness, silent, stroking each other. She had made love to no one since the morning she'd left Jude's apartment. On that day, with a hesitant dawn deftly tinting the Seine, a night such as this by the Hudson was unthinkable. But then again so was Max, and the collapse of her home, and her immense fortune lost, and Parisian promises become leaves in the wind.

All that remained then was this, and the stone mill in the woods, and Max – Max betrayed in the end, for he had loved her as no other. He'd made no effort to hide it. Nor, though he had tried, had he been able to disguise a deep and abiding mistrust of his son.

What had been done though was done. Violent longings remained. She would walk with the son toward the abyss yawning ahead.

And so the hours passed, and the bustle of hotel sounds vanished, and the streets below emptied, and even the river moved on discreetly, keeping its counsel, far too wise to defy time and the tides and the desperation of lovers.

Only the slam of a door down the hall startled Caroline out of her reverie.

"The last train's gone!" she exclaimed.

"Of course the train's gone."

"You'll have to call me a taxi."

Mikhail smiled, caressing her still. "And where shall I tell him to take you this hour of night?"

"My guest house. Antonin will be waiting tomorrow."

"I have Antonin's number. You can call him in the morning. Your lawyer's bringing you in," Mikhail murmured, "simple as that."

"But it isn't so simple."

"Isn't it?" he asked, bending to kiss her again.

Unevenly: "No."

"What part of that kiss was so difficult, tell me."

She looked up at him but made no answer.

"*Tell me*," he insisted.

Still he heard no response. Instead she turned and stared fixedly at the bridge. A heavily laden barge lumbered upstream.

Lights of a freighter slowly moved toward the Narrows. Finally, as a gentle rain began to strike the window beside them, she said, "It is you, Mikhail. You are leaving today. You haven't told me but I know it. Before I came here I knew it – and it was all right with me then. I – things were unfinished."

"And now," he asked gently, turning her around to face him. "Have you finished things now?"

"What I had to tell you – you have heard."

Taking her face in his hands, he said, "Have you no more to say to me, then, Caroline?"

She had not intended to say "I do, Mikhail. Yes."

But the words were fashioned somehow so that Misha responded, "Stay the night with me, then. We can call Antonin when you awaken. I'll tell Max I've postponed things."

"But the yacht sale…"

"There will be other yachts."

"Your trip to London…"

"I was only going because you stayed away."

"Ah, Mikhail," she groaned, yearning and foreboding mixed.

"Yes or no, Caroline."

Sounds of a plane taking off into the night skies grew fainter. Everything appeared to her fainter, indistinct, as though the intricate web taking shape had already begun to cloud things. "Yes then," she repeated, as another betrayal began to form in that web. "Yes, Mikhail, since it must be."

They made love again, many times, before she called Antonin.

"But you will need me tonight, won't you, Caroline? After the music, I mean…"

"Yes, yes of course, Antonin."

"I will be waiting then."

"Thank you."

"Out in the courtyard," he added, though he had never in all those months waited anywhere else.

"I am always so grateful," she managed, and then she heard herself murmur "goodbye" and "thank you again" and then it was done. She had lied to him too, as Misha had told her to do – as she had lied to Maximilian – and all traces of the woman Jude had betrayed disappeared.

Then she returned to Mikhail's bed, for it was early still – hours before Max would be waiting, stretched out on his daybed, looking out over the courtyard.

Antonin, meanwhile – far too restless to sleep – had moved to his own window.

He looked toward the end of the street, where a thickening mist covered the river. He strained to see northward, where the arc of the bridge lights resembled tired stars. For a long time he listened, hearing the now-heavy rain splash on the metal staircase outside his building.

At last he turned, walked to his windowless kitchen, waited there for his coffee, then reentered his living room – also his bedroom, dining room, workroom, and study.

He had already made her two tables. Carefully covered, they were pushed up against the wall next to his worn, brown plaid couch. Today the headboard would follow.

"Yes the headboard," he thought, "since she won't be needing me this morning. I can cut something fine today – intricate – since she won't be needing me," he repeated.

The rhythmic grinding continued well into the afternoon.

Caroline was by then approaching the library for her rest. She had arrived right on time for the morning's session with Max, had rendered his phrases exactly, had taken her break with him, her lunch with him, not for a moment betraying the fact that nothing could ever again be the same somehow between them, nor her fears that he had somehow guessed that.

With a sigh of relief she opened the door to her small room.

"Misha," she gasped, "what are you doing here?"

"My father lives here," he reminded her, flashing his disarming smile.

"But that's just the point…"

"Are you going to leave the door open?"

After a moment's indecision, she locked it securely behind her.

"Much better," he murmured.

"Misha, we can't here…"

He was undoing the same blouse he had removed the evening before.

"Where then? I'll meet you…"

"Your hotel room."

"They'll never believe the same lies…"

"Then up at my own house."

"With Antonin in the driveway?"

"He will be gone by eleven."

Tugging her skirt up, Mikhail answered, "I was a boy the last time I waited for Antonin Onegin," and then he pressed her against the door and made love to her standing up, placing his hand over her mouth when he knew her pleasure was near, and then his own followed, fiercely.

In the brief time remaining, she didn't want any clothing. They simply lay down on her bed, and he talked of the sea and she talked of her books, complementary voyages, or so it seemed, until a brief fifteen minutes were left.

She washed herself carefully then, dressed with even more care, took immense pains rearranging her hair.

Thus, as she walked up the steps toward her afternoon session with Max, she imagined, somehow, he could be deluded one more time.

She hadn't counted on her lingering scent, which no ablution could eradicate.

And yet Max chose to doubt senses honed over a lifetime, studying her as she bent over her notebooks beside him – lovelier somehow than he had ever seen her before.

He also chose not to notice that Caroline had on the same clothing she had worn on the previous night, and to believe, after all, that the flush which had at last begun to recede from her neck was due to her passion for words – sharper perhaps than a woman's need for a man's bed.

Hence he too was serene on the following day, for she had arrived bright and refreshed from a night at Todd's Farm, and their work had gone well until lunch.

And then again came her rest, during which time she did not rest.

Half in fear, half in anticipation, she had passed through the library, opened the door to her small room, closed it behind her and had found Mikhail waiting. She'd made no protest this time – the moments they could steal were short – and she had begun to covet his wild needs with a desperation approaching his own. It had happened quickly. Each time he had loved her, more of her had been awakened, or more precisely reawakened – for he knew there had been another, and she was holding back from him still – yet he also knew now that abandon was in her nature, and that hunger defined her – and he was determined, come what may, to own this fierce creature, body and soul, making her lose herself in the process, as he himself was now lost.

But this second time Max was sure. As she came up to him he was sure, despite the soap and sang-froid and her fine French perfume. She had just left a man's bed, although he did not know where, and, as yet – though he suspected – he did not know whom.

From that moment on, Maximilian was obsessed. Nevertheless, even then, he managed to hide from his mind what his heart could not bear – that fact that he had wanted her exclusively – not as a father might dote, or a kindred soul care – but with a frightening physicality that had been there from the start. He had known such a thing once before, only back then he was young still, and the adored girl but a child, and now there were only a few sunlit days left, and the beloved woman had come to him, unexpectedly, as though to make up for that first spring, turning this autumn sweet, so that the smell of her preferring another was more than his pride and his love and his lust could endure.

Consumed as he was then, he would have to consume her. He would destroy in his turn, for the wound had gone deep.

First and foremost however – and this he planned with a cool precision which belied the emotions which gave him no respite – he would have to have proof, a few details at least, something to justify actions otherwise unendurable.

On the following day, he invited Misha to lunch.

He noted her fine eyes with care, taking care not to show it, and repeatedly saw just a confounding serenity – blended still with correctness – whenever she'd answer his son, or serve him some sauce, or laugh in her soft way at some tale from his travels.

Mikhail, in his turn, remained cordial throughout, even gracious on occasion, nothing more, nothing less – as his father would have expected – for although she worked in his home, she was somehow always a guest.

So seamlessly wrought, in fact, was the concealment of the lovers, so incontrovertible their composure, that Max was tempted one more time to deny what he knew – perhaps even bury his plan – until she served his son coffee and passed both milk and sugar his way, as a bride would have known after several mornings together, and thus his fine monogrammed plates did indeed speak in the end, for they had had only tea in their luncheons before that, and Misha had taken it black.

Max carefully sliced the Black Forest cake by his side, offered more coffee, a bit of fruit from the centrepiece bowl, and then in a negligent tone said he thought he'd extend, by thirty minutes, his afternoon's rest.

"Are you not well, Max?" Caroline asked abruptly.

"Yes, yes I'm fine. A little more tired than usual. We've been working hard, after all." Caroline nodded, handing a plate to Mikhail. "Sleep a little extra yourself, Caroline. There won't be a sound to interrupt you. Elsa's gone off to the market. Antonin's taking my car for a tune-up."

"I suppose it will do me good."

"Until five-thirty then," she heard him reply as she closed the door carefully behind her.

Mikhail was too discreet to follow her downstairs directly.

"Our usual brandy, Max?" he asked instead, genially.

"I think I will, Misha. It might help me sleep some."

Twenty minutes elapsed before Maximilian drained his glass. Mikhail took his leave – another fatal misstep, for he felt compelled to add at the doorway: "I've a client to see now back at the Riverside Suites. Tomorrow for sure I'll stop by again, Max."

Had he not told this last lie, Max would never have known the truth, for Mikhail could have remained in the living room, reading, leaving Caroline to her rest and Max would not have been sure. If he did not leave now though, it would be undeniably clear. He had followed Caroline into the library.

Only one thing remained. Somehow Max managed to stand at the window, eyes on the courtyard, watching who came and who left through the only door to his house.

Mikhail never left, and no calls were made or received to postpone any engagements, for Max had carefully left the receiver on his desk phone off the hook. By the time Elsa arrived, just past five, Mikhail had not emerged and it had exhausted Max to stand there, staring down into the courtyard, like a child on Christmas Eve determined to know, once and for all, if Papa Noel were indeed just a myth.

Anyone else but his son he might have accepted – no, not accepted, but acknowledged with begrudging grace, in some fine fragile way, for she herself was so frail and at the same time so fierce, recalling his wilful Cecilia – and he had thought them so different, and in the end they were one and the same, and the same boy had stolen them both, and thus he too would have to suffer, although he knew it would take all he had left in the doing.

The chance did not come right away. On the following morning, like the unanticipated snowfall when she had slept far too late, Caroline failed to appear.

"Mikhail's contractor has arrived," she said when she phoned.

"Yes, of course," replied Max.

"First time he's been to Todd's Farm."

There was a moment.

"I'll need to show him the woodlands, the footbridge…"

"The mill too, Caroline," Max replied then, astutely. "Best to see a design right on site for the first time. In the fullest sunlight," he continued. "You may not again have such a chance."

"I will take your plans with me," was her answer, spoken softly. "Until tomorrow then, Max."

"Goodbye, Caroline."

The builder had started four days before that – Max had been told by Antonin – but she had lost her way by that time, as Misha had since the beginning, and hence she too blundered, telling one lie too many, never suspecting that Maximilian suspected, wanting only to have one full day with Mikhail, deep within the abyss – although she had struggled before she had joined him there.

They spent that full day in each other's arms at her guest house. By the time darkness fell, Mikhail knew – perhaps the only thing he clearly saw – that he would never again return to Europe. That would mean parting, and he could never leave her.

"I can work from here," he'd said abruptly, lying beside her in the bedroom where once before he had undressed her and bathed her, with no other needs late that night than to bring her cold form back to life.

His needs on this night though were different.

"My father is here, after all; my clients come often; I've a quick trip to make to London this week, but that's it," and then he stopped all of a sudden, feeling her hair on his shoulders, for she had raised herself up and was touching his face as he spoke, as if to trace his next thoughts and thereby, in some way, to keep them unuttered. Her attempt was in vain. He had made up his mind.

"You are here, Caroline," he concluded, with a most elegant simplicity.

"Mikhail…"

"All you would have to do – this will take time, I know – is to love me as I love you."

As though surprised by the sound of his own words he again paused. Then, for they had long since passed denial's point: "Which I will do all my life, if you were there by me, trying."

It was admitted so frankly, from a man who had never managed any such words to a woman, that she was able to hold only a particle back, nothing more, as he made love to her one more time before he went to her kitchen and prepared breakfast as dawn broke.

And yet that particle will remain, he somehow knew in his heart, and the thought filled him with dread as he drove out through the gates, planning the next time he'd see her, never seeing Antonin's car, backed off into a lane just to the west of Todd's Farm.

Nor, on the following day, did he go to see Caroline in his father's house.

"Tomorrow's Sunday," she had warned him. "Elsa's day off, Mikhail."

"What better time?" he had murmured.

"It is too risky," she'd insisted. "Maximilian might need me."

"Perhaps so," he'd agreed. "I'll go to the opera instead, since you won't let me have your song."

Mikhail made a point of calling his father from the opera house, four-thirty p.m. sharp, Caroline's rest time exactly.

"That's right, Max. *Otello*. Then dinner with Adrian Heller. Yes exactly," he laughed, "that overpriced shipbuilder who's come to dine with us several times. I'll have to miss your concert though."

"Stop by tomorrow then," Max replied. "There's music here always, you know."

Warning chimes in the lobby announced the start of Act II.

"Without fail, Max."

"'Til tomorrow then."

Mikhail took his seat. He studied the crowds, the fine chandeliers, the mysterious underworld of the musicians. He was enormously pleased.

Stressing as he had his absence, above all on Elsa's free day, he was convinced he had allayed any suspicions – no doubt subconscious – lingering still in the underworld of Maximilian's head. That such misgivings might exist he had an inchoate recognition, for it had not been lost on the son that they loved the same woman – nor had he been unaware, since that fateful interview beside Winchester's Green, of his father's lingering resentment. Now above all times, he knew, Maximilian had to be duped.

No easy matter, Misha reflected, as the opera house dimmed. Max was a master dissembler, a man of great passions, explosive when angered, unforgiving when hurt. And yet – testimony to the clouded perceptions his own passions had created – Mikhail thought, watching the huge wine-toned curtain ascend, that with that one simple phone call he had deceived such a man.

Iago's aria began.

Mikhail listened intently to his dark and defiant "Credo in un Dio crudel." *Exquisite blasphemy*, he judged, *this believing in a cruel god...Morbid*, he thought. *False on this day above all.*

And yet, on this day above all, he was moved to the depths of his soul by Otello's song near the end of the act. Against his own will, it seemed, he pondered this farewell to joy on his way back to the Riverside Suites. "Ora e per sempre addio," he sang again and again to himself as he walked. *Now and forever goodbye.*

He put the key into the lock and still the melody lingered. He undressed and stared at the river and recalled the night she had come to him and how her body had gleamed under the glow of the bridge lights, and then for some reason Otello's great torment returned, like a malevolent vale, so that in the end sleep escaped him, as it was eluding Maximilian then, and each in his own room poured another brandy to quiet his nerves.

⌐ ℂ ⌐

Within a matter of hours, as though a lifetime had passed since they'd parted, Mikhail had taken Caroline in his arms and laid her down on the bed.

It was Monday, her rest time, ninety minutes remaining, and they were in her sanctuary behind the library door. The door to her small room they had neglected to lock. All but their needs they had neglected by that time, and thus he had forgotten to cover her mouth when her pleasure was near, and again when his own came, and hers once more, so that they never heard Max on the staircase for the first time in a decade.

All she would ever remember was his form in the doorway, and Mikhail's weight no longer crushing her hips, and then a blow to the son's face, palm of the hand dealing a second blow on the return swing, so that Mikhail staggered and hit his head on the wall, blood oozing out of his nose, then from his mouth and then two more blows – these with Maximilian's cane – before Mikhail slumped down onto the red velvet bed, vaguely seeing the outline of Max moving toward him.

"No more!" Caroline cried.

Max felt her clasping his knees.

"It is I who have caused this," she sobbed, and then he looked down at her, naked, as he had always wanted to see her.

"Max, please, let the next blows be mine."

He raised his thick cane into the air. She lowered her head to blunt the force. Her wild curls streamed about, vain attempt to protect her, for he was lost to all reason, wanting only satisfaction.

And yet that last blow never fell. She looked up at him a second time, half in terror, half in anticipation.

"Max," she wept.

"Don't touch her, Max," Mikhail managed, staggering somehow to his feet.

The cane was still in the air.

"If you touch her I will kill you."

After a moment the cane fell with a crude thud to the floor. She was clasping his knees still.

"Move away from him, Caroline."

"No. No, I do not have to. He will not harm me. He is done harming."

Again she lowered her head, not in surrender this time, but almost – Max would remember this later – almost in a loving way.

Max would also remember her hair, streaming about his knees as she had awaited her beating, for the image of other heads had appeared to him in that instant – hairless heads, forcibly shaved at war's end – women who'd loved the wrong men, German babies to prove it, so that guiltier neighbours could deny much darker collusion.

Jean-Luc Onegin had also appeared, at least the fear in his eyes before his turn was to come, although those eyes were black, and the kneeling woman's were mauve.

Worst image of all was his own face, reflected in the mirror behind her – nothing at all remaining of the hero of the Resistance, for he had become of all things the tormentor, mouth slightly upturned, hand raised to abuse, heart inured to the pain he seemed about to inflict with some joy.

He had stared for a moment at that face in the glass. Then, without the help of his cane, he managed to turn, leave the lovers behind him, move through the library, make his way up the stairs.

Half-dazed still, Mikhail heard the fall directly above him, and then a woman's voice, "Mikhail, let me go to him!" and then he lifted her, knowing she could not lift herself, and placed her carefully on the bed and said, "I will go, Caroline."

He found Max face down on the floor by his desk.

Kneeling beside him he said simply, "Max" – nothing more, as he turned his body around and found a weak pulse still.

"Elsa," he called then. "Elsa, come quickly!"

"Elsa is out," whispered Max. "I told her to go."

Mikhail's head began swimming again.

"Go now yourself…"

"Where shall I go, Father?" Misha cried – the first time in his lifetime he had said anything other than "Max." He resisted the urge to vomit as he reached for the telephone.

"No hospital," managed Max.

"There is no other way."

"No hospital," Max insisted, eyes wide open now and very wild, so that Mikhail saw in them recollections of physicians who could not be trusted.

"I have a colleague" – his breath came short. "Ollikainen, Central Park West."

"You need a doctor."

"He is also a doctor."

Mikhail guessed that they had worked together once, unbeknownst then too to officials. He searched through the phone book. Nicholas Ollikainen arrived at once.

"I'll be all right," Maximilian managed as he was lifted onto his daybed. "Elsa was out. I thought a burglar came in…I'm an old man, Nicholas. I – old men hear things. It was the stairs, not a thief that gave me this shock."

This last was said fuzzily, for Dr. Ollikainen had by then injected him with a powerful sedative.

"I'll be all right," Max repeated. "Mikhail will be here."

☾

"Mikhail," said Dr. Ollikainen, closing the heavy door behind them, "You yourself need attention…"

"I'll just wash up some, get a bit of rest myself…"

Laying a hand on his arm, Ollikainen interrupted.

"Tell me what happened first, Mikhail."

Only at that moment did the pain begin throbbing again behind Mikhail's eyes.

"I can be trusted to help you."

"I know that."

"I'll need the truth, though."

"The truth is" – Mikhail leaned against the banister – "the truth, Dr. Ollikainen," he went on, making an effort as though to remember, "is that there really was a thief and Max surprised him on the staircase...I put my key in the lock at that point and walked through the hallway."

Ollikainen studied Mikhail's face as he continued.

"There was a terrible struggle. Max tried to help, but fell down. I prevailed in the end and the burglar ran off. Max was by then as you saw him."

"How did you get him upstairs?"

"I...I carried him."

"Alone?"

"There was no one to help me."

"I see."

Mikhail's own condition would not have allowed that. Both men understood it, but Nicholas Ollikainen pressed him no further. For the sake of the father, as he had done in the war years, he offered his skills and asked nothing more.

"I will come by in the morning," he promised, having dressed Misha's wounds. "Until then I suggest..."

"Wait..."

Ollikainen looked up.

"There is another. I – my father's assistant. She heard the scuffle of course."

"Where is she now?" interrupted the doctor, for it was the one piece of the puzzle that had been missing until then.

"Small room beside the library."

"Show me."

"Let me go in first."

"As you wish."

Caroline's door remained opened, just as Mikhail had left it. She too was as he had left her, though she had covered herself with the paisley silk robe. Her eyes seemed wild, wider than ever. Her hair was soaked with perspiration.

"I have a doctor," whispered Mikhail.

"No –"

"He is a friend. He has already seen Max."

She sat up abruptly.

"Max is resting," he murmured, smoothing her hair back. "Max will be fine," he repeated, not convinced in his heart, but he could feel her trembling as he held her. "So it is you now. Please...let Dr. Ollikainen come inside now. He has been told there was a thief tonight. He will be faithful."

She nodded wearily. Mikhail waited in the library. After about fifteen minutes, Dr. Ollikainen reappeared, carefully closed the door behind him and said, "She needs a hospital."

"She will not go."

"Her state of shock is most grave."

"Then you must do what you can, Doctor – here, in Maximilian's house. You know he would want that."

Their eyes met.

"A break-in like this, after all..."

"I will sedate her," said the physician, interrupting that long gaze.

On his way through the archway Ollikainen met Elsa Varig returning.

"Good evening, Miss Varig."

"Has anything happened?" she asked uneasily.

Ollikainen made no answer.

"Doctor, please tell me."

"There was a burglary..."

"God in heaven!"

"Monsieur Max attempted the stairs."

Elsa stared at him, horrified.

"I have sedated him. The girl as well, who happened to see it. As for Mikhail – Mikhail will be fine, near as I can figure, although the scuffle bruised him up a bit. I will know more in the morning."

"I must go."

"Go. Yes. I think they could use you in that household."

He could not tell if she guessed – as he had – what had in truth been stolen that night.

⁓ ☾ ⁓

"Whisky again," Antonin ordered at a bar he had frequented in years gone by. He thumbed again through the day-old paper he'd found, stared at the television flickering over the shelves, watched the crowds passing the grimy windows beside him – and still he couldn't get Misha's last-minute phone call out of his mind.

"Max has some guests in – colleagues from Litchfield," he'd been told. "They have insisted on driving Caroline home. Well, it's on the way, after all."

Litchfield was not, Antonin knew, on the way to New Salem.

"So you can have some time off. Her attorney's to drive her tomorrow, it seems. Paperwork to go over…" Misha's voice had drifted a moment. "Forms. That sort of thing."

Stunned, he'd replied no more than a confused "Day after, then," to which Misha had answered, before ringing off quickly, "A day or two more perhaps. I'll be in touch, Antonin. Rest in the meantime."

But Antonin could not rest. He who had waited for years in a jail cell found waiting even an hour then unendurable. Why hadn't Max phoned himself? Had Misha really dialled from Maximilian's house? Worse – and it was this last which gave him no peace – were the guests in from Litchfield to take Caroline anyplace?

Well, it was possible. The ride, the forms, the attorney – all even probable, he repeatedly said to himself, deciding to varnish her nightstand. After an hour he'd thrust the brush into its coffee can, reached for his coat and gone out.

Another hour had passed, then a third – and then, sipping his fifth drink, he'd glanced at the clock at the back of the bar. Max would be serving cocktails. The concert would start soon, followed by coffee perhaps and then brandy, and then the guests would depart, although Caroline would not leave – not yet – not for another half hour – he had figured it out by then. She'd wait with Max for a bit, out of courtesy, partly, mostly caution by then, and then she would follow Mikhail to the Riverside Suites.

With increasingly indistinct speech he recounted his thoughts to the stranger beside him, as though in the retelling he could confirm the details, and then, somewhat unsteadily, Antonin stood.

"Let me call you a cab."

"I'd rather walk," he replied, giving the same answer, savagely, when the bartender made the same offer.

The walk in fact did do him good, for the rain had at last stopped, and it was twenty blocks to Maximilian's house. By the time he arrived, his speech was no longer thick, nor his vision blurred. The chaos within, though, had not subsided as he stood in his usual place looking up at Maximilian's house. There were no lights on in the living room. From the second-floor windows there was no music to be heard. He checked his watch and observed that it was only eight-thirty.

Intermission, he thought, and so he waited, not hearing a sound, not a note – not once her laughter over the clatter of saucers and cups, not even Mikhail's banter, and then he made his decision. Though he had rarely moved from the lamp-post, and though he had been advised, absolutely, that his services would not be needed that evening, he walked up the pathway and knocked on the door.

"Antonin!" exclaimed Elsa Varig, as though she had never before seen him on that threshold in the darkness.

He noticed that she did not step aside.

He made his way past her anyway, leaving her speechless a moment. She had wanted to say, "What are you doing here, Antonin?" or "This is not the time, Antonin," for she had overheard Misha phone him earlier, and now, facing him in the entryway, she could see that he had spent most of the night in some bar.

Very cautiously then she merely observed, "We didn't expect you tonight, Antonin. Let me fix you some coffee."

"I'm okay."

"Stay with me while I eat then."

She prepared a small bit of supper, which he barely touched. She finished her coffee, which he declined. He seemed uneasy, as though straining to hear music, footsteps, some sounds of life in the eerie silence around them.

Finally he announced he would go upstairs to see Max for a bit.

"Antonin, go tomorrow. Monsieur Max is exhausted."

"Too tired to see me?"

"How could you think so?"

He glanced at the door. Misha had warned her to say nothing of the evening's disasters – events he had described to her as he had detailed them to Ollikainen. Whether or not Elsa suspected more, as their physician had, nobody knew. She was prepared to protect Max, come what may.

"I will go anyway," he decided.

"I'll hurry ahead and light the lamp."

In the few moments she'd gained, Elsa reached Maximilian's room and whispered hurriedly, "Mikhail, Antonin is approaching."

Antonin brushed passed Elsa, looked around quickly and was horrified to see Max on his daybed, Mikhail by his side.

For the third time that evening, as calmly as he could manage, Mikhail told his false tale of the evening's events.

For the third time that evening, he failed.

Mikhail sensed this at once, though for a while neither man spoke, both of them off their guard facing one another, Maximilian between them.

"She saw it all, you say Mikhail?" summarized Antonin finally.

"She saw it all, Antonin."

"Max descending the staircase?"

"Max confronting the thief there."

"And so now she is sleeping?"

"With a little help from the doctor."

In the renewed silence Antonin reflected. From time to time he looked at Maximilian's face – ashen, even in low light, seemingly lifeless against the immense mound of pillows. He glanced again at Misha's face – swollen, even in low light, with ugly blue marks

over one eye and two sharp cuts surrounding his lip. And then –
this time correctly – he put the pieces together. Max had never, not
for a moment, been duped by Mikhail. When the chance came he
had seized it, staircase notwithstanding, though in the end, Antonin
guessed, the effort would cost him his life.

But what of Caroline? Had it occurred in her room? On the
staircase as Misha'd insisted? Was she indeed still in that room
sedated by the doctor Mikhail'd called?

The clock he had made struck twelve; he stood and filled a glass.

"You may not need that whisky," ventured Misha.

Antonin drank with gusto, taking a second one along as he
returned to the kitchen.

The house was utterly still, dark throughout save for the lamp in the
library where Mikhail sat, somewhat dazed still, keeping vigil while
Max and Caroline slept. After about an hour he heard steps in the
hallway. He listened, carefully placing his cup down. The steps
paused; the house fell silent again, and then the door to the library
opened.

"Antonin! – What are you doing here?"

"Don't you think I belong here?" His voice had become thick
once again, his step extremely unsteady. "Don't you think I read
books, Misha?"

"Of course you read books," Mikhail answered, fully alert now,
and very wary, for he could see as Antonin tried to speak that he was
moving toward Caroline's room.

"*You* didn't read tonight, though, did you, Misha?"

"Antonin, you've had too much to drink."

"Steadies the nerves."

"Look, why don't we both go into the kitchen?"

"The place where I fit in, you mean?"

"Fine. Then we'll both just talk here."

"I didn't come here to talk."

"Well then tomorrow…"

"I came to see Caroline now," mumbled Antonin.

Cautiously, Misha moved to the closed door leading to Caroline's room.

Unevenly, Antonin moved to the same spot.

Again, as they had across Maximilian's bed, both men faced one another, Antonin's face partially shadowed, until at last he took one more step and warned: "Get out of my way, Mikhail."

"You know I can't do that."

"What I know" – Misha felt himself shoved – "is that you can't stop me."

Again Antonin pushed, both immense hands gripping Mikhail's shoulders.

"This time I'll have my way," he said hoarsely, "not like you did though…"

Mikhail clutched the hands grasping him. His own seaman's grip was strong, his lean body forceful, his will even more so in this room as again the men found themselves face to face, no longer expectant, not even silent, straining as though with one terrible groan, both of them desperate, both determined.

It was Antonin who staggered back as Mikhail wrenched himself free. He paused, his breathing laboured. Disoriented more than angered he looked around, then stared hard at Mikhail, and then anger alone surged – resentment which encompassed far more than this room so that he raised his hand slowly to deal the blow that was needed – the one which would open doors that had remained locked to him for a lifetime.

To his surprise, it never fell. Instead he felt Mikhail's hand once again blocking his arm, his weight again forcing him back, his sailor's arms hurling him sideways against the wall by the door.

Books from the shelves above tumbled down, tipping the lamp as they crashed to the floor. Startled, suddenly in the darkness, both men remained motionless, once more expectant, Misha more than ever focused, Antonin more than ever confused. He sensed Misha approaching, smelled his sweat in the shadows – or was it some other man's smell – two maybe? – he couldn't be certain – things were all so obscure, untested, as he himself had once been on that first night in prison, not having yet learned to strike the first blow or be lost, hurt or be hurt, so that there in Maximilian's house – so strangely darkened, so vacant, he followed instincts learned dearly, price exorbitant still.

The last thing Mikhail felt was Antonin's woodworking knife, plunging deep into his chest.

Elsa Varig had heard nothing from her kitchen in the back of the house. As she moved toward the library with a tray of desserts for Mikhail, she wondered why the lights were out. Thinking that Misha had returned upstairs briefly, she switched on the hall light and entered the library. With a cry she saw Mikhail's body on the rug, crumpled beside the inner door as though guarding it still.

"Misha," she repeated, kneeling beside him.

"The burglar returned," he said hoarsely – last words he managed that evening.

 ⁓☽⁓

Late into the night Elsa was questioned by the police, who had followed the ambulance to Maximilian's house. Relaying all that she knew, she told of the thief who'd returned, of Max still asleep in his room, of the assistant asleep in her own room, of the doctor who'd been in attendance and who would come back in the morning.

Of the assault weapon she said nothing. The police noted in the record that the thief had escaped, weapon in hand, and could not possibly get far on foot.

In this last assumption they were correct. Antonin Onegin was in Riverside Park, crouched inside a subway maintenance shed at the end of the walkway. His one call from a public booth had been to a prison mate, recently released, who for a fee could be trusted to drive him out of the city. Within an hour he was across the Mid-Hudson Bridge, heading north by northwest into the Adirondacks.

He was still on parole, thirty-six days left to freedom. Or rather up until then on parole, liberty up until then within reach.

All in the past, he realized grimly, immense woods like eternal night spreading in every direction around him, deserted roads like coiled springs climbing without end. He would have to vanish now over the border, never again to return.

Ollikainen closed the door softly and rejoined Elsa in the kitchen.

"Did you tell her?" she asked, wiping her hands repeatedly on her apron.

"Some things, yes," said Nicholas guardedly as he sat on a stool by the window. Behind him, reluctantly, morning had dawned cold and raw. "I told her Max would survive, as in my opinion he will, though I did not add that the time remaining would most assuredly be short. I also told her she was well, which she is, and very strong –" here he considered aloud, as though to himself in some classroom: "Most remarkable, really, given the circumstances."

"But of the burglar's return last night?" Elsa burst out then, for she had summoned Ollikainen again after having found Mikhail gasping for whatever was left of his life on the floor. Nicholas had done what he could, saw there was no choice but to call the hospital, later relayed to the medics the story Elsa Varig had told him, no more believing what he was saying than he had believed Mikhail earlier. Some domestic explosion – long time in coming – had occurred in Maximilian's house. As to the details, he was not as yet certain. Max and the girl had been sedated. They could not have stabbed Mikhail. Elsa Varig, he knew, would have laid down her life for him. That left only one suspect, whose name Dr. Ollikainen never once mentioned as the ambulance sped away. If by some miracle Misha survived, if he then chose to press charges and make his private life public – well, it would be out of his hands. If he did not survive – a far more likely scenario – he himself would not be the one to break Max with his suspicions. In any case – and his heart

402

ached with sadness at the cross-purposes defining one's lifetime – Antonin Onegin would mostly likely make a mistake, Mikhail would die in the meantime and Max would learn soon enough that one of the boys he had loved had murdered the other.

"But of the burglar's return," Elsa insisted in the most extreme agitation. "Does Mrs. Devereux know yet? – I mean about Mikhail. Does Monsieur Max know?"

"The girl, yes. I judged her strong enough to hear it. I thought it best, in fact – now, while Mikhail lives still. As for Max..." Nicholas sighed, slipping his stethoscope from his neck. "No. There I judged differently. A second shock now would take whatever life that remains."

He stood, reached for his bag, and, not without effort, for he himself was older than Maximilian: "Tomorrow, Elsa. Tomorrow I will tell Max whatever news I must bring."

Misha was in the recovery room when Caroline reached the hospital. He was there still at midnight, twenty-four hours after Elsa had found him. Not until noontime the following day was he tranferred to the Intensive Care Unit.

"You can go in now," the attending physician said in a kind voice to the strangely silent, pale woman who had not moved from her chair outside the surgical wing.

Caroline stood quickly.

"Fifteen minutes."

"I understand."

"He is not lucid yet."

"He will know I am there," she said, moving as though in a dream through the double doors into the hallway beyond.

It seemed odd to Donovan Heller that Mikhail failed to appear in the lobby of the Savoy Hotel, London. Not four days ago, in the Plaza Hotel, Manhattan, they had agreed on this meeting in England to finalize a yacht sale with long-time British clients. After waiting an hour, the clients had gone. Heller had called the Riverside Suites, Misha's club, Maximilian's house. Only then did he learn that Mikhail was near death.

"But I was with him on Sunday."

"He was assaulted on Monday," replied Elsa Varig.

"May I call the hospital?"

"He is too ill to take calls."

"Day after tomorrow, then, if I may."

"Day after tomorrow? No...He'll be in surgery one last time day after tomorrow."

Her voice sounded grim. His chances seemed slight. Donovan said he would phone at week's end. With a heavy heart he prepared for dinner with his old client's friends.

He had never met his hostess, but had heard that she was lively, well-connected, herself a woman of means. She was also independent, her third marriage having ended like the previous two, in divorce.

"You will like Cecilia," said Jamie Parker, Donovan's client. "She's rather impossible to resist. Also rather impossible," he added, for he himself had courted Cecilia in the past.

The taxicab stopped in front of a pale grey stone town house. Beyond the heavy oak doorway was an elegant hallway, beyond the hallway a living room filled with flowers, guests and sounds of chamber music somewhere. Moving with ease among it all, more striking past fifty than in her wild golden youth, was Mrs. Cecilia Matson Montgomery.

Neither Donovan Heller nor any other guest would have known this was Mikhail's mother. The terms of her divorce from Maximilian had been harsh, all rights to the boy, the sandstone house by the sea and the d'Olivier name surrendered. At first she'd been unconcerned. *Let him keep what he wants*, she had thought, relieved to be gone from Nice and Hélène and that rain ceaselessly lashing Provence.

Yet it was not long before an odd yearning took root in her strange wilful heart. She wanted, just once, to see Mikhail Alexander. She wrote to Maximilian's attorney, through whom all correspondence passed, and received word that the request had been denied. She wrote again. Again she was refused. The war came to an end. She sent the boy Christmas gifts, birthday gifts, every package returned unopened.

After six years she sent no more gifts. *Schoolboy now in Provence*, she assumed, certain that Maximilian would never send the boy far from Nice.

The odd yearning subsided. She was in her prime, not yet thirty, ready to put the whole business behind her.

Six more years passed – wild years like the earlier ones, only the parties went longer, the cars and men faster.

She married again – one of the faster men – himself twice divorced, two sons of his own. Within a year he had found a mistress. Cecilia pretended not to notice. Instead, desperate to have this man's child, she was determined to avoid another disastrous separation.

It was not to be. Twice she miscarried. Pregnant again she went to Geneva, where at a world-class maternity clinic she was delivered of a daughter, stillborn.

Her second marriage was over. She was forty, her beauty no longer angelic, but moving toward handsome. Men courted her, more than ever it seemed since her father's death had left her sole heir to James Matson's fortune.

Of Mikhail Alexander she thought little. He would be through prep school, she surmised, kind and gentle, like his father, although perhaps, also like him, capable of a great revenge. From time to time she wondered if Max had lied to him – surely the boy had asked for her, if only once – saying that she had died when he was born.

On her fiftieth birthday, Cecilia married a third time. It lasted less than a year, although she was grateful when the end came that the divorce was discreet. They parted amicably, if not as friends, at least satisfied, each having gotten what they were looking for in the affair. He had made friends, social contacts and a generous settlement. Twelve years his senior, she'd felt once more like a girl. The feeling was not to occur again in her lifetime.

She sold her father's estate, then the fine house in Cannes, and then began, yet again, a new life on her own: Cecilia Matson Montgomery, generous hostess, supporter of the arts, friend to those of talent and promise. The d'Olivier surname and that brief windswept summer to which it belonged, seemed by then like some fable, told to her once as a child.

Hence it was like a knife plunged into her own breast when she overheard Jamie Parker say during dessert, "No, I did not sign those contracts today. The sale may not even go through. Donovan, what do you think?"

"I fear for the worst," was his answer, and then he relayed what he knew, sketchy details after all, but ghastly in outline, before he concluded in a sombre tone: "Of all people Mikhail. Mikhail d'Olivier. Touched by the stars if ever a man was, stabbed in his father's library – all of it likely to end at Metropolitan Hospital."

Cecilia made a fruitless effort to remain with her guests. As the plates were removed she retreated, murmuring something about a servant taken ill, then she went up to her room, knelt alongside her bed and sobbed. The sounds recalled cries she had tried vainly to stifle when Misha had finally pushed his relentless way out of her womb.

Her old yearning returned, not to be denied this time. She stood and walked to the phone and called Manhattan, Information.

⸓ ☾ ⸍

"No, no there is somebody already with him now," said the attending physician in the Intensive Care Unit. "Unless you are a close relative," he added, having seen the woman's bronze eyes darken almost to black.

"I am his mother," said Cecilia.

"You may go right in."

In the three days since Max learned of the thief's return to his library, he withdrew not into his room, which for a decade had already become his home, but into profound silence. Elsa mistook his introspection for grief; his physician described it as exhaustion; Max, though worn and saddened, had in fact spent that time deep in thought.

Thus Ollikainen was startled to feel a hand on his arm as he stood to leave that third night, for the grip was strong, the voice fervent. "A word, Nicholas, if you've time..."

"Of course, Max."

"You say there is hope still for my son?"

The physician moved his chair back to the daybed.

"Some hope, Max...yes. Depending on tomorrow's surgery. What could be done the first night was done. Mikhail needed more, though, that was clear too from the start. Earliest possible day, given his weak state."

"So it is to be tomorrow," Maximilian repeated, as though confirming his own thoughts.

"First thing."

Max stared again at the courtyard. A steady rain dripped from the awnings, sloping from winter fatigue it appeared. The empty walkways were slick, the fountain superfluous.

"I'll look in later then, Max. Ten or so."

"Wait," he heard as Max turned back from the window. Ollikainen remained seated alongside the daybed. Max listened until the last of the chimes from Antonin's clock echoed out in the hallway; then, betraying no emotion as he leaned in: "This thief who appeared..."

"Reappeared."

"Has he been caught?"

"He seems to have vanished."

"Do they know who he is?"

"Another mystery."

For a moment, as though he would study some document's fine print, Max fixed his eyes on the doctor.

"Why call it a robbery then?"

"Because, Max," said Ollikainen, steadily meeting that gaze, "that is what your son said."

"The burglar returned," confirmed Max.

Nicholas nodded.

"So that is all the police know."

"That is all Elsa told them."

Absently, Max fingered the braided lapels of his robe. Ollikainen's chair creaked in the silence. Once again suddenly, though in an uncoloured tone still: "Unusual, Nicholas, wouldn't you say?

"A thief returning you mean?"

"That very same evening."

"The police say it happens, Max."

"I suppose."

Elsa's uneven step could be heard crossing toward the front door. Beyond, with a heavy thud under the awning, a delivery boy let his stack of newspapers fall. Max glanced outside, watched the boy cut the twine, reflected a moment, turned once more.

"That knife they found, Nicholas…"

"It was never found, Maximilian."

"Perhaps Misha described…"

"Misha said only three words," repeated the doctor. "Of that fact I am certain."

"You have asked Elsa?"

"Many times."

"And you are satisfied?"

The front door slammed as Elsa returned. She crossed the tiled entryway back toward the kitchen, sounds of her movements receding across the patterned carpet of the living room.

"You and I both know that I am," was the physician's reply then, for the house had become utterly still once again, surrendering nothing more.

"Yes. Yes, I do know that," Maximilian acknowledged. "And Nicholas, need I say on this night..."

"You should rest on this night."

"Nevertheless..."

Ollikainen snapped his bag shut – definitive end to the exchange.

"As I said I'll look in," he repeated, reaching for his hat as he stood.

"Tomorrow...Look in tomorrow. First thing if you can," added Max, easing his head onto the mound of pillows beneath him.

Nicholas stood, turned and glanced one last time at Maximilian – eyes closed, hands folded, heart and mind both racing now – there'd be no stopping that, he well knew.

"Rest, Max," he repeated.

$\smile$ ☾ $\backsim$

"Monsieur Max, are you ill?" asked Elsa hastily, answering his insistent ring.

"No. No, perhaps just too impatient, Elsa. Come in."

"May I bring you something?"

"Please."

"Your usual broth?"

Max shook his head.

"Tea then, this evening."

"No. No, this evening, I think – please take the seat alongside – that's it, good. This evening," Maximilian went on, "I should prefer hearing the truth from you, finally."

Elsa Varig turned pale. Max continued to stare. She tried to lean away somewhat, out of the arc of the courtyard lamp just beyond, but Max had positioned the chair so that even the tip of its tall ladder back remained harshly lit. She looked to the left, toward a painting of Nice over the dresser; she looked past the daybed into the courtyard, then to the right at scenes of Provence on an antique triple screen.

And all the while Maximilian's gaze followed her, silently, until in the end she had no choice but to lower her head. Even then Max let some time pass, as though in deference to the rain, heavier than before, rhythmically striking the windows. The noise seemed strident to Elsa, the time endless as she remained with her head down, right hand absently stroking the pronounced veins in her left.

And then once again Antonin's clock chimed in the hall. Maximilian waited, counting eight strokes. Soundlessly then, he reached and placed the weight of his own right hand on hers, stopping its movement.

This left Elsa staring down at Maximilian's powerful fingers. They remained in her lap, holding her hands beneath them – no pressure, no pain, just a reminder, as the clock had so poignantly noted, that time and her options had by then both run out.

Desperately then, head down still, she murmured, "What do you need to know, Monsieur Max?"

"How it was done."

"Nothing more?"

"We will see."

With that Maximilian let his hand slip away, ever so slowly, as he resumed his position on his daybed. It was a pledge of good faith, they both knew, although she dared not yet raise her head, staring instead at the crease made in her skirt by her old hands and his huge one.

Finally, though still barely audible: "With his woodworking knife."

Calmly, though almost whispered as well: "And where is that knife now?"

"I tossed it into the river."

"And where is he now, Elsa Varig."

"That I do not know, Monsieur."

"Elsa, if we are both to survive this, *I must know where he is*."

"Monsieur Max," she cried out, "if I knew where he was I would have gone to him – I would have made some excuse, asked for some time off, anything – but I do not know, and so I wait as you do – I wait for my son as you wait for yours – I found only his knife, Monsieur Max – and that I kept to myself, as Mikhail did, for as long as he could."

She blinked her colourless eyes, then lowered her head once again.

"You must forgive me, Monsieur, for not telling you sooner."

In her chestnut hair he saw her mother, Anna Berg. Her controlled, raspy voice resembled her lover's – Jean-Luc Onegin – and the hoarse voice of their child, for whom Max lost his leg.

"What's to be done?" she cried out once again.

"Hush Elsa, be still now. I must think."

Max looked away, not to the courtyard this time but back to his large room, half shadowed now – his immense desk with its books, papers, reminders, recollections – the pen which had rendered his life and its passions, one and the same even now.

"Monsieur Max" – It was Elsa's hand now reaching out now for Maximilian's – "should the worst happen tomorrow…"

"Should my son die, you mean…"

"Beloved Mikhail…"

"Misha," was how he rephrased it, as if trying to remember someone he had known only briefly.

"Should the worst happen," she repeated, since he had added no more then, "I will be gone when the sun sets, because my step would remind you each moment, morning and evening, for the rest of your days of the thing that my son did – and yet you would tell no one what my son did – for the sake of your nurse you would be silent, Monsieur Max, of this I am certain…"

"Be *still*," he commanded again, harshly this time, for so few minutes were left, and he would lose none of them – he would not lose his son, nor Anna Berg's grandson, and he would not lose the girl – above all the girl – though it had seemed odd to Elsa and Dr. Ollikainen and to himself above all that he had never once asked for her.

And yet they were all that remained.

"Should my son die," he went on, in his desperation forcing

efficiency still, "you will remain here, as you always have, ElsaVarig, do you understand me?"

"Monsieur, *please…*"

"You will say nothing. When they question you – and they will again – you saw nothing on Monday, *do you hear me?*"

This last was accompanied with a startling thump on the table, for she seemed indeed not to have heard him.

"You saw only my son, gasping for life, and heard only his words, *The burglar returned.*"

Mechanically, Elsa nodded.

"There was no murder weapon," Max went on, sternly still. "Nothing you found in any case. If you were seen in the courtyard – which is likely – you returned for an item you dropped from your marketing bag. If you were later seen down by the river – also a probability – you needed some air after such ghastly events. You felt you could go then since the doctor was here. The doctor was here still, was he not?"

"I – no…no he was not, Monsieur."

"For the love of God, Elsa!" Max said, with a second resounding crash on the table.

"I mean yes – yes, if you say he was, Monsieur."

"We are speaking of *your* sworn recollections!" Max cried.

Dimly then, though her hands were still shaking, Elsa began to see what it was that he wanted. Max, steadier now, repeated his question with exaggerated precision. His intensely blue eyes seemed to cast a spell on her as he waited, forcing phrases he needed to hear to take precise shape inside Elsa's distraught head.

Finally, with barely a hint of conviction: "The doctor was here, Monsieur, yes."

"Anything else you recall?"

Once again their gaze met. Once again that strange force from him as she reached back toward a scene with increasing fluency invented.

"I remember the marketing bag…the item, I mean. That special tea that you need, which is why I felt I must go."

Max urged her on.

"I found it under the archway, out toward the sidewalk."

Max kept rolling his arm.

"It is now in the cupboard. Next to the biscuits…your pills. I put it there myself, Monsieur, when I came back from my walk."

Max seemed dissatisfied. Elsa straightened herself. Then, almost with indignation: "Feel free to send someone to search if you like. English tea. Top shelf next to the stove."

A faint smile played at long last across Maximilian's face.

"No, no that will not be necessary. I am satisfied, Elsa Varig. And very sorry to have disturbed you. You may go now."

Elsa rose. Turning, she felt again that same large hand on her arm – a gentle touch this time, leaving its own imprint too in its way.

"I'll take my coffee at eleven, Elsa, as I always do."

⌐ ☾ ⌐

Not until late afternoon on the following day did the d'Olivier telephone ring. Max was informed that his son was alive, at least for the moment, having survived a complicated, experimental new procedure wherein the heart itself had been repaired.

"The next few days will decide," he had also been told, "assuming, of course, that by some miracle he can hold on through the night."

"Monsieur Max has some hope now," whispered Elsa to Dr. Ollikainen when he arrived for his visit that evening. "I saw it on his face today. You'll see it for sure now as well."

Ollikainen saw far more than hope when he reached Maximilian's room. Stunned, he found Max at his desk, fully dressed, as though awaiting a visitor.

"Guests tonight Max?" he asked, trying not to betray dismay at what he considered ill-advised haste. "You mustn't make so much effort."

Maximilian leaned forward, all traces of the exhaustion that had marked his face days before vanished.

"Nicholas, you must help me."

"Always, you know that."

"You must help me leave."

"Leave?" stammered Ollikainen, recalling cattle trains – Kindertransport connections – *leaving* always a metaphor for what could never again be recovered.

"Max, what are you saying?"

"I want to go to the hospital."

"But you're so much improved, Max…"

"I want to go to my son."

Ollikainen sat back, stupefied. Max had not left his house in twelve years. For ten of those years he had never descended the staircase – with the exception of whatever had happened which he had chosen to call theft. The effort had nearly killed him. Now he seemed determined to do it again.

"It is impossible," said the physician.

"It is imperative."

"Later perhaps…"

"*Tonight*," Max insisted, reaching beside him for his cane. "With or without you I will go tonight – to see Mikhail one last time, if that is how it must be."

He stopped all of a sudden, gazing beyond Nicholas toward some far distant thing.

"I must ask his forgiveness."

In a gentle tone Nicholas answered, "He is unconscious, Maximilian."

"He will hear me."

"And should you not – I mean – should the effort prove too much – as I believe it might…"

"Then it is you who will do it. You must say simply, 'Max was on his way here to ask your forgiveness.' He will know what you mean."

It was clear then to Dr. Ollikainen that Max would not be dissuaded.

Having seen the physician's tag on Ollikainen's jacket still, the head nurse waved him on into the Intensive Care Unit. To Maximilian, standing slightly behind, she said, "Name of the patient you have come to inquire about?"

"Mikhail Alexander d'Olivier."

"Only immediate family members, sir – I am sorry."

After a moment, as though the concept were unfamiliar, Maximilian responded: "I am his father."

The nurse looked up at him. Large and powerful still, he was clearly unsteady, not so much old as long-lived – more like a grand-father than the father of the young man in 3A.

"Forgive me, sir. Please go right in."

"Thank you."

"His mother is already there."

Max stood rock-still by the desk.

"Come, Max, while there's time left," called Ollikainen, who was holding open the double doors.

Still Max did not move.

"Are you all right, sir?"

"I – Yes. Fine – You must be mistaken though," he insisted, gesturing toward the chart with his cane.

The nurse consulted her list once again.

"No, no mistake here. Cecilia Matson Montgomery, in today from London," she added, more than ever perplexed by the man, suddenly rooted as he seemed to his spot by the doorway.

Finally, more like a gasp than a query: "Is she alone?"

"She is not."

Max leaned his weight on the cane. He had heard that she'd married. Perhaps she was there with her husband, or an escort – and then suddenly – the possibility made his blood freeze – another man's image took shape, for it would not be unlike Antonin to risk everything, as he himself had, to come back one last time and ask for forgiveness.

After a moment: "Go on ahead, Nicholas."

Ollikainen did not go. He let the door close behind him, watching Max keenly, astonished to see him mustering strength and a counterfeit calm one last time.

"The man is dark," Max went on to the nurse, "fortyish?"

"It is a woman, sir."

All feigned composure disappeared. For the first time since she had clasped him – stripped and defenceless – he remembered her name. Then came her eyes, and that ornate old world script, and then passions and a matching obsession which had defined his own star-crossed life.

"Full circle," he murmured.

"She has been here every day, some nights too I believe, since the patient arrived. I don't believe they are related..."

Ollikainen moved toward Maximilian.

"Max," he said discreetly, "this has all been too much."

"No."

"Let me in go for you, speak for you. Whatever you want me to say I will say..."

"It is no use," Max insisted, having somehow seen clearly that it would come down to this in the end, though he had never imagined it would be here, in this place, and that they would be together at last in that room, and how on earth would he face the one, whom he had pursued with such a vengeance for so many decades, or the other, whom he had almost killed the past week.

In the end, Max never faced either.

He was about to enter Mikhail's room when he saw them both there – Caroline to the left, Cecilia on the right, both facing away from the curtained screen near the door. Caroline was silent, though now and again she leaned toward the bed to smooth out the sheet or check the tubes in his arm. Cecilia never once moved, transfixed there, it seemed, by the face on the pillow before her.

Her beauty, Max thought, was more than ever astounding – riper now, to be sure, no longer the body that had swung toward a cobalt Cannes sky for him once – but that very ripeness was more arresting, as though the decades had softened her heart instead of removing her youth, and the years had turned to gold the brazen indifference of an early grace. Nevertheless, Max was aware, not a shred of the old insane desire for her remained. Just this stunned awareness of her beauty, still undiminished.

The patient moved all of a sudden. For an instant he opened his eyes, and then again he lay motionless, deep and unnatural sleep somewhere between life and death.

"Mikhail," Max heard Cecilia say then – still that compelling murmur he remembered precisely, only this time it was not caprice, not some passing whim like a house or a gem or a man's desperate heart she desired. This time she wanted her son. He had opened his eyes, briefly, and she would not be denied; he had wanted life once again and she would secure it, whatever the cost. The confession was long overdue, after all, the reckoning unavoidable, and in any case, though the effort might break her, they were unlikely ever to meet again on this earth.

"Mikhail," she repeated, bending still closer. "Who knows if you could ever, even in health, recognize the voice that is speaking. I spoke to you only once, long ago – the morning I held you."

Misha's eyes remained closed. The room was utterly still, save for the rhythmical beeping of the monitors overhead.

"I was afraid of you then, Misha. I was afraid I would drop you, or hurt you, for you had hurt me so, born as you were with such a vengeance, as if you knew I was not ready. Yet you were flesh of my flesh. You would have your own way. Resilience would be your destiny – that much at least I saw that day – that one single day – for I was so lost and you seemed so sure, and I remained lost, and I am willing to bet you have never been lost."

She passed her hand over his forehead, gingerly, as one might quickly touch a newborn.

"No, you have never been lost, not once, and though I tried to find you, over and over again, I knew in my heart I would never succeed. My gypsy ways would be yours – that and your father's great pride," she added resignedly, "but at least one thing remained from that summer in Cannes – *one thing*," she insisted, her murmur now ardent, for she knew she had only this chance left, and she knew he could hear her somehow, just as he could hear her sobs when she had told no one else he was inside her.

"*You will not be denied, Mikhail.* That's what survived from those days, what I've come to tell you on this day. Though I would give up my life in exchange for yours now – offering I was too scared to make long ago – you've no need." Her hand remained near his head, hovering indecisively a moment before she let it fall back on her lap. "My stubborn heart's yours, son," she whispered. "On your own you will live."

And with that perfervid prediction, as abruptly as she had started, Cecilia fell silent.

Only then did Caroline turn, knowing at last the identity of the woman who had been waiting beside her that night. Cecilia felt herself burning, in fact, under the intense gaze of the girl. She faced her in turn, steadily, only then noting the cream and gold cameo pinned on her dress.

"Yes, it was yours once," Caroline murmured, fumbling to unpin the brooch. "You deserve it again, Cecilia Matson, for if he lives, it will be a mother's doing. And besides – besides," she repeated, tripping over the words as though they were a bone caught in her throat, "I haven't the right. I only wore it this week so that he would focus on something, *anything* – see at least one thing he loved…"

She reached out her hand to return the cameo to Cecilia. Cecilia closed Caroline's fingers around the elegant brooch.

"I don't know who you are, my dear."

"Please…"

"But I know who gave you that gift, and though he was angry with me once, and for most of his life after that, I know too he would want you to keep whatever was left of those days."

Caroline shook her head.

"Believe me," insisted Cecilia, "he will not make the same mistake twice. I could not love his son, and for that I was never forgiven. I suspect you have done the opposite. This time though he will forgive."

A nurse entered and began to move the screen from the doorway, but Max put his fingers to his lips so that she stepped back for a moment – it would be a moment after all, and her routine check could be made after she stopped in the next room – and so she silently retreated, and Max remained where he was.

He saw Caroline pin the brooch back onto to her dress. He saw her smile at Cecilia, somewhat shyly. He saw Cecilia return the smile, wisely, for Cecilia had never, not once in her life, ever been shy.

"It is a very long story," was all Caroline managed.

"Such things always are," was Cecilia's response.

Both women fell silent.

Max remained still unseen.

Yes, yes it was a long story, he reflected, begun in an orchard above Cannes in the arms of one beauty, ending in another secluded spot, yearning for another woman, desperately, so that he almost killed her. He studied her profile as she faced away from him, toward Mikhail. She could still arouse his desire. He took a step backward and left, not making a sound, and found Ollikainen waiting at the nurses' station behind him.

"Did you speak to him, Max?"

"There was no need."

Ollikainen stood, fearing the worst.

"What he has needed to hear all his life he has heard. Or maybe I needed to hear it. In any case, the boy will live, of that I am certain." He stopped. "Full circle," he murmured again, and then, along with surging relief, he felt a tremendous exhaustion.

"Come," said his colleague kindly, "Let me take you home, Max."

~ ☾ ~

Misha felt not exhaustion but increasing strength as time passed – resilience part natural vigour, part recollection, perhaps, of a voice heard decades before then, part awareness perhaps of those flowers filling his room – were they hydrangeas? – he couldn't be certain – everything was a blur, but their deep hue fixed on him whenever he opened his eyes, until on the third day he had managed to smile, and on the fourth say her name as he was wheeled from the Intensive Care Unit into his own room.

His mother never saw that room. There were only two worlds she was destined to share with the boy, she guessed: one the protection of her womb, the other exclusive, mysterious, vital fluids passing again into his flesh – a strangely not dissimilar place. Beyond that space she had no claim. She had relinquished it once, only to reenact its ontology here, and now she would again retreat, not lost and desperate, like the first time, but resigned, even wistful, certainly wiser.

Hence she never heard the phone ring in Mikhail's private room, nor did she see Caroline answer it hastily, only to hear Elsa Varig say, "You must get a message to Mikhail. As soon as he can understand, you must tell him these words, and only these words, exactly as I will now say them."

She lowered her voice before pronouncing them, stressing each phrase exactly: *A colleague of Antonin called. He is well, although he is away, and must stay away at least for a time…due to parole obligations.* Can you deliver that message?"

"Yes. Yes, I can," Caroline managed, astounded still by the unexpectedly urgent call, its quick, cryptic words.

"Mikhail will understand," Elsa went on. He will grasp every-thing, *but only if you say it correctly.* Shall I repeat it?"

"I – no. There is no need. I have heard you well, Elsa Varig. I will say exactly what you wish, as you have said it."

"Good."

Caroline longed to ask for Max. Her heart ached for news of him, of his health and his days, and his nights, and his heart – yet she felt she hadn't the right to even mention his name.

Suddenly though, Elsa offered: "This very same message I have relayed to Monsieur Max. He has been greatly relieved by the news. He is also heartened by the daily reports that are phoned in from the hospital. Both boys, he now knows, will survive this ordeal."

And that was all. No word of her. No query as to her health. Not even a hope that in some new life she would somehow be well. Yet Max had to know she was there. The hospital would have reported it. How else would Elsa have known that she could be found there, beside Mikhail, as she had been for ten days?

It was all too clear, Caroline saw. Max didn't even want to hear her name. Never again could she go back to those rooms she had come to cherish as she'd once loved her own home. They were both now, fittingly, cinders.

Misha will be pleased though when I tell him, she thought. *Yes, he will be pleased, for it must have seemed odd to him that Antonin has never appeared, not even once, to wait and give comfort or at least ask during these days. Now he will know. Parole obligations...I must remember the term exactly when he awakens tomorrow. Perhaps his head will be clear enough to hear the words as I say them.*

If not, decided Caroline, smoothing the sheets out again, *I will say them again, and again the next day, over and over again, until he is pleased.*

She needed only to say them once. Mikhail fixed his gaze upon her as she said, softly but clearly: "There has been word from Antonin. Elsa Varig received the call."

Mikhail stared at her.

"Well not exactly from him – but from a colleague, a trusted friend, it appears – and he relayed to her what she said to me, and then she insisted I tell you exactly."

Word for word Caroline repeated Elsa Varig's mysterious message – at least to Caroline it had seemed odd, or perhaps merely unlike the stolid housekeeper's daily detachment – but for some reason Mikhail took enormous solace in the strange words.

He lay his head back on the pillow, closed his eyes and slept a deep and dreamless restorative sleep, knowing at last that Maximilian would not have to forfeit all of the souls he had protected.

⌒☾⌒

"Cecilia!" said Roger Gachet, in his broadest, most expansive tone. "I have cancelled every appointment…"

"Really there was no need," she replied, offering her hand with a frank charm honed to perfection over the decades.

She had been met in the main lobby of La Ronde, having stressed that her flight to London would depart at six-thirty, that she had only one hour, and that she needed a gift for an old friend – a physician who had arranged for her immediate entrance into Metropolitan Hospital, Intensive Care Unit, Manhattan.

"Good God, Cecilia…"

"No, no, all's well. I…it was a friend. Mikhail d'Olivier. Our families have been close for decades. I simply felt I should be here."

They went directly to Estate Treasures, floor two, where Cecilia glanced at the flatware, the tea sets, the cut crystal goblets, the elegant jewels. She selected a gold antique frame, then paused again at the case with the rare black pearl necklace and matching pearl ear clips.

"A king's ransom, I should imagine."

"Well, in the vicinity."

"Someday, Roger," she answered winsomely, taking his arm as they walked back downstairs. "I just might surprise you. You might walk into a room and find those black pearls round my neck."

"Nothing surprises me," he said in a rare burst of candour. "Ah, Claire! Do come and meet Mrs. Montgomery – a valued friend of La Ronde."

With a satisfied nod he felt compelled to add then – after all, the McCallister pair was a most exceptional acquisition – "Miss Tierney is also a valued friend at La Ronde. She is my assistant."

Cecilia offered her hand. Claire basked in her ravishing smile. In the oddest of ways that smile was somehow familiar.

"Mrs. Montgomery is in New York on an errand of mercy – hospital visit – old friend of the family. She has promised she'll stay a bit longer the next time."

"Hopefully, Roger."

"At least young d'Olivier is doing well."

Claire stared at Roger.

"I met his father once – I'm sure I did," Roger went on. "Well that was years ago, ten at least…"

"Was there an accident?" Claire blurted out.

Like Roger, Cecilia was taken aback – more by Claire's sudden pallor than by the intrusion.

"No – no not exactly."

"Then he is ill," she pursued, her statement clearly a question.

"Do you know Mikhail?" asked Cecilia. She was disturbed by Claire's Tierney's insistence and did not pretend to the contrary.

"We have some mutual friends. Our paths have crossed on occasion. Can you tell me what's happened?"

"Mrs. Montgomery has a plane to catch…"

"*Please*," Claire repeated. Her tone was so plaintive, her blue eyes so grave, that Cecilia paused for a moment, studied Claire keenly, and guessed something more intimate than mutual friends had united them once. Delicately then – it was a day for reparations after all: "Mikhail was attacked in his father's home by an intruder. There has been complicated surgery. It is my firm belief that he will mend quickly."

Too stunned to reply, Claire merely nodded.

"Yes," Cecilia insisted in a calm voice, laying a hand on Claire's arm as they stood in the doorway. "He will be fine, I expect, as the weeks pass."

Claire managed a quiet "Thank you" before Roger announced that Cecilia's car had arrived.

"Dearest Roger," murmured Cecilia, "for now *au revoir*."

Roger kissed her and promised to send the frame to Metropolitan Hospital that very day. Thus it was that Claire discovered where she could find Misha that evening.

"May I see him?" Claire asked the head nurse. "I won't stay but a moment – unless he is sleeping, or very uncomfortable."

"He is awake – but uncomfortable. There is somebody with him."

"I can come back then."

"No, no. You may also go in. Visiting hours will end in five minutes though. "

The door was slightly ajar. Claire pushed it a little more and stood at the threshold, as Maximilian himself had done also that week. Like Max, she had seen Cecilia that day. Now, also like Max, she stood transfixed by the other woman. The woman did not see her. She was bending over Mikhail, adjusting his pillow, speaking tenderly in a low voice. His face turned toward her, away from the doorway. He reached up and touched her, smiled and then closed his eyes.

There was something about that mass of black hair, that long and lithe body – something oddly familiar about the woman – though Claire had not yet seen her face.

"Mikhail," whispered the woman. "I'm going to lower the blinds. The setting sun might be too much."

She stood, made the adjustment and returned to the chair by his side – never once glancing back at the doorway behind her, where Claire was standing, rock-still now, having at last seen the stranger's face – *Half Moon*'s face – more unique in its strangely compelling grace than even Jude McCallister had rendered it.

For a moment or two Claire Tierney remained there, too astonished to leave, too astounded to speak, images of the past year swirling around in her head – Christmas bells, a beaded bag, Mikhail's loafers disappearing down the sidewalk beneath her window, Mikhail loving another. That this other returned his love was clear from the way she bent again over his face, letting her hair brush against him so that he could caress it, as the sea lingered with love along the quay in Honfleur, where Jude McCallister no doubt remained, still hoarding his treasure.

Puzzle at last completed, she initially thought, the colliding images told all: Half Moon had left Jude for Mikhail d'Olivier.

And yet – given Jude's fierce love – how could that picture be right?

Victory was hers, she remembered Jude saying. In the end he was wrong, concluded Claire grimly. Victory was Mikhail's, as always, for hadn't she too fallen prey to the vagabond charm of this man?

Without a word she backed away. Her high heels echoed down the hallway. So too, in her head, did the promise she had made to Jude McCallister on the Normandy coast. She would never speak of their meeting – that had been her commitment – and because it had mattered so to Jude she would not now renege.

Besides, she considered, nursing her own hurt, the time had come to forget. Mikhail would survive. He would have his Half Moon. Jude too would survive. He would find another.

I too will find another, Claire promised herself as she hailed a taxi outside the hospital.

And so Caroline never learned of Jude McCallister's catastrophe, of his long and desperate fight for life again, of the love that consumed him still – and her too perhaps, unacknowledged, although Claire could never have known this last fact. Nobody could. Caroline Devereux had been too hurt to confront that possibility.

⌐☾⌐

"You're a queer one, Onegin," Simon Rand muttered as they continued north on the deserted highway through Québec province toward Labrador. High winds from the east brought the distinct smell of salt. Off to the west were the Laurentians – mountains like walls, Antonin thought, with sheared-off trees recalling rows of barbed wire. "I mean, first you make me call that house again."

"I paid you."

"The place where you *did* it..."

"I paid what you asked, Rand."

Simon Rand shook his head, disbelieving, as the battered blue pickup lurched ahead into the darkness.

"To let some housekeeper know you're doing just fine," he said under his breath. "You call this *just fine*, man?"

"You missed a meal on the way?"

"Jesus."

"Anyone hear that call?"

"No."

"Searched your car at the border?"

"You just got lucky, man, that's all."

"One more call…"

"No more calls."

"Whatever the price…"

"Look," Simon said sullenly. "Take my advice. Forget those folks. Nobody gets lucky twice."

Antonin turned toward the salty winds from the east. Slowly the sun set and the highway curved toward the salt and then a roadside stand appeared in the distance.

"Stop at that store," Antonin said all of a sudden.

"We have enough food."

"*Stop,*" he insisted, and since a third of the journey remained to be paid still, Simon Rand stopped, and Antonin went inside, still carrying Rand's gun, and when he returned, not more than five minutes later, he announced calmly: "At Port Ste-Catherine there will be a phone. Here are two thousand Canadian dollars. I will be needing you to make that call then."

Either way, Simon knew there would be no turning back. Antonin Onegin had risked everything for a phone call, which would have to be made now, come what may, though he knew enough never to ask what had occurred in that God-forsaken store by the woods.

"Metropolitan Hospital. Here is the number. The patient's name is Mikhail…"

Simon Rand darted another glance at the passenger next to him. He loomed so large that he seemed out of place in his truck, as though he belonged to the Laurentians off to the west.

"Dead or alive still – that is the only thing I need to know," continued Antonin, his voice a low monotone like the encroaching darkness of the Canadian forest.

The wad of bills stuffed into the space between them felt suddenly thick to Simon.

"You'd better hope he's dead, man, that's all I have to say."

Antonin made no answer.

"If he's alive still he'll hunt you down…"

"There's the town up ahead."

"Or have the parole board do it for him."

Simon Rand slowed his truck. Shrouded in fog, a painted red phone booth was barely visible through the trees.

He turned off the lights, opened his door and felt Antonin's hand on his arm.

"No names, Rand. No road map. Just a report on the patient."

"Right."

"d'Olivier."

"You told me that."

"I'll wait for you here," replied Antonin, slumping down in his seat.

It seemed a long time to Antonin 'til Simon walked back toward the truck, wad of bills in his vest, ignition keys in his hand.

"Alive and well," Simon pronounced, slamming the thick door beside him.

He started the navy blue truck up under the fir trees shading the corner.

Antonin laid his head back and closed his eyes and slept a deep and dreamless restorative sleep, knowing at last that Maximilian would not have to forfeit all of the souls he had protected.

⟡

The full moon turned pale as Caroline reached the south bank, making the woods unfamiliar somehow, trackless almost in winter's irresolute light. Relieved by the sound of the falls, she moved on. Once inside the mill house she sat on a stool by the door, sounds of the wheel ceaselessly turning behind her.

"Even here it's all changed," she reflected. Workmen had gutted the rooms; wiring had been installed; plumbing and fixtures were already in place. And yet she felt only sadness seeing her mill taking shape. The stubborn stones of the place, transformed by Mikhail's money and Maximilian's designs, had brought only discord, as she had.

Mystified, she pondered Antonin. There had been just that one message and Mikhail seemingly glad for the words, although never again since Elsa's call had he mentioned Antonin's name. She herself had had no word from him. Only the headboard had arrived, shipped the morning he'd vanished. From her perch near the doorway she could see it propped against the hearth wall. She shuddered, recalling the heavy sound of his boots the day they had walked round the mill.

"I think it is good," he had pronounced on that day.

Where is he now? she wondered, and then once more she shuddered, despite the new heat in the house, and hurried on back toward the river.

Crossing the footbridge, she made her way to the guest house – soon to be gone as well, she thought pausing alongside the dirt mound, for her new tenants would be arriving, as scheduled, in little over a month.

Off to her right was a slope that had once been wide porch steps. To her left was the orchard, trees so recently peach-toned, branches ice-blue now, like the stars. Suddenly thoughts of a tree house occurred – a schoolboy in hiding, an architect smiling, songbirds coaxed into a tune so that she quickened her step and then quite without warning – his face had eluded her since the stabbing though she had tried to recall it all week – she heard a voice like ebb tide in Provence as once more she stopped.

A space that sets someone free, Caroline – that is the best place, it whispered, and then at long last she saw him – not as he'd been on the first day, with a paisley ascot and his dignity, extending his hand and his home and in the end, she now knew, what had remained of his heart – but as he had been on that last day, towering over her, cane raised above her, face ashen with rage, then remorse, then a mortal reluctance to hurt anymore.

She turned away from the thought, rushing on toward the walls that surrounded the guest house. Taking her key from her purse, she saw a single envelope in her mailbox.

"Antonin!" she exclaimed, for she had never accepted the fact that he had not tried to contact her – even once – during the past desperate days. Here for sure was an explanation.

The explanation came from another.

Dearest Caroline, she read, still in the distant blue light of the stars.

I haven't the right to call you that, much less to write to you, not even to think of you, and yet I have of course, day and night, as I have thought of my son, whom you have loved well enough to ransom back his existence – having kept a vigil, I am informed, until the critical stages have passed. For that I must thank you.

Yet it is not to thank you that I write.

I write to ask for forgiveness.

It was a madness born out of love, no point denying it now – love of life long denied, love of beauty, love of Misha, my homeland, his mother – all of it so long ago – all rendered so perfectly, as you once assured me it would be – you with your elegant face, for which I was not yet prepared in spite of my years, although I got used to its pallor, and came to rely on its presence, and then I deluded myself into thinking that what I felt was something akin to what a father might feel.

Of course it was more than what a father might feel. And of course – now I know – it could not be – wanting to keep you like that, frozen in time by my side, locked in the darkness of days come and gone. You were right to want more.

Enclosed is a cheque for these past days. You have earned it.

I would not dream of asking you to return, for I know you would never again appear by my side, although it is my deepest desire – that and seeing my son well again, and Antonin Onegin safe.

Hence, when you are ready, please call Anatole Kramer. I will tell him to be expecting your voice, and to find you the superb position your rare talents deserve.

His father and I – you may have divined this – were colleagues. It has all come full circle.

Paul Maximilian d'Olivier

Post Script:

I have loved you more than all the other beloveds combined. There is no need to let me know if and when you forgive me. I shall feel it the moment it happens, and my soul will be relieved of the profound sadness it now feels, peace no longer denied me.

Winds were brisk the next day, billowing clouds high and swift, sunlight intense on the surrounding slate rooftops. Out in the courtyard, Max saw, two small boys tossed a ball by the fountain. Antonin's clock chimed eleven. He heard a knock on his door.

"Come in, Elsa," he called wearily from his daybed.

"It is not Elsa, Maximilian."

He raised himself slightly and looked toward the door. Caroline felt of all things suddenly shy.

"I have brought pens, Max," she said in a small voice. "And should we need…"

"Come to me."

"Notebooks…"

"*Come,*" he cried hoarsely, holding his arms out.

Neither would ever remember how she had rushed to him then, how she had fallen down on her knees, recalling that other night, until at last he said, "No more, Caroline. No more tears."

"Max," she repeated still.

"I wrote to you."

"I read it."

"And in that letter I said to you…"

"I know what you said to me."

"Hush, then," he insisted, terms of endearment he had not used since the year before Mikhail's birth coming easily now. "Hush and

430

be still now…yes…that's it," he confirmed, voice more than ever like the changing of Provençal tides.

Soon that voice too drifted off until there was only the wind in spite of the heavily draped room, and then even the wind evanesced and a billowing cloud momentarily darkened the room so that Caroline raised her head and saw him observing her still and whispered, "Yes, Maximilian. Everything's possible now."

That very day they resumed working, Max recollecting at an almost feverish pace, Caroline rapidly filling her pages.

Later, though, rereading the scenes she had rendered – France in the war's final months, Resistance at long last triumphant – Max again became strangely silent. Several times he returned to her pages, several times he looked away from them – not so much dissatisfied, Caroline thought, as for some reason disheartened. She did not press him, however, but merely waited as she had always done whenever he'd search for words or events or – more frequently when he'd fall silent – his own place in the picture.

He seemed to have found that place after some time had gone by. Whatever the picture presented, though, gave him no pleasure – not even a glimmer of satisfaction. "The work is unfinished," he murmured, and still Caroline waited, for he had not yet turned back to her, eyes clouded now with the contemplation of this last clearly disturbing thing.

"A postscript perhaps…a translator's note," he went on indistinctly.

"Max, what are you saying?"

"Something to indicate that the patriot…hero for want of a better term…never really existed. Well for a time he existed – handbreadth's time only, though – that's what the record must say. You will not need me to dictate," he added jaggedly, refusing to face Caroline still. "You will never forget what you saw."

Max said no more then, grateful for the fact that the room was in shadows, glad for the sunset long since come and gone.

But Caroline no longer took refuge in darkness.

"What it is that I saw, Maximilian?"

Max made no answer.

"What, Max?" she persisted.

Finally, not so much wearily but like midwinter's valiant light simply extinguished: "I wanted my way, Caroline. I nearly killed for it. I believe I could have killed – gladly," he confessed, turning at last to her so that the next words, uttered with a sudden violence, were , although whispered, like the roar of a great wave bursting abruptly upon them. *"I was no different from them, that's what you saw."*

The great wave receded. But for that firm, mechanical marking of seconds out in the hallway, there was absolute silence. Indeed the courtyard, the archway, the home-going crowds on the street all seemed to have fallen utterly, unexpectedly still.

Until Max heard or thought he heard the rustle of Caroline's skirt in the dimness, her hand drawing the table lamp nearer, her murmured "I nearly died for wanting my way once, Maximilian," these last words clearly discerned as she turned ever so slightly and switched on the light alongside.

Max was astounded – not by the sudden glare, nor by the fact that she had removed her shawl in the darkness – that she had done in the heat many times – but by her next forthright, unrepentant, unequivocal, "Reminders remain, as you know."

He had never asked her how it happened; she had never offered any details, having recorded for him only how it felt to be burned, nothing further until that moment – until she had turned on that lamp, so as to be heard more distinctly, recounting for him then in a most dispassionate voice how she had danced, and had fallen, and had still wanted music, and had gone up in flames for her passion.

"All for a song," was her bittersweet coda, "harmony strictly forbidden, for I had already transgressed on the day of Communion – but I was a devious girl, and I wanted my way, and would you then write an epilogue calling me one of them, Max?"

"How could you think such a thing?" he groaned. "You had not wanted to harm."

"Neither did you. You wanted your way, but your way is a fierce one, as mine is, and so you mistake it for cruelty's way – but that is a cold path, admitting no passion, just the infliction of pain, which you are unable to do."

"I beat my own son."

"You settled an old score."

"I would have beaten you."

"Never, Max, not in your lifetime, which is why I asked for the blows I knew would never descend."

Max shook his head.

"And even if they had – had you tried once, or twice – it would not have made you one of them," she added.

"Where is the line drawn?" he cried.

She reached into her bag.

"Here. Your Catullus."

He took the leather-bound book from her hand, its softly lined pages filled with the script he now knew as he knew his own past.

There they all were – every lyric he'd ever longed for – songs of ecstasy, words of passion – renunciation, introspection, understanding, renewal.

Caroline leaned in to him as he studied her renderings.

"He wanted to hurt out of hurt, Max. Who in a lifetime has not done the same? And what impertinent soul would write an epilogue to Catullus?"

$$\sim (\sim$$

They worked together throughout the winter, into spring, and Antonin's name was never mentioned. Caroline longed to ask Max but felt she must wait. *When the time comes, he will tell me,* she said to herself as the days passed, sensing a dark thing had happened, and that Max and Elsa and even Mikhail knew, although not one of them would speak of it.

She was only partially right. Antonin's fate since the stabbing was unknown to them all. There had been only two calls – one from Simon Rand, anonymous, to the hospital – one from Antonin to his mother, from a public phone booth on the highway. That he was armed, and had robbed twice, and was desperate, nobody knew. He had merely assured Elsa that he was well, and would be gone for a while.

Not for a moment had Max believed it. He knew Antonin's nature – fierce in his affections, volatile in his anger, easy prey to those who would offer help in exchange for unholy dependence. Forced to move now among them, Max knew, Antonin was at risk. Yet of his concerns he said never a word.

Neither did he ever mention that he knew Caroline spent her rest time at the hospital each afternoon. After all, he now understood, he owned a part of this woman no one else could ever claim. He would wait. There was much to be done still. He was accustomed to waiting, feigning forbearance.

☽

On the last day of March, Mikhail was released from Metropolitan Hospital. He did not return to his father's house on 86th Street. Nor had he any inclination to revisit his rooms at the Riverside Suites. Luckily, Donovan Heller had offered *Land's End*, his Riverdale home overlooking the Hudson.

"I won't be needing it, Misha," Heller'd insisted. "I'll be in training for America's Cup. That boat you sold me better not leak, by the way."

"It won't."

"I'd also like it to win."

"That I cannot guarantee."

"Then at least take my house. It'll bring me good luck."

With a wan smile Misha'd agreed. Caroline took him to his new home. All this and more Max was aware of, for he had never failed to call the hospital every day since the disaster. Yet not a word about Mikhail – not even a whisper of Antonin – was ever exchanged with Caroline.

⟩☾⟨

Land's End was just that – glass and timber, like the bow of a ship, jutting out onto the shoreline. A tall row of pines sheltered its entrance from the street. A long curving driveway wound around to the deck. Below, moving unhurriedly toward the Narrows, the Hudson in all its splendour passed by.

Surveying the scene, Misha sank onto the sofa. "It is not possible," he murmured, "that I am here, alive, soon to be well, soon perhaps even to sail…"

Caroline sat down beside him. He turned her face to him and kissed her – a gentle kiss, nothing more, and said, "Now you must go. Max will be waiting."

"Yes."

"Will you come back today?"

"During my rest I will come."

"Tomorrow?"

"No. Tomorrow the Mortimer Bannisters arrive at my guest house. Changing of the guard," she said with a smile. "My lovely mill house awaits."

"Furnished?"

"Finely."

He suspected sparsely but made no answer.

He was right, although the rooms Max had designed were absolutely perfect in form and function. Antonin's headboard had pride of place on the second floor, framing the new bed she'd bought to replace the ropes no longer trusted. Next to it was the pitcher, centred still on the nightstand. On the opposite wall was a mirror – oval, freestanding – beside an antique armoire she had found in a shop near Maximilian's house.

In the hearth room below, the high-backed benches had remained, as had the wooden table, the copper pots on the mantel, the sturdy sideboard on the opposite wall.

Books she had removed from the guest house were stacked in the grain room, transformed into the study Max had envisioned. In time, Caroline planned, whenever Antonin should return, she would have bookshelves and perhaps a table to read at.

Of the semicircular building overlooking Rodin's house she recalled nothing.

From the steps of the guest house – his new home – Mortimer Bannister waved.

"Thank you again," called his wife.

Caroline too waved, then continued on down the south lawn. There was new grass on the dirt now – small lime-green feathers swaying with gentle, untested allure. For a while she just stared at the scene, as Misha had looked at his whitecaps and rock cliffs. She watched a red fox race down the slope not long ago a veranda, glimpsed a wild turkey take flight, heard the clatter of deer crossing the planks of her footbridge.

And then in the quickening wind the orchard gate banged abruptly, sending a few raucous jays scrambling into the sky. Startled, a hoot owl warned of spring's false-hearted charm; dampness rose up from somewhere deep in the woodlands; and Caroline shivered, not so much from cold as from a presentment of finality.

Intimations of Immortality, she reflected, recalling Wordsworth as she too crossed the bridge, for it was Wordsworth Maximilian had conjured on the day she had met him, and somehow it now seemed prophetic that he had again come to mind.

By the light of a new moon she arrived at the mill house. Restless still, thinking of final things on her bench by the great hearth, she took paper and pen from her bag.

In the event of my death, she wrote with her usual care, *I deed the land of Todd's Farm to the town of New Salem, forever to be preserved in its natural state. As administrators of this preserve I name the family of Maximilian d'Olivier, and his descendants, including Antonin Onegin,*

who together shall have sole authority over the use of the property's
buildings – guest house and mill house, gate house and sheds.
  Caroline Contini Devereux

At her attorney's the following morning, Caroline had her
will duly witnessed and signed. She then felt a great peace. Life
was surging beneath the earth on the farm she so loved, and she had
made sure it would have its day, as she had had hers there, for
somehow she felt that what she had known there was all behind her.

Maximilian's response, though, on the following morning,
surprised her. "It cannot be, Caroline."

"Well I don't see why not."

"The trustees, I mean…"

"Max, it won't be a burden. The town will take care of the grounds.
The homes can be rented. An occasional visit, nothing more…"

"I am not speaking of burdens."

"Then why refuse me?"

How to tell her what only Mikhail and Elsa Varig knew?

"Why?" she insisted, placing her hand on his arm so that he was
reminded of the day she first came to him, more fervent by far than
even Anatole Kramer had warned.

He considered a moment. It was no use, he perceived – no
sparing her now from the second half of that fateful evening downstairs. She was bound to learn somehow. Best to hear it from him, to
hear it gently…

"Has Mikhail spoken to you, Caroline, about the night he was
stabbed?"

"He has never mentioned that night."

"Not a word about what really happened down in the library
while you were sleeping?"

"Nothing," said Caroline, suddenly seized by unease. "I thought
perhaps he could not remember. It was Dr. Ollikainen who told me
that a thief had reentered. Well of course I knew then Misha had lied
with that verb – for all our sakes, Max." Nervously she folded and
unfolded the handkerchief still in her lap. "Antonin too has been

kind, though. More than kind. Life-saving as well, Max, I can never forget that…Max?"

But Max was suddenly at a loss. He took the handkerchief out of her hands, not knowing what else to do then. For a long time he studied it, as though its navy and wine-toned initials might offer some clue as to how to proceed. She saw his immense hands stroke the cloth, his large white head bent down, as though defeated, or waiting – she was not sure which – nor did it matter at that point, for she had surmised that a great sorrow had at last bowed that fine head, and in her wish to relieve it, the fear in her heart disappeared. Thus it was she who broke the silence that had descended upon the room.

"If there is something else I must know," she replied, "I must know it at once."

Max was unable to answer.

"There is nothing on earth I wouldn't do to help, Max, you know that."

Ah, to lay hold of the words, even a few ones –

"Nothing can ever hurt us again," she whispered, taking his hand. "We have lost almost everything but each other."

"He is gone," Max said at last, also a whisper, head still bent down.

"Gone?" Caroline echoed, her voice so small he would have mistaken it for a memory had she not left her hand in his.

He nodded.

"Do you mean he is dead, Max?"

Desolate, facing her finally, as though through some distant lens: "To the best of my knowledge he is alive. We will not see him again, though. He can never come home."

Silent, wide awake in her mill house that night, Caroline relived every detail of the story Max had with effort recounted that afternoon.

"She had been comely then," he had remarked, remembering Elsa Varig's face. "Not the beauty her mother was. No, certainly not Anna Berg's face, but in her frail, uneven way there was charm, and, shy as she was, not seeking love, she found it.

"Jean-Luc Onegin found it too, seeking it less, betrothed to another by his parents as he was at that time.

"Well their love could not be, that was all. And yet there it remained. Few in Nice knew of their son, born to Elsa that same year. For Anna Berg's sake I swore to protect him. I swore to keep Elsa. I…Jean-Luc I lost," Max had reminded her, feebly, and then he had added no more, for of the woodworking knife and Elsa's lies, and his own, and Antonin's flight with its two telephone calls he had already said much.

And all the while gravely, with her face fixed on his, Caroline had remained silent. From time to time she had nodded, leaning in on occasion so as to hear Maximilian's hoarse, halting words more distinctly. Not until he had finished, 'til he had looked away sadly – as though the panorama of those past years called to him still with insistence, though he could no longer make answer – did she speak. Her voice, cool and gentle, was nevertheless no longer small.

"Where is he now, Max?"

"We have been told that he is in Canada."

"Nothing more?"

"Labrador. Lancaster Bluffs, or so Simon Rand stopped by to say last week. Elsa let him in through the kitchen. God only knows what Antonin did to make that man's trip worth the effort."

At that point she had moved, or rather shifted her weight in the chair so that the lamplight fell on her face. Max had studied her then, finding everything she had not said in her deepening expression – eyes that were not serene, not even accepting, but clearly determined, pallor heightened slightly by conviction rather than passion, mouth remarkably firm, as though pain and compassion had cancelled each other out on those lips, leaving behind just the strange almost shining resolve which defined her.

She would not judge – that was clear – for it was not in her nature to judge, only to love, and she would love Antonin Onegin until the end of her days. He had tried to kill Mikhail. He had bowed Maximilian's head. And yet whatever she could do now to save him she would do, come what may, for she had been once as he now was: lost and desperate on foreign soil, covered in the heat of summer, until a hot July wind had brought a song in her direction, and she had surrendered everything for a kiss.

April was mild, dusty rose dogwoods lining the walkway leading to Maximilian's door. These Caroline paused to admire nearing eleven one morning, when abruptly a stranger brushed past her – head bent down, hat lowered over the heavy brown scarf around his neck though the warm sun was high. For some reason she watched as he walked briskly on, hugging the sides of the archway until he disappeared into the crowds. When she arrived upstairs, Maximilian was on his daybed, anxious, unopened envelope in his hand.

"Leave your coat by my desk and make sure you have bolted the door," he said. "I want no interruptions while you read this to me, not even from Elsa – above all from Elsa. Whatever she needs to know I myself will tell her later."

Caroline studied the envelope – smudged, one edge torn, addressed in rudimentary script, *M. d'Olivier.*

"No postmark, no address, no return address," she mused aloud.

"Antonin Onegin would know better than that."

The wafer-thin paper suddenly felt like a stone in her lap.

"Hand-delivered this morning. No doubt many hands were involved. Again God only knows at what cost," murmured Maximilian.

For his sake Caroline steadied her hands as she removed the faded blue page.

Dear Max, she began.

I am at Sagamore Knoll – white clapboard house on the high coastal road. It is a dairy farm. There is also an orchard. There are fir trees for export. *I help out with the chores – in exchange for my rent – but my main job is the highway. Heavy snows fall through March. The winds are always very strong. I clear the roads and so work is steady. Also I have a bit of woodworking on the side. I've sold a clock, like the one I once made you, and a headboard, like another I made. So you are never to worry. Please tell my mother…Also tell Mikhail…I will see none of you again. That is my sentence…For what I have done I am sorry. I will be sorry forever. Do not* – Caroline broke off –

"Caroline," Max urged again.

Do not tell Mrs. Devereux. She always thought I was good.
Antonin.

Neither Maximilian nor Caroline spoke for a while.

"Perhaps you should keep that," Max said at last to her softly.

"It is yours."

"It is ours."

"Nevertheless," she replied, refolding the paper and placing it into its envelope, "you will want to look at it, over and over again, and he would not want me to."

They did not work then on his memoirs. Caroline moved to the window and stared at the fountain which endlessly reached for the tangled pale blossoms of cherry trees arching above.

"Go on out there now, Caroline – off into that fragrant, frail morning soon to be gone as all such days must. But for now it is there. I should like to think of you in its midst. Later, toward sundown, I should like you to bring – well, just the scent of the day in your hands."

When she returned she found Maximilian at his desk, working not on his memoirs, but on some other project that absorbed him. He looked at her, smiled, then bent back down over his papers.

"No, no leave your notebooks for now and come sit by me," he said, sensing her move toward the daybed. "I've come up with a plan. It'll take doing. Everything's possible though – I'll make certain of that."

He made an adjustment on his pad, saw that Caroline was seated before him, capped his pen carefully and said, "I have a colleague in Québec. Didier Franck. Excellent attorney. I know I can count on him to do me this one final favour. I have helped him once or twice in the past," he added quietly, then said no more of French days. Instead, forcing efficiency: "I plan to set up an account – money to be deposited, monthly, from a fund I'll establish. Antonin's name cannot appear. He is wanted by the authorities. Armed robbery, two counts. The first, I understand, over a phone call of all things. The second, also due to a call, involved a homicide near Niagara."

This last Max said in an uncoloured tone which he hoped would hide his anguish and perhaps blunt her pain. It had done neither, they both saw, when their eyes finally met again, briefly.

Nevertheless, Max went on: "I cannot trust Simon Rand – not with this kind of cash. Trust funds take too much time. It will be May soon and there won't be snow on the roads. And, as for those woodworking jobs..." He sighed. "Antonin seeks perfection. He takes forever to polish. The boy will need cash before long, before hunger sets in, and then desperation, and – well, it must be done, that is all. Didier must find a courier. One who can be trusted to reach the border. I will search here in the meantime."

"You can trust me, Max."

It was uttered so softly Caroline thought perhaps he had not heard her, for Max went on speaking as though she had said nothing.

"There are a few still whom I can call – who will take my money to the border..."

"I can place it in Antonin's hands."

"They'll have to meet near the Falls..."

"I will have to meet no one."

He was about to continue when he felt her hand on his lips. It was the first time she had touched him there.

"That phone call was made for the sake of us both, Maximilian, though he must pay with the rest of his life for his sin."

"Caroline, it is unthinkable."

"He will not harm me."

"Nevertheless..."

"Please let me go, Max."

He turned to her. Her eyes shone with that brilliance again – strange fervent wilfulness, Allessandro had called it. Max remembered her telling him when she had described her ill-fated dance. He remembered their first day, when she had assured him she could render his life, and that he would be pleased by the results, for she had studied much, and could be counted on.

"It is too far," he decided aloud.

"Simon can take me to Sagamore Knoll. I will give Antonin the money. Didier will by then have prepared an account, to be opened by me in Goose Bay, Antonin Onegin having the right to draw from it, every month. In the meantime," she added kindly, "he will not starve. There will be no desperation."

Max felt his heart torn in two. The sight of Mrs. Devereux would resurrect Antonin – he knew that – and resurrection, of all things, was what the boy needed. She could bring him forgiveness. She could fill his next weeks with food.

She would also be at grave risk, transporting a great sum of money, relying on Simon Rand – no, no it could not be done. She would have to be denied. Besides – this fact too was now clear – he himself needed her near him.

"The distance is great," he heard himself say again. "You are already" – he paused. He had wanted to say "frail," but she had interrupted with "determined."

"Caroline…"

"I beg of you."

"I cannot allow it."

"'It is my deepest desire.' You said it yourself in your letter. And…and a woman can heal sometimes, Max, when everything else has been tried and everything else has not worked and I've seen it happen – we have both seen it happen – although you have chosen never to speak of that day – and yet your other boy lives."

It was then that Max knew. Somehow she had learned that he had stood behind that white curtain, Metropolitan Hospital, hearing Cecilia speak for the last time to their son.

"Yes…yes, some things, I suppose, belong to Eve in the end."

Caroline recalled Vianne stroking the statue that had bedevilled Rodin.

"First of May, thereabouts. Everything should be ready by then. I – can you be ready by then?"

"I can be ready tomorrow."

"No, no I'll need a few weeks. Ah," he said, with a sudden sharp intake of breath, "You've made me choose, Mrs. Devereux."

"I have helped you make up your mind, Max," she said, placing the letter back into his hands.

It only remained to tell Mikhail of her departure. A full week passed though, and Caroline said not a word. Four more days went by, and still she kept silent.

He'll be relieved, she reasoned a fortnight before her departure. *It was for us after all, for our sakes his ordeal. Tomorrow I'll tell him*, she vowed as her thoughts drifted off and *tomorrow* turned into *the day after next, without fail – weekend the latest –* and at last there remained but the last week of April.

By then the sunsets were languid, spring still uncommonly mild, Maximilian's memoirs unfinished, the long trip to Todd's Farm with his new car service endless. Tired as she was, she was unable to sleep on those rides. Sleep eluded her still alongside the water wheel turning, rest at last hers with the moon fading over the ridge.

Not once in those weeks, though he too was exhausted, did Maximilian ask her to stay. The little room that had once been hers was, by unexpressed mutual understanding, nonexistent.

And yet there it remained, just off the library, which was just off the hallway, through which she passed every morning and again late each night.

And there its memories lay, as though sealed by some higher officials banning all conscious intrusion.

And so the days passed, and Misha swiftly recovered, and with each new sign of strength in him, Caroline left for some other time, surely more opportune, any mention of her departure. Indeed she left for another time any real conversation with Mikhail, or more precisely, any dialogue with herself which like her red velvet room remained out of bounds.

Tomorrow, she promised herself, once again indistinctly, as the car left Maximilian's on the first day of her last week. Before long they were just climbing the Heights, bridge long since in the distance, Land's End too left behind, or so Caroline thought eyes half closed in the darkness, images blending.

Suddenly though, as the car rounded a curve she saw one sole, unmistakable house jutting out on its point, double doors open still to the offshore spring night wind, shimmering deck lights still on like some fine ship at anchor.

Just as abruptly then Land's End too vanished, and all was darkness again, or rather confusion within as she repeatedly turned only to see the empty parkway stretching behind. Its desolate path seemed like the hospital hallways she'd come to know like her home. The image of Mikhail there – Mikhail everywhere – could be avoided no longer. What he had suffered came into focus: his endurance, above all his silence loomed large. He had protected them all, and had paid dearly for the attempt. She yearned to touch him again, although up until then – although he had kissed her in the hospital, and when he'd arrived at Land's End – she had not returned to his bed.

What had she been afraid of, she wondered, as the lights of an elegant cruiser moved downriver. Max could no longer be betrayed. They had made their peace on another plane. He owned a part of her no one else did – and the rest, like so much now between them, had remained unexpressed.

It was not Antonin. Within two weeks she would see him, and he would be as he had always been, and she was not afraid of him.

She was not afraid of the voyage, for she had travelled much in her life.

She was not afraid of Elliot, who had at last forfeited his claim to her – not just the demand for her land, but the far deeper domination begun in the fire he'd repaired.

Partly repaired, she reflected, recalling how, naked at long last, she had looked at herself, first time in a mirror, second time on a cloth, finally in the eyes of the artist who'd fashioned both model and masterpiece, neither before even remotely imagined.

Had she been able to now, she would have reclaimed what he'd taken. It was past repossession. She had surrendered, like Antonin, what could never again be redeemed: innocence, trust, devotion so overwhelming she would have killed to preserve it. Jude had taken it all. Jude was hoarding it all still, wherever he was.

Victory was his, she acknowledged then, ruefully, and with this admission came understanding. What she had feared was inflicting more pain on Mikhail – pain to his body, still slowly healing; pain to his heart, a far more terrible thing, for he loved her as she had loved Jude once, and – matching half of the coin – he had loved no one before that, though he had made love to many. This last fact had been revealed to her not in the heat of their mid-winter's passion but in the emerging spring moments they had shared together as he recovered. She had felt it in the touch of his hand, a glance, a brief smile in her direction as she had stood by his hospital bed. Mikhail had surrendered as she herself had once done.

Bittersweet triumph, she said to herself, for at last she was aware that she could not give back completely, though she would give whatever was left.

Mikhail was watching the boats pass, lying on the deck overlooking the river, wanting nothing more at that moment than whatever was left.

She would not appear though, he knew. Since she had moved into the mill, she never stopped in after work. Besides, she had already been by that afternoon. The day had been mild and they'd taken tea on the deck. She had brought flowers, books from his father's library, news of the memoirs, the mill house, the guest house, small things.

Nevertheless, despite her affection, always so artless, and her kindness, never with limitations, she had seemed to him slightly distracted, at times almost aloof, as indeed she had appeared to him during the past weeks at Land's End.

Ironic, he had thought that afternoon, watching her walk away toward the car that would return her to Maximilian. What they had never had was now theirs – privacy, leisure, a house to themselves whenever they wished – and yet now she was distant and he too now felt fear. Like her he was scarred. For months she had been a nurse, a devoted one – expert – but not a lover, not once. She could perhaps not return to what a lover would feel. By his hospital bed she could have hidden this change. Passion would not have been expected. Here at Land's End, though, she would have to confront it. For sure it was this which had kept her away, Misha'd decided, turning back to his house as she'd driven back to his father's.

And yet he'd stayed restless. He tried to sleep, as he often did in the late afternoon, but sleep had not come. Day became evening and he returned to the deck. Stars he remembered as though they were his children filled the sky. A tourist boat passed, listing ever so slightly as visitors jammed the deck to see Manhattan's own stars appear.

Mikhail sipped his cognac. The music and laughter diminished as the boat disappeared. And then there was silence, save for the waves lapping against the shoreline under the deck, so that when at last Misha heard another sound he was startled. Visitors never came late at night, unannounced. And yet he knew her step, and so he turned, and his heart seemed to stop as she approached him and he heard her say: "I wanted to see you again, Misha, before this day was out, although I was afraid I might disturb you, and yet I continued, for you know how insistent I can be."

He was still stretched out on his lounge chair. She seemed to blend with the constellations above her.

"I have been waiting all day for you to disturb me," he murmured, and though she had wanted to speak to him – it was time to tell him, she had decided, abruptly instructing the driver to turn off toward Land's End – her purpose blurred as she felt her skirt moving up, and his experienced hand parting her legs, and then – not unlike what she had come to say that night, or that low, drifting boat that had recently passed – her panties too were soon gone, for he had pulled her down to him and had kissed her, over and over again, until he had aroused the one thing that had always vanquished her stubborn heart.

She straddled him to let him enter her, and then she moved against him, ever so gently, and he said simply, "At last."

Not until they had made love again and lay resting in his bedroom overlooking the water, did Caroline tell Mikhail of Simon Rand's visit, Antonin's house in Lancaster Bluffs, Maximilian's decision to continue to care for the boy.

"He still calls him 'the boy,' Misha," she said, "although Antonin Onegin has managed to escape what would have surely entrapped a far lesser man."

"He has paid a huge price for that night," said Misha, soberly.

"As you did," she replied, lightly stroking his scarred chest. "Max has too, of course."

"How is he?"

Evasively: "He keeps to his schedule. His work is nearing completion. First draft, of course, but he has omitted nothing. It will need little revision."

Misha seemed satisfied and made no answer. Caroline never mentioned that the strain of these past months – Maximilian's passion, his trip to the hospital, his recollections, which he was now telling quickly, forcing himself to push harder as the days and nights dwindled – had all taken their toll. He would often pause crossing the room; he would pause as they ate; he would stop as she rendered, searching not for a word but for the breath to shape its sound. Above all, she noticed, the music had changed. Over and over he wanted the final quartets of Beethoven. Not six months earlier, his favourites had been the first.

It was almost as though the strength, which was receding from him daily, had been transferred into his son, who was recovering with astonishing speed. And yet since the night when his blows had rained down upon Misha, father and son had not spoken. Unseen, Max had gone to the hospital. Unofficially, Misha had asked for Maximilian. But a line had been drawn. Something in both had been broken, perhaps never to mend.

He must go to Max, Caroline thought as she lay beside him that night. *When I am in Labrador, perhaps. It might be easier then.*

She still had not told him of that trip to Labrador, however. The fact that Max planned to get money to Antonin was all she had said. Misha had never asked how. He merely assumed Simon Rand would be taking the funds.

It was a matter of days now though, no longer weeks that were passing. Nearing midnight, as though in reminder, a freighter's horn echoed. Caroline's voice seemed to blend with its diminishing cadence when she finally said, "It is I, Mikhail, whom Max is entrusting with the money."

Misha was stupefied. Surely he'd heard wrong. Surely Maximilian – no, no as bold as he'd been in his lifetime Max would not have devised such a plan.

"It will be just a few days," Caroline ventured, reading his thoughts.

Max of all men. Max who never misjudged…

"Simon's returned to Goose Bay and will be meeting my plane. Well the last of the planes. I'll be stopping in Halifax, Nova Scotia, then on to Goose Bay, Labrador. Return trip the same. As for the memoirs…"

So it was true then. One final chapter. Razor's edge still for Max, who had no doubt enlisted whatever colleagues remained to play parts in this last scene.

Fog rolled in from the Narrows. A bell buoy sounded not far from his deck. Searchlights from the top of the bridge rhythmically broke through the clouds until at last he felt Caroline's hand on his arm – a tentative touch, a question, a caress in the dark which seemed to plead, "Tonight of all nights, Mikhail, answer me."

How to tell her he knew those seas well – Fundy's immense tides, Labrador's cliffs, the massive icebergs offshore, the fine ships he had known forever lost off Gaspé.

Max is a fool, he was tempted to say.

"When is this to be?" is what he said.

"Sunday."

"Which Sunday?"

"This Sunday."

No, no Max wasn't a fool, Misha decided. Max was a master. Before the start of June's thaw, well before summer's warmth – heroics to cap off a lifetime remembered.

Mikhail turned from her then, disdaining more comment. He stared at the cruise ship downriver, lights strung like beads stem to stern. He heard a police vehicle pass in the park by his house, a bus on the corner slow down. And then the car disappeared, and the ship's lights went out and only that hand on his forearm remained.

"Tell him I've pressed no charges," he said, facing away still.

"That he already knows."

"As to the knife…"

"It is gone."

"Caroline, you are mistaken."

"I have made no mistake, Mikhail."

Misha turned back and in a hard voice insisted, "Surely Max told you. I was unable to take that knife."

In a soft voice she answered, "Antonin's mother did. She tossed it into the river."

The room felt to Misha as though they'd set sail somehow – landlocked dimensions irrelevant, perspectives as on a long voyage distorted.

"Elsa Varig?" he managed.

Caroline nodded.

"Elsa?"

"Yes. Yes, all those years beside Max, inside that house, next to the boy, never saying a word. The boy, Mikhail – and this too Max told me – the boy was Anna Berg's grandson."

"Anna," Mikhail murmured after a moment – Anna whom Max had adored, or so he had heard, for of his first years in Nice he had only vague recollections. Not even Hélène's face was clear, though of his grandmother's beauty he had for years heard reports. His own mother – and this too he had heard, for he had never once seen her – had also been lovely. She too came to mind then as past and present, like mirrored images in the river, lost all clear distinction. Of their recent reunion, he had retained no conscious recollection. Something, he knew, had saved him from extinction. He had attributed it to his youth.

"And so you see, Mikhail," he heard Caroline say beside him, "the boy too was loved, although he never believed it – and now he must know it – now or we'll lose him, and it is for this Max is sending me, or rather letting me go because I begged him. I said others could bring him the money, maybe even forgiveness, but what Antonin needed – what Max could only let *me* bring in his name..." She was about to repeat *love* when Misha's mouth found her mouth and his arms wrapped around her and he finally whispered, "Dearest, enough. Go, since I see now you must."

They fell asleep in each other's arms – as they had done the first time at the Riverside Suites – until dawn coloured the Palisades amber, and the sky turned pearl grey in the mist, and the pale river stirred.

Similarly intertwined they remained every night, but the week would not stay for them, and like the tides their time passed until one last sunset remained.

He made love to her then with a desperation he had never known. She had returned what she could give – nothing more, nothing less. Finally he had dozed, although sleep eluded her in the darkness. Her bag was packed, carefully placed by the entrance. A large sum of money had been cautiously tucked inside her purse. So too a letter, written by Mikhail, to be hand-delivered to Antonin when she arrived. The moment seemed far away, and yet also quite near. On the following night she would land in Goose Bay, Labrador. At some point thereafter, assuming Simon Rand kept his word, she would be met at the airport and taken to Sagamore Knoll, wherever that was.

Deepest night's stillness, which was strangely unlike peace, descended. Nothing disturbed the waters. In time a fine sloop passed by, just before sunrise, when Misha had at last awakened, and at last Caroline slept.

He disentangled himself from her arms. She stirred, then fell asleep once again. He walked to the window, watching those elegant sails catch the flame-coloured light.

"It will all end as *Serenita* did," he said to himself then.

"I will phone you," she promised, tearing herself from his embrace as the last call was announced for Flight 406, New York to Halifax.

The last thing he remembered was the tortoiseshell comb in her hair.

☾

In the April light Honfleur harbour was bursting with colour – red and pink roses on the railings; ivory blossoms on the trees; turquoise and gold and white shutters thrown open, matching the painted boats rocking below them, impatient.

Jude too was impatient. As he had done in his past life, though, he arranged his paints and his brushes with care, moved his easel a bit, repositioned his chair, stared at the scene to be rendered.

"Today of all days you will paint splendidly, Monsieur Jude."

"Yes I believe I will, Marie-Claude."

With a glance at the sky, a final adjustment to his chair, he picked up his palette, sat down, and began.

High noon came. He rested. Late afternoon's light called. He returned to his canvas. A child trying new skates paused to stare at the boat taking shape on his cloth. A group of fishermen followed; the deacon of Ste-Catherine's passed; a woman with oysters for sale turned – and like the boy they all stared and like Marie-Claude they all smiled, for Jude McCallister's work had never been finer.

Dr. Le Brun had foreseen this spring day, Jude remembered. How long ago his prediction now seemed – Christmas bells pealing, a mess of eggs on his chest, Théobald's fervent assurance that his art would be not just saved but renewed.

The words had seemed laughable, even cruel. They had proven prophetic, though, for Jude McCallister's suffering had remade him as an artist. Even the enforced abstract phase, while Germaine had worked him to exhaustion, had reshaped the way he perceived what would find its way to his cloth. He had always been a colourist. His outlines had always been bold. These qualities now had been pushed to new limits, as he himself had been pushed, and in some deeply subliminal way, his art – whether abstract or representational or one of myriad styles in between – had been forever transformed. He had burst the boundaries of past achievements to reach astonishing levels of renewed self-expression.

The breakthrough, of course, had not been wholly artistic, tied as it was to his continuing physical rehabilitation. Jude could at last move around the quay, down into the cobblestone streets, out toward the sea, up to the mariners' church on the hillside behind him, and the sight of him on these walks, stronger with each passing week, had filled Dr. Le Brun with a justified, keen sense of pride.

Except for one thing.

Jude evinced no desire to return to Paris, to his home, to any life other than the routine he now had – Germaine, Marie-Claude, the rented rooms of Dr. Meurice. He did not seem to understand – perhaps he preferred denial – that this arrangement could not last forever. Jean-Paul Meurice would be returning; Germaine du Pannier would need a rest.

Honfleur of course would remain, and if Jude truly wanted Honfleur – if Normandy were to become his last and greatest inspiration – some other accommodations not far from the harbour could be secured. But it was not the harbour Jude sought – not even its brilliance, suspected Le Brun. Jude wanted the house, the room, the pattern which for him had become life – dependency, Théobald realized, more lethal by far than the morphine Sœur Eugénie had been forced to remove.

Le Brun pondered this problem as he waited at the piano bar of the Hôtel de Crillon, hearing the excellent harpist interpret some of his favourite Cole Porter tunes.

Competent, Le Brun decided, *but none of Jude's fire there*, for as he listened he remembered how Jude had on occasion set the room ablaze, blending perfectly with the same harpist, as though some harmony that had eluded her occurred alongside him.

Again and again his thoughts drifted back to Honfleur, to Germaine, to a far more perilous harmony.

Rebecca Chase signalled a break. As she passed, Le Brun put his glass down.

"You played exquisitely, Mademoiselle."

"Thank you."

"Have you a moment?"

"Alas, no."

"I am a friend of Jude McCallister."

As if he had struck her with those words, Rebecca Chase stared. She had not heard from Jude since the previous summer, and though she was accustomed to his ways – though he had often gone off to his lone secret places – he had never before vanished, without a trace, leaving his home by Rodin's house for almost a year.

"Jude is well, I hope," she said breezily, taking the seat Théobald offered.

"Yes and no."

"Yes and no?"

"Well, you know how these things are," Théobald answered evasively. "Some paintings fail...some paintings succeed. A man like Jude..."

"A man like Jude will not accept failure."

An elderly couple stopped by their table to compliment Rebecca's music. Théobald took the welcome respite to think through his position. Whatever demons awaited in Paris, he decided, would have to be confronted by his patient if his recovery were to continue. Perhaps this woman could help – at least stir in him some old desire, not for his old life, of course – that would never come back – but for more meaningful things: colleagues, music, inspiration, independence.

Yet how to arrange such a thing?

Impossible, Le Brun reflected, as still more patrons stopped by. *After all*, he reminded himself, *I have sworn never to betray the thing he most treasures.*

Rebecca's new pianist joined them. Another colleague sat down. Fifteen minutes soon passed and Rebecca Chase finally stood.

Suddenly Théobald asked, "Will you be playing here again next Sunday?"

"If I am not playing elsewhere," she answered, determined to appear as elusive as Jude himself had been for almost a year.

"We shall speak again then, Mademoiselle."

"Perhaps, Monsieur," she replied, turning back to her harp.

I'll have a week at least, considered Le Brun, as the pianist too gave his hand and chandelier lights dimmed above. *More than enough time to ask him if he will see her. If he says yes, there is hope. I am sure she will go to Honfleur.*

Rebecca was by then playing, wistfully, *So Nice to Come Home To.*

MINUET

Seaborne clouds covered the Hudson as Caroline's plane climbed.

No signs of the sea though, she mused as the hours passed and a continuing greyness more like forgetting than sleep sustained the frail craft droning on over the water.

So profound was this dulling of recollected dimensions that at the end of a sudden descent through the clouds, Halifax, Nova Scotia like an abruptly recalled face surprised: blue and white coastline exceptional, deep-water harbour supreme.

Here Caroline waited, walking the long wharf in winds surprisingly brisk for late spring. East of the narrows, she sensed, for it was once more obscured, a vast and impatient sea brooded. She thought of Antonin, forever trapped by those seas, of Misha who had traversed them, of Misha's ship claimed by them. She pictured the Hudson, a fountain, the water wheel next to her mill house, ceaselessly turning.

And then the continuing flight to Goose Bay was announced.

To the north, as her plane made its way, icebergs like oversized passenger ships passed; in the distance the sky paled; westward the mainland's raw, desolate beauty appeared – sheared-off spruce coastline, lakes and vast timberland rising from Labrador's granite coves.

Finally, lulled by the sound of the steady propellers behind her, Caroline slept. When she awakened her plane had touched down in Goose Bay, Labrador. As she stepped onto the frail metal staircase pulled up to the aircraft, she saw that same stubborn light poised uncannily over the stillness.

The terminal was one large, oak-paneled room – coffee shop, newsstand and baggage claim areas deserted. A circular bench in the room's centre was empty. Several men stood at the bar in the alcove marked *Airport Lounge* near the rear, but Simon Rand, as Max had described him, was not among them.

Undecided, she stayed in the doorway. There was a public phone booth near the counter, but she had no number for Simon, no address in Lancaster Bluffs, nor, in any case, could she mention Sagamore Knoll. She was to be met, that is all Maximilian had said, and so she watched an Air Force plane land, a second take off, the last of her fellow passengers drive off toward the highway. In their turn flight crews and personnel disappeared down the road, which, after a slow descent, dissolved into seemingly endless forests of pine.

By then she had taken a seat on the bench. On the floor by her feet was her single small suitcase, under her shawl a slim leather purse, unobtrusive she thought, though ever so slightly it bulged with the cash sent from Maximilian. She pulled her shawl tighter, felt several times for her suitcase, heard the lounge jukebox repeatedly playing somebody's song.

And then the ticket agent closed his counter, switched off the light overhead and slipped out a side door to his car parked by the building.

Which left just those few trucks in the lot farther down, *Blue Moon* once again playing, and footsteps approaching Caroline's bench from behind. She turned and saw mud-spattered work shoes alongside her suitcase.

"Let's go," Simon Rand said. "No more planes due 'til morning."

Caroline was astounded. She had not seen him in the alcove.

"I was in the men's room," he added flatly, as though he could read all her thoughts. "Waiting for the place to clear. Always does at this time. Take your bag and let's go," he repeated, firmly this time, so that Caroline stood and with a brief "thank you," followed him out to his truck.

No further words were exchanged as the navy blue pickup rumbled onto the highway.

Heading east again, Caroline judged by the salt smell and the slant of the light on the trees. Winds stirred as they passed little settlements to the left, a wide lake to the right, the omnipresent vast forests beyond them on both sides.

Inside the truck, silence deeper than fog reigned. Outside, in time, settlements, cabins, and camp sites disappeared; the highway gave way to a two-lane gravel road; Caroline glanced at her watch and saw that a half-hour had passed.

"It must be quite hard, Mr. Rand," she said, clearing her throat, "to maintain unpaved roads when the snows come."

"Ain't easy."

Renewed silence, save for the crunching of tires on the gravel, and the wind.

"Does he know I'm coming?"

"There'll be a contact soon. That's all he knows."

"Tonight, though, I mean…"

"Less said the better. What if you didn't show, or got robbed, or something worse happened –"

"I – yes…Yes, I understand. Antonin would be disappointed," she answered, to which Simon made no reply.

The lake narrowed to the proportions of a long curving inlet. The smell of the sea became stronger. Unexpectedly then, in a lowered voice as though there were other passengers in his truck, Simon Rand finally did say, "There was a homicide back in Niagara – you heard?"

"I did hear."

"Wasn't no homicide. Customer near the store pulled a gun on him, that's all. Self-defence, pure and simple."

Simon Rand shook his head.

"All for a telephone call, can you believe it?"

Caroline looked away.

"Couldn't eat for days. Managed to sleep though that night – after he'd heard the man he had stabbed would survive…Well, he was always a queer one," Simon concluded, and then again he fell silent.

The little inlet became a bay, swelling wide toward the sea. The truck slowed.

"We are here, then, Mr. Rand?" asked Caroline faintly, eyes fixed on the icebergs drifting by in the distance.

"Soon," he said as they waited for a bus to pass. At the next crossroads they stopped, then veered northward again up a long coastal dirt road. Suddenly, as the truck stopped again at the top of a bluff overlooking the sea, she heard gruffly, "There."

In the glare of the headlights Caroline saw a white house, two-storied, with a wraparound porch leading to an annex to the right of the entrance.

Sagamore Knoll, she read carved on a hand-painted sign near the truck.

"Will you wait, Mr. Rand?"

"Got one more errand to run. I'll be back at this spot in one hour, though, exactly."

"Thank you."

"Thank Mr. Max. Primary deal is with him. Get you back to your room in Goose Bay by eleven. *Eleven,*" he repeated, "and since he's only paid me half to date, you'll see my truck again, right by that sign straight ahead, ten-ten the latest."

And with that he was gone, leaving behind what was by now the familiar echo of truck tires on gravel.

Caroline looked around. The yard was dark, although flood lamps lit up the house and the drive leading around to what appeared to be back fields, a tractor, a barn in the distance.

Seems deserted, she thought, again pulling her thick shawl around her as she made her way to the porch. She knocked, called Antonin's name once or twice, heard only the wind in response.

She walked around to the back. A flock of geese passed in the arc of the floodlights. She continued on toward the tractor, isolated vehicle at the end of the driveway, where once again lamps lit up the barn and the silo beside it. Beyond, but for unfamiliar constellations of pale distant stars, earth and the dark sky seemed as one.

So disorientated was she by the sight, so loud the sudden cry of gulls swooping down to the sea, and the moan of the wind lashing the bluffs, that Caroline never heard the heavy work boots approaching. Not until they were quite close did she turn, startled first by the noise, then by the sight of a man slowly advancing, head bent down, hat pulled over his brow, eyes on his boots as he walked so that he too, for the moment, was unaware of another person on the drive.

She would know him anywhere, though she could not yet see his face. She knew the stoop of his shoulders, the slow and hesitant step, the way his large hands swung, ever so slightly, as he made his star-crossed progression through the troubled paths of his life.

She did not call his name out, nor did she move toward him, for he looked up at last – was that a vaguely remembered perfume? – and saw her standing there, much as she'd been on that first night, when she had appeared under the awning, and some of her hair, just as now, had come undone and was blowing across her temples and he had heard her call softly, "Antonin?"

Now she said nothing. She merely stood in the squash-coloured light of the flood lamps, taking in the sight of him, large as the landscape – one with it almost, so fitting did his presence seem.

"You, Caroline?" he finally managed.

She nodded.

"*You?*" he repeated, as though she might vanish at any moment as the seagulls had done.

"Why not me?" she answered. "It isn't so far, after all."

By then he was next to her, folding her into his arms as he had done when her house burned, and she felt suddenly safe and relieved with her head on his shoulder, against the roughness of his pea coat, for his embrace was a sheltering thing, and his love without limits.

They remained thus a moment, neither moving, although the aspens around them and tall grasses swayed.

At last she looked at him, and he remembered hydrangeas in his rear-view mirror, and such a pale face, despite its radiant smile, and then he too smiled when she glanced around her then and said, "We seem to always meet on driveways."

"Yes," he said, thickly.

"This is the nicest one though."

"Nicer than Todd's Farm?"

"Yes," she said, looking around one more time. "Yes, in its own way, Antonin. Because it suits you, I think, as my home once did me."

"You still have the land, though."

"I do still. And the mill. And the guest house –"

She stopped, fumbling under her shawl for the bulging black purse. "We'll speak of all that tomorrow. There's not much time left tonight. Simon Rand's due back soon and…well…take what's inside this," she continued abruptly. "It's from Max."

"Max," murmured Antonin, running his fingers over the leather grain.

"Be quick, Antonin. It's in an envelope, but mind the wind. Inside the house might be better."

"Yes. Inside the house. I'll go in first and get lights," he said as they walked 'round to the porch.

Two hurricane lamps cast a rose-tinted glow through globes of cut cranberry glass near the door. Caroline entered, recalling a similar dimness – humid streets, hotter house, monogrammed plates displayed on ornate shelves. Here in the shadows she saw a huge stone double hearth. Behind the hearth were stacked logs, a wood-burning stove, copper pots over the pantry against a brick wall in the back.

Left of this pantry there appeared to be a workroom – weaver's loom, benches, a colourful textile in progress.

"Owner's wife works in there," Antonin offered, "unless she's planting in April or helping her husband with the harvest."

"So it's a couple then…"

"If you don't include me."

"Do they not include you?"

"They have their suppers out here," he went on, as though she had not spoken, pointing to a round, heavy table to the left of the entrance. "Living room's to the right – that dark space behind you."

Caroline made out a sofa, two chairs, a table between them with an oversized wooden radio.

"Every night they hear music…" Antonin smiled one more time, and said in a voice more like Provence than the Arctic, "Always reminds me of Max."

In the days that would follow – unimagined that evening – she would remember that smile, like Borodin's song Christmas Eve – quick and simple, unforced. Few were the occasions when it had ever graced Antonin's mouth, and yet in this forbidding land, exiled more than in his father's house, it had played twice upon his lips, both times without reluctance – and thus Caroline wondered, watching him place a kettle above the embers in the back hearth, if he had at last found his own space – the one which sets a soul free.

"I don't often eat here," he confessed, bringing a tray to the table.

"Why don't we go then where you do eat?"

"That's in the annex. Two rooms off the side porch through that low door by the staircase. Tomorrow we'll go there."

He placed his cup down abruptly.

"You're coming back tomorrow, aren't you?"

"Yes. Yes, of course I'll be back. Mid-afternoon thereabouts – if it won't interrupt things."

He said her name, nothing more, although it sounded like a reprimand.

"I meant your duties, the owners…"

"The owners are gone through the spring. Same trip every year. Hunting, fishing, basic provisions to be fetched."

A rising night wind rattled the windows. Antonin listened, as though hearing some strange, whispered confidence there.

"This'll most likely be their last trip, though. They're getting on. They want to leave, sell Sagamore Knoll by the fall and move into town, and...well, I suppose nothing lasts forever." He shrugged, feigning a practiced indifference, and then he fell silent, and she knew she was right about the space that had freed him.

"I shall have to see it all tomorrow then," she said firmly. "Not just the house again, but the annex, the barn, above all the meadows. You know how I love meadows."

"Yes."

"The wilder the better."

"Supper afterwards, Caroline. We'll eat as we did in your guest house, last Christmas. I will cook for you, as I did that week. Will you be staying a week now?"

"No."

"Two perhaps?"

Barely audible: "I'll have to be leaving day after tomorrow."

"Ah," he replied, heartsore at the thought of his exile.

She put her hand on his arm.

"Max will be waiting. He'll want a report on my trip, on this land, about you most of all. That's why I've come. It's not just the cash in my bag – which is for now, for six months, for whatever you need. Max was desperate for you to have it long before winter set in, but he's also made other plans. First thing in the morning I'm to meet an attorney in town – well the main office is in Québec, where an old colleague of Max works. They've set up a fund for you, and I'm to finalize things, and start an account in the bank, so that every month while you live money can be deposited from Québec and then mailed to a post office box here in town." Her voice grew intense as she spoke, her shining eyes deep in the flickering light.

"You won't have to worry now, Antonin – never again will you worry," she repeated, her words coming still faster, for just a few minutes remained and of these things she could not speak once

Simon Rand's truck appeared. "Max is determined for you to be at peace," she concluded, "as he too is at peace, since what went wrong is long gone and what remains is his love."

There was absolute stillness. He placed his own hand – callused, immense – on her slight one and said, forcing the hard phrase: "It is too late, Caroline."

"It is never too late."

"The time for kindness is over."

"Why not let Max decide that?"

The twin lamps flickered low, close to extinction, and in a matching low voice Antonin said at last, "Because there remains one more thing."

"He knows it all, Antonin."

"Back in Niagara…"

"Including Niagara."

"Then you must know of it too."

"I know all that Max knows. More, as a matter of fact, for I know you were assaulted first. Simon told me today. I guess he thought I should know it wasn't your fault after all."

"And yet you came up here assuming it was."

"I came up here wanting to see you."

"And Max sent this money assuming it was."

"Max has lived long and seen much."

Simon's truck turned onto the driveway, headlights casting a bright, unforgiving light into the room. Within an instant the lights were extinguished, leaving only the glow of the lamps inside their cranberry globes, and yet the moment had been enough for her to glimpse the tears falling down Antonin's wide, sunburned face.

"Nothing but trouble," he murmured, as if he were alone in the room. "Trouble and then some, since I made Max lose his leg."

"One is prepared to lose much in a fervent embrace."

"It wasn't that under a train."

"Ah, but it was," she replied. "You were all that remained to him then – you and your mother to follow – for your father was gone, and your playmate too, sent to England on another train, and your friend's mother, Cecilia, lost before that afternoon."

Something like ice breaking offshore seemed to split in the silence.

"How is my mother?"

"She is with Max still."

"Good."

"As her own mother once was."

Antonin nodded.

"She tossed your knife into the river."

Antonin's grip was suddenly firm on Caroline's arm.

"When did she do that?"

"After the ambulance came for Mikhail."

"But the police must have insisted…"

"She said she'd found nothing, though they repeatedly asked her, and so she waited 'til midnight, long after they'd left Max, and then she slipped down to the Hudson and from its shores it was done. Max didn't learn of her lies until many days later. He figured it out for himself, as a matter of fact. It was Elsa's mother, after all, who'd taught him survival."

Headlights again flashed insistently into their dim space.

"You must go now," said Antonin, moving his hand from her arm after a moment.

"Until tomorrow," she murmured.

She stood, reached into her purse, and placed Mikhail's letter on the table. The envelope was unsealed, fine ivory vellum, navy blue border, addressed simply, *Antonin, Sagamore Knoll, Labrador, Canada.*

"Perhaps – after I leave tonight – you'll want to read this, Antonin."

Even now, so few letters exchanged, none received in his jail cell, he instantly knew the firm, confident script.

"Yes," replied Caroline nodding, pretending to take no note of the immense hands that were trembling, "written by Misha, last evening."

They had not mentioned his name since she'd arrived. Everything else she had discussed – openly – but this, unlike the killing in Niagara, went far back in time, love and despair both mixed in the thrust of that woodworker's knife, regretted the moment it found its way into Maximilian's son's heart.

"You have read this?" he managed.

"It was not addressed to me."

"But he is well, I've been told."

In order to learn that, Caroline knew, Antonin had paid more than the thousands he'd robbed.

"Yes. Yes, he is well. I expect he has assured you of that in his note."

His eyes slowly met hers.

"For now, goodnight, Antonin."

She turned and opened the door.

"Caroline?" he called suddenly.

"Antonin?"

"Let me fetch you tomorrow."

"You have your work to do here."

"That can wait for a day."

"And Simon's been paid for two trips…"

"He'll take the same money for one."

She glanced apprehensively toward the driveway. Max had arranged things, precisely, and Simon did not seem like a man who made last-minute changes.

"My own truck knows the road," Antonin persisted. "And I can come whenever you need me, and…and I would love to drive you," he added humbly, "one final time, Caroline."

A gust of wind blew into the house as she stood on the threshold. More than ever, he thought, she looked fragile, almost unearthly – a slim silhouette, dressed completely in white, shawl and long skirt billowing back in the wind, endless black night stretching forever beyond her.

"Outside the bank," she said with sudden decision. "I will be finished by three."

"I will be there then."

She hurried away toward the truck. Antonin stared at the taillights as they disappeared into darkness. Then he walked into the house and reached for the envelope on the table.

⁓ ☾ ⤵

Conversation seemed superfluous, as was always their way, at the start of their ride on the next afternoon. Caroline even dozed – that was also their way – and he had always liked it when she'd slept near to him, certain no harm could come to her then.

When she awoke she looked around at the barren mounds to the north, the rock-strewn shores to the south, the patches of ice clinging still to the sides of the mountains. A cold rain had threatened since noon. The overcast sky had turned livid.

Could there be snow tonight? she wondered, then quickly banished the thought, for it was May 3rd after all – and yet the Arctic was so near to them.

Rain or snow, she decided as the sky turned still darker, *there will be dinner soon with Antonin – and that will please Maximilian, and perhaps Misha more so, and I most of all will be pleased, for it will give me one more night in this place the French called Land of Cain, dirt nobody wanted – although Antonin wants it, which is why I have done what I have done.*

Drowsily, she looked at him.

"I have a plan, Antonin."

"You have always a plan."

"Yes, but this one concerns you."

He steadied his truck on the dirt road.

"You must buy Sagamore Knoll."

"Dearest Caroline," he exclaimed, and then in an instant he was sorry, for not once in his tattered days had he ever said such a thing.

She took no note of his discomfort, sitting up suddenly, fully alert now as the truck lurched off the highway onto the gravel road that led past the lake.

"It can be done, Antonin. In fact it *has* been done –"

"What are you saying?"

"You tell the owners you want it, simple as that. You do want it, don't you? I mean, not as a mere place to live in, but as I've wanted Todd's Farm – as I've needed its trees and stone walls and sometimes fierce river."

Antonin nodded, recalling those woodlands and, strangely, these new ones he loved.

"Well then," she insisted, "the owners know you already, and they trust you, and if they want to leave by September, before the snows come, they'll take a fair price, no question about it, and so I've left a down payment with Didier Franck's colleague in town."

She had no money left, Antonin knew, and so he was mystified as she continued, "As an attorney he can act for you – Max has seen to that."

"Caroline…"

"You won't have to come forward."

"How have you done this?"

"Everything perfect, discreet."

"*How have you done this?*" he repeated, for he was suddenly fearful, not for himself, but for her, for the wild heart inside her that matched her black, untamed hair.

"Antonin, it was easy."

"It could not have been easy."

"Look at me."

"I am driving."

"Then pull to the side of the road now and look."

He did as she asked and still he did not understand, until she at last said, in a bright tone, triumphant: "My earrings – don't you remember them?"

Pierced diamond studs, he recalled. She had never worn them before this trip. In fact, now he remembered, he had been surprised when he'd seen them. Must have been all that remained of the heirlooms, he had decided. As he looked at her now, he saw she was without them. In an instant he knew what she had left with the attorney.

"Foolish girl," he murmured tenderly. It was as close as he had ever come to speaking like a lover.

"I don't see why, Antonin. I didn't need them and you did."

He longed to touch her but didn't dare.

"What I did need once, desperately, was a friend when my house burned. That friend I had, day and night, by my side. You shall now have your own house. Yes. Finer than mine was," she ardently added, "for it will know only your love, no disillusion. I will ask Max…"

"There is no need to ask Max –"

"I mean for the payments, an increase…"

"No, Caroline."

"You can't mean you will refuse me," she stammered after a moment, as the lake alongside turned steel grey under the clouds.

"No," he repeated, and then she withdrew from him, slightly, and he sensed once again he had wounded, this time the one he loved best.

Remorse again overcame him. Because of her he had lost himself, and then he had found himself, and now she was there beside him, for only this evening, with only her comb left, eyes uncomprehending – yet still so lovely, like the bunchberry dogwoods with their purple blossoms by the side of the lake.

How she resembles them, he reflected, *defying the wilderness to make an offering, bright and beautiful, fleeting.*

In the end it was those dogwoods which made him recant, and let her again have her way, for as he watched her watching the buds open, he at last understood. She had loved him as he had loved her all along – not in a flamboyant way, not like some tropical plant, but like those sturdy mauve berries that preferred a silence like the Arctic.

With the first frost they would vanish, long before summer's end. No matter. They would appear once again in the frail warmth of the spring, needing no coaxing in April, no pruning, knowing the fierce, rocky land would let them be when it was time.

So it was with their love – unsullied steadiness that needed no declaration, no proof, not even the brush of a hand. They had already joined, body and soul. They had embraced once beside her cinders, once again beside his tractor, and both times she had rested her head on his shoulder and he had sheltered her, and in the sheltering there had been peace.

"Caroline," he said softly.

She turned to face him again, hurt still clouding her eyes.

"I can make the payments," he managed.

"But the initial one…"

"That you have given me, as you once gave me fine books, and I will keep both gifts. Afterwards" – he felt the warmth of her smile now – "there will be income from the dairy farm; I will sell fir trees in December; I'll have what Max sends, what I make in my shop. Yes. Yes, I'll have a shop," he added, his voice fervent as well now. "The whole annex will be a shop. People will need my things, you'll see, or the things I'll repair for them, and even someday perhaps, if I've managed to save well, I can return to you…"

With her hand on his mouth, she stopped him.

"My gifts are not loans, Antonin, unless you want your headboard back."

How he would love to have kissed that hand, gently, before letting it go once again, but he did not, and so she took it away, and he started his truck up again and headed eastward, out toward the sea.

◟ ☾ ◞

There was a steady rain falling when they reached Sagamore Knoll. Caroline found a slicker – immense on her when she slipped into it, but Antonin simply smiled and said, "Suits you," and then together they crossed the soaked meadow into the barn, where she helped with the chores. By the time he was finished, a sharp wind had come up.

Antonin stared at the sky. "Nor'easter," he murmured. "We'll be in for heavy rains before it blows over."

"How soon will that be?"

"Hard to say. Storms like this sometimes stall from the Labrador Sea down into the Gulf."

"That's my flight path, exactly."

"You may not get out then tomorrow."

"Day after?"

"Depends. Fog can follow the rain as the temperatures rise. They won't fly 'til that's gone. Too many mountains to clear; too many icebergs east of the cliffs."

She nodded, but made no reply, leaning hard on his arm as they wandered on toward the woods. Thunder rolled off in the distance, as though in some dream play, for it seemed then to Caroline that nothing could harm them under the intertwined branches of tamaracks, balsams, birches and spruce trees that formed a fine roof high above.

After an hour they were back in the house, faces and hands drenched, hats gone in fierce winds that swept over the fields as they ran.

The hearthside was warm, though, supper unhurried as they spoke of the things that remained: Elliot's engagement to Susan, the will Caroline had made, the land trust she'd formed.

"And the mill?"

"Suits me."

He smiled as she told of the orchard, the guest house, the foot-bridge, and then there was silence. He seemed to want to speak of one more thing, but stood instead and turned the old radio on and of all things the sound of Strauss filled the room – waltzes they'd heard Christmas Eve in Maximilian's house, and hence it could no longer be avoided.

"How is Max?" Antonin managed.

"He is about to complete his memoirs."

It was not the answer to his question and she knew it, but the one he had wanted she dared never say. Max was dying – that was clear to her before she left him, and thus she had said to him, over and over again, that she would return, mission accomplished, before a scant three days had passed. It was for this, she believed, that the threatening storm had unnerved her. She was anxious to reach him in time.

Lightning forked in the sky. Static became silence as the transmitter died. The lamps dimmed to a spark, rallying gamely after a moment, so that Antonin said, forcing a cheerful tone,

"Perfect timing. We can each take a globe and have a glance at the annex. Mind the low doorway," he added, as she followed him past the staircase.

His two small rooms were amazing – one filled with stains, cloths, brushes and knives of all lengths – one by far sparer, with only a bed, a small dresser, a bookcase half-filled, a low table on which were the things he had fashioned already.

She passed her hand over the smooth tray, studied the intricate curves of the clock, examined the contrasting tones in the precisely cut chess board, picked up the rectangular frame with its old photograph cut to size.

Two children – no more than five she surmised. One of the boys had black hair and black eyes; the other was fair, with a smile that could conquer the devil. A fine house, colour of sandstone, stood in the sunshine behind them.

"Sent with the note you brought," Antonin fumbled, and then he added no more, nor did she ask then for more, since what had had to be said had been written, and Antonin had been absolved.

I am glad, Caroline thought, as Antonin's truck rumbled along the dirt road back to the airport motel, *that Cecilia's earrings found their way here*. "For having kept a vigil beside my son," she had written on the white card enclosed with the gift sent to Misha's hospital room. Cecilia never forgot a favour, much less a miracle.

Two miracles, Caroline mused, *two in the end*.

"I will come again in the morning," Antonin interrupted as she reflected.

"No…"

"Just to be sure your plane gets off."

"Max will not want that. He made a point of it. 'Customs officials,' he told me. 'I do not want Antonin in the vicinity.'"

Since he made no reply she then repeated, more firmly, "You must respect Max in this. Otherwise, Antonin, everything will have been in vain."

Outside the airport motel their parting was brief, achingly so, for neither could endure anything longer than a quick third embrace, even fiercer than the first one outside what had once been her home and the second outside what might soon become his.

"Not really leaving," she insisted. "You'll be receiving a letter next spring, when the bunchberry dogwoods are blooming again, and there'll be payment enclosed for a clock, which I'll be needing for my mill house."

"So the letter will be instead of a visit."

"No," she laughed. "Advance warning, that's all. The buyer will follow. A year from today, more or less. Four little seasons, nothing more, and perhaps it won't rain, and we can go deeper into the woods, and maybe plant something there, for of course it will be yours by then..."

She stopped. Their gaze met one last time.

"Go now, Caroline," he said thickly, releasing her quickly, lest he should engulf her in some dark way, for his heart, like her hair, was as wild as the wind.

He would of course return in the morning. He would park where he was now, well to the south of the airport motel road, out of sight of officials, within view of the flights taking off. He would know when she left. If she did not leave, he would be there for her.

⁓ ☾ ⌐

Caroline did leave, after a delay of nearly two hours, when a lull in the rainstorm parted the clouds and allowed the pilot a window to get his plane off the ground.

From his secluded spot in a pine grove close by the highway, Antonin watched her go. The departure disturbed him – not the fact of his solitude, which would from henceforth be his portion, but the pilot's bravado, gauntlet thrown into a storm that had not yet spent itself – Antonin was sure of it – for after only one winter he had learned the prime rule of survival in this bleak and unapproachable, unforgiving Land of Cain. Nature here never gave quarter. On the fools or the proud men who presumed otherwise, it could without mercy take revenge.

Caroline's plane veered toward the Labrador coast. Below was the lake, steel grey now among the pines, where she and Antonin had stopped and he had agreed to keep her diamonds; after that she saw the mountains, defiant and brooding, and then the hills, spare and brown, tumbling down to the shoreline where one or two settlements fronted the ocean, midnight black in the rain.

The pilot climbed; turbulence followed; headwinds made sleep impossible as they crossed the Labrador Sea, rounded Newfoundland's north peninsula, and began to descend into the airport at St. John's.

After the spare and remote proportions of Goose Bay, thriving St. John's seemed enormous. Caroline longed for some rest, but who knew how long the stopover would be?

I'd better call now, she decided.

"Yes, I'm fine," Misha said in a jubilant tone, relieved beyond measure by the sound of her voice. "Yes, Max is fine too. I spoke with Elsa today…No, I have not been to visit. I'll call him now, Caroline, yes, and tell him you're on your way. – God, how good those words sound. When you've rested we'll both go."

She understood that he meant, *It might be easier then*, although she knew it would not be, and that they would have to meet without her, whenever Misha was ready.

Hence she merely said, "Fine…fine, dearest," and told him quickly of Antonin, and of the place which seemed to suit him in its strange way.

"This Sagamore Knoll, Caroline, is it far from the sea?"

"Not as close as *you'd* like, but not far – and it will be his soon. I – he's making arrangements with the owners," she said, adding after a moment, "He has read your letter."

"Ah."

"The photo's framed already."

An announcement interrupted.

"Mikhail, I have to go. The plane's taking off after all."

"After all?"

"Well, the weather's been filthy. But it must be clear to the west, or we wouldn't be going. You must promise to call Max..."

"I will."

"Tell him all about Antonin, and that I'm so happy he's well, and...and goodbye, Mikhail..."

"I'll meet your plane in New York."

"If you can."

"I'll be there."

"So will I."

"I love you, Caroline."

Static ensued, and then another announcement in the room, and by the time she could return the phrase, their connection was gone.

⠀⠀⠀⠀⠀⠀⠀⠀⠀⠀⠀⠀⠀⠀⠀⠀⠀⠀᷄ ☾ ᷅

An odd stillness reigned in the cabin during the overlong crossing. It continued as the plane descended – a sensation felt rather than seen – for after a lull the heavy rains had continued, and in the total absence of visibility all land seemed to have vanished.

A gust of wind rattled the aircraft, the cabin went dark, and at the last moment the pilot veered upward as a sudden wind tunnel engulfed the plane. The rapid ascent sent boxes and suitcases from compartments above onto the floor.

Caroline was in the first row, seat 1A. Neither hers nor the compartment over the man beside her opened. Yet she felt his hand grip her arm as the plane seemed to shudder, then again sharply descend as its wing scraped the tip of what seemed like tall cliffs densely veiled in the fog. The plane lurched toward Northumberland Strait and the mainland beyond it, where the pilot hoped to land his now damaged craft – if he could get past the Strait – in Moncton, New Brunswick.

He was unable to do so. Caroline saw the left wing dipping and rising just past her window, heard the engines grow louder, felt the horizontal rocking grow stronger, and then – after the plane appeared to hover a moment, undecided – the cabin tilted abruptly, and a steady diagonal decline began toward the sea.

The gentleman in 1B said in a low voice, "My God, forgive me."

Caroline leaned forward, oddly detached, staring outside the window of seat 1A, First Class section, Trans Canada Flight 407 from Goose Bay, Labrador. The overhead compartment above 1B burst open. Caroline stared outside still.

"Ah, there it is," she said to herself, as the plummeting aircraft fell through the last, low level of clouds, and the sea had appeared, not sapphire blue as it was when she had soared over these waters two days before that, but pearl grey and cool nevertheless.

"God forgive me," she heard one last time, and then only a shattering sound and then bliss – indescribable – not cold, but heavy and thick and salty and warm, and then darkness came fast upon the absence of feeling.

"Is the sea always so warm here?" Rebecca Chase asked, intrigued.

"No," replied Jude. "Honfleur's been especially hot these past weeks. That's what they tell me, at least," he went on with a slight laugh. "I've never been here in May."

They were seated together on the cobblestone steps that led from the tiny town plaza down to the harbour. Rebecca's pale green sundress was tucked round her knees; her long bare legs dangled in the water; the auburn ribbons on her hat fluttered behind her, blending with the matching curls of her red hair in the breeze.

She tilted her face to the sun, holding on to her hat as she leaned back on one elbow.

Jude opened his sketchbook, took a crayon from his pocket and started to draw. "What are you sketching there, Jude?" Rebecca asked after some time had passed.

"You."

She turned to him.

"Well, not anymore," he said with impatience.

"Sorry," she answered, facing the sea once again.

In the returning stillness Rebecca thought of the past remarkable week. Only eight days before, Saturday evening as promised, Dr. Le Brun had reappeared at the Hôtel de Crillon. "Monsieur Jude will see you, if you've the time, Mademoiselle."

She'd been about to demur when he'd said, "Before you decide, I must share a few things with you – things only a doctor would know, but I can't do it now and I can't do it here. I'm on call until twelve. Could we meet for a drink then?"

She had been absolutely astounded, not having guessed before then that Le Brun was a physician – Jude's physician, it appeared – that he had returned to the Crillon with the express purpose of finding her, and that Jude's year-long absence had been a crisis.

"I – Yes. Twelve-fifteen will be fine."

They had agreed on the Café Rivoli, not far from the Madeleine church. Even Théobald, who knew things no one else knew, was unaware of the irony, for it had been in that bistro, at that same table facing the plaza, that Jude had read and reread his short letter to Caroline, asking her to be his wife, never dreaming that within minutes his letter, his wallet, his whole way of life would be gone, never to be retrieved. Of these events, remembered vividly as he had recovered, he had said not a word to his physician. Hence in choosing this bistro, thereby setting in motion a second chain of events which would in ways as yet unimagined bring his patient's life slowly full circle, Dr. Le Brun was as much in the dark as Jude himself had been the year before, seated in the same place, fashioning different plans.

"This table suits you, I hope?"

"It is perfect, Doctor, thank you."

Le Brun had nodded, ordered a late supper for two, and then in low and carefully measured tones, so as to blunt the effect of what he had come to impart, he had described Jude McCallister's ill-fated walk through the Champs-Élysées, the struggle that had ensued, the hospital room overlooking celestial-toned windows, the boats of Honfleur, also vividly tinged.

His tone throughout had remained calm, his demeanour controlled, for he'd been determined to cause no more pain than the story itself would inflict.

The endeavour'd proved fruitless. Though she had tried not to show it, Rebecca was overcome, from time to time shaking her head, indistinctly repeating, "It cannot be, *Mon Docteur*."

"*Hélas, Mademoiselle*, yes. Jude himself, should you agree to a visit – but no, now that you know the facts, you may prefer not to go."

Rebecca'd made no reply.

"Perfectly understandable."

Still she had not answered.

"I will merely tell Jude…"

"Tell Jude I am coming."

Le Brun had looked closely then, trained as he was to miss little, even in shadows. "You are sure, Mademoiselle?"

"I am sure."

"He is not the same man."

"He will always be the same man."

Wearily, the physician had smiled.

"I meant, Mademoiselle, that Jude is now a better man. Certainly a finer artist, one and the same in his case."

"Yes."

"Which is why he must no longer hide. He himself knows it now. He has let me speak to you – that in itself was a triumph – and your visit will be a beginning. Mind, I expect no more than that."

"I understand."

"You need never return to Honfleur."

Rebecca had also smiled then.

"Just let him see in your eyes that what has occurred has not diminished him. The rest he will face in due time. All he needs now is a friend."

They had agreed then she'd take the earliest train the following Sunday out to Honfleur. On his way home Le Brun had recalled his excursion the previous week to Honfleur. "Out of the question," Jude had said flatly then. "No visitors, Théobald."

"She is hardly a visitor."

"Then why insist?"

"I do not insist. I only suggest. You have a friend who cares to see you. You have worked for years side by side. If for no other reason you owe her some courtesy now."

"Courtesy!"

"Do you think calamity has exempted you from common decency, Jude? Dr. Meurice returns in late fall. He will be needing Marie-Claude. Germaine du Pannier will have to rest. It has been hard on her, this routine –"

"It is her job, is it not?"

"It has been her job for three decades and then some."

"Nevertheless –"

"Nevertheless she has been here."

Angry, appalled more by his own words than by Le Brun's insistence, Jude had returned to his paints. Ebb tide had shifted as he mixed, dabbed his palette, readjusted his easel, once more faced Le Brun.

"Théobald, I spoke harshly. Forgive me. I'm just not ready, that's all."

"When you are ready then, Jude."

Drawing up a chair, Le Brun had said nothing further, but merely watched as the charcoal sketch was slowly, superbly filled in with bright hues. So intent had he been on the process, in fact, that he had been startled when Jude tossed the brush down and cried, "Does it mean that much to you, Théobald ?"

"I take some pride in your achievement."

So simply said, the words had disarmed Jude.

"Not just the bones set or the head fixed, but right there on the cloth." Le Brun had added – "Yes, I take pride in the fact that you are once again in that place, and I take pride in the fact that you have much more left to paint, and that I will always be a part of it, in my small way, for I was fortunate to have been on duty when you were brought in from the Pavillon in Paris, and I will count myself even more so when you return to Paris, unafraid. I will sign off then, on this assignment. Until that day, as your physician, I will not rest, Jude, you know that."

"You mean as my friend you will not rest."

"Either way, I'll grow old waiting."

"Théobald…"

"So will you see her?"

Jude had looked again at the harbour – at the peach and cream and clear turquoise houses, the white and red roses, the black and green sailboats, all rendered uniquely on the canvas in progress. But for the friend at his side, he well knew, that and all the other cloths filled in since his beating would have remained without image.

"Do as you wish, Théobald," he had said at last with a sigh. "For the sake of those works where you've so rightly seen your own reflection."

"Small reflection."

"Only prepare her," Jude had added hoarsely.

"That will not take me too long."

Two days later Jude had had word that Rebecca would be visiting on the following Sunday.

Clutching Le Brun's directions, Rebecca Chase had walked the cobblestone quay, spotting at last the narrow, half-timbered house he had minutely described.

No sign of Jude, though, she had reflected – a fact she'd found odd, glancing around the bright, colourful scene, recalling that Jude, at least the Jude she remembered, would have found such unique light irresistible.

He may perhaps be painting inside, she had decided, making her way toward the home of Dr. Jean-Paul Meurice.

At the doorway she'd stopped. She had promised Le Brun there would be no sign of surprise – nothing, at least, that Jude could decipher, yet in that absolute Sunday stillness, as she'd pulled the string for the doorbell, she had felt suddenly fearful.

Jude would miss nothing – of that she was certain – no matter how breezy an entrance she could possibly manage. It was his business, after all, to capture expression. Hers would tell all – this too she well knew – for they had made music together for over a decade, and he had learned, on the wing, to take his cue from her eyes.

Of all times on this day he would take the same cue from the same place.

And yet on this day he was indoors. Perhaps he could not as yet move toward the quay. Perhaps his physician, for the sake of the patient, had told but half of the story.

"Oui, Mademoiselle?"

Behind, in the dimness, there'd been no sign of a painter.

"Rebecca Chase," she had told Marie-Claude, producing not her card but Le Brun's, which had suddenly seemed more appropriate.

"*Ah, oui*...Please come in. I'll tell Monsieur Jude."

Rebecca had sat by the window. The house had seemed even more silent than the deserted quay just beyond.

And then she had heard Marie-Claude's voice, speaking low in a room that seemed to adjoin the salon. After a moment – no mistaking that sound – she'd heard a murmur which was Jude's reply, and then the sun had shifted somewhat so that the salon had suddenly brightened, and Marie-Claude had reappeared.

"If you will follow me, Mademoiselle. Monsieur Jude has been waiting."

Ten seconds – twenty perhaps – before Rebecca had moved into what had appeared to be, at first glance, a consultation room, nothing more.

And then she had seen the paintings.

Some were already framed, most still just cloth, all magnificent interpretations shaped by a mind at the height of it powers. How to account for this fact? – for the artist was seated, close by the window, vivid blanket across his knees, silence and shadows around his chair, face and hands deeply marked by the struggle he'd been through. His fine eyes were still sunken, his grey hair had receded, his complexion, though he had worked often in sunlight, still a disturbing chalk white.

Ah, but the paintings around him – brilliant abstracts, shimmering seascapes, portraits of fishermen, children, Marie-Claude over and over, little Germaine many more times – and then that last one – propped on an easel – hauntingly beautiful, called simply *Half Moon*. Rebecca had stood for a moment beside this last work. She'd seen that face once before, she believed – she wasn't sure. A crowded room, dimly lit – that was all she could conjure. That and a song's refrain: *La Vie en Rose*, she thought, though even this fact was unclear. All she knew for certain was that the model, whoever she was, naked and scarred and disturbingly alluring, had inspired Jude McCallister's masterpiece.

Making an effort then she'd looked away, only to find herself stunned once again by the profusion around her. Everywhere there was harmony, as though Jude the musician had merged with Jude the painter in a violent transmutation which had exalted him.

She would never remember how long she had studied these works. She would only recall that she had finally turned toward the man in the chair who had said nothing yet.

I will see all I have lost in her face, he had told himself at that moment.

But what Jude saw when their eyes met was everything he had become. In the time it had taken Rebecca to take in the sweep of his achievement, she no longer saw the frail figure she had first glimpsed in the shadows, but rather a man who was fundamentally more compelling than ever.

Moving toward him she had studied Jude's face, although still he'd said nothing, enduring her scrutiny that Sunday morning, with only the church bells as witness. He had agreed to this meeting, after all, come what may, so that he was surprised when she had stopped, and then smiled, and with a winsome simplicity asked, "Why, Jude McCallister, have you kept yourself so far from us?"

"I have been working," had been his reply, said with his own smile at last – a shy one, having felt in her greeting, above all in her frank gaze, that what he had most feared did not obtain. He had indeed become the person Théobald had predicted – changed to be sure, having surrendered much in the past year, yet in the relinquishing, paradoxically, having gained mastery over the most elusive and challenging aspects of his work – one and the same with his life – so that the grace notes in the former reflected the latter's renewal, and restored life, in its turn, had found its dazzling way onto his cloth.

This had been promised to him by his physician. It had been confirmed in the firm grasp of Germaine, the solicitous affection of Marie-Claude, the gentle, perhaps even inviting caress of Rebecca's hello.

Filled with relief then, like a modest athlete embracing a defeated opponent, Jude had struggled to stand.

"Don't Jude, please –"

"But I must."

"Why must you, Jude?" she had asked tenderly, taking the hand he had offered.

"Because, dearest Rebecca, you have come a long way. You are my guest after all. First guest I've had, as a matter of fact, since I was beaten and left for dead a year ago, nearly, off the Champs-Élysées."

And then again he had smiled, no longer shyly but rather in wonder. He had mentioned the thing. His words had called forth the ordeal, making the fact of it palpable – incomprehensible pain swiftly granted clear and definitive shape – as though the horror, like one of his sculptures, had been completed. It stood apart from him, although it would always be his. It could be glimpsed in its entirety, but no more than its entirety, and though never grasped, perhaps someday accepted.

"Someday, perhaps," he murmured, as if his deepest insights had been a conversation he had shared openly with Rebecca.

"For now," he went on resolutely, "I should like to show you Honfleur – at least the quay, which we will have to ourselves, since Mass in the mariners' church has begun."

"If you will promise we will come back here, to these paintings –"

"We will come back here to these paintings."

"And if it won't tire you."

"I walk the quay every morning. Afternoons too, when the sun's high and warm. In between I paint what I see. Wherever it happens."

"Show me wherever it happens."

"You mean you want me to paint now?"

"Yes."

"With you here?"

"What's wrong with me here?"

"Rebecca, you haven't come out to Normandy to watch me paint in the sun."

"How do you know, Jude," she had answered, linking her arm into his then, "what I have come out to Normandy for?"

"Done!" said Jude with a flourish, dropping a pink pastel crayon into the cardboard box by his side. "Well, of course nothing is ever done. Everything can be improved, but the light's gone by now, and you've been so good here on the steps" – he stopped.

"Rebecca, your feet must be freezing."

"I wanted to keep them in the water."

"But I was not painting your feet."

"Believe it or not, Jude," she laughed, "we tourists happen to like the feel of its tides on our flesh."

"Well even so –"

"We also like to see paintings."

"Mine isn't perfect."

"My songs aren't either."

"Let me dry off your feet first."

"If I can then see your picture."

He rubbed her ankles, her arches, the delicate feet that matched her fingers, so often observed yet for some reason never noticed as she had touched her harp beside his piano.

"Are you warmer now?"

"Much."

"Shall I show you your portrait?"

"If you feel it is time."

"When is it ever time?" he asked with a sigh, handing over his sketchbook.

The work was exquisite, above all its colours: red hair that resembled the sunset, pale green sundress, bright auburn ribbons trailing behind in the breeze. As for her face…no, it was not really her face but the *fact* of her there he had captured, contented and vivid like the bay he had filled in around her.

"As I said," Jude repeated, "one can always improve things."

Rebecca Chase shook her head. She studied the painting some more. Then, reflectively: "As soon as you can, Jude, whenever you can – you must return to Paris. You have agents there, colleagues – a dear friend or two," she added, placing her hand on his arm. "What you have painted here, after all…"

"A woman, the harbour…"

"What you have painted," she insisted, "cannot forever be hidden in the home of Dr. Jean-Paul Meurice. It must be played at some point, like a song, or it remains merely a score."

Incoming tides teased the first step where they sat. Over the waters, with gusto, Normandy's flag waved.

"Harmony should not be hoarded," Rebecca concluded, "that is all, Jude."

~☾~

Conflicting emotions beset Jude as he walked back from the train toward the house of Dr. Meurice. He had lingered long at the station. She had never looked prettier.

"I will see you again, Jude, I hope," she had said as the incoming local had slowly arrived. "Paris awaits while you wait –"

"In the meantime," he had heard himself blurting out, "will you come back to Honfleur? I mean while the trees are in bloom still."

"They'll have turned by next month."

"Next weekend then?"

Sounds of a baggage cart clattering past had drowned out Rebecca's answer. Her hand on his and above all her smile, though, had led Jude to add, "There's a Saturday local that'll get here by noon. You could return on the Sunday express. Marie-Claude can arrange one of the rooms up on the second floor." He'd felt her hand on his still.

"Less of a rush that way. I mean it isn't easy to find the right tree for a sketch. I intend to sketch of course."

The conductor had called out for boarding.

"If you can stand it."

Rebecca had jumped onto the car stairs. Over the train whistle she'd called, "All day long if you like, Jude," and then she had waved, the train lurched out of the station, and like the whole afternoon, Rebecca Chase resembled a dream.

But she was not a dream, Jude reminded himself as he carefully moved down the quay. She was a woman, a friend, trusted and trusting, which is why he had mentioned Marie-Claude, and the second floor, and the clearly artistic purpose of the visit he had proposed. She could feel secure in her return trip, knowing he would respect her, never guessing what he himself barely grasped.

And yet there it was, he reflected, pausing outside the bistro alongside his house. The scent of her close to him on the steps, her frank green gaze during dinner, their many duets over the years – all of it had aroused a need he had thought would never return to him.

Even this need, though, was uncertain. Perhaps it was all in his mind, not in his limbs, a foolish projection, not a potential, and thus, he considered, unlocking the door with his large key, it was perhaps best, after all, that he had made things clear from the start.

They were not at the start, though; this too he considered, placing his scarf on the hook by the door. She had loved him for years. She had come to him willingly still. In her eyes he had seen himself fashioned anew, as Théobald had predicted.

Vainly he tried to read by the low lamp near his window. As the hours passed the only clear thing was the snap of the wind in the rigging of a sailboat nearby.

He switched off the light, but remained in his chair. Nearing midnight, off in the distance, he heard the last Deauville train's strangely provocative whistle.

Perhaps it is time, after all, he thought as he crossed to his bed, paintings in profusion around him.

He turned his face to the wall, waiting for sleep to come quickly, easel and portrait and former days consigned to the darkness.

Bell buoys like chimes marked the hours. Sleep at last came nearing dawn. Among his fragmented dreams, he recalled only his masterpiece.

꙳ ☾ ꙴ

Overlooking the Hudson, Mikhail scanned the skies for any trace of the violent storm that had blown over the coastline that afternoon.

Finished, he saw with relief, tracing the arc of the clouds drifting on down past Land's End.

The odd thought occurred to him then – mariner's fantasy – that he wished he had sailed to Nova Scotia to bring her back from her journey. After all, he remembered, she had called him Jason on that dark Christmas Eve car ride, and he had thought of Medea, and indeed within weeks – the parallel vaguely disturbed him – she had awakened in some foreign land, like the Princess of Colchis, bearing her own fleece of gold.

Well it is over now, he reflected. *She has delivered the money, my letter, Maximilian's forgiveness. She will be back with us this evening.*

He checked and rechecked his watch. Within minutes his car

would arrive. In late Sunday's light traffic, as he had planned, he reached the terminal with time to spare.

Two policemen stood by the arrivals counter, Trans Canada Airlines, though they said nothing to Mikhail as he continued, in what were clearly high spirits, to the information desk directly ahead.

"Flight 407. Due in from Halifax. Can you tell me the gate, please?"

"Family member, sir?"

"I – not exactly. Well hopefully," Mikhail added, flashing his fine smile. "Soon. ... Yes. In the near future."

Something odd in the attendant's eyes – avoidance that did not quite mask concern – gave Mikhail a sudden chill. He glanced at the board above them. The day's recent arrivals had already been posted. The evening's departures were listed in order. Only one line was blank, as though this particular aircraft had never left Halifax, never intending to arrive in New York.

Mikhail looked away from the board. The huddled figures around him suddenly came into focus. He saw desperate faces. An elderly woman was weeping.

"It cannot be," he murmured distractedly.

"We are awaiting further details..."

"But the passenger called me –"

"All we know for certain is that there was a storm en route."

"Rain, yes, I heard."

"Violent rains."

"We had them here, around noon."

"In which the aircraft lost control, attempting Charlottetown airport. The pilot veered off toward New Brunswick."

There was a moment before the attendant concluded softly, leaning over the counter so as to place his hand on Mikhail's arm. "To no avail, sir...I'm sorry."

Mikhail stared at him, like a child trying to read the signs on some foreign train platform.

"The plane is lost, then?" he stammered.

"It would appear so, sir...yes."

The board, its one line empty still, prompted the next anguished question.

"And the passengers?"

"We are hoping there will be survivors."

Mikhail sank against a stone pillar behind him.

"Here," said a policeman, "There is a room to the right, for friends and relatives only…"

"I – no," replied Mikhail, crumpling into a chair by the pillar, all vestiges of the vigour that had returned to him since the surgery seeming to seep from his body like the sweat now appearing under his eyes and on the top of his mouth.

The policeman steadied him with a firm hand.

"Thank you…You needn't. – I'll be all right."

"Best if you let me take you in with the others now, sir. At least for a short while. There'll be reports as received, coffee and food of course…medical help…"

"Yes…yes, if you think this doctor can help her," was Mikhail's vague, incoherent response as he stood slowly, like a transplanted child still.

"He'll help however he can…Come. That's it's, now. Door's right this way."

Misha's airport vigil began five minutes later, 6:00 p.m. precisely, estimated arrival time for Caroline's plane.

Five hours later, most of the facts had been learned. On an immense detailed wall map, the site crash had been identified – sixty kilometres north of Prince Edward Island. In spite of the rains, even heavier after the crash, planes from Charlottetown, Moncton, Halifax, and St. John's had combed the rough seas at once from New Brunswick to Nova Scotia. Fishing boats had ventured south from the Gaspé Peninsula, ferries westwards from Les Îles-de-la-Madeleine. Finally, darkness approaching, parts of the fuselage had been sighted. Baggage, boxes, debris from the cabin had followed. Floating in calmer waters at last, along with seat cushions, air vests and pieces of clothing, bodies of the passengers had appeared off those same Îles-de-la-Madeleine.

Strangely, while the grim facts had been explained in that plain, grey square room, Misha had become calmer, more focused. Much of his strength had returned as the rescue attempts had been detailed, for he knew those seas well: Labrador Current to the north, Gulf Stream to the south – the first lethally cold, the second a strange, narrow strip of surprisingly warm sea making its sinuous detour around Prince Edward Island.

One could survive in that strip, Misha reflected, repeating the phrase obsessively – sometimes aloud, most times in his head, returning again to the wall map next to the blackboard, tracing and retracing points of latitude, longitude, air patterns, sea currents. *One could survive here…or here – or even here,* he decided, moving his hand along an invisible line northwest from Prince Edward into the Gulf of St. Lawrence.

I myself swam there once, off my boat, he remembered, fixing a pinpoint on the map with his left index finger. Though it was well off the course of the estimated crash site, he took a curious, almost sensual delight in the recollection, conjuring it repeatedly as the darkening hours passed.

Nearing eleven, all but four victims had been recovered. None of those found had survived, so that what had at best seemed a slim hope at sundown had by midnight become fact. Some of the mourners around Mikhail wept inaudibly, some uncontrollably, some embraced those – friends or strangers – who were seated beside them.

Mikhail neither wept, nor ate, nor spoke to anyone in the room. Dazed, he merely sat in a chair, hearing the count of recovered bodies increase, staring at the blackboard, the podium, the microphone, the fluorescent lights overhead.

Finally he stood up and walked a third time to the map. A seating plan of the aircraft had been posted beside it. Lists of passengers had been issued, along with any identification that could be provided by boarding pass copies.

Four bodies missing still, he reflected, two of them flight attendants, two of them passengers, seats 1A and 1B. He looked at his chart bearings – accurate, unassailable – like many a landfall he had correctly projected by the tentative light of the stars overhead. He looked again at the plan of the aircraft. Mrs. Caroline Devereux had not yet been found.

"Will you have some tea, sir, some coffee?" an attendant asked softly. "Is there someone you wish us to call for you?"

"There is no one," answered Mikhail, absorbed in his observations.

"Perhaps our physician here…"

Mikhail shook his head, eyes fixed on the map still.

"To those who are alone," he insisted, "he is especially helpful."

Mikhail turned at last, clearly shaken, but unable to grieve yet. Not on that evening. Not with four missing still.

"I am a sailor," he finally answered. "I've been alone many times, in rough seas and calm ones. I have lost much, have seen others lose more, and know that the ocean will have its way when it is time – but only when it is time."

"We will of course do our best, sir – dawn to sundown for days if need be."

"I don't think you'll need days," Mikhail murmured, turning again to the map, running his fingertips along the line he had traced before in the Gulf of St. Lawrence.

By midnight, most of the mourners had made their way through the door to what had once been their lives. By twelve-thirty, save for the attendant, he was the only one still in the room.

"At the first news of anything we will call you, sir."

"I don't mind waiting."

"There are no searches in darkness."

"Yet there are fishermen, sailors – night crossings on ferries," insisted Mikhail, gesturing with an unsteady hand toward the map. "I'll need to know, don't you see?"

It was increasingly clear to the attendant that Mikhail needed, at the very least, a bit of rest and some food.

"As I said, sir, we will alert you at once. You can even sleep here if you like. We have a small place upstairs."

Mikhail glanced above him, eyes sunken, face haggard, trying to picture the small place where he knew sleep would not come. There was no place that evening where sleep would come – that he knew also – but Land's End, at least, was alongside the river.

I will go home, he decided, not because the river could take him to where she was waiting – deep in his heart he had begun to sense that improbability – but because he might feel her presence more deeply over the waters there.

In thirty minutes, exactly, Mikhail's car pulled away from the terminal.

At least the poor man will rest now, thought the attendant, slowly turning the lights out, spent himself by the vigil, finally making his way toward the exit.

It was not rest, however, that awaited Mikhail as he rode toward Manhattan. Indeed, he was not even headed for Land's End at that moment. He had instructed his driver to go to 86th Street directly. In spite of the hour, Max would have to be informed. He himself would have to deliver the blow. Though he had not seen his father since other blows had fallen in that place, he was the only one now who could tell Maximilian that the woman they both loved had most assuredly been lost.

Odd, Mikhail thought, pausing in the deserted courtyard below Maximilian's house. Lights were on still in the living room, the dining room, the place called Mikhail's bedroom, although he never slept there – even behind the curtains pulled tightly closed in Maximilian's room. On occasion a long concert could last until midnight. Receptions for guests and musicians might even follow 'til one. But it was well past one and there were no sounds from the house – not a note, not a word, no echoing laughter of departing guests on the stairs, so that Mikhail shivered in the solitary dampness. Had Max already been told about the crash of Flight 407? Did he know, after all, that she had not returned to Manhattan?

Unlikely, Misha decided, focusing still on the windows above the cascading fountain. Had he known, Max would have called the airport. He would have asked for details, for Mikhail, for information about Mrs. Devereux. He would have sent Elsa Varig. Tonight of all nights there would not have been silence in that grand house.

Quietly, then, for since his father had struck him, Misha no longer carried a key to the house on 86th Street, he knocked at the heavy front door.

"Mikhail," exclaimed Elsa Varig, her features drawn, her face pale. "How did you know of this?"

Behind her, descending the staircase, Dr. Ollikainen appeared.

"Misha, I am so sorry. For all of us this was unexpected. Above all for you it must have come as a shock."

So Max has heard after all, Mikhail thought. But how? Max got his news from the papers. He had no television in his house. Elsa Varig's radio rarely played in her kitchen. She would not have known of Mrs. Devereux.

Dully, after a moment: "How was my father informed?"

"Informed?"

"The crash occurred after noontime. It has not even been half a day."

Ollikainen's eyes deepened as he met Mikhail's gaze.

"And after what he's been through…"

"Mikhail…"

"Of course we have all been through much. But at his age – and with his work so hard, and…and he felt deeply for her," Mikhail stammered, "which is why I thought I should be here when he was told. – We both know how it was, Doctor, you and I…I mean with Mrs. Devereux. Not that all hope is lost. No, no we must stress that to Max."

Gently: "We cannot stress that to Max."

"Well, I don't mean unduly."

"Max is gone, Misha," said the physician. "Your father died this afternoon."

Mikhail stood rock-still in the hallway, his expression blank, the words unclear as he heard them, head beginning to throb. His vigil at the airport seemed to be taking place once again, here at this entrance, although now he was one of the mourners who had left the terminal dazed, having had positive identification.

He slumped down onto the pale silk settee tucked into a curve by the stairwell. He studied Elsa Varig's sensible shoes, firmly planted on the floor beside him. He stared at Ollikainen's black physician's bag, placed on the last step nearby. Finally, as he fixed his eyes on the intricate pattern of the hall's cream-coloured carpet, he felt Elsa's hand on his shoulder.

"It was very peaceful, Mikhail. I was with Monsieur Max."

Misha looked up at her, absently.

"And I was summoned soon after," added Maximilian's physician. "No signs of a trauma, no stroke. A simple passing away from a life lived so fully, for such a long time, to…to whatever called him at that moment."

Mikhail grasped, at that moment what it was that had called him.

"When did it happen, Elsa? Can you remember?"

"Well it must have been about…"

"No, no, exactly," cried Misha. "Can you recall this *exactly*?"

"As a matter of fact, yes. Yes, I can…I had gone in to inquire if Monsieur Max would take lunch in his room. He seemed to be sleeping so calmly I was reluctant to disturb him. In fact, I sat down by his daybed – just in case he should wake then. I remember the trees outside his window – white dogwoods in bloom. And I remember his satin coverlet, green like the leaves under those blossoms. It was moving rhythmically, ever so gently, as he breathed softly in his sleep. And then just at that moment, Antonin's clock in the hallway chimed, two p.m. exactly, and I turned to glance at it through the doorway – I have always favoured that clock, as you know – and when I turned back toward Monsieur Max, I saw that the coverlet was still – utterly still – though the breeze through the dog-woods had not stopped – and I knew then he was gone. Yes, just like that…From one moment to the next…While Antonin's clock chimed."

Mikhail was shattered, as though felled once again by Max. The impossible had occurred. A storm had washed over the coastline, taking them both on its way – not in succession, Mikhail understood, overwhelmed by the cosmic improbability of the fact, but in some mysterious coalescence more like destiny than happenstance.

No – no that could not be, he told himself, and yet he knew it was true. He looked into Elsa's face. Only a tentative touch answered his long searching glance – a brush of her hand on his cheek, nothing more – as though to confirm the words she had said and the fact that she would watch over him still, although the others were gone.

And then another touch, a firmer hand on his shoulder, prelude to the quiet voice of Dr. Ollikainen, who was still standing beside him. "We were colleagues since I was fourteen. Your pain is mine, Mikhail – a small portion only though, I know that…I am sorry."

Mikhail made no answer, but merely nodded in mute acknowledgement, fixing his gaze on the courtyard beyond the windows ahead.

The fountain gleamed in the moonlight. The white dogwoods glistened. How often had Max stared at both, Mikhail wondered, while she too had looked out, monogrammed pen in her hand, preparing to render the thoughts taking shape? Yes, of course, it had happened. Concurrence, not coincidence. One view, one book, a love that would not endure dissolution, a heart that somehow knew she was gone – for the hall clock had chimed twice then, and her plane had plunged toward the sea at three p.m. Atlantic time – two p.m. in New York.

Apparently, neither Elsa nor Ollikainen knew as yet of the loss of Flight 407. And yet Max had divined it – Max who knew secrets no German officer had ever imagined, who could envision any beauty, shape any space, sense any betrayal, feel any passion. In the lost and private Mrs. Devereux, he had found these things mirrored, rare and precious reflection, although the days remaining were few when she had come into his life. Of course he had known when such a heart had disappeared.

Turning at last from the scene, Mikhail said simply, "I will go up now, Dr. Ollikainen."

"If you are strong enough," interrupted Elsa.

"I am strong enough," Mikhail answered, though he had endured one vigil already that evening, unbeknownst to the others. "It is you who must rest, Elsa – at least a little bit if you can – and you, Doctor."

"There is no need."

"I would prefer it."

"Then I'll be back before daybreak," Ollikainen responded, understanding that Mikhail had to go to his father alone this last time, for he had stayed away most of his lifetime, and the past could not be recaptured.

"Until tomorrow, then," Mikhail answered, turning to climb the curving staircase behind him.

Approaching the daybed, Misha was startled. Maximilian bore no resemblance to the man he remembered. His features were calm, his expression peaceful, his wide brow cleared of the pressing concerns that always seemed to hover there, slightly beneath the surface.

Misha pulled up a chair – Caroline's chair, he vaguely remembered, although it too seemed in some way fundamentally altered, as though it had been reupholstered, its dark wood refinished. Then, for a long time, he studied the odd contentment that had refashioned his father's face.

Increasingly, it made him angry. Such a look was out of place. What belonged on that face was what had always been there – fierce striving, intensity, restlessness, love of life, yearning, disappointment, lust for beauty, impatience.

And that other thing, Misha decided. *Above all, that one thing should be there, and it has vanished, almost obscenely.*

Misha was thinking of rage. Max had been a violent man. He had seen and done the unspeakable to free Provence from its captors. He had wounded Cecilia with a vengeance that would have exhausted a milder man. He'd lost a leg to keep those he hated from harming a friend's boy. And he had tried to kill his own son.

All that anger was gone, like yesterday's rain, not a trace of it left on the man for whom desperation meant living.

Try as he might then, sitting beside Max, Mikhail couldn't picture the precise colour of his father's eyes. He tried to recall how they'd been at the station, when someone had pried him away on the platform. He tried to recall them under the elm tree when they had spoken years later on Winchester's Green. Finally, as Antonin's clock chimed four a.m., he tried to recall them one last time, as they had been only last winter, with Mrs. Devereux pleading, clasping his knees.

Useless. No colour surfaced in Mikhail's recollection – no tint, no shade, so that he was glad at last to see pale streaks of light colour the sky. Ollikainen would be returning soon, within the hour, Mikhail guessed, hearing the clock toll four-thirty.

During that hour Mikhail studied Maximilian's face one last time. The oddest thought occurred to him then.

Perhaps, he reflected, Max was only pretending – not that he was alive still – that of course, Mikhail knew, even in his exhausted bereavement, was not possible. But was there not one more sham that could be enacted that evening? A final part to be played by the master dissembler? Yes – yes he was sure of it. That contentment, like some paste applied by a dowager on her way to a masked ball, was a cover-up, nothing more. Max was no more satisfied in eternal darkness than he had ever been in his lifetime. He had gone with the one soul who could match his. But with her he would yearn still, though no longer alone, for it was his nature, as it was hers.

A week to the day since the private memorial for Maximilian, Misha stared down at a serenely blue Northumberland Strait. His flight from Halifax, Nova Scotia, would arrive shortly in Charlottetown, Prince Edward Island. At eleven the following morning, out by the north capes, a memorial for the victims of Flight 407 was to be held.

All but two bodies had been recovered, though rescue attempts had continued from dawn to daybreak throughout the past week. Among those finally found, there had been no survivors. The missing passengers, seats 1A and 1B, forward cabin, First Class, overlooking the left wing, had been presumed lost, for even in May – despite the warmth of the Gulf Stream – hope had at last dwindled and the rescue had been suspended.

And yet how beguiling it seems still, Mikhail said to himself, as the aircraft prepared for a perfect descent over the coast. *Nothing has changed since the day I first sailed here.*

He crossed from the terminal onto the access road, then reached the highway past the next hill. Here he turned north, heading in the direction of his oceanfront guest house. He could have taken a taxi but preferred the long walk, traversing the island on his own, *dead reckoning*, he considered ironically as the warm Maritime sun declined.

A strong breeze came up, stirring the pine groves lining the road as he passed. It was a strange sound, Mikhail thought – not really mournful, just inconclusive, and thus it unsettled him, so that he was glad when the terrain steeply rose, and the cresting road widened, and the pine groves gave way to a remarkable vista of the valley below.

Like a fine patchwork quilt expertly stitched in rare silk, earth the colour of topaz, jade green, dark ruby red, and citrine covered the land. Silver-toned silos gleamed in the sunset. Copper-hued rooftops shimmered beside them.

Today an artist's palette, Misha reflected, stopping to gaze for a moment. *A week ago bruised, black and blue in the rain.*

Slowly he made his way down the curving clay roadway. He passed what appeared to be lonely white houses, and then evening came on, and parlour lamps followed, and he wondered about the lives sheltered by the simplicity of those lights.

He followed the road as it veered toward the north shore, leaving behind the lone sturdy homesteads. It was what he had wanted – to approach the red coastline alone, by the light of the stars, mariner still in his heart – a heart he feared might split in two as a pale crescent moon hovered over the path straight ahead.

The Gulf of St. Lawrence appeared. Immense and deserted, its shoreline continued for miles beneath cliffs that appeared charcoal black in the night.

Misha walked on, coming upon a staircase that led down to a wide cove below. He paused, then made his way to the sand and sat on a large rock facing the sea – last chance for such quiet, he knew, for in the morning, farther on up the shoreline, the other mourners would gather. Their grieving would be public, their farewells official, their final glimpse of the sea a shared glance that would no doubt bring them closure, although Mikhail knew he would find no such consolation. Nevertheless he would go, giving if not receiving the support that he needed, for he had come to the island not just for this service, but to perform another last rite, which he owed to Maximilian.

On the next day, Misha rose early, preferring to walk the last miles of coastline. By the time he passed Tracadie Bay, nearing the site of the service, he saw black cars passing him slowly. The sea was by then a deep blue, the surf a contrasting white, the capes a deep, vivid clay red, the dunes beyond a combination of dark grass and pale sand.

Mourners had gathered on the broadest of these dunes. The service was simple, conferring if not peace then a nascent acceptance in the hearts of those huddled together. Only one woman stood apart – not so much disconnected from the others but from the situation. Misha remembered her vividly. She had stayed a long time at the terminal, as he had, waiting in vain for some news. Her husband had been the man in seat 1B. His body had never been found. Like Mikhail, then, she stared vaguely toward the whitecaps while the service continued. The day seemed unreal to them both, the moment – in an odd way – inconsequential, as though its significance, so poignant to the others, bypassed their own hearts, leaving them heavier than before.

In forty minutes, the group had dispersed, some singly, some on the arm of a fellow mourner. Mikhail lingered, seated on a slight ridge in the dunes. Among those who passed was a couple he did not recognize – at least not at first. The man was tall, handsome, grey-haired, very distinguished. The woman was striking: tanned, blonde, beautifully dressed in a black chiffon dress that moved in concert with the wind. Not 'til they climbed the stairs did Misha remember that he had indeed seen that face before…Dr. Elliot Devereux. Featured on the cover of a medical journal at Todd's Farm.

"Come, Susan, let me help you," Elliot said as he offered his arm to the stunning woman beside him. Mikhail sighed, watching them disappear hand-in-hand. After all her fierce struggles, the days remaining to Caroline were to be few after all.

The beach was suddenly still, completely deserted. Misha took off his shoes and socks, rolled up his trousers, opened the small leather bag he had slung over his shoulder. He removed a fine silver urn and held it a moment, feeling its warmth in the sunlight. He thought of Maximilian's funeral – so very private, so simple, the only stipulation being music, to be chosen by those who loved him, as was the place for the scattering of his ashes, at whatever time deemed appropriate.

His father's will had been simple as well. He had provided astutely for Elsa, as well as for her son. The house, and the rest of his large estate, was left to Mikhail Alexander, with one significant, poignant exception. He had asked that Caroline's name, as co-author, precede his own on his memoirs, and that the large advance he had received, along with all future royalties, be hers alone, to be dispensed with as she might choose. He had, of course, learned of her own will, so recently made, so seemingly prescient, with Todd's Farm to be maintained forever as a natural haven in the event of her death. Hence, and this had clearly been his father's intention – so that the irony overwhelmed Mikhail as he sat in the strong offshore wind by the bay – Maximilian's long life and Caroline's land – both so rich, so filled with their passions, were from henceforth entwined, one sustaining the other.

Mikhail stood, still holding the urn, and walked toward the sea. The ocean shelf at this point was exceedingly high. Bathers could wade far into the sea and still have the tides barely cover their legs. This Misha did, solitary wanderer into the crystal-clear waters, until at last the surf brushed the edge of his trousers. For a moment he waited, and then, feeling the strong breeze increase, he opened the urn and scattered the ashes of Maximilian. The current would take them north by northwest toward the mainland, he'd reckoned, gauging the wind patterns exactly. It was what Max would have wanted: to have been near to her still in those mysterious seas.

He himself turned and once again chose the long walk back to his guest house, although this time he crossed the roadway, passing small ponds and blue inlets and newly planted clay fields, leaving the dunes forever behind him. He was glad for the clouds which steadily thickened, cancelling as they did any potential for the reappearance of last evening's pale moon, although blue herons lingered, visible still in the lengthening shadows – long-legged, disdainful – recalling a bargain he'd made once, paid in full, leaving him afterwards lost.

Lost again he left the island, first thing the following morning. Elsa would be receiving him in the house that was his now on 86th Street – home at last, but too late, or so he thought then, for it was devoid of all meaning.

༄ ☾ ༄

Antonin Onegin spent that morning in a tiny secluded Moravian church near Goose Bay. Unobtrusive, motionless, he remained alone in the last pew, for from the newspapers he'd learned that a service for the crash victims was to be held that day on Prince Edward, and it was the only way he could think of to participate in the memorial.

There in the silence he remembered how they had stopped by the lake en route to Groswater Bay, bunchberry dogwoods scratching their windows, her eyes full of hurt, her earlobes at last bare.

He recalled her departure the next day. He'd taken no pleasure in his supper after she'd left him then, no solace in the waltzes the old radio played, no satisfaction in the clearing of the skies nearing nightfall. It was too late for her – he was sure of it – despite the benevolent stars which had reappeared, one by one, over the Labrador Sea.

He'd left the house at that point, troubled and restive. By the light of his lantern he'd passed the barn – dark and silent, then entered the woodlands, also utterly still. Here he had wandered, waiting for the time to pass, for at eleven, concluding the music, the nightly news would be reported.

By ten-thirty he had returned to his chair next to the radio. At eleven exactly, he'd heard reported, in a sombre and official tone, what he had already, in clear, prescient detail, perceived in his heart.

"Confirmed," he had said then, or perhaps that was the groan of the wind in the evergreen trees as he'd slumped down in his chair.

And then that last week had gone by, and all passengers, including Mrs. Devereux, who was missing still, were announced lost – a fact that did not surprise Antonin, since he had known it from the beginning, from the moment she had walked away toward the airport terminal road.

Most of that week he'd remained in the house, having completed his chores before daybreak each morning, and then again after sunset. Wistfully he had thought of Mikhail, who would no doubt be in attendance at the memorial on Prince Edward. As yet he had had no word of Maximilian's death. Thus he had thought of him too, there in the grand house, wondering how he would survive the loss of the soul he too loved best.

Oddly, and this Antonin considered standing out on his church steps after his own private service – he could not conjure Caroline's image as she had been in that grand house. Her presence – vividly hued, palpable almost – had remained for him in the Maritimes.

Jude had painted well all week, palette mostly gold, auburn and green. He felt especially well the next weekend in fact, waiting in the sunlight for the local train due in at noon.

"Rebecca!" he exclaimed, with a blend of welcome and surprise in his voice, for he was still astounded by the fact that more than his frame seemed to be mending.

She stepped down from the vintage, wine-coloured train car, her own colours that day being red, navy blue, and the straw-coloured tones of her skin.

"Well didn't I promise I'd come?" she asked as she approached him, arms laden with boxes, face still framing that smile that recalled late nights on the Right Bank.

Somehow she managed to free her hand and take Jude's; then she gave him a gift for Marie-Claude, another one for Germaine, a small tapestried suitcase.

"You must have found me much recovered," Jude replied with a wry laugh, "to have burdened my hands so – one of which still holds a cane."

"I have found you much recovered," was her answer.

"Well," he said after a moment, somewhat awkwardly, not from the boxes he was balancing but from her presence so near him, "let's be off then."

"On second thought, Jude, I should perhaps carry the presents."
"Nonsense…"

"Keep the bag if you like, but I can't have you mixing my gifts up, which you'll do, beguiled as you'll be by that quay you love so."

One more time she smiled, and with an engaging insistence took her gifts back, for she had not counted on that heavy cane, and thus they returned, passing blue languishing boats, to the half-timbered house of Dr. Jean-Paul Meurice.

Jude was clear on two points as they pulled the bell string by the doorway.

In spite of the changes the past year had wrought on his face, his hands, every part of his limbs, Rebecca wanted him still.

More important perhaps, in spite of those changes – and the awareness was as sudden as it was forceful – he still wanted a woman.

Jude's driver took more than his usual care on the sinuous road leading north from Honfleur. After an hour's climb, as instructed, he stopped at what seemed to be the highest point overlooking the sea – vast meadows dotted with apple trees to the right, sheared-off cliffs to the left dropping down to a sliver of beach washed by immense surf.

"This'll be fine, Marcel," Jude said as he looked up the hill. "'Til sundown then, thank you."

He took his sketchbook and cane. Rebecca took his arm. Together they climbed a gentle knoll in the fields until the land levelled off slightly and a warm afternoon sun slanted upon the grass, unobstructed.

"Yes, this is fine," he repeated.

Rebecca spread out their blanket. Jude arranged his supplies. Steadily then – even at the start utterly sure of his way, she saw – he began to sketch the spectacular scene.

Unaware of time slipping by, he continued. He filled in the coastline, cliffs, meadows and sea in the distance, hand every now and again coming to rest by his side, not out of fatigue, it appeared, but because he seemed to be deciphering sounds of a surf long since hidden from view far below the steep headlands, yet still somehow present, audible nearly, in the scene slowly coming to life on his pad.

And all the while Rebecca remained silent, half reclined on the grass beside him, hearing as well those mysterious sounds, seeing none of their secrets.

The day's warmth disappeared. Jude seemed not to notice, perceiving just ever-deepening shade turning the white headlands ochre. He switched from pastels to charcoal, listened intently again, chose a pencil, a pen – never saw Rebecca stand, remove the navy blue ribbon that fastened her bright hair, move through the grass toward the edge of the cliff.

Not until a brisk offshore wind billowed the sheets of Jude's pad did he turn and suddenly see that Rebecca was no longer beside him. Puzzled, he looked around, only to find an endless succession of empty green slopes in a steady retreat from the sea.

Shading his eyes, he turned back. Directly ahead, the road was deserted. Southward he saw a lone stand of beech trees, seaward branches sheared off like the pale cliffs below. To the north, framing a steeper bay, clumps of junipers huddled together along the continent's jagged edge.

A vague unease overcame him. He reached for his cane and made his way, much too fast, across the uneven terrain toward the top of the bluff. Below him were bathers – minuscule figures stretched out on blankets along the sand. Beyond them were more figures, even tinier – solitary swimmers floating atop the water or stroking forcefully through the heaving sea. The fact occurred to him, briefly, that one of those swimmers might be Rebecca, but then he concluded, as his concern for her deepened, that the only stairs to the beach were cut into that northern bay, barely visible from where he was standing – surely too far for her to have walked in such a short time.

All of a sudden he felt unsteady, so close to the edge of the cliff. Images assaulted him – torn strips from a canvas, footsteps behind a pavilion, Christmas bells pealing behind strips on his own head.

"Rebecca?" he called, forcing himself to look directly beneath him, but only his own voice was returned in the echoing wind.

Twice more he called, twice he heard only the wind in response, so that he decided to turn to the north, planning to make his way down that staircase somehow, for the only place she could be, he had decided, was somewhere among the swimmers who had ventured out past the bay.

Presentments of loss made his heart pound as he walked, or perhaps that was the surf below – his senses could lead him astray still he knew – so that as he caught his breath he leaned on his cane and blamed himself bitterly for having brought Rebecca so far. She did not know the landmarks, was unfamiliar with the pathways, had absolutely no experience with the sudden drops at the edge of each cliff.

Again far too quickly he pressed on to the north. Off in the distance was more scrub dotting the foothills, and what appeared to be an abandoned stone shed between wind-twisted oaks. As he passed it he saw that it had once been a dovecote, no doubt empty for decades, yet somehow still standing, though most of the windows were shattered and cracked red tiles had begun to tumble over the steeply pitched roof.

Jude at last reached the staircase. He was about to descend when all of a sudden he stopped, looked again at the dovecote, and reflected that somebody might be inside there – lost, exhausted, perhaps just curious – perhaps forced to go in.

He retraced his steps toward the shed. The front door was ajar. He pushed it still farther, taking time to adjust his eyes to the musty dimness inside.

Half on its hinges, the door banged as it swung against the wall behind it, startling the figure standing by an open window at the opposite end of the rectangular room.

"Jude – however did you find me?"

He was too stupefied to answer.

"You were painting so intensely. I didn't want to disturb you. I just slipped away."

"Slipped away?"

"Well yes…Yes I did. I figured the sun might go down, and the stars might come out, and there you might be still, sketchpad still on your knees – so I decided to sightsee while there was light left."

Far more slowly than he had walked in the last ninety minutes, Jude moved away from the entrance and crossed toward Rebecca. Even in the half-light, she could see a surge of conflicting emotions passing over his features – relief, exhilaration, disappointment, most of all anger.

"Well not exactly sightsee," was her clumsy rephrasing. "More like explore...wander about –"

As he approached she also saw, clearly, the grey exhaustion in his face. She turned away from him then, aimlessly passing her fingers over the dusty windowsill beside her, shame welling up inside her, for it was a long distance from where he'd been painting to the dovecote where she'd found refuge, and he had crossed it hurriedly, in a state of high tension, judging from the sweat gleaming still on his temples.

Shame turned into remorse. Though she had expertly hidden this fact, her explanation had been disingenuous.

She'd felt ignored while he'd painted – worse than ignored, inconsequential, absent almost, and it had both rankled and surprised her as she lay in the sunlight beside him, for it was something she had not felt on the previous weekend, when it was her own portrait that had absorbed him, something she had promised him she could never feel when he was sketching – an emotion she had never experienced when they had played together at the Crillon. Well, at the Crillon, after all, as when he had painted her in the harbour, Jude had been focused on their interaction. In Étretat things had been different. Out on that knoll was a Jude who had once more unnerved her, for though his body had remained beside her, he had in his unique and incontrovertible way disappeared. Off he had gone, as he had so often done in the past, once again with a mistress – the one he loved best this time, she suspected – his work, the view, the thrill of the brush in his hand, his compulsion to shape come what may. With a sigh she had understood. He had emerged from his ordeal fundamentally unaltered. His canvas came first still – everything else, including his women, forever subservient to one overriding compulsion.

The insight had wounded her, far more deeply than she could have imagined, for she too was an artist, and a fine one, yet she had never been vouchsafed the concentration, perhaps even fine madness that distinguished Jude's genius. Piqued, she had left him there – jealous of his devotion to an intangible with which she could never compete, angrier still that such a commitment would never be hers.

Not until that moment, though, under Jude's burning gaze still, was she completely aware of what she had done. Her face coloured deeply. Jude perceived it at once, for he never missed any tone, not even in such failing light.

"I am sorry," he managed, thinking that his appearance, weary and unexpected, must have frightened her, or that his tone, rough and impatient, had with good reason offended. She was his guest after all. It was not his place to impose demands.

"No, Jude," she answered, dusky remorse still on her cheeks. "It is I who am sorry, making you walk so far, worrying."

She saw that his cane had been left by the doorway.

"Here," she continued. "There's a small bench by the window. It won't be dark for a while yet, and you can rest, and I can rest, and…and you must forgive me for today, Jude, even if you cannot do so yet today."

Sinking onto the bench: "A misunderstanding, Rebecca, nothing more."

That was his way, Rebecca reflected as she sat down beside him. It was not the first time Jude had occulted whatever had wounded him, body or soul.

Late afternoon sun filtered unevenly through the shattered panes. Jude remained silent, watching a jagged prism of light moving imperceptibly across the floorboards.

Suddenly, as though seeking absolution, Rebecca reached down for his hand. She raised it to her lips and kissed it, regret and tenderness and desire all mixed into the moment, so that he looked up at her, surprised by the gesture, and then he smiled shyly, for his hand, uniquely spared outside the Pavillon, had not touched a woman since then.

She pressed his palm against her cheek, closing her eyes as if to record the sensation exactly, and then she moved it again to her mouth, kissing the palm this time, murmuring, "I above all people have hurt you. I am sorry."

The dovecote once more was still.

The rainbow-like prism dissolved.

"Never again, Jude, though, I promise."

How comforting, Jude reflected, was her quiet assurance in that increasingly dim place. So much had been uncertain these past months, and though much had been recovered, there was still that one thing – it often awakened him with a start as though the harbour waters had risen and rushed over the quay into his room.

He took Rebecca's face in his hands, recalling vaguely that he had kissed her before this, Sacré-Coeur's dome alongside, Montmartre's streets spreading like star-points toward the city below. He had pulled away on that evening, loving another. It was all now behind him.

Fleetingly, nevertheless, as though in some forgotten dream, Rebecca's tongue in his mouth recalled Caroline Devereux in his arms, shortly before his own arms had been broken, and Mrs. Devereux had disappeared, or he himself had gone away – one and the same in any case, given the circumstances that had occurred – and so it surprised him that in this stone covert, this woman – statuesque, outspoken, as distinct from the reed-like reticence of the iris who had loved him so fiercely that she was willing to burn for him – it surprised him that he had become now so urgently aroused.

"We have to go now," he murmured thickly.

"Yes."

"It will be too dark to walk soon."

"I suppose it will," was Rebecca's answer, although neither seemed able to stand at that moment, for as he had spoken Jude was caressing her red curls, gently at first, then with more firmness, and then he suddenly grasped her hair so that he bent her head back as he found her mouth again, fiercely this time.

He would have made love to her then and there, his concern for her having become intense need, his fatigue having waned, or perhaps just forgotten – it no longer mattered – but a violent gust of wind intervened, throwing the broken door back up against the stone wall, sending last season's stray leaves swirling around their ankles.

Startled more by the absence of light than the noise, Rebecca said, "Night is falling, Jude."

He turned and saw tentative stars framed in the doorway.

"Yes," he responded, his voice hoarse and thick still.

"And the road back is rocky."

"You have learned much," he acknowledged, pulling away from her, somehow. "We must get you home now – back to the harbour, before the paths on the edge of the cliff disappear."

They walked toward the doorway. At the threshold he stopped and drew her against him one last time, although he did not kiss her then, fearing he would lose resolve and slip off her sundress and lay her down on the floor and ease himself on top of her, in spite of the isolation of that lonely place, for he knew now his ordeal had not left him powerless to make love to a woman again.

On the contrary. After the struggles of the passing months – after the long sleepless nights and the longer days of despair, his own body had become if anything more insistent, his own hunger, always intense, was now if anything more acute.

"Don't go upstairs tonight, Rebecca," he whispered, letting his fingers wander down from her face to her neck. "Unless you want to. I won't follow you...although I could," he said with a smile. "I could climb up to the roof after today's walk."

It was she who smiled shyly now as she reached again for his hand, though she did not raise it to her lips this time, but instead, fixing her eyes on his, pressed it gently against her breast. He traced its outline beneath the thin gauze of her navy blue sundress.

"If you promise to do that again I will stay with you, Jude."

"That and whatever else you may want of me," was his straightforward answer, for it was no game they were playing now, no improvised tune in a fine lounge on the Right Bank, but instead – for her, the realization of long-cherished hopes; for him, the allaying of long and lingering pain. She was determined to have him. He was determined to love one more time. For the present, as for most of his life – with the exception of one hot summer's encounter – he knew only desire.

And yet perhaps…perhaps with the passing of time…

So Jude reasoned, if reasoning could be applied to the surge of longing within him. So too Rebecca projected, if something akin to clear plans could be applied to her calculations. Thus, each turning over that same word *perhaps* as they walked, they made their way down the darkening path to the car which had returned for them.

⌒ ☾ ⌒

Jude took a brass key from his pocket, unwilling to pull the bell string and disturb Marie-Claude at that hour. They stepped softly inside. He closed the door carefully, stood for a moment in the silence, then took Rebecca into his arms, kissing her deeply there by the entrance, once again letting his hands trace her languorous form.

"Come," he murmured, leading her into his room.

She remembered the first time she'd entered that space – had only a week passed since then? – afraid of what she might discover then: a ravaged man, unrecognizable, unable to paint well again. Instead she'd been staggered by the paintings, the genius, vigour reclaimed with such effort.

Now again she was staggered, not by the paintings – these she could not see in the shadows – but by that same force that seemed to want not just her body but her soul, her essence, heart and mind and limbs in conjunction.

There was nothing rough in this power – that was the strange thing. "Are you comfortable?" was all he had asked after he had undressed her and placed her down on his bed and lain down beside her – far less clumsily than he had imagined he could do – and when she had nodded he had caressed her a long time, wanting his hands, not his eyes, to fix in his mind her voluptuous shape – her full breasts, her wide hips, her long and delicate fingers, her long and powerful legs. Again and again he'd kissed her mouth as he did so,

511

then every place he had touched, and then he had parted her legs, kissing her long and deeply there too before he'd positioned his weight on her body, thinking of nothing but her body, forgetting his own limbs and their previous numbness, feeling at that point only a wild rush of life as he repeatedly entered her with a need which could have wounded but for the gentleness that had somehow remained, so that she made no objection, not even when he turned her over and gripped her with a strength that surprised them both, and thrust with a force that made him forget pain and the colours of pain and even the sounds of the sea by his window and the tearing of cloth and irretrievable loss.

They fell asleep intertwined on his bed, surrounded by paintings, silence, dreams, and the outgoing tides.

⟳ ☾ ⟲

"Jude," murmured Rebecca, stirring in the suddenly bright light, "it must be noontime by now."

"Ten past two, to be exact."

"I've missed my train!"

"There'll be another."

"But I've got to play tonight at the Crillon! Come…help me dress."

"As I recall there wasn't much."

She smiled. The herbal scent in her hair, now familiar to Jude, resembled burnt umber.

"I'll ask Marcel to drive you."

"No…"

"You can be in Paris by six."

"Jude, if I make the three-thirty…"

"If you make the three-thirty, I can't make love to you again."

"Then come to Paris next week."

"You know I can't do that."

"Why can't you do that?"

Jude ran his hand through his hair. Rebecca felt suddenly awkward, though she had tossed off her sheet and was sitting next to him, naked.

"I am not saying leave, Jude. I only say visit – come and see me – because I can't come back right away. I am committed at the Crillon for the whole of next weekend. After that an audition…" Her words trailed off as he kissed her. "I'll have to impress them…" Again a long interruption. "Your agents await, Jude," she murmured. "They're planning a show of your new works, I've heard."

"From whom have you heard this?" he tenderly asked as he again laid her down beside him, and she made no response but the one he sought with increasing insistence.

By the time she had left Jude had agreed – something which before that weekend would have seemed unthinkable – to return to Paris within two months. To be sure there would be demons in Paris, spectres lying in wait in his head, if not somewhere else. It was a risk he was willing to take now – slow steps, a tentative risk, but there'd be Rodin's house, and his eyeless marble neighbours waiting, and Rebecca Chase would never be far, and perhaps, in the end he would not always need the seaside home of Dr. Jean-Paul Meurice.

⌒ ☾ ⌒

"Pity the rain hasn't stopped," observed Lucien Barthes, standing at the top of the steps in Honfleur.

Viktor Graff scanned the waterside shops. With a collector's eye he saw some studio doors open still. "One quick stroll," he insisted. "I might find just the right thing."

"Viktor, we can't just stare into their houses."

"Lucien, have you ever met an artist who won't sell a painting?"

With that they were off, pausing from time to time beside an open atelier as rose-filled verandas dripped onto the cobblestones underneath. Lucien's spirits seemed to lift as they walked – barely perceptible change, but one which pleased Viktor. It was for this, after all – and not really to buy a picture – that he had suggested Honfleur, perhaps even Deauville, Paris a mournful place still for his friend since he had learned of his cousin's death in a plane crash off Prince Edward Island.

Over a month had gone by since that crash. Her body had never been recovered. There had been no closure, no end to the false hopes, no memorial in Europe, save for the grieving in Lucien's heart, and the simple service he had arranged near Raphael's house at the church of St-Louis-en-l'Île. From that day to this one, when Lucien had agreed to accompany Viktor to Honfleur harbour, Caroline Contini's name had never once been mentioned.

"Here though, if anywhere," Viktor thought as a warm onshore breeze stirred, "past sorrows might soften."

Rain dwindled to mist moving in from the sea. Boats at anchor rocked gently. Lucien stood at the end of the north quay and watched day like the tides recede. By the time he turned back, harbour lights had come on – ceremonial tapers, it seemed, shimmering by the hundreds across the serene bay.

"Why not stay on for supper?" Viktor suggested, seeing his friend clearly beguiled by the sight. "We can still make Deauville by ten."

They recrossed the north quay, rounded the steps by the plaza, strolled again toward the ocean along the south side of the bay. Passing a narrow half-timbered house, Viktor stopped. Next to the house was a bistro, its menu carefully placed in the window.

"Looks promising, Lucien, what do you think? I say we try it...Lucien?"

Viktor turned. A few steps behind him, Lucien had also stopped, looking as though he had seen a portent inside a neighbouring doorway.

Uneasily, Viktor approached the doorway. Then, although the room was in shadows, he too stared, transfixed by the same painting propped up against the back wall.

"It cannot be," Lucien breathed after a moment.

"Yes...Yes it is she," Viktor confirmed, stunned by the ironic fact that of all people there, looking as if she were alive, looking indeed more vibrant, if that were possible, than when he had met her the previous summer, was Lucien's cousin – slender, scarred, dressed in rope sandals, nothing more – her wild black hair loosened, her outstretched arm beckoning though not in a lewd way – more with a mixture of joy and surprise, emotions hauntingly captured by the artist, at the time clearly enraptured.

Jude had not seen them. Facing away from the doorway, he was intensely sketching Germaine.

"Though I don't know the artist…"

"I do," murmured Lucien. "We met a year ago in Paris. I was with my cousin. He made a sketch of her at the theatre. He also plays" – here Lucien stopped, overcome by the memory of that evening at the Crillon, when she had fixed her eyes on the musician and he had returned her gaze, piercingly, though not a word had passed between them. And yet something had happened – some essential communication had occurred – so that she did not seem surprised when he had sketched her at the Comédie-Française, arm reclined on the railing, watching Cyrano wooing Roxane.

"Lucien, let's leave…"

"Piano," continued Lucien, vaguely completing his sentence as though his cousin had encouraged him.

"I saw a place in the plaza…"

"I'll join you."

Viktor considered. As the studio darkened, the artist put down his sketchpad.

"We may as well both go in," Viktor sighed, sensing there was a story which had remained to be told on that day, and that in the telling it perhaps, Jude McCallister might offer the comfort that until then had eluded his friend.

"Yes of course I remember you," said Jude politely after Lucien introduced himself.

The man was much altered – the fact was not lost on Lucien Barthes – though day's waning light cast but feeble light into the room.

"We came out to Normandy to buy a painting – not that we expected such treasures," added Viktor sincerely as he looked around.

Jude noted that Lucien had walked directly toward his easel.

"Have you been working here long?"

"Not before Christmas."

"And so this particular portrait…"

"This particular portrait was done late last summer."

Lucien turned, gazing again at Jude's face, seeking something in its features – facts of her last days, perhaps even consolation, for sure a common recollection.

There was nothing.

He turned again toward the painting.

Viktor too looked at the portrait called simply *Half Moon*, staring in spite of himself at the markings rendered so unflinchingly as to make burned flesh compelling.

Jude simply watched the two men watching his painting. He was determined to maintain control of his hard-won emotions, to show no sign of that seemingly indestructible ache that had suddenly surfaced.

Rain began again past his window, mist shrouded the sailboats, Caroline's cousin continued to gaze at his painting, and then in a voice that resembled his own, surprisingly, for he believed he could withstand any and all pain by then, Jude said, "How is she?"

"How is she?" repeated Lucien, vacantly staring at Jude.

"I assume all is well – that Mrs. Devereux has made her peace with her life, her house, her husband…her duties, as she once called them," Jude added not without rancour, at once regretting the tone, knowing he hadn't the right to cast blame.

Viktor guessed then that in spite of the obviously intimate

relationship Jude McCallister had had with this model, he was unaware of the crash off Prince Edward Island.

Lucien, too, slowly realized that Jude did not know; that he'd heard little or nothing about Caroline's life during the past year, months that had been anything but peaceful: homestead burned, husband and fortune lost, all too brief independence…

Suddenly, he was at a loss. How to tell the artist, with his cousin's image before them, that she too was now gone, along with so much else in her life?

"Lucien, is she not well?"

Helplessly, Lucien looked at Viktor.

"Lucien's cousin was lost in a plane crash last month. I – we are all deeply grieved," Viktor went on gently – and then he too broke off, noting a terrible pallor spreading across Jude McCallister's face, seeing his eyes become dim, watching him study the portrait as though to give the lie to what he had heard, to confirm that Caroline was alive still – for did she not fairly speak on the canvas? Was her vivid body not still before them? Had she not remained in his room, arms outstretched, welcoming, although she had not written – not once – and he too proud to write a second time, knowing the letter would have to be different, for by then the man had also changed?

It was then that Lucien knew, seeing this man who had fought so, that his own sadness was but a shadow of Jude McCallister's grief.

Viktor was also aware, though he had intended to try and buy that magnificent portrait, that Jude McCallister would never part with it.

"Come," he said instead. "Sit down, Mr. McCallister. This has been a terrible shock."

"Yes. Yes, I will sit down."

Rain splashed on the window beside him.

"I should be grateful for any more facts," he managed with dignity.

Lucien then related, as much as he knew them, the turbulent events that had followed Caroline's return to America.

Jude listened intently, saying nothing, nodding from time to time as though to convince himself that what he was hearing had in point of fact taken place.

She had indeed reinvented herself – that was what most impressed him. Her awakening had not been fleeting. In the end it had redefined her, so that dependency on anything or anyone after that had disappeared.

Not without pain did Jude come to this conclusion, for its concomitant reality was that as she had made this change – as she had left her husband, her house, her former ways, her former friends – she had apparently also decided to leave Paris behind, and the man who had sketched her, whom she had promised to marry, and the large semicircular house overlooking Les Invalides.

Confusion passed over his face – a mixture of sadness, regret, grief, disbelief – and then, having learned the mechanics of self-mastery which in the absence of contentment sustained him: "Thank you. Thank you both, very much. I am glad fate brought you here, to my portrait, which I will cherish now more than ever."

☾

Jude dragged his easel out onto the cobblestone walkway. He placed his table beside him, arranged his paints with great care, aligned his brushes and pencils, prepared his treasured palette. By sunset, however, his dampened rags had erased almost all of his efforts. He'd found no charm in the basin, no allure in the boats, nothing at all for the next several days. Finally, thinking to paint the ancient and picturesque square, he walked up to the mariners' church on the hill. There he worked several more days, canvas rubbed clean by his rags nearing sundown – no paintings completed, no sketches in progress.

Seeing him walk down the quay so exhausted, Marie-Claude would prepare him a fine Norman supper. After that Jude would read, or listen to music, or open the doors to hear the deeper harmony of the changing tides in the bay. Finally, because he still had to push his limbs first thing in the morning, sleep would come to him in his studio.

It was never a benediction.

Fitful and nightmarish things would seep into the darkness, so that again and again he would awaken, long before daybreak, lost in the dim space around him, wanting only his paints, and his model.

Dr. Jean-Paul Meurice was due back in August. The month before, as he had promised, Jude prepared to leave Honfleur. There was much to be done – return trip arranged, apartment in Paris to be opened, body to be strengthened still, works in progress to be completed.

These remained unfinished – an irony Jude often pondered during his final days in Honfleur. He had recovered so much by the beautiful harbour: not just his hands and his legs, but a magnificent new way of painting – a fact he was humbly aware of – and now of all times, in all places, creativity had vanished.

Still, Paris awaited…Perhaps there, perhaps in time paintings as yet undreamed of – and with this thought he would return to the task at hand as his days on the Normandy coast slowly dwindled to one.

This last morning dawned bright – offshore winds crisp, cobalt skies clear. As Le Brun had predicted, his goodbye to Marie-Claude caught in his throat when she gave him her hand, and yet he was able to thank her, and present her with her portrait, and two views of the harbour, which she had greatly admired, in her frank Norman way.

His farewell to Germaine was agonizingly brief, for he found speech impossible and so merely clasped her against him, holding her fiercely for a moment – a fact which pleased her own breaking heart then, for she took pride in the clearly restored strength he had fought savagely for – struggle she had insisted upon. He murmured her name at last; nothing more. She drew back from him a bit, nodded, and merely said, "You are going back as I said you would, Monsieur Jude. A storm-tossed ship, righted at last."

Of the fact that there was hurt still there – some new hurt whose source she was unable to identify, she said not a word. In time, she suspected, that too would be righted.

Long after he'd left she found her gifts in a parcel left by a courier in her home – a stunning portrait of her in her Norman dress, a painting of her home, another one of the ocean at the end of her broad lawn, and – oddly enough, a portrait of the painted wooden statue of Saint Ann in the mariners' church.

With great tact Marcel turned south just past the Arc de Triomphe, avoiding the more direct Champs-Élysées as he continued on to Pont de l'Alma along avenue Marceau. Off in the distance, below the Quai d'Orsay, Jude could make out the spires he had come to know like his own hand from his hospital window.

The car slowed, making a last turn. To the left were the columns of Pont Alexandre, to the right the grand Esplanade leading to St-Louis-des-Invalides. The sky was a blend of gold, burnt sienna and black, like the strangely calm river beside them.

Jude braced himself for the sight just ahead – the glorious dome, Rodin's house, his garden – everything that had inspired him over the course of his lifetime as an artist. How much would be changed now, he wondered? Would the Seine still inspire? He could not say. He hadn't painted in over a fortnight. He might never again paint, he allowed, shuddering at the sudden cessation, which, in spite of Germaine's hands, had refused to be mended.

The car stopped by his building. Jude peered through the windows. When he reached for the door handle, finally, the strangest sensation overcame him: amid the bustle of home-going crowds all around, Honfleur's endurance resembled a dream – its bright silence a seascape perhaps, some lost cherished painting, vaguely remembered.

⁀☾⁔

Without so much as a glance at the stairwell beside the frail elevator cage, Jude walked directly to his apartment, took out his keys and was at last, after almost a year, back in his own home. He paused in the hallway a moment. Resolutely he turned toward the living room on his right.

Undisturbed, he reflected with some surprise, as if the paintings and sculptures done in some other life, by some other hands, should have disappeared with those days. The piano too was unchanged, he saw, running his fingers along the keys as he crossed. He repositioned a sketch or two on the wall, straightened a book on the shelf, then slowly opened the doors that led onto his terrace.

Twice he made an effort to step out onto his veranda; twice he decided against it, not because he had left his cane by the doorway, but because another scene had appeared superimposed upon the vista below him, lights of the city became a match in July's heat, darkening sky an immolation.

He returned to his hallway, ignoring his changing room, walking on to the studio where he had worked for almost three decades. This, Jude suspected, would be the most difficult space, and so he was again surprised, pushing open its wide door, to find himself facing the room with unexpected equanimity. He looked at the loveseat, the rose bowl, the fireplace mantel across. Perched above it was the bell jar, lovelier than ever, Jude noted, despite the catastrophe that had threatened, almost a year ago, to shatter its fragile allure. He passed directly beside it, opened the doors to his terrace and was glad when the telephone rang and he could once again avoid the sweet night.

"How good to hear you at last, Jude," he heard a woman's voice say. "I left a few things for you…very few, I'm afraid. After work tomorrow, though –"

"Rebecca, you needn't –"

"But I want to. I can't wait to see you."

"I've missed you too, very much," Jude managed after a moment, partly because he was aware she needed to hear those few words – partly because he was lost.

He hung up the phone and turned again toward his hallway, bypassing the kitchen, the dining room, the guest room – all of them of no interest. It was the door to his bedroom that beckoned insistently – the only remaining real challenge, Jude was clear on this now, and so he continued, walking in his halting way, until he stood by his large bed, where she had found herself, once and for all time it seemed, unashamed.

He glanced out the window. A million stars had appeared to rival the lights far below. She was now one with them all, a thought which gave him no peace, for there it remained still, and the persistence disturbed him: that lingering, unworthy rancour. He had awakened her for some other life, for some other man to be sure – a transaction, like the sale of his paintings, in which he had had, in the end, no significant part.

This reality was unassailable. Every letter that had arrived at his home had been forwarded to him in the hospital, or to his studio in Honfleur – instructions carefully followed by his housekeeper at the request of Dr. Le Brun. As for his periodicals – and Jude received only two art journals each month – these had remained at his home, for Jude could not read long works in the first months, and in the later months, finding a new art, he'd had no time and less interest. Hence, to sort out his mail over the course of the past year, there'd been two baskets in his office – one for correspondence, one for magazines, the former emptied each week and forwarded to the artist, the latter filling slowly with the few journals that arrived.

Jude had glimpsed this full basket as he had passed by his study. He had also seen, wincing, the empty basket beside it, for he knew he had opened its letters, and not one of them, in any season, had been postmarked Todd's Farm.

He returned now to his study to pick out a journal – any one from that basket would do – so long as the coming night could be endured.

He turned on the lamp by his desk, seated himself beside it, reached into the basket, pulled out a few samples.

Nothing of interest, he reflected, distracted and restless, listlessly thumbing through each of the pages. He picked up his pencil and made some designs on his blotter. He rearranged his fine pens, ran his hands through his hair, studied his paperweight – a round onyx piece he himself had once sculpted – and then he reached down and pulled out the last magazine.

It was then that he saw it – very bottom of the basket – the incorrect basket, as it happened, for it was not a journal but a letter.

An odd presentment overcame Jude. He took out the letter – pale blue vellum, faded somewhat, postmarked the previous September. He knew at once who had sent it, knowing her hand – that elegant script, and her perfume, which lingered still, faintly, on the slightly crushed envelope.

What he did not know – there was no way he could have guessed this – was that Caroline's letter had been mistakenly delivered to Jude's neighbour across the hall. The elderly lady had at once brought it by. She had knocked and called out and announced that she had a letter, wrongly delivered. In response from the kitchen, she had heard Jude's housekeeper call, "Very kind of you, Madame Tourine. Please, if you can, put it in the basket in Monsieur's office. Second door to your right. I'm washing the floor inside here and my hands are soaked."

A few minutes later, Vera emerged from the kitchen. Madame Tourine emerged from the office. Mrs. Devereux's letter had found its way into the emerging pile of journals, lost there among them, never to be retrieved until Jude McCallister discovered it on the night of his homecoming.

With a hand now unsteady he held the envelope and simply stared.

Had she rejected him? Accepted him? Strangely, since she was now gone, the second alternative seemed worse, unendurable – testament to the inscrutable, ineluctable star-crossed paths fate had decreed for him.

He passed his hand over her name above the return address on the back. Then, with excessive precision, he opened the envelope, removed its one single sheet, and read:

Jude,

I arrived safely, and all is well here, and the farm is beautiful in September. So, I imagine, is the terrace garden outside your studio doors. I hope you are painting, long into the sunset, and finely.

The pickers have come to the orchard and were all finished by nightfall. Heavy rains fell thereafter – nearly a week as I remember – so that the river rose over the footbridge and I could not get to my mill.

I have been to the guest house though – every day on my walks through the north fields, no longer in bloom.

In fact I've spent most of my time during these storms in that house, for I have books there I treasure, and cider and jam from the trees to put up, and the view of the ridge to the west is unobstructed.

By now, 17 September, your retrospective is due to open. I know it will be a success for you, both in a personal way, and, of course, in terms of your profession. All my good wishes for a stunning review go with this letter.

Caroline.

P.S. The letter you sent me somehow got lost on the way.

P.P.S. I hasten to add then, since I know you must be wondering, that what you explained to me in your apartment on our last night was true, every word of it, for no sooner did I leave you than life elsewhere lost all meaning, and even this dirt I adore is foreign sand to me without you, so that home to me now is where you are painting – as you insisted it would be, which is my answer to the question that somehow got lost on the way.

Staggered, Jude remained in his chair, motionless silhouette by the low light of his desk lamp. After some time he looked down. He read and reread Mrs. Devereux's postscript – agonizingly simple addendum – straightforward agreement to what had been fervently asked, and then seemingly, without explanation, rescinded.

By the time he looked up he had confronted it all – not just the words but their meaning, her tone, the fact of her there in his house on this night, unendurable alternative. He had not wept once since his beating – not in the hospital, when he learned what he would have to face if he were somehow to survive; not in the ambulance, when a life such as his own seemed no longer worth the effort; not even in Honfleur, when he had at last unwrapped the image he could not face until then.

Now, clutching her note still, Jude wept bitterly. He could have spared her such pain. He could have written again – not until Christmastime, to be sure, when he was lucid at last, and his hand could move some – but it was precisely at that point when his own pride had intervened. How to ask her to return to the man he'd become? Even a visit would have repulsed her. Becoming his wife would have been unthinkable.

Ah, but had he known of her letter, his pride would have crumbled. He would have written once more, or have asked Théobald to write – an explanation at least, not necessarily an invitation, so that she would have been free to do as she wished – which, he now knew, having read *life elsewhere has lost all meaning* – would have meant returning, for a love like hers could not die, although she herself could, and it was too late now for the correspondence which somehow might have saved them both.

He felt the room suddenly darken – a sensation of beauty retracted. Puzzled, he turned and saw that the lights above Les Invalides had gone out. He stood, very slowly, and walked at last onto his terrace. Stars filled the sky still, though the city below him had dimmed. Silence like ground fog seeped across small streets, the squares, the slow-moving river beneath its deserted stone bridges.

Off in the distance, some far corner behind Rodin's garden, it seemed, accordion sounds drifted back toward Jude's terrace. Instantly, he knew the song. He lingered a moment, then turned and reentered his house and closed the doors tightly behind him. Nevertheless he could still hear, wilfully almost, diminishing echoes of *La Vie en Rose*.

Dieu seul saura, Susannah Joubert Pellerin said to herself, wondering in her native French. She stared at the menacing clouds overhead, then at their livid reflection in the Gulf of St. Lawrence below. *God alone knows*, she repeated.

She walked toward the cliff at the edge of her yard and scanned the trees she had planted to gauge the force of the winds.

Perhaps another storm like that last one – perhaps just some rain. We could be lucky this time if it moves west toward Québec.

She sighed, shook her head and went back to removing her clothes from the line. Yet still the gathering clouds caused her to look up again, anxiously.

Serge would know, she reflected. Her husband could always predict how these things would turn out. But Serge was away, having already left, as he did each July for six weeks of fishing around the Labrador Sea.

She shuddered to think he may have sailed into this storm. *No. No, Serge knows his way. Every year the same route. He won't be caught unprepared*, decided his wife then – confidence not without merit, in fact, for there was little the ocean could do to surprise Serge Pellerin. He had spent decades fishing in dangerous and unpredictable seas, and yet every August, in fair days or fierce ones, Serge Pellerin made it home to Rocher aux Oiseaux.

Tiny Rocher aux Oiseaux – her island, as Susannah called it – lay far to the south of these Labrador shores, midway between New Brunswick to the west, Newfoundland to the east, Québec to the north, Prince Edward Island to the south. Only fishermen's Île Brion and a small archipelago, Les Îles-de-la-Madeleine, lay between Prince Edward and Rocher aux Oiseaux, so that Susannah's island, a speck on the map, was surrounded for miles by an ocean sometimes benign, sometimes malignant, either way lifeline to the island's seven inhabitants – all of them French-speaking, all with roots to the Acadians who had managed to stay in their homes after the fall of Québec and the end of French rule in Canada.

Fiercely independent, capable of enduring extreme winters and isolation, these descendants of lighthouse attendants lived in a world of their own. Their aptly named land, Rock of Birds – home to hundreds of species of migrating birds each year – was jagged, steep, washed by tides that invaded the many coves of its shoreline. Here and there, suspended it seemed over some steep sheared-off cliff, a house might be seen hugging the edge of the island.

Point Guetter, Susannah's stone cottage, perched sturdily above one of these deep coves, was aptly named also, for *Lookout Point* faced the ocean at the highest point of the island. Far to the south, miles beyond the minuscule Îles-de-la-Madeleine, were the tall red north capes of Prince Edward Island.

Rarely, if ever, did Susannah sail to the Madeleines, though her husband's boat took him to their shores every August for provisions.

Provisions also arrived, May to October, in packet mail boats from the Madeleines. Thereafter, once November's storms began to seal off Rock of Birds, packets were often forced to turn back to the mainland, not to return until spring.

Thus it was the cold, even more than their language, that set the inhabitants of this island so uniquely apart. The surrounding waters would freeze until March, layers of ice alone defining the shoreline, deepening snowdrifts obscuring each cove.

Indeed, were it not for the ribbon of warmth around Rock of Birds – *Notre Bénédiction, Our Blessing*, as the islanders called the Gulf Stream – even these last few Acadians would have been forced to abandon their world.

Instead, with each spring they discovered salvation: a near-tropical anomaly that forced the earth to give quarter, breaking up ice on the beaches, leaving no more than a trace of snow on high ground.

The process was swift, the change from April to June astounding. Land became fertile; fishing was plentiful; even a swim was delightful off the coves by each homestead. Like the rarest of wines this magical respite was savoured, for all too soon would come autumn, and though the Stream would persist still, its effects would be cancelled by the Labrador Current, forcing its frigid midwinter's path to the south.

Susannah thought with dread of approaching September, then quickly banished the fear, faced with more pressing concerns. Serge was away. A new storm was perhaps due. The house and grounds had to be secured, the woman to be cared for. Not that she needed much caring for now. She was anything but demanding – always polite, always anxious to help, and yet somehow helpless, utterly lost.

Yes, that's it – utterly lost, Susannah reflected, watching her, unobserved, before taking the wash in. *God only knows who she is, how she arrived here, where she was going.*

Again, folding the wash in her kitchen, she pondered these questions, thinking back to the worst storm that had ever battered Rock of Birds.

Serge had gone down the staircase that led to the cove directly below. In a matter of days he'd be off. For weeks he'd been preparing his boat, marking his charts, making repairs to his equipment – yet on that morning he'd been uneasy, repeatedly checking the line where sea and sky intersected. There was something uncommon in the darkening clouds – colours he himself could not gauge. All he knew for certain was that they would not escape whatever was in the making north by northeast of their shores.

By five, the rains had begun. Serge had already covered his boat, having removed what remained of his gear to a deep cliff-side cave at the edge of his beach. On more serene summer nights, he and Susannah had often dined in this cave, savouring the day's catch under seemingly endless white skies. That evening, however, he'd climbed the stairs hurriedly to join Susannah up in the stone house. By nightfall, they'd heard the surf pounding their beach, incoming tides stopping just short of the cave as gale-force winds tossed uprooted plantings about. By dawn, save for diminishing winds, the storm had passed through. Light was beginning to pierce parting clouds, although the waves were immense still, and the billowing sky appeared unconvinced.

Susannah had risen first, crossed to the edge of her lawn, then made her way down the steps. The sand was dark brown still, littered with crabs upturned, branches from the shrubs above, shells, seaweed, a bell buoy torn from its marker.

Nevertheless, in spite of the wind and the high churning surf, this new day was slowly but surely becoming benevolent – truly a sea change, unique to these shores.

She had remained by the stairs a moment, scanning those shores. The fishing would be exceptional in the weeks to follow, at least…*Housekeeping too*, she had sighed, for Serge was determined to sail when he could, no doubt within days, and the encumbered beach with its cave would remain hers to clear.

A week's task, perhaps more, she had projected then, picking her way toward the boat. She could barely make out its storm-tossed name as she'd approached…Ah yes, there it was: *l'Inattendu*. *Unexpected*. For some reason she stopped, recalling the day Serge had named his boat. *Napoleon's motto*, he had explained then, having spent most of his years sailing in capricious seas. *Always the unexpected occurs.*

A distant foghorn had sounded. Susannah had looked toward the sea, then again at the boat. With brisk winds swirling still round the cove, she'd felt a deep, sudden unease. Something seemed to be draped over the hull – clothing, cushions perhaps, even sails from an overturned boat –

No, no that was no sail, she had at last seen, taking a few more steps forward.

"Susannah, wait!"

Soundlessly, Serge had just crossed the damp sand. Like Susannah he'd stopped, disbelieving, staring in spite of the name he had given his boat, for there, crumpled against *l'Inattendu's* starboard curve, was a body – face toward the prow, hands over the face as though to protect it from the surf and the tides and the long gaze of strangers.

"*Attends*," he had warned again, kneeling alongside the hull. Then, urgently: "*Vite*, Susannah! *Quickly!* The woman's alive still," he had proclaimed, incredulous still, turning her white expressionless face toward him. "Yes. Alive," he had repeated firmly. "For the moment at least."

Gently, tides once again surging, they'd moved the stranger into their cave.

"*Frottage*, Susannah, quickly. I'll build a fire."

Susannah had already reached for the woollen blankets stored on the cave's high shelves. Expertly, even as the fire caught, she had removed the woman's soaked, shredded clothes and begun to massage the limp form, ice-cold despite the warm ribbon of *Notre Bénédiction*.

All morning long she had worked with precision, her kneeling form shadowed in the flickering firelight.

Serge too had worked expertly, preparing the herbal ointments Susannah had needed.

By noontime, when the woman still had not stirred, Serge had relieved Susannah, massaging more firmly, marvelling at the deep and delicate tracery of scars his fingers found.

All this and more Susannah remembered as she paused in her kitchen, ten days later, and stared at the stranger in the chair just beyond.

Violette, they had caller her, astonished, when she had at last awakened toward sunset and had stared at them both with vague and unknowing eyes that were deeper in hue than the wild purple phlox in the vase just above them.

"*Pas Violette*," she had murmured, repeating this twice before drifting back into a deep sleep. "Not Violette." Toward midnight she had again opened her eyes. Repeatedly after that, gathering strength with the fire's heat and the strong broth Serge had prepared, she had briefly awakened.

"Tomorrow perhaps we can take her up to the house," Serge had said nearing daybreak. "In the meantime she will be safe. The tides have begun to recede. We will stay with Violette."

"Her name is not Violette."

"No – no of course not. But at least we know that. And that she herself knows it is wrong. That may be all she can remember. But it's a beginning. More words will come when it's time."

Serge had been right. By sundown the next day, the woman had begun to speak. She had thanked them for their attention, had praised the food they had prepared, had savoured the warmth of the cave – all in fine, perfect French though it was clear she was neither Acadian nor from provincial Québec. It was also clear she had forgotten everything up to the moment she had awakened in their cave by the sea.

"Everything but the fact that she is not called Violette," Serge had repeated, taking comfort in that speck of consciousness, assuring Susannah that the rest would follow somehow.

He had assured her again, one last time, as he was repairing his boat just before his departure.

Four days had passed since the storm. They had moved her up to the main house, as planned, the day after they'd found her. They had given her the front room, facing south over the Gulf. She had grown stronger, had gone out into the yard, had begun to help with the chores, had never ceased to admire the beauty of the island rock, now her home. Not once, however, had she mentioned her life – whatever it was – before she'd been washed up on those rocks.

They had asked her, of course, when she appeared strong enough to speak of it.

"Where are you from, Mademoiselle?" Serge had said gently.

Susannah had waved her hand and warned: "Don't, Serge, not yet."

"There may have been others," he'd whispered.

The woman had simply stared at Serge. Suddenly then she had shaken her head, although her violet eyes expressed not a hint of emotion. "I was sailing alone."

Serge had leaned in to her.

"It was foolish, I confess it," she'd said, noting the wonder on his face. "In a rainstorm like that I should have been home."

"And where is home?" he had pressed her.

She had only frowned, leaning back in her chair, closing her eyes once again, veiling whatever pain lay behind their incredible hue.

No further details had ever been offered to Serge and Susannah Joubert Pellerin. Several times they had tried, but always in vain, for Violette – she had come to accept this name, although she was somehow sure it was incorrect – could not remember flight 407, Trans Canada Airlines, destination: Halifax. She had no recollection of the aborted landing en route, no picture of the shattering impact that had split the plane along the wing line, just behind the first class cabin, upending both sections in a vertical equilibrium – one final miraculous balance – before the sea swallowed the splintered pieces.

She had seen it happen, had heard the roar of the water as it drowned out the passenger's screams, had felt the annoyance of rising debris in her path. Later there had been voices – three of them – two calling, one groaning, all ending in darkness. Everything seemed to have ended in darkness, she had reflected, floating, clutching a cushion of some sort. There'd been a vortex of air along the wing line – that she vaguely remembered – just behind the first class cabin, which had sucked out the passengers in 1A and 1B, along with the attendants braced for impact in the two seats across the aisle. And then, as night fell, even this last scene had faded.

All that had remained was that annoying debris: suitcases, trays, something that felt like the doll of a child, something larger, curved, hollowed out deeply within.

"Ah," she had said as she'd reached it, recalling the boat her father had made when they had vacationed in Montevideo. "My canoe's come this way."

She had clung happily to its sides while it had carried her slowly from the concentric circles eddying still around the multiple plunge points.

Then her arms had grown tired. Twice she had tried to climb over the sides; twice she had failed. The sea around her had grown rougher, causing the object to pitch and roll in the waves, so that when she had tried a third time, she had been scooped inside with seeming ease. The rain had stopped – another mercy – or the sheared-off nose cone that cradled her, barely, would have filled to the brim and sunk too in its time. Instead it had rapidly moved in the still-churning sea – current stronger than ever in the wake of the disaster – taking her northward around the Madeleines toward the southern shores of Rock of Birds.

Not too far from these shores she had passed out from the strain, never sensing the nose cone tip on its side in the waves, so that when it too finally vanished she had slipped out, like a fish from its net, tossed onto the beach by the tides, not to come to life again until Susannah found her at Lookout Point.

It surprised Rebecca Chase that Jude did not make love to her the night after his return from Honfleur. As scheduled, she had arrived with flowers, groceries and a fine bottle of wine. Taking the parcels from her he'd kissed her deeply, front door still open behind them, partly because it was not in his nature to bestow a perfunctory kiss – partly because he had known, since the previous month, that she would expect such a welcome.

And yet Rebecca had sensed at once that the embrace had fundamentally changed. Everything that night had seemed altered. Though he'd been gracious throughout, even at times affectionate, Jude had remained distracted during their candlelight supper. She'd guessed its source lay in what had no doubt been a wrenching farewell to Honfleur.

Thus, when asked politely about her audition, she'd answered merely that it had gone well, declining to add that the position, should she obtain it, was with the Vienna *Volksoper*, beginning September the latest. Also kept deep within was the fact that she was prepared to leave Paris, but not without Jude McCallister.

It will be best for him, she had reasoned, watching him stare at the flickering candles. His work had flourished in Normandy, far from the Champs-Élysées. It would flower again in Vienna among other fine artists, musicians – above all with her, whom he had long accompanied and whom he had at last begun to desire, or so it had seemed just a few weeks before.

"Truly beautiful, Jude" she had pronounced when they had returned to his living room for a brandy. The piano, she noted, remained covered with a silk damask cloth. Curtains, tied back, allowed only a partial view from the French doors.

"The paintings are all yours, I see."

"Well, they have to hang somewhere," he said with a wry smile.

"And the sculptures?"

"I like to fiddle."

"How well I know," she'd replied, taking his arm as they approached the veranda.

"Shall we step out, Jude?"

"I – no, I don't think we should. I've only just gotten back, after all. Things are still somewhat disarrayed. And it looks like rain over the river," he'd observed, looking out over a clear, absolutely cloudless sky.

"Then show me the rest of the house," Rebecca had said breezily. Heights, no doubt, disturbed his frail equilibrium still.

Slowly, they'd walked down his hallway. "My study," he'd said, with a slight wave of his hand toward the antique polished desk facing away from the veranda. "Changing room," he had murmured, with barely a nod to the right this time. "Also doubles as my office, when there are no models around."

"Then this must be where you paint," Rebecca had said, reaching the last space.

"Whenever I paint."

"Whenever dawn breaks, you mean."

"I mean whenever I paint."

She'd slipped her arm from his, and, since the door was wide open, walked directly inside. From the threshold she'd heard, "I haven't had time to arrange things."

"Well, it looks fine to me," she'd declared, rejoining Jude in the doorway, having seen no new paintings in the room. Either they had all been shipped to his agents, in preparation for the new exhibit, or he had not painted at all in the past weeks. She guessed correctly the latter, though misjudged the reason.

"Off to the left – well you've seen most of the left," he went on. "Two bedrooms, dining room, kitchen – standard fare, nothing more."

With that he had guided her back down the hallway, so that she caught just a glimpse of a small room – guest room, she had supposed, between the dining room and what she presumed to be Jude's bedroom, door closed securely.

Back in the living room, certain the topic would please him, she had brought up the exhibition.

"A month from today," Jude had replied offhandedly. "Not much time after all."

"Will you be adding new paintings?"

"They will be showing what they have."

"Ah."

"Still," he had added quickly, "it's not a small body of work."

"Not at all…"

"And I am particular about presentation – wall space, proper lighting. I'll be working each day with Auguste and Armand."

For the foreseeable future, it appeared, Jude did not plan to paint. In fact it wasn't clear what he planned, thought Rebecca, as the increasingly awkward evening lagged.

"Jude, I must go," she had finally said, nearing ten. "I've got to practice in the morning. Tomorrow night, as you know, my usual Sunday at the Crillon."

She paused and then added, "Why not join me? Last chance perhaps to hear the old songs there."

"I don't think so, Rebecca. I – you don't mind, do you? We could meet afterward," he had added then, irresolutely, having again seen hurt colour her features.

But the master painter had discerned wrongly for once.

"My place, then, Jude," she had replied, having expected his demurral. "You haven't been there since – since last June, I believe. I'll pick you up after work."

Jude had considered – pause akin to the moment before a musician bends to his instrument. He was back home after all, with no chance to turn back. If not yet the Crillon – if perhaps never again that crystal and gold space – then surely Montmartre's heights which recalled Étretat's cliffs could be faced. Once, after all, she had returned his kiss in that room overlooking the hills. He had loved another then. That other was gone now. Tomorrow for sure then…tomorrow he could make amends, return Rebecca's affection, return more than affection, for had she not in Honfleur taught him once to forget?

⌒ ☾ ⌒

En route to Frères Durand the next day, Jude took a slightly circuitous route, thereby avoiding Café Marianne. On occasion he paused, catching his breath by the bookstalls lining the river. At Pont Royal, he stopped once again – not to rest this last time, but because the sight of the Louvre across the Seine caused a swirl of emotions to rise up within him – joy at the recollection of masterworks known like his own hands; shame in the fact that he could not paint, or would not paint; awe in the contemplation of lives resolutely committed to gifts of the spirit, recompense incorruptible; and finally – yes, stubbornly – pride in his own work, such as it had been until then.

Hoping to dull the image of future days without such achievement, he turned his attention to the river, churning and swollen from record-breaking weeks of rain. So relentless, in fact, had the past springtime storms been that for the first time in decades the riverside towpaths were completely submerged.

A stand of willow trees close to the water's edge caught his attention. First, as always, he was primarily aware of colour – black, gold, and citrine under a near-turquoise sky. Shapes then intrigued him – tall, slender trunks, intertwined branches, languorous leaves arching downward, as if exhausted from the constant rain.

Had he been able to, Jude would have painted those trees then and there, but he'd left his sketchbook behind inside the locked trunk by his door. Still, as though drawn by some strange force, he continued to stare at the lowest branches of the willows. They too were submerged. Their interlocked forms, waving beneath the river's surface, were no longer yellow but dark charcoal black, undulations almost erotic, Jude thought, thickening mass strangely familiar.

He forced himself to look away, but there was the cathedral, and a lady at the end of the bridge selling flowers the colour of plum wine and bells pealing like laughter under the arches of Place des Vosges and Mrs. Devereux was everywhere.

Time was the only hope that remained, Jude understood grimly then, time and his gallery work – no longer creation, but somehow still shaping – and Rebecca, so devoted, whom he would see in the evening, finding, perhaps, a semblance of peace in her arms.

꒷ ☾ ꒦

"Lovelier than I remember," Jude said as he stepped into the prow-shaped living room above Montmartre hills.

"Let me open the windows, Jude. The night is warm still…"

She felt his hand on her arm.

"Rebecca," he murmured, "if I've seemed distracted, I'm sorry. My return here has been…unexpectedly…"

"Splendid."

"Nevertheless –"

"More than splendid, Jude. Miraculous. But you're such an impatient man," she went on, a touch of the old playful tone in her voice. "Everything has its time, you know." She smiled warmly. "Including my supper, though that won't take long. Let me just fix you a drink –"

"Rebecca, don't fuss so."

"We're celebrating," she insisted, turning down the lamp by her harp. "This'll be enough light, I think. The best lamps are outside."

Jude sipped his scotch and stared out at the city. An absence of feeling, which he mistook for contentment, overcame him. The beauty of Paris, which he mistook for his home still, overwhelmed. Thus, by the time Rebecca returned, bearing a refill and sheet music so as to play her harp while they waited, he had managed to dull the memories that had repeatedly surfaced that afternoon.

She played for about twenty minutes, carefully avoiding any songs they had done together at the Crillon. Jude longed to accompany, fill in some chords at least on the wing as he had often done, an imagined audience enraptured. It was not to be – and he knew it – and so he simply surrendered to the summer evening, and the scotch, and the harmony of Rebecca Chase.

Dinner in her little dining room off the salon was intimate, its mood as quiescent as that last song Rebecca had played, Gershwin's *I've Got a Crush On You*. Not until they were nearly finished did Jude glance again toward the windows. After a moment, abruptly, he turned back and in a forced way picked up the thread of their conversation. Rebecca followed – they had played together for many years, after all – but she had noticed that now-familiar shadow pass over his features. Refilling his wine glass, she stole a glance at the windows. She found nothing, save for a shimmering half moon rising over the city.

After a while she rose, cleared and served fine French cognac in the little alcove beside the dining room, which also served as her bedroom. Jude emptied his glass and took her into his arms. When he heard the folds of her taffeta dress fall to the floor, he stepped back for a moment, admiringly, as though he had never before seen her statuesque form. He continued to gaze as she stretched out on her sleigh bed, positioned directly beneath the window. Slowly, as though in a dream Jude lay next to that form – statue which had somehow come to life, it appeared – voluptuous, beckoning, starkly white in a shaft of pure light onto the bed.

He himself was in shadows. With a practiced hand he traced her fullness so vividly outlined in such unique light.

And then the light moved, having finally cleared the last rooftop across, so that Jude turned and looked up and again saw, unexpectedly, that lonely and insistent ice-blue slender moon.

The old turmoil recurred. He felt a violent surge, as though the Seine were once again bursting its bounds, spilling not over the stones but seeping somehow through his limbs. Somewhere deep in those limbs, the slight thread he had clung to throughout the day's disillusion snapped. The renewal he'd hoped for, he saw, was never to be.

But it must be, he thought – *passion, Rebecca, his work...it must be* –

This last he said aloud so that Rebecca asked, "What must be, Jude?"

"You – *you* must be," he gasped, *"life again."*

Here he broke off and took her face in his hands and kissed her hard, vehemence verging on anger. Indeed, what surprised Rebecca then was the ongoing roughness – absolute and uncharacteristic absence of tenderness – with which he began to touch her.

Instinctively she recoiled. He was, after a year, again a powerful man, and she sensed that something within him had unravelled, or was about to unravel, and that they should stop while he could stop, not understanding he'd long passed that point – that he had passed it that afternoon, when all else had failed him, and now he would not be refused, not even dictated to – but instead he himself would subdue, so as to heighten his pleasure, which in his desperation he confused with life.

His breathing came harder – not from exhaustion, but from the increasingly fierce arousal her growing resistance had stirred. Pressing his mouth on hers still, he moved his hand to her neck, which he encircled, unaware of the pressure his fingers had caused, just for a moment, before they moved down to her breasts, which he caressed roughly as well, so that she managed, "Jude, enough," but it was by then not enough. He pushed her legs apart and forced his hand up between then, and then in a flash he remembered that night by the Pavillon, only now he was no longer the victim, but the one filled with vile lust – horrifying imperative which was strangely compelling as he entered her, thrusting repeatedly as she pushed against him.

"Enough," she gasped a second time, feeling herself invaded rather than cherished, although in some vague way as she struggled there in her sleigh bed, she was also aware that the things he was doing sprang not from a need to abuse, but from an urgency akin to madness.

"Please, Rebecca," she heard him thickly reply. "Please let me finish this," and Rebecca grasped then that she could stop him at that point – but only at that point – even sensing in that last distant rational plea Jude's need to be stopped, an almost subliminal hope to have permission to proceed denied him – refusal wherein lay a last chance to save himself.

It was withheld. In the end Rebecca did not deny Jude. What she had resisted as violation all of a sudden became her own chance to subdue, conquering not as muse but as woman, enslaving not the painter, whom she knew was beyond her, but the man, driven already to drown the year's pain in her.

Hence, in that millisecond while he waited, the man never did hear words which resembled "Jude, no more," but instead, murmured somewhere beside him in the darkness, Rebecca's equally savage, "Take what you need, then, Jude. – Finish."

He did, and was forever lost, overcome by his need to forget, turning her over and again forcefully thrusting, no longer with violence but with desperation, until at last Rebecca felt him shudder repeatedly against her back and she knew he had finished whatever it was that had possessed him.

And then there was silence. He moved his weight off her and rolled to the side of the bed nearest the nightstand. She lay beside him, staggered not just by his lust, which had strangely resembled revenge in the end, but by her own need to possess, which was perhaps as an utterly conscious decision in its own way more brutal.

But she felt no remorse. Thinking herself the victor, once again she misjudged. To be sure, she correctly assigned Jude's continuing silence to shame, perhaps even self-loathing. She knew he would blame himself fiercely now, giving himself no quarter, for though Jude might be complex, intense, highly sexual, consumed by creation, he was not a cruel man. Love to him was not annihilation, sex not exclusively feral. A passion for beauty defined him, not the senseless destruction of form, so that this night, which resembled defacement, was anomalous, atypical, bizarre snap of a spring far too tightly coiled in the year since his beating.

All this and more Rebecca astutely surmised. She also believed that in showing himself at his worst to her, paradoxically, Jude

McCallister had been subdued. Guilt, which she preferred to think of as gratitude, would forever remain, ensuring a loyalty which better behaviour might not have secured her. Desires of the flesh – always a dark and vehement thing with this man – would also remain. Thus, deeply indebted, profoundly obsessed, Jude in his body and soul would from henceforth be hers, Rebecca concluded.

But she had erred. Because in stature of soul despite closeness they were profoundly mismatched, she thought Jude would continue to trespass where he had so ruthlessly trod. He could not. Lying there in the darkness he wished it were otherwise. He longed to be able to love this person he'd hurt, to love her again, rather, for he still cherished her, feeling more than ever beholden – in that respect Rebecca'd judged rightly – but he knew himself better than that. He had shown himself at his worst to her and would never again risk the exposure. Nor would he risk harming Rebecca again – certainly not with his hands, never again even with words, a chance remark, the slightest gesture that might offend.

And yet…

Yet once before it had happened. Once before he had been stripped bare, displaying a cruelty he had not believed possible, hurting a woman almost as deeply as he had come to love her in the days that had followed. He had had reasons then, to be sure – not excuses but reasons, just as on this night there had been causes. On this night too then, perhaps…

"Cigarette?" he heard in the shadows beside him.

"Thank you."

No more than these words were exchanged as they smoked side-by-side, thinking, readjusting, while a midnight blue sky draped itself gently over the rooftops.

Rebecca's thoughts served only to confirm her conclusions.

Jude's, on the contrary, left him more than ever lost. Everything past and present, all future projections, thoughts themselves seemed distorted as though he were viewing each concept through shattered stained glass. His resolve to protect Rebecca whatever the cost was all that remained clear – but how to begin? What to say to her now? She'd need more than friendship; he could offer no more; his own needs would return – that fact too he perceived despite the increasingly splintered reflections around him, so that what remained in the end was what he had feared at the start: hurting the woman beside him again, and what failed him still in the dark were the words and of all things his hands, fearing to touch her as he did, and his eyes, unable to see himself leaving her after what he had taken, unfocused on anything else after what she might...

"Jude?"

The sound, barely recognizable, seemed to come from across some immense gulf.

"I should like you to know that I know," she said from that far distant place. "I mean that the year's come and gone – each day taking its toll, and...and tonight was no different – tonight you paid still," she went on, as Sacré-Coeur's chimes began tolling midnight, or perhaps those were Christmas bells pealing, thought Jude indistinctly – bells when achievement seemed possible still.

"Jude, *listen*," murmured Rebecca, sensing him slipping away to a place that wasn't hers, nights she couldn't claim. "Tonight too's come and gone – not in a way to be reprised but we've known other nights, you and I...other ways" – here she paused 'til the top of the hillside was silent and then in a voice Jude thought strangely no nearer, though she had managed to find his hand across the abyss: "I've been your friend here in Paris...more than your friend in Honfleur – either way harmony's possible still if we try."

This last she said softly, almost a murmur, although its resonance lingered distinctly, like the echoing comfort of harp strings played expertly close to Jude.

"You needn't answer me now;" – this too he heard clearly – "what went before matters more than tonight, Jude – just so you know," Rebecca repeated, and with that she fell silent, and Jude felt exhaustion which he mistook for relief, and heard forgiveness which he misjudged as forgetting, and was more than ever beholden.

Rebecca too felt relief. She'd steered clear of the storm. They'd moved ahead slowly, speaking softly awhile, hand in hand on her sleigh bed. They had agreed to meet for supper after her second audition the following night. Thus, reasoned Rebecca as though sight-reading notes on some long-undiscovered score, if in his tumultuous state Jude's path was not clear to him yet, then at least the foreseeable future, destined perhaps to include no more than the next night, had been charted. Time and her vigilance – indeed, insofar as Jude's heart was concerned she sensed a mission not unlike that of Germaine's – would heal whatever hurt still remained.

Rebecca remained at the window. She watched Jude make his slow way toward the cabs down the hill. She heard one lone chime toll, then two and then in the stillness the city appeared but a mirror image of the heavens as, mixed in with the stars, images of her past with Jude recurred: duets at the Crillon, walks by the Seine, Jude's previous visit when he had seemingly loved another, Marie-Claude leading the way into the consultation room where he had waited.

How long ago that day seemed! How overwhelming the paint-ings, the artist in half-light, above all his portrait – that haunting achievement. Vividly too it took shape as she gazed at the rooftops, the chimneys, those pale wisps of clouds drifting across a waning, mysterious, indecisive half moon.

And then suddenly, as though clouds in her own mind had parted, she looked again at that clear light, and, thunderstruck, saw at last she'd misjudged. Like one who wrongly reckons the star-crowded sky, she'd been blind. *Half Moon*, he had entitled it – nothing more than that, save for the date, summertime of the previous year, and the place, Paris, and then his signature at the bottom – barely visible – as though the artist, among all the facts mentioned, had been the least significant factor.

But there was nothing at all insignificant about that portrait. Nor, she realized dazed still recalling the night's calamitous outcome, had there been anything random in the debacle. Jude had glanced twice through her windows – once while they were dining, never again to appear light-hearted, a second time as he'd lain down beside her, never again to recapture control. She had assigned the cause to the hands of attackers in the Champs-Élysées. Now, as though staring at Jude's masterpiece itself lighting Montmartre, she knew. It was not his ordeal but a woman who had unleashed his rage in her sleigh bed.

That was all she could grasp though – that and the fact that Jude had surpassed himself in that painting, reaching a perfect blend of matter and form, spirit and subject, colour, line and proportion rarely, if ever, vouchsafed an artist – even to one such as Jude. She herself, as a musician, had on occasion experienced vaguely analogous flights. She had heard grace notes as she had played, things that were not in the score, or the harp, or her hands, but which had appeared unbidden, floating above and beyond her performance, making it perfect. For this reason she had assumed that such a unique, indefinable thing had occurred the previous summer – that Jude had been granted the finest of grace notes, and that he had bowed to them humbly, creating his finest work.

Half the tale to be told, she ruefully saw now. Jude had indeed surrendered to inspiration. The grace notes had come not from his muse though, but from the woman.

Rebecca thought back to the scene and the date on the portrait.

The scene she knew well. Offhandedly Jude had displayed it during the tour of his apartment on the previous evening.

The time, too, she could identify. *Half Moon* had been painted near August, she figured, judging from the flowers that were barely visible in the portrait's background on Jude's terrace. Hence – and the calculation made her shudder – the artist's masterpiece had been completed within weeks – six at the most – of the attack in the woods off the Champs-Élysées. He had been left for dead by the Pavillon. But for his days in Honfleur, he had painted nothing after that, nor, apparently, had the fierce love affair continued.

This was the one piece of the puzzle Rebecca could not decipher. How could Half Moon have vanished just when Jude needed her most? The fact that she *had* disappeared – like the realization that she was no model – was clear to Rebecca. It was also apparent, judging from the gaze that was at once filled with wonder and longing, that the woman, whoever she was, returned, perhaps even surpassed, whatever feelings had inspired the artist.

Yet Jude had spent almost four months alone in his hospital room. On his own he had gone to Germaine in Honfleur. He was alone still, despairing, when Dr. Le Brun had approached her, a matter of weeks ago, at the Crillon.

Clearly, Rebecca reflected, Jude was still in despair. But was he alone still? Had Half Moon returned to Paris? Did this explain the changes she had perceived in him – the badly hidden embarrassment in his apartment, his surging conflicts in hers?

Like the identity of his subject, the answers to these questions remained a mystery to Rebecca.

And yet she needed to know. The viability of her calculations made in the stillness beside Jude could be sustained only in the guaranteed absence of Half Moon.

Not just sustained, she perceived with ever-sharpening insight, but enhanced. After such colossal rejection – and Half Moon's change of heart had to have been that – Jude would be more than ever attached to a new love, above all one to whom he remained deeply indebted, who understood him in his explosive passions, subset of his genius, and who was prepared to accept, if not excuse, such inevitable complexity.

She slipped at last into her sleigh bed, having promised herself to know all by the end of the following evening. Jude would be vulnerable after all, defences not yet re-established. Even in the crowded bistro he had chosen hoping to avoid a more intimate, potentially bruising encounter, he would not hold out for long.

⤷ ☾ ⤶

The little restaurant on the Left Bank was a safe choice, thought Jude as dessert was brought to their table overlooking the river. Behind him was the Place St-Michel, sidewalks filled with students heading on up the hill toward the Sorbonne; to his right was the Pont St-Michel, busy as well with crowds en route to the Right Bank; far from sight were his old haunts near the Delacroix studio, his own workroom overlooking Rodin's house, and, above all, Place des Vosges with its wind and identical homes and superfluous light.

Fortunate too was the fact that Notre-Dame blocked any view of the old Hôtel-Dieu directly across the Seine, and that in the sudden rain the bookstalls had emptied and the quayside walks were devoid of lovers embracing.

Things had gone well after all. Rebecca'd seemed if not buoyant then at least undisturbed. He had maintained an air of courteous if not enraptured attention. Rebecca's audition had provided a reliable subject of professional interest – one in which he'd found refuge as awkward pauses had lengthened, and to which he returned now, as renewed silence occurred.

"Tomorrow's audition will be your third then," he offered.

"Third and last, Jude, I hope."

"So the decision will be made then and there?"

"Latest the weekend."

"Ah."

"By then I'll know where I stand."

Gingerly, Jude reached for his brandy, as if another word might break the glass. Carefully, Rebecca stirred her coffee, declining to return to the topic at hand. After all, she herself was not sure she was prepared to leave Paris. Less clear to her still was whether Jude McCallister would follow.

At the moment in fact, it seemed he had even ceased to follow the conversation. In the thickening mist the bridge lights had come on, and, as he had reached for his glass, he had seen their reflection in the window. The sight appeared to have cast a spell on him. Rebecca sipped from her glass, folded her napkin, smoothed out her skirt and waited. Jude turned and stared at the bridge that led to the island where Dr. Le Brun had remade him.

The waiter approached with more coffee.

Rebecca waved him away.

Jude gazed still at the Seine and Rebecca stared still at Jude and at last shrewdly discerned on his face not brutality recollected but a profound, indefinable ache, not unlike mourning.

She looked as well through the glass. The plaza had emptied; the bridge walk was shrouded; nobody was approaching on the darkening quay.

And yet Half Moon had appeared again – Rebecca was sure of it – judging shrewdly once more, for Jude had indeed seen Mrs. Devereux, vividly, not on that bridge but as she'd once been on that bridge: long, sheer pale skirt almost diaphanous in the lamplight, form-fitting turtleneck which she insisted would have to do, violet eyes never once leaving his face so that the spaces around him had blurred to nothing, and, nearly beside himself with the urge to paint her, not yet knowing that this included touching her, he had said fiercely, "Wear whatever you like. Just as long as you come."

No, there was no way Rebecca could have observed these things. Jude himself had barely been able to sustain his focus on them. Indeed, he had blocked it all out for so long that he never imagined such a safe bistro could so vividly conjure that first night.

"Jude," murmured Rebecca.

And yet there it was, perfectly coloured as only a painter's remembrance might be.

"Jude, *please*..."

There they all were in fact – the sittings, the struggles, his portrait finished at last – the failed one, not the fine one: witness to ruthless obsessions and a cruelty that had resurfaced only the previous night.

Vaguely, as though from a distance, he felt increasing pressure on his arm. When he finally turned, he saw Rebecca's hand on his sleeve, and, looking up, found her green eyes fixed not on his arm but his face.

Never before had he seen such a deepening malachite hue in those depths. Nor had he ever found such a combination of control and compassion there, distance at war with devotion it seemed – mixture he would have painted, despite her overall softness, in bold strokes.

"Who is she?" he heard, or thought he had heard.

"Who is she?"

"The woman you saw."

Staggered, Jude could make no reply.

"I don't know her name. – I know what you've called her," Rebecca went on in a tone as close to neutrality as she could muster, though she allowed her hand to slide down from his arm and rest on his hand, protectively.

"*Half Moon*. Your masterpiece. The one you won't let out of your sight. – I suspect she won't let you out of hers, Jude, although perhaps once she did, and now regrets her betrayal, and it is for this…*for this*," she repeated, speaking rapidly now having seen the colour drain so completely from Jude's face, "that I ask such a difficult thing. – *I have to know, don't you see?*…I'm willing to wait, try to make up for things past, love you however you like, Jude – but Jude," she insisted, her voice matching that strangely combined hue in her eyes, "I'm not willing to share. You wouldn't want that from me. You wouldn't want that from *you*. I – one thing only remains," she said abruptly, sensing the protective hand about to tremble. "I need the truth tonight. Spoken or not it will invade other nights anyway…we both know that now –"

"Half Moon is dead."

It was Rebecca this time who thought she had heard wrong. She stared blankly at Jude, but as he did not repeat the words, she slowly processed what remained of their cadence until at last she understood. The truth was hers now, as she had insisted it must be. Of all the responses in the world, it was the one she had never foreseen.

"Jude, I am so sorry."

He nodded.

"Forgive me."

"You are not to blame."

"For insisting, I mean – forcing you,"

"I insisted last evening."

"Still –"

"You had every right to know now," he concluded. His eyes, not in the least unkind, remained on that now fragmented green tone. His expression, less troubled than she had ever known it, was neither serene nor matter-of-fact, but simply relieved. He had given shape to the fact. There it was finished, like one of his sculptures, polished in the wheel of expression so that it could be placed, like a porcelain bowl, in its completeness to remain undisturbed. Rebecca *had* deserved to know, that gaze seemed to say, since with her intuitive gift she had somehow divined much, and since he had with a matching barbarity forced her too, and since, not to be denied, Mrs. Devereux was after all gone.

And so the revelation was done – finale Rebecca recognized not in the ensuing, definitive silence, but feeling Jude's hand slip away from under her fingers.

He did not slip away though – that fact too she numbly realized as the waiter appeared and began to refill their cups and Jude said with his usual grace, "No – no I don't think I will have any more. Unless the lady…"

"I'm fine."

"Just the cheque then, please."

Haltingly, after a moment: "Thank you, Jude."

The faintest of smiles brushed his mouth, as though to concede he had complied, for better or worse, with that one thing of which she said he had need.

But was it for better or worse, wondered Rebecca alone, dazed, en route to Montmartre in the back of a taxi. Here Jude had offered no clues. There'd been no break, no formal parting – not even an awkward vague promise to call sometime soon.

On the contrary. All politeness, or perhaps with no other choice in such despairing isolation, he had proposed dining together again in a few days in order to celebrate her audition and its doubtlessly fine results. He had waved as her cab pulled away, no hint of weariness in the gesture. To be sure, his hand never again had touched hers as they'd carefully made their way through the narrow restaurant aisles, the rain-soaked square, what remained of the night's conversation. Still, he had seemed if not blithe then not bitter, if not renewed then not resentful – signs from which a lesser mind might have found solace.

Rebecca, though, remained shaken as the cab slowed to a stop above Sacré-Coeur. While it was true that her rival could no longer threaten, she sensed that Half Moon, no longer living, would have more of a presence than she could have alongside Jude.

Jude, all the while, was also alone, not in a cab but standing beside the statue of St-Michel in the square. Looking again at the globes on the bridge, he thought he was going mad, for he felt Caroline's presence still, palpable, calling him everywhere.

$$\backsim \; (\; \backsim$$

It was as Jude had predicted. Rebecca's audition went swimmingly. That very week she received an offer from the Vienna *Volksoper* – a job she had wanted for a lifetime, decision to be made within a fortnight to fill the suddenly vacant assistant harpist's position.

"Two weeks, Fräulein, that is all we can allow you," Direktor von Bergen had insisted. "A burden, I realize…"

"Maestro, I understand. Within two weeks you will have your answer."

Two weeks, she said again to herself, running her fingers along the strings of her harp as she stood. A very short time, after all. There would be her apartment to let, her colleagues to part from, Paris to leave behind…

No – none of that mattered. Only Jude mattered, she knew, as she lay down on her sleigh bed.

He has only just heard of her death. The wound is still raw. It will heal, she said again to herself, *but not here, not in France. She is everywhere here.*

Again, Rebecca'd judged clearly. Half Moon was everywhere, stronger in death than in life, invincible rival so long as Jude stayed in Paris.

"*L'Inattendu arrive toujours*," murmured Jude, recalling the motto as he approached Napoleon's tomb in St-Louis-des-Invalides.

"Yes," Rebecca said thoughtfully, linking her arm into his, "The unexpected does occur."

It had been a week since she had told Jude of her audition, her offer, and the decision she'd made to leave Paris. He'd listened attentively – intrigued almost, asking about performance dates, repertoire, planned tours, recordings. What he had not said was what she most wanted to hear, though: that he would go with her to Vienna.

But he had not refused. He knew only too well her position was sound. He *should* go – make the effort at least, see if Austria like Honfleur could provide inspiration, bring forth new paintings, any paintings, something he feared might not happen in Paris.

He understood too what she had diplomatically avoided. Paris crippled him still. Though he might allow, or rather hope, that recollections, like colours, could fade over time, above all in strong light, he sensed the former might never be granted him, and in the latter, since Lucien's visit, he had painted nothing at all.

"Well you needn't decide now. You've still time," Rebecca'd confirmed as stones on the path crunched obligingly under her feet. "You can always follow me after I go."

"Yes, of course," he'd agreed, sinking his cane with a steady precision into that gravel as they advanced.

Inwardly, though, Jude had not been so sure. If they did not go to Vienna together, he guessed, he would never go to Vienna, making Rebecca's firm deadline his too; the best he could do was delay, postpone six days at the most, for he was still deeply divided. She filled a void in his life – one which loomed large at the thought of her leaving. They had dined twice since that night by the Place St-Michel; they had gone to a concert, two lectures; she'd been obliging, solicitous, undemanding in her companionship – but that was all it had been. Not once since his trip to Montmartre had he made love to Rebecca. Not since their dinner overlooking the bridge had they ever mentioned his portrait, its creation, or the woman who had inspired it.

What then would Austria offer? How to find peace in Vienna so far from the place he'd called home most of his life – the only home he had owned, repository of recollections which, though admittedly painful, he seemed perversely to cherish?

Perhaps an end to the pain, Jude projected, turning away from Rebecca's taxi toward his own doorway. Companionship, he considered, stepping from the antique cage elevator into his hallway.

And so six days became one – Rebecca Chase still determined, Jude still divided, neither daring to broach the subject that like a stone weighed on their hearts.

Jude, in fact, seemed determined to spend their time in other ways – concerts, museums, galleries, day trips – anything, Rebecca believed, to divert their attention from what was consuming them both.

Even on the last day, when they met for a late lunch in the Marais, Jude abruptly, with a forced brightness, filled yet another lengthening silence with, "Why don't we stop in at Musée Carnavalet? Have you ever been there?"

"Years ago."

"Just down the street a bit. Well worth another visit."

Within minutes, they were inside the old mansion, moving through period rooms depicting the capital's history.

An odd choice for this last day, Rebecca reflected, for she could not tell, as Jude paused by each room, if he were saying farewell then to Paris, or to her.

They reached the windowed second-floor gallery where Rebecca paused by a music room off to one side. Among its priceless antiques was a small, eighteenth-century harp. For a long time she stared at that harp, thinking of times long gone by, imagining days still to come. So intensely did she gaze, in fact, that she was startled when an antique clock on the mantel tolled fifteen minutes 'til five.

Smiling, Jude murmured, "Stay here, if you like. I'm going around to that set of rooms on the main street façade."

He approached an immense elegant space, also overlooking the courtyard, and then he too was moved – not by a harp but by the fact that he had entered Madame de Sévigné's apartment. Facing him was her portrait; across from him, one of her daughter; between them – strangely palpable once again, as though in distance yet more clear – he saw another face: smiling, wistful, choosing as the one she liked best house Number One, Place des Vosges.

She never lived far, Jude thought he heard Caroline say in the stillness, and then he recalled with a sharpness that had eluded him since his beating how he'd sensed exile that first night in Caroline Devereux's days.

At long last he knew. No matter how many detours he took, what distractions he chose, suddenly, unexpectedly, there he would find her. The city he loved so was hers now, forever. Ironically life for him now seemed possible only in exile.

He moved back to the music room. Rebecca had gotten permission to remove the red velvet roping and examine the harp. Unobserved, Jude watched her bend toward the instrument, lovingly, as once again, the reliable clock on the mantel chimed five.

Once again startled, Rebecca turned. Seeing Jude waiting she smiled, passed again around the roping and joined him in the corridor. And then again there was silence, and both of them stood there, saying nothing, until finally Rebecca managed, with a last look at the harp and a glance at the clock and then a long steady gaze at the man she would have, at all costs: "You see, Jude, it is time."

Alone, home again in his apartment, Jude walked down the main hallway. There was the vast salon, with its untouched piano. Facing it was the kitchen, unused. Next to it was the dining room, never filled, and across from it the changing room, always closed.

Taking a few more steps he stopped. On his right were pristine cloths, unopened boxes, solitary painting wrapped still on his easel; on his left the master bedroom, which he preferred not to examine.

He walked back to his study and stepped out onto the veranda. The Left Bank, the Seine, Rodin's house, Les Invalides – there they all were still, all devoid of meaning, though they were filled with more lights than there were stars in the heavens.

"Yes, it is time after all," Jude thought as he stood there. He would call Rebecca, as promised, at noon on the following day. She would be calling Vienna at three. By then she would know that he planned to go with her.

⌒☽⌒

Nearing dawn, as her husband had prepared to set sail at long last, Susannah Joubert Pellerin'd grown uneasy. Two weeks had gone by since the great storm's upheaval – a fortnight, nothing more – and yet Violette, for so they still called her, had recovered her strength with remarkable progress.

But that was all she had retrieved. She had remained without recollection. Not for a moment could she remember a single detail of her past, not even her true name, and though on that first night she had acknowledged that "Violette" was a mistake, she had in time come to accept it as the only word that might fit.

She had also confirmed after that first night what they had guessed from the start. She was not from the islands, not even from the mainland, for in her elegant French there was a distant inflection, resonance almost antique, out of time.

She had read widely – that was also clear – and knew every *Lieder* Susannah would sing whenever Serge played their old spinet after dinner'd been cleared.

"She belongs to somebody, Serge," he would hear his wife whisper those nights – words she'd repeated emphatically as he continued to stock *l'Inattendu* that last day.

"Schubert," she had insisted, passing along a box of supplies… "Schumann – one does not learn those notes in isolation."

Serge had nodded, carefully stowing his nets.

"One does not teach oneself French, Molière –"

"Of course not," Serge had exclaimed, facing his wife at last. "But what else can we do? She's like a child still."

"You should perhaps take her with you."

"Into the ocean?"

"Into the Madeleines."

"That is still the ocean."

"Nevertheless…"

"Violette is not well yet," he had pronounced. "The sensations of the sea…the recollections – it might all be too much."

"But isn't that what she must do now? *Recollect?*"

"Not in a harsh way, Susannah. Not into the sea yet."

Serge had stared out over the ocean – shimmering, though still slightly unsteady. "Besides, I can't just leave her alone on some landing. I'd have to go farther – Newfoundland…Prince Edward Island. Yet even there what would I do? Advertise? And if nobody claims her? Take her to an asylum?"

Susannah'd shaken her head, horrified.

"So you agree. There's no choice. We must be patient, take our chances, hope she'll remember," Serge had concluded, growing tender as he saw concern deepen his wife's charcoal eyes. After all, he was going away for a month, sailing alone, as Violette said she had done, into the wild Labrador Sea. Not without reason was Susannah always fearful upon his departure – above all on this day, when he was leaving her on her own with an immense responsibility.

"*Tiens,*" he'd said gently, folding her into his arms, "there'll be no storms while I'm away. Violette will have peace. She will not be a burden – you'll see. You will come to rely on her in the end."

Susannah'd nodded, somewhat calmer, then continued to help pack *l'Inattendu*. Directly above them, out on the lawn by the stone house, Violette was resting on her favourite swing chair. Surrounding her was the ocean, stretching forever in every direction – utter absence of humanity in its dark numberless waves.

She'd felt a deepening peace. Such gentleness in those who had found her, such a fine dry breeze on the heights, all of it like a dream – perhaps it was a dream…but no, no there was Susannah, arms filled with empty boxes, reaching the top of the stairs.

"Wait! Let me help you," Violette had called, hurrying toward the steps.

Susannah'd smiled, in spite of herself, at the earnest face of the stranger. Serge had perhaps been correct, after all. She might come to rely on the girl.

"Not now, Violette. A few more days perhaps. Then we can gather fruit, put up the jam, plant the bulbs that arrive. You'll be much stronger by then."

"You have been very kind to me, Susannah."

"Rest a bit more," had been Susannah's response.

Violette had returned to her chair. Lulled by the sound of the waves, she had slept.

By the time she'd awakened, mid-morning, Serge had long since sailed off.

Lookout Point was full and peaceful for Susannah and Violette in the next weeks. They spent their mornings gathering fruit from the trees Serge had planted; they took their lunch on the lawn under the mild Maritime sky; as afternoon's sun poured into the kitchen, they put up the berries they'd chosen.

Rest would then follow, and then supper, and then they would sit in the parlour, Susannah softly conversing about a life lived intently in an oddly fulfilling isolation, Violette nodding, understanding, vaguely recalling a similar solitude.

From time to time they would read.

"Choose what you'd like," Susannah would urge on those nights. "My collection is small…"

"It is lovely."

"But the books are all fine – from an old manor in France."

Repeatedly, for some reason, Caroline would walk to the book-shelves, run her fingers along the tooled spines of each book, and choose the letters of Madame de Sévingé to her most fortunate of daughters.

꙳ ☾ ꙳

For her late afternoon rest, Violette always chose the swing chair by the edge of the lawn. Here she would read a bit, or stare at the sea, and here, after a few days, she began to notice a plane overhead, banking southward, always on the same path, always near sundown. She could hear its approach even before it appeared, so that after a week – drawn to it strangely – sensing the low airborne rumble grow louder, she would look up and scan the skies and wait for the aircraft to break through the clouds. Carefully she would follow its descending trajectory. Long after it vanished she would continue to gaze, wondering about the passengers, thinking them prudent to have travelled together.

"Safety in numbers," she'd murmur, recalling that foolishly she had sailed alone, in the roughest of sea storms, from…from where, she would insistently ponder, and then her thoughts would trail off, like that plane overhead.

All she knew for certain was that she was not from this island – her French was too different. Nor was she from the mainland. Serge had said it lay far to the north across an immense Gulf. How could she have crossed an immense Gulf, so far from the north?

Repeatedly she tried to picture it – the harbour, the town, even a sign with the name of the place in her head. Repeatedly it refused to be conjured, so that in the end she was always glad when Susannah would appear, touching her shoulder, ever so slightly, saying that supper was ready, for Violette's efforts ended always in failure, leaving her tired from the strain, and unidentified still.

꙳ ☾ ꙳

A steady rain descended on Rock of Birds toward the end of July. Susannah had seen those clouds gather, taking her wash off the line, scanning the waves to gauge the force of the wind, fearful of a reenactment of the past month's immense storm. And yet, as Serge had predicted, these rains tapered off nearing sundown the next day.

"Violette, we can go out now," Susannah announced with relief, peering out through the parlour window. They had not left the stone house since the previous morning, and though the earth was still drenched and the ocean uneasy, Susannah longed for a walk on the beach while light remained.

Violette, she understood, would not accompany her to the cove. Though she was well enough to manage the staircase, she had always demurred when Susannah suggested they go for a stroll on the sand. In time, Susannah had stopped insisting. After all, she decided – and the thought was increasingly comforting – Violette would be always be waiting on her swing chair by the edge of the lawn.

And yet – yet so strange, mused the much older lady, barefoot by then, taking her time-tested path through the receding surf. *So enraptured by the horizon, so terrified still of its shores.*

How clearly she'd seen. There was indeed a confounding ambivalence inside Violette's head. She could remember coming to life in the Pellerin cave: shadows on the stone walls, flickering lights, warmth, mounting resentment – this too she remembered – for her reappearance had been reluctant, even angry, given the fact that only moments before then, seconds perhaps, she had been called into another world, an eternal space, devoid of loss and discomfort and the onus of accountability.

She could also recall – maybe again only a dream – that once before it had happened. Once – perhaps on the mainland, perhaps not – she'd had a glimpse of transcendence, something exceptional, only to be recalled to its temporal counterpart by one who would not be denied.

"Where does it go?" Violette wondered aloud after supper that evening.

"Where does what go, Violette?"

"The plane that passes toward sundown."

"Charlottetown, Prince Edward Island."

"Ah."

"Every day?"

"Every day."

"Where does it come from?"

"It comes from the mainland."

"The mainland is large, I've been told."

Susannah rephrased her answer, forgetting, on occasion, that the stranger had no point of reference.

"Montréal. West of this island. From there to Prince Edward Island."

"I see," Violette murmured, though it was clear she did not.

"A circle route, Violette. Most precious, believe me. We couldn't have mail without that plane."

"I haven't seen any mail…"

"You will. A packet boat comes toward the end of the month, bringing mail, sometimes a letter from Paris."

"Paris," echoed the stranger.

"Far from here."

Violette heard her sigh, as if the stark reality of her isolation had become suddenly palpable to Susannah.

"Yes, yes it is always a wonderful day when the packet boat comes," Susannah continued, summoning her uniquely defining mixture of optimism and submission.

"I have a sister in Paris. For a time she lived here, but Dominique found it hard. She returned to France in the end – not to La Rochelle, the old Huguenot port where our people still live, but to Paris, new friends, new life, new art supply shop on the Left Bank. Every summer she writes. Of course other things too reach our shores after May…Magazines sometimes come, sometimes a letter for Serge, but in July…" Susannah's eyes glowed like hot coals as she leaned in.

"Tulip bulbs, Violette! Directly from Paris. Well not directly," she corrected herself. "First they clear Customs, back on the mainland – Montréal most of the time."

Stars began dotting late-darkening skies as she spoke.

"Quite an event, future tulips from Paris."

Violette stared at the moon rising over the Gulf.

"I love the news too, Violette. Old news, of course, but it's news nevertheless. In fact," she confessed, leaning in still toward the stranger, "I even iron the papers, so that they look just-arrived. It pleases Serge when he returns. He's missed so much out at sea."

"Viens, viens vite, Violette," Susannah called as she ran toward the stairs.

"Hurry," she repeated, and Violette hurried, although she stopped at the top of the stairs, wishing of all things she could follow her good friend, but the beach remained out of bounds in her head, and so the best she could do was wait, clutching the railing, close by the edge of the cliff as July's packet boat ever so briefly docked in the cove.

"Susannah, let me carry the box."

"No."

"But you must. It is heavy. I am strong now, Susannah."

"If you like, Violette," conceded Susannah, for the box was indeed large, and it pleased Susannah to see Violette growing sturdy.

Throughout the late afternoon, the package lay by the hearth, unopened – as the stranger was – while Susannah prepared an exceptional supper.

The dishes were cleared. The parlour was tidied. Susannah finally cut open her parcel, murmuring as she sorted through mounds of crumpled newspapers that served as packing. "Two letters for Serge...a catalogue, a magazine from La Rochelle – ah, here it is," she exclaimed, finding an envelope, paper-thin tissue, navy and red border, marked *Par Avion.*

"Didn't I tell you? My letter from Dominique!"

Violette listened vaguely – always that curious veil on her eyes – while Susannah imparted, as though they had always shared some blood, news of her sister, her recent visit to La Rochelle, her art supply shop on rue du Bac, facts about Jude McCallister.

He lives nearby, I am told. Susannah read clearly. *Somewhere close to Rodin's house. His recent work's due to open. I enclose a clipping of the event. Also a brochure on the works – quite remarkable, really, given that brutal attack – rare in the Champs-Élysées – which left him for dead toward the end of last summer."*

Violette tried to remember the Champs-Élysées.

⸙ ☾ ⸙

Lookout Point was in darkness. Violette stood by her window and gazed at the lawn, the chairs, the pines and the ocean, all citron-toned in the light of the moon. Then, nearing midnight, she slipped out of her dress – one of a few Susannah had lent her – and slipped into her bed, from which she could still see the horizon.

But for the outgoing tides there was absolute stillness. Never before, since she had come to this island, had she felt such a silence – an almost unearthly quiescence – sea, sand and stars one immense, repetitive sigh.

Then again, she reflected, never before on Rock of Birds had she been awake at this hour. Susannah had always retired promptly at ten, having turned down the parlour lamps and fastened the shutters shortly past nine.

Tonight though she had wanted to talk, to read and reread Dominique's letter, remember her parents, her wedding, her long life with Serge.

Intently, the stranger had listened – partly because she knew, even after so few weeks, that the little packet boat from the Madeleines was like a locket worn round Susannah's neck, bearing connections – partly because she herself had no connections; and so Susannah's intrigued her.

And yet I must sleep, Violette said to herself, as midnight became one, and then two, and the murmur of ebb tide reached her, wide-awake still in her bed.

Must be the task that awaits, she decided, for she had agreed to unwrap the packet's tulip bulbs, first thing in the morning, pressing the newspapers into a pile to await *l'Inattendu's* return. It was all she could do – for the moment – to repay Susannah Joubert.

Shortly before dawn, the last of the stars disappeared. Violette slept at last. Only that pale moon remained – discreet yet all-knowing, shedding a reticent light on the scene as though it alone understood, in its indifferent way, that the newspapers cradled not just next April's garden, but the stranger's forgotten connections.

☽

Only a dozen left, observed Violette, piling the newspapers onto the table. She had already unwrapped many bulbs with great care, and, just as precisely, had ironed each wafer-thin sheet. With a glance out the window she guessed she'd have time still, for Susannah was still at the hand pump, wash left to be hung on the line.

She laid the next newspaper flat – dated two months before – and began smoothing it out to prepare it for pressing. Suddenly, passing her hand for some reason over that same sheet again and again, she heard a strange rushing sound. She turned toward the window, fearfully this time but no, there was no storm, only brisk winds and bright sun and then again that strange noise – not out by the stairs, but inside her head, she unsteadily realized – a surging almost, as though the sea had forced its way into her cave after all, in its wake trailing remembrance.

She looked back down at the paper. With the palm of her hand she smoothed it, picked up the iron, put the iron back down and fixedly stared. The photograph came into focus. Disbelieving, she continued to stare. *She knew these people* – a few of them anyway – pictured among the crowd at a service on Prince Edward Island.

She read and reread the headline, *Memorial for the Victims of Trans Canada Flight 407*. She examined the article which recounted, in detail, the crash of that plane. She turned the page over, finding additional pictures – victims presumed dead, their bodies never recovered. And then she reached for the table. Her breath began to come hard. Sweat poured over her temples, her cheeks, the curving tendrils on her neck. Centred on the page she saw herself,

Caroline Devereux, exactly as she might look in the oval mirror on Susannah's dresser. *She was that dead woman.*

No, that was impossible. She was in Susannah's kitchen, unwrapping the last of the tulip bulbs.

But why was she also in the *Montreal Times*, dated a full eight weeks earlier…?

Why "presumed dead" under her face? Such a strange word.

Why was Susannah taking so long to finish the washing?

She ran to the window. Susannah was pinning clothes to the line still.

"Grey, finely cut, somewhat tattered," Violette murmured, disordered, seeing a skirt and matching jacket swaying with the rest of the wash newly hung.

She staggered back to the table, half expecting to see the photograph gone. The picture was there still – only now, with that rushing sound louder, other vague outlines took shape and then vanished – not on the page, but in her head – the shock of impact, debris, a canoe that her father had built or perhaps it was not a canoe…something larger, smoother, with a hard metal surface. Where she had been, where she was going – even a hint of these facts refused to be summoned – and yet her story was there, her past, her whole life – of this she was certain – not in the newspaper's words, but in its photo, in the group assembled at the memorial on Prince Edward Island.

She sank again into the chair, bent her head over the faces, ran her fingers once more over the slightly blurred features. For what seemed like a long time she waited. Noonday's brightness burned through the windows. Susannah's kitchen seemed vast, the ocean beyond without measure, the sound in her head most unbounded of all.

"Can you not speak to me – one of you?" she cried out in desperation, and then she folded her head in her arms, wanting to weep, but the people were there, and must at all costs stay dry, and besides, they might call to her, or whisper, and she would know at last, and so she remained very still, barely daring to breathe, her face on the paper, until – she was not sure at first, for it was less than a whisper, she did hear a sound – not like the noise in her head but more like her given name – the other one – "Caroline," murmured by a voice remembered, murmured by several voices, all familiar, and so she raised her head up and listened, staring again at the people, and the people slowly, one by one, like bulbs from abroad ever so gently unwrapped, revealed themselves to the stranger – no longer a stranger now, never again in her lifetime a stranger, for at long last she knew.

"Yes, yes, now I know," she repeated, tears streaming over her face at last, unchecked, unavoidable, sent by sadness and joy and stupefaction, and wonder.

There was Elliot Devereux, with whom she had lived on Todd's Farm. Next to him was Susan Foreman, whom her husband had said he would marry. Somewhere between them, invisible, yet clearly remembered, was a house gone, a fortune lost, a set of priceless black pearls, a sheet of paper at last signed. There was also a guest house, an orchard, a mill by the birch trees…

Ah, but of course there was the next face, waiting his turn to speak, for he had much more to impart. Mikhail…Misha…golden even in his sadness, who had loved her to desperation, and whose affection she had returned, but not in the same way, not in the way he had wanted – even this she remembered, for there'd been another before him, someone who'd come between them somehow, and as she considered this she'd heard music of all things, and recalled a great man, a great house, monogrammed elegance –

"Max!" she cried out, loving him still.

She searched for this man whose passionate life she had rendered. His face was not in the picture, leaving the puzzle unfinished, and so again she studied the photo, glancing at last at the shorter article beside it, bypassed until then, which recounted the career of Paul Maximilian d'Olivier, who had died peacefully in his sleep on the day of the plane crash. He had wanted no service, no memorial. His ashes were to be strewn, by his son, at a place deemed appropriate. His son had selected the Gulf of St. Lawrence.

"Max," she repeated, this time barely audible. "Misha," she whispered, as though he could hear her. "Dearest Mikhail – such anguish – to have lost us both that afternoon."

She returned to the short piece, carefully reading and rereading each phrase until she sensed him near her as well, no greater distance than his daybed.

"But of course you had to go, Max, did you not? – for I too was gone, and it was one life after all, and somehow you guessed what no one else could have known – that it was over, completed, as your story at last was."

She stood and took a few steps toward the screen door facing the back fields.

"Max?" she called into the wind, for it seemed to her that she had been wrong, that she had not sensed him beside her, that he was out there instead, out beyond the staircase, the cliffs – palpable still, powerful, brushing aside everything but his need to create and its social concomitant, a hunger for justice.

"Max?" she repeated.

Her only response was the sea.

"It is fitting," she sighed, scanning the limitless Gulf of St. Lawrence. He had fought by the ocean in Nice; he had returned to it in the Maritimes. Along the way they had met – their first interview was more vivid than ever – he, still insisting on perfection, she, boldly promising to provide it, both somehow knowing they would never again be apart. How she had loved him!

And yet it was not he who had kept her from returning Mikhail's love, although he had tried – that memory too sharper than ever – and in the process he had hurt his son, as had that other man, whose name still escaped her as she returned to the table, for he was not in the picture, though she recalled he was star-crossed and brooding yet somehow dear to them all.

She scanned the photograph closely, one more time, searching for that brooding face. It was not there. She looked at those presumed dead. Antonin was not there.

"Antonin," she repeated, surprising herself by the sound she had made. Tears again filled her eyes. Of course he was missing. He could never leave Goose Bay. Yet she had left him contented, as Max and Misha had wanted, as he had never been before then – not once – for her errand was clear to her now, like the lake where they'd stopped near the place where he lived. It had all been completed out by the bunchberry shrubs.

She leaned back in her chair. Still disbelieving, as one who had lost all hope might feel, suddenly rescued, she closed her eyes for a moment, awaiting immense relief.

Peace did not come. Something was missing still, some fundamental part of her being. "Last piece of the puzzle," she murmured, eyes closed still so as to see past things distinctly, "and yet I remember them all – I am sure of it, even the missing ones, even those long since gone."

Indeed, she remembered them clearly – a wrangler who'd loved her, a father who hadn't, an uncle who'd claimed her, only to leave her bereft. Yes, even that she recalled – her little bedroom above Raphael's room, the noise of Rome in the streets, nothing to do but submit to the heavy step in the stairs, no place to go, until that letter from Yale came.

And then she was saddened, there in that kitchen, recalling, not without effort, that the physician who had repaired her had damaged her too in his turn.

She thought of the scars that were left – bittersweet vengeance upon the doctor – marks on her neck, her ribs, swords on her hips, matching swords on her thighs. She unbuttoned her blouse, slipped her skirt up a bit, and, for the first time since she had come to Rock of Birds, Caroline touched them, the four of them, counting falsely, for it was this that had eluded her, the fifth one, which, she believed, belonged in another place. It was the name of another thing – something fine, not a scar on her right breast – and so it could not be remembered, for she had sworn to forget the artist and all that pertained to his life and the solemn, stubborn oath would not give way.

She felt herself growing tired. The day's revelations had drained her, body and soul. And yet...

She again scanned the photo. *There is one more*, she reflected, *or something about one of these – something essential.*

Exhaustion made her unsteady.

I must remember...I must. They will have spoken in vain if I don't. They will not rest.

Repeatedly she conjured Mikhail, Max, Elliot, Antonin. She remembered the horseman, Jesús, and Allessandro, her father, and even tried, in desperation, to find her mother, who was absent, and so again there remained only Raphael Contini.

"Raphael it is you," she said hoarsely. "You have not revealed yourself fully, or I have forgotten – yes, I have forgotten – something important, or lovely, or vile perhaps – I do not know, though once I knew, yet now it hides."

Forcing herself, she recalled Raphael – her life with him, so unhappy – his life with others, frequently also disturbing. Yet there was one he had cared for over the years come what may – a mistress he'd stayed with, a woman in Paris, wherever that was, on a pretty island that led to a bridge and from there to a large sunlit room, a veranda...

She stopped. The tissue-thin envelope was still on the sideboard. As if a blow had struck hard, that rushing sound started anew. Weak as she was then, she stood.

But I know no one in that place –

She crossed to the sideboard. The envelope remained unsealed, its pale blue pages tucked inside. There was no need, after all, to take out the pages, for she recalled every word Susannah had read the previous evening – the chatter, the gossip, above all the art supply store on the Left Bank with its news.

Such odd news, she thought, running her fingers across the red and blue border, the words *Par Avion*, the stamp with its black and gold burnished dome – elegance vaguely remembered, Caroline thought, as though some corrective lens on the stamp had suddenly sharpened its background – half-hidden streets, sculptor's home alongside, walled garden, night falling, eyeless forms in the dark facing a woman facing…what? – Caroline couldn't say. There were no houses left to be glimpsed, nothing more to be touched, once again nearly a void except of all things the sensation of smell growing stronger – smell of cinnamon, roses, turpentine, paint, cloth, sweat on his limbs – "Jude!" she cried out, and in that one word, or perhaps in the scents which were one and the same with that word, the solemn, stubborn oath gave way, since there could be no forgetting.

The house became utterly still. Caroline placed the letter down. Next to it was the catalogue, bearing a recent picture, along with the clipping, which reported the artist's recovery and immanent return to Paris. Caroline reached for them both.

There he was – no mistaking it – his beautiful face, worn now, haggard from his own ordeal, eyes with knowledge of evil unknown to most men.

Had he known she had written? Probably not – not in the autumn at least. Her letter would have arrived after the attack – this much she gauged from the few details in the clipping. He, of course, could not have written, certainly not in the beginning, and then later – she shuddered at the thought of his beating – later he wouldn't have written. Never, battered and broken as he'd been, would he have asked her to come to him, convinced he'd have nothing to give in return.

How little he knew her! How little she'd known herself! And yet how foolish they'd both been, for it was now surely too late. He was returning to Paris, lionized once again, on the arm of a new love, the article seemed to imply, shaping his life once again.

Unbidden, perhaps even forgotten, she could not intrude on that new life. It would be enough for her to know he had loved her, that he had not betrayed her, that he had survived – as she had – nearly insurmountable trials.

Again and again she stared at his beautiful face.

"It will be enough," she repeated. "Yes, it must be enough," and then she turned to the catalogue and studied his work and saw she'd judged falsely, thinking his suffering had marred his talent. If anything – though in style it was vastly different – Jude's art had become more compelling, his expression far bolder.

And yet, Caroline noticed, there was something which had not changed. That indefinable yearning had remained. It was there in each painting – in the abstracts, the portraits, the impressionistic interpretations of Honfleur's lovely harbour.

She looked again at the portraits. *No images of his new love,* she mused.

Why would he not paint his new love? – Jude who had painted her over and over, who could not resist putting on canvas whatever his hands had found pleasing, seeking essential beauty. Why all that longing still, more insistent than ever, informing his new works? Why, above all, the unmistakable nostalgia that still deepened his pale eyes?

The rushing sound slowly receded until it was no more than a whisper. Then, just as suddenly as it had begun, the noise ceased completely, replaced by answers to Caroline's questions – partial ones, very tentative still – like a door opened slightly on a room still in shadows, or that red velvet curtain, slightly parted, revealing a dimly lit stage and Roxane waiting still. Jude too was still waiting, it seemed, not for her perhaps, but for something – something his new love had not provided – the only thing that could hold him: inspiration.

Oddly enough, it did not feel like her own hand again undoing her blouse. She wasn't even conscious that she was searching, that she sensed something still missing, final piece of the puzzle, something even in darkness known for a lifetime yet on this bright day still unrevealed, maybe just fiercely denied still, maybe imagined and if so, was it all just a dream? – were Jude's hands...?

"Ah no, not imagined," Caroline murmured, leaning her head back as her fingertips traced what he had finally painted, what she remembered at last in such vivid detail that she could almost touch the damp canvas, smell the paint and shapes and colours of Jude McCallister's masterpiece.

He had not painted its equal since then – the fact was only too clear as she looked again at the paintings to be displayed in Paris. Powerful as his work had become, brilliantly revitalized despite his ordeal – perhaps even due to that pain – he had not lost himself in great love only to find himself in a more sublime place, surrender which for Jude as both artist and man, Caroline knew, suddenly recalling Jacob's paradoxical victory, remained the only hard path to triumph.

No, Jude had not found that path. He had not come upon passions to match his own, needs like his, yearning to mirror his own restless mind. Once, yes – it had only taken a glance – the thing had occurred. If they had only looked again while time remained! If he had but written! If she had rewritten! If she could only say now – but she could say nothing now, for he was in Paris and she was on Rock of Birds; he was alive still, she on the other hand – it was in the papers, there'd been a funeral – she was gone, vanished, lost to everyone everywhere but to herself on this island, tattered suit only left, nearest telephone across the Gulf of St. Lawrence.

She stopped. The notion staggered her. She tried to put it aside, but the concept returned insistently, like an overture's main theme.

Presumed dead.

The word no longer seemed odd, unattractive. She repeated it over and over again to herself, hearing in its finality something increasingly thrilling, unique: proscribed yet irresistible analogue for renewal.

More than renewal. Against all odds rescue, resurrection, for could one not, presumed dead, preserve? Could one not save one's land? Woods? Mill house forever remaining though nature alone would preside? *Might not second chances appear?*

The possibility seemed remote, yet within reach – alluringly closer in fact as time passed and she stood clutching the sideboard, motionless, eyes fixed on the incoming tides, their relentless progression no longer disturbing, their fathomless depths of all things now her friend.

As though to a friend, Caroline listened. Waves tumbled onto the beach, disappeared, others formed, disappeared, and still the surf followed its secretive path, reticent, undeterred. So, Caroline saw, could it be with her own days. She had lost everything, even presumably life, and yet closely guarded, clear paths remained – tracks which could with some care be erased as the tides skilfully, always, reversed their direction.

Caroline considered this. Barely daring to breathe, she turned the phrase over and over again in her head – inconceivable, irresistible, increasingly imperative words: *second chance*. Once, in her pride, she had retreated from such a thing. He had demurred too, in his pain. Improbably now, here – at Lookout Point on the way to the Arctic – it had come round once again – briefly perhaps, perhaps already too late, yet among the limitless possibilities resurrection presented the only one which seemed to matter.

But had she the right to do this? To remain Violette? To leave Caroline Contini Devereux buried at sea while she refashioned herself come what may? And would he then come to her – knowing – for he would be the only one who would ever know?

She could not say. She might receive a message, "I cannot join you" – nothing more than that, or "I cannot join you, though I have loved you as no other." Or silence alone might be the only reply, affliction worse than her day of Communion, for she would have sought the affront to both body and soul this time.

And at this last thought she faltered. She could not bring herself to the brink – last of the cliffs she still feared – unsecured hazard of body and soul once again, risk with no guarantees, without even a hint…

She looked again at the paintings, the catalogue. There was his image still and the yearning – but not the answer to this final, essential question.

She dared not open the letter. It had been sent to another. She was certain, however, that she recalled it exactly, and that the assurance she wanted was not to be found there. Nor was it to be seen in any photograph, catalogue, detail perhaps overlooked in the kitchen.

Outside, perhaps. Out in the bright noonday sun and the wind.

She crossed the lawn and reached the taught line stretched through the poles. She fingered the skirt, almost dry in the breeze. She touched the back of the jacket, placed toward the sea, then slipped though the linens so as to face the grey pieces, only possessions remaining, or so she thought until she turned and looked again at her suit.

Only then did she see it, pinned with care onto the lapel – Maximilian's cameo, which must have remained where it was as she'd swirled through the Gulf Stream, which Serge and Susannah must have safeguarded, and which, for some reason, Susannah had deemed appropriate to have replaced on the lapel this afternoon.

Caroline shielded her eyes, not from the high, midday sun poised directly above, but from the moment's refulgence – clarity glinting on both present and past scenes. Vividly she recalled Max recollecting those past scenes, voice low and throaty sometimes, other times sweeter than wine with emotion, sensuous as the sea either way as he spoke fervently, and she wrote ardently, and, because it was time after all, fate having brought them together to reenact not just record past events, side by side they bore witness to that leap off a rope swing, that unexpectedly wild, despairing embrace which had caught Max off guard but to which he had returned willingly, no guarantees…"*Coûte que coûte*, Caroline, did you get that? *Whatever the cost,*" he had insisted, forcing himself to conjure that fateful spring's longing, its mounting desire, above all the prescience of hurt which could not be avoided.

And all the while she had solemnly nodded, not because she had heard Max distinctly that day, but because he had told far more than a tale and she knew it; he had described far more than a face, plumbed much more than his pain, acknowledging finally, splendidly, the life-altering force of overwhelming attraction.

Hearing a sound behind her – no longer a surging but more like stones washed by ebb tide – Caroline listened. "Yes…Yes, I would do it again," she thought she heard that same seaborne whisper confess somewhere over the Gulf. "In spite of it all I would do it again, Caroline. In fact I did do just that, the afternoon Anatole Kramer sent the unexpected back into my life."

In the still-brisk onshore winds, Caroline sank to her knees, pulling the grey suit down with her. It had all come full circle – a perfectly configured shape, like the oval cameo that had been transferred Christmas Eve, witness to all the risks Maximilian had taken – the passionate choices, the imprudent connections, the far grander loyalties, the concomitant deep hurts. This one superb piece – oyster white and pale brown with a most intricate golden halo – Max had cherished above all things. It had also survived, not worn and tattered like her suit, but shimmering like the whitecaps off in the distance. Its serene face – enigmatic allure not unlike the unknown – was not hers to decipher. Yet how to turn from that fine, ivory gaze, wrought so expertly decades before this day, compelling, unascertainable grace calling still?

A sudden chill filled the air. Within weeks it would be autumn, Caroline realized, one full year since that burned-out September.

"Autumn," she repeated, recalling Serge Pellerin's description of hidden Acadian harbours along Prince Edward's south shores. "If I cannot reach Cap-Egmont before the crossings become impossible, I'll have to stay here 'til the ice breaks…April perhaps."

Long before then – she was sure of it – Jude McCallister would have vanished.

☾

"Mon Dieu," exclaimed Susannah Joubert, rushing up from the tool shed, seeing the stranger on the grass, head still bent down over the clothes pulled from the line.

"Violette!" she called loudly, but diminishing winds and the waves carried her voice out to sea.

"Violette," she repeated, touching her shoulder as she did so, until at last the stranger looked up from the crumpled fabrics she was holding. Her eyes seemed filled not just with colour but understanding – breakthrough Susannah had hoped for when she had pinned the brooch on the jacket that morning – and yet so intense was Violette's gaze, so deepened the hyacinth hue in those eyes, that Susannah feared she had unlocked what should perhaps have been left undisturbed.

"Are you all right, Violette?"

Caroline turned away, running her fingers along the delicate filigree surrounding the face on her pin. She seemed to be gazing at something quite clear, and yet distant.

"*Pas Violette,*" she said softly.

"Yes, yes I know you have another name."

"But it is a beautiful name – like Rocher aux Oiseaux, Rock of Birds – something I can take away with me when I go, as I must soon – something that will always recall your kindness...this island...the miracle of our meeting here."

She paused, lovingly smoothing out the suit on her lap.

"I should like to keep it."

"Keep it?" echoed Susannah. "But what about your other name, the real one? What about your surname, your past life? I felt for sure today you had remembered..."

"I did remember. I remembered everything this morning, though I will never know *why* it was then," Caroline added haltingly. "Only that it occurred as my clothes swung from the line, beckoning right where you'd left them, and then the whole picture took shape – slowly, sometimes resistant – until at long last I was sure – things were finally clear – brighter, perhaps than the day's light when I left the house and walked toward the cliff and saw my brooch on the jacket you'd hung."

As though to savour what remained of that now-waning light, Caroline glanced around. Then, gently, taking Susannah's weathered hands in her own: "You saved the cameo for this morning, and I know that, and for the rest of my days I will thank you, Susannah."

The front lawn fell silent, onshore winds momentarily stilled, late day's indecision matching Susannah's wistfully slow smile.

"I…well of course I am honoured. And *Violette* suits you, immensely. Nevertheless…," here the old woman stumbled, for the stranger, who was no longer that, appeared essentially altered, although her features were unchanged, as if in recollecting she had renewed herself, and the backward glance had brought completion.

Yes, that was it. What had before been mere vagueness – lovely childlike compliance – had in a matter of hours become wide if not fully-shared knowledge, and the change was astounding, and more than ever Susannah felt she did not know the nameless woman – and more than ever she was at a loss, partly because she was still accountable for her welfare, partly because she had come to care for her, profoundly, as a mother might love a dear special child, from whom she was soon to be parted.

"Susannah, what is it?"

Susannah tried but made no answer.

"*Tell* me, please, you *must*, while there is time left –"

"*Who are you?*" Susannah heard herself cry then, fiercely almost, clutching the hand that held hers still.

Momentarily, both women were startled. Caroline had not expected such an abruptly passionate query. Susannah had not anticipated such a powerful surge of emotions. Unaccustomed still to their lingering force – or perhaps that was only high tide suddenly cresting below – she drew her hand away slowly.

"I mean…Serge is due back any day. He'll have to take you back home. Your friends will be waiting, your people. You'll have to tell me where they are, where you live, so that the trip can be planned, the crossing made before September, and…and I will miss you so," she exclaimed, once more abruptly, for she had not planned to say that and yet the thought of icebound days just beyond the horizon recalled Dominique who had left, and now again loss – this time the one to whom she'd once given life.

Compassion filled Caroline's heart. She too had known loss, over and over again, the ache of last partings, ensuing dull, throbbing solitude so much worse than farewell.

"I am…I…" It was her turn to falter. She reached again for the hand slowly withdrawn. Pressing it against her cheek, she closed her eyes, motionless, as if the evening too might be seized. Then, with a mixture of tenderness and something frail in the sound, like a young branch resisting fierce winds: "I am Violette Todd, a lady who sailed alone – very foolishly, I confess it – from Prince Edward Island."

"But that cannot be your home. Your speech is not Island English, nor Acadian French, nor even that vague French from the mainland. – No, that cannot be your home," she repeated, pity again welling up in her eyes, for she began to think then that Violette had only partially, or incorrectly, remembered, and did not wish to tell her so, fearing to inflict such an immense disappointment.

Caroline smiled, touched as much by Susannah's kindness as she was impressed by the fact that words, in the end, would always define her own path.

"You are wise, Susannah, as always, and have guessed correctly. My home is not on Prince Edward. Yet it is the place where I live now, the place where I sailed from."

Susannah nodded, expectantly.

"I am a writer. Sometimes I translate. My home is wherever my fountain pen takes me. At the present time it is Cap-Egmont."

"The old Acadian harbour?"

"That is where I'll be staying."

Susannah turned toward the Gulf, surveying its always intriguing wide, turquoise band. She recalled the evening Serge named his boat. She remembered the morning she had discovered the stranger. Softly, like still-diminishing winds in the cedars, she sighed, *"Notre Bénédiction."*

"And what is this blessing, Susannah, which you seem so to cherish?"

"An ocean current, nothing more than that, Violette, closest thing we come to destiny here on this island no one ever discovers."

"Vite, Susannah! Venez vite! Another packet," Violette called two weeks later, running back to the house from her chair where in the afternoon sun she had rested.

"Never another so soon, Violette."

"But just look," she insisted.

"Serge!" Susannah exclaimed, knowing those sails like her own name, though the triangular canvases were barely visible still, way off in the distance.

"Serge," Susannah repeated, this time much softer, amazement and welcome both in her tone, for she was always surprised, despite the name of his boat, to see him returned from the Labrador Sea.

"But is it Serge or is it not?"

"It is Serge."

"Then you must hurry."

"L'Inattendu will take its time."

"Susannah, please let me finish here. There's a strong wind on the beach. You'll need your shawl from the parlour – and your bonnet's by the doorway – and here, give me that apron...Much better," pronounced Violette, and Susannah smiled at the young woman's fussing, though she began to smooth back her grey hair and roll down the sleeves of her blouse.

"In the meantime I'll take the fruit in, tend to the kitchen hearth, warm the fish stew you prepared...

"Go," she entreated, watching the triangular canvases quickly grow larger.

"You will be staying with us, will you not, Violette?" asked Serge that night after supper had been cleared. "I can see that Susannah has come to be fond of you..."

"Very fond," murmured Susannah.

"Very good," echoed Serge. "For as you say, Violette, home is wherever your fountain pen lies, and your people the books that you find, and…and we have pens here, and books to last through the winter –"

"Serge," interrupted Susannah.

"We can even send out for more when the May packet arrives…"

"Serge," she repeated, more insistently this time, so that her husband stopped, looking from one woman to another, guessing at last that Violette Todd would be leaving, and that it would have to be soon, while the crossing was safe still.

Nevertheless, as he pushed his chair back a bit he felt compelled to add softly, though he sensed the futility of his proposal, "You know, Violette, since you remember everything now, and so clearly, you could reconstruct Cap-Egmont in your mind – bring it to life, so to speak, here on Rock of Birds. Your days would be undisturbed. You might even find –"

"I have to go, Serge. I have no choice, although I promise you I will return someday – many times I expect." Her smile resembled September in the fire's waning light. "You will grow tired of me, Serge, wait and see."

"Never," was the old sailor's reply, for the stranger – she would always be that to him – now seemed a part of his Acadian house. So it had always seemed to him, even in the beginning, in her vague days, perhaps because fate had chosen their hidden cove for her salvation, perhaps because her eyes matched the phlox in his yard, most likely because his wife loved her so, and they'd had no children, and he himself was feeling weaker, perhaps only weathered, either way longing for youth in his house, earth's sweet, unimagined revival half a long year away still.

"Never," he repeated, and then he blew out the candle so that they could all get some sleep.

☾

Seated for the last time on her swing chair, Violette watched the moon coming up over the Gulf. The air was still; the night mild; the sky filled with numberless stars.

Many things came to mind: her farewell from Susannah, only hours away now, so that with each passing moment that profound ache in her heart – pain one might feel upon leaving a mother, she guessed – continued to deepen; her farewell from Serge, whose uncanny sense of the sea after six decades and then some seemed to her then, like Maximilian's exact sense of space, less a practical skill than a gift of the heart. She thought of the grey sandstone place in Provence which was not so very different, after all, from Point Guetter overlooking the Gulf – waters that now sheltered Maximilian himself, depths that she too, for a time, had of all things called home.

This brought to mind thoughts of her crossing. Her dress was all ready. The boat was all ready. Serge had prepared their lunch, a simple dinner, supplies for her to keep on Prince Edward. He'd marked his mariner's charts minutely, though the route was more familiar to him than any hidden path along the rocky shores beyond his cove. Still, he insisted, every contingency had to be considered. Nothing untoward could mar this return trip – nothing unexpected, he repeated, forgetting for once the name he had without sentiment given his boat, for he was determined to travel securely over seas that had once tossed the stranger among the rocks and debris and upturned crabs on his beach.

Mostly, though, Violette thought of the errand ahead.

Where is he now? she repeatedly asked herself. Would that one message she planned to leave with Frères Durand ever reach him? And if it did would he care?

Within a day she would arrive on the coast by Cap-Egmont. The day after that she would call. In less than a month she would know.

So softly did Serge approach that Violette did not sense his presence until he had taken a seat on the chaise longue beside her. Even after that, for what seemed like a long time, night's undisturbed quiet prevailed.

"The sea is calm, Violette," she finally heard in the silence.

"Very calm."

"A very good omen."

"Yes."

Once again silence. Finally, in the pale moonlight, discerned Violette, Serge inclined toward her, about to say something urgent it seemed, only to sit back directly, having said not a word.

After some time he tried again, faltered and again sat back down.

"Serge, what is it? Have you something to say to me? Does Susannah need...?"

"It is not what we need, Violette –"

"What you'd like then."

"What *you* might need," he said cautiously, steering with mariner's tact toward what he perceived was a delicate theme. "When you arrived you had nothing – no wallet, no purse. We presumed they were lost."

"They were lost."

"But not everything's gone –"

"Oh no, Serge. No," she repeated in a voice which she hoped sounded buoyant. "Everything's all where I left it. Undisturbed. Waiting still to be claimed."

Long slender clouds momentarily covered the moon.

"I need only arrive," she went on. "Matter of hours...a few calls at the most." Here she paused, like the moon too momentarily lost. Then, brightly again: "Land legs – that's all I'll need to find first, Serge."

"I see," Serge said in the darkness, tone as neutral as he could manage.

Again they fell silent. Stubbornly round the moon those tenuous clouds remained. Violette's chair ever so slightly rocked as she shifted her weight, passing her hand over her neck, wishing she could add something specific – bank accounts, money that might be transferred, but she had already held back the facts of her Trans Canada flight and would not further deceive.

But how to tell Serge the truth? How to say there remained only the cameo she planned to part with at long last, having no other choice – that she had seen this fact clearly the morning her past life had returned, everything flooding back to her as she had clung to her skirt and her jacket and the oval brooch on its lapel? She could not admit to such need, though she had known on that bright day, with an absolute, resplendent certitude, that Max would approve of the plan – no, more than approve – he of such passions and fearless of all risk – he would urge the endeavour, for so Violette had conceived it – an endeavour, not a sale, not the thing she had refused to do in Roger Gachet's office.

"So you've an account on the island," Serge confirmed, still in that undecipherable voice, still in the darkness.

"Not an account *per se*, Serge –"

"Friends?"

"Hopefully."

"*...Hopefully*, Violette?"

Slowly, words of all things eluding: "I – one does not circulate much on assignment. And – and my last assignment was a long one. ...Memoirs. A book. It is over now," she thought to add then, but at the sound of the phrase the thought struck her like salt spray, so that her voice too disappeared.

Still, she believed Serge had nodded. She heard the chaise longue creak beside her and knew he had reclined once more. She assumed she'd convinced him. She began to swing gently.

But he who could gauge a storm's force long before it had stirred even one leaf was considering, weighing her silence, her words, both the ones she had spoken and, more important, those she had left like becalmed seas, postponed.

A light breeze picked up. Like that full opal-toned moon finally clearing the clouds a good sign, Serge decided. All the night's portents were fine – winds, currents, tides, warmth – odd that she had no knowledge of the Gulf Stream's warmth this time of year...Stranger still her many questions about Cap-Egmont – where to stay, how large the village, how far from a seaport, the highway. Why never a word about her books, her work, no concern for those who might be concerned?

With an inward sigh, Serge conceded. Susannah had been right. For whatever reason – perhaps only his wife who so loved the girl would have divined this – Violette had remembered everything only to hide once again. Or rather remain hidden. He himself could not say. He had not seen her that windy morning, had not witnessed the radiance which had so stunned his wife, the joy at once palpable, vivid, yet when expressed, so carefully phrased.

"And why keep the name we gave, Serge?" Susannah'd whispered shortly before he'd come out to join Violette on this last night. "Why nothing else, never a question about wallets, her purse –"

"Not ours to say."

"Maybe not, though since that morning I've guessed – more than guessed, known somehow. Mind, she must never suspect, Serge, at least not now...Now, perhaps after dinner when you've some private time, just give her this. Tell her I'd like her to have it. Violette will understand," his wife had added then, simply, placing a book from their library shelves in his hand. "Yes, she will find what she needs here."

And with that Susannah had stood and gone to her room and Serge had glanced down and seen the volume of Madame de Sévigné's correspondence left for the girl who'd been loved as a daughter on Rock of Birds. After a moment he'd opened the book, feeling what he thought to be a page marker toward the beginning.

He was mistaken. There between chapters, he'd found neatly folded the Canadian bank notes Susannah had managed to save over time. "For some unforeseen thing," she had always insisted, year after year carefully placing her money in the French porcelain box by her bed, "though what that might be on Lookout Point by the sea – *Dieu seul saura, Serge...Dieu seul saura,*" she had always, without variation, sighed in conclusion.

God only knows, Serge said again to himself, stealing a glance at the swing chair as he reached for the book by his side. *One thing alone remains clear. Even by the light of the stars I can see it myself now. She will have nothing but this when she goes.*

Lovingly, Violette fingered the worn, gold-lettered volume.

"A remembrance," Serge offered hastily, "Nothing more…"

"Far more that than, Serge," she managed. "All those nights while you sailed, other nights too before I came here…one night above all –"

She stopped. The quickening breeze had turned over some pages. Stupefied, she stared at the bills carefully tucked into the binding.

Finally, spoken so softly that the sound might have come from the grass swaying in the summer wind, "I can't take these, Serge."

"They are not from me."

"Then you must say –"

"Only what Susannah has told me to say: that the little gift is from her, and that you would understand, once again finding whatever it was you might still be needing in there, and…and that is all, Violette. I cannot undo what has been done – or rather prepared for. – Yes that's it," he repeated, marvelling to himself as he spoke of things he himself had not fully grasped 'til that moment. *"Planned.* Carefully, over the years, as each packet boat came with her gifts in July…You were the unforeseen thing she was expecting."

Here Serge paused, stood, heard breaking waves on the rocks by his cove. Then, with a nostalgia that in a man of far lesser endurance would have resembled weariness: "The seasons of waiting are over. Come, Violette. We must all rise with the sun."

⁓☾⁓

Dawn broke discreetly, indigo clouds giving way to pink streaks on the horizon. Susannah was standing, slightly behind Violette, having helped pack the last of the provisions into the boat. Serge untied the ropes which moored *l'Inattendu* to the cove. And then suddenly – there on the beach where they had found Violette – silence.

"We are ready," announced Serge, his tone official, commanding, like a well-seasoned captain about to slip out from some grand port.

Awkwardly, Violette turned. Susannah made no reply when Violette said her name, barely audible above the tides, though they were falling, and very quiet.

"Come," Serge called out. "Come now before we're stranded."

Violette repeated her name once again.

The only response was the breeze, respectfully gentle on this occasion.

"Goodbye then, Susannah. I will come back to this cove, you know that."

Susannah nodded. Violette reached, and was surprised by the force of the old woman's embrace which engulfed her then, long and fiercely.

"*Au revoir, Violette,*" she answered finally, releasing her. "*Chez nous – Point Guetter – toujours ta maison.*"

"Yes," Caroline murmured. "Yes I know that this will always be my home – Lookout Point, overlooking the Gulf." And then she repeated, most tenderly, "*Au revoir, Susannah Joubert.*"

L'Inattendu made its way across the inlet that led out of the cove. Susannah was clearly visible, waving repeatedly from the beach. Even from the open sea she could be seen still, for she had climbed the steep steps to the high ground, and again waved beside the swing chair at the edge of the grass.

Little by little, her small form receded, then vanished. Rock of Birds then diminished, before it too disappeared. *L'Inattendu* alone was left then – *Unexpected* – heading south by southwest toward Prince Edward Island.

☾

Nearing day's end Cap-Egmont harbour was silent, its weary boats rocking at anchor, its boardwalk deserted, light onshore winds sending rippled reflections from the overhead lamps into the bay. Sea and a billowing sky were pearl grey in the stillness. Out past the sandbar, now and again, Northumberland Strait heaved a sigh.

Serge Pellerin too sighed as he took a last look at the scene. Violette had long since left. At least it seemed to Serge a long time, though at the most ninety minutes had passed since they'd said something that resembled farewell, some small stifled sound whispered into the wind as a setting sun tinted the tides burnt sienna.

He had wanted to dock at a busier wharf up the coast. She had persuaded him to continue to this remote cove near the point. He had wanted to walk with her toward the guest house. She had insisted on going alone.

Well, at least, Serge reflected, untying the ropes that had secured his small boat, *we went together into the tackle shop. We found out where the guest house was, more or less. Above all she seemed happy*, he remembered, as *L'Inattendu* slipped away from the dock toward the sea.

Slowly but surely the harbour receded. He recalled how she'd stood close by the last shed on the dock, hand raised to the wind – so frail, he had thought as the boats and the lamps and her slender form once and for all disappeared.

By nightfall he had cleared the Narrows, leaving the sandbar behind him, turning northward again into Northumberland Strait. Though he continued to hug the shoreline, he no longer scanned its inlets and roadways, for he knew they would not meet again. Fate had intended her to alight for a moment on Rock of Birds, like the rare species that nested only a season on their cliffs.

He reached North Cape by midnight, where he dropped anchor, prepared for morning's return to the Madeleine Islands, and at last surrendered his body to sleep, and to dreams that confused him.

⌒ ☾ ⌒

Caroline had by then made her way through the pine groves behind the harbour, turning west, as instructed, onto the winding clay roadway when she emerged. She passed a few clustered homesteads as the road steadily rose, then dipped, then veered sharply southward, leaving the sea far behind.

Here the settlements dwindled, giving way to red, gold and malachite fields on her right, curving sienna ploughed strips to her left. Save for the breeze there was absolute stillness. Not even a homestead remained on the horizon as she advanced, walking rapidly still, sensing the road curving back down toward the sea as the last bit of day lingered, like a porch lamp waiting.

And indeed, with the sounds of the sea off to her left now quite distinct, she made out not one but two porch lights off in the distance. Approaching, she saw a pale yellow farmhouse set back from the road. A red barn flanked one side; aspen groves flanked the other; another barn, also bright crimson, was centred behind them, marking the start of precisely tilled fields.

The little compound was approached by a narrow clay drive-way. From a mailbox alongside the road, a wooden sign swayed in the breeze, hand-lettered name visible still in the dusk: *Journey's End*.

"Journey's End," she repeated, glancing at the paper clutched in her hand.

She looked again at the house: white intricate trim on the porch and gables above; bright red front doorway; long, dusty grass lining a gravel path to the steps.

Vacancy, she read on a smaller sign as she slowly walked up these steps.

The room was on the second floor – that gabled window which had so intrigued her overlooking the open front porch. It was a large space, simply furnished, its few oak pieces oversized. The chairs were upholstered in a faded cream-coloured chintz: intertwined leaves and dark red carnations that recalled gardens she had long ago tended. The four-poster bed had a matching crewel spread.

Caroline closed the door, opened the casements and sat down on the bed. Beyond the windows she could see the roadway, beyond the roadway fields of now-familiar red and gold hues, in the distance a clay pathway leading down to the sea.

"Journey's End," she murmured again, and then sleep overcame her.

Nearing midnight she awakened, surprised to find herself still fully clothed, still propped up against the pillows in the utterly dark and unfamiliar room. Hurriedly she undressed, closed the window, then slipped beneath the spread this time, soothed by the crisply starched sheets. Again sleep came quickly, while a steady rain dripped from the gables above her window.

All that was left of the rain shortly past six the next morning was a light mist on the fields and heavier fog over the sea.

"Will it rain again, Mademoiselle, do you think?" Caroline asked as breakfast was served by the tall parlour windows overlooking the porch.

Honorine Vallère, manager, chef, and owner of Journey's End, as her mother before her had been, gazed at the brooding Northumberland Strait.

"No," she replied with decision. "No, the storm barely touched our shores. It has moved south now, to Nova Scotia."

"Ah."

"The day will be damp though. You'll need a shawl."

Caroline nodded.

"Though it will only take you ten minutes to get to the gas station at the tip of the coast. They have a telephone there – bright red booth, like my barn, close by the side of the road. – Only for local calls though. Here on the island. Coins, nothing more."

"But surely there must be another phone –"

"To contact the mainland?"

"To call Paris."

Honorine frowned.

"Well there's a phone at the general store. You could reach an operator – not right away sometimes – but if you're willing to wait, reverse the charges, wait some more for her to ring you back there."

"I can't wait!" Caroline blurted out, surprising them both in that quiet front room. "It's already noontime in Paris! I...the place I'm calling – a gallery – closes early on Saturdays. And besides" – here she fumbled – "It wouldn't do in this case. Reversing the charges I mean. I can reimburse someone, anyone," she added fervently. "All I need, just this once, is to borrow a phone – a phone that's somewhat nearby. I might not make it in time if I walk back to the wharf."

"I wish I had one, Mademoiselle."

Caroline turned away, all brightness drained from her face, so that her customary pallor seemed all the more remarkable. She had not expected this setback. Frères Durand was never open on Sundays. The call would have to wait two more days, and already she had a nagging presentment that she was – or very soon would be – too late.

"St-Timothée!" exclaimed Honorine.

Startled, Caroline looked at her.

"Old Acadian priory up in the hills. Père Gabriel's been the abbot for years there. He has a phone, Mademoiselle."

"Is it far?"

"Not if you hurry. If you go now – turning straight to the north at that fork in the road, you can reach the church in thirty minutes."

"And if Père Gabriel is not there?"

"There are always priests there."

"May I tell them you sent me?"

"If you like, Mademoiselle. But there will be no need. They will help you – you'll see – at the church of Notre-Dame de Grace.

Caroline reached for her shawl. As she rushed for the door Honorine called, "Remember, white clapboard, brown trim, tall wooden steeple. You'll see the steeple from a distance…"

"Thank you," Caroline called back, already hurrying down the pathway.

Honorine watched until the young woman was out of sight. She had indeed turned correctly, and was by then heading northward along a steep and uneven clay roadway. As she moved inland through continuing mist, the rolling countryside grew more verdant, the red and yellow fields sparser, the smell and sounds of the sea increasingly faint.

Finally, off in the distance, piercing the grey sky, a tall wooden steeple appeared, and then the tolling of bells could be heard, eight of them, so that she knew it was exactly one p.m. on the rue du Bac, Left Bank, off the boulevard St-Germain, Paris, France.

꙳ ☾ ꙳

It surprised Jude McCallister to hear his telephone ringing first thing in the morning on a Sunday. He was even more startled to hear the voice of Auguste Durand, breathless, somewhat relieved, glad at last to have found him.

"Auguste, what is it – what's happened?" he asked, concern quickly supplanting amazement, for the brothers Durand knew he always painted in the mornings, and – unaware as they were of his inability to create anything since his return to Paris – they would be most reluctant, save in an emergency, to disturb his studio time.

"No, no it is not such a crisis, Jude – at least it did not seem so when it happened, and yet it was all so strange – so unusual," murmured Auguste. "We received a phone call at the gallery – yesterday, just before closing."

"Auguste," replied Jude, with an irritability of which he was not proud, "that is hardly a reason –"

"Ah, but it is," countered Auguste, and then he stopped, momentarily, for never before had he contradicted his most celebrated artist.

Jude McCallister remained silent, aware of the significance implied by that fact.

"The lady seemed so distressed, Jude…"

"Lady?"

Jude thought at once of Rebecca. On that very day, noontime, as he had promised, he was planning to call her, and thank her, and accept her invitation to Vienna. Something untoward had happened – an accident, illness, but no – she had his private number. She would have called him directly, having no need of the brothers Durand.

Jude sensed what had by then become a familiar confusion – someone he had forgotten – a model, a patron, a woman whose portrait he had agreed to paint.

"Yes – yes a lady, long distance, from Canada."

Jude felt an odd sensation course through his body.

"Prince Edward Island, to be precise, wherever that is," added Auguste. "All she wanted was to find you if I could, get word to you somehow – really it was so peculiar. She insisted I tell you she was well – no, *spared* – that was the term she used, and that she was waiting still, though she did not say for what – presumably a painting you once offered to send her, and for which perhaps she had paid, and which was perhaps still in our possession – we just did not know – so much this past year has remained closed to us after all."

"Yes," managed Jude, though he would never remember sinking into his chair at that moment.

"We assured her we'd call you on Monday, nearing sunset, but it just wouldn't do – she kept repeating that phrase – despite the fact that you had a mistress, she acknowledged…Jude?…Are you still there, Jude?"

"I am here, Auguste," whispered Jude.

"Interrupt you we must," she instructed, "sunlight or no light, and at that point we asked for her name – she had spoken so forcefully, you understand – and she said simply, 'I am Half Moon.'

"Well we were stunned. I mean we've seen the portrait, Jude – the masterpiece – the one you wouldn't part with, though God knows we could have fetched you a fortune for that work."

Auguste Durand then heard a voice ask – perhaps it was only late summer's wind on the Seine – "Is that all she said?"

"No. No, of course, I wanted some proof – identification – something before disturbing you.

"We will need to know more than 'Half Moon,' I insisted, and she replied – I believe I got all of it – there was some static, and one could hear organ music in the background –

"'I am the lady he painted when the bell jar almost fell after Nero the cat jumped off the mantel and then there was no choice but to render me as I was, once and for all, though I had denied him until then.'

"Well something like that, Jude. Close to that in fact. Quite close.

"'He may wish to paint me again,' she went on. 'I do not know. Once, I remember, it was his deepest desire. You are his agents after all, and so I felt obliged to let him know that I am waiting' – no, *'spared'* – she used that word again – 'as he too has been saved.'

"And then she gave an address – the guest house had no phone, she explained; and yet still she would wait there, by the sea, until the leaves turned, after which time she would know – she would be sure – that you had gone somewhere else."

Here Auguste paused again, anticipating Jude's answer.

There was only silence.

"Well," added Auguste, increasingly uncomfortable, thinking perhaps he had said too much, or too little, and, deciding to err on the side of disclosure, since there was so little left, he concluded, "there *was* one more thing."

"Go on," he heard vaguely, as though from a distance.

"She said you could write if you wished – if you were not coming, if you wanted to tell her, so that she would not wait.

"'Half Moon,' she repeated, 'that name alone will suffice, in care of Journey's End, Cap-Egmont, Prince Edward Island, Canada.'

"Ah – a coda," Auguste corrected himself. "I was to tell only you – no one else, and you were also to tell no one. Well, of course, we divulge nothing of your private life, you know that, Jude – which is why I called you directly. I tried twice yesterday –"

"I was out walking," said a voice which no longer resembled Jude McCallister's.

"And now again this morning, though with my apologies, for I know you are working, and yet it all seemed so strange to us, so compelling. You have painted nothing like *Half Moon* before or after in your career."

"I don't expect I ever will."

"Well it's been barely a year after all."

"Just about."

"There'll be more to come, Jude, many more."

"Yes."

"Whatever's filling your days now," said Auguste, anxious by then to ring off, yet feeling obliged to encourage, "your very next *Half Moon*'s no doubt in progress."

"...Yes," Jude repeated.

"Goodbye, then, for now, Jude."

Dazed, Jude placed the phone back in its cradle, unaware of his surroundings, detecting nothing then of time and space.

At last he managed to stand, walk into the hall from his study, turn again into the studio where he no longer painted, stare in numbed disbelief at the mantel, the bell jar, the rose bowl, the ornate mirror above the loveseat.

Slowly he crossed, unlocked the French doors, stepped onto his terrace, gazed at the city below.

Midday's light played on the railing, the roses, Rodin's house, the river...Above all the river. Ceaselessly, westward, it forced its way through Norman farmland, passing apple trees, ancient manors, Rouen's soaring cathedral, Honfleur's painted bay; then it found the Atlantic, still making its own way, though part of a far greater thing from there on, from Étretat's cliffs to a tiny province in the Maritimes.

Eastward too it traced its own steady path, down toward Dijon, source not far from Bern, Zürich, the Austrian border, Vienna.

Sunday bells announced the last Mass – noontime – at the church of St-Louis-des-Invalides. For a moment or two, as the reminder lingered in the afternoon light, Jude remained on his veranda, transfixed by the river – destiny's waters in either direction – and the matching glory of the magnificent dome.

"Yes – yes, it is time to leave Paris," he decided.

He returned to his study and looked at his calendar...24 August.

He made one telephone call.

NIGHT MUSIC

More than the usual chaos surrounded Orly Airport's international terminal. Not even the roar on the runways drowned out the confusion around counters, gates, ramps and the cluttered spaces between them. Flight cancellations interrupted announcements; final calls echoed; nothing could be heard precisely as residents returning to Paris collided with crowds departing at summer's end.

Jude McCallister paused. He was glad he had packed so little. His right hand – by far the steadier – gripped his mahogany cane; his left held a small suitcase containing his sketchbook, brushes and paint tubes, a change of clothing or two, a zippered toiletry bag. More than that, he well knew, he could not possibly manage, although he had tied a windbreaker over his shoulders, despite the still humid weather of Paris. Canada could be cold, he had heard, so near to September.

"Can I help you, Monsieur?" asked an old porter kindly, seeing the clearly perplexed and slightly disabled man by the door.

"No, thank you."

Within moments Jude reconsidered, for his pride, like his past life, had been abandoned in the apartment he had closed that very morning – a mere four days after the phone call he had received from Auguste Durand. The flight would be long, the connections exhausting. He was already beginning to feel the effects of the efforts involved – a strain Dr. Le Brun had advised postponing a bit, but one he had decided to risk, come what may, before the last week of August coloured any more leaves along Canada's shores.

He turned again to the porter. Then, motioning with his cane into the crowds: "Perhaps…after all – you might direct me. Air France, Flight 590, Paris to Montréal, connecting to Halifax, Nova Scotia, from there to Charlottetown, Prince Edward Island."

"Follow me. We'll bypass the queue this way, head on straight to the counter, move from there to the gate."

Jude nodded, though he declined to allow the attendant to carry his suitcase, which, after all, he would have to hold on to the rest of the way.

The attendant too nodded – out of politeness, not from conviction – for he could not imagine this man ever reaching that tiny, remote Maritime province.

⁓ ☾ ⁓

Jude looked down from his window and stared at the river – towpaths and bridges and willow trees greatly diminished, though still to scale from this height, like tiny models in a child's game. He stared more keenly as the plane climbed, so as to fix the precise moment when, without warning, the slender blue ribbon would vanish.

The moment did not occur; the Seine would not be dismissed; and at the thought of its wilful beauty Jude smiled, for there it remained, no longer one graceful arc slicing a city in half, but purposeful still, serene, curving securely through Norman pastures.

Fitting farewell, he reflected, recalling his lurching ride alongside its waters, the smoother return trip to Paris, the improbable, intervening rebirth of the previous winter. More than ever those days seemed like a dream, perhaps a tale told to him once as he gazed upon great red-roofed manors, citrus green orchards, dusky sienna fields – each in its turn passing beneath him, everything fading like youth and ambition, everything smaller, even Rouen's shining streets – even, although he continued staring long after they'd vanished, the soaring towers of its cathedral.

One thing only remained. Oddly enough, though just a speck by the sea now, this place alone appeared undiminished still, every detail unaltered, each bright colour precise. *Like the sea it shelters, enduring,* observed Jude, glimpsing – he guessed for the last time – the precious bay of Honfleur.

No sooner witnessed, the scene disappeared. Jude's plane veered northward abruptly, passing wide windswept knolls where once he had spent the day sketching. Soon these fields too disappeared, and then again the plane banked, and white sheared-off cliffs appeared, marking the continent's edge – and then, sharply ascending, his aircraft soared over the Atlantic, blindingly splendid in possibilities.

Cabin lights darkened. Jude put his head back, longing to rest some, but the events of the last days played and re-played in his head. He remembered his numbed disbelief throughout Auguste's conversation, the decision he'd come to out on his terrace, the call he had made to the airlines, reserving the first available ticket.

"Round-trip, Monsieur?"

Ever so briefly he'd paused.

"No. One way only. Prince Edward Island. As soon as possible."

Not until he had said this, expression shaping still inchoate perception, was Jude completely aware of what it was he had decided. He was leaving Paris, most likely forever, since it was clear, though he did not yet know the reason, that she could not come to him.

Starting all over, he mused. *New workroom, new colleagues, only my paints and my brushes...and even this dirt I adore is foreign sand to me without you,* he heard a voice in his head interrupt, echoes of a tender confession on faded blue paper – and then again he remembered the Seine, which would not be dismissed, and his own stubborn passion, perhaps even stronger than hers. He'd had no choice after all. A one-way ticket was all he required – that and a few days to prepare his departure.

Of course, in addition, there'd been three calls still to make. The final two – their words also replaying as clouds like smoke puffs passed his window – had been the hardest.

"Yes, of course, I'm quite well, Armand," Jude recalled having insisted, surprising the crisp younger twin with his mid-morning phone call.

"Change of pace, nothing more…Can't say for how long. Paris can often fail one in August."

"Jude, you should rest some."

"I will."

"Take your time."

"That is all that is left."

"Well, yes. Yes, of course. But you've only returned," Armand had protested, unsettled, sensing an odd finality in Jude's tone.

"Only again to disappear," had been Jude's breezy reply, and then to his surprise he too, casting about for the next words, had momentarily lost his stride.

"As always, Armand…"

"As always, Jude – not a word."

"I am away. That is all."

"Yes."

"For a while this time."

"But how to contact you?"

"Whatever paintings I wish to sell I will send. They will come through my physician. Letters included, Armand, I promise," Jude had added then, recovering kindness if not his buoyant tone, for he had worked fifteen years with the brothers Durand, whose efficiency, never mistaken for devotion, had nevertheless remained keen.

Armand had managed a courteous, befuddled, "Thank you."

His elder twin, hearing that afternoon of Jude's call, knew he would never again see his most celebrated artist. Solace remained though – considerable comfort – in the continued prospect of representing him.

"You can't be serious, Jude," Dr. Le Brun had exclaimed.

"I will be leaving in four days."

'But such a long trip!"

"I will manage."

"Jude, you must be prudent," was Théobald's careful response.

"Do you not think I am strong enough?"

"I think you should wait."

"Because I'm an invalid still?"

"Of course not."

"Then why should I not go?"

The reasons were many, Dr. Le Brun knew, why Jude, who still grew fatigued after brief walks through Paris, should not make this trip.

"Théobald?"

After all, his patient had only recently begun to live independently of Germaine.

"Are you there, Théobald?"

"Paris has patrons," Le Brun had offered then, lamely.

"I have painted nothing since I returned to Paris."

"These things take time."

"I haven't much of that left."

"Inspiration will come Jude, *believe me*."

"Nevertheless I must go."

"To an icebound Canadian island?"

"Yes."

"But how will you paint there?"

"Constantly. Skilfully. As I have never painted before in my life, Théobald. *I have no doubt of it*."

Again Le Brun had reflected – not, this time, in order to contradict Jude, but because he had heard something he once believed he would never again hear in Jude's voice: conviction – no, more than conviction, uninhibited fervour. In a flash he'd reviewed the past year's long struggle. The one constant – and there was only one thing which had never altered – was the painting Jude would not part with. *Half Moon* had gone with him from the Left Bank into Normandy, from Honfleur back to Paris, ever-present companion in the days of his exile. And yet at the start of this phone call – Le Brun had considered it odd – Jude had asked if he might leave the precious portrait with his best friend for safekeeping.

All of a sudden that best friend had known. Jude had no need of his painting. His model had found him.

"Jude –"

"Please don't say no," Jude had interrupted. "Because I should like – I should like to think, Théobald…that I might be leaving with your blessing. That is all."

Another long silence – another struggle deep within Théobald. Right reason argued for caution; his heart, more forceful witness, disagreed. As physician he had obligations; as a friend, he was fiercely devoted.

In the end, recalling Germaine's words, he had come down on the side of incontrovertible truth. *The miracle he must do himself, Théobald. Deep in his own heart.*

"Go with more than my Godspeed, Jude," he had said then. "Go with confidence. You will never be stronger. And go quickly. Waste not a moment, for fate has a way of gainsaying even the soundest prognosis."

Peace like a rare Parisian snowfall had fallen then upon Jude.

"I will take heart in those words."

"Take heart in whoever awaits."

"So you have guessed then."

"I have had a passing acquaintance with your head, Jude, remember? Not every thought of course," Le Brun had added with a slight laugh, determined to hide the deep sadness of parting. "On occasion, though, here and there an insight" – He stopped, having masked nothing. "Will you be back?"

"I wish I knew."

"Ah."

"Perhaps, from time to time, on my own I'll pass through."

"And the lady?"

"I suspect she cannot come."

"Pity."

"Yes."

"I should like to have seen her."

"You have already."

"So I surmised."

"Many times this past year."

"And each time I just stared. Such expression, Jude…So unique."

"She is indeed very fine."

"I meant the portrait."

"They are one and the same."

Jude paused. Then, with much effort, a coda: "Théobald, I was to tell no one. Those were my sole instructions. I know only my destination, and that she is waiting, and that she was not, as the papers presumed, lost with the others. For a lifetime you've kept my secrets. This too you must honour."

"Forever."

"Because," continued Jude quickly, fearing the weight of the next words would cause him to stumble, "try as I might, I could not vanish from you, Théobald – leaving no trace, no explanation, as I must do with the others. No, not from the hands that saved me. She would not want me to. I will say simply, whenever I find her – I will say there is one…and only one" – here at last he did falter.

"Who again says hello," Le Brun had gamely supplied.

"In return I will send –"

"There is no need."

"Sketches. Letters. Notes to Germaine enclosed, Marie-Claude, Sœur Eugénie, Dr. Meurice. Yours alone will bear a postmark. To the others, when it is time, you must simply say…"

"That you are painting, Jude, splendidly, in the place you work best."

꙳ ☽ ꙳

Only Rebecca Chase had not been surprised by Jude's call. In her heart, all along, she had known he would not go to Vienna.

"I must go though," she had managed evenly. "I've no choice."

"Of course you must."

"A chance like this, after all –"

"Once in a lifetime."

"Like you," she had answered, reaching still for that blithe tone. Jude had made no reply.

"Will you stay in Paris?"

"No; no, I don't think so."

"Once again wandering –"

"It is my nature."

"Except for one summer perhaps."

"My home is my work now," Jude had responded, bypassing the inference, "wherever it takes me, so that Vienna would not – I mean for the two of us" – Suddenly, fingering the coils on his telephone wire, he had murmured. "Rebecca, I'm sorry."

"Don't be, Jude."

"I had hoped…I mean once I recovered…"

"I'm very glad to be making a new start. And such a good one! You must come hear a concert."

"Yes. Yes, I must."

"In a year, two at the most, I will be principal harpist," she had proclaimed, feeling instantly foolish for the transparent self-promotion.

"Herr von Bergen is lucky."

"Time will tell, I suppose."

"It always does."

Silence had followed – something akin to the stillness after the last perfect note of a remarkable performance, and then Rebecca had suddenly felt a gnawing impatience to be off, and the receiver had felt suddenly heavy in Jude's hand.

"Stay well," she had concluded. "You have fought hard for your health, Jude."

"Play well, Rebecca. You have fought hard for this chance."

Jude's response had fallen damply. He could share nothing more with her, least of all the truth, so unexpected, and so he had said her name one more time, nothing more.

"All the best," had been her rejoinder – a jarring note, falsely played, but he had repeated her vale, gently, and then it was over.

Jude's plane pierced the last wafer-thin coating of clouds, leaving France and its steep Norman cliffs far behind – Étretat, Montmartre, the Champs-Élysées, the Crillon – yes, even the Crillon, although the lady who'd overpaid for his song waited still.

How he would find her, he was not at all certain. Yet he was convinced he'd succeed, just as he firmly believed he could endure the twelve-hour crossing ahead. After all, there would be a break on the mainland – Montréal Airport – and then another short respite in Halifax, Nova Scotia.

Montréal, as it happened, exhausted him further. Like Orly terminal it was chaotic. Many flights, including his next one, had been delayed several hours. The bistros had closed. The counters beside them were under construction. Jude had declined an available wheelchair, unexpectedly offered, though the walk was extensive from one gate to the next.

Not until midnight was he was airborne again – ninety turbulent minutes to Halifax. At two in the morning he touched down at Charlottetown airport, its tiny terminal deserted, darkness like velvet drawn over the island's bright fields. Again, unsolicited, he was offered a wheelchair.

Pale now and very unsteady, he considered a moment. He recalled the day he had arrived in Honfleur – the harbour, the boats, above all his driver, efficient and kindly, preparing to wheel a stretcher out of the ambulance across to the quay.

Have you no chair? Jude had asked then – how well he remembered winter's tenuous light – *something with wheels so that I might arrive... less defeated?*

No, he would not take a chair now, and for the very same reason.

"I'll take a map, though," he told the attendant, "if you have one. And the phone number for a taxi. And" – he glanced at the scribbled note in his hand – "directions to Cap-Egmont if you would."

The attendant's eyes widened.

"Is it very far?"

"Well, yes. Yes it is. Perhaps not in distance – the island is small after all – but the road follows the shoreline…and in the darkness, Monsieur, so late at night after all…"

"Dawn will follow," Jude insisted, despite the crushing fatigue he could no longer conceal.

"I will phone for a cab, then."

"I am obliged."

Jude was soon seated in the lone taxi that had pulled up to the terminal. Within a brief quarter-hour, lulled by the car and the quiet and the thickening salt winds, he felt himself giving way, as though deeply sedated, falling again into that dark place he'd come to know well that previous winter.

Dawn, he reminded himself – *a matter of hours, nothing more.*

The thought gave no comfort. Cap-Egmont loomed unfamiliar, out of reach. Journey's End seemed just that, aptly named – some dreamscape finale.

"She will be waiting," Jude murmured.

"Did you say something, sir?"

"Nothing," he answered, as though from a distant place.

He tried to picture her waiting, standing next to some window, then corrected the image, for of course she would be sleeping.

No matter, he thought. *There'll be a lobby…I'll tell the clerk* – his projections fragmented. The clerk – if one existed – might not receive him at such an hour. Certainly no one would call her. His taxi would have left by then, like the remaining shreds of his resilience.

Rain moving in from the mainland began. Jude sank back down into his seat. He closed his eyes once again, mesmerized by the sound of rubber blades on the windshield, comforted by the thought of a bit of sleep and its renewal.

Sleep refused to be summoned. Perhaps he had passed the point where such a thing could occur. Perhaps he recalled his lack of vigilance off the Champs-Élysées. Whatever the cause, with his head on the backrest, Jude McCallister remained aware, ever so vaguely, of his precarious place at this time, on this road, along this heretofore unfathomed shore.

Soon even this mindfulness waned. Only the scent of thick pine groves remained, and the salt and the sweet, heady smell of wet sand near the cab. He remembered Deauville. He remembered Honfleur. He remembered of all things the blissful drip into his arms which Sœur Chantal would provide. And then, startled by the image of that hospital room, he opened his eyes. Something was wrong again, he was sure of it, someone again was approaching from…from where? There wasn't a house or a light or a car to be seen for miles, only the dark, which he felt he must avoid at all costs, or perhaps surrender to it – he was not sure, he could not say…if he could only just sleep.

"Is there a place I could stop nearby?"

"A restaurant?"

"A hotel if we come to a town."

"No town here for miles."

Jude slumped again in his seat. The driver glanced in his mirror. His passenger's head had fallen back onto the leather. The face was ashen, immobile, his fitful sleep laboured as they moved on in the rain.

⁀☾⤸

"Bit of luck you've had, sir," Jude heard, startled by the sound of the driver's voice in the darkness. "Seven Pines has a room. Pretty deserted in fact, old and in need of repairs as it is. Still, so far out on the point, it was the best I could do."

Jude lowered the window. All he could see was one lone house in the woods. All he could feel was overwhelming fatigue.

"Thank you," he managed, surrendering his suitcase as he struggled to get his bearings and then eased out of the car.

They walked in silence up the long driveway. Jude paid the fare, or what he thought the driver had said was the fare.

By way of farewell the driver said only, "Rain's due to clear out just past dawn. Tomorrow's drive should be fine."

He placed Jude's bag by the door.

"Thank you again," Jude called into the wind as the taxi moved onto the road leading eastward – without him – back into Charlottetown.

Jude was led to his room.

The clerk disappeared.

Without removing his clothes, Jude fell onto his bed, sounds of a strange sea and the strong scent of cedar filling his room.

Not until noon on the following day did he awaken. He lay utterly still, watching the brisk offshore breeze blowing the curtains back from his window. He could hear seagulls nearby, the surf even closer, a lone raspy lawnmower out past the porch. He stood and walked to the window, not knowing what scene would await him, for the only sensations he could remember were fear and the strong smell of pines in the distance. Hence he was unprepared for what then overwhelmed him – what would always undo him – colours so fine that his heart filled to bursting and his arms longed for his model and his hand yearned to paint once again, for now he at last understood, gazing at the rich gentian blue of the sea, the contrasting red of the earth, the green and gold fields and pale dunes in the distance, why she had chosen of all places this one – island more like a canvas than a minuscule province surrounded by water.

The exhaustion, the doubts, the previous evening's disorders melted away. Warmth filled his room, or perhaps it was strength that Jude felt, he couldn't be certain – he wanted only one thing now. Strangely enough, he felt time running out on him.

Tides were again rising when he walked to the desk by the stairs. An old weathered clerk looked up, confused, as though surprised to see a guest appear.

"No, no there's no phone here. But about a mile down the road..." He stopped, looking closer at Jude. "I'll send my son. He can phone for you there. Shouldn't be more than an hour."

Shortly past three Jude was again on his way, heading due west into the sun once again, passing the port town of Summerside, which brought to mind Normandy's grace, then moving inland through vivid fields that resembled primary tones about to be mixed. Twice, on the misty clay high roads, the driver took a wrong turn. Twice he retraced his route, finally reaching Mont-Carmel on the windswept Acadian coast just past five. While he refuelled there, Jude consulted his map.

"Cap-Egmont's the next town. We can ask someone there."

The car made a long slow descent, rounded a sudden sharp bend near the shore, then slowed to a halt by the half-hidden wharf where, not six days before, Serge Pellerin had said goodbye to Violette.

The brisk wind had strengthened, snapping the tricolour flag – Évangéline symbol, colours of France – floating over the harbour.

"Journey's End, was it, sir?"

"Yes. Local guest house."

The driver disappeared into the tackle shop beside the docks. Jude remained in the taxi. The afternoon sun slipped away, indifferent to Jude's impatience.

"Not far at all," confirmed the driver, turning the car onto the dirt road cresting directly behind the harbour. They passed the same clustered homesteads Caroline had seen on her way, heard the same vivid silence as red and green fields replaced woodlands, came at last to a yellow farmhouse set among aspens and wheat fields and two crimson barns.

"Stop," called Jude suddenly. "There's a sign on the grass there – next to the driveway."

"Shall I check, sir?"

"I'll go."

"But it might not be Journey's End –"

"Still," Jude replied, oddly drawn to that pale house with its white trim, red roof and intricate mouldings surrounding the gables, "I could use the slight walk."

He made his way toward the sign swinging fast in the wind, read the ornately carved letters, then walked back to the car.

"Journey's End," he said simply, in a tone which he hoped sounded calm, but his hand trembled as he paid for the ride and took his small bag from the back of the cab.

The taxi backed out of the driveway and disappeared.

Jude remained some moments longer, facing the suddenly deserted road. Directly ahead was a winding clay path slicing through twin seaside fields – one the colour of lemons, one a rich apple green. Both meadows rose in the distance – a barely perceptible swell, then obligingly fell and disappeared into the most undiluted, indescribable colour of blue he had ever seen – deeper than morning's rich gentian, softer than navy.

So there it is, he thought, disbelieving, *the sea she has chosen to face. And all along I was facing it too, on the opposite side, only in that place the waters were restless, pounding immense cliffs, and here they are wise, and no longer struggle, and their reward is a celestial tone, clear and eternal, surpassing even the rose on that cathedral façade.*

He turned and walked up the drive to the porch. The red front door was unlatched. He pushed it open with care, finding himself in a small central hallway. To the right was a parlour; straight ahead was a staircase; to the left, through an archway, was an octagonal space, once used for dining, now the reception room.

Honorine Vallère looked up from her large desk. Under the archway she saw a tall grey-haired man – clear and expressive blue eyes, mouth with faintly upturned expectation, face weathered by life, she imagined, more than the sun, for the complexion was pale, remarkably pure, yet burnished tracks of experience seemed to colour his features. His body was strong, though only recently so – this too she surmised, noting the fact that the man held a cane in one hand, so that as he approached she sensed that his force, which was strangely compelling, came more from his heart, or his head, or wherever determination took root, than from bones or limbs or muscles or the sinews of form. He was uniquely attractive.

"Can I help you, Monsieur?" she said with a strong French inflection – unmistakable Acadian echo that made the question seem out of time.

All of a sudden, at the end of such a long trip, standing before the person who could direct him to Mrs. Devereux, Jude found himself at a loss. He knew so little, after all. She had said to write if he were not coming and that simply *Half Moon* on the envelope, care of Journey's End, would be enough. But how to ask for *Half Moon*? On an envelope, maybe, for she would have checked the post every day, long before it had been sorted. Besides, the house was not large – five or six bedrooms at most. Had she not gone for the post, the owner herself would have shown the note to each guest. Caroline would have claimed it.

"Do you need a room, Monsieur?"

"I – no. That is, yes. – I mean I'm not sure, Mademoiselle."

Honorine placed her pen down, folded her hands, and looked up.

"I suppose I do – yes, after all," Jude went on, having realized in that brief silence that should the worst happen – should he have erred, should she have vanished – he could not return 'til the next day.

Honorine reached one more time for her pen.

"There is a vacancy on the second floor," she said.

"Ah."

"A very pretty room."

The delicate dormer, remembered Jude. Its shape had intrigued him. "Yes, there is a lovely room under the gable. I'll take it."

"*Hélas –*"

"Whatever the price."

"It is already occupied."

"Well then another," answered Jude sharply, vexed by the delay, and his indecision, and all this aimless talk about rooms.

Honorine inclined her head. "I believe Monsieur will be happy with the room I have mentioned. Right next to the gabled one. Also faces the sea."

Jude waved his hand with impatience.

"Just your name," she continued, swinging around a large leather-bound book so that he could add his signature to the register.

"Don't you need my address?"

"No."

"A night's pay in advance?"

"Nothing. Not in Cap-Egmont. I will be paid at the end of your stay. Journey's End, in the meantime, will be your new home."

"Very kind of you," murmured Jude, regretting his previous tone.

She turned the book back around, then produced a large antique key.

"Your room is ready. Whenever you wish, you may go up."

"Thank you."

"Your suitcase will follow."

"There is no rush for my bag."

A substantial pause followed. Jude lingered still by the desk. He glanced around at the hall. He peered twice through the long double windows onto the porch.

"Something else perhaps?" Honorine ventured.

"Yes. Well not something…Someone. I am looking for someone. One of your guests, here. – A lady."

"There are several, Monsieur."

"She is expecting me."

"I was not informed."

"Neither was I!" Jude burst out at wits' end.

Honorine refolded her hands.

"Not 'til last week, I mean. After that" – he faltered a moment. Save for the surf in the distance there was absolute silence in the guest house.

"Caroline Devereux," he at last heard a voice which resembled his own pronounce, first time he'd said her name since she had left him the previous summer.

"You are mistaken, Monsieur."

"Mrs. Caroline Devereux –"

"We have no Mrs. Devereux."

"But she is staying here –"

"Not at the present."

"*I tell you she called. It'll be a week tomorrow.*"

Honorine thought, ever so briefly, of the woman who'd run to Père Gabriel for his phone. No, that woman was Violette Todd.

"One week exactly," Jude repeated. "Saturday last."

Honorine carefully turned the oversized pages.

"I am sorry, Monsieur. The lady you seek was not in this house then."

"*You are certain?*"

"Absolutely."

Hummingbirds, softly droning, suspended themselves alongside the window, making an effort, it seemed, to overhear Jude's next words.

"*Half Moon,*" he finally managed.

Honorine looked at him, quizzically.

"She might have used that name perhaps."

The large yellowed pages made a brittle sound as Honorine checked.

"There's been no *Half Moon*, Monsieur."

"A lovely woman…tall, very pale." Jude made an arc in the air as though to conjure her beauty. "Perhaps if you check one more time…" He watched Honorine search. He saw her shaking her head. He repeated, vaguely this time, "It'll be a week tomorrow…tall, very pale…" And then abruptly he stopped. It was no use. He had made a mistake, or perhaps Auguste had, or perhaps a cruel joke had been played. Yes, that was it. Another barbarity.

Honorine's form grew indistinct. Jude's mind raced over the past days, over the past months. It was all now a blur. The walls seemed to be closing around him. He needed to think. Out on the porch perhaps…perhaps in the air. He turned and walked toward the archway.

"I will be back," he said in a changed voice, leaving his suitcase beside the desk.

Honorine nodded, having seen in his fine eyes, in just those few moments, anticipation falter, then vanish, replaced in turn by despair.

"Out on the porch," she heard him repeat a few times before he disappeared into the hall.

Jude did not reach the porch. At the screen door he stopped, his path seemingly blocked by a volley of unanswered questions. Who on this earth would have inflicted such a blow – intentional, carefully planned, directed solely at him and therefore worse than the ones in the dark by the Pavillon? Only Théobald understood how he had valued that painting. Well, the brothers Durand also knew, and Claire Tierney and most likely Rebecca had guessed. And yet, Jude reminded himself, not even Le Brun knew the name of the model. Only Lucien, and of course Viktor, had the keys to that secret, discovered by chance on the quays of Honfleur.

…Lucien? Not in a lifetime would he have traduced his dear cousin.

…Viktor? Not in a lifetime would he have inflicted pain on his friend.

Which left Caroline Devereux. She alone would have known the details surrounding the making of her portrait. She might have told someone – a whispered confidence to a false acquaintance, a cry of anguish to a sympathetic one.

Jude stared through the screen at the green and gold fields and clay paths and cerulean sea in the distance, forever hoarding its secrets.

Not in a lifetime would Mrs. Devereux have recounted that morning in August. She was on this island, he was sure of it. Somewhere near Journey's End. And she would remain where she was until the leaves fell, of that too he was certain, although he guessed now that she was here with another name – one he might never recognize.

There was a creaking sound on the porch as an elderly gentleman settled himself into an old wicker rocker. Ever so slowly, the sun inclined toward the horizon. In the ensuing embrace the sea blushed a soft mauve, the china blue clouds became rose, the spruce green of the pines darkened to something like indigo – and all of a sudden Jude turned. There was a way still, he realized, rushing back through the archway.

"My suitcase – have you sent it up?"

"I will do it directly."

"No! Not yet. I'd like to open it –"

"Here?"

"There is something I need now."

Honorine could only think of some critical medication.

"It will not take a moment," Jude urged, fixing his gaze on her intensely.

Honorine was suddenly fearful, no longer of illness but its opposite, a strangely forceful vitality that had overtaken the man, drawing her into its sphere. She produced the small bag, which she had moved behind her desk, then watched him open it hurriedly, search through its meagre contents, take out a sketchbook, pencils, his tin full of crayons.

Too stunned to speak at that point, she simply stared as Jude sketched, taking his time but wasting no time, tossing one crayon away, finding another, reenacting this procedure over and over again, as though neither shape nor the lines that produced it bore the main burden of importance. He seemed to be after colour. The rest would follow somehow.

Colour, she said again to herself, hearing the sound of each crayon dropped back into its tin. The room then fell silent, as Jude retouched a few lines with a charcoal pencil from his pocket.

"Here," he announced, neither hopefully nor in triumph, but with the dispassion of a physician absolutely certain of his conclusion.

"This is the lady, Mademoiselle. It is she who has called me. Perhaps I said the wrong name – I do not know – but this is the lady. She gave the address of your guest house. I should like to find her...I *must* find her. She has been waiting."

Honorine stared at the sketch. The likeness was haunting – not just the face but the hyacinth eyes, the midnight black hair, the translucent pale skin, the dusky rose knowing mouth.

It was indeed that same woman, as though she were right there before them – ardent, insistent, about to rush down the road to place a phone call to Paris.

Honorine nodded, still astounded, then looked up once again.

"The lady you seek, Monsieur, is Violette Todd."

Jude leaned his weight on the desk.

"You will find her there, on the beach, if you cross the road by the fields. She spends most of her days there, sometimes her evenings, though for the life of me…"

"Go on."

"…what with shores so deserted now, I cannot imagine what she is thinking. Yet she just watches the tides change, or takes long walks in the surf, or sits with a book on a blanket, or writes in a notebook. On occasion, at nightfall, I've gone down to fetch her. I was afraid she would miss her supper, or lose her way in the dark."

Jude reached for his cane. A slight smile played on his face.

"I'll go today, Mademoiselle. I shall fetch Violette."

He closed up his bag, turned and walked toward the archway.

"Your sketch, Monsieur," Honorine called.

"It is yours," Jude replied. "Imperfect gift, truly, for I can never repay you."

꩜ ☾ ꩜

Jude stopped at the roadway, waited for a truck to pass, then made his way through the fields, eyes fixed on the ocean, shimmering in the distance like aquamarines tossed to the wind.

When he reached the rise in the earth he suddenly paused again. The sea's horizon was visible still, but the shoreline, the beach, the meadows dissolving into sand were obscured. Only the hillock remained, and in a matter of moments Jude would pass that knoll too, and the fields and the road and his old life would vanish, and the tides and the sea and surf would reappear – and the woman.

He let his cane take more weight. The old anxiety surfaced. How changed would she find him? He thought back to Rebecca, who had entered his house in Honfleur and had seen his paintings and had turned to him and had wanted him more than ever. Ah, but he had never held Rebecca before then, had never loved her to desperation, had never painted and pursued and tormented her until at last she had revealed herself – once and for all uncovered, so seemingly frail, yet so terrifyingly strong, having been scarred more by life than any flames on her flesh.

Image upon image flooded his memory. Everything circled back to the mirrored salon of the Hôtel de Crillon, where she had paid such a great sum for him to take notice, and where, when he had finally looked, he had seen his own soul.

He murmured her name. His anxiety subsided. She too had been plunged into hell this past year. Like him she'd been felled, left for dead in the dark, as though pitiless gods had punished them both for the way they had loved, without limitation – shameless, overt and near-blasphemous thing.

He was much altered. Perhaps she was too. No, he reflected – only he could have changed. Time might pass, envious deities pursue, but she would always resemble the nude he'd once painted, beauty which had eluded him until he had met her, love also unknown 'til that day.

He thought again of his painting, left with Théobald.

He thought again of Théobald.

You are strong enough, Jude, he remembered. Indeed, he could swear he'd heard the phrase again, vaguely, though it may just have been the surf on the other side of the hill.

Either way, Jude responded, half to himself, half into the wind, "If you think so, Théobald," and thus he decided – no longer thwarted by the earth's rise, or the greater obstacle of his own unease – that he would walk on toward the beach, and find the woman at long last, and present himself as he was now, for she herself had once done the same, and it could not possibly cost him more than the price she had paid for her agonizing, self-fulfilling, passionate revelation.

He walked over the ridge, followed its steady slope downward, came upon a staircase, paused once again at the top of the steps.

The beach was wide, Jude saw – not like Étretat's blanched narrow sands, although like Normandy's outpost, it was almost deserted. The tides were on their way in – swift but unruffled, so that small groups of clam diggers hastened to finish their task. A few families shared picnics. Older boys crouched by a sand castle in progress, or played cards near the steps, or braved the nearly autumnal Gulf Stream for a late summer's swim. Scattered among them were sunbathers, catching the last of the day's warmth.

Jude stared at these last for a moment, none of whom he recognized. He shaded his eyes and scanned the beach several times, staring again when a woman appeared, rounding a sand dune to the north, also heading for a swim.

It was not Caroline.

"Is there another beach past that bend?" Jude called to the boys playing cards. One of them shrugged.

"Just a large private house."

"Nothing more?"

"A few docks."

"Private too?"

"Part of the house," said the boy. "Only their own boats go there."

"Thank you," Jude murmured.

The boys returned to their game. Jude surveyed the beach one more time. The sand seemed fine, the terrain flat, save for a large wide grey rock to his right, strange and solemn in such a place, and a few smaller ones on his left.

I have missed nothing, he told himself, holding on to the railing from his vantage point at the top of the stairs. *Caroline is not here.*

As it happened, Jude was mistaken. He could not possibly know she had spread her blanket next to that large rock, on the opposite side, where its reliable shade had offered some shelter from the glare of an earlier sun.

A last glance at the shoreline revealed nothing more. Dismayed, Jude turned back toward the ridge.

Tomorrow, perhaps, he mused, although he sensed with a vague dread that should he fail to find her before then, he would never again see Caroline's face.

At the top of the staircase he paused. Cool shadows had spread from a stand of pines at the end of the path, casting the fields in a grey tone that almost matched the large rock which had so strangely intrigued him. Perhaps it was the shape, or the fine polished texture – Jude would never be sure – but he turned one more time, remembering rows of menhirs in Bretagne – huge, immemorial stones he had painted. He recalled age-old dolmens, painted too many times – altar-shaped rocks of prehistoric rites, and then once more he thought of fate, and jealous gods, and time passing, and then he observed that the tide was coming in quickly, and then Caroline stood, as though to scan the horizon.

Clearly visible beside the rock, she removed her white wide-brimmed hat and unclasped her hair, which seemed to welcome the moment as she raised her face to the wind. She wore a simple white blouse and long flowing white skirt, partly obscured by the rock, but which now and again billowed back in the breeze.

She did not see Jude, though her face was turned slightly in his direction. She merely stared at the ocean, as if she were sounding its depths, even from the rock where she stood, or decoding some fathomless script in its surf – Jude could not tell, so overwhelmed was he by the sight of her – so unexpected, so lovely – she who had haunted his days and stalked his long nights, there before him like a naiad, rising on unfamiliar shores.

He continued to stare, taking in what he feared might be merely illusion – fragile substance of art – as he had done once before then, watching her in her box at the Comédie-Française. The angle now was the same, the pose identical – arm reclined languidly, not over a railing this time, but on a large grey stone rock, head tilted slightly, eyes looking forward, seemingly fixed on eternal things. The palette only had changed – here indigo blue, there velvet red, glint of the sun replacing a thousand taper-like bulbs, wheat-toned sand by her feet where intricate carpets had been – and Jude was glad, all of a sudden, that he had left Journey's End with his sketchbook inhand still, for there was nothing to do now but sketch, as he had done on that evening, knowing of no other way to introduce himself, properly.

She remained there, unmoving. He coloured his portrait with care. When she sat down again he was almost finished, and so he himself sat, and with the crayons he'd stuffed in his pocket, he filled in the background.

He put no name to it when it was done.

☽

"Have you a minute?" Jude called again to the boy by the stairs.

"Well, we're just dealing a hand –"

"Time enough then to take this picture to the lady beside that rock."

The boy turned toward the stone. There was no lady in view.

"The other side," Jude insisted. "Here's a dollar if you hurry."

The boy approached shyly. Jude tore the sheet from his sketchpad. The portrait, offhandedly offered, made the boy stare once again, not at the rock now but at the picture, filled in as it was with the magic of the island, known to him since his childhood, overlaid splendidly with some other thing, which he had yet to discover, and so he had no name for its yearning.

"But only if you hurry," Jude added then, firmly.

The boy was back in a minute, seated beside his friends, taking his cards up, having left the gentleman's sketch.

Jude waited a moment, wondering if she would stand, but she did not, and so he made his way down the steps and moved toward the rock on his right.

Caroline saw a shadow cross the sketch she clutched in her hands. She knew at once he had approached, casting that darkness instead of signing his name, but for some moments she remained very still, utterly silent, until at last she looked up and fixed her gaze on his face, as once she had done before beside his piano, eyes still filled with the things they could not hide on that night.

"I was sure you would know the artist," Jude said.

She merely nodded.

"Do you recognize the man?"

Still she said nothing, although she stood, very slowly, as she had done when he'd seen her, although now she no longer gazed at the sea but into his eyes, equally deep, and then she raised her arm, deliberately, as one might do in a dream, and traced his mouth with her fingers, and touched his fine silvery hair, his temples, his cheekbones, and then she replied, barely audible in the rising night wind, "It is difficult, Jude. You are more beautiful than ever."

～❨☾❩～

Jude vaguely remembered flowered wallpaper – red and green blossoms on a cream-coloured background – or perhaps it was Caroline's mouth, which he insistently kissed on the landing of the staircase at Journey's End, or the green clasps on her blouse, undone in haste in her bedroom, or her white skirt in a moment unbuttoned.

Indistinct too were the moments it took him to lay her down on the crewel spread, and the exact colour of the comb he then removed from her hair.

He only remembered, precisely, the tone and texture of her markings, which he traced without rushing, as a sculptor might feel the surface of a fine work, completed.

Also he recalled how she began to move when he kissed the places he'd touched, and the fact that she resembled her portrait, and that when he entered her it was like the first time, as though they had never been parted, except that now he did not have to instruct her. Now she understood the remarkable power her body possessed, and was unashamed of it, as he rejoiced in his own force reclaimed, so that she was not so much consumed by his unsparing need as completed by it, made of the same thing as he was.

Not until midnight did they return to the rock where he'd found her. Save for high tide's assurance, there was absolute stillness. Reclined on the stone, Jude sat facing the sea. Caroline lay on the blanket, with her head in Jude's lap, losing count of the stars suddenly crowding the sky.

"Jude..." Her voice trailed off.

"I am here."

"For how long are you here?"

"For however long you remain."

"I can never return to Paris," she confessed at last, simply.

"So I've surmised," he replied, stroking her hair.

She turned her face up to him, searchingly.

"One-way passage, all used up," he went on with a slight smile, slipping away from the rock and onto the blanket beside her. "Might as well stay."

"Jude, *listen*. You should at least know –"

"What should I know?" he asked tenderly.

"I cannot leave."

"I do not care."

"Still –"

"This alone matters now," he insisted, "this and whatever nights may be vouchsafed to me still, exiled like you now, contented." She felt his fingertips on her neck, heard his voice also trail off... "Oceans away from a world I have also forgotten."

She knew he meant his ordeal – place not for a moment forgotten, although he said nothing more, for his mouth had once more found hers and his hands the half moon on her breast.

"Only this, Violette," she heard him repeat after a while, after he had slipped up her skirt and was once again moving his hands across her body, insistently.

"How do you know that name, Jude?" she whispered.

"Persistence," he answered thickly.

"How did you find me?"

"I painted you."

"No, I mean here."

"So do I," he replied, parting her legs so that he could enter her in the moonlight.

September passed quickly. October was brilliant. Jude painted often that autumn – the house itself, flint-toned fields in a storm, crimson paths to the beach, vacant ridges at daybreak. Abstracts too filled his workroom – an improvised studio adjoining their bedroom, itself crammed with landscapes and seascapes and above all else portraits: fishermen at the shoreline, Honorine at her front desk, schoolchildren in the damp sand, Père Gabriel by his church.

Mostly, though, Jude painted the woman, for as such, unidentified, she had appeared to him in his dark days, insistent object of longing when he could not yet shape her name, and later, when he could – creature of more obscure desire.

He preferred to paint her naked, with only her comb in her hair, although she often appeared in his seascapes – now smiling cryptically, now darkly pensive – of one mind with the island in either case, Jude McCallister judged.

On many occasions, while he sketched, there would be absolute silence. Other times they would speak – pliable sounds, blending in with his brushstrokes – of the dwindling scent of the pines, for example, or the uncommon cold of the surf, or the goldenrod meadows recently razed to the earth's height, or Trans Canada flight 407.

"And so you left him in Goose Bay?" Jude inquired one afternoon when she spoke again of this last thing.

"Yes – yes I did."

"Willingly?"

"I had no choice."

As he sketched she was nude, her leg tossed over the arm of a white wicker loveseat, her reflection repeated in the triple mirror behind.

"Max was waiting, you see. I mean at the time he was waiting. He died the same day I did."

Jude filled in his canvas with rust-toned reflections of the meadow's rise, clearly visible from their window. She had already told him of her resurrection in Susannah's house on Rock of Birds.

"I learned of both deaths the same day – his in New York, mine in the Gulf."

Jude nodded, stepping back from his canvas.

"It was time, after all. He had completed his story, one and the same with his life, and so the last conjured pages – I know this now – meant no more days to be lived – not by the man recollecting – not by the woman who wrote it. Same tale, as I've explained, Jude…I should like to say parallel, except that the lines met somehow."

"Much love in the meeting?"

"Yes."

"Love for Antonin also?"

"Much."

"Father and son, I assume."

"No. Not officially," replied Caroline, feeling strangely and suddenly, of all things, exposed. "Though it ran deeper than most blood ties," she hastily added. "Which is why I took such a long trip, so quickly. Antonin needed Max. Antonin always needed Max. Without that, I think, Max would have been long since defeated."

Quietly, Jude continued working. Caroline also fell silent. Up until that strange pause, barely perceptible, she had spoken freely, knowing that Jude's queries were never a challenge, but rather a sounding of his model's soul, much as he would caress her body, which as both artist and lover he never ceased to explore. Thus of her days without him he'd heard everything – or what he had thought to be everything – until that unique hesitation so late in the season, so unexpected, as though the wings of a dove had inadvertently brushed her mouth, stopping the next thought.

He had not mentioned the moment, although he'd observed it, for at the time he had been shading her cheekbones, and had noticed the dusky confusion which had coloured them, momentarily.

An instant, two perhaps at the most, and her customary pallor had begun to replace that rose tone. But by then Jude had guessed.

The image of something as yet undisclosed – more likely someone still guarded – had surfaced, uninvited, ever so briefly tinting a translucence betrayed.

It does not matter, he told himself firmly, cleaning his brushes as she swept up some stray wisps of hair with her comb. Had he not already told her as much? Had he not insisted, drunk with the sight of her on their first night, *I do not care, Caroline?* And had she not willingly still, despite his demurral – though he had never once asked her – had she not already shared much with him, without the slightest guile?

He knew her false name, for example, and the secrets it guarded – how she had had to forfeit the old one, saving the land of Todd's Farm in the process, making her peace with the days spent beside Maximilian, closing the door on his house and the exquisite book they had together made.

He knew that Antonin, star-crossed, had remained by her side, solitary guardian when fire again ravaged her life, and that in exchange for his kindness she had left him his own house.

He even deduced over time that this had not really been kindness, though she herself had not mentioned the chaste yet wild thing that had bound them together.

"I needed him too, Jude," was all she had said of her journey to Goose Bay and the diamond studs left behind. "Not the way I needed Max – no, not that strangely destined congruent reliance – but in another way, equally forceful. I suppose we were both Monday's children," she had concluded, her tone suddenly wistful. "Misfortune's siblings, joined from the moment we met."

Recalcitrant, still-golden leaves drifted down past the window behind them. Mechanically, Jude continued cleaning his brushes. Looking back on it he suddenly realized that she had never mentioned the reason for Antonin's exile. "Parole violations," was all she had murmured, and now, as she reached for her drape, he again guessed correctly. Antonin's sudden departure, so permanent, was somehow linked to her discomfiture, so badly hidden that afternoon.

It does not matter, Jude repeated, watching her move to the window to feel the breeze on her body. Desire intertwined with a stubborn unease overcame him so that he too stood and crossed to her and turned her around to face him and kissed her deeply. He had promised to keep her secrets, every one of them, and if there remained one she would not – most likely could not – impart yet, he would wait, respecting her silence, leaving her heart undisturbed.

He removed the drape from her shoulders – of its own accord it had fallen the first time, he remembered – and led her away from the window and made love to her with a desperation which reminded her of that first time, before Maximilian, before Antonin...before any other man was ever imagined.

ᴒ ☾ ᴖ

They lay intertwined as autumn's weak light disappeared – Caroline drowsily quiet, Jude pondering his obsession with a hidden occurrence he had no right to unveil.

Perhaps, he decided, feeling her stir toward him, it was the fleeting India pink that had suffused her cheeks while she'd paused – colour so comely, yet to her clearly unwelcome, as though some profound lasting thing that had occurred in his absence had to be hidden at all costs, not from him but from herself.

The half moon on her breast pressed against his own chest; the crossed swords on her ribs moved ever so slowly, like their sheer curtains at sunset, for by then she was breathing deeply, having fallen asleep in his arms.

Jude too tried to rest, although he failed. Like a groundswell his suppositions rose over the silence as she slept. He could have accepted, not without effort, some deep attachment she felt obliged to withhold from his own heart. He found it hard to ignore a passion she herself could not confront.

Still, lying awake in the darkening room, he reminded himself of his fervent pronouncement down by the beach when he'd found her.

I do not care, he told himself firmly yet a third time as sleep at last overcame him. *Wherever it is you have been, Caroline, I do not care.*

Caroline, however, cared deeply. On more than one occasion she had wanted to speak of Misha – not every detail perhaps, but the fact of him, his existence. Time and again she had tried. Yet for the strangest of reasons, she could not even mention his name. Even stranger – as she slept then, so profoundly, she dreamed of a deck overlooking the Hudson and a beautiful ship passing Land's End on its way out to sea.

☾

Jude stared at the ocean while Caroline dressed for dinner. He had resolved to set aside the insecurity that had unsettled him that afternoon. After all, he himself had shared only a portion of the year that had intervened since she had left him in Paris. Of the assault on his body he had spoken candidly once, nearing nightfall, while he had been painting her on a deserted sand dune. The telling had been brief, his voice throughout monochromatic, most of the brutal details – unendurable even in retrospect – omitted for both of their sakes.

On another occasion – sunrise out by the back barn – he had described the ride into Normandy, Honfleur, Marie-Claude, the home of Dr. Jean-Paul Meurice. Once again the account had been unadorned, its outlines rendered in blurred form, for as such the first days remained in his memory still, and though the ensuing spring with its resurrection would forever remain starkly clear in his head, Jude could not find the words to express the transcendent miracle wrought. Hence, of Dr. Le Brun he had said next to nothing. The few times he'd tried he had faltered, and so, toward the end of September he had merely shown Caroline the magnificent abstract he had been working on throughout the fall – elegant navy and crimson and curving white shapes, framed in ornately carved bronze-toned wood.

For a long time she had stared at the painting – finest work he had done since he had arrived in the Maritimes.

"Théobald?" she had finally asked.

"How did you know?"

"Because it's all there, Jude…Not all that he is, of course. You could perhaps never paint that, but I can see all you've said up 'til now."

"I haven't said much, I'm afraid."

"I haven't needed much."

With that she had turned and looked again at the painting. A lone blue jay, intrigued, had remained motionless, silent – watching them from behind the remaining two leaves on the slender white birch past their window.

"I love him too, Jude, you know. Not only because he has kept my secret, and my portrait, but because he saved your head, and your hands, and sent you back home."

"Paris was no longer my home."

"I meant back to me."

He had smiled vaguely, but said no more, for what remained was Germaine, whom he could not speak of yet, so immense was the weight of her hands pressing still on his heart – and Rebecca. Germaine, he suspected, he would someday describe to Caroline. Rebecca would never be mentioned. For a time his reluctance on this matter disturbed him, and then he had come to see he was right, not because any vestige of their short-lived passion remained, but because it had happened, the thing had existed, however fleetingly – interlude brief and resonant, like her harp strings. He could not now relay its outlines. Not even a hint of this intermezzo would he convey to the woman beside him. She would not judge him – of that he was certain – and yet she had struggled with such a fury to reclaim not just herself, but him too, that somehow he wanted even their grim separation to remain as she had believed they had been, undisturbed by the intimation that for a time he had wanted another.

Why then, he wondered, pausing on the staircase on their way down to dinner, *why was he still so reluctant to grant her a similar dignity?*

~ ☾ ~

Jude and Caroline, sole guests for supper that evening, were at their customary table, overlooking the porch and the starkly bared maples no longer shading Journey's End. The sea was at rest. Delicate clouds, resigned, were passing into the night. All around there was peace, island quiescence that ruled every autumn – poignantly brief reign – six weeks, nothing more, between summertime's languor and hard, barren November.

Only Jude felt excluded from this overarching tranquility. Caroline too, perhaps; he could not be certain. Twice she had turned toward the bay, as though searching for something, or someone, on the distant horizon.

Well she has done that before, he thought, briefly convincing himself it was only the sea which had called her. Indeed, from the first moment he'd seen her, standing beside that grey rock on the sand, she had often seemed drawn to some hidden allure in the tides. Sometimes at night, when she thought he was sleeping, she would silently rise and walk to the window and fix a curious gaze upon the ocean beyond. Other times on the ridge, thinking herself unobserved while he worked, she would stare at the same scene, making what had always seemed to him to be some uniquely strange contact with the indecipherable surf. In time he came to believe that she did in fact hear and see things forbidden to other souls, given her plunge into its Gulf and the selective welcome it had provided. He himself had heard in the tides mysterious greetings late at night in Honfleur, having also been spared alongside the same sea, though on its opposite shore.

All this and more Jude considered as Honorine served their coffee. Caroline turned a third time toward the now-charcoal horizon. Jude studied her profile with a painter's precision. He thought back to his studio overlooking Rodin's house, to those weeks when he had tried to paint her, searching in vain for the one thing he needed – her soul, without which his work was doomed to failure, and which she had so fiercely withheld from him. He thought ahead to the future, to the day when she might lament her starkly precipitous choice – passion so like her – to abandon everyone, everywhere, except for him, for the rest of her life.

This last haunting image remained as they strolled the beach after supper. Already perhaps – but no, not so soon. She would not be regretting so soon…In future days, maybe. He took her slim hand in his. They walked on in silence. What had happened, Jude wondered, as he had sketched in their bedroom that afternoon?

"Shall we go in now? You seemed tired."

"With such a beautiful moon, Jude?"

"Well I only thought –"

"Unless of course *you're* tired."

"I'm fine."

"Then let's just sit on the porch. It will be too cold soon for such things."

They settled themselves in the flickering light of an antique gas lantern alongside the door. The harvest moon grew gigantic. A few island cicadas, defying fall's frost on the lawn, managed to fill the crisp air with a tune.

Honorine's wicker rocker creaked in atonal response. Jude always chose this white chair, its collapsed tufted seat, deeply worn along one edge, matching the day he'd arrived: red, green and gold tones. Caroline for some reason favoured the swing chair beside him. It had always pleasured him to watch her sway there, ever so gently, although seasons ago its matching cushions had been removed.

He took her hand once more, pleased with the moment, pleased with her nearness, confirming again to himself, *Only this matters.*

As though in agreement, beguiling fireflies danced. A hoot owl called from the pines several times. The hardy cicadas played on.

And then Jude heard a voice that resembled his own ask, "Did Maximilian have any children?"

The swing chair came to a halt.

"Besides that strange bond with Antonin –"

"I never said it was strange."

"It was a bond, though."

"Well, yes…"

"Deeper than blood you said."

"I did say that, Jude," she agreed after a long pause.

"Which left me wondering," Jude persisted, "if there were perchance any others."

Sensing Caroline stiffen, he at once resolved – perhaps it was not too late – to say no more on the subject.

"A son, for example."

Caroline made no reply.

"You mentioned he'd married."

"Very briefly."

"Cecilia, I think…"

"Over before it began, more or less."

"Ah."

Stillness returned to the porch. Off in the distance the tides changed. Jude saw that the swing chair remained immobile – rigidly so – as did the woman beside him.

Why have I done this? he suddenly asked himself, despairing.

How has he heard this? she repeatedly asked herself, feeling her strength fail. *No, he has not heard. He has somehow divined that I have loved another, and that that other had to have been flesh of Maximilian's flesh – not Max as he was, so near to the end then, but Max as he'd once been – since I alone knew who he'd once been.*

She felt a tightening in her chest as Mikhail's image – precise, disturbingly palpable, superimposed upon Maximilian's, seemed to appear there in the darkness. Earlier in the day the same thing had happened, while Jude had been sketching her and conversing with her and had said that small phrase, *father and son*. Not until now though, since she had made her decision on Rock of Birds and had turned from the newspapers on Susannah's table, had she seen Misha so distinctly.

At the sight of him her heart ached. Her head throbbed. She had loved Misha once, yes, desperately, convinced Jude cared no longer.

But now, here, on this night, with Jude seated beside her – what was Mikhail doing *here*?

She longed to turn then to Jude, to cling to him as if she were drowning once more, but she could not reach. He could not help. He himself had stirred up those waters again – the irony pressed on her temples – with that repeated phrase, *father and son*.

Confusion mounted within her. Although the air had turned cold, she felt the rising sensation of heat out on the porch – suspicion of embers not yet extinguished, she guessed distractedly – a barn perhaps…her house…that searing reflection of Mikhail, left behind without so much as a word.

Recognizable dimensions of time present and past seemed to blend. Mixed in with the night wind she heard a strange fervent Welsh tune. Instead of the sea air she tasted something like sweat on her mouth, on her brow, sweet mysterious warmth after such cold in her mill house, sweet like the smile that came into focus at last – Mikhail singing, golden, like youth always triumphant, pushed aside in Susannah's kitchen – *what was he doing here?*

"Misha," she whispered.

Jude turned to face her.

"Mikhail," she repeated.

"Caroline, did you say something?"

"Mikhail Alexander Matson d'Olivier – Maximilian's son," she said clearly a third time, for Jude had wanted to hear it, and now she had said it, and from henceforth, she knew, there would be no turning back.

"A son," she insisted. "Maximilian had a son."

"Fortunate man," managed Jude.

"Yes; yes, he was."

The surf seemed unbearably close all of a sudden.

"Just about Antonin's age?" Jude asked.

Caroline merely nodded, remembering the photo now framed in Goose Bay.

"I thought so," Jude murmured, and then he slipped her hand from his in the darkness, brushing distractedly at a moth that seemed to be hovering near her forehead. After a moment it vanished. She refolded her hands in her lap – at least Jude thought they were folded until the moon shifted slightly, clearing the porch roof, bathing the love of his life in a pitiless glow, pale reflection of the way he himself had unmasked her. The fact dawned on him as he caught sight of her clasping and unclasping her hands – a fierce and repetitive gesture which also involved gripping her wrists, so fine and slender that her fingers encircled them, nails overlapping her thumb, digging into her flesh, involuntarily. With a sudden horror he recalled he had grasped those wrists too once, forcing her to drop his scissors, but not until after she had ravaged her image, something she now seemed to want to do once again, though there was no painting to deface now – only the model.

"Caroline," Jude said quietly.

She made no answer.

"Caroline," he insisted, reaching over to stop her hands, and in that touch she was recalled to the present moment, and a powerful anger welled up inside her, as it had once surged in his studio, for both times he had tormented her, forcing her to remember what she had preferred left untouched. In Paris, though, there'd been cause. His work was at stake. But now, here, with her choice clearly made, what right had he to decipher things she herself could not grasp – *what right?* They had lain hidden 'til now, like Anne-Sophie's letters in Raphael's box. But for Jude's persistence, Misha might have remained unresolved.

Jude tried to unclasp her fingers – metaphor for his probing, she thought, and so, angrier still, she pushed his arm away and suddenly stood and moved toward the edge of the porch, gripping a slim painted column to steady herself.

"Yes," she flashed, "Yes, Jude, they were the same age, both misbegotten, only with Antonin you could see it at once, slouching the way that he did through his days. With Mikhail it was different."

"Caroline, it is enough now –"

"Golden," she persisted, caught in the undertow of her recollections, "kissed by the gods people said, sent off to safety in the same war, refusing thereafter to take his rightful place in his father's heart. Thus he too remained lost. We were all lost in that house. – *Lost*," she repeated, her voice now so desperate that Jude tried to stand, thinking to move toward her, but she put out her hand and said, "No, there is no need. I have not finished yet," though what she really meant was, "No, it is not time. I do not know yet."

Her hand, no longer gripping the column, visibly trembled.

"Misha was christened in Nice – typical late afternoon Provençal baptism – high tides, bright sun. I remember these details for I rendered them carefully once. I repeat them now to you, Jude – though like the tides those days soon passed – because you have taught me tonight on this porch that nothing has changed since your veranda. Whatever the cost, you must see."

How well she knew him! He could make no objection. He simply stared at her frail face, wishing that she would stop, or that the now-silent cicadas would start, but they seemed to have vanished, and she seemed determined to continue, destroying them both in the process.

"Caroline, I beg you. Come to me. Let me undo the things I have said –"

"No! That cannot be. What you wanted to know you will hear, for despite the ocean you've crossed and the sorrow you've witnessed, you have a great need for facts, Jude, come what may." Her breath began to come hard. "I met him at Maximilian's –"

"I asked out of love," Jude cried. "I was wrong."

"Out of love he pursued me," she echoed, unsparingly, "though he could have had any woman, anywhere, and frequently did before last winter's misfortunes. I resisted at first. It proved too hard after a while, all at sea as I was, shining and bright as he was, blessed with fair winds all his life, sleek like the fine yachts he sold. His father feared this and tried to kill him. His playmate discovered this and almost did."

Jude buried his face in his hands, sorrow filling his heart – sadness for her, for himself, for the delicate idyll his pride had stubbornly shattered.

"Not that they wanted to protect me, Jude. No. Make no mistake there. They wanted what I gave Misha. Max with his great heart and Antonin with his great hurt – both of them fearing to trespass, but Misha feared nothing, and you were long gone I thought, and so I let him love me – yes, I did, over and over again, and we were discovered – I have never been clever with essential things, as you know, with the result that" – in spite of her efforts her voice finally caught here – "his playmate is forever in exile, and his father died on his daybed, unattended by me."

The precipice, glimpsed once before in his studio, loomed again at their feet.

"My plane crashed that same day. Mikhail's grief must have been crushing. He had wanted to spend the rest of his days with me, loving me as he did, and yet you could not be supplanted. Not even by Maximilian's son. What had begun out on your veranda had not been completed yet."

Her hand was calm now, her voice no longer uneven.

"Be content now with your facts, Jude. They have cost me more than you'll ever know."

She moved away from the post she seemed no longer to need. The last of the leaves on the red oak tree drifted into the wind.

"Such an odd thing," she added vaguely then. "The road not taken inflicting such pain on us both."

Jude watched her walk down the steps and disappear at the end of the drive.

⤵ ☾ ⤴

The night had turned cold, the air uncommonly still. Jude listened, hearing only the sea in the distance, and, close to the porch steps, Honorine's cat moving among the dried leaves. Caroline had not returned. With an ache in his heart he remembered her parting words. He remembered her voice, coming in little hard gulps as she had described Mikhail. He remembered Rebecca – not the morning she had entered his studio and had gazed upon his paintings, greeting him with such a clear love, but the afternoon she had vanished on Étretat's cliffs. That night had been the beginning of a briefly passionate liaison. This night, he feared, had been a finale.

He made his way down the drive to the deserted roadway beyond. But for the light by the hand-lettered sign there would have been absolute darkness, for the moon was now veiled in clouds that resembled smoke drifting in from the Strait.

At the highway he stopped. To his left were the vast groves of pine trees she loved; to his right were the dunes, dear to her also, stretching for miles by the coast. Straight ahead were the steps leading down to the sea.

Jude chose to search by the sea. In the choosing he shivered, not at all certain why. This was not, after all, Étretat. These waters were calm, save in a bad storm, and – but for its secretive rocks – this beach was level. Above all, Jude reminded himself, Caroline was not Rebecca. She knew every inch of this shore, every path through the sand. Indeed, it had often surprised him how she seemed to advance so precisely, without really *observing*, as though, having once known the fathomless depths of the Gulf, she could never be lost along its tame, shallow rim.

Why then this fear that refused to subside? The beach was absolutely secure. He was just overwrought. She was just past the ridge. There by the steps he would find her, or close by the dunes or the surf or some safe windswept place in between. *Madness such indecision*, he told himself firmly, making his way down the clay path toward the barely visible ridge.

At the foot of the staircase, though he adjusted his eyes to the moonless wide vista, he could distinguish no outlines. The black expanse of the sea seemed to have merged with the beach. Even the dunes to his right were gone, somewhere – he couldn't fix their location precisely, and so he stayed where he was, leaning against the railing, straining to hear a sound that might guide him…Off in the distance, ebb tide…beyond that, a foghorn…somewhere near to him, ceaseless, the swaying of sand grass.

K . L . V I D A L

Jude moved toward this last sound, guessing that it would lead him across to the south dunes. From there he would continue directly, straight down to the shore. The tides had already changed – a fact he gauged more by the wind than by sound. In little less than an hour the sea would seep in over the sand. In just under two it would cover most of the beach. As fast as he dared then, Jude crossed onto the dunes. There he rested a moment, getting his bearings as he sat among the murmuring reeds.

Oddly, their rustle disturbed him. *Slender and enigmatic stalks,* he thought, *deceptively frail things – self-possessed, swaying, never breaking…always surviving.* He recalled how they'd whispered, indifferent, keeping their counsel as he'd painted the dunes last fall. He recalled Caroline Devereux, hoarding her secrets as he had tried to portray her uniquely mysterious beauty in Paris. And then like the tides, unwonted images followed – the Left Bank, the Seine, the match he'd held out, her challenging gaze as she'd lowered her palm. Yes, that was Caroline Devereux, unbreakable will which gave the lie to her grace – solitary, self-sustaining, sand grass in the night wind.

Max had known this, Jude suspected, for she had spoken often of the heat in that house, the sweat on those books, her insistence on perfection – no time off, no mistakes – her tempestuous employer surprisingly pleased at the start, then hopelessly lost.

Antonin had also known. How else to explain that violent week by her charred house, sheltered only by her driver, who must have been made of some similar force, who gave up all hope of peace for the chance to possess her those days, his own way, shielding her from the violence neither mistrusted?

Jude thought of them all as he made his way toward the sea: Dr. Devereux, Susannah, Roger Gachet, Serge Pellerin. Each had in vain tried to possess the unyielding soul he now sought, so that Elliot had abandoned her, no match for that force, and Susannah had been abandoned, never knowing by what force. Serge had perhaps guessed; Roger had for certain known.

"Mikhail," murmured Jude as he reached the shoreline at last. "Misha," she'd called him. Golden. Unerring. Unafraid even of Max. He above all men would have known her, for he had undressed her, and made love to her, and it was in such intense physicality that Caroline's passion found its purest expression. Had not the mere recollection of this pleasure driven his own hands to frenzy under a half moon in Montmartre?

He waded into the tides – careful slow steps in the no-longer placid Strait. Twice he called out her name, but like everything else on this ambivalent night his voice disappeared. Finally he had no choice but to make his way back to the beach, where, in the frail glow of the moon which had ever so briefly reappeared, he scanned the shoreline for clothing, footprints, any remaining trace of her on the damp sand.

There was nothing.

He re-crossed the dunes, found the staircase again and sank onto the steps there, exhausted.

Jude was startled when he awoke to hear the tides cresting – not far from the staircase, he judged – though it was too dark still to see the shoreline. He felt the air still sharply cold on his hands. He saw layers of rose tinting a no longer black sky as, slowly, outlines of the bay seemed to step out of the shadows.

Jude did not stand. Perhaps he needed more light, perhaps he felt numb from the cold, or the wind, or that dull ache in his heart – he could not distinguish.

I will know more with the light, was all he promised himself, sensing the ridge, silent and steep, beginning to loom large behind him. He watched the railing beside him take shape, counted the steps as they appeared, noticed the outline of a child's toy dropped by the staircase. Finally, ever so slowly, like an old servant reluctantly summoned, the dunes emerged out of the darkness.

Still Jude McCallister waited. He stared out over the sea, navy blue and quite visible now. He studied the clarified stone of the jetty off to his left, scanned the surf straight ahead, shook his head slowly, murmuring "useless," having deciding another walk on the beach would reveal nothing more. She was not to be found there, nor, he had at last guessed, was she to be found by the highway, inside the pine groves, or out past the barn behind Journey's End. As she had done before, more than once, Mrs. Devereux had vanished. It was her way, he reflected, remembering sounds of his heavy door closing only last year in Paris when both painter and painting had been abandoned. He recalled Rock of Birds, at least as much of her resurrection as she had recounted, and realized now that in that renewal she had carefully, brilliantly, wilfully erased a lifetime.

Parallel moments, he recognized ruefully. Swift and passionate partings, abrupt and similar choices – and now again it had happened. Somewhere she had found shelter, or what she would make into shelter, in her own time, on her own terms, keeping her distance, her counsel, her wits, her resolve. He would never see her again.

The vividly layered sky became a monochromatic pale blue. He heard the soft tides begin to retreat from the dunes, a fisherman's trawler heading out past the jetty, the diminishing cries of a gull chasing the wind. Mixed in with these sounds was Caroline's vale that morning in Paris: *We should have been satisfied with la vie en rose, Jude. It is always a mistake to try and see things distinctly.*

⌐ ☾ ⌐

One thought only sustained him as he moved back toward the meadows. Once before, perhaps for the first and last time in her life, he could not say – she had come back to him, freely. He had returned to his apartment to find her waiting for him in the stairwell. Now again perhaps, while he had been searching for her by the shoreline, she had retraced her steps to Journey's End. She might be seated still on the steps there, same scent of her perfume filling the hallway, same timid unspoken 'Hello' to be whispered.

Jude hurried on toward the rise and saw the path stretching ahead – clay which was not quite dark red in the dawn, but rather more like a thin charcoal strip through the fields. Beyond, off in the distance, he could make out the roadway, the guest house, the barns – still somewhat vague, and then behind them the pine trees, nothing more than a blur.

It was that blur which made him stop again. The pines belonged so to this place. Fiercely, as though to no other earth they were rooted – sentinels guarding the passage out to the Labrador Sea. Try as he might to recall a different world, another day, wanting that same welcome now, that same woman waiting, he knew in his heart it could not be. Once and once only had such an encounter been granted him. Cavalier poplars were lining the Seine on that day. Those were Acadian evergreens lining the bluff up ahead, Maritime clouds parting above them, strange island rocks on the beach, not menhirs in Bretagne –

And then abruptly he turned, for it had occurred to him in that instant that he'd just walked the same beach without seeing that rock. No doubt he'd passed it – several times, close perhaps – he could not say – he hadn't Caroline's unearthly orientation on a dark beach with the tides out. Besides, there'd been mist, later fog, so that the chiaroscuro of sea-dawn had obscured even the dunes 'til after he'd wakened. By then he had ceased to watch, ceased to hope, focusing more on past scenes than on the unfolding grey present. And yet the one thing he needed – last to emerge from the darkness, perhaps, because of its battleship halftones – had appeared. Somehow he'd missed it, thinking only of Mikhail – Misha, she'd called him, remorse and envy intertwined in his heart as he remembered.

He still thought of Misha, although now he missed nothing as he descended the steps and crossed the beach slowly, as he had done on the day he'd arrived. The sand drifts had shifted during the heavy winds of the night, so that the beach felt more than ever uneven under his feet. He stopped to listen before he rounded the rock. Surf and sand grass and wind filled the air – nothing more. Still, he walked on.

If I find you again, Caroline he thought resolutely, *I will hold on to you forever…No*, he corrected himself, as a flock of geese, silent and grave, made their elegant way through the lightening sky, *No, never again tightly. Letting go when it is time.*

There where he had seen her the first time, Jude did indeed find
Caroline, huddled against the rock on the damp sand. Her head was
bent down, her arms clasped round her knees, her long untamed
hair undone. He could see that she shivered. He could hear that she
wept still.

"Caroline," murmured Jude.

She seemed not to hear him.

"Look at me," he insisted, "Look at me so that I can see your
face, dearer to me than my life."

She raised her head slowly. He knelt down beside her. Her eyes,
mauve like the tentative sky, seemed even deeper in the matching
light. As he brushed the tears from beneath them, he remembered
again that violent struggle beside his failed portrait. He recalled too
what had followed – absolute silence – both of them stunned by the
hurt he had inflicted. And yet he had willed such a thing. He would
have done anything to keep that image, failed as it was, intact. To
keep the one that succeeded he'd staggered back from the dead.

"How I have loved you," he managed, murmur borne instantly
out to sea by the wind. Two more words, something like "...Such
desperation," trailed off behind them.

By then he had drawn her against him. Her curls, damp and
thick, mixed with his own fine grey hair. Her breath was moist on
his cheek. Her heart beat with a frightening force on his own, for
she trembled still, strangely, though whether from cold or the night
endured or some other darkness he could not tell, and so he merely
said, "No more, Caroline....Hush. There is no need," and as he
rocked her he again recalled Paris – not the morning she'd left
him, bruised in body and spirit, but the last time she'd lain beside
him, face and hair wet just like now, fearful of daybreak, knowing
deep in her heart somehow – though they had promised to be
together again, six weeks the latest, before October had stripped the
last chestnut trees lining the river – that fate even then had other
plans for them both, and that nothing would ever again be the same.

How prescient had been her misgivings that morning! He had been left for dead by the time the chestnuts were bare; she had been stripped of all but her pride. Now again here she was, seemingly lost in his arms.

"Caroline," he repeated, holding her even tighter as the offshore wind sharpened. "Be still now. It's over."

There was only the wind in response.

"The pain I have caused you is over," he repeated.

She moved away from him slightly, and, still saying nothing, raised her eyes to meet his. Fleetingly, as on that first day, he saw the expression that had haunted his days since she had first stared at him by his piano. Nothing before or after had so bedevilled him as an artist. No one had ever bewitched him so as a man. Why such a thing should have been so he had never quite understood. He had painted hundreds of faces before that brief glance at the Crillon, countless expressions of sadness, anger, pride, hope or despair, and yet her face alone – those immense eyes with their intimate knowledge of extreme good and evil, that barely perceptible smile, the inexpressible pallor – suffering's legacy with its dusky rose overlay of survival – above all the understanding that had passed between them, wordless, definitive – her face alone from that moment on gave him no quarter. Though he had once caught its allure – lavish, mysterious grace notes on his canvas – and though he had many times since then pressed his still powerful body into her frail one – she had remained somehow *unattained* – exotic, incorporeal siren song in his head, elusive and irresistible shape in his hands.

He never *would* truly have her, that much at least he now grasped, even if he had never, most likely could never, define the nature of her attraction. He suspected this very enigma to be the source of her power, for in her nearness, even when he could not see her, he painted as he was born to paint, and in her presence, when at last he could touch her, he surrendered to pleasures never before imagined in his experienced nights.

How foolish he'd been all along! How blind not to have understood! It had taken the previous night, with its agonized search, to make him at last see. From that first mirrored glance, he had wanted what could never be.

"I was wrong," he said abruptly, as though she had carefully followed the silent train of his thoughts. "You can never be claimed, not even by me. You must be loved, that is all, sometimes fiercely, other times at a distance, but always, always..." He stopped. He had said that word once before and the fates had laughed at them both. Now, understanding somewhat the ways of destiny and Mrs. Devereux, he knew better, and so after a moment in a quiet voice, he merely added, "Come. No more tears. Let me still love you. Let me take you with me when I leave Journey's End."

There followed silence akin to the moment when those beautiful migrating birds had vanished off to the south.

"So you are leaving, then," Caroline answered, first words she had spoken since he had found her crumpled against her grey rock.

"As soon as possible."

She nodded vaguely.

"Will you come with me?"

She shook her head.

"And yet you waited all night for me, Caroline –"

"Nevertheless –"

"Not where I thought you might be. No, that staircase was another night, a different world, and this beach is far from them both. Still..."

"I cannot leave."

"You cannot leave the island. But you can leave Journey's End."

"Jude, what are you saying?" she asked distractedly.

"That it is time," he replied, "that is all. That you need places not filled with my paints and my rags; that I need a space where I can impose my will on my cloth, not on your heart – which would in any case resist me."

Weakly she smiled at him, or perhaps it was daybreak – Jude could not tell, for both were so beautiful – coal black and cream tones, Tyrian violet, patches of cameo pink and dark rose – yes that last was her mouth – he could no longer resist it. His lips searched for hers, kissing them lightly at first, then parting them with his tongue so that he could kiss her deeply, for a long time, relief and desire mixed in his embrace. He kissed her hair and her neck and her breasts and then again for a long time her mouth, until at last, drawing away from him a bit, she whispered, "Jude, for this night I am sorry," wishing she could have added, "for those other nights, too, the ones spent without you," but the words would not come and she stumbled and this too he sensed so that he too drew back slightly and with a wistful expression took her face in his hands.

"Hush, Caroline. I said no more. To the end of my days I will regret holding a match to you, as I will regret to the end of my days how you have cried on this night. Never, never again – I swear to you," he pronounced, knowingly tossing the gauntlet down to the fates with his words, risking it anyway. "I will find us a house," he went on, "more like a farm – right on the sea, where you can have a garden, and books and an orchard, and whatever else gives your heart wings, and I will paint what I see – mostly you, I expect, wherever I'm looking, whether you're there beside me or not."

"Such a place does not exist."

"If it did, would you go?"

"It is not here, Jude."

"*Yes or no, Caroline.* If you follow me, the rest will come also, in its time. And if not –" here he too fumbled. "To the end of my days, that will be the third thing I regret."

Aspens lining the south side of the bay swayed in the wind. Sails of a lone ship, barely visible, passed in the distance. Through a wisp of stray hair Caroline stared at them both for a while. Then she turned back to Jude. His left hand, no longer shattered, still held her right one. At the thought of his beating she shuddered – broken days somehow endured for her sake, for the sake of his art, one and the same still she knew, as she had once before guessed under the poplars inside Rodin's garden.

She raised the now-restored hand, pressed it against her cheek, and said simply, "Yes, Jude, I will follow you."

He raised her face to his and kissed her.

"But first you must find this place –"

"I have already seen it."

She smiled – an expression tinged like autumn leaves with nostalgia – for he was in love with this place, wherever it was, and meant to have it, come what may.

"White clapboard main house," Jude went on, moving his hand as though he were sketching. "Long stand of pine trees… lighthouse… small guest house. – Well I don't expect many guests," he said with a slight laugh, "but it will do for your books, pens –"

He stopped. The day which had dawned with such a sharp chill had turned even colder. Within weeks it would be December, yet at the thought of this place overlooking the sea – beauty unique and eternal, like the sculptures once housed beside him – Jude felt a surge of new life, as if the next month were April, and pale citron grass had replaced piles of dun-coloured leaves beneath maples, and the next precious seasons were his, unencumbered, all of them mild, not one of them borrowed.

"Yes, I could paint well in that lighthouse. It's been abandoned forever, but the view of the sea's fine, and the second-floor windows look out over the main house, and beyond it a lawn, a high wall, wide sloping sand dunes leading down to the coast."

Caroline closed her eyes, trying to picture this scene, for it seemed possessed of some rare, unspecified grace, some indefinable thing from her past – grandeur not unlike the beauty that had endured at Todd's Farm perhaps – perhaps that walled garden with its eyeless stone statues Jude himself had recalled.

"Last farm on the highway," he said as though reading her mind, "just past Dutchman's Rock."

"There's no house on that bluff."

"Tucked into the point on its own secret bay," he announced, not without pride, for he knew she would be happiest in the most private of houses. "Jason himself – even some latter-day fine and exceptional sailor would be hard pressed to find it. Only the light-house stands out."

Caroline tried to banish the suddenly stark image of Medea. Instead, after a moment she asked, "Has the farm got a name?"

"It is called *Sans Souci.*"

"*Without a care in the world,*" she murmured half to herself.

"It was that sign which first caught my eye," continued Jude eagerly. "Now more than ever, I think" – suddenly he was interrupted by the intrusive calls of returning gulls – "now the name suits us," he concluded simply, having determined, throughout his vigil the previous evening, that he would allow nothing to disturb the peace of whatever days might still be theirs.

Thus, by the time he took Caroline's hand and led her back up the staircase and over the rise toward Journey's End, he had dismissed Max and his son as though they had never existed. After all, Max was in fact gone. So too was Caroline, as far as his son was concerned. Whatever memories had coloured her face on the preceding day were just that. From henceforth, he would not give them a thought. She too in time would forget. Already, he believed, recalling her simple, beguiling *Yes* when he had asked her to follow him, she had no doubt begun this forgetting.

The sun warmed his shoulders. He remembered how she had kissed him. Slowly they crossed the roadway.

"Mind, the farm needs some work, Caroline."

"I hope so, Jude."

"I thought you would."

"It is my specialty, after all."

"Yes. I remember…Restoring life to the earth."

She smiled – pensively, or so he believed – but made no answer.

"It is not something one forgets," he added softly, and then they walked on in silence toward the porch steps.

꒰ ☾ ꒱

Almost a year to the day since Jude had first mentioned Sans Souci, the farm was indeed brimming with life. Marigolds, gentians, white roses, and lilacs lined the porch of the old windswept main house. In the small orchard a harvest of apples awaited; near the shore beach plums had ripened, and unannounced, toward the end of the spring, great flocks of blue herons had arrived on the dunes. There they had stayed – self-contained, stately things, silent, experienced, ever-watchful in the yellow heather.

All this and more Jude could see from his lighthouse – everything but the place that most intrigued him each day: Caroline's library, two stone rooms, once a secluded guest house, hidden at the end of a circuitous trail through the woods.

"We'll be needing to have those trees pruned a little," he had suggested when they'd first moved to the farm. "Certainly widen that pathway a bit."

Half-heartedly, she had assented, but with the changing of seasons, she had planned other things. Finally Jude had guessed she would never clear out those pines, preferring, for some reason, their dark and tangled obscurity to the brightness of the fields beyond. *A place like her mill*, he had decided, watching her disappear into the trees each afternoon, not to reappear until after the sun had dipped low in the sky. At first the sight of her so entombed had unsettled him. He would watch for her, fretful, until shortly past sundown she would emerge, walking across the meadows with that sensuous, swaying step that she had. Little by little he worried less, even in winter, when any semblance of a path through the woods was obliterated by the snow. Unerringly, he suspected, she knew her way through those pines, just as she could still move with ease through the heaviest fog into the roughest seas for a swim.

Not until well after nine on a summer's night would she take this long swim, needing no more than the glimmer of light that remained so far north. Afterward, face to the seaside breeze that never abated on the bluff, she would sit beside him in the gathering darkness of the main house front porch.

Jude cherished these moments. Even more than his lighthouse, it was this rambling shingled main house he loved. Gabled, asymmetrical, its wraparound porch bulging in half-circles at the corners, it had been furnished simply – unadorned island style that recalled neither Todd's Farm nor the Left Bank in Paris, but rather Susannah Joubert's Point Guetter. It had been Jude, though, exclusively, who had travelled beyond Dutchman Rock for whatever was needed. Caroline had preferred to remain, as she put it, buried at sea.

"Well in a way it is really so, Jude," she insisted, late on a cold autumn night. "No one can find me here, surrounded on all sides by water."

"No one is looking, Caroline," Jude replied gently. "Sans Souci is your home now, yes, and the island forever your boundary, but almost five seasons have passed since that crash in the Gulf. You could venture with me into Summerside – even Charlottetown. One photograph in the paper, after all – a paper from the mainland, eighteen months ago almost –"

"Jude, I cannot."

"Not today perhaps."

"I am happy here."

"But afraid still."

"Yes," she said vaguely. "Yes I am." From the edge of the bed where she sat, high on the top floor of the main house, she could see Northumberland Strait, brooding and black in advance of a storm. "What I have done, after all –"

"Chosen life."

"What I have done," she repeated, "could be undone in an instant. One false step, then recognition, and then…" She stopped, turning away from the window. "All that I cherish would be destroyed, Jude."

Jude made no answer. It was not the first time they had spoken of this. Often throughout the past year he had renewed his proposal, hoping to convince her to put her strange fears aside, leave the confines of their farm, explore the hauntingly beautiful island – even the cove around Dutchman Rock, a matter of hours, absolutely secure. Each time she had refused him. Beyond their gates she might be seen; Todd's Farm would again be at risk; Elliot's claim perhaps resurrected; her word from henceforth in doubt. "Above all your peace, Jude – forever gone, and our fragile felicity shattered. It isn't worth it. I am happy here. That is all."

Not for a moment, though, did Jude believe her conclusion. She was not truly happy. Indeed, since the day she had vanished into the darkness at Journey's End, she seemed to him to have become increasingly, unpredictably anxious.

Utterly mystifying, he often mused watching her, for he himself was at long last contented. That night by the grey rock seemed to him to have happened decades ago, if it had happened at all. Never again had she coloured so strangely, or gazed at the sea so intently, or mentioned Max or his house or his projects – or his son. All that remained of that evening's confession was her palpable, unacknowledged anxiety – in this impending storm clearer than ever, so that when a shutter below them banged in the rising wind, Caroline visibly started. "It is nothing, my love – just a storm coming on," murmured Jude, taking her hand as clouds from the mainland moved in.

A few northern lights lingered like lanterns awhile. Side by side, silently, Jude and Caroline watched them. As they did so Jude pondered, more than ever at a loss. Even along the north capes – he had checked this himself more than once – there were no signs of the now-forgotten disaster, no indications of continuing interest, not even the smallest memorial out on the dunes where the service had taken place. Their tiny island was at peace. He was too. Surely it was her fate to share as well in this fulfillment, and so he said softly – more like a refrain than an ending, for he was hoping this time her decision might not be so final, "Caroline, Prince Edward's pathways won't hurt you. I have painted their every mood, understood each of their seasons. I'm sure if just this one time –"

"You have never painted better, Jude."

Jude understood. He let the subject go, gracefully, taking up the topic she had deftly offered him in its place. It was not one which displeased him. Part of his happiness at Sans Souci stemmed from the fact that he *was* painting so well, fluidly – mind, hand and heart in unexpectedly fine concert.

"Yes, I have been satisfied," he said with a comely pride, for he remembered only too well the bitter struggles of his last year in Paris, and had never since then approached his canvas without respect for the reappearance of inspiration in his life. "Island magic," was the only way he had ever answered her astonished reactions to his new work. On this night, however, holding her hand still, for she seemed to be receding into some other place even as he caressed her, he added, "that and you by my side, Caroline."

She left her hand in his, but made no answer.

"Théobald, too, of course," Jude went on after a moment, "somehow still by my side, in his own steady way, even at such a great distance…Every work shipped to him sent on to the brothers Durand…letters sent back in return…" Jude paused, as though savouring rare vintage wine. "One came today as a matter of fact."

Caroline was not surprised. From her window that afternoon, she had seen Jude walk out to the roadway. He had remained a long while by the gates. On his way back to the house he had paused, gazing off at the sea, the pines, the main house, the Acadian flag next to his lighthouse – colours of France he had never replaced.

"I hope the news was all good –"

"Mostly a report of a major exhibit. First one the gallery's held since I left. I mean of my own work – my new things."

Jude's new black cat, Danton, uncurled himself on the dresser. He stood and stared at the sea and like the incoming tides seemed disturbed by the storm. All of a sudden he jumped, one long perfect arc, and landed next to the window. He brushed the panes as he paced, and then abruptly he sat, for there was no exit.

"Do you miss it, Jude?" Caroline suddenly asked, recalling a similar moment, already two summers past.

"Paris?"

"Paris. Your colleagues. The Left Bank. Rodin's house."

"I would yearn for its splendour I think, if you were not here with me now. But Paris without you – no, I have been there without you. I painted nothing. I tried, but I failed. Here I try and succeed."

The regal red oak by the porch swayed, scraping the side of the house. Jude turned and looked long at Caroline, who seemed to be listening to the sound intently.

Lovelier than ever, he thought, as he reached up and removed the shell comb he had made for her hair. She smiled. He drew her against him, kissed her mouth lightly and felt her lips tremble.

"Come, you are cold."

"It's the wind."

"Let me cover you."

Rain began falling, lightly at first, like a shy suitor tapping at the window. Jude went on speaking low – of Théobald's work, Marie-Claude, Auguste and Armand, the well-mounted show at Frères Durand, Inc.

Motionless, Danton remained facing the sea, as though he were being painted.

"So you can see I was right, Caroline. Mystery painters retain their allure. One of my paintings sold in a day as a matter of fact. Even Auguste was surprised."

Languidly Danton turned and fixed his bronze eyes on Jude.

"Well, the whole thing surprised him. One single buyer, completely unknown, just as secretive as the artist. Had the painting removed at once from the gallery walls. Took it away with him that very day, back to wherever he came from."

"Which painting was it?"

"The landscape I did out by the tool shed last fall."

"Jude, that wasn't a landscape."

"Mostly a landscape then – grass and gullies and trees and the violet sky. Well, of course, the focus was you. The focus is always you, Caroline, whether you're in the painting or not. That time you chanced by, and sat on the wheels watching me work, and your colours were one with the sky and the sea and the earth and there, unexpected, was the painting I wanted."

He smiled, lay down beside her, brushed a stray wisp of hair from her neck and went on, "Call it a portrait if you like. To me it remains a landscape."

"We should have kept it," she insisted.

"I can't keep every work I paint of you," he laughed. "I would sell nothing! No abstracts, no landscapes – not even plums on a table. Besides, paintings were made to be loved. I was pleased to find out somebody else was so pleased."

Noiselessly, Danton stood and with a turn of his elegant head followed the arc of a hawk out to sea. Caroline lay in silence under the blanket and thought, for some reason, of Serge Pellerin...Serge, voyaging always. Serge and his boat, *L'Inattendu*.

Jude again felt her fear, vague unexpressed thing under his hands.

"Be still, Caroline. Your journey too is at an end. No harm can come to us here."

She took his hand from her neck and kissed it, but again made no answer.

"You'll see," he promised, as she settled herself against him. "Someday, whenever the time comes, you'll make your way through those gates, free of the past with only the future to think of."

"Someday," she sighed, or perhaps it was just the sound of the surf past their walls that Jude heard, a lone breaking wave on the sand – he could not be certain. Nor could he guess how long they lay there in silence, watching the last of the northern lights vanish.

She is peaceful now, dreaming, he thought, while again that red oak tree scratched at the house as though seeking shelter. Danton paced restlessly, seeking the opposite. Sleep at last overcame Jude.

☽

Off in the distance, en route to the west capes, midnight's packet from Borden passed. Its lonely horn echoed as it disappeared beyond Dutchman Rock. After that all Caroline heard was the sound of Jude's breathing – undisturbed at last, rhythmic, recalling his brush strokes when he was working securely.

She rose and crossed to the window. Thunder rolled over the Strait, like the groan of a heavily laden ship leaving port. Ever so briefly Jude stirred, searching for her there beside him, finding her in his dreams perhaps, for he did not awaken.

She turned again toward the sea, its waters heaving against the horizon, uneasy, as she was, feeling the weight of the storm moving in from Québec.

The slow lights of a steamer passed, and then the last mainland ferry crossed, and a careworn barge followed, and then in the darkness Jude's breathing was peaceful once more, his sleep no longer troubled, despite the ponderous sound of the rain on the porch.

Caroline shivered. Rivulets ran down the freshly planted front lawn. The wooden steps to the beach, the shore, even the sandbar beyond Dutchman Rock faded into the mist. Only the lamp in Jude's lighthouse remained, casting a pale, valiant glow on Sans Souci's walls.

He will not come tonight, she decided, though whether relieved or disappointed she did not dare then examine. She merely remained where she was, absently stroking Danton, who rarely approached her, but who for some reason on this night had found his way to the red velvet loveseat beside her.

Then, without warning, on the other side of the tiny, multitudinous rain-streaked panes of glass, despite the fog and the wind and the slanting seaward sheets of rain, he appeared – image that had increasingly haunted her since she had moved to Sans Souci. The face was suntanned – it was always so – the eyes fixed and deep, the fair hair slightly tousled, the firm mouth slightly upturned in a faintly quizzical smile.

"Why do you follow me?" she whispered.

There was no answer.

"Why now, *here* – after so many months?"

Still only silence.

"Why can't you let things alone, Mikhail?"

649

Not a word, only the rain and that same silent stare, that same golden face, insistent, unyielding – apparition so vivid that she'd even reached out once last spring, vain attempt to retain what she knew could never be touched, for in that instant he'd left her, just as he had vanished while Jude had been sketching her, bare leg tossed over the chair in their small gabled room at the top of the stairs in Journey's End.

How well she remembered that fateful day in Cap-Egmont – first time she'd seen him since his troubled eyes had looked out at her from a newspaper in Susannah's kitchen – first and last time she had thought as she'd posed, so that out on the porch she had finally spoken, and in the confessing had thought to dispel the strangely palpable sensation of Mikhail's nearness.

It had not been dispelled. Clearer than ever it had returned to her down by the rock that dark night, retreating only when Jude had approached her, vanishing altogether when he had mentioned their new house. For the remaining brief weeks of that beautiful autumn there had been peace. Sans Souci had been purchased, the land cleared, the house fixed. *Misha will not reappear*, she had thought, but she had been wrong. He had returned the first time Jude had left her alone on the farm.

The day had been windy and cold, December's sky burdened with heavy snows on the way, and as she had stood on the porch staring out at the sea she had suddenly thought of Todd's Farm's veranda, and her long Christmas gown trailing snow on the steps, and a man she both liked and disliked lingering in the doorway – confident, smiling, smitten, determined, saying goodnight after a kiss she had twice denied, then at last not so reluctantly given – and suddenly there on the hard crimson path by these new steps – she had never realized how much he looked like Max – there was that same bold young man, come again without warning, as he had come to her room at Journey's End.

Mesmerized, through the snow which had started, she had returned his intense gaze. He'd seemed to take a step toward her, then stop; she believed he had called once – but no, it was the wind through the pines which had repeatedly whispered, as he himself had, a year before then, "…other half of the coin, Caroline, you'll see."

A month had passed after that day. Jude had left her again, wanting to sketch Charlottetown Bay. Still, having begun to feel secure, she had gone deep into the woods to her guest house, where in the warm glow of her lamp she had reread Catullus and had looked up from the poems and had seen him watching her, wordless.

Wordless again in June – a year to the day since mourners had gathered out on the north capes for the victims of Flight 407 – he had followed her walking the surf, Jude not yet back from a trip to the Cavendish shores. After that he'd come frequently to the dunes, now walking beside her, now waiting ahead on the sand just a bit, always the same time of evening, Jude always absent.

At last she could bear it no longer. Come the first frost of autumn, she no longer went down to the beach at the end of the day.

Jude had noticed at once. Within a week he'd remarked, "You've stopped taking your long sunset walks down by the beach," and she had responded, "Well with night falling so quickly now," and he had considered it odd, knowing she loved the sea best of all in fall's gloaming, but had said no more.

Misha had stayed away after that – six full weeks – and she had begun to think she had outwitted him, closing her world off, limiting her walks to strolls with Jude, working before noon in the orchard, never venturing after dark into her library deep in the woods, for she had grasped, reviewing the year that had passed since she had moved into Sans Souci, that preferring to make his way, on his own, by the light of the stars no doubt, Misha had never appeared to her while the sun was high in the sky still, or when there'd been workmen around, or above all – but for the first time, when she'd been posing nude by the window at Journey's End – with Jude McCallister near.

She had also concluded – though for this there had been no proof, just intuition – that her precarious peace could be preserved only so long as she stayed within Sans Souci's walls. Beyond those stone walls, who could say? Down by the harbour, for instance, among the returning sailors at day's end, she could without warning be confronted with that confident face. Or she might see him out on the highway, find him in some deserted cove, or even – and this above all things she feared – encounter him as she had done the first time: defences down, no way out, no way to hide her confusion, and Jude there beside her, sketching, silent, more than ever observant.

To be sure, Misha had stayed but a moment at Journey's End, but it had been long enough to betray her somehow, conveying to Jude inadmissible things she herself had not seen. She still had not seen them. Whatever they were, they had returned to some fortified place in her heart, buried as deeply as she was behind her stone walls and excuses and a daily routine which for over a month had not failed her.

Safe, she repeated, still stroking Danton, *here with Jude in my bed, far from the shoreline, the highway, the harbour...safe with Jude.*

A branch tumbled down from the oak tree onto the porch steps. Danton uncurled himself, making an odd hissing sound.

"It is nothing, Danton, be still," Caroline said.

Danton would not be still. He stood guardedly, waited, and suddenly leapt from the loveseat onto the polished floor, where once again watchful he waited, unmoving, until his black form seemed to disappear as he crouched down by the window.

All this and more Caroline saw as though in a trance, so vividly had it again brought to mind Jude's apartment in Paris. One after another, images of that morning took shape – a bell jar, a drape, high-heeled rope sandals, a comb removed from her hair. She remembered Jude's hands on her hips, positioning her trembling form. She remembered relief when at last she was naked, all defences in vain. And then at the sound of reluctant leaves thrashing about in the wind just beyond, she was recalled to the present time, and watched her reverie evanesce, and glanced up at the window again and was suddenly horrified.

"No," she whispered wretchedly. "It cannot be."

She put her hand to the glass. He would not leave. She begged him to go. He merely smiled, a little more knowingly, so that she closed her eyes, forcing away the image, but the insistent rain on the porch roof mimicked his perseverance. The walls around her began to spin – vertigo that recalled the stiflingly hot, mirrored changing room in Jude's McCallister's apartment. She was forced to reach once again, hoping to steady herself, but the glass she touched now was cold – not like the warm window she'd opened in Paris, so that the sudden contrast made her open her eyes and stare straight ahead again into the Maritime rain and Misha was there still, silent, inscrutable, not even a small hint of blame in his slightly ironic smile, more than a trace of desire in his glance.

"What is it you want, Mikhail?"

There was no answer.

"Please, Misha, *I beg you* –"

The only response was the snap of Jude's flag in the wind, and, in the distance, the approaching drone of the night flight from Paris. She pressed the back of her hand against her mouth to stifle the sob that arose, and then out over the Gulf, over that treacherousand beguiling warmth where she had once somehow survived even death, lightning lit up the sky, outlining Mikhail's insouciance – or was it forgiveness – she could not tell – it was so dark once again – and in an instant thunder would follow, and perhaps Jude would awaken – and then hoarsely, "Thank you," she whispered, touching the glass a third time as Misha began to recede into the storm, and relief like a wave poured over her flesh, and like a wave it did not last, for when she removed her hand from the glass, thunder, like Mikhail, having come and gone quickly, another face had replaced his.

This one, unlike his, was repeated over and over – a seemingly endless, identical series of uneven images filling the streaked tiny panes.

This one, unlike his, was inside – pitiless, unavoidable, perfectly accurate dispite the prismatic distortion.

This one was Caroline Devereux, as she was now, in this place, as she had been before, in another place, body indelibly marked, heart absolutely unchanged, mind no longer misguided, knowing the truth at long last.

"Come away from the window," Caroline heard Jude say behind her. She felt his hands on her shoulders, her neck, his breath in her hair. "Come away," he repeated.

He led her back to the bed. She lay down beside him. He bent down and kissed her, barely touching her mouth first, for he had seen her tremble as he had spoken, and had surmised, wrongly, that it was the storm which had unsettled her.

The slight touch on her lips became longer, more fervent, yet he made love to her gently, much as he'd done after untying her sandals, his portrait of *Half Moon* completed. The occasions were not dissimilar. As he had then, he wanted her now to have pleasure so tender all recollections of pain would recede, for she had seemed to him lost once again as she had been on that morning, and once again as he entered her, he wanted her to find herself.

He could not have known it had already been done. She had seen the truth there by the window, as once before, beside a palm tree in the lobby of the Riverside Suites, she had viewed yearning over the Hudson and had identified its shape – a woman – damaged and passionate wanderer – matching half of the coin. On that night she had waited. On another day she had chosen. Choosing had not meant forgetting.

In vain then – how clearly revealed in that flash of lightning over the dunes – in vain her daily routine, her escape, the narrowing circle of self-imposed exile. He who moved best by the stars, needing only the compass of his determined will, would not for a moment accept without proof that ambiguous taunt *presumed dead*. Should he be searching still he would find; should he be reaching now they would touch; and, if Mikhail willed it, once again they must meet, as they had confronted each other before, not so unexpectedly, in the Riverside's revolving doors.

…Not so unexpectedly. She had groaned at the thought. She had put her hand up to erase it and yet there it had stayed, black like the hair framing each face in the window, reality far more disturbing than Mikhail's perseverance. The dreaded encounter was inescapable; until it occurred he would haunt her, receding politely on occasion, not so politely on others, never distant, never disheartened, supremely confident in his tenacity...*and all along, since the day she had chosen on Rock of Birds, she had counted on this.*

The revelation had staggered her, as though that same flash of lightning had coursed through her body. And yet...yet, she had confusedly wondered – last desperate futile denial – how could such a thing be? She had barely considered him in Susannah Joubert's house, barely given Maximilian's son a thought as she had refashioned her life. One backward glance, perhaps two – no, more than two she'd been forced to admit as Danton had once again hissed at some shadow and, no longer blind, she had recalled having studied the mourners a third time, Jude's brochure to one side, only to fold the paper abruptly, heart filled to bursting at the sight of him mourning, grieving not just for her but for his father, both lost the same day.

But they had not both been lost the same day and she knew it. More, and herein the seeds of deception – *self*-deception, for there was no one left to be lied to that morning – Mikhail knew it, or rather would not rest until he'd disproved it, for he had sailed twice round the world, tested seas larger crews would have feared, understood currents across the Atlantic and would have remembered of all things *Notre Bénédiction*. He had perhaps often encountered this warmth, never without marvelling at its uniquely sustaining depths, its swiftly moving progression, forces which could have blessed one more person one last time – one sole survivor presumed dead.

Diminishing sounds of that lone steamer's horn in the bay had recalled Caroline back to the present then, back to her bedroom, her windows, knowledge at last in the eyes of those multiple images staring back at her standing there, all of them unforgiving.

And with good reason. She had solemnly perjured herself on Rocher aux Oiseaux – newspaper crumpled, head turned away, eyes suddenly closed and the thing had been done, the lie told to herself, a profound love like a plank in the sea swept away, and a man such as Max, or his son – more and more they seemed as one to her now – had been dismissed.

No, not dismissed; postponed, she had finally grasped, for it was all she could do in the blinding sunlight that day when they had both been revealed – Misha and Jude resurrected *together*, both gazing out at her from photographs clutched in her hands, both chastened, both altered, both wanting her still – somehow she'd seen that.

What she had refused to see, or rather what she had occulted having momentarily glimpsed, was a far more poignant reality: she had wanted both men in return.

Two faces, two loves, one dilemma…one lifetime left to her. On an improbable island, an unacceptable decision, and in recalling that choice now from her vantage point eighteen months afterward, she had again remembered Maximilian – not Max as he'd been in Provence but Max in Manhattan, like her resurrected, reappearing unseen outside a hospital room, facing an earlier love and the woman who had replaced her.

Two faces, two loves, one dilemma…no more days left to live. Max had walked on, placing his old but still-powerful hand over his lips so as to silence any and all who had seen him standing behind that hospital screen. Only the cream and gold cameo had survived to bear witness. He had not had to choose. For the first and last time in their strangely congruent lives, the parallel lines of their lives had diverged on Rock of Birds – unacceptable reality she had preferred to ignore on that lawn, seeking instead validation for blindness, finding his rare but assured touch in the wind, hearing him counsel her, *Do as I've done, Caroline.*

Again the irony was overwhelming. Embrace life she was sure she had heard in the surf on that morning, yet the unforgiving selection offered in Susannah's kitchen had been anything but life-affirming. It finished nothing, guaranteeing still less, leaving half of her days restored, half destroyed, half of herself fulfilled, half forever denied, so that in the end there remained no alternative but to split slowly in two, coming asunder in a beautiful place called of all things *Without a Care in the World.*

All this and more Caroline considered as she lay sleepless in the continuing rain beside Jude. And yet from self-knowledge had come at least resignation. She'd made her choice so as to be chosen – she knew that now – just as she understood she had burned all of her former life's bridges but one.

If it is to be crossed, let it be now, she decided. Ineffectual Sans Souci's walls after all. Truth and the mariner's image had found her, even in Jude's bed. A matter of time before the man himself followed.

☾

The following day dawned clear, bright, sharply colder with a hint of fall's end in the air. Jude went off to his lighthouse just after dawn. Just after noon he emerged, announcing he would take a few portraits to be framed at the art shop in Summerside.

"Is it far, Jude?"

"Not if one could get there directly."

"But one can't?"

"No. There's only the coastal road."

Caroline frowned, trying to trace the sinuous route in her mind, and as he approached her Jude smiled. She had arrived on the island by sea, after all, and had remained secluded at Journey's End until he had brought her to Sans Souci. What little she knew of the unexplored province she had learned from her books and her maps. Of her ill-fated flight over the island she recalled only black clouds.

"Road's mostly deserted this time of year," he explained, "miles of shore to the south, misty farmland up north – sand dunes, harbours, and then finally Summerside, tucked into its own bay."

"Sounds beautiful."

"Nothing lovelier."

He kissed her quickly and reached for his parcel. "I should be home just past dark. No later than nine."

Through the open doorway she could see that he stopped, as though fixing the tones of the sea and the foam and the oyster-white sails of that elegant ship passing by.

"Jude?" she called uncertainly, and then she too stopped.

"Something you'd like, Caroline?"

"Yes."

"Tell me, then."

"Take me with you?"

He thought he'd heard incorrectly – rustle of trees yearning for Indian summer, perhaps, so quietly had she spoken.

"Yes, please, take me along, Jude. I should like to see what you consider the loveliest thing in the world."

He turned and looked hard at her. Climbing the last step, he approached and with the back of his fingertips traced the sensuous curve of her lips, as if adjusting a sketch he'd just made. Then, with a strange mix of tenderness and regret, he replied: "Second loveliest, Caroline. Let's be off."

☽

Not until late afternoon, as Jude's car rounded the last bend in the shore road, did Summerside's wharf come into view. In a brisk northeast wind, the lone crimson leaf on the City Hall flag swayed. Whitecaps like brushstrokes on navy blue canvas dotted the sea. Westward the sun lay undecided on the horizon.

Jude and Caroline parked at the edge of the long crowded dock – content, for a while, to watch the fishermen stretching their nets out to dry, stacking their traps in neat piles, hauling tarpaulins over their trawlers in advance of the evening. Off in the distance a slow freighter passed; close by a launch approached; passengers disembarked; and then a solitary fishing boat pulled up to the jetty.

L'Inattendu, Caroline suddenly thought, though when she looked closer she read its name, *J'attends*, carefully painted on the stern.

"*I am still waiting*," she repeated.

"Did you say something?"

"Only the name of that boat."

"Curious, but appropriate," was Jude's lighthearted answer. "That line near the tackle shop seems to be endless."

"Shall we dine there?" she asked.

Jude made no answer.

"Unless you've got work waiting."

"I do not work in the dark."

"Then why not stay, Jude?"

He looked around the wharf quickly. "Well, it's not Chez Marianne off the rue de Varenne…"

"It will be to me. I haven't dined out much since then."

"Very well," he said softly, recalling his detours the previous summer – vain attempt to forget how life had been before his ordeal.

"Come," he said abruptly. "A fine supper awaits us."

Just past nine they emerged from the old shingled café. *J'attends*, in the meantime, had put out to sea once again. Evening descended on Summerside Harbour.

꙳ ☾ ꙳

Within a fortnight Caroline could venture, unaccompanied, beyond Sans Souci's walls. Often she drove down to Cap-Egmont on the coast. Some days she helped Honorine prepare Journey's End for the winter; some days she walked to the wharf in search of varnish and canvas for Jude; most times she worked in Père Gabriel's orchard.

"Violette, you must not fret so over each branch."

"They are unruly, Mon Père," she replied late one gold afternoon.

"So are my parishioners."

"Yes, but I cannot help that. Here at least I can assure you some excellent pies for the winter."

"Do you think pies will win over my flock, Violette?"

"They cannot hurt, Père Gabriel."

He smiled, turning back toward the path that led to his white clapboard church.

"Don't be too long in that fruit tree," he called back. "The sun goes down quickly now."

Caroline heard the gate close. The orchard was suddenly still, save for the rustle of a determined breeze across the ripe branches.

The chill of December seemed to be weighing anchor just off the coast. Caroline prepared her harvest.

�☾⟩

"You're sure you don't want me to drive you," Jude said, watching Caroline reach for her shawl. "The rain's supposed to get heavy."

"I don't mind rain."

"Well, no, of course –"

"And I can't lose my way."

"It's pretty straightforward."

"So I think you should work, Jude."

He nodded.

"Unless you don't want to work."

"It's not a question of want, Caroline. More a matter of…"

"Need, Jude, I know."

"Need…yes. Which can be postponed." He fumbled – reluctant for some reason, to see her drive off into another storm. "It's a distance to Charlottetown – not in miles, to be sure, but the coast's never straight, as you know, and at this time of year…"

She stopped his mouth with a long kiss.

"I should be home before dark, Jude."

"I will be waiting."

Turning south at the end of their drive, Caroline recalled their parting.

Odd, she considered, *how like Mikhail's words in that Newfoundland phone booth they'd sounded.*

Odd too, she reflected, turning her wipers to high as she passed Summerside Harbour, *how they recalled that black boat, come into port here last month, just for the evening.*

⟨☾⟩

"I hope you're not closed yet," said Caroline hurriedly, placing her rain-soaked umbrella into a bright copper stand by the door.

"We close when I leave, Madame," replied Monsieur Daniel du Lac, proprietor for half a century of Daniel du Lac, Fine Antiques, number fifteen Great George Street, a block from Charlottetown Harbour. From behind his desk at the other end of the shop he waved a long elegant hand, as though surveying vast lands from a throne. "Feel free to browse if you like."

"Thank you," she murmured, although she remained at the threshold a moment, undecided.

Daniel du Lac glanced up twice after that. She was still standing there, clearly uneasy, looking around the small crowded space. Finally she began to move through the nearly impassable aisles, glancing now at a silver frame, now at a pair of bronze statues, now at a faded edition of the complete works of George Eliot. She ran her finger routinely over a large silver rose bowl. Ever so briefly, she admired a porcelain figurine.

Keen-eyed, courtly – more than ever astute despite his eighty-two years, Daniel du Lac pushed his green visor back so as to see her more clearly. *Lovely*, he thought. *Very lovely. Certainly not a tourist this time of day. No islander either, not in that flowered shawl.*

She studied a tall crystal lamp, an ormolu mirror, a set of Belgian lace napkins.

"Gift for a friend perhaps?" he finally asked from out of the shadows.

"No – no, I don't think so, Monsieur."

"Something for you then, Madame."

She shook her head in reply.

Monsieur du Lac was intrigued, on his guard, entranced – he was not sure which, for the late afternoon had turned strangely mauve in the rain, and as she'd demurred the stranger had smiled at him, vaguely, though with unspoken understanding, as if she too, like the fine things in his store, belonged to another time, and in that moment he'd almost believed that her pale face and violet eyes and dusty rose mouth matched the slender, surprised girl on his demitasse cups, painted with care in Napoleon's time.

By then she had turned, having completed her half-hearted tour of his shop, and was looking intently at a dark bookcase next to his window. He watched her, increasingly baffled. She had come into the shop for a reason, he was sure of it, yet she seemed reluctant to disclose it. He stood, not without effort.

"As I said there's no rush," he confirmed, though whether to please her or to pose a challenge he was more than ever uncertain.

Caroline made no answer, clearly entranced by something displayed on the shelves. In fact, recalled Monsieur du Lac, she had been staring at the case for some time that afternoon, standing on the brick walkway just outside his window, seemingly unaware of the rain dripping down from the awning above.

"I would be happy to unlock the glass doors, Madame –"

"No," she replied abruptly. "I – no, thank you. There is nothing inside the case."

"The case itself then."

"The clock above this case, Monsieur."

Daniel du Lac was surprised. The clock had been placed in a high place, overshadowed by costlier items beneath it, surely invisible from the walkway, barely discernible now by the low light of his fringed lamps.

And yet she had found it, the one mysterious piece in his shop, its untraceable beauty matching hers in an odd way – parallel charm which could never escape a man devoted for decades to the allure of exceptional form.

More than ever intrigued, he threaded his way to the window. She remained facing the shelves. They stood side by side for a moment, looking up at the curious, fine, understated, perfect clock.

"Beautiful," she breathed.

He nodded.

"Is it very old?"

There was no answer.

"How old would you say that piece is?" she repeated.

Daniel plumped up the tapestry pillow on the wing chair beside him. *"Hélas,"* he began, straightening the pillow's fringe with exaggerated precision, "I could not say, Madame, exactly."

"More or less, then."

Again Daniel delayed.

"Approximately," she insisted, with a precision he found surprising, given her vague, almost ethereal beauty, and the fact that her eyes – as though mesmerized – never once left that clock at the top of his bookcase.

"That particular piece," he said at last with reluctance, "is not, strictly speaking, antique. The provenance of little value. As to its future worth..." He stopped. The late autumn day seemed to have changed places with night, and the edges of his awning were blowing about in the cold wind, and she was still staring at the piece – a stranger so out of time, as though from another world – the clock absolutely brand new, from a shop far to the north.

"May I see it?"

"Well, I don't believe in this light –"

"It will be enough," she replied, fixing on him, by way of entreaty, that same fervent gaze with which she had stared at the case. "I can take it down. You needn't trouble yourself. It won't take me a minute."

He could see it was no use. She would have her own way and examine the clock.

"I will take it down, Madame," he sighed. "It is deceptively heavy."

Caroline sat on the loveseat beside the front window. She ran her hands over the face of the clock, opened the slender door below it, felt the sumptuous curves of the broken pediment along the top. The wood had been polished to perfection, the roman numerals painted precisely, the brass knob and handle rubbed to an elegant sheen.

And all the while she said not a word, as though, sightless, she were finding her way through some far-distant, well-known woods. Monsieur du Lac too remained silent – not because it was his policy never to hurry a client, but because it had all been so odd: the resemblance of her frank allure to the piece, the seemingly spellbinding effect the timepiece had on her.

Increasingly, he was unsettled. On the one hand he feared some unsavoury intrigue. On the other he was a firm believer in the irresistible force a finely wrought object might possess. He'd built his fortune on the inevitability of such mysterious fascinations. Hadn't he once watched a client drawn, as though by a power beyond his control, to something so small as a uniquely bejewelled spoon?

Ah, but there'd been a difference. That little spoon was an investment. Sizable future profits enhanced its rare beauty. Besides, the collector was a provincial solicitor, known to him for a lifetime – not this disturbing, persistent, hauntingly beautiful stranger.

She continued to gaze at the clock. He continued to ponder, arranging and rearranging three silver goblets on the table beside him. He heard the old bookseller lock up his shop alongside. He watched as the lamps lining the walkway went on, one by one, so that the grey sheets of rain became iridescent in their narrow arcs.

And then he made his decision. He would say next to nothing about the timepiece, draw her intentions out, make sure he had not been placed in some carefully laid trap. After all, he was not on sure ground in this case. For all he knew the clock had been stolen, or smuggled, or sent to his shop to transmit something illegal.

"Unusual piece, is it not, Madame?"

"One of a kind," Caroline murmured, though she had seen its replica in Antonin's annex at Sagamore Knoll.

"I could see from the outset you were drawn to it. Well isn't that always the case with such things? So beautifully made…so distinctive."

"It seems absolutely brand new," she interrupted.

"Well, yes. Yes you might say it is new. New to me, that is…"

"Just acquired?"

Monsieur du Lac shrugged his thin shoulders. "A week perhaps. Ten days. Certainly nothing more."

A strange expression came over the woman's face, as though a third figure, unexpected, had silently joined them. Her remarkable pallor became almost translucent. She moistened her lips to keep them from trembling. She tried to speak several times, only to falter. At last she turned her face slightly, so that only her profile could be seen by the light of the lamp on the table beside her. Half-hidden thus in the shadows, she struggled to subdue the feeling of fate closing in.

Her efforts failed. Stronger than ever was the sensation of past and present on the verge of colliding. First the presence of Misha somewhere down by the docks – invisible form so vividly clear she'd walked the quay in the rain, waiting, but he had failed to appear. Then she had crossed toward Great George Street. The wind had turned sharper as she had passed the fine doorways, the rain heavier, but a semblance of calm had returned to her heart until she had reached the corner and paused and peered through the windows of Monsieur Daniel du Lac's shop and now here in her lap was a work she would know as she knew her own hands.

Clutching the clock still, she looked out the window. Rivulets ran down the cobblestone street toward the dock. A pale slender beam from the lighthouse pierced through the gloom and somewhere a foghorn responded and then an elegant boat made its way toward the narrows, its rigging black in the mist like the sails of a pirate ship.

Mrs. Devereux knew at that point. Come what may, the dreaded question had to be asked. Folly to try and avoid what could not be postponed.

She turned back from the window. Her eyes, dark as black plums now, fixed on the pale blue bespectacled ones of Daniel du Lac. She leaned in to him, laying one hand on his arm. "Was this delivered by hand?" she inquired.

Daniel was startled. More than ever he felt threatened, foolish, at risk, off his stride...and yet –

Yet how she resembled that clock – polished, fine, with a deceptively strong force in the slender grip that would not release him. He thought again of that beautiful spoon with the fine ruby handle. He remembered the buyer's bright gaze, so like this woman's intense stare, so like the shimmering droplets of rain on the windows behind her, or perhaps those were the glistening gold and dark bronze and intricate silver pieces around her – he could not be certain – nothing at all seemed as it had been up 'til now – and so heard himself stammer, "It was shipped by the craftsman. I say craftsman, Madame, though it may just as well have been a woman. As I said I don't know. There is no more to tell. No history, no provenance..." He stopped, confused, regretting the whole sorry business – the strange letter received, pictures enclosed, his sudden decision to take in the clock, unsolicited, as if it were a foundling left on the wrong stoop at midnight.

No – no, it was not the way he did business. Things in his store came through regular channels. He must have been mad to have done what he'd done.

And still that grip on his arm, that incongruous ardour akin to electrical current passing between them.

"Monsieur du Lac," he heard in the shadows, "Everything has a history."

As if to confirm her observation, the little spotlights built into his ceiling shone approvingly on his many treasures. Their focused glow resembled his profits – steady, predictable – respectability's lifetime rewards. Only the beautiful clock in her lap was in darkness, worth next to nothing, and yet it was the thing he loved most of all in his shop.

He had had it only a fortnight. Still, there it had been, silent at the top of his bookcase, high above the pendants, the fans, the marcasite bracelets, the intricate chains...An old man's one folly, that clock. Homage to the unexpected. In the autumn days of a long and decorous life, a smile, a wave, a parting nod to the romance of life. He had promised to part with it, but had hidden it in the shadows instead, where no one could possibly find it, where no one would want it, and yet of all days on such a dark day she who so resembled the piece had appeared, and had discovered it, and had wanted itas he had wanted it, only more fiercely, for she had known instinctively what had taken him decades in his shop to learn: profits, papers, documents signed in triplicate – none of these played any part in the allure of a fine piece. The fascination was in its inner life, secrets a craftsman shared only with his material, whispers heard only by like hearts – days, decades, centuries later perhaps – sole verifiable provenance. He had suspected hers was just such a heart the moment he'd seen her – vague and lovely and determined, like that Seurat he'd once owned. Hence he'd been on his guard, fearing exposure, ridicule, contraband of all things, anything but the truth. And yet there it was. Folly to try and avoid what could not be postponed. The woman must share in its story, for she had already heard, standing beside it, the clock's unspoken desires. His own precious time with the piece, brief as it was, had come to an end.

He turned away from the bookcase, met her unsettling gaze for a moment, and then in a low voice supplied: "I received a letter – one sheet, nothing more, recently come with the Labrador post. It contains, such as it is, the full history of this clock. It was meant to be shared. These things always are. And yet...yet I will tell you," he felt compelled to add then, no longer with caution, but with something like wonder as he stepped away, "It is not the way I do business."

With that he turned and shuffled back toward the rear of his shop. He fitted a key into the centre drawer of his desk, untied the worn string wrapped in every direction around a bundle of papers, and thumbed through his uneven pile.

"*Ah! Voilà.* Near the bottom for some reason. I suppose it never occurred to me that you would come into my store...I should have known better," he muttered half to himself, crossing back to the loveseat where Caroline waited.

He replaced the clock in her hands with a crisp pale blue envelope. As though in a trance, Caroline stared at the postmark. Then she opened the envelope, took out the carefully folded letter, and read:

Dear Mr. Daniel du Lac,

I have heard of your shop. I have seen pictures of your windows on the back of a journal which arrives every month at a library here. These windows are very pretty. Especially I like the way you have arranged your tables and lamps. Also I like the green awning over your doorway, and the lanterns that look like full moons on the walk. I am glad the red maples out front are full too. This way, I expect, summer's sun will not fade your things.

I write of these things because they are very important. I have a clock I would like to sell. I have made it myself. (See enclosed photographs.) The order was taken a year ago. The clock was promised to a lady. She was on her way to Charlottetown, but is no longer there. Still, a promise is a promise. I can see that your shop is on a beautiful street. I can also see boats down the block — tall masts in a harbour. They are also quite grand, so I know the right person will buy this. It will find its way to the right house. One fine day, in such a fine place as yours, my clock will be found.

You are the first person I've asked. Whatever you think it is worth you can charge. You can also keep the money. The clock was meant to be a gift, but the lady would object — I know this — so if you like the clock, you can return to me, when you are able, two dollars Canadian, for postage, care of Didier Franck et Fils, Goose Bay, Labrador. The money will reach me.

If you do not like the clock, you can send it back to me, above address the same, c.o.d.

Respectfully,

A.O.

Silent, immobile, paler than ever in the dusky, receding late autumn's gloaming, Caroline read and reread Antonin's letter. Monsieur du Lac meanwhile moved a small crystal bowl on the table beside him. He readjusted a picture frame. He wished he had wound the clock, so that its ticking, at least, would fill in the silence.

The only thing not foreseen, he reflected, glancing out at the drenching rain obscuring Charlottetown Harbour. *It is not a fine day.*

Finally he heard the rustle of a fringed, silken shawl, the refolding of the single blue sheet into its envelope, and then a soft, oddly uneven voice beside him confirm, "So you see, Monsieur, it is exactly as predicted. I happen to like rain. I always have...I am the right person."

Not until then did Daniel du Lac turn. For a long time he studied the stranger. More than ever her eyes shone, conveying even in half-light a deep and mysterious joy mixed in with amazement, as though – unexpectedly – she had come upon some fabled world, long-sought, long-hidden.

He was absolutely correct. In the lines of that one heartfelt note – like one who at last finds a constellation's shape in the heretofore hidden arrangement of pale, reticent stars, Caroline had traced an outline, admittedly vague, but at the same time revealing, of Antonin Onegin's days in exile.

He was well – clearly she'd seen that. He could not have made such a clock in the midst of calamity. Maximilian's legacy also seemed undisturbed, for Didier Franck et Fils were still the conduits for any funds sent to Goose Bay. Perhaps he had friends. There did not seem to be enemies. And once again in his life there were books.

The image had brought back Manhattan, how there was always a book on the front seat of Maximilian's car, how he had read beside her every evening during that dark week in her guest house – lives too quickly gone, like a Labrador summer's night, and yet he had somehow found a library – she remembered the building exactly, across from the bank in Goose Bay – and clearly he felt at ease in there.

Yes, clearly, she had reflected, sensing no hint of the desperation which had in the past impelled Antonin to such violent ends. He was willing to forgo money from the sale of his clock. He was willing to offer it publicly, though prudently, safeguarding his identity, but with an obvious pride in its worth. Finally there was the letterhead – most critical revelation – centred at the top of his page, announcing simply, but with befitting pride, *Daedalus, Fine Woodworking, Sagamore Knoll.*

So he at last has his shop, she had said to herself, closing her eyes for a moment as she had leaned against the bay window, *and finally somehow that farmhouse, for he would not have used the land's name if it were not his to use, nor could he put a shop in the annex if the former owners still lived there.*

And then she'd remembered his face – wide and warm, flushed not with the sunlight, but with the plans he was making, having accepted her earrings by the side of the bunchberry shrubs.

People will need my things, you'll see, he had predicted humbly that day.

Indeed she had seen, there in the pretty window of Monsieur du Lac's store. Monsieur du Lac had seen too, although only in pictures, and yet he too before long had decided, *Yes this person's work I must have, whoever Daedalus is, master of intricate craft in some faraway shop.*

Images of that shop, that house with its wide porch, those vast fields bordered by tamarack stands and the cliffs beyond crashing down to the sea crowded her recollections, so that for a while Great George Street, Charlottetown Harbour, the tiny island she now called her own home vanished each in its turn. Not until a door in the confectioner's store alongside slammed, and footsteps rushed down the rain-soaked brick pathway, was Caroline abruptly recalled to present dimensions. She looked around for a moment, smiled faintly, touched the clock gently one last time, and then, placing it on the table beside her, said, "Monsieur du Lac, I will pay whatever you ask."

Daniel shrugged. "I can ask nothing, Madame. You've seen the letter."

"I have."

"He does not want money."

"Yet I am sure he could use it."

"A gift – those were his instructions. For the right person. Well, there we've complied, I suppose, rain notwithstanding. Nevertheless, that still leaves…" He stopped. She was staring again.

"Why not one more piece?"

"Because he never sent one more piece."

"It wasn't time, don't you see? Now it is time," she said, leaning in to him again with that confounded fervour of hers. "When you send the money for shipment, you could ask to see more things. I know you would like them. I know others like them. People will pass by your window and stop to gaze and come inside.

Some will leave with his work; some with another's work. Either way life will fill up your shop here, you'll see."

Daniel du Lac glanced round at his shop, every inch of it filled with priceless things from the past.

"They'd all be new," he began.

"Beauty has no age."

"I'd have to redo my old sign."

"Why not let Daedalus make it?"

He took a long look at her. And then one last time he sighed. Two foundlings in one month, both come in out of the rain, just before winter, neither to be denied.

"Then it is settled?"

"I suppose so," he said, his canny business sense telling him he was defeated the day he took in that clock, his devotion to beauty touched by her suddenly radiant smile.

"Splendid. Here then. Two dollars Canadian for shipping, one hundred more for the next piece. It need not be for me. Perhaps it will be – who knows? I don't live here in town. Others may see it first and want it keenly, as I did."

"I do not think so keenly," he said dryly.

"In any case, they must have it. Charge whatever the craftsman suggests. My hundred will be for the next order then, and the one after that, and so on and so forth. Everyone will be happy. I myself might be lucky. I might chance past your store, and something from Daedalus may have that day come in. And if not..."

"You can come in anyway."

"I should like that."

"You needn't always –"

"No, certainly not. We could, on occasion, simply talk. If you were not busy, I mean. I would not want to interrupt."

A slight smile at last played on Daniel du Lac's face. All she had done that afternoon was interrupt.

"Come at this hour, Madame. I am never busy at this hour. I am closed on Sundays, of course..."

"Of course."

"But any other day…"

"Thank you."

Monsieur du Lac stood, then paused for a moment, feeling that this transaction, about to be completed, was in a strange way just beginning, and that the clock he was about to part with had a history still to be played out in his store.

"Yes, well now to the details," he murmured.

"Ah yes, the money."

"That too," he replied. "First though, I'll have to wrap this…"

"Oh, no need to wrap now."

"Madame," he said firmly. "You cannot take this clock out into the rain under your arm. Besides, you are not from town. It will take you a while to get back to your house. Even with tissue it could break…"

"But I am not taking it, Monsieur du Lac."

"Not taking it?"

"Not taking it with me, I mean."

"I see," he replied, although he did not.

"I'd like the clock to remain a gift – a present I promised last year, but…well, I couldn't find the right thing, and now I have, and…" She stood, glanced outside, saw that it had long since turned dark, and took a small notebook from her handbag.

"Here. I will write down the name, the destination – all very simple – and when you have time, you can prepare my gift for shipment. The place is not far, though you'll have to be sure you don't miss the next northbound packet."

She wrote quickly, without hesitation. Daniel stared at the sheet she then offered. *Serge and Susannah Joubert Pellerin*, he read. *Point Guetter, Rocher aux Oiseaux, Canada*. He pondered a moment. "I've never heard of this place."

"Nobody has," replied Caroline cryptically. "Except maybe the boatman."

"Well, we've missed September's ship."

"October's then."

"It will have to be October. November's can't make it sometimes. Anything later always turns back."

Caroline's eyes once again deepened. Vividly she had pictured the ice and deep snow drifts soon to surround Serge and Susannah.

"No need to worry," Monsieur du Lac added briskly. "I myself will make sure your present gets on that packet. I'll save all the receipts, any notes sent in return. The boatman always waits for these…Any card to enclose?"

"I – yes, if you have one, so that they can see your address here, and they will know that I'm still here, right on this island, as I said I would be."

Caroline thought for a moment. *For Serge and Susannah,* she wrote. *This clock I treasure above all my possessions. Hence I send it to you, whom I can never repay. Know that I am well, and very happy, and will never forget you, and will write again, and send whatever you need. You can always write by return packet. Monsieur Daniel du Lac will save your letters for me.…All my love, Violette.*

There remained only the money, briefly recorded, and a farewell, not so brief – and Caroline was off, at least 'til the next time she passed down Great George Street.

Over and over again, slowly making her way along the slick, winding road westward, Caroline relived the events of that extraordinary day.

Of Antonin's life she had learned much. To be sure there were details remaining, but the deep, underlying anxiety she had felt for him over the past year had, like a stubborn December storm carried at last out to sea, greatly diminished.

Lessened too, for the moment, was the deep yearning she had long harboured to reach across the Gulf of St. Lawrence somehow, if only one last time, and enfold Serge and Susannah Joubert Pellerin in her arms.

All that was left…

All that was left on this strange misty night at least was the seemingly endless ride home. She passed Summerside Bay, Mont-Carmel, Cap-Egmont, and then for a long time – sole car on the highway – continued along the sloping, deserted Acadian coastline, Northumberland Strait one vast dark place on her left, silent Évangéline farms equally black on her right. Finally, just past eleven, off in the distance she made out Dutchman Rock.

She had never been out so late, by herself, since she had come to Prince Edward Island. She had never driven so far, never approached Sans Souci in the darkness, never left Jude so alone – for his muse, she well knew, made her exit at sundown.

The lamp was on still in his studio. More lights were on throughout the main house. *I am glad he is waiting*, she thought, feeling again that recurring confusion, as though another face, without warning, had been superimposed upon the one on that clock.

The constellation that was Antonin's life had been traced well by Caroline Devereux – remarkably well, though there was no way she could have imagined the fortitude he'd had to summon before those shimmering distant joys she had perceived had become real. Nor, from such a distance of time and place, could Caroline have ever guessed that Antonin Onegin, master craftsman, had found of all things in his exile, love.

It had not come to him easily. Overwhelmed by the crash of Trans Canada Flight 407, he had at first stumbled, despairing, into an all too familiar inferno. He was unable to read, sleep, get through his chores without exhaustion, continue his woodworking in the annex. When in a month, after receiving word from the law offices of Didier Franck of Maximilian's death, date and time the same as Flight 407's crash, he walked unsteadily to his room in the annex, not to be seen again for two weeks.

What he had eaten then, nobody knew, but when at last he emerged, having heard imprecise sounds of the owners' return to the main house, he was a haggard, unshaven, shell of the man he had been.

Drink, they assumed had sustained him, if sustained could be applied to the pale shaken figure with matted hair and sunken eyes who appeared in the great room one evening, work boots unlaced, shirt unevenly buttoned, overalls badly stained. He mumbled a greeting, nothing more, then went out toward the woods.

"Drink," they confirmed after he passed, leaving a lingering acrid smell more distinctive than sweat.

"Lived on it, seems," muttered Adela Mackenzie to her husband.

"Ain't had much else," agreed Cyrus.

They were right. Antonin had survived on whisky – never once touched since the night that had set this calamity in motion. Had the owners of Sagamore Knoll not returned in fact, had he not heard them stirring each morning, rushing to begin tasks they had assigned him in what he believed was some distant past, he would have welcomed a slow, certain death there in the back rooms, unaccompanied.

Indeed, incoherently, from time to time in the annex he prayed for this, the only benediction he deemed himself worthy of.

It was not to be. Unanticipated things remained. In the end it was an odd thing – absence of song in his house – which called him forth from his stupor, for never had the owners been without music after dinner, and yet, since they returned, he never once heard the radio. There was only the owner's low murmur out there on the sofa, and now and again, though this was extremely unclear, another sound – a woman's voice, barely a whisper, more like a breeze in the pines.

At first he dreaded this voice, so frail and vague did it sound – phantom of Mrs. Devereux returned to accuse him perhaps – perhaps Elsa Varig's ghost, colder than ever, discreet still, come to warn him one last time. Whatever it was, desperately seeking silence, Antonin drank harder. And yet there it remained.

After a week, fear turned to loathing. Seven nights in a row, and nothing but conversation, unintelligible, seeping in through his barred door – no songs, never a radio, just the blurred far-off sounds of Adela and Cyrus Mackenzie, voices he recognized still, and that soft dreamlike whisper, completely unknown to him.

In a rare lucid moment toward the end of the second week, Antonin concluded that the old radio had broken. On another such moment he thought, *they've lost someone too in that crash. Music would only disturb them.*

On both counts he was wrong. The wooden radio worked perfectly well. The Mackenzies were not in mourning. They did know something, however, of Antonin's grief, for there had been rumours of the service he had arranged at the Moravian Church.

"Must've been somebody close," Adela concluded as the days passed. "God only knows *who*, though."

"Could've had kin here –"

"A hired hand from nowhere?"

"Could've had a good friend."

"Couldn't make a good friend. Never said more than two words, and those with his head down. Still, we agreed on a fortnight..."

"Only decent."

"Two weeks to grieve, not a day more – and no pay for the time," Adela reminded him, pushing the phrase with increasing force through her thin compressed lips as the allowed fortnight slowly dwindled to one night remaining. It would be coming on soon toward harvest, after all – by the look of things biggest ever, God be praised, and if Antonin Onegin could help still, well fine, he could stay, last two week's rent deducted up front end of June, fair being fair with a man likely as not to be more of a hindrance then help as time passed.

From behind his locked door, strangely enough – for by then his lucid moments were just about nonexistent – Antonin somehow guessed that his days in the annex were numbered. Not that it mattered much. The farm was sure to be sold. No one now would take his offer. Besides, every inch of the place would remind him of her – meadows and woodlands, gravel driveway, cranberry globes.

"Better this way," he told that strange, unsympathetic, unkempt man in the mirror. "I can leave her thick hair behind me, her voice..."

He stopped. For some reason his finger was pointing at some dark thing behind the strange man. He stumbled up close to the dresser. His finger managed to touch what it was that he yearned for – cedars out by the main road reflected in the glass before him, cedars bending ever so slightly in spite of their height and their independence, tangled web smelling of spruce resting once on his shoulder.

He closed his unfocused eyes. Her black hair was still there, more than ever distinct past the lawn, though not so distinct as her voice – by now he was sure it was hers on the other side of the doorway, although the sensation was not so clear as that pain in his chest.

A suddenly sharp offshore wind from the Labrador Sea rattled his window. Vague scenes in his mind began to collide. Nice turned into New York which looked like Winchester's Green, for some reason fenced in barbed wire.

He sank to his knees. Seagulls like ghosts laughed at the sight of him kneeling there, cowed like a child on the soiled threadbare hooked rug, while scenes from his life like a dream-play changed places. Searchlights became stars over a water wheel turning, and megaphones blaring resembled crows in a pear tree, and then a stalled train, gigantic, grew even larger when he opened his eyes.

Stricken with terror, he stood. The sudden movement made his room, the road, the sea off in the distance spin. He tried to fix on something, anything that would keep the vortex from dragging him down with it. All that appeared to him was a small oval frame – for some reason that was not spinning – and so he staggered in its direction and picked it up and forced his watery eyes to focus on two little children. He raised his hand and caressed the face of the fair one, who seemed to smile back at him, and then, very gingerly, he touched the face of the dark one, who merely stared back at him, passing no judgement.

He placed the oval back down, took a few breaths without pain, and held onto the dresser to steady himself. Slowly that too ceased to spin – first the top narrow drawer, then the wider ones underneath. Finally he was able to grasp the handles of the thin drawer and pull it toward him. Way in the back, under his mufflers, he found the letter she'd brought in her purse from that fair boy, which in his condition he could never reread, but which he held close against him.

How strange the accuracy with which he recalled every word in that note. Strange too, after a moment, the precision with which he reached for the leather pouch, hidden beneath his gloves, filled with the money Maximilian had sent. Some of it still remained – most of it did in fact, for he had spent next to nothing since she had left him, save for the bottles of whisky he'd purchased in town. Those too were all there, most of them empty now, lined up on the floor next to his bookcase.

He managed to cross to that bookcase, stop, then once again steady himself holding onto its shelves. Arranged there, he saw, were richly bound leather volumes. He could in no way make out the titles, but he remembered the name, *Leatherstocking Tales*. He also remembered Simon's Rand's outrage as they were about to drive to the border.

"You got to take *books* with you, man? You ain't even got money."

"I can get cash when we need it."

"Onegin, we need it now."

"There's a roadside store up ahead. We'll have it then," he had insisted, words which remained crystal-clear in his mind, even now, interrupted only by one more sound – a scratching noise at the window.

Making a slow, fearful spiral Antonin turned, half expecting to see the phantom of Mrs. Devereux out on the porch.

There was no one.

He stood rock-still waiting. The scratching resumed in the wind. He lurched toward the window and saw the stiff branch of a juniper brushing against the now grimy pane. Struggling, he opened the window. A rush of cool evening air met his face.

He grew increasingly lucid – partly the effect of the breeze blowing into his room, partly the sudden image, unexpectedly vivid, of another window, other branches, similar grating sounds, even stronger winds coming up.

"My earrings – don't you remember them?" asked a triumphant voice in his head.

"Foolish girl," replied the echo of a lost man's uneven words.

"I don't see why, Antonin. I didn't need them and you did."

The man's response was unclear; the woman's words were precise.

"…Your own house, Antonin. Finer than mine ever was."

Despairing, he turned away from the window.

"You tell the owners you want it, simple as that, Antonin."

He stared at the dirty space, smelling of smoke and self-loathing. He saw the stripped bed and stained clothes and piles of woodworking shavings from what seemed like another life. And not for a moment, as he did so, did that voice cease to speak to him, fierce and wilful, beloved – also from that other life.

"You *do* want it, don't you?"

He ran his hands over the dust on the once-golden spines of his fine books.

"Antonin, *answer me.*"

A heavy truck passed in the distance. Two hawk owls called from the tamarack trees, and a pair of jays seemed to answer, and the clock she had loved so chimed with persistence beside – flawless, unerring, like the diamonds she'd left him, and the words she had said on that day supplanted the timber wolf's howl in the woods, *You cannot mean you will refuse me.*

The night had turned even colder. He crossed back to the window and put his face to the wind again, this time directly, inviting sweet berry scents to replace the dank taste in his mouth, the salt sting of the sea to clear his unfocused gaze.

The woman's voice echoed a moment, then grew fainter and fainter, not so much disembodied as filling the vast land around him, fields and meadows and woods and cliffs sweeping down to the sea – voice neither finished nor present, but like stars caught in the birch trees content with eternal spheres – somehow still wild though, unyielding, nothing at all like that whisper outside his doorway, which was a pliable, shy thing, firmly rooted in this world, as he himself was at long last.

Mrs. Devereux faded into the night. No bitterness, no remorse, no empty bottles lined up on the floor, he now knew, could bring her back into his life.

Strange, the odd peace that he felt; stranger still his sudden decision, for she who had loved the earth so, perhaps the sea more, she who preferred night storms to calm days, forests to walkways, books to conversation, music to books – she who had ransomed all she could still claim so as to be sure he would have these things, always – ocean, dirt, lightning, woods, a library, a radio – she would always be near him, *so long as these things remained his.*

He placed the half-empty tumbler on the nightstand, splashed a bit of water onto his face, dressed, straightened his room and emerged into the parlour.

"Evenin', Mrs. Mackenzie," he said as he passed her, unsteadily.

"Good evening to *you*, Antonin."

"Evenin', Mr. Mackenzie."

"Better than others, I reckon."

Antonin paused, then walked out the back door. He passed the old barn, the tractor, the silo, then crossed through the meadows on his way into the woods.

Deep inside these thick woods – his head was increasingly clear as a hint of frost tinged the lichen he tried in vain not to crush – he remembered a third figure, silent, nearly crushed also, seated between the Mackenzies.

Clean-shaven, prepared, Antonin was at his post in the barn on the following day, a few moments before dawn.

The door had creaked as he entered. He'd been surprised to find it unlocked. Still more had he been startled to see someone inside, carrying bundles of straw toward the stalls. Carefully he had moved forward. Finally he had recognized, vaguely, outlines of the woman he had glimpsed on the previous evening, when he had made his way past the sofa, taking his first uneven steps into the cool night.

"Hello," said the woman.

Antonin managed a civil nod.

"You must be Antonin."

"Yes."

"Antonin Onegin," she went on brightly, as though they were at a dance and the next waltz were theirs.

"Yes," he repeated, increasingly puzzled by the stranger's presence inside the barn before daybreak.

"I thought so." She put the bundle of straw down. "Cyrus Mackenzie told me about you. His wife Adela described you. So I knew you at once when you came out of your room late last night."

"I don't expect I resembled –"

"Oh yes, I knew you at once," she insisted. "You look more rested now, that is all."

With that she smiled and held out her hand. "My name's Eliza."

Antonin wiped his own hand on his overalls before taking hers. "Eliza Barlow. From Saskatchewan."

Odd, Antonin thought, how she had emphasized the province more than the surname.

"We'll be working together some, leastways 'til the harvest's in. After that –" she picked up her bundle – "who knows?"

She walked away toward the horses, some of them already stirring.

Antonin stayed where he was. He had imagined so many phantoms in the past week, heard so many voices, that he was unsure about this encounter. He tried to recall it precisely as he too turned to his chores.

The woman was young, fair – more like a girl, he decided, no more than twenty. One could not say she was tall, yet she appeared somehow sturdy – broad shoulders, broad hips, pale brown hair braided into a crown on her head, expressive brown eyes which seemed somehow older than her years.

Mostly he remembered her brisk, artless manner. He had concluded she was related to the Mackenzies somehow – granddaughter, niece perhaps – yet how unlike the reticent owners of Sagamore Knoll the frank young girl seemed.

Absolutely unlike them, he once more reflected, eating his lunch in the shade of his tractor, parked out by the back field.

He was still pondering this, crumpling empty wax paper back into his brown bag, when again she appeared, as she had done just past dawn – without warning, unlikely.

"Hello again," she said cheerfully, seating herself beside him.

"How did you get here?" was his response, quickly regretted, for it must have made her feel unwelcome, which she was not, and his nature seem rude, also untrue.

"Well I had an hour's break, just like you…"

"Yes, but still…"

"So I just thought I'd stroll."

"Eliza," Antonin answered, suddenly feeling older, much wiser, almost paternal, though not quite paternal – "one does not simply stroll through such a meadow."

"Why in heaven's name not?"

"Well there's the grass for one thing –"

"Isn't it grand?"

"I didn't mean high."

"I didn't either."

She brushed away a mosquito.

"I meant the colours – goldenrod, spruce, sky like a navy blue blanket over it all."

A light breeze stirred the earth.

"Just like the prairies," she added, unable to mute the wistfully strong note that coloured her voice.

Antonin guessed that Eliza was homesick. And yet how could that be, given her buoyant directness? Well it was possible, he reflected, despite the difference between her ways and those of the owners. The steep sheared-off cliffs, the rocks in the earth, the smell of the sea could have made the mainland seem more distant.

"You'll be back soon," was his mumbled reply. Instantly, the words had surprised him. Wasn't it only the day before this that he himself seemed past comfort?

"Perhaps, Antonin."

"Nothing unlikely about it. These fields'll be ready for harvest after next month."

"A month and a half, I should say."

"As I said, not so long."

"As I said, yes and no."

Silence spilled into their space beside the hunter green tractor.

"You'll be staying on then, with your relatives?"

"The Mackenzies?"

He nodded.

"They're not my relatives."

"No?"

"Good glory, no."

"Well, I just assumed –"

"Oh no," Eliza emphatically answered, "I have no relations. The Mackenzies just found me. Well not on some doorstep. I placed an ad in the paper. Same one I place every spring – last five springs at least, six maybe. I'll have to count."

"The number doesn't matter…"

"Oh, but it does, Antonin. It matters immensely. It has to do with – I mean the reason I followed you out through this grass now…" She stopped. High noon shone on her face. She looked up at him, steadily, having no need, it appeared, to shield her dark eyes from the light. And then in a voice soft like the breeze she said, "I knew you at once late last night. I saw myself in your eyes when you walked out that door. Only I was ten when I remember myself. Ten! Can you imagine? Yet it's as clear still as yesterday's rain."

Suddenly awkward, she turned and gazed at a patch of blue sky over the cedars. "Well there'll be no rain today, that's for sure," she pronounced, and then she fell silent.

Surprising them both, Antonin broke the stillness. "Go on, Eliza."

She picked a primrose from the grass beside her.

"Please," he insisted, and then again there was silence until he murmured, somehow finding it bearable, "I don't remember yesterday's rain."

"I know," she said, nodding, gazing again at the cedars. "That's why I followed you out to this field...It's all happened before, Antonin."

"But we've never met..." He broke off. So much, after all, had gone unrecorded in his brain. Perhaps he did know this girl. Perhaps he knew her too well –

"No, we've never met," she assured him, as though she had read his thoughts. "And yet it's happened before," she repeated, brushing aside a strand of pale hair that had escaped from her braid. Then she fell silent a third time and looked away from the cedars and stared instead at the lone vivid blossom clutched in her hand still – and then, barely audible, because he had asked once more, she continued quickly, so as to end quickly. "I knew us both when you passed last night, Antonin. That was *my* door I heard slam – well mine was the back door, not a side door, and there were police all over in the kitchen and I thought at first I was in trouble because I was late coming home from school and that they'd had to go looking for me and that I'd be punished but no, no they were not there to scold me, or send me off without supper – they were waiting to tell me that my mother was dead."

"I am sorry," he murmured.

"Thank you." Her tone had become flat, monosyllabic, in striking contrast to her earlier brightness. "You'll find this queer," she went on, "I mean to you I'm a stranger, and strangers don't speak of these things on first meeting...Thing is, though, you have to talk when you must, and I have to talk now, today, because it's today that we're in, and tomorrow, who knows? – and besides..." The sun shifted slightly. Eliza's face was now shadowed when she looked again at Antonin, finally, "...you're not a stranger to me. The Mackenzies had told me you'd lost a friend in that crash, but I was sure it was more because you looked just like me by that door, *stricken*, and so I figured it out. 'They are wrong,' I said to myself. 'It wasn't a friend. It was far more than a friend. It was *the* friend, and now there's only despair left, like I had.'"

"Eliza," murmured Antonin, half in sympathy for her, half for himself.

"As a matter of fact" – she leaned in to him slightly – "I knew even more. I knew you felt it was your fault. I could even see that when you passed – yes, absolutely, because when my mother died – they found her hanging from a tree out front – I was sure I had done it, although of course that would have been a strange thing, because I was in school as I said, but in another way I *could* have done it, I mean I just never knew. All I was sure of was that in that whole year since my father'd left, I never once saw how unhappy she was, how desperate – it must have been plain as day – and I must have been blind, or very selfish. I wasn't a child, after all…"

Antonin took her hand – for no other reason than to tell her she was indeed still a child then – and it never occurred to him that he was touching a woman he'd never met 'til that day, and it never occurred to him that he had never once taken Caroline's hand, except to nurse her back from her delirium the day Dennis Ballantine left.

"I should have seen it," Eliza continued. "We were alone in that house for a year and ten days – nobody else for her to talk to, nobody to look at her, really *look* at her…and I missed my father I guess, and maybe instead of looking I was blaming her because he'd left us, or maybe instead of looking I was just playing with the other kids, while she kept losing every job she'd find, because she'd never worked, and wasn't clever, and couldn't save money, and I wanted to play."

Eliza paused, although she left her hand inside Antonin's.

"I'll never know," she repeated, her voice almost drifting away. "I'll just never know. I only remember believing I could have kept her from hanging there – and nobody could tell me otherwise, and so I stopped eating, because I wanted to go wherever she'd gone, only I didn't have the nerve to hang from that tall tree, and besides somebody might stop me, but nobody could make me eat, and so I did almost die. I was in a hospital, and then in a clinic, and then in an institution, and then one day I wanted to live – Yes, Antonin! Simple as that," she confirmed, feeling Antonin's gaze burning into her own. "I peered through the window of this new place, a hospital near Prince Albert, on the first really cold day of autumn – and Antonin," she breathed with a sudden flush, "if you could have only seen the colours – I remember them to this day – not the blue and the green and the gold of the plains, mind, but red and purple and bronze – aspens and fir trees and spruce and at night you could hear the wolves, and in the day there'd be caribou off in the distance, and moose and bison – at least I think you could see those. I was seeing all kinds of things then that weren't there at the time."

"Yes," Antonin managed.

"That just the point!" she cried out. "I *knew* you'd know. I knew it last night when you appeared, so unexpected, and all of a sudden I decided to find you, first thing this morning, and so I asked the Mackenzies what time your workday would start and they told me dawn in the barn and I told myself I'd get there sooner although Adela Mackenzie said, 'Mind you don't spend your day talking, Eliza. You have come out here to work,' and I told her I wouldn't talk, but she couldn't see me when I left because it was dark, and she can't see me now, because we're on the shady side of the tractor, and...and besides..."

Eliza appeared to have run out of breath at last, or to have no more need of it, having finished what she'd wanted to say then, with the exception of her final words: "Neighbours of ours took me in for a while. For two full years I went to school, winter and summer. I had to catch up. I'd lost six terms, after all. After that – I was fourteen – I put an ad in the paper. I needed a job. I knew the neighbours couldn't keep me, not unless I paid them. Well the only job I knew I could do – I'm like my mother I guess – was work outdoors – fields, prairies, mountains, it didn't much matter. I could stay on through each harvest. School never starts 'til after harvest in Saskatchewan and so that's how I made it. I finished high school this

June. I'm done with it, Antonin, I mean with the past. Only the future's ahead, God knows where, but it's a good feeling to have it done with."

Antonin heard himself answer, "You were done with it in Prince Albert, the moment you wanted to live."

"You were done with it yesterday," Eliza softly responded.

She suddenly reddened. "Well that's about what I came here to tell you, Antonin, though I was a long time in doing it, I suppose. I've got to run now. Adela Mackenzie will scold."

And with that Eliza slipped her hand away, stood and said, "'Til supper," and vanished.

ᵔ☾ᷢ

Many suppers that summer were shared by Antonin and Eliza. Most evenings they ate on the porch, seated at a white wicker table alongside the annex. Adela Mackenzie thought it unseemly.

"Where else can they eat?" muttered Cyrus the first night. "You haven't once let him sit at our table…"

"No good'll come of it, Cyrus, you'll see."

"We'll see."

Adela was wrong in the end, and Cyrus of all folk was right, since a great deal of good came that year to the hired hands at Sagamore Knoll. With the last of their chores done they would often return to the steps just past Antonin's door. There they would sit side by side in the gloaming, speaking of many things, watching the sun slip with reluctance beyond the woodlands west of the farm.

Over the clicking of her knitting needles, Adela would peer at them, nightly, through the slats of her drawn parlour blinds.

"Can't for the life of me imagine how they can talk so past sundown."

Cyrus would turn up the radio, making no answer.

Antonin and Eliza would speak more freely at that point.

Sometimes they'd describe the day's chores behind them; other times they'd plan for the work that awaited. Most times they'd speak of their own lives – recent things, distant things, insignificant moments, shattering recollections.

By midsummer, for example, Eliza could remember every detail of Antonin's childhood. She had heard about Max, the train bound for Dachau and Mikhail Alexander, sent off to safety in London. She knew of the tension between them, and how they had struggled fiercely in Maximilian's house, and how Antonin had had to run.

"He didn't die though, Eliza," Antonin confessed late on a cool, starless July night. "Although the knife wound was deep, he was strong. Still, I had to leave."

"But if he didn't press charges…"

"There were other things."

"What other things?"

Lights of a logging truck appeared in the distance.

"Self-defence," Antonin mumbled, and then his next words mixed with the rumble of the truck staggering up toward the cliffs.

"Eliza, listen," she heard him continue as though from a distance, "I didn't mean to kill, but I had stolen, on parole still, and…and the man died, and…" Here Antonin faltered.

For what seemed like a long time the front porch was silent. Finally he looked up again, feeling Eliza's intense gaze. Her soft brown eyes seemed to see things he himself could not clearly define, or perhaps, once identified, never truly accept. When she at last spoke, her words, so thoughtfully chosen, so carefully weighed, seemed above all so simple. "It is all in the past, Antonin."

"Yes."

"Things will work out for you now, you'll see."

Slowly he nodded, not because he believed in himself, which he did not yet, but because her ways, like her frame, were always so sturdy, and yet the overall impression was one of compassion. It was a gentleness he had always longed for, and had only found once in his lifetime, in Caroline Devereux, despite Maximilian's fierce loyalty and Elsa Varig's devotion.

Oddly enough, though – and this often perplexed him – of Mrs. Devereux he had never spoken. Eliza knew he had lost a friend – *the* friend, as she had put it – in that crash off Prince Edward, but that was all she knew. Whether man or woman, comely or plain, young or of a certain age, she had no idea. Nobody did. Antonin had never mentioned her name in the memorial service arranged at the Moravian Church. Still less had he discussed her with the owners of Sagamore Knoll.

"Someday I will tell Eliza," he often promised himself, yet though he had confessed, not without effort, his darkest crimes to her willing heart, he found it impossible to mention Caroline's name, nor the part she had played in those dark things, nor, above all, her strange and mysterious beauty. He preferred to leave that fact buried, as she herself was at sea now, although from time to time it would surface to startle his bright days or haunt his profound sleep.

Only the presence of Eliza Barlow made this endurable – not just her kindness, but the fact that she too had endured much.

He knew, for example, of her first months as a hired hand out on a large farm in Manitoba – how she had been teased and tormented by the two sons of the owner, how with a friend they had followed her out to the fields one evening in August, how they had taken their turns with her there.

"I was fourteen, Antonin," had been her sombre conclusion, over something that sounded like a deep groan from Antonin Onegin's throat.

"And yet the next year you placed an ad," he had managed to answer, his voice filled with pity and a desperate yearning to shield her.

"I had no choice."

"Did you return to Manitoba?"

"No."

"Did you ever tell the neighbours?"

She shook her head.

He took her hand, much as he'd done once before by his tractor, without even thinking, for he could not very well place her heart in his palm, and yet he wanted to, if only to erase its raw wounds.

"I am sorry," he murmured, as he had done the first day they'd spoken.

"I was in Alberta the next year," was her response.

"Was that any better?"

"They were very kind to me."

"And the year after that?"

"Vancouver, British Columbia." She smiled weakly. "I guess you could say I worked my way westward."

"And yet here you are. About as far east as it gets."

"Yes," she repeated. "Now here I am."

He did not dare ask about the future, for he remembered she'd said "God knows where," that first day, referring to days yet unknown. Hence he said nothing, nor did she break the silence, which was often their way.

And yet, lying alone in his annex that night – Adela made sure that Eliza slept in the spare room, across a thin wall from her own bed – Antonin pondered. *I am done with it all*, had been her coda that first day. It was clear she would not be returning to her neighbours' house in Saskatoon. It was also quite clear she had nowhere else to go.

He marvelled at her resilience. He wondered at her uniqueness. Mostly, for some reason, he resolved to work hard, as he had promised Mrs. Devereux, not only because Caroline had left him her diamonds, but also – strangely it was all of a piece – he desperately wished to be worthy of Eliza's unwavering, unconditional trust.

☾

"What is it that you are reading?" Eliza asked one evening in August, putting her needlework down.

"*Pathfinder*," replied Antonin.

"You were reading something else when I first came."

"*Last of the Mohicans* then."

"Looks like the same book to me."

"Same author wrote it."

"Ah."

"And it's got the same hero."

"Is he wonderful?"

Antonin thought for a moment

"Yes. You'd like him. Travels all through the wilderness, with a faithful Indian friend. Lots of adventures."

"I meant the author."

"Oh him," Antonin smiled. "Fenimore Cooper. Sort of like Natty Bumppo."

"Natty's the hero?"

"Well, that's one of his names."

"He has different disguises?"

"Different adventures. Some of them so remarkable the name of the deed was forever attached to him. *Hawkeye*, for instance. *Deerslayer*."

"*Deerslayer*," murmured Eliza, gazing away for a moment. "I used to see deer from my window up in Prince Albert. Sometimes there'd be elk, sometimes other things."

Antonin laid his book down. "You should have lots of names too, Eliza. You've had more adventures than Natty."

"Perhaps I will someday."

Her voice, Antonin thought, was uncharacteristically shy. So was the way she reached then and touched the now-polished letters on the spine of his book.

"Has it got pictures?"

"It has pictures."

"I thought so."

"Watercolours."

"Could I look at them?"

"Books are meant to be read," he said gently.

"Well, yes I know, Antonin."

"Books like these above all."

She nodded. He studied her face, suntanned, so youthful, a blend of knowledge and wonder that touched him deeply or unsettled him, he was not certain which.

"Why don't you start with the best one?" he suddenly asked.

She shook her head.

"But you read beautifully. I heard you reading to Cyrus when he took sick last week."

"Not such a fine book."

A hawk, lazing about as though on furlough, drifted above them. Antonin suddenly stood. "I'll go and fetch you that book," he said.

Later on, by the low light of a gas lamp alongside her small bed, Eliza opened *The Last of the Mohicans*. For a long time she gazed at the first page. She studied the title, the fine fancy letters, the author's elegant name, the firm ivory paper. She turned to the next page – pale-tinted waterfalls, woods, a huntsman off in the distance, a maiden.

Surrounding this scene was a wide cream-coloured border. This too she looked at, for there was writing inside the border at the top of the page – beautiful writing, more beautiful than the title page – a most elegant ornate script, done in a velvety black ink.

For Antonin, she read. *Who loves books, bridges, wild things, and the Hudson Valley. Merry Christmas. With all my heart, though you deserve so much more,*

Caroline Contini Devereux.

Stupefied, Eliza stared hard at these words. She passed her hand several times over the strange old-world writing, reading and rereading its astonishing dedication. Then, soundlessly, she closed the fine book.

"So here it is then," she whispered, for now she knew the last thing, the name Antonin could not share – not only the name, but the person, the face, the identity, the friend of friends who had been lost in the Gulf.

Lost, she reflected. *Presumed dead, worse than dead – a haunting forever mystery.*

These facts and more she had learned late the previous spring, seated in her school library, holding the *Toronto Times*. There on the front page she'd read the account of Trans Canada Flight 407 and its ill-fated passage from St. John's: destination Manhattan. She'd seen a picture of Prince Edward's north capes, the mourners on the dunes beside them, the photographs on the back of four passengers, presumed dead. Caroline Contini Devereux was one of those missing. Caroline Contini had been the love of Antonin's life.

She remembered the woman exactly. Drawn to it somehow, as had the other students gathered around her, half a continent and then some from the Gulf of St. Lawrence, she had stared again and again at that face – frail, intense, heartbreakingly beautiful – out of time almost, like her script.

"So this was the woman you loved, Antonin," Eliza confirmed still in a whisper, as though the handwriting were a photograph, the velvety ink her thick hair, the inscription to Antonin an embrace out in the back fields.

Had they been lovers? Of course, she decided. How else to interpret those passionate words above the huntsman? Who but that woman could have left him as lost as he'd been?

She turned out the lamp.

With all my heart, clearer than ever, remained in the darkness.

She pressed her face to the wall. The lovers would not be dismissed – he so immense, never rough, just somehow untamed – she so improbably fragile, almost unearthly.

…An improbable pair. Absolutely unlikely. And yet…yet perhaps not so unlikely, Eliza thought as she lay in the stillness, and Caroline's image grew even more detailed, above all her gaze – penetrating, not cruel, filled with some dark thing nevertheless, some knowledge of happiness linked to despair – mirror image of the heart inside Antonin Onegin.

Cora must have been like that, thought Eliza. *The woman Natty Bumppo loved*. She recalled Antonin's eyes, glowing hot like the setting sun, as he had described *Hawkeye*'s devotion to the beautiful, beleaguered woman.

"You will like this part best, Eliza," he had said, placing the book in her hands as they'd said goodnight on the porch steps. "It is sad, yes, but very beautiful, you'll see."

Had he wanted her to read in this inscription everything he could not mention? No, clearly not. He could not have guessed that the paper had reached her, so far away and alone as she'd been.

I myself will never mention it, Eliza decided. *It will be enough for me to know that he was loved in that way once, by such a one as Cora was, and that he loved deeply in return.*

A sharp night wind rose over the Labrador Sea. Sleep eluded Eliza. Burdened, confused, lost as she had never been, with the exception of Manitoba, she tossed and turned on her thin bed. She did not know yet – before long she would grasp this – that she loved Antonin perhaps as fiercely as Caroline Contini had, though in a different way, more than ever repressed now, for it involved a comparison that made her own handwriting seem rudimentary, her own courage wanting and her self-reliance inferior to some finer, more frightening thing she was not yet prepared to acknowledge.

Nevertheless there it was, unrecognized, keeping rest firmly at bay – a longing to touch him with her strong, sunburned hands, a yearning to have his even stronger ones stroke her back in return, even in places that had been invaded by other men once, during a late summer's harvest she had sworn she would never remember. Indeed, by force of her great will, and an even stronger endurance, that season had come and gone, along with its shattering pain. Never, she'd vowed, never in her lifetime would anything that resembled desire soften her sturdy heart – and so it had been until this summer, with its yellow days in the fields, its half toned evenings by the wicker table, its silvery nights on the steps of the annex under those strange northern lights, mysterious things, shining not just on the grass but on Antonin Onegin, who was always beside her, large like a cedar – shining too on this vague need within her, although this remained hidden, for she had sworn to dispense with it, and hence refused to believe that at long last she loved with a great, unsettling, almost overwhelming physicality.

No, she could never accept it. Physicality was not in her scheme of things. She preferred to think of such passion as Caroline's province, much as books were that lady's portion and beauty her birthright. She would not have believed – indeed she preferred not to believe, since such a supposition would have left the door open for some future encounter involving her own flesh – that Caroline's bond with Antonin had been of a different sort, that physicality had not formed a part of it, although great passion had, and that now, unbeknownst to her, physicality formed an immense part of what Antonin was feeling, lying on his own bed in the annex, thinking of Eliza.

"No – no I will never tell him," murmured Eliza drowsily, at long last.

No – no I will never touch her, decided Antonin, restlessly still.

August was spent much like June and July at the Knoll. Eliza had finished *Pathfinder, Deerslayer* and *The Prairie* by then; Antonin was rereading *The Spy*. Their routine was established, undisturbed on the surface, but only on the surface – for change was everywhere in the air toward the end of the summer, season of sudden reversals so close to the Arctic.

Crimson borders, for example, like the edges of fine books, outlined the maple leaves down by the driveway. Eliza had need of a sweater out on the porch of an evening. Two new signs had appeared on the farm.

One, hand-carved by Antonin – gold letters outlined in red so as to resemble the maples – had been centred in the annex window. *Daedalus*, it announced. *Fine Woodworking, Sagamore Knoll*.

The other, stuck deep into the ground at the end of the drive, had been painted by the Mackenzies in uneven black letters. *House and Land for Sale. Inquire Within.*

Once a day, sometimes more, cars would pull up the driveway to inspect the house and the land. The sight of these cars always seemed to unsettle Antonin. The fact that they pulled away, often quickly, seemed to please him immensely.

Must think new owners would fire him, Eliza reflected. *And somebody's bound to buy soon, what with the harvest so good, and the orchard so full, and all those fir trees to sell.*

She was surprised then, on the first of September, to see that the sign at the end of the drive was still there. She was also surprised to see Antonin, so close to harvest time, taking on extra chores. Instead of lingering on the porch late at night, he would return to his work in the annex. Instead of resting on Sundays, he would drive off in the pickup to paint some man's barn, fix someone's well, lay some new gravel onto the roads before the first snowfall hit.

"Antonin, you will exhaust yourself," Eliza ventured one evening.

"Just for a short while, Eliza." He glanced at the sign by the road. "A couple of weeks, nothing more."

She nodded, then went back to her book.

Never before had he noticed such a strange shadow pass over her eyes.

"Eliza, we will be fine," he assured her, and once more she nodded, although the cloud was still there, and then again she bent down to her book, and he suddenly longed to use something other than words in order to comfort her, but after a moment he turned and disappeared around the corner.

It seemed odd to Eliza, recalling his words as she took her late evening's stroll, always alone now, that Antonin had included her in his optimistic projection. After all, she had struggled mightily to conceal from him, at all costs, her increasing anxiety at summer's end. Her contract with the Mackenzies expired November fifteenth. Hired hands for planting would not be needed 'til spring. In the meantime, she knew, she could not return as an orphan, age twenty, to the house alongside that old tree by her first home.

The facts were painfully clear. The days remaining were few. She would have to find something – kitchen work, laundry work, service with room and board somewhere, whatever wage might be offered.

September passed quickly. The nights became colder, the days became shorter. Eliza resolved every evening to place an ad on the following morning. She promised herself every Monday to spend the next Sunday searching.

She did none of these things. Where in Goose Bay, in winter, would a new servant be needed? Well maybe child care, but she was a farm hand, just out of school herself. Besides, Antonin would have to drive her into town. She was loath to disturb him. She was reluctant to bring up the subject of their imminent parting. For the first time in a long time she was paralyzed by the unknowable.

Antonin, on the other hand, appeared to be working even harder these last weeks.

Perhaps the Mackenzies can't keep him either if the house doesn't sell, she thought. And the house did not appear to be sold. The sign was still by the road. No one who'd stopped had ever returned for a second look – a fact which greatly perplexed her.

Such a beautiful place. Why would nobody want it?

Slowly she guessed the truth. Things she considered advantages seemed just the opposite to potential buyers. They would step out of their cars, feel the chill of the winter already rising from cliffs below, think of the icebergs to follow, then turn away from the house and orchard and fields and the tamaracks blowing eternally out on the bluff.

It was all so confusing. Antonin's chances, admittedly slight with the Mackenzies, would likely as not be reduced with new owners. For his sake, then, she was gladdened whenever Sagamore Knoll was rejected. For the sake of the house, she was sad. Solutions everywhere seemed to be wanting. Hence she just let the days pass, with uncharacteristic indecision, and marvelled at Antonin's efforts, the reasons for which she could not fathom. Antonin himself did not see them. All he wanted to do, before her contract ran out, was to make enough money so she could go where she liked, take her time, find the right job, make it through Canada's winter.

She would resist his gift, he knew. She would demur, and postpone, but in the end she'd have no choice. She would have to accept it, as he had taken Caroline's diamonds, not out of need – he could never picture Eliza hopeless – but from reluctance to see any hurt in his eyes. Goodness was in her nature. Not once did he allow himself to consider it love.

Neither, in those last weeks of autumn, did he allow himself to consider leaving Sagamore Knoll. He had contacted Didier Franck. Caroline's diamonds were exceptional – more than enough for a fair-market down payment, some even left over to last through the next year. And yet he had waited. He'd have no chance, he well knew, should a more handsome offer appear.

October turned grey and windy. The more handsome offer never appeared. Antonin redoubled his efforts, for Eliza had to be provided for, and Sagamore Knoll had to be secured, and it never occurred to him, consciously, to intertwine the two needs.

Nevertheless they were joined, on a night neither imagined, November deadline approaching, unexpectedly bright skies.

It was after eleven. Eliza, still strolling, was passing that annex sign, *Daedalus*, hearing Antonin grinding and polishing, cutting and shaping, working and reworking. Something important no doubt – a favourite table someone had broken, a baby's chair somebody needed.

Her heart filled with pity. Under a jumble of stars and a platinum moon reclining on the top of the aspens, everything seemed to be resting. Everyone seemed to be sleeping – everyone but Antonin, who was working harder than ever.

"Antonin!" she heard her own voice exclaim as she pushed open the annex door. "You should stop. Daybreak will call us both soon. What are you making there that can't wait?"

He looked up abruptly, also astonished, for she had never once entered his annex. Nor had she ever looked so comely, there in the glow of the lamp in his doorway, sleeves of her white blouse rolled up over her arms, face colouring deeply, though whether from shyness or sunburn he could not decide. Her light brown braids resembled a corona coiled round that moon past his porch.

"Something I promised once, nothing more."

"Is it expected tomorrow?"

"Yes and no."

"Antonin, don't confuse me. Not more than I am already –" she stopped, colouring even deeper. He looked up a second time, against his will he would swear, and smiled at her standing there – weathered yet inexperienced, artless, fervent embodiment of all that was new again in his life.

"Are you confused tonight, Eliza Barlow?"

"Well, yes...Yes I am. Change of seasons, I expect – you know, fall almost gone, winter days coming, Sagamore Knoll up for sale, and who knows if the new owners...such a beautiful place – I would hate to think of it badly tended – unloved, I mean – one has to love land, you know, or it won't love you back...these fields above all – I saw it at once – fruit and balsam and syrup and grain..." Again she stopped. "Foolishness, I suppose, to think of the fate of a tree."

She put her hand on the doorknob. "I'll be going on up now." She felt herself burn under his gaze. "You should rest too," she repeated. "It is late."

"It *is* late, Eliza. That's why I have to finish, tonight, almost the end of the season. Then I will rest."

"Sleep well, then," was her answer, as she turned back toward the screen door.

He too turned away – the effort was greater – lowered his visor, and began again with his sharp knife. Thus he never saw that she had paused at the threshold, and was looking down at a handwritten note, dated that very day, left on his table by the entrance, addressed to *Daniel du Lac, Fine Antiques, Charlottetown, Prince Edward Island.*

...Prince Edward Island. She felt a suddenly vivid chill though she had not yet recrossed the threshold. Failed landing. The north capes. Death unaccepted haunting his nights still...Antonin making that piece for a phantom.

Impossible. For sure it was somebody else. Antonin could not still be so lost.

She glanced back at him. Antonin could not see her. The note was open on the table. She knew it was wrong, that if he turned and saw her reading he might never forgive her; that she was perhaps better off, after all, in the dark.

Dear Mr. Daniel du Lac, she began.

Quickly she read the brief letter – and then a second time, heart filled to bursting, she reread the middle lines.

The clock was promised to a lady. She was on her way to Charlottetown, but is no longer there. Still, a promise is a promise. I can see that your shop is on a beautiful street. I can also see boats down the block – tall masts in a harbour. They are also quite grand, so I know the right person will buy this. It will find its way to the right house. One fine day, in such a fine place as yours, my clock will be found.

Antonin's eyes were still shaded, his head bent down, his shoulders hunched over his work. And so again he was startled, feeling a feather-light touch on those shoulders, hearing Eliza's voice once again, no longer tentative.

"I can mail that clock myself, Antonin, from Goose Bay, while you wait out in the truck."

He stared at her, making no answer.

"It will never make up for her, I know that – I mean my helping you – but it might be risky for you to be posting things, in such a public place – and besides, you will know that someone who cares for you deeply held on to the package and carried it for you and sent it along on its way. And then you will be too. It will be finished. You will have done what you promised, like Natty Bumppo, remember? – when he sets Cora free in the end, though it costs him so much, and he knows there'll be pain to endure still, but he has no choice – no, he has to do it – I remember his words exactly – they're in the first book that I borrowed…*what cannot be avoided must be accepted* – that's what he said, Antonin."

She took his hand as he had once taken hers, gently, but full of purpose – "other things too, Antonin, but you know so much more than I do, so I don't have to say any more – I mean about Hawkeye, except that" – she fumbled – it was to be their parting, she was sure of it – the thing she most dreaded was upon her – and she was getting through it somehow, because it was helping him, whom she loved as she'd loved no one else in her life, not even her mother in days gone by, and so she quietly added, "Mind, these are Hawkeye's words too, not mine, Antonin – I would not speak such fine things" – she stopped, drew a deep breath, found the courage to fix her eyes on his, and said from memory, "God bless you. Think of me sometimes when you're on a lucky trail," and then she fell silent, and looked down and saw she was holding his hand still, and she took a step backward and tried to withdraw it but found she could not, for he would not let it go – he felt himself drowning, confronted with such tenderness, so late in his life, for the second time in his life, so that he pulled her against him, to steady himself, to steady her too because she too now was trembling, and seemed suddenly frail to him there, as his first love had been, although Eliza had always been sturdy.

She felt his mouth on her mouth, and to her surprise she responded, parting her lips for the first time in her young years, allowing his tongue to touch hers, since it was vaguely clear to her then that it was that which he wanted, and then it became vaguely clear to her that it was that which she wanted, and so she did not move away when she felt his hand on her breast.

Instead, with an instinct akin to a prairie sunflower's inclination, she pressed herself against him and there was that drowning sensation again in his head when he felt her skirt in his fist, then felt it sliding along her leg as he pulled it up, then heard himself murmur, "No," and saw himself pulling back and letting go of her skirt, gripping her shoulders instead – too fiercely he feared, but he had to hold on somehow, steady himself anew, for as he had kissed her, this woman-child who adored him, he had seen in an instant that he could not take her that way, not in his annex, hired summer help in his bed. She would have recalled Manitoba, and that shattering farm on the mainland, where no one had loved her, and here in the Maritimes he loved her, and he would take her, yes, over and over again, but as his wife, nothing less.

"Listen to me," he managed, his voice thick with desire and with the effort he'd made to subdue it.

"*Listen*," he repeated, fixing his gaze on her so as to steady her still, seeing that she continued to tremble, and that both her face and her neck were now flushed, and that she herself knew it was neither confusion nor shame, but rather passion which had brought that hue, "I have worked late all these nights – here in the shop, out on the roads, in other men's houses – fixing, building, repairing, so I'd have money for you."

She shook her head.

"Although I knew you would do that –"

"No, Antonin –"

"And that you would say that –"

"I cannot take that money."

"*Please* hear me, Eliza..."

"I didn't earn it," she cried, her colour scarlet now, because confusion was back in her head, and she was thinking he had figured that if she took that money he could make love to her, and thus she could say that she'd earned it, and she wanted to run from him and he sensed it and became desperate, for it was all coming out wrong.

"I can't let you have it now, don't you see?" he too cried. "I can't give you *anything* that will help you leave. I have to give you things that will make you stay – the fields that you love, the fruit trees, the house – yes, all of it. Sagamore Knoll. I plan to buy it. I have the money. I've had it for months now..."

She stared at him, speechless, sudden fear crowding her eyes – not for herself, but for him, and so he said kindly to soothe her, "It was a gift, Eliza, my love – nothing you need be afraid of – those dark days are all the past, as you yourself said one time."

"A gift?"

"Well, you know Max provided..."

"Yes, I remember. Every month."

"Caroline too left me something."

"More books?"

"No," he said with a slight smile. "Almost as fine though. So that when the time came I could buy Sagamore Knoll."

"How she must have loved you," breathed Eliza.

"Yes…as you do."

"I've tried to hide it."

"You've done it badly."

Her head was spinning.

"Well the time to buy never came – at least not right away. It wasn't for sale at first, and I hadn't proved myself yet, but now I have." He paused. The next words, as yet unspoken, seemed already astounding. "Hard to believe it. People think I am prompt, and very strong, and reliable, and that my hands are unique."

"All that is true, Antonin."

"Perhaps, but I had to prove it to me, to the Mackenzies…to you most of all, although I didn't know this last part 'til tonight. I thought if I just sent you away –"

"Please don't send me away –"

"You'll have to marry me if you stay."

She was too stunned to reply.

"Because that's what I want now. I'm sure I wanted it when I saw you at daybreak that first time, but I was so blind, or I thought you'd say no, and you can still say no, Eliza, and you can still have the money I saved, and I will not make love to you tonight – no, nor any other night before you go, because that would trespass against you, and I could never trespass against you, although I could make love to you with desperation – if you were my wife, I mean, and you do not have to answer now anyway. You can think, take your time, and even if you do say yes – whenever you say it – I will not touch you until we are married. That is how it must be, although I hope we will marry soon – there's a Moravian church that I like, and besides, it would kill me to wait long." He paused for a moment. "That is all."

He had dropped his hands from her shoulders – when exactly, she could not remember – and his arms looked suddenly awkward and in need there beside his powerful body, and so she looked up and him and touched his cheek and said simply, "Yes."

Adela and Cyrus Mackenzie accepted Antonin's offer the following morning. Four weeks later, Antonin married Eliza. Caroline Contini had by then walked Great George Street, in a late autumn rainstorm, and had found Antonin's clock. It was on its way to Lookout Point, Rock of Birds, care of Serge and Susannah Joubert Pellerin.

Mikhail Alexander had also seen the same clock, there in the window of Monsieur Daniel du Lac. And so his story too came to an end, although it turned out, as full circles do on occasion, to bring about not completion, but once again the unexpected.

RONDO

Although time and the Labrador Sea had forever divided Caroline from Antonin Onegin's world, she had formed a clear if general picture of his refashioned days in exile.

With Mikhail it was different. There had been no clues, no letter placed in her hands, no handcrafted work to decipher. Only her yearning had remained to remind her of the man she had once known – imperfect guide after all, based as it was on an image at first submerged, then denied, then intermittently and reluctantly glimpsed crossing the back roads of her recollections, so that whenever she had imagined Misha invading the seclusion of her new home on Prince Edward, he had come to her golden, untroubled, as though the world they had once shared had remained forever unchanged, as if the remarkable music in his father's house lingered still in those rooms.

Nothing could have been farther from the truth. After the memorial on Prince Edward Island, with Caroline and Max both gone, Mikhail's life bore no resemblance to the suntanned insouciance of his earlier days. *Emptied*, he would often say to himself, watching the stars come and go over the Palisades facing Land's End. Even Antonin was forever lost – Elsa's carefully veiled words relayed to him in the hospital room had made it clear – so that as that first summer passed and Misha'd seen the boats, one after the other, slip from their berths in the Hudson to warmer ports south of the bay, he was, for the first time in his life, like a rudderless ship at sea, utterly lost.

In time I will heal, he would promise himself as the weeks passed. *A season of peace with the coming of autumn perhaps, a bit of rest in the winter.*

With the coming of autumn, Misha's depression increased. September's crisp light on the Hudson unnerved him; the spectacular cobalt blue sky seemed out of place. Mostly he found the cliffs facing Land's End disturbing – their precipitous drop, the riot of bronze and magenta on once predictably green trees. It was all much too close to a scene he preferred not to remember – ruby red fields, yellow dunes, confused mourners facing a splendid, becalmed, supremely indifferent cerulean sea.

Best to leave now, Misha thought as those leaves on the opposite banks one by one fell. The world was large; he was young; oceans as yet unseen beckoned still –

And here his listless thoughts would drift. He had no desire to return to London, to the Caribbean, to his old ports of call. He could not bear the thought of the Riverside Suites, where once, far into the night, she had waited for him in the lobby. Finally, although the thought of the library with its red velvet room off to the side threatened a hurt deeper by far than the wound left by Antonin's knife, he returned to his father's house – for so he still thought of it. There, at least, Elsa Varig would be waiting. He could at least fill up her days for her, fill up the rooms, reduce the silence where once musicians had stayed long into the night.

In time, his attempts proved successful. By the end of September, Elsa resumed her duties with even more than her usual precision. By the end of October, Mikhail decided to follow her example. He returned to his work, determined to lose himself in its demands. He travelled, sold a yacht in Barbados, made several new contacts, renewed some old friendships. The only place he avoided – and this with a scrupulous vigour – was Todd's Farm, Connecticut.

And yet there it remained – uninhabited, wilful – images of its neglected acres surfacing unexpectedly in Mikhail's mind. By an old mill in the Caribbean he recalled the house Max had designed; crossing a river in Wales he remembered a footbridge, a stream, a wheel ceaselessly turning. In time he grew to expect these unwelcome reflections. He prepared in advance for them, forced each down in its turn, faced away gamely, planned a new trip or two. Always, the same justifications obtained. *Todd's Farm will endure. The town will arrange things. Creatures will soon make their home where her own place once stood.*

Not even upon his return to Manhattan, where he had promised to spend the holidays with Elsa Varig in the old empty grand house, did Misha consider making a visit to Caroline Devereux's place. Such a thing would take time, after all. Days, perhaps weeks, would have to be spent behind those stone walls, where only the land had been deeded to the town of New Salem. Everything else had been left to the d'Oliviers – trust agreed to by Max, commitment the son now found onerous, an imposition, so that he hoped for heavy rains in November, better still early snow – storms thick enough to blanket the back fields, the orchard, the guest house, his obligations.

As though in spite, late November was suave. It was especially mild the day after Thanksgiving, when Misha returned from an aimless walk in the park to find a note on what was now his own desk in the library.

Misha,

Walter Reston from New Salem phoned. Urgent. Please call him as soon as you can. I wrote the number below.

Elsa

Turning the letter over absently, Misha considered…Elliot Devereux's lawyer. Only once had Caroline mentioned him, the night before her departure – something to do with the trust Max and his son had accepted. "It can never trouble you," she had murmured.

"There can be no claims on my land now. My husband has sworn this in writing. Walter Reston has a copy. The original, safe in my mill house –"

He had silenced her with a kiss, not wanting to hear of her will or his father or any sad tasks to be done in her absence. He refused to think such things possible. She had broken away, perhaps sensing them immanent.

Half a year ago, Misha reflected sadly, staring at the note in his hand…Yes, that was Elliot's attorney. Whatever he wanted had to do with Todd's Farm. Whatever his client had signed was in Caroline's mill. A trip to that place had to be made after all, decided the sole surviving trustee of the neglected Devereux estate. Fate would have its own way in these things.

A few languorous boats were still sailing the Hudson when Mikhail left New York on the first of December. Northward, the leaves seemed to be dancing on borrowed time as he made his way through the woods leading on up the ridge – sole car on the road in spite of the sun's almost sensual warmth. Nearing day's end, he descended the curving back roads and in the distance finally glimpsed the walls he'd tried so hard to forget.

He stopped, opened the gates, passed through the pillars and parked by the guest house. Beyond, at the end of the gravel drive, there was only the strangely shaped mound that had once been her main house. The grass was yellow and tall, waving like wheat in the exceptional wind. Here and there wildflowers, still stubbornly blooming, managed to thrive intertwined with the grass, so that as he approached, Misha reflected, the effect in such light was like a Provençal canvas hastily painted in Nice.

There was absolute stillness. At the edge of the mound, he could see field mice darting into the grass. A red fox followed on down toward the river; a partridge strode out of the orchard; black squirrels chased up a lone oak beside him and then once again silence, propriety, no hint of the fire that had destroyed the Devereux home. Only this new world remained, with its new inhabitants, as though the old place and its elegant parties and cherished possessions had been but a winter's sleep.

Why then, Mikhail wondered looking around him, was Caroline's face all of a sudden so hauntingly vivid? Never before had he sensed her like this, an almost palpable thing, body and soul one with the grass there – no, not one with the grass, presiding over the grass, as though it were still some grand hallway.

Memories, he decided, wading into that tall grass. *Memories. Nothing more than that.*

And yet there was something more. Try as he might to refuse them, images of her survival in the Gulf Stream recurred – scenes he had refused to consider since his return to Manhattan – only now the suggestions were stronger, the details more realistic, causing Misha to shudder at last, not from the fact that the sun had shifted again, but because he desperately wanted to call Caroline's name – madness that had never occurred to him, not even on the north capes of Prince Edward, when he had sat alone on the dunes, scanning the Gulf stretching before him, sensing only her absence.

Here it was different. Here he sensed only her presence. Indeed, in this secluded place teeming with life, in this eerie warmth where there should have been frost, ice, perhaps even snowdrifts by now, Mrs. Devereux's death seemed preposterous – a hoax perhaps, an oversight, some misunderstanding about to be clarified. He tried to tell himself it was natural – illusion made forceful by the fact that she'd lived here, danced on the very dirt beneath the grass waving invitingly still – and then he did call her name out, and when there was no response he called a second time, and then fear overcame him, for never before, not even on long seafaring journeys alone in becalmed seas, had he mistaken mirage for the beautiful scene represented.

He resolved at once to leave the meadow – the farm if need be – and yet as one under a spell he remained where he was, picturing not the home, forever gone, but the woman, who seemed if anything more vital. Not until the sun suddenly dipped below the poplars did he at last turn away. It was December first, after all. Warmth notwithstanding, night would fall quickly. There was the mill to approach still, the signed paper to find – one quick look, a few steps, door tightly shut again, and the thing would be done. He would be back in his car before dark, back in Manhattan by seven…back in those purposeless, vacuous days in his father's house – or so he perceived things from the stone bench in the orchard where he suddenly found himself seated, for it was there that his steps had taken him as he had emerged from the grassy mound, lost, undecided, unable to make his way down the back field toward the woods.

The uneven gate, off its hinges, had easily opened. The orchard paths were quite visible still, in spite of the weeds forcing their way through the cracks in the slates, and the remnants of fruit and dried leaves on the stones. Bits of fruit could be seen on the trees too here and there – pears mostly, clinging with a strange tenacity to the bare, intertwined limbs, although now and again a small, brittle sound on the clutter beneath them announced their surrender to the quickening wind – coolness Misha did not feel, overcome as he was by the tangled, unkempt, abandoned spaces around him.

Of all things disarray, he groaned…*utter neglect in the place she loved best*. And then with his face in his hands he tried to forget the promise he'd made to maintain what was left of her farm – attempt interrupted by the sound of a turtledove taking flight from a hemlock beside him, and the recurring sensation of Mrs. Devereux's nearness.

He opened his eyes, looking around distractedly for signs of autumn's disintegration, time passing, death at last claiming its due. He saw just the reverse. Even in this place, behind these abandoned walls, giving the lie to decay and what might be presumed lost, he saw life. Wherever he looked there was life – next year's buds tightly locked, some shiny brown chestnuts partly unopened, a glistening garden snake making its undisclosed way, two spectacular pheasants poised by the gate.

Mikhail stood, more than ever unsettled, for the sky had already deepened and there remained still the footbridge, the river, the wilder banks on the opposite side. Hurriedly he made his way toward those woods, guiding himself by the sound of the falls as he carefully moved through the trees, passing night creatures biding their time on the damp moss, finally coming upon the darkened mill by its great wheel in the clearing.

The little door creaked as he opened it. He passed through the hallway and entered the hearth room, hearing only his steps on the floorboards, and, through a window which had come unfastened overlooking the deck, the wheel's ceaseless revolutions – sound that unnerved him, bespeaking continuance as it did. He crossed decisively to search through her desk by the doorway. The signed paper she had insisted she had left in her mill was not there. Nor was it in to be found in her study, the kitchen, or the narrow storeroom between them.

Which left only her bedroom. Here, as in the hearth room, in spite of the dust and the dampness, everything was exactly as she had left it: in the armoire a few clothes, on the dresser things he preferred never to see again in his lifetime – a silver hair brush, a shawl, gloves she had slowly removed on their first Christmas car ride.

The nightstand alone remained – Antonin Onegin's work – left 'til the end in the vain hope of avoiding it. There toward the back of its sturdy compartment, he found a slender plain folder. He unfolded its one sheet of paper. Astonished, by the beam of his flashlight, he read:

I, Elliot Devereux, forfeit all claims to Todd's Farm – guest house and mill house and the river between them, pastures and orchards and the birch grove between them, stone walls around them, grass underneath them, weeds growing over the house no longer remaining – and I, Caroline Contini, forfeit disclosure of the above craven thefts, until the day of my death, and all claims to my pearls, black set of five, along with the opals, the rubies, and the fine lapis necklace set in white gold. Like my home, they are gone with the wind. The land remains mine, and any buildings still standing.

Below, in the old-world script he knew well, was her signature. Below that, in a bold, firm, clear hand – that of her husband. At the very bottom, date and place of signing, Todd's Farm.

Even the river seemed to fall silent as Misha studied that brief, impassioned agreement – final, resounding bargain struck by one who would not to be denied. Facts that up until then had been vague were now clear. Her master plan – black pearls, opals, and lapis – would have bought time, a new start, saved her from ruin. The gems disappeared, the new start annulled, the thief tracked with a bedrock persistence he knew only too well in her, and the end game – she was not above blackmail – played out with style, desperation, and wit – combination not foreign to her.

Misha turned off his flashlight. A brilliant moon spilled through the stark trees onto the veranda, so that when he looked again at the paper he could easily see Caroline's signature – oversized, like her passion; intricate, like her body and the analogous workings of her restless mind. There was no need to reread the bargain. Like each rock and blade of dried grass he had walked on that day, it was engraved in his mind, forming in turn yet another clear picture – this one of himself, lover who for too long had indulged his own private grief, friend who had forsworn the one favour asked of him.

Both errors needed redressing. What she had saved so impressively he could no longer imperil with a negligence she would have considered far more wounding than theft. And at the same time, Misha decided, making his way through the trackless thick woodlands, the disrepair of his own days could no longer go unattended. He would manage Todd's Farm, yes, but from a distance – only way to keep up her land and his spirits, preserve her buildings and his equilibrium, save what she dearly loved and at the same time let it go.

As good as done, he reflected, moving under the archway into his father's courtyard beyond. Workers, a foreman, tenants for the guest house would be found. Come the spring, summer, autumn the latest, he would return to the place – farm and his heart both repaired, past behind him at last, harvest of rich future days guaranteed.

The elegant fountain, sparkling beneath holiday lanterns,

seemed to be murmuring in agreement as Mikhail crossed toward the doorway. On the following morning, though far less smoothly, Walter Reston also agreed to the plan.

"Just so it gets done," he said in a thumping voice that resembled a gavel. "I represent the town, as you know."

"I did not know."

"I sent a letter in May."

"I was away."

"Another in June, sir."

"Prince Edward Island," Mikhail managed.

"Ah yes. Yes, of course…such a sad end for Mrs. Devereux." Walter coughed, audibly shuffled some papers. "Nevertheless, Mr. d'Olivier, one must press on. Insurance, you know. Repairs. Restoration. It's been allowed to run down."

"It will be neglected no longer."

Reassured, Walter Reston rang off. Relieved, with a brief smile in spite of himself at the bitter irony of it all, Mikhail pondered. Caroline's words had proved on all counts exact. *There can be no claims on my land now.* The affair had not, after all, concerned Elliot Devereux. And yet the rescued agreement had in its own way saved Todd's Farm.

He glanced one last time at the vivid, baroque script on that agreement, slipped it back into its envelope and placed them both carefully – along with the past, he firmly promised himself – inside the library safe.

Safe, too, was his master plan, Misha reflected with some pride toward the end of the year. Workmen had begun clearing Caroline's land. He himself had gone twice to Bermuda, drawn up contracts for two yacht sales, accepted many of the invitations that always managed to reach him wherever he was. Elsa saw the change instantly when he returned to New York. A hint of the old warmth had begun to appear, replacing that subsurface melancholy which had darkened his earlier summertime efforts.

On Christmas Eve, as a matter of fact, Mikhail rang up Claire Tierney at Gallery La Ronde, midtown, Fifth Avenue.

Nativity bells tolled five-thirty as Mikhail made his way into La Ronde's glistening lobby. Roger Gachet was not surprised. Gentlemen always slipped into his store Christmas Eve, just under the wire, last-minute gifts for a wife, or a client, or someone they preferred to call one or the other.

"No, no," Misha said affably. "I'm simply here to wait for Miss Tierney."

"Ah," murmured Roger, deflated. "She should be down soon. Right now she's on Two, estate jewels. You could join here there…"

"I'll wait here."

"As you wish."

"Browse a little perhaps."

"By all means," said Roger, rallying. "Contemporary art's here on First. Recent acquisitions. All very beautiful," he added in hushed tones, though there was nobody else in the store. "I'll tell Miss Tierney you're here."

"…Beautiful indeed," Misha reflected, pausing by each of the finely framed paintings in the large salon to his right.

Two in particular caught his attention. Thought totally different in style, they were both by the same artist and had been clearly conceived as a pair.

"Jude McCallister, Paris," he murmured, reading the signature at the base of both works. Their dates were the same, July of the previous year. The colours in both seemed to blend, although the one on the left was a vivid abstract in mauve, black, gold and cerise, while the companion piece, done in the same hues, was an elegant still life – flowers, a vividly fringed shawl, French doors, a terrace beyond.

Mesmerized, Mikhail stared at this work. He had seen it before – he was sure of it – but no; no, that other painting was a portrait, its photograph torn to shreds by the model herself on a car ride last Christmas.

Misha moved closer. He reached out his hand, as though to confirm his conclusions by lightly touching the work, then stopped, knowing there was no need. There indeed, was Mrs. Devereux – not by the half-opened door, or shadowed out on the terrace, but in the incredible colours Jude McCallister had reproduced.

Stunned, Misha turned to the abstract. Caroline Devereux had been painted there too, he perceived, although the canvas was filled with pure form, no recognizable shapes, just sumptuous vessels for the same glorious tones.

"Extraordinary, are they not?" whispered Roger Gachet, who had in his practiced, inaudible way, materialized.

"Remarkable, yes," stammered Misha. "I...even the framing..."

"Designed by the artist."

Mikhail nodded.

"We've only had the works a season. There has of course, been much interest, above all the still life – but alas –" Roger sighed. It always pained him to discuss limitations.

"They must be sold as a pair."

"Well, yes. Yes, how did you know?"

"Sailors see things few people find," laughed Claire Tierney approaching. She held out her hand, greeting Misha with a well-rehearsed, confident grace. Mikhail, off his stride, fell short of her tone in reply. Roger, eyeing his paintings remarked: "Your friend is quite taken with these McCallisters, Claire."

"Roger, it's Christmas. Don't be fretting so over my pair."

"*Your* pair?"

"It was Claire who arranged for the acquisition," Roger explained. "She feels a certain...how shall I say...?"

"Attachment," supplied Claire.

The large room fell silent. Mikhail's eyes strayed back to Jude McCallister's work. Claire's eyes studied Mikhail.

"So they are for sale still," pursued Misha.

"Absolutely," proclaimed Roger.

A clerk began locking the entrance. Chandeliers in the lobby dimmed. Silence again filled the space, and then:

"Would you mind if I bought them, Claire?"

"*Mind*, Misha?"

"Well, I wouldn't want…I mean if you're all *that* attached –"

"She'd be delighted," said Roger.

"Thrilled, yes," Claire confirmed after a moment, having recovered a manner as seamless as her close-fitting silk suit. "A perfect match, Misha, really. Elegant buyer. Beautiful paintings –"

"Then it's settled," announced Roger, stifling the sigh of relief which had almost escaped like steam from a valve.

"Settled," repeated Claire, turning away from the pair Jude McCallister had been willing to exchange for the portrait of *Half Moon*, never in his lifetime to be surrendered.

Later, over a drink at Café Pierre's most intimate table, she pondered the irony of it all. The pair at last in Mikhail's hands. Mikhail's hands having stolen the love of Jude's life. She was almost tempted to describe that windy night in Honfleur. Twice she was on the verge of revealing her visit to Mikhail's hospital room. Of both events she said nothing. She would keep the promise she'd made to the artist by those quays on the Normandy coast. She would also keep, deep in her own heart, the fact that she had glimpsed his model at Mikhail's bedside a matter of weeks after that, the fact that she knew the woman's name, Caroline Devereux, as reported in the news accounts of the Trans Canada Maritimes crash, and, as also reported, the fact that Half Moon was dead.

This last was the most compelling reason for Claire Tierney's silence. Like Rebecca Chase, who was about to make her debut as principal harpist with the Vienna *Volksoper*, Claire Tierney knew better than to compete with a phantom.

They parted awkwardly by the fountain in front of the Plaza Hotel, air kiss on both cheeks, tourists passing on dreamily, hand-in-hand toward the city lights.

Claire turned back one last time, shaded by the awning outside a glittering, now-deserted Bergdorf Goodman's front entrance. Misha was striding northward, blending into the crowds alongside

Central Park. He appeared to be in a rush, although he had not mentioned any engagement.

"But then again he would not have," Claire reminded herself.

Purposefully, she turned south and began to walk toward her apartment.

Forever lost…Misha murmured the words over and over to himself as he stared at the paintings which had been delivered that night from La Ronde. *Presumed dead*, he repeated, increasingly doubting the phrase as he studied both works.

He looked again closely the next day, and the day after that, and as the week passed, Mikhail's fragile, incipient peace disappeared. His old fixation returned, renewed, for now it was a double thing, encompassing artist as well as model. He became restless, unable to concentrate, enduring long holiday dinners and still more endless receptions, leaving them all much too soon so as to return to his house and his paintings. In his sleep, strange vivid dreams would recur – splashes of colour, unrecognizable shapes, a beautiful woman, half-dressed, trying vainly to call to him from the deck of his storm-tossed sailboat *Serena* – and always, superimposed on these scenes, undulating as though on a banner in the lower left corner, Jude McCallister's name.

On occasion the madness occurred to him to try to locate Jude McCallister, though to what end he could not guess. Perhaps just to look at him, unnoticed. Perhaps just to speak, in general terms, so as to hear his voice, watch his expressions, understand the source of an attraction which for Mrs. Devereux had remained, even as late as the previous Christmas, clearly irresistible.

Other times Misha'd recoil from the thought of ever meeting Jude McCallister. *I know who he is now. That is enough. Anything more and I might*… Here he would stop, shuddering at the thought of his mind retreating still further.

Finally, toward the end of December, though he vaguely sensed his compulsion might have catastrophic results, Misha decided. He would track down – if not the artist, who might prove impossible to locate – at least whatever pictures he could find bearing his distinctive signature. Through the painter, he reasoned, he might put an end to his folly, or rather his madness, as he increasingly viewed Caroline's lingering, nearly palpable face. He needed perhaps but to see that face painted in years gone by, rendered repeatedly by the man she had once loved so fiercely, to release him from longing, bondage, to force acceptance of the fact that like the others she too was gone.

Nearing five New Year's Eve – again these late holiday calls never surprised Roger Gachet – Mikhail telephoned La Ronde.

"Regrettably, no…no we are not his agent," he heard.

"Well then who does represent Jude McCallister?"

After a moment, as though he had just swallowed an immense pill, Roger replied, "You could try Frères Durand, Paris, France."

Within a week Mikhail was in Paris. A day after that the twins made a sale: a portrait of Caroline Devereux, not nude this time but dressed simply in a long white sheer skirt, white blouse, high-heeled rope sandals again. The work was untitled, signed McCallister, clearly dated – no location.

Misha had stared for a long time at that portrait.

"May I ask when you acquired this work?" he had finally managed.

"The portrait is dated, Monsieur," Auguste had replied, all discretion.

"Yes, yes I see that." He'd run his hand over the frame. "Three years ago, autumn."

Again a long silence.

"Curious piece."

"We have others, Monsieur," Armand had hastily offered. "Other McCallisters, even. Honfleur, Trouville…"

"I've seen them both."

"Rouen, Deauville, the cliffs near Dieppe…"

"My only interest is this work."

"Well, yes. … Yes of course such élan –"

"I'll take it."

Armand was staggered. Jude had asked a king's ransom for the picture, as though to inhibit just such an impulse.

"The offering price, Monsieur –"

"The offering price does not concern me. I am sure it is fair. I wish to return to New York with it. Tomorrow. Can it be readied so soon?"

The nonplussed frères Durand had taken a deep breath in concert.

"You will have it this evening," Auguste had promised with a slight bow.

"Delivered to your hotel." Armand had added, inclination identical.

There remained but the paperwork, completed with dispatch, the farewells, hastier still, and then, just as quickly as he had appeared, Misha had vanished, leaving the twins more than ever in awe of their reclusive celebrity painter, who clearly could still cast a spell.

A cold rain had begun to fall, turning the late afternoon streets gunmetal grey as Mikhail blended into the crowds along the boulevard St-Germain. He passed d'Orsay's damp, stone façade, the French Institute's dome, partially hidden by low clouds, the bookstores, the bridges, the blur of pale, unknown faces distorted by steam streaking the old café windows overlooking the Seine.

By the time he crossed Place St-Michel, day's light had faded. Tiny Viviani Square alongside St-Julien-le-Pauvre was deserted. As if in some dream still he paused, opened the wrought-iron gates of the square and found a secluded bench under an elm tree facing the river. Here he remained for a while, vaguely sensing the rain dripping onto the dried leaves behind him, indistinctly seeing Notre-Dame's spires as, through a fog, he had seen many a tall mast passing before his own ship of an evening.

On this evening though, alongside this quay, he was unaware of the cold and increasingly raw winds. One thing and one thing alone consumed his attention, causing him now and again to murmur, incredulous, lingering over the words so as to make their full import somehow comprehensible. *Alive…She is alive.* Not only alive, but still beautiful, vibrant – he repeatedly turned this fact over too in his mind, recalling the haunting expression that still marked her features, that same vague smile somehow poised between hope and nostalgia. With what flair had Jude captured that smile! With what seeming ease her wide eyes! A matter of brushstrokes, nothing more than that – though more than enough to give the lie to that other phrase Misha'd never truly accepted.

"Presumed dead no longer," he murmured as darkness fell over the square and the city. Certainties only remained in this dimness; all doubt had vanished; all false assumptions were gone; for there'd been a small piece of evidence she had neglected to hide, or had forgotten to hide, and he alone would have known it. He alone would have recognized that cameo pinned to her blouse. Unique, irreplaceable, it had belonged once to his mother. Max had presented it to Mrs. Devereux on the previous Christmas. Thus, along with his model, the artist had made one mistake – a simple one – a most insignificant detail – but Mikhail was accustomed to sailing by the light of the stars, and the fine jewel on this painting shone brightly.

So too did the false date carefully noted in the lower left corner. Three years could not have possibly passed since the picture's completion. Its delicate model was wearing a gemstone received shortly before her Trans Canada plane crashed.

One thing only remained, Misha saw, still facing the silent, inscrutable, now black river Seine: the location so deftly omitted beneath Jude McCallister's name.

Back in New York, undisturbed in the secrecy of the secluded red velvet room, Mikhail studied his portrait. The scene was part landscape, part portrait. The surroundings were charming, oddly out of time – perhaps a deliberate note – roses and lilacs, a stone well, a pair of wagon wheels casting their shadows onto a field.

Off in the distance, behind what seemed to be poplars, a patch of sea could be seen – done again, Misha thought, with a few brushstrokes at most. Indeed, the whole scene had a curiously imprecise aspect to the execution – everything somewhat out of focus, so that the overall effect was both striking and vague.

Except for the figure. Here there was nothing but absolute clarity, as though a photograph had been taken of Mrs. Devereux by those wheels. She was seated, or rather half-seated on the edge of the crossbar. Her hair was unclasped, billowing in what must have been a brisk wind. Her skirt seemed to rustle; her hand appeared raised to smooth it. That was Jude's genius, to make static cloth speak of wind, beauty, desire, evanescence. And they were all there, these things – sensual breeze, luxuriant meadow, beloved face resigned and yet somehow still yearning – impermanence everywhere concretely rendered.

Again and again Misha returned to this last thing. The more he stared at the painting, the more he perceived intimations of transience – in the intertwined shapes cast by the wagon wheels on the grass, in the clouds suggesting not rain, but a knowledge of rain, in the fact that the well seemed to have outlived its time at long last, for there were no ropes from its roof to the stones at its base, no buckets for bringing forth water.

In short the painting seemed as troubled as did the woman on the crossbar: lady at home in her new surroundings, wherever they were, yet at the same time unsettled, conscious of exile, unwilling to part for a moment with the only thing left to her – Cecilia's once and future wedding gift.

It was perhaps to suggest this contradiction – happiness that was neither fulfillment nor disappointment – that Jude McCallister had so finely shadowed his work. Or perhaps Jude himself had had a presentment of a similar outcome in his own days, or perhaps he remembered it from his past life – or perhaps it was simply the salient feature in life, as the artist perceived it.

Whatever the source, the brilliant and deliberate chiaroscuro in Jude's painting haunted Mikhail's days. The more he studied the work the more it confounded him. Was its diluted splendour indeed the artist's worldview represented? Or was it, as he had first thought, Mrs. Devereux's own ambivalence?

In time, he decided it was as he had first thought. The restless landscape so strikingly rendered was but a reflection of the yearning that had deepened her fine eyes. Perhaps most poignant of all, the artist had known this. Though it must have grieved him to do so, his destiny was to depict whatever was clearly before him, or else create a flawed painting, and Jude McCallister was not a man to let a work of his fail. Before him, wherever the scene, was a woman conflicted. He'd had no choice but to render this longing.

But a longing for what? Perhaps yearning was simply her nature – bittersweet inevitability, just as Jude's fate was to paint whatever he saw. Or perhaps…perhaps –

Here Misha would stop, and force himself to turn away, turn out the lights, close the door to the little room, the heavier door to the library.

The thought would not be dismissed. The possibility that she loved him still gave him no quarter, no respite, so that after a month he cursed the obsession that had led him to Frères Durand, Inc.

Better by far to have only suspected survival. Hope would have faded in time. I would have let her go. Now, so long as that curious ambivalence suffused her beautiful face, there could be no letting go. The old fixation – finding out if she lived still – was replaced with a new one: finding out where she lived. After all, not unlike Jude, dead reckoning was his destiny, although the testing came mostly in darkness, out on the ocean, not in the daylight, next to a canvas. Still, the result was the same. If Jude had been able to paint her so clearly, he should be able to find her.

Elsa felt pity seeing him study that painting each evening. She herself had never approached it. Indeed, ever since Antonin's disappearance, she had never forgiven Mrs. Caroline Devereux. Whenever Mikhail was not in the house, she left the velvet room closed, disdaining even a glance at the woman who still bedevilled her household.

Even when he was home, even when he was in that room, as he so often was until night cast too many shadows on the little alcove with its portrait over the bed, Elsa never once entered that space. Should there be a phone call or a package or any information for Mikhail, she would speak softly from the doorway.

Thus, late one evening in August, after he had returned from a yacht sale in the Caribbean, Mikhail heard from the threshold behind him, "Supper will be ready for you in ten minutes, Mikhail. I've set your usual place –"

"The dining room, yes. I'll be right in, Elsa, thank you."

The library steadily darkened in advance of a late summer storm. Misha turned on the small red fringed lamp and sank down on the bed as a last ray of sunlight spilled onto the wall from the library window. The painting seemed suddenly different, almost new, bathed as it was in the crimson glow of the shade and the even warmer, fragile, burnt umber gleam of the sun. He had never seen it in this light at this time – half daylight, half evening, half rainstorm, half clear skies. In short, he had never observed it in tones matching the painting's ethereal setting, the model's uncertainty, the artist's deliberate imprecision.

And then there it was – not in the sea or the stones or the lilacs or even in the woman's face: what had eluded him until this moment.

He touched the canvas as though to confirm what he'd seen.

"Dirt…yes," he said, almost in wonder. "What she always used to call her land."

Indeed there it was – a small patch, barely visible, impressionistically rendered by the artist at the base of the poplars – a dot, nothing more, seeming afterthought toward the left of the picture, a third of a brushstroke overshadowed and almost invisible next to the brown of the tree trunks and the blue slice of sea alongside. In fact, Misha remembered, he had once or twice noticed that mark, had thought it a leaf perhaps, perhaps an apple, for it was a strange tone – neither crimson nor brown but the dusky sienna of clay – and it did not occur to him, since yellow-green grass covered the rest of the landscape, that that stroke represented neither fall fruits nor stray leaves but the earth, the land all around them – driveways not in the picture, walkways hidden behind walls, fields nimbly excluded from the scene but most assuredly everywhere, for how well he knew them all, the clay lanes and paths and rock cliffs of Prince Edward Island.

"Supper, now, Misha," Elsa repeated softly, from the threshold.

"Thank you, Elsa. I'll be in straightaway."

Mikhail stood. One last time he stared.

How did this escape me? he marvelled. *Well, it's a minuscule mark, after all, like the blurred artist's name in Claire Tierney's photo.* The thought also occurred to him then that his mind simply could not, or would not, remember that long lonely walk toward the north capes, nearing the plunge point of the aircraft, bearing his father's remains.

Now it was once again vivid – not just the roads from his sad walk, but the harbours and coves and tiny wharves seen from his boat many times. Yes, he knew this Maritime province. He had simply refused to consider the fact that she might be secluded there still, even waiting there still, hiding perhaps from herself as well as from him.

Before the end of September Mikhail was in Charlottetown. He had bought a new boat, hoping to sell it that year in Bermuda, but instead, strangely drawn to the beautiful ship, he'd been unable to part with it. On the first fine day of autumn, he rechristened her in Manhattan. Slipping out through the Narrows soon after, he set sail east-north-east – *Serena II*'s maiden voyage – destination: the Maritimes.

So late in the season, he knew, he would be heading into notoriously unpredictable seas. Ships far grander than *Serena II* had foundered off the shores of Nantucket, Nova Scotia, Cape Breton, Prince Edward – and as he had named his new boat he had remembered his favourite – the steady one, charmed vessel lost to the same ocean's spite once, same strange time of year. He had even pondered the wisdom of giving this untested lovely thing the same perhaps fateful name. He had considered others, had even ordered life preservers with a different choice, but when they'd arrived, and he'd seen their midnight blue letters, *Nocturne*, floating like undisturbed sleep on their pale cloudlike spheres he had said, "No, there have been enough dreams," and, recalling how she had called him Jason once, decided instead to dare his own destiny and rename the yacht after the one he had loved so – steady one, painted in gold like fine fleece on her sleek oyster-white hull.

Battered somewhat, badly stained, the letters were nonetheless visible as *Serena II* made her way finally into Northumberland Strait, through a hard driving rain, vestige of the last of the violent storms from Labrador down through the Gulf of St. Lawrence that had assaulted the North Atlantic for almost a fortnight.

Well past sundown Misha dropped anchor in the relative calm of Hillsborough Bay. Off in the distance, in what he perceived to be clearing skies, he could see the flickering lights of Charlottetown Harbour, where he preferred to dock under the guidance of sunlight the following day.

For now he would rest. He lay in his stateroom, hearing sounds which over the years had become more familiar to him than his heartbeats – diminishing raindrops on the upper deck, a foghorn off starboard, church bells in the distance, ebb tide turning round – a movement he gauged only vaguely by *Serena II*'s changing drift, for by then he too had begun drifting, into profound sleep.

Morning dawned cooler, untroubled. Beyond the narrows Misha could make out the swell of the land rising up from the bay, masts of another ship languidly rocking, spires on a hilltop, tall pines. He gazed unhurriedly at the sight – scene which after such black storms recalled many an illusion traced on the horizons of becalmed, more southerly seas. Only the drone of the harbour patrol launch recalled him to present time, present needs, and yet he lingered awhile, leaning against the railing, pondering an awaiting encounter perhaps more tempestuous than the waters he'd passed through.

He returned to his stateroom. Through the portholes above his bunk he watched dawn's last trace of mauve disappear, then layers of peach and cream vanish, and then, without a care in the world it appeared, translucent blue skies filled the space.

In the matching tranquility of the bay, *Serena II* barely moved. Contentment ruled over the waters, like angels carved upon a tombstone, causing Mikhail to return to the question which had from time to time surfaced throughout his long voyage, and, before that, on occasion back in his father's house.

Had he the right to do this? Invade such carefully contrived exile? She had, after all, *chosen* to remain missing. She had never once called Land's End, much less the d'Olivier house. Her only contact had been made, somehow, with Jude McCallister.

The man she had wanted all along, he reminded himself bitterly, momentarily persuaded that contentment suited her, reflecting that real love would not disturb hard-won peace, turning away from the windows until *Serena II* tossed in the wake of a passing ship, and the spell of the harbour's tranquility was broken, and Mikhail knew its peace for what it really was: resignation at best – false and fleeting surface calm, fortitude notwithstanding.

Within an hour he had readied his ship and weighed anchor and began to move through the Narrows toward the beckoning wharf.

For the next fortnight Misha remained moored in Charlottetown Harbour, refilling supplies, refitting his boat, strolling the cobblestone streets of the town.

He did not expect to meet Caroline. She would never have made her home, he well knew, among the summertime crowds of the port's narrow lanes. Nevertheless he searched every doorway, walked every inch of the quay, traced and retraced his steps through the wooded park beside Battery Point. He studied the mansions overlooking these trails, the pale, careworn cottages on the opposite side of town, the weathered islanders grouped around chapels and markets and the old red-brick law court.

There was never the slightest sign of Mrs. Caroline Devereux. Nor was she ever in any of the restaurants Misha frequented – some nights by the harbour, others up near the college, other times farther out, in remote country inns set back from the highway.

And yet she is here, Misha would tell himself back on *Serena II*, turning the lamp down in his cabin, preparing his next day's excursions. It was no longer obsession, but fact. She might have gone northward to some wilder shore, inland perhaps to some lone hidden homestead, but she had not left Prince Edward. This was her home now, this province hoarding its gemstones – rare sheltered space of mysterious charm in the Gulf. Sometimes he sensed her tantalizingly near; other times, unaccountably, he felt she'd withdrawn, though never for long and never too far on an island where nothing, not even Acadia, was ever truly remote.

With this thought he would sleep at last, fitful unnerving thing, disturbed now by the groan of some low-riding tanker, now by the recollection of her wild, wilful heart pressing on his.

A third futile week passed. Misha resolved to search elsewhere, charting a course around Prince Edward's perimeter, passing as close as he dared to the turbulent north capes, scanning the homesteads en route.

On the day before his departure, he needed a few more supplies. He chose to continue along Great George Street, guessing he might not soon have the chance again for such an invigorating walk. Thus it was that he came upon the shop of Monsieur Daniel du Lac, Fine Antiques.

⌒ ❨ ⌐

"Unbelievable," murmured Daniel du Lac.

"Isn't it?" breathed Mikhail, staring up at the timepiece carefully centred at the top of the bookcase. "Almost in darkness – everything else in the store so well lit – and yet it caught my attention…"

Daniel managed to nod.

"Seemed to call out to me as I stopped past your awning to have a look at the harbour from the top of the hill."

Daniel took this in silence, overwhelmed not by the clock's beauty, as the stranger had mistakenly thought, but by the appearance of the stranger himself – again almost closing time, again his shop empty, again the same seemingly irresistible allure touching an unsuspecting, chosen heart. At that very moment, in fact, he'd been preparing the shipping papers to accompany Violette's gift on the next northbound packet. Ever so briefly he'd paused, trying to imagine this unknown place, Rock of Birds, and had looked up from under his visor and had seen Mikhail out on his walkway, motionless, staring into the shop. The little brass bell above his doorway had rung. The stranger had entered. Like a recurring dream, the next sequence unfolded exactly as it had done on the previous day, causing Daniel du Lac to watch spellbound as the man wandered about his crowded store, casting occasional disinterested glances at things, taking his time toward the window, stopping at last by the bookcase next to the grey velvet loveseat.

At that point Daniel knew. His strong presentment the night before had been right. The transaction he had concluded then was in a strange way only beginning, and the clock he was about to part with had a history still to be played out in his store. Hence, forgoing the customary initial formalities he'd merely stood, and had made his way down the aisle, and along with the stranger had gazed admiringly upon the timepiece, and was not surprised when the gentleman asked at last: "May I see that clock, Monsieur?"

He had expected those words. He could have predicted their intonation. And yet Monsieur du Lac was surprised all of a sudden to feel his resigned heart resisting. Perhaps, after all, this was not the man fated to complete the circle of the clock's path. His sudden appearance, his demeanour...all of it maybe happenstance. The timepiece was technically sold, after all. It might fall as he reached, suffer some damage as the gentleman looked. The delicate balance, the woodwork...

Daniel was glad when a small group of tourists stopped to admire a pair of bronze statues displayed in his window. He had a moment to think. In that moment resistance hardened. The timepiece was spoken for, simple as that, and should have been removed at once from the top of the case.

And yet there it had stayed. *For safekeeping,* he had said to himself, casting a last backward glance as he'd locked up on the previous night. In his heart, though, he had known otherwise. Almost a week remained until the packet's departure. Plenty of time still to wrap, fill out the papers, reserve a place on the boat, carry the gift to the dock. Meanwhile the clock would be his. Whenever he wished he could look up, admire its grace, its indefinable blend of force and fragility, which for some reason seemed like love to him, as he vaguely remembered love to have been half a century past, before his young bride had died, and their newborn the next day, and the buying and selling of old things had filled up his days.

"Might I have a look?" Misha repeated.

The tourists glanced up at the name of his shop, then again at the statues, whose blank indifferent stare seemed to disdain such frank longing. The bookseller locked up his shop alongside, nodded genially toward the antiques store, then followed the tourists on down the hill to the wharf.

Daniel by then had made his decision. He turned to the stranger and in a voice that he hoped sounded resolute said: "Well, I would love to oblige, Monsieur, yes –"

"Splendid."

"And any other time I would have – any other day that is, but on this *particular* day –" He straightened his perfectly placed plaid bow tie – "no, no I cannot take it down. Not today. You're too late."

Misha glanced at the door, slightly ajar still, its hand-painted, rectangular "Closed" sign swaying uncertainly. Then he looked hard at Daniel.

"Tomorrow, then," was his answer. He was piqued and made no effort to hide it. "What time do you open?"

"I – well it's not a matter of time, you see. More like circumstance, I should say. Yes…that's it. I am sorry to disappoint. It is out of my hands."

"The clock has been sold, you mean."

"The clock has been promised."

"And yet there it is still, displayed to the public."

"Not really displayed, no," countered Daniel, creating and collapsing a tent with his hands by pressing his fingers together, "and certainly not to the public. It was about to be packed in fact, shipped off on its way this week –"

"Then for God's sake while there's time left," exclaimed Mikhail, out of patience, "what's the harm if I look?"

Daniel sank down on the fine silk bergère near his door. In the last rays of the sun his grey wisps of hair seemed like a bronze crown. Yet there was nothing golden about his face, Mikhail thought, for the pale, stoop-shouldered man seemed suddenly older and as fragile as the Venetian glass carousel on the table behind him.

"Please," Misha said after a moment, regretting his earlier tone, "let me at least have a look, here on the loveseat, where there's some light still. Just a few minutes. That's all the time it'll take. No, no stay right there. I can take it down myself. You needn't trouble yourself."

Daniel was startled. He felt his shop suddenly filled not with things but with sound – complicated harmonies vaguely expected – as diminishing echoes of the gentleman's voice merged with the memory of Violette's passion, and, like a descant above them, a towering grandfather clock near his desk began slowly chiming the hour, seven p.m. *All of a piece*, the old man judged as he counted, *two missing halves of the coin – solitude, sundown, same exact soft insistence, same exact fervent words.*

He sighed. He had been right after all. With a surrendering wave of his long, pale, veined fingers he said, "Well if it matters so to you, Monsieur –"

"It does."

"Take the piece down if you like."

The dignified tolling ceased. Daniel watched as the stranger ran his hands over the clock. He was not surprised to see the man touch the face lovingly, feel the polished wood carefully, follow the curves of the pediment with more than a connoisseur's interest. He was not intrigued by the silence that seemed to invade his store once again. Nor was he in the least puzzled by the length of time this meticulous, quiet, intense process took. In fact, when at last the man did look up, darkening shadows by that time spilling onto the loveseat, Monsieur du Lac was prepared for the barely whispered first question.

"This piece is not old, is it, Monsieur?"

"It is not."

"Nor was it made here on the island," Misha continued – not really a statement, but a question, Daniel du Lac knew, since he had been expecting it.

"No."

The stranger's eyes deepened until they resembled dark topaz.

Gemstones, thought Daniel. *Even that is the same. Nothing left to do now but provide the same explanation*, he reflected, and so still in that even tone which was neither mistrust nor disinterest, but more like the acquiescence of a golden leaf descending, he recounted the story of his letter received, the note sent in reply, the clock in its turn shipped, the curious attraction he had felt from the start for the timepiece.

"I know I needn't explain to you why I felt as I did, Monsieur. These strange affinities are strong. I wanted to keep the clock, simple as that, though even I didn't understand why at the time, and so I hid it up in the shadows, on top of the bookcase right where you found it, but to no avail. It was not destined for me. Just as you saw it today, out from under my awning there on the walkway, someone else saw the very same timepiece, at about the same time in fact, yesterday, and then *voilà*..." He snapped his thin fingers. "Love at first sight, Monsieur – *le coup de foudre*," he repeated in French as befitted such elegant, overwhelming attractions, "the clock desired, claimed, its shipment arranged, further commissions assured – all in the space of an hour."

Daniel turned and pointed out toward Great George Street, as though to fix for them both before dark the exact location of this most extraordinary convergence of strangers, so he did not see the colour drain from Mikhail's face, nor how his tanned, weathered hands seemed to hold on to the timepiece to steady themselves.

"The only real difference, Monsieur, was that at the time it was raining, *pouring* – well if you were in town then you remember," said Daniel fluidly, having by then an almost superstitious belief that the fate of his cherished clock rested exclusively, albeit temporarily, on his own scrupulous participation.

"A small detail, perhaps," he allowed, "but in reality…" He stopped, stunned by the change in the stranger's demeanour – anticipation turning his tourmaline eyes almost black, the handsome, gold face suddenly pale. Everything else he had predicted – woman and man pulled as they'd been in the same remarkable way toward his shop – so that he had believed, falsely, it was the fate of his clock to elicit such parallel yearnings. Now with this changed man before him he knew. It was not the future of strangers fated to be linked by A.O.'s fine hands. It was the histories of acquaintances waiting to be renewed.

Discreetly, Daniel glanced at the grip the gentleman had on the clock still. *No, not acquaintances*, he decided. *Far more than that in this case.*

Which brought in its turn a dilemma. Having decided not to obstruct whatever remained of the clock's fate to be fulfilled in his store, Monsieur du Lac had his heart set now on seeing it through. Yet there was so little to add. Concerning the timepiece, he had relayed all he knew. Concerning the woman, the story was different. Indeed, the story was missing, for she had revealed next to nothing. That blithe farewell, her smile, her promised return – all of it strangely opaque – no last name, no address, past and future days blurred, present tense absent, as though time and belonging belonged to others somehow, undefined spheres and transience her portion.

He felt the gentleman's hand on his arm, sensed his intense gaze once more. He recalled Violette's grip, her fiercely determined

K . L . V I D A L

eyes. *Monsieur du Lac*, she had insisted then, *everything has a history*.

"But that's just it!" Daniel heard a voice which resembled his own exclaim. "She had none."

The stranger stared at him blankly.

"Even less than the clock in your hands! At least I know where that came from, why it was made, how it found its way to my shop. With Violette, on the other hand –"

"Violette?"

"History vanishes. No place or date. Only her name and her vagueness and the clock's destination. Even her name's not complete," Daniel murmured, chagrined, but then he considered and smiled in spite of himself and said, "Well in her case perhaps one had no need for more...*Violette*," he repeated after a moment. "Not really a sound, more like the one thing you see the first time she glances your way."

He gestured in the direction of a Limoges figurine on the mantel. "Yes. Just like that," he confirmed, as though the porcelain head had nodded back, and Misha knew then it was Caroline Devereux on Great George Street in the rain on that day – so pale and fine was the elegant statue, so enigmatic the smile, so undecided the immense and perfectly painted hyacinth eyes.

Only her name was now different, and as again that grandfather clock in the back of the shop began chiming, Mikhail pondered this. He recalled the Trans Canada crash, the memorial out by the north capes, the dwindling references as the months passed. By now, it appeared, Caroline Devereux felt secure, safe enough to stroll Charlottetown's narrow streets, something she could only have done – having survived not extinction but far more cleverly presumption of death near these shores – if she had buried her past along with that wreckage, reinventing herself in the process, not just present and future days, but also her name, emblem of all that was gone.

The measured tolling once more ceased. Monsieur du Lac looked around. Seven-thirty p.m. – closing time long delayed, evening descended, not a tourist or sailor or merchant left on the walkway, and still the mysterious Violette to describe. Like fine sand through his fingers, the image resisted even the hold words might have. Yet those phrases were all he had left. Few as they were, he would offer them to the stranger, as the clock had been given to him, unsolicited – a gift, those had been A.O.'s instructions – although the right person turned out in the end to be two.

"As to the lady," Daniel began, "Well you can see it all there in the statue. Elusive somehow, despite the precise form, as though the artist set out to make her deliberately vague. Of course in this case we have no artist. Still," Daniel went on, gesturing once again in the direction of the figurine, "Violette comes to mind. She was all contradiction – cast in the same paradoxical mould. She paid handsomely for a clock she had no plans to keep. In an anonymous note she was incredibly moved. Her manner was polished; her allure uncontrived – I should like to say out of time, like the things in my shop, yet one sensed earth in her nearness, ripeness like beach plums. No, no that's not quite it…"

He removed his spectacles as though to find just the right word. The image escaped him. He sat back in his chair, about to apologize for his failure when all of a sudden the gentleman said, "Please don't disturb yourself. I can imagine the rest."

And with that he proceeded, to the astonishment of Daniel du Lac, to give an exact description of the woman who had come into his store on the previous night – her face, her form, colouring, height, pallor, fragility, strength – everything down to the water dripping through her thick, tangled hair; the comb which of course failed to hold on to that hair; the cameo fastened securely – no doubt to some brightly-toned flowered shawl.

Of her extraordinary markings, distinctive enough in themselves so that no other description would have been needed, he said nothing. They were as one with her flesh to him, one with her soul; he barely remembered them, and besides, anyone could have made mention of those vines like curls on her neck, whereas what he had had to describe, things at once palpable and intangible, only he would have remembered. Indeed, he had done it with such a passionate clarity that he seemed to be painting a sketch, filling in tones with a striking palette of mauve, peach, rose and black crayons, so that now and again Daniel just nodded, amazed by the breathless, perfectly accurate rendering.

When he was finished, still holding Antonin's clock, Mikhail rested himself against the loveseat, much as the woman had done after reading and rereading the note postmarked Goose Bay. Daniel himself did not stir, moved as he was to the very depths of his soul by the stranger's frank yearning, so like Violette's sensual grace. More than ever he was convinced it fell to him somehow to link the two things. More than ever he felt ill-equipped. To be sure, he had clasped many a set of fine pearls in his day – but gemstones like these lovers' lives…ah, there he was at a loss, out of his depth. He had shared all he could with them both. What was there left to disclose?

He turned to the window. The barest curve of a slender white moon hung over the masts in the harbour. The barest hint of dried rose petals remained in the pewter bowl by his chair. They seemed as one to him in the stillness – one thing distinctively fine, uniquely Old World – that elegant mark near the sky, the scent of a trellis long-vanished, and then for some reason, mixed in with them both was the vague image of something else curved, baroque, redolent of the past, midnight blue like the sky.

Mikhail saw the old man sit up. His pale blue eyes shone. He uncrossed his long, thin, slightly bowed legs, and in a triumphant tone said, "There is one last thing. A card to be sent with that clock. Violette left it unsealed – told me to read it in fact, since anything mailed in return was to come back to my shop…I will retrieve it."

The sight of that note nearly undid Mikhail, so distinctive the script, so poignant the dedication, *For Serge and Susannah…whom I can never repay.* He stared at the signature – one word, simply – *Violette.* He read and reread the promise to write, send whatever was needed, return to Daniel du Lac's shop for anything sent in reply – all very careful, everything veiled – one thing and one thing alone unmistakably clear: whoever they were, Serge and Susannah meant all the world to Caroline Devereux.

And yet, thought Mikhail mystified, they had come only recently into her life. With the exception of Antonin, she knew not a soul in the Maritimes on the eve of her departure.

Daniel offered no clue here. "She never spoke of them. Just that she'd searched over a year for the right present for them. As for the rest –" he shrugged – "I know no more than you do. I'm to save any letters, that's all. Violette said she'd pass by – no, *chance* to pass by – those were her words."

"Then she's from town?"

"No. One had the sense it was far – that she came rarely to town, if at all."

A long silence followed. Fretfully, Misha stared out the window, then at the table beside him. His eyes fell on the envelope beside Caroline's card.

Serge and Susannah Joubert Pellerin. The last name meant nothing.

Point Guetter. Lookout Point. The place was unknown to him.

Rocher aux Oiseaux. Rock of Birds. He sat up and looked closer. North-northeast of the Madeleines – the picture was vague still – west of the Newfoundland mainland, due south of Québec's remote eastern coastline, dead in the centre of the Gulf of St. Lawrence.

Yes, he was sure he was right. He had passed its sheer cliffs one spring, off his course in a storm. It had seemed to him lifeless, forbidding, yet for some reason he had never forgotten its adamantine endurance. *Strange fortress lost to the rest of the world*, he had thought sailing by, although even in fog he could see it had not been abandoned. Already the Gulf Stream had warmed the waters around it, and already the rarest of beautiful migrating birds had passed the prow of his ship on their way to its shores.

Islanders only had eluded Mikhail on that voyage, for he had passed Rock of Birds to the east, off its wildest shore, where among the caves and sheer cliffs there had been no sign of settlement – no boats, no harbour, not even one homestead.

And yet it was there all along, realized Mikhail, thunderstruck, *no doubt facing south, no doubt made of stone like the island beneath it – sturdy, enduring, lonely place, Lookout Point*.

The irony overwhelmed him. Of all the places on earth to have offered shelter that night, of all the grand islands he'd passed in his lifetime – one minuscule, overlooked, battered speck in the sea: Rock of Birds.

Even the outline of Serge and Susannah began to take shape. *Acadians*, Mikhail guessed, judging by the name of their house. *Elderly, tested by life*, he also surmised, for only the old, attached to a land loved in distant, far sturdier years, stayed on in such stark, oddly cherished isolation.

As to the rest of the picture – no, those outlines were vague still. Whatever had happened during that violent storm off Lookout Point – however long Violette had remained on *Rocher aux Oiseaux* – Serge and Susannah alone could bear witness. They alone would know where she'd gone. Most likely they'd brought her, having heard something of her future plans – plans, Misha rightly suspected, which had been offered only selectively by a survivor already presumed lost to the rest of the world.

Still, sparse as those facts might remain, Misha would hear them all now. Candidly, despite the months come and gone, Serge and Susannah would share what they could with him, not out of courtesy to a stranger who'd come unexpectedly to their island, but in open confidence to a friend who'd crossed the Gulf of St. Lawrence with Antonin's clock.

꜡ ☾ ꜆

The rain was not much more than drizzle by the time Mikhail took the large, carefully packed box from Monsieur du Lac's hands. They were standing again at the threshold, door again slightly ajar, rectangular hand-painted "Closed" sign still undecided.

"How to repay you?" Mikhail managed.

"The clock was meant to be a gift. Those were A.O.'s instructions. I have merely found – how shall I say? – a worthy courier, that is all."

He glanced again at the sky, felt the suddenly brisk wind that had followed the storm, presaging perhaps another, and added simply, *"Dieu vous garde, Monsieur."*

"Yes. Yes, thank you...Godspeed to you too, Daniel du Lac."

As he watched the gentleman disappear down the hill, Daniel mused: *I never did find out his name. Violette left only half of her own. A.O. sent only initials.* He sighed. *And yet the circle's been closed. The necklace is clasped. Who remains still to wear it – proudly or sadly or briefly or perhaps not at all – mine not to know, I suppose.*

He felt a twinge of regret in his old heart, sadness upon completion, or perhaps it was just that old weary ache in his limbs the night dampness brought on.

He turned out the last of the lamps in his shop. The sign continued to sway as he slammed the door shut and turned away from the harbour, up toward the park near the top of the street, down to his own empty home by the sea.

☾

Under clouds the vague colour of quartz at day's end, Cap-Egmont's harbour was especially lovely. The wharf was secluded, the boardwalk near-empty, the anchored ships small enough so that the jumble of intertwined masts could not hide the muted though still-brilliant island palette. Green, gold and copper-toned meadows caught the diminishing light to the north; southward the sea was at rest, its untroubled waters a dusty rose shade that resembled the sky and Caroline's mouth, as Misha recalled it.

Serena II was also quiescent, keeping its counsel, languorous dream-ship at the end of the dock.

Indeed, everything about the past week resembled a dream, Misha reflected, reclined on a deck chair overlooking the harbour. He thought of his walk up Great George Street, his departure the following morning bearing Antonin's clock, his arrival at Lookout Point, his return to Prince Edward – not back to Charlottetown but, as Serge had directed him, to this remote western cove on the Acadian peninsula.

The sea route had been exact, unerring, for little more than a year had gone by since Serge himself had left Violette Todd by this very same boardwalk, same indecisive time of day.

"Such a strange parting," he'd murmured, seated beside Mikhail out by the steps on the edge of his lawn. "She was resting right on that swing chair – yes, right where you're seated now, Monsieur, and it was a night just like this – clear and silent and crisp – but I was troubled. I knew by the time the tides changed she'd be gone. I also knew she had nothing – just that pin she was prepared to part with at long last.

"Well, of course, that could not be. We gave her some money – a trifle, although she protested." At the recollection, Serge had smiled briefly..."Proud. Just like my Susannah. Sand grass and cedar, I'd often think, watching them work side by side. One rooted here by the rocks, one destined to sway with the tides. Star-crossed meeting, if ever there was one."

"Mind you, she loved us," Serge had added after a moment, running his hand over the pediment of Antonin's clock.

"Still, from the very beginning I knew. There'd be no keeping Violette. Although it would soon be November, last packet 'til spring-time, April for some reason seeming each year more distant..."

Once again Serge had paused. Silent for what had seemed a long while, he had gazed at the Gulf stretching below. Then, suddenly straightening himself: "No. Back to the sea she must go. Come daybreak *L'Inattendu* sailed with her like a naiad reclaiming her kingdom...Well, in a sense it *was* her domain," Serge had confessed, leaning in toward the stranger. "I came to believe that, Monsieur, given her strangely protected path through the Gulf, that long, deep forgetting sleep from which she awakened – twice – once in our cave, as I have explained to you, once again on the lawn, as Susannah's described.

"What went before – I know just what I've said, nothing more. She was sailing alone in that rain...Most injudicious of her...She returned again to what seemed a precarious solitude. It was her wish. I could not interfere. I left her where she had chosen – a wild Acadian coast like the one she swore she could never forget."

By way of conclusion, Serge had let his hand slowly fall from the clock onto Mikhail's chair, for there had been no more to impart. He and his wife had told Mikhail all that they knew, as Misha'd predicted they'd do, overjoyed as they'd been with the remarkable clock, the treasured letter attached, above all the knowledge that Violette, safe in the Maritimes still, was well, unchanged, undiminished, had never forgotten them.

"We will see her again someday, I am sure of it," had been Susannah's brief coda, for she had been silent out there on the lawn beside Mikhail, reliving in her husband's narration their brief summertime idyll.

Perhaps to confirm this, high over the waters above Rock of Birds that pale moon had appeared, slender still, casting its tentative glow on the suddenly fierce incoming tides. By the time those same tides had turned, Misha'd set out once again, south by southwest as Serge had so carefully charted. By the following sunset he had reached Cap-Egmont.

All this and more passed through Mikhail's mind as he reclined on his deck chair, docked at last in the place he had sought for a lifetime.

$\smile$ ◖ $\smallsmile$

"Well as it happens, Monsieur, Violette Todd did stay here once," confirmed Honorine to the stranger come into port on the previous day. "In fact she stayed quite a while, perhaps even two months, but a full year's come and gone since those days."

"So she has left Cap-Egmont."

"She has."

By way of reply the stranger stared out the window toward the now-deserted shore road. In those brief moments Honorine studied the man: crisp, open-collared white shirt, dark tan trousers, navy pullover tied with unstudied grace round his shoulders. Such artless appeal had in fact been the first thing she'd noticed as he'd

approached – the winsome confidence that had put her at ease,
even made her want to oblige him, that spontaneous smile, which
had made her colour somewhat. He had been visiting friends, he'd
confessed. There remained one he'd still hoped to see before his return
to New York.

"Close acquaintance – friend of the family. Well in recent years
we've lost touch." Again that fine smile. "I'm only berthed overnight.
A day or two more if this storm hits," he'd added, and Honorine had
felt suddenly sad, not for the rain but at the thought of his leaving.

Nevertheless she'd been cautious. She had admitted to all she
could say in fact, knowing that Violette Todd prized above all things
a private, nearly reclusive existence in her remote, walled estate out
past Dutchman Rock. Even among the old Acadians scattered along
the coast she had been reticent, preferring to visit the harbour, the
abbey, the guest house alone, intermittently – never for long stays.
Indeed, as far as Honorine knew, no one but Monsieur Jude had ever
been inside Sans Souci's walls.

Still, as she continued to study the stranger, who continued to
study the empty beach out past the road, Honorine felt conflicted. If
there were a way she could help, give at least the farm's name this
one time, the general area –

Alas, there was none. She fumbled, fingering the tassels on the
key to her antique desk drawer.

"The fact is, Monsieur…"

"I understand," said the gentleman, suddenly turning back as
though he'd been reading her mind all along. "After all a year's a
long time. You have been very kind."

Startled, Honorine made no answer. Something was different.
Something had changed in the few silent moments just passed, for in
the gaze that met hers now, in those exceptional opal eyes, there was
a deepening fervour which had replaced all insouciance.

"I know I called her a friend," those urgent eyes seemed to say.
"I know I said we'd lost touch, that I'd be sailing tomorrow perhaps,
perhaps not, depending on fate and the seas, one and the same
in these parts – and it was all true, every word…*but Mademoiselle,*

there's so much more. My life and hers and no doubt a third hang in the balance of this one thing I've asked, and which I know that you know – you are her friend now – you could not have spent so much time with her here and not be her friend now – and now I need her address, nothing more, for with that I can find her, and without that, although I know she's not far, I may not. At least not 'til the winter. Certainly not once the snows come. After that who can say? Springtime comes late to these shores. She may have gone off once again. Again to have lost her! *I've come so close, Mademoiselle*."

All this and more Honorine seemed to read in the deepening gaze that never once left her face. She half expected him to continue, this time aloud as he stood there before her, but instead he just turned and made his way toward the hall.

"Wait, Monsieur! *Please!*" she called.

Mikhail turned to find Honorine hastily writing on a pad of paper beside her.

"*Voilà*," she pronounced, not without evident pride, for she had in those moments solved her dilemma. "This is where you will find Violette. Not today perhaps – maybe not for a while if it rains. But come Sunday for sure. Yes. If you go then you will see her."

Perplexed, Mikhail stared at the paper she quickly tore from the pad.

"Abbaye St-Timothée," he read aloud. "Père Gabriel Beaumartine."

"Violette's fond of the place. Whenever she can she helps Père Gabriel with his trees. The orchard's not big, but on his own –" Honorine smiled – "well, the pastor's not as young as his fruit, you might say. And those trees are his life. And Violette understands trees. Or perhaps, as she says, it's the other way round. 'Trees understand me, Honorine,' she insists. Either way, she'll be there."

The parlour fell silent.

"*Allez-y, Monsieur*…Go on," she repeated, for the stranger seemed suddenly rooted to some preferred spot on the carpet. "Once the storm hits, there could be rain for a week." She turned for a moment and studied the grey, brooding Strait. "*Allez-y vite!*"

Honorine remained standing beside the large picture window. How like the woman he sought the man seemed as he moved down the road – vigorous, undeterred, buoyed by youth and its seemingly endless possibilities, favoured with beauty and its universally granted exemptions. His appeal had lingered long in the room, like perfume. Vividly it brought to mind another late autumn entrance, another man – older by far, self-contained, proud, face tempered more by life than the sea. That morning too she would always remember – the careful, deliberate walk, the delay, the ensuing confusion, the despair barely kept at arm's length.

So very different, Honorine mused, staring out past the porch at the increasingly troubled breeze. Suddenly she recalled the unique force in Jude's hands, the unsettling depths of his eyes, that unvarnished longing beneath his decorum. It was all there again today, she reflected – different man, to be sure, different grace, strength from the sinews as opposed to fortitude's resolution – but in essentials, in that mysterious urgency that threatened at any moment to break through well-conditioned bounds – yes, the moments were strangely one and the same.

Full circle somehow, surmised Honorine, not without an increasing, indefinable sense of foreboding. And then she turned from the window and the once-more deserted fork in the road.

"Yes, that is so, Monsieur," affirmed Père Gabriel stoutly. He was perched on the steps of his church, rocking back and forth on his sandals, which he wore over socks in the autumn, black woollen tips visible beneath the long, ample folds of his chocolate-brown habit. His arms, also ample, were tucked deep into the tunnels of each opposite sleeve. A tan rope belt surrounded his extremely robust waist. Indeed, Mikhail thought, in spite of his years, everything about the abbot was extremely robust – wide face, wider smile, wide ring of white hair crowning a deeply tanned head.

"Mademoiselle Honorine was correct," he went on. "We should be lost without Violette. No apple pies…no fruit tarts."

Extricating a large hand, he waved ceremoniously in the direction of the orchard.

"Well you can see how she frets there – all summer long in the sun, even in rain sometimes now, what with December so near and my flock always hungry.

"'They come to nourish the soul, Violette,' I say. 'Cider and jam, Mon Père, pies and your Bible,' she answers, always with mischief like plum wine in her eyes."

He brushed off a leaf which had drifted onto his shoulder. Then, philosophically: "She may be right after all, Monsieur. The winter is long. My feast day banquets are welcome. Sunday Mass seems more crowded these days. Who can say?"

Noon began to toll slowly from the bell tower above them. Père Gabriel waited, then glanced around in the sudden silence that for some reason always surprised him after the last chime had faded. He sighed and gazed out past his orchard, out toward the rolling hills no longer a bright July green but a dustier tone, sadder and wiser it seemed, like an infantryman returning home.

"Yes, yes, of course you may wait. Wherever you like. There's a bench in the orchard, up against the wall behind the blueberry shrubs. Follow the pathway inside."

Again his large hand found its way into the sanctuary of his ample sleeves. "You won't have to wait long. Not by the look of those clouds. Violette won't take a chance on a sudden storm upsetting her fruit."

And with that Père Gabriel began rocking again on his well-cushioned sandals, as though surveying his kingdom, which clearly included those clouds, and Mikhail turned and walked toward the gate to wait inside the orchard for Mrs. Caroline Devereux.

☾

As the priest had predicted, Misha did not have to wait long. That tango-like step of hers was unmistakable, that swaying progression which had bedevilled him as she had moved beneath her gown around his father's living room, Christmas Eve.

There'd be no gown now, Misha imagined, hearing the rusty gate creak as it opened. No long gloves, no sapphires – perhaps just that cameo, maybe not even that – in any case he was perhaps too far to see that much, too shaded by the intervening leaves... too overcome all of a sudden by the sight of her turning to lock the gate behind her, stopping to caress the cat that had slipped in beside her, pausing to gaze at the sky as the abbot had done, to assess the heaviness of the clouds and the precious time remaining.

She could not see his bench. She was looking east; he was off to the north; there was nothing between them at last but once-flowering trees and that absolute stillness again after the bells had announced the half-hour.

If anything, Mikhail saw, she was more beautiful than he remembered her. Much was unaltered – same thick black hair hastily caught at the back of her neck, same slender form, same strangely luxuriant grace. Much, though, was different. Her uncommon pallor, after so many months so far north, was even finer, almost crystalline. Her languorous step, while still light, seemed to him slower, more deliberate. Above all her face registered something he had only glimpsed in Jude McCallister's work. It was not in her eyes, though they appeared deeper and more immense than before, nor in the still slightly upturned curve of her sensuous mouth, nor even around the stray curls mixed in with the permanent vines on her neck.

No, Misha decided, after she had sat down to fill her basket with fruit that had fallen during the night – no, the yearning was everywhere. Her remarkable beauty was suffused with it now – imprinted, one might almost say, stamped with a blend of desire and contentment, regret and resignation, satisfaction paradoxically formed of undisguised longing. Jude had somehow seized hold of this contrast, rendering even its disturbing allure – but he had offered no explanation. Perhaps he could find none. Perhaps he dared not probe for it. In any case there it was – the ambiguity he had expressed in that falsely dated, fine portrait, only the contradiction was far more striking on the live model's features, in her form, in her movements as she stood and moved up the ladder and reached for whatever remained on the branches.

All this and more Mikhail pondered, for he was unable to go to her, as though he, like Jude, had been unaccountably blocked by the very enigma that had lured them both to its source.

And yet he could not remain so. Unlike Jude he had only this moment, this one chance to grasp what was there before him, decode the beguiling yet distant loveliness that caused him to falter, in spite of himself, as she made her way back down the steps and resumed her place on the grass.

The bells tolled once more, but only once more. Caroline too heard the chime. Pushing away a stray wisp of hair from her eyes, she looked again at the sky, stood once more and with decision moved on to the next tree, determined to make the most of what remained to her then.

At that point Mikhail knew. Perhaps even more than her painter he knew. *Purpose*, he finally realized, defining for himself with incontrovertible clarity what even Jude had preferred to leave blurred, unexamined. *It is that which she's found here, that which remains here – not happiness, not even fulfillment, certainly nothing that can obscure the ambivalence that shadows her features. Nevertheless there it is – purpose – the next task, the next tree, life to be lived in an orderly way, fruitfully, according to rules she herself has configured, limits she of her own will imposed.*

Light filtering through the branches defined her more clearly as she moved on. Her long, flowing skirt was wheat-toned; her low scoop-necked top the colour of wine; around her waist she had tied a vividly floral fringed shawl, so that somehow, thought Misha, she seemed to be one with the last, richly hued days of the fall.

No, he corrected himself. *Belonging to no season, really. Out of time, as she was when I knew her, only more so in this place – this churchyard, this island, this remote French-speaking soil untouched too by time present.*

But time present was passing. St-Timothée's orchard slowly grew dark under thickening clouds. Gusts of wind rattled the gate. Piles of dried leaves swirled up and around Mrs. Devereux. And still, not unlike the first time he saw her passing under the archway into his father's house, Mikhail stayed where he was – unsettled, unseen by her, beset once again by the conflict he thought he'd resolved outside Charlottetown Harbour...*Had he the right?* Such purpose as hers must have been bought at a high price, such fruitfulness dearly acquired. It was perhaps her privilege to have it remain undisturbed.

A crackle of lightning sliced through black skies over the church. Steadily, though with a quickening hand, Caroline worked on. Struggling, Mikhail reached for that same equanimity, or at the very least resignation, only alternative left to them both, he began to believe, nearly convincing himself as the first heavy drops fell – and then the orchard gate creaked once again and Père Gabriel appeared on the path. He called her name softly at first, then in a sharper, far more canonical tone, until at last she appeared, or rather descended a step from the top of the highest, still heavily laden tree, parting some branches to find the abbot motioning impatiently from the wall.

"Quickly now! Gather your things!"

She remained where she was.

"Come, Violette," he cried out. "Come along. *Come down at once before who knows what strikes us both.*"

Once again Caroline vanished, only to reappear and make her way down the tall, wooden ladder. It was his church after all; the sky belonged to his gods, her face seemed to say, resignation alone remaining there – no trace of ambivalence now – acceptance defining her features, her movements, even the way she removed her shawl from her waist and covered her head with it before she picked up her basket and crossed toward the abbot.

So intent had Père Gabriel been in reclaiming Violette that he never even noticed Mikhail. Indeed he seemed to have forgotten him, stepping aside as Caroline slipped through the arch before he pulled the gate shut behind them with a resounding finality.

Sounds of their footsteps receded. Misha remained on his bench, letting the rain soak him through, grateful for the sudden drenching which had both interrupted and resolved things. Purpose, he now knew, had not been Caroline's choice. Purpose had been imposed from without – by time and the passing of seasons, by the demands of those who loved her, like Jude, those who admired her, like the abbot, those who remained indifferent, like fate and approaching December.

The end result was the same. Mrs. Devereux had been disarmed. If this was her wish, or, more precisely, if she had accepted the fact as unavoidable, there was nothing more to be done. He would go not in peace but resigned – yes, at long last resigned, but let the finality be of her own choosing. This much they both deserved, Misha decided, irresolution turning to vapour like the fog rolling in from the Strait as he stood.

Water splashed noisily from the fruit trees onto the gravel. Lightning again forked, seeking the church spires. "Yes I've the right – more than the right," he said in defiance of who knew what lay in store for them all. "We are obliged now to meet. I know where she comes when she can, and the rains can't last forever."

⌒☾⌒

"Just the varnish, Raoul. That's all I'll be taking this time, unless by chance those cloths –"

"Monsieur Jude's lucky day," Raoul interrupted. "Lucky night, I should say, Mademoiselle. Day's long since gone, though one couldn't say when in this mist."

The clerk turned, leaned back as far as he could and squinted up at the wall clock over the counter.

"After eight," he managed to read aloud, disbelieving. "Well, I've been running all day. That supply ship from Halifax came in a day early. Wanting to keep ahead of the storm, I expect…"

Absently, Caroline smiled.

"Needn't have rushed so," muttered Raoul, squinting still as he studied the uncertain clouds over the bay. "Worst of the rain's passing us by. High winds later on, that's for sure, but no flood tides, you'll see. Drizzle perhaps still, maybe some fog…"

His small voice trailed off like that storm, imprecisely, for Raoul was old. He could never remember exactly *how* old, though he could name every boat come into port in his lifetime, track the course of a storm before it had formed in the Gulf and recall that his grandfather had run the shop before Canada became Canada, a fact he was fond of repeating, mostly to British tourists. Beyond these vaguely connected spheres, Raoul's expertise waned, his thoughts blurred.

"Ah yes, Monsieur Jude," he reminded himself. "Varnish and cloth. Lots of both. I left them out in the storeroom. I won't be a minute."

With that Raoul vanished behind a tattered black curtain. Caroline crossed to the window and stared out at the boardwalk, its wooden grey planks shining like steel in the glistening rain.

All of it so familiar by now, she mused. *Every fisherman known to me, most of the trawlers, the launches, the sailboats, home port ones at least –*

"Here we are, Mademoiselle – right where I put them. Well, not exactly right where I put them…Mademoiselle?"

Caroline made no answer. She seemed lost in reflection, as Raoul himself was so often, and so he thought nothing more of it, but simply placed the cans and the cloth on his counter, took out his pad to write up an invoice, recollected, put down his pad and said,

"I forgot. This was already added to Monsieur Jude's account. He prefers to stop in for his bill every month, check any boats just come in, stay on to sketch if the scene strikes his fancy…Most of the time it does. He painted that houseboat last year. Left the picture with me for Christmas."

A delivery van that had been parked just past the shop window pulled away.

"You needn't pay for this now," Raoul went on, as though Violette had turned back and were standing before him, fishing into her bag for her purse or a pen or a cheque book, whereas in reality she had not moved from her spot by the window – only place in the shop from which one could see the end of the deepwater dock, hidden from the entrance by shade trees and sheds and the van that had just moved.

"Why not drive round to this side, Mademoiselle? Not so many steps to the car. I could just load the supplies into your trunk and then *voilà*..." He stopped, seeing at last she was paying him no attention. Slowly he made his way across the shop and stood beside Violette, who still appeared unaware of him. He followed her gaze out in the direction of the end of the deepwater dock. Then, after a long, almost reverent pause, he breathed,

"Beautiful, isn't she?"

Caroline nodded.

"Docked just past sundown last night."

Still no reply.

"Quite a sight, Mademoiselle. Quite a sight watching her sail through the Narrows in that light. Crew of one, I was told. Unbelievable."

Staring ahead still, Caroline managed somehow, "Islander, do you think?"

"No. – No, that much I knew at a glance. 'That ship's not from here,' I said to myself, locking up for the night. No place even close, sleek and grand as she is, untroubled still by the winter. Still, just to be certain, I checked. – Well of course it was dark by then. Difficult to read anything let alone fine golden lettering by the light of that low boardwalk lamp. I got as close as I could though. Long enough to see the name...make out home port." He tugged on his old worn lapels as he continued to stare, announcing at last, "*Manhattan*! Can you imagine? Can't remember when a boat's docked overnight here from Manhattan. Certainly not this time of year."

"Are you open?" a customer asked abruptly from the entrance at the other end of the shop.

"Yes, yes of course. I – we were just looking. What can I do for you?"

Raoul turned away, shuffled back to the counter, produced a few hooks and some lines. Another customer entered, looking for rain gear. After a moment a third left, carrying an extra life vest.

By then it was almost eight-thirty. Suddenly Raoul remembered Monsieur Jude's varnish and cloth.

"Mademoiselle, I'm so sorry…forgive me."

He turned, about to cross back to the window, and was surprised to find Violette gone. She had left through the side door. Jude's supplies too were gone, Raoul saw.

He moved to the window in time to see Violette stepping out of her car, reparked at the edge of the deepwater dock. He watched as she stood for a moment and stared, reading and rereading the name on the stern of the ship, it appeared. Then, as though in a dream, she moved toward the berth and stepped onto the ladder.

"Are you still open?" a fourth customer called from the entrance.

"Yes, yes of course," answered Raoul, making his way back to the counter, forgetting about Mademoiselle and her strange fascination.

⌒☽⌒

Mikhail was lying in his stateroom, three steps below the ship's main salon. He was trying to read – no longer Catullus, which he had placed back on his shelf when he had returned from Père Gabriel's church – but Shakespeare's *The Tempest*, with its magical island where past and future change places.

He heard a step, or so he thought, on the ship's starboard deck. For a moment or two he listened, but heard no more. He returned to his book, making another effort to concentrate, sensing again he would fail, when once more he heard steps.

This time he was sure. He sat up on his bed. There was somebody aboard his boat, not on the deck this time, but in the cabin, passing through the main salon, approaching his stateroom. He stood, about to walk to the doorway when Caroline appeared on the threshold before him.

She merely stared at him, paler than he had ever seen her, save for that one frozen night in her mill.

He too was silent, for though he had already studied her that day, he was taken aback by her sudden nearness, well past sundown, deep in the swaying cabin of *Serena II*.

He made no move toward her. She remained where she was, unsteady still, not from the movement of the ship but from the sight of him, whom she had last seen in an airport in Manhattan, eighteen months earlier, whose voice she had last heard in a violent rainstorm in Newfoundland, and whose last words to her then, broken by static, had been "I love you."

Yes it was Misha, tanned and weathered from his voyage, not just this one to the Maritimes, but the previous ones, the seasons of mourning and chaos, the final decision to find her, the struggle thereafter to leave her in peace.

He himself had found no peace – she saw that also at once – though it was no longer the grief she had seen in the newspaper that marked his face, but another hurt which she feared was bitterness, but which, when he finally spoke, she recognized as the thing that had always been there, just never so close to the surface – yearning bedrock and deep, like her own.

"I still do, you know," were his words, barely murmured there in the cabin, as though a year and half had not happened, and the conversation of that last phone call had yet to be concluded.

She nodded, tears welling up in her widening eyes which remained fixed on him as he approached her, for she could not approach him – she feared she would fall if she moved, dissolve into the waters around them as she had done when her plane had plunged into the Gulf – and so she was grateful to find that she did not have to move, that he had taken her into his arms and was holding her tightly against him.

She let her head fall onto his shoulders. He ran his hand through her hair, thick with salt and the damp night.

"Yes, Caroline, I still do. I love you desperately. I never stopped, not for a moment, although you did. I suppose you had to…"

A muffled groan escaped from someplace deep in her.

"You have not found it easy though, have you, my love?"

She shook her head.

"Not even in the beginning?"

"It was never easy," she cried, first words she'd uttered since she had entered his stateroom. "I thought it would be at first. I was convinced time would heal – that you had been spared. *I thought I had set you free, Mikhail.*"

He stepped back from her slightly, and, with just a trace of irony, smiled.

"Do you really believe I've been free, Caroline?"

She made no answer.

"I came up here needing to know," he insisted.

"I stayed up here fearing to say."

"Say it now."

"Mikhail…"

"Before I sail again –"

"Are you sailing again?"

"The sea is my home, you know that."

The moment both feared and sought was at hand – inevitable admission she had avoided, craving it still, reckoning long overdue.

"No, Misha," she whispered. "Not for a day have you been spared. Neither have I."

She felt his mouth on hers suddenly, his steady arms holding her even closer to stop her from trembling, and at last she did stop, deeply returning his kiss because in that hidden cabin which resembled her red velvet room she felt sealed off from time, and in those forbidden dimensions removed from the shoreline she seemed lost in space, and because she had set no one free on Susannah Joubert's lawn, least of all herself.

She tried somehow to break from him.

"Not yet," he protested, for her kiss had proved stronger than any compunctions he'd felt pursuing her, and her embrace sweeter by far than any pleasure remembered, and like her he was lost.

"Misha," she gasped. "We can't."

"We have."

"That was before."

"I meant just now."

"I came to explain things!"

"Is that what you came for?"

"I saw your new boat. I mean it might have been yours. I – it was growing dark." Her pallor vanished, replaced by a deepening flush. "I thought perhaps just a word…" She stopped. His eyes remained fixed on her, as with the passing of each season they had never ceased to torment her.

"A word, then," conceded Mikhail, although he did not move away this time. "A word, Caroline, if that's what you came for."

She tried to resume, faltered, took a step backward, and realized she was against the door still.

"Two if you like…I am not in a hurry."

Another attempt, another stumble, and then, mixed in with her failed words, music drifted down from the houseboat alongside.

"*Easy To Love*," murmured Mikhail.

Vaguely she heard the lyrics filling the small space between them.

"Like you, Mrs. Devereux."

"Misha…"

"Is it still Mrs. Devereux?"

A substantial pause. "No."

"You have married then."

"…No."

He smiled. "What else have you got to tell me?" he whispered, tracing the outlines of her mouth with his fingers. "Tell me," he urged. "You came to explain, after all."

Haltingly: "Your face appeared to me."

"I too have had dreams."

"Not in my dreams. I would have accepted you in my dreams."

"Where then?"

Laughter from the deck of the houseboat floated into the cabin.

"Where was I not allowed?" he insisted, pursuing the vines down her neck.

"By my chair while I posed."

"Where else?"

"Out on the porch…The dunes. Even the pine groves at night."

He kissed the vines he'd caressed. "I would beg you to leave me…"

"Foolish girl."

"I dreaded each passing ship –"

"*Serena II* is not a passing ship."

Swaying harbour lamps cast a flickering glow on her face as she raised her eyes to him, slowly.

"You should not have come back, Misha," she warned him.

"You knew that I would, Caroline."

"Nevertheless –"

"Your choice was false from the start – a decision that left me free to find you," he said before he kissed her again, pressing her up against the door of his cabin. She struggled – he had expected it – doomed attempt to deny not his needs but her own.

What he had not expected was her strength. She fought his unyielding insistence with a desperation that astounded him.

"Slender reed, it is useless," he murmured, slipping his hand from her neck down to her breast, where he allowed it to linger. "This time I will not go."

Her resistance aroused him. He reached down still further, gathered her skirt in his fist, pulled it up to him and pushed her legs apart. She stifled a gasp. His left arm tightened around her; his right hand remained where it was, fingers strong and salt-worn like the sea in her – fierce, unforgiving caress so that with a violent jerk she wrenched her mouth free of him. There was no room. He caught her mouth as it moved and bit her lip – that full enigmatic lower lip that had without remorse taunted him, beckoning from vivid abstracts, portraits, a still life, his nightmares.

She managed still to resist. It made no difference. He licked the bright ruby droplet that had appeared on her lip. He licked the vines on her neck, wrapped a mass of her hair around his hand, pulled her head back and stared at her.

"God, Caroline," he said, stunned by the fact of her there, the fact that she fought him still, fought herself in the depths of his sailboat named *Steady One* where the only choice left was the one she had already made, back in Susannah's house.

"You waited all night for me in the Riverside Suites. You waited all year for me here, walking the harbours, the boatyards, Great George Street – no, don't pull away – I know it all…I know you loved once before me, and that you thought he had left you, and so you let yourself love me, and then Jude – don't, Mrs. Devereux – *it is useless* – there is very little I don't know."

He unfastened her blouse. She was naked beneath it. She was always naked beneath her clothing – lingering habit from the hot, covered years – so that as he whispered, "Stop fighting, beloved," he had already found the half moon that had bedevilled his nights. "Move instead with me…*kiss me*," she heard him insist as he pulled the comb from her hair, and then her skirt too fell to the floor, and *Oh, Lady, Be Good!* mixed in with the song drifting down, and then other sounds filled her head – murmurs which resembled the sea on the night she too sailed alone…"I bought his abstract because I saw you there. I bought his still life because I saw you there. I bought that last portrait – falsely dated – yes, even that I alone know – you were wearing your brooch," he confessed, not without triumph, as her slender arms encircled his neck at long last. "Yes, Caroline, I have them all. You alone remain. Yes, just like that…move with me. – *Yes, Jesus, that's good.*"

She would vaguely remember lamps by his bed turned out, the taste of him or the sea in her mouth – unsparing insistence wanting something withheld from him still, seeking again between her breasts, her legs, and again when he faced her away from him, not yet fulfilled.

He would always remember breakers cresting like storm tides when she cried out his name once and for all, gripping the powerful hand that held her tightly against him, surrendering that last stubborn particle of her soul to him, never before relinquished.

And then, save for the music that floated down still through the indistinct night, *Serena II*'s cabin was silent.

The harbour too was at rest. Laughter and the tinkling of glasses on a nearby deck drifted into the wind. The last of the lobstermen's trucks rumbled up the clay road. A car that had stopped by the tackle shop turned, moved past the boats in their berths, and vanished into the night.

꒰ ☾ ꒱

A cloudburst had suddenly soaked Charlottetown Harbour, interrupting Jude's work for the day. Seascape unfinished, he had waited at the foot of Great George Street, hoping for late afternoon's light to return.

Only the threat of more rain had darkened already volatile skies. Resigned, he had packed up his paints, found a harbourside bistro, ordered supper and brandy and lingered awhile in autumn's uncertain allure. Leisurely then, for he had told Caroline not to expect him 'til midnight, he had made his way westward along the long, winding shore road, completely deserted so late in the season. He had not intended to stop on the way, but as he had rounded the final, steep curve and had seen Cap-Egmont in the distance – last of the trawlers wandering into the harbour, lamps burning still in a few of the sailboats just berthed – he'd changed his mind. He would pick up that varnish and cloth after all. Despite the veiled, troubled skies which had seemingly thickened, he could perhaps work in his lighthouse first thing in the morning.

"But Monsieur Jude," Raoul had replied, bemused, "your supplies have been called for."

"Tonight?"

"About an hour ago."

"Are you quite certain?"

"Mademoiselle Violette came around."

Jude had glanced up at the clock…Odd for Caroline to have come into Cap-Egmont so late. She had planned to leave Sans Souci before noon, hoping to spend the day helping Père Gabriel. The afternoon would have been tiring, the drive back even more so.

"…Thank you, Raoul."

"Goodnight, Monsieur Jude."

A fragrant, soft rain had begun. As he had crossed to his car, Jude had pondered. The day had been mild, after all. She could have gone on to Journey's End, joined Honorine for tea, supper, an unhurried walk down to the wharf...Last chance of the year for such pleasures perhaps. Yes, for sure that was it.

He had even turned at that point, thinking perhaps to catch sight of them still on one of the covered benches around to the back of the shop. He had looked back up the boardwalk, beyond to the shore road, beyond that to the meadows and homesteads and dark, precise ridges slicing the damp fields in half. He had heard old Raoul locking up. He had remembered Honorine never left her guests in the evening.

He had also remembered then, standing in the arc of a harbour lamp next to his car, that Caroline had of late resumed her long sundown walks on the dunes. Not a week had gone by, in fact, when she hadn't taken her car and ventured still farther – Summerside, Borden, even as far as the north capes. But for that first trip to Charlottetown (losing track of the time finding a clock, of all things!) she had always come home before dark – restless still to be sure, on occasion silent, distracted – but no longer fearful. It had made him happy to see she had put the past year of struggle and strange doubts behind her.

And yet for some reason on this night he himself had felt anxious. He'd gotten into his car, started the motor, switched on the radio and, not knowing why, had lingered still.

Easy To Love had begun. The last ferry had left. Tall swaying masts had recalled couples dancing. Imperceptibly, as a layer of fog had discreetly covered Jude's windshield, the scene had become indistinct, blending with similar vigils, similar yearnings – that first trip to Charlottetown, darkness, Sans Souci silent, heavy rains while he'd waited; that other fall night at Journey's End, buried passions acknowledged, desperation until he had found her – never again to possess her.

No; no, it was best not to dwell on such things. Better to lower the windows, invite time present back into the car. He breathed in the cool air, closing his eyes for a moment, recognizing the next tune – song he had played under the crystal lamps of the Crillon, words mixed in now with the lone cry of a gull, the gentle lapping of tides…*Oh sweet and lovely lady be good*…yes, those were the notes, the complex progressions, the lyrics…

Once more he looked round. Of course she'd gone walking. Nothing but dark empty rooms on the bluff. Here by the ripening meadows on such a sweet night, such life!

The wharf had become almost uncannily still. The last of the trawlers had docked. The last of the traps had been stacked. Slowly the lobstermen's trucks had gone off, each in its turn. *Only one left*, Jude had thought, gazing abstractedly at the end the quay. *Only one left and that car hidden 'til now.*

Strange how his own footsteps had resembled another's as he'd made his way toward that car. Stranger still how he had known it at once, even beyond the last of the harbour lights – how he had known it would be empty, unlocked, keys still inside as though it were parked by its own home. And then – even this last had surprised him – he had turned. Against his will he had turned to look at that home, and, with the unendurable deliberation of one in a dream, he had stared, and had automatically nodded, benumbed, and had murmured somehow in a voice not at all like his own, *Ah, yes…there it is at long last*, for there it was at long last, poised, secure in the tides, aware of its own unassailable grace. Gently it rocked, slow and sensuous drift, at one with the waves reaching down under the docks. There it was at long last, not unexpected.

The mist had thickened again. Jude could barely make out the careful lettering on the stern. He'd had to move toward the steps a bit.

Serena II, he had seen. Bold, slightly curved script. Golden, he'd thought.

As for home port…no, that he could not see from where he stood. The night was darkening still, or so it had seemed to Jude then, and those letters were smaller. He'd had to walk down one more step.

Manhattan, he'd read. Fine, deferential script as befitted a courteous guest...Nothing more on that line.

As he had gazed he had seen the lamp in the lower cabin go out. He'd heard the last of the lobstermen's trucks disappear. He'd felt the quickening wind on his face, through his hair, after that on his shoulders, his back, for by then somehow he had turned and had begun walking away and vaguely this time he had known his own steps, and vaguely this time he'd sensed he had reached the opposite end of the boardwalk.

And then Jude's car too had disappeared up the clay road toward the cliffs.

☾

From his chaise longue on the deck, Mikhail watched billowing clouds part, come together again, drift on languidly toward the mainland. The rain had at last tapered off. Caroline had just left.

He finished another cigarette, stood and walked to the railing. Flickering lights pierced the dark – kerosene lamps burning low in a few of the fishing boats still, starboard glow on a barge heading north, candles in the parlour window of a farmhouse up past the shore road.

He thought back to his father's house. December...nearly two years ago. Candles there too in profusion, champagne, the music of Haydn, presents under a tree. Her gift had been thoughtful – an intricate sailing ship poised in a pale green glass bottle. His gift had been heartless – a bell jar that had left her defenceless.

It was what he had wanted – a chance to wound the woman his father adored, bruise the creature Antonin lived for, hurt the household where he had never been more than a guardedly welcomed guest. Never could he have foreseen how on that first Christmas car ride the fates would repay his blithe meanness. *Sailor's chords* – that was all he had said at their journey's beginning, turning the radio on, hearing *From the New World* symphony start. *I hear the earth in it, not the sea*, she had stubbornly countered, as though her dirt, that farm she so loved, would forever protect her.

The irony of it all struck him like salt spray there by the railing. In the end it was the Atlantic which had received her, saving her in the process, and now it was his ship she was prepared to call from henceforth her home.

How it had cost her, that final surrender! How she had fought that last barely audible *Yes* in his arms, the splintered *Yes, I will go with you, Mikhail* – unconditional capitulation like the yielding of body and soul which had preceded it.

She had managed to sleep some before then, pressed up against him on his narrow bed. Motionless, he had lain beside her, pondering the decision he was about to demand. It was perhaps heartless to force such a long-postponed choice so abruptly. She deserved time to think. He could delay his departure...A fortnight. Maybe even a month. December's worst storms were still far to the north.

As he'd debated he'd watched the arc of the harbour lamp sweep her nude form – a repeated caress of pure light which had annoyed him. He'd heard the rain like an insolent rival tapping on the portholes above her. He'd wished he had remembered to close the window alongside, finding the breeze which had made its way to her body distasteful.

Not another chance in this lifetime, he had reminded himself. *Nothing left of my lifetime without her.*

The coastal patrol launch had passed, stirring his boat in its wake. Caroline too had stirred then – barely perceptible inclination, yet it was a yearning that spoke not just of her needs but his own...Matching half of the coin. He had seen it clearly from the beginning; she had perceived it dimly over time; in between those two points, Jude McCallister had reappeared to claim her once more in this place.

How he had done this, Mikhail couldn't guess. Susannah's story had ended with Violette's sudden departure. Serge had left her alone on these docks – one final bittersweet wave under violet skies, deserted clay roadway rising behind her. Within a few weeks, though, with *Monsieur*, as these islanders called him – the implied deference verging on awe had repelled Mikhail – she was hidden away on some high coastal road, lover and model and closely-guarded, adored muse.

Jude, it is you who would not be denied, Misha'd said half to himself then, half to the last of the northern lights which had managed to shine through the clouds onto her hair. Increasingly too, those stars had unnerved him. Like the rain and the wind and the lascivious arc of the lamps on the boardwalk, they had whispered of one who'd returned for what was no longer his own.

Could he have answered them, Mikhail would have flashed: "She was free when we met. Her husband had found another. Jude McCallister had done the same – presumably far deeper wound. And yet once more there he is – out on his bluff called of all things *Without a Care in the World* – there he is with his farm and his paints and the woman he once cavalierly abandoned. Compelling allure to have made his way back with such force into her life."

But since Misha could not so reply, he'd merely stared out at the rain that had lingered, begrudgingly, leaving long, silvery streaks like fine hair on his portholes. Deep in his heart, meanwhile, irresolution had dwindled. She had come down to the wharf on her own, after all. Here on his ship, away from the pull of the earth, she had forgotten France and her former life. Here on his ship then he would force her to choose.

Jason, he'd thought, bending slowly to kiss her. How fitting the name she had used. It was his destiny to take her from him, as it was Jude's to take his one masterpiece from her defiant heart and splendid form.

At the touch of his lips she had stirred, moving still closer. Her slender arms had slipped round his neck, her slumbering form dissolving into his own as though she would be lost in his flesh – no, desire far more transcendent, subliminal longing for absolute union not even her violent passions had ever expressed.

He had remained utterly still, darkness and the lapping of waves and the unequivocal choice in her beckoning dream washing over his wakeful heart. If he could only sail with her at that moment, slip away from his moorings without causing pain! If she could only keep dreaming, passing into his life undisturbed, undivided, sustained by the deep love those few silent moments had forever confirmed.

…Impossible passage. She had known from the start it would have to end in this way; that the reckoning she had delayed could not for all time be postponed.

A second light kiss, even a third and still she had slumbered against him, as though warding off wakefulness and the reappearance of some vague, unforgiving dread, silenced for only a brief time in dreams.

Pondering this, Misha had heard a premature wave breaking against the prow of his ship, the sudden splash of a fish seeking escape, Susannah's Joubert's mystified voice in his head, *No, Monsieur Mikhail. There is no more to tell. Mademoiselle Violette simply remembered her life and was gone.*

But there was something else. A last piece of the puzzle remained – whatever it was that had compelled her to honour Jude's prior claim, secretly, despite the fact that well after that broken affair she had once more found deep love.

He'd watched her tranquil beside him, but only tranquil in dreams – exemption which had troubled him deeply, for though he would risk all that he had to sail with her come the dawn – present and future days, peace, his ship in December storms, his never-before humbled heart – one thing and one thing alone he would not hazard then, not under the fairest of skies. He would never risk breaking her. Whatever it was that had remained undisclosed – and vaguely he sensed this – might just possess such a force. It could not remain unrevealed. Come what may, he would put the last piece of the puzzle of her mysterious days into place.

Silently then, he had reviewed what little he'd learned about Jude the past year. Repeatedly, the same sketchy portrait emerged, the same blurred montage of a driven, reclusive, nearly iconic world-class painter. That he was difficult, sometimes harsh, demanding more of himself than of others – everyone seemed to agree. That he was also extremely appealing was also well known.

A man of singular grace – those had been Auguste's words. *Charming, utterly charming*, had been Armand's echo, encomium which had lingered in Mikhail's mind long after the delicate ship's clock had chimed – ten-thirty p.m.

After another hour, *Serena II*'s drift had changed. Currents too had adjusted; a brisk offshore breeze had come up; northern lights were fast fading, and Misha was still at a loss. There was no choice remaining. He would have to wake her and ask her, although for some reason he guessed nothing would ever again be the same.

"Not for me," he had insisted, feeling her wondering eyes fixed on him, sensing even in shadows the elegant visions that had so recently taken up lodging there evanesce. "For you – for your sake alone have I asked. *What was it that took you from me?*"

Only the groan of his ship's heavy ropes made reply.

Fervently he had repeated the question, and yet still there'd been silence, save for that one final song floating down from the houseboat nearby – blurred lyrics, intermittent in the lingering rain, but unmistakably *The Man I Love*.

Strangely, Misha'd reflected, she had seemed to be listening more to the music than to the echo of his passionate words. He'd been about to touch her in fact, force her to reply once and for all when he had felt her touch him, hands in the darkness tracing the outlines of his face, his shoulders, much as a sculptor would fix in his mind an image he feared he was about to lose for all time – and then at last the song had ended, and suddenly she had held him with a force he would not have thought possible before that night's passion, and then, turning away so that she seemed to be addressing not the man she so wanted, but rather the depths of his discreet and most beautiful ship, she had at last, in a strangely controlled, monochromatic voice, recounted the story of Jude McCallister's walk through the Champs-Élysées, his pause by the dark and deserted Pavillon, the staggering agony that had resulted.

Nothing in his tumultuous, wandering days could have prepared Mikhail for what he had felt as he'd grasped – to the extent that anyone could have understood – Jude's ordeal. Jaggedly, for these things too she had told him, he had at last pictured the moment not even Susannah had witnessed – bright, late summer sun in that kitchen, past time nonexistent, present time but a dream, future incomprehensible until the floodgates of memory had poured back into Violette's head names and places erased by the Gulf, and a chance letter reread – brochure enclosed – had restored the man she'd once loved, loving her still it appeared, although by then shattered.

Homeward-bound, the last mainland ferry had passed Cap-Egmont harbour, jolting *Serena II* in its wake. Misha had felt the shock as if it had occurred in some vast space within him. Within moments he'd felt a surge of emotions like crosscurrents filling that void: first and foremost compassion, sorrow resembling love for a man so unspeakably felled; then, although he had wished it were not so, pity gave way to something like awe in his heart – admiration for Jude's endurance, his desperation to paint, live, find the woman beside him whatever the cost to a body so stunningly willed back to vigour. Up until then Misha'd considered such overriding obsession his province. Now, unexpectedly, he had come face to face with a yearning so boundless he'd felt his own longings belittled.

This had enraged him. Though he had met the man through his art, never in person, he believed he had taken his measure. Now, as ever invisible, Jude seemed to have changed in proportion, in stature. He had grown. From worthy opponent, he had turned into invincible foe. No way to crush such a man. How to wrench a beloved from arms so fiercely reclaimed? How to insist on his own rights when she had so clearly, and perhaps not without reason, returned to Jude's prior one?

…Perhaps not without reason. Over and over, like a scratchy old tune replayed, he had considered the concept, hoping at least for understanding, resignation, if not total acceptance.

In vain. The same eddying swirl of emotions had surged, this time with more force. She had been lost after all – nothing left but the courage to love one more time, only to learn that Jude wanted her still, that it was all a mistake, like her death an illusion, finality merely presumed.

Yes, one had to feel pity. One even had to admire her resilience, her fortitude, self-deception so thorough she had been able to function superbly, albeit briefly – time enough to reach back to the man who had painted her once, more than enough time to dispense with his replacement.

And with this last thought, begrudging respect and compassion had vanished, leaving in Mikhail's heart that same swelling anger which had remained in the end to define his feelings toward Jude. She had reinvented herself at the expense of his own peace, condemning him to a grief more ironically painful than the one she'd emerged from, for Jude's ordeal had occurred – her sadness was valid – whereas from henceforth he would be mourning a death which had never, in fact, happened.

You had no right, Caroline – no right, he had almost cried out then – roughness that would have recalled the way he'd just loved her, harshness with much darker intent though this time, for he had found himself wanting to humble her, repay his own hurt in kind. In fact he remembered he *had* called her name out – strange feral noise not so much uttered as escaped from confinement. He recalled too that he had then raised his hand, and that she had not averted her face, whether too proud or too wretched for such inconsequential self-defence he could not say, for at that moment another face had appeared to him there, other hands wanting a parallel justice, stopping just short of identical blows across that same beautiful face, so that in the end, like *Serena II*'s still straining ropes, Misha had groaned and had murmured "Max" and had lowered his hand and said merely, with a breaking simplicity, "How I have loved you, Caroline Devereux."

Not until then had she wept, brutal sounds too filled with the pain she had caused him, pain she had caused herself, suffering every-where – Jude at the hands of assailants, Mikhail at the hands of his father, his brother – all of it senseless, all of it somehow her doing, collusion with fate her own fate, she believed, feeling a haunting remorse both deserving and groundless, anguish recalling Communion day's failures.

Such a crossing of stars! he had thought hearing those sounds, solace escaping them both for a while until he had finally managed, "Hush, Caroline. Be still now. No more," and then he had once again pulled her against him, feeling his hurt and her pain become one as he held her, his rage merge with her anguish, his need to avenge and her fear slowly fade, intertwined, leaving behind what had always been there, what would never recede: one shared, darkly secret despair.

Slowly, her trembling had ceased after that. Wordless, the lovers had remained unmoving, pressed up against one another in the dark.

Wordless, but only Caroline had found respite. Misha'd been only too keenly aware that the time remaining was short, that their minutes alone in this harbour were passing – borrowed, at best, for the duration of one already half-spent night – and there was much to be done still, much to be prepared, for in that last, silent, inexpressibly wretched embrace he had determined his rival was not Jude, but her pity for Jude, and had guessed rightly that Jude in the end would despise such compassion, and thus Misha'd decided – with the puzzle at last completed – that he would set sail come the dawn, as he'd planned, and that before then, as he had planned, he would ask her to choose.

Now, tonight, he had judged, convincing himself with her quiet beside him that taking her quickly was justifiable, not merely expedient. Jude's life had been lived after all. He had seen much, possessed more: talent, wealth, fame, seemingly endless inspiration – legacy grander by far than all the others combined, insuring as it did what few men could ever hope to possess: immunity from transience, age, insignificance – privilege reserved for the gods, sole province of art and its only true recompense.

To be sure in his youth, from the few facts that were known of the man, love had been intermittent, disappointing. So had it been in his own life, Misha'd reflected, as in Maximilian's before him. Yet even there Jude the artist had encountered exemption, even in broken dreams passion enough to bring many a priceless canvas to life.

As for his masterpiece – ah, that passion was different, exalted, as was the woman who had inspired it. That kind of love came but once in a lifetime, if it ever came in this lifetime – desire not unlike art, fulfillment beyond surfeit, and even that Jude had known. Even Caroline Devereux had come Jude McCallister's way, as though by birthright of genius and irresistible charm.

So Misha had reasoned, if reasoning could be applied to the blurred images that had passed through his mind as Caroline lay in his arms. How lovely the grace of her body against his! How unequivocal her inclination – all secrets shared at last, all shame subsided, night and the rain and relief only remaining.

Desire stirred again in his heart, quelling resurgent envy of Jude, for his own weathered hands had their own force, he knew, and his experienced touch could confer their own joy.

She'd heard her name murmured again, she believed – she couldn't be certain – sounds of the sea had engulfed them both after that, and she was glad for the weight of him, glad when his needs had spent themselves deep within her, not unlike surf seeping into warm sand, indissoluble union, unspoken witness to the fact that what had drawn them together when she had believed she was free was far more powerful now, when she had nowhere to turn.

"Turn to me," he had whispered, still holding her tightly against him. "For all the days that remain, turn to me."

She had drawn back a bit, perhaps not comprehending, perhaps not willing to focus on what it was he was asking.

"Yes, it is time," she had heard him insist then. "I mean to sail with the dawn. You and I both know I must. We both know too I can never come back."

The ensuing pause had been brief, absolute, but within its confines Misha'd sensed triumph, felt Jude retreating, ever so slowly, like a sister ship passing at midnight on the horizon.

Inexorably, he had pressed on. "And we both know one last thing, Caroline. Never, not for a moment, in all the years that remain to you both in this place, will your pity be enough for him."

"It has never been pity."

"Hasn't it?"

Again there was silence – not because she was sure, and ashamed to admit it, but because she was not sure, and afraid to examine that.

"Compassion, then. Kindness. If it has not marked your lives yet, as you say, that is only because it has been well concealed. In any case it will come. Jude is not a man to be deceived. He has already been forced to paint things you have tried to suppress. Itis his genius and the price he has had to pay for that gift, source of his talent and his torment and you will never decrease the former, only increase the latter as the years take their toll on you both – on his dreams, on your youth – and he sees in the eyes he once cherished what it is he has become."

Shaken, confused, torn, filled with desire, Caroline had not replied. Steadily, with a dead-on reckoning refined over thousands of miles, Misha'd concluded,

"It will be too late for him then. Time will have passed him by – time and the chance to return to the one place he lived richly – no, you cannot deny that his years spent in France were grand ones, that he had there what few men ever enjoy, what still could have been his but for the fact that fate momentarily crushed him, forcing him to chose a confinement you have already found meagre haven at best and at worse, unendurable pretence."

Suddenly Misha had stopped, startled by sounds of a rowboat, the rhythmic dipping of oars into the waters of the bay near the edge of the deepwater dock.

Caroline had not heard this interruption, nor did she hear the steps of the watchman continuing on to the boathouse, nor the fact that all music had finally ceased on the houseboat nearby. There had been only the picture Misha had painted, and the sounds of the last Paris-bound flight, via Toronto, over the water, and finally, after stillness had returned to the cabin, as though beckoning from some dark secret space deep within her, Misha's irrefutable, irresistible, "Set him free, Caroline," whispered repeatedly into her hair. "Set him free."

⸽ ☾ ⸾

Had the night watchman, making his desultory way around the boardwalk – for nothing untoward ever happened in Cap-Egmont harbour – chosen to shine his lantern through the windows of *Serena II*'s starboard cabin, he would have observed a passionate couple – gentleman unknown to him – in a long, fervent, seemingly decisive embrace. He would have seen the man stroke her hair, the woman repeatedly nod, a kiss, another nod – the man at last throw himself back on his bunk as though in a state of immense, long-delayed relief. He would, of course, have had no idea as to the source of this sudden and obvious happiness on the part of the man, nor could he ever have guessed the extreme agitation which had preceded what was clearly a capitulation on the part of the woman. All that and more had remained undisclosed, for it was neither the custom nor the duty of Cap-Egmont harbour's night watchman to peer into the staterooms of the boats docked in his bay – above all visiting ships, grand ones like this one, to which all courtesies would be due as to a journeying prince.

Hence he was long gone, making his way toward the boathouse and the trawlers pulled up beside it by the time Mrs. Devereux had reached for her clothes in preparation to return, ever so quickly, to the house on the cliffs just past Dutchman Rock.

Mikhail had made strong objection to this brief final visit, sensing some vague but palpable threat in it.

"Darling, it's late," he had argued. "The roads are deserted. Jude will have long since gone to sleep, thinking you've stayed with Honorine. You wrote as much in the note you left, didn't you? You can just as easily write again now – just as easily and with more grace, sparing you both a needlessly painful farewell."

She had continued to gather her things.

"Come the dawn – before if you wish – I'll have the letter delivered. Any one of the coastal supply boats go past Dutchman Rock at that time."

"Mikhail, no," she had answered at last. "No, this I must do now, tonight, in that house. It cannot be avoided."

Turning, she had caught sight of her face in the mirror behind Mikhail's bureau. For a moment or two she had studied the image, as though surprised by its features. Vaguely then, for the cabin was still mostly shadows, she'd seen the reflection of Misha approaching. Their gaze had met in the oval, glass which seemed to be watching, passing no judgment.

"It cannot be avoided," she had repeated in a strangely subdued voice, as though to those distant observers.

Gently he'd taken the comb from her hands, and, tying her hair back, replied only, "Then at least promise you'll come back down right away. Tides will be swift in the wake of that storm. We'll have to get out past those Narrows just as soon as there's light."

Somewhat wistfully, he believed, she had smiled. It had made him reach for her as she moved to the threshold. Then, with an oddly unsettled heart he had observed, holding her tightly against him, "Nearly two years since that first Christmas kiss on your porch, Caroline…and that vagabond soul of yours still matches mine."

As on that snowy night which seemed to them both so long ago in this cabin, he'd kissed her deeply. "Again," he had murmured, and she had done as he'd asked, as though in a dream, for she was lost, and he was right; she was at sea and he in home port and nothing had ended in those nearly two years – there had been only beginnings, false starts, resurrection that had offered no refuge.

"Go now," he had said, freeing her. "I'll be here waiting, 'til daybreak."

Silently, with the same solemn gaze as when she'd first entered that stateroom, she had nodded, and had traced his fine suntanned face with the tips of her fingers once more, and then she had turned and walked up the steps to the salon.

Mikhail too had turned then and had sat back down on the bed, watching her as she had passed through the hallway into the salon beyond, watching her still as she had suddenly stopped, and had also begun to stare, not back at him but at the starboard wall of his cabin, at two paintings placed over the sofa – pictures she would have known as she knew her own markings – one an abstract, the other a still life, both done in the grand years, as Misha had called them, before the artist's ordeal – both, she well knew, in the artist's own way, portraits of her.

For a long time she'd looked at them, unaware of Mikhail's gaze, which had never once left her face, suffused as it had slowly become with something he had never seen there before, or had refused to recognize. Certainly he had denied it on this night. And yet there it was, despite all the lies and half-truths and dreams he had told them both in the dark – radiance indescribable, as though she were not so much contemplating those works as reflecting them, or rather the workings behind them, as though she were one with the paintings, not as observer or as model or even as muse, but in some finer capacity, some far grander role, *as though she were somehow co-creator.*

Staggered, Misha'd considered this concept as she had continued to gaze at the pictures – the disturbingly rich tones, the distinctively sensual shapes, the precise yet elusive rendering of things both quotidian and immortal.

Yes, he'd been right. Remarkably, one more piece of the puzzle – hitherto unimagined by him in spite of his efforts, no doubt unperceived by her still in spite of her keenness – had remained unseen. Now it could not be ignored. Her face transcendent even in shadows expressed it ineffably. Not only were those paintings clear reflections of the woman beholding them, but somehow, just as vividly, she in her turn reflected the force that had made them. She was their mirror image. They were hers.

Why this should be so Mikhail had not instantly grasped, but it had come to him quickly – a rush of understanding not unlike the windy, mysterious morning Susannah Joubert had described. As he'd remembered moments in his life with her, other moments she had shared with Max, with Antonin, with Serge and Susannah, even with Monsieur Daniel du Lac on Great George Street, he had seen that life was art to Mrs. Devereux, existence a canvas, indeed many cloths – bliss, bereavement, dreams, disillusions – everything part of the *œuvre* she lovingly shaped out of her days and those of the strangers who crossed her unique path, never again to be strangers, touched as they'd been by that electric combination of intellect, will, and compassion which, far more than her beauty, defined her.

This then was the truth, what really bound her to Jude McCallister. She was one with the man, understood him as no one could, or had, or ever would. He with his hands, she with her striking allure and tenacious attachments – both of them worked on the same plane, both in the service of an ideal few could imagine, let alone bring to pass. How cataclysmic that first meeting must have been for two such souls! How preordained from then on their indissoluble interaction, for Jude would have recognized not only beauty in Mrs. Devereux, but, as in his own case, the power to create beauty. Indeed, in the end, it was precisely this duality which he had so exquisitely captured, bringing forth that matchless, unsettling, unforgettable portrait in Paris.

Almost against his own will, Misha had pictured that moment – intense sunlight no doubt on the scene, intense struggle for sure in the moments preceding the scene, for Caroline was not a woman to reveal herself blithely. He had imagined Jude's feverish hands, longing to touch as well as create, yearning to ravish and as well as render more perfect. Of course out of that fateful convergence of forces had come *Half Moon*, the masterpiece. Of course others would follow. Without exception, whatever the subject, Jude would from henceforth paint her – partly because he would always be reaching for that felicitous interaction of forces, partly because as creator he was no longer alone, condemned and solitary wanderer, but one of a larger whole which he had at last understood, having seen his own hands in her heart.

Caroline had long gone by the time Misha had reached these

conclusions. That strange almost unearthly silence of the earlier night had returned to his cabin. And still he had remained on his bed, staring off into the salon where she had stood rock-still for so long, entranced.

It was this last which had staggered him – not the fact that they both loved the same woman – it was in Caroline's nature to be desired – but the fact that she had loved them both in return, unconditionally, with such exceptional, fierce, paradoxically exclusive passion.

Incomprehensible contradiction. Each love was unique, each man distinct, yet the overwhelming attachments were on a par. It was her fate – sombre destiny – something he had mistakenly considered to be impossible when, hours before, in reviewing the many riches of his rival's blessed life, he had reflected on Mrs. Devereux. That kind of love comes but once in a lifetime, he had concluded. Looking back now with her gone, he had seen he'd been wrong. *That kind of love could happen twice to the fortunate few* – fortunate only if it occurred sequentially, progression which was not displacement, chapter begun after the last one had finished.

Caroline had not been among those so graced. One profound love had become two on Susannah's lawn – error not of her own choosing, mistake of the gods perhaps, more likely malevolent stroke, punishment not for her beauty – time after all, would erase that finesse – but for her temerity, her imitation of them, her facility for creation. Hence it had befallen her to be forever divided, condemned to parallel passions, each in its own way sole and exclusive expression of her tumultuous heart. And hence it had befallen to Mikhail to have at last found what he had most desired: an answer to his most pressing question that evening. It was not the one he had wanted. Like everything else on that night, it had merely presented one last aching dilemma.

To sail with her would mean to break her. To leave her behind would be to return her once more to that ambivalent world, Sans Souci of all names, exiled forever from the kingdom of peace, as he himself would again be, once again sailing, hunting, rootless, seeking a place of his own on the high seas of all worlds.

The choice was his to make, his alone now, and the hours remaining were few.

Anxious to reach Dutchman Rock, Caroline drove far too fast, forcing herself to ignore the night's distracting, metallic palette, willing herself to focus instead on the road's hairpin curves. Concentration proved futile. The tides were too loud; the winds in the wake of the storm far too strong; above all the shimmering coastline confused her – that curious malachite surf far below, the silver-tipped barrier reef, the whitecaps, the waves, Jude McCallister's face at each bend in the road, all those chrome-coloured dunes.

Dazed, she drove even faster – reckless speed even for daylight, she knew, but there was much to be done still, much to be said, and all that remained was what remained of this night – strange iridescent expanse which had become a blur as she climbed, a brilliant comet streaking past, clouds nothing more than a trail of indistinct tones, beach far below an occasional glistening sheen.

Only a sharply outlined pale moon at the top of the ridge was intermittently clear, and, in spite of the time that had elapsed and the things that had happened to him, Jude's face strangely unaltered, as it had been in the grand years.

She tried to turn from that face, shut out the image before her as she had attempted in past months to turn from another gaze, other eyes seeking hers, and then her car struck a stone and suddenly swerved.

It was the final sharp curve. The road doubled back to the right but the car lurched to the left, as though with a will of its own it would seek out the sea, comforting depths off in the distance, not unfamiliar. She made out the guard rail, some hemlocks, a narrow rocky ledge beyond, and then in one last, blinding flash she saw the Gulf, bejewelled arms thrown wide in welcome.

Her own slender arms struggled, stiffened against the wheel, and then relaxed, no longer needed, resistance once more on this evening in vain.

Darkness and a fierce wind surrounded both car and driver at the top of the ridge. Hemlocks and junipers flanked the vehicle and the lady; spruce and boxwood and intertwined bayberry leaves hid them from sight in the secluded overlook just to the left of the curve. Not even the horn had sounded at impact – violence blunted by the dense yet pliable tangle of pines which had slowed the car down as it careened over the roots and hard ground, forcing it to come to a halt in a cushion of privets just before the edge of the copse. Save for the wind after that, and the sound of the wipers which of their own accord had begun to sweep the car's windshield, silence returned to the small private space.

By the time Caroline raised her head, tides were high. The ocean's rim was still black; the shoreline jade green. In between was the sandbar – ever narrowing strip sharply dividing these shades. Breakers intermittently tumbled onto this reef; others spread from the surf onto the dunes, whose precise form beneath the sheer drop of the cliff Caroline could not see. Nor could she see the steamship making its slow, distant way to Québec, hidden as it was by the swaying cedars bent down over the wall. Yet it was the blast of some horn which had awakened her, she surmised, some boat en route to the mainland. She never thought to envision another thing, a closer horn, one lone southbound car speeding on down the cliff behind.

Indeed, she could think of little for some time. She was too stunned by the jolt with its momentary blackout, its absence of feeling, sound, loss of control – or was it will? – too overwhelmed by the fact of her body still there, still in the car as before, still intact, no doubt bruised, shocked, but still whole.

Even these critical facts took some time to determine. Only in stages was she able to grasp what had happened, judge the effect of the impact – crash which had been thwarted so simply by a jumble of trees, or perhaps not so simply by fate – she could not say. Nor could she ever assess the part she had played in the thing. Clearly she *had* played a part. She had at some point decided, at some point surrendered the wheel, embracing the sea once again, gladly, without the slightest compunction. Perhaps she had seen no alternative then. Perhaps she had wanted none.

Bewildered, shivering more from the shock than the cold, she forced herself to consider this fact. Could she have averted that headlong rush of her car toward the sea? Had she viewed the attempt as futile? Found it alluring?

Only the wind made response. But for the stars and the beam of her headlights shining doggedly at the guard rail ahead, all was in darkness. Even the moon seemed to have stopped in its tracks, reclining stubbornly on the horizon, unwilling to shed any more light on the scene. And yet Caroline needed to know. She who had functioned so supremely for most of her life in the dark now craved above all things light, understanding. She could make no movement without it, no attempt to start up again, if such a thing were at all possible still, for that last treacherous curve had doubled the night back upon itself. Nothing was now as it was, or as she had believed it would be. Her enigmatic surrender at that bend in the road – complicity or resignation? – had shaken not just her body but also her will, or more precisely her perceptions of what remained to be willed. One thing only was clear. Whatever she had glimpsed at that last hairpin curve – image that had dissolved in a blinding flash as the car swerved – had to be summoned once more, its stark truth without fear confronted, its correlative implications acknowledged. Therein lay the key, she suspected – the road which remained to be taken.

Thoughts became more precise as time passed; sensations sharper. Sounds of the cascading tides, soon to crest, reached her distinctly from the base of the cliff. *Serena II* would be rapidly rising. Misha would be preparing to sail. Jude would be waiting, perhaps sleeping, certainly not working. Well, of course, he never worked in the evening. Tomorrow though – or rather today – a matter of hours – she tried to envision that new day, the full light, Jude in his lighthouse, freed at last from the past and its precipitous choice made in pain, all the world his to roam once again, its many wonders his to depict.

The sight refused to be conjured. There remained only the sea, and off in the distance, gathering clouds, the pale moon, the tiniest sparkle of stars one by one fading.

Caroline closed her eyes, resolved to dismiss those unsettling, diminishing lights, determined to imagine sunrise, patiently waiting, with all of its colours and possibilities. No scene came to mind, though – no fragrance other than that of the pines in the copse, no sounds compelling enough to drown out the surf and the wind and the scratch of that juniper branch on her window.

And yet tomorrow must come, she reflected, unsteadily. *Light will dawn, spread, spill onto Jude's studio floor. Leaves will stir. Ships will sail –*

Thoughts broke off. Once again that stiff juniper branch – or was it the scrape of Jude's knife correcting a tone, the bristle of brushes on cloth, pen strokes on paper…? Hard to decide in the dark. Such a compelling noise, so close to the car – right alongside, it appeared, not far from the throbbing pain that had begun again in her temples.

Eyes closed still she leaned her head on the driver's side window. It was ice cold, dulling the pain of the scraping which now seemed to be on her own flesh, her face, even her breast, fit retribution somehow, above all on this night – no, no that was another time, she reminded herself, other side of the world, other end of her life, nothing left of it now but those markings, that half moon, that masterpiece never to be sold or displayed in his lifetime – bargain struck by two strangers in Paris, agreement faithfully kept by the artist thereafter. Even in exile – even from her, she recalled as the tides continued to swell, he had tenaciously guarded that portrait, refusing to unwrap the package sent by his doctor from France. *To be opened when I paint something that approximates its allure* – that was all he had said the day the parcel had reached his new home by the sea. Strange, the combination of pride and nostalgia in his voice as he had placed the sealed box against the wall by his studio door. Stranger still his brief coda…*One is not always vouchsafed such a thing twice in one's lifetime.*

Suddenly, with that unexpectedly piercing recollection, the imagined sunrise Caroline had sought so keenly took precise shape in her mind: brand new day, intense light, Jude in his workroom – oddly unlike his lighthouse – canvas made ready, paints and brushes at hand –

And here the image fragmented. Although sensations remained – sharp smell of turpentine, texture of canvas, occasional dripping of primary stains on a cloth – the painting in progress for some reason vanished. Redrawn, retouched, rubbed, erased and corrected, it was left unfinished, or rather abandoned, carelessly covered, dawn by that time having become dusk, artist by then having returned to the main house.

Unnerved, Caroline tried to dismiss the whole scene, forget the drop cloths, the paint carts, the vague resulting presentments of something untoward having already occurred in that lighthouse. Instead – if she could but picture him working! – she followed Jude back in her mind toward the main house he loved – porch where his spirits revived, turret where on occasion he sketched, room at the top of the stairs where at long last he rested.

No sooner envisioned, this conjured scene splintered too. Even in sleep Jude seemed frustrated, restive, as though only in dreams, and only then piecemeal, could he glimpse what it was he had tried so fiercely to seize in the sun. Not since Paris had he appeared so defeated, since the night he had burned her, the mornings thereafter when cloths had been left untouched and paint tubes unopened and Jude McCallister silently, but without exemption, had a long last ceased working.

Caroline shuddered, though whether from shock still or the sudden shadow passing across her face, she could not say. She sat up abruptly and peered through the window. There was no one, at least not near the car, no face she could see, no form alongside. Carefully, she lowered the window. The overlook seemed deserted, the road empty behind her, the rocky ledge straight ahead – no, that narrow strip remained hidden, despite the slim beam of her headlights. She could not see past the hemlocks and shrubs lining the ledge of the copse.

And yet she found herself drawn to that place, heard her unsteady steps making their way over the broken branches and rocks toward the tangle of privets overlooking the Strait. *There for sure some fresh air*, she had confusedly thought as she advanced. *There at least recognizable sights, sandbar, the sea...above all the dunes.*

But the dunes still remained hidden, out of sight directly below the sheer drop, although the roar of the surf soon to crest onto their seaward sand seemed, like the wind, even at such heights, strangely inviting. As one might in a trance she moved on, passing the hemlocks, out of the beam of her headlights, away from the cedars and pines onto the bright, hardened ground by the edge of the cliff at long last.

"Ah there they are still," she breathed, looking straight down at the distant though comforting undefiled strips of white sand. *Still in place, self-possessed and pristine – even from this place sublime*, she judged, fixedly staring for what seemed like a long time, disdaining to reach for the guard rail, raising her face to the sharp westerly winds, soothed by the sounds and the scents and the familiar salt taste left by the currents of air on her mouth.

Against her will she closed her eyes. She pictured tall, slender sand grass, enduring, remembered deep trackless drifts, warm and soft on bare skin, sensed agitation subside and the long shadow cast by past scenes diminish. She dared not move in fact, disturb the moment's imperceptibly spreading contentment, quiescence which was not peace, not even resignation, but nonetheless stasis, absence of striving, anticipation not unlike the patience of a great swell at sea destined to break on the shore in its time.

Lightly she grasped the guard rail, absently tracing and retracing the metal's smooth surface, its circular shape, sturdy and cool to the touch.

Suddenly, like a favourite line of music played in a strange room, the sensation beneath her fingers compelled her attention. Something in the texture, the shape, in the play of her hand on the curve – repetitive gesture that might recall a sculptor's review – made her at last open her eyes. She turned, sensing somebody back toward the pine grove it seemed, or perhaps back toward past days remembered one last time...

All still unclear, yet still oddly familiar, she thought waiting there by the ledge until the next fierce gust of wind died away, and then she indeed did remember the voice, the exact words, never once over the seasons diminished, never across the miles indistinct.

She took a step away from the rail, disbelieving almost, half expecting to hear not the Atlantic but the banks of the Seine stirring around her, so clear did the whole scene become all of a sudden, so unaltered the moment. Above all the face was unchanged, tangible almost, more arresting than ever on this remote bluff of all places, oceans away from the room where she had first seen Vianne, sightless and beautiful girl in Rodin's house. The student again seemed to be guided by inner mysterious light, moving assuredly in a darkness which was forever her portion, seeking, running her fingers over the surface of strange phantom statues, finding at last with her hands what the artist had seen in his heart. Her radiant face then became distinctly triumphant; her unseeing eyes shone; her movements appeared more than ever secure, absolute, as though that sixth sense of space she possessed had been honed by her examination of the sculptor's intentions, her discovery of the beauty he'd sought, the truth he had expressed.

She seemed to approach at that moment, smile vaguely and then, as a night hawk soared out from the top of a cypress tree near the car, and the last of the slow-drifting clouds broke away from the moon poised beyond, Vianne disappeared. More than ever the little copse, suddenly flooded with light, resembled the cool, silent garden alongside Rodin's house, although aspens now stood where tall, eyeless figures had once been, and a great vaulting sky had replaced Les Invalides' dome.

What thereafter remained was what had remained on that night, nothing more. Nothing more would be needed, for then as now it was all. Then as now, more insistent by far than the sea with its tides washing over the dunes far below, were the echoes of Vianne's insights, lingering still on the heights. Eve had sinned, yes, but not in the Garden of Eden, not shamed by desires of the mind, the heart, powerful needs of the flesh. Here, now, in the workroom of the artist, finite dimension not unlike Eden reserved for the creation of undying things, she had transgressed, turning away from the sculptor, withholding what she alone could provide – irreplaceable conduit as she had become for priceless gifts the gods were prepared to bestow on him, uniquely.

In the end he could not work, or live – it was the same for him, no René? Vianne had concluded, repeatedly touching Rodin's statue, decoding the artist's desperation as he had sensed inspiration withdraw.

I expect you are right, the guide had agreed before his group had moved to the rapturous lovers intertwined in *The Kiss*, leaving Mrs. Devereux behind them, staggered, unobserved and alone in the museum's darkening rotunda.

Once again Caroline felt herself left behind in a deserted, suddenly darkening space, as though lights somewhere had been dimmed, time somehow had run out. Glancing around, she saw that the moon had finally vanished into the Gulf, leaving the sea and the sky dark, the copse now in shadows. As though a museum had indeed closed, silence then spread through the grove. Mist like a sheet covered the car, obscured the pathway around it, hid that last hairpin curve in the road past the shrubs.

By then it no longer mattered. By then Caroline knew what it was she had seen at that place. Splendidly they had appeared, poised in a perfect arch: hands the sculptor had called of all things *Cathedral* – place of grace, Vianne had insisted, sanctified lodging, stained-glass mirror of truth and its beauty, vast and empty and silent in the absence of inspiration.

Unevenly still, no longer from physical shock but from the far greater impact of revelation, Caroline made her way back to the car, caught a glimpse of the roadway beyond, and at the sight of the choice implied there wearily sighed – small splintered sound like a twig snapping somewhere – knowing only too well what had occurred as her car had veered toward the sea. *Behind me a pledge to sail I could never forswear. Ahead a duty to stay I could never annul. No other way out*, she understood grimly, having once before sensed herself desperately, irretrievably lost.

Again, the irony was overwhelming. To sleep forever in her cold mill house had beckoned seductively once on Todd's Farm. To crash unseen here like a wave on the beach had presented itself with an even greater allure...Parallel impasse, antithetical ending. It was Misha that night who had found her, who had given her life back to her, warmth from his warmth sustaining them both in one fierce, vital embrace, for he would not be denied. It was to Misha now that she must return, parting from him forever in one fierce, final embrace, to give Jude his gift back, for he would not be denied.

Yes, Misha, to give him his gift back, she could hear herself telling him back at the end of the deepwater dock. *That and the love I have for you still is all that is left. The love will endure. Absent or present, with the passing of years, the changing of tides...* She could almost feel his gaze on her as she faltered here, made a second attempt, stumbled again only to manage no more than a wretched, *As it was from the start, Mikhail, from that first glance in your father's forbidden red velvet room, so it will always be for me. Dark, secret buried thing. Not a day's respite without you.*

Misha would still remain silent, *Serena II* restless and ready behind him. He would never know, or rather never again believe how she adored him, of that she was certain. At least he must understand the powerful thing that was keeping her back on the island, making her take back her promise, parting her from the man who had haunted her dreams, even in exile – and so she would stammer on, reaching for Mikhail's arm which would not reach for hers in return.

Can't you see, Misha? she'd beg despairingly then. *It would not be that way for Jude. Nothing would ever stay the same – I mean with his work, one and the same with his life. We were mistaken before.*

The ship's ropes would groan again, untimely reminder. Still he would make no response, at least not at that moment. Someday perhaps he would know the effort those few halting words had required, the price she would have to pay for them in the endless days, far longer nights, still to come. For the present though, on this night, he would not understand. Their time together would have run out. All she would be able to add then would be this last jagged, *Yes, mistaken. It is not pity but its opposite. It is the way that I love. I have loved you like that, Misha, so that it has become my fate to be forever divided, my heart like the tides forever denied peace – but a choice had to be made and I have made it, and you will sail now and you will always have me somehow in the sea. Perhaps that is why the sea saved me – to leave me there for you always to find me – but he will not find me up in his lighthouse unless I am someplace nearby, model and muse to him still for some reason, reflection of what it is he must force onto his cloths...*

The words trailed off in her head, but the meaning remained. Her car managed to start, move slowly onto the road, turn once again and again hundreds of times, it appeared, descending, no longer climbing, heading south back down to the wharf.

Somehow she would get through the next hour, she told herself firmly, convey what had to be said, survive the wrenching, resulting, final separation.

As it turned out, there was to be no anguished parting, no need for a speech, no explanations, no final wrenching goodbye. As it happened, when Caroline rounded the last bend and saw the harbour at long last, Mikhail and his boat were both gone.

Stupefied, Caroline looked at the ropes which only hours before had strained under the weight of the seemingly restless ship, and now, carefully coiled round their posts, resembled the houseboat beside them, languidly settled. She stared at the steps which had led her before from the falsely safe haven of the deserted boardwalk to the surreal, dark dimensions of Mikhail's cabin. Those steps now seemed confused, as she was – purposeless, dangling from the docks to some indeterminate place. The thought even occurred that if she were to move toward that ladder, walk down ever so carefully as she had done earlier, she would encounter *Serena II* just as she'd left it, only submerged now as she herself had once been in those seas.

But of course that was not possible – not with the ropes left behind in such meticulous form, not with the wharf bumpers retied to their posts and the berth so untroubled, intact, like a tidied hotel room awaiting the next guest.

No, Misha was gone. Alone, somehow against the tides and strong winds, as he had done all the seafaring days of his life, he had sailed.

She scanned the horizon out past the Narrows – sole, treacherous path to the Strait. The water was briefly tranquil, undisturbed by the trailing wake of a ship, the fading of lights, the delayed break of a wave nearer shore. Even the bell buoy's warnings had ceased, for like everything else on this suddenly changed set, the mist with its lingering rain had disappeared. A baffling, almost sinister absence of sound had replaced them.

Into this strangely malevolent calm, footsteps intruded. Caroline reached for the ropes marking Mikhail's now-empty berth. She did not move as the steps approached the end of the dock, nor when they stopped close behind her, nor even when she heard a man's familiar voice say, "There you are, finally. Well, of course, I expected you here. I have been waiting awhile, walking all night almost, or so it seems, and yet I didn't see you pass by –" the man paused when Caroline turned. "Forgive me. I didn't mean to frighten you. I thought for certain you knew me –"

"Yes, yes, of course I know you, Pierre. It's just that so late – I was distracted. Such a strange silence…"

"It is a strange night. I can't recall when the dock's been so still." By then the guard was standing beside her. "Well it's better than rain, I suppose. At least this didn't get soaked. I can deliver it as I promised." Caroline felt a slim envelope pressed into her hands. "There's more," he went on, patting the oversized pockets of his pea coat. "Ah yes, *voilà*. I was to give you this too – no one else, not even the next guard." He thrust a thin package into her hand. "The gentleman said you'd be back – guaranteed – that I was to watch out for you until dawn…*Daybreak, Pierre* – those were his last words before he shoved off – except that he thanked me and paid me – and before I could protest, he had jumped back into his boat, which seemed to be slipping away without him almost, so that he had barely enough time for a wave and then he was off."

Pierre gazed off in the direction of the now desolate berth. He shook his head slowly, still disbelieving.

"Never saw anything like it. Crew of one in the dark, fighting the currents, gone before you could say her name almost... *Serena II*...Last things that remained. Fine golden letters floating out there on the waves, almost right where they should be, it seemed, and then they all disappeared toward the Strait – boat, sails and master – as if I had dreamed that night sailing and only those trinkets I gave you remained." He pushed his cap back and shrugged. "Well now you have them – that's the main thing. Duty discharged, as they say," he confirmed, reaching again for his lantern. Then, with a last backward glance at the sea as though he too would be gone to mysterious ports: "*Hélas*, not my last for tonight. I've a few rounds to walk still...*Bonne nuit, Mademoiselle.*"

The night watchman's steps, like his words, trailed off into the dark. As though in a dream – for she too at that moment felt the distinction between sleep and wakefulness blurred – Caroline moved to the bench by the side of the shop where in the pale arc of the lamp her trembling hands turned to all that was left of *Serena II*'s passage.

Beloved, she read,

I can almost picture you as you read this, for you will have returned to the harbour in Cap-Egmont as I begged you to do, wanting you forever with me.

You will be there on that bench by the tackle shop; the moon will have declined; the first hint of dawn will be hours away still. Only by the light of that tall lamp will you be able to see my words. I myself can barely see them, thwarted not by the dark but by a more profound sadness welling inside me, blurring the words, the page, everything but your face as I saw it for what I knew then would be the last time.

I am in my cabin, just about ready to sail, writing by the light of that lamp near my bed. It is where I was seated when you walked unsteadily from my room, promising to return before dawn. It is what I had insisted you had to do – choose on this night, set a man free whom you pitied, sail off to new lands with a man you still clearly loved.

I was wrong – or more correctly, only partially right. That we will both always love as we have since the beginning – fiercely, even to madness and perhaps beyond that – I no longer doubt. That remains true. That will always be true – incontrovertible fact like the tides, and just as relentless.

What was not true – though at the time I said it I believed it – was that only compassion remained in your heart for a man you once loved. I suppose I wanted to believe this. I longed for it to be true, Caroline, so that you would come with me – sail without shame, free in your own heart at last. Not until I saw you turn and suddenly notice the paintings on my wall, not 'til I watched you stare with such a mixture of anguish and rapture at the work of the man I believed you no longer wanted, did I know I was wrong. For my sake I had asked you to leave him; for my sake you had agreed, trusting me, trusting your love for me, mine for you — all of which have remained undiminished, none of which have diminished the hold Jude still has on your heart and always will.

What I had asked you to do can never be – you might come with me but never gladly – something would always remain to pull you back to this island, Paris, Honfleur, wherever it was he had gone off to paint, or to try to paint and most likely fail, for I suspect you have been more than model or muse to such a man as he is. I suspect the only truly grand years for him have been the recent ones, the rare days since you met – such astonishing things these random first glances! – there it all was for him – whatever it was he was seeking in your remarkable ways – found at long last, and forever.

All this and more I saw in your face as you gazed at those paintings, which were, of course, portraits of you. And yet here you were in my ship, ready to sail with me as I had insisted, arguing with a desperation which you confessed had been your own pain since the day we first met in my father's house, and unremittingly ever after, so that you gave yourself to me secretly in that same house, secretly in your mill house, secretly in your dreams when it was no longer possible for you to see me, having survived in the sea only to have learned that Jude too had survived, that you had loved twice, and completely, and always would, time and the changing of scenes notwithstanding.

It is your fate – that was clear to me watching you watching his work not ten feet from my bed. You could never choose, Caroline. You might decide, yes, but you could never forget. None of us will ever forget. But I can at least take the burden from you, gently, under cover of darkness, choosing for both of us, releasing my ship, restless thing, from the last of her moorings here in your harbour, releasing you in the same moment from a crushing dilemma that would only break you in time.

Stay where you must, so that he can still paint, and you, with that powerful force that you have, still create. If I could remove the longing that will return to your days, the nostalgia he will be condemned to depict, the yearning that will from henceforth resume its old place in my own heart – willingly I would do these things too – but it is not in my power. Still, the sadness I feel is receding, and something else like the sea rising beneath my ship is taking its place – something beyond resignation, more like peace at long last, for in a strangely intimate way, I am taking you with me tonight. All that I needed to know I have learned; all that I have ever felt has been returned – nothing withheld from me, nothing denied me, since all along, you have loved as I loved, dearest proud fierce thing, and here on my ship you could no longer hide such an immense and enduring and fine need. It is enough for me. Wherever I find myself, in whatever harbours never before imagined, ports still undreamed of – it will always be enough. It will always be you, Mrs. Devereux. There will be no other love.

Mikhail

It was a long time before Caroline managed to open the slim package still in her lap. Inside she found Mikhail's copy of his favourite poet – Catullus. A bookmark had been placed toward the end of the volume. She opened the book to the place and saw, centred on the page, one of the poet's last beautiful lyrics – written, as the beginning pieces had been, to the love of his life. And yet it was not, like those earlier poems to Lesbia, a startling cry of erotic passion. Nor was it filled with the rejected lover's disillusion, as the middle lyrics had been. There instead was, in essence, Mikhail's vale – conclusion to everything he had managed to write in his final letter before setting sail.

If ever anyone anywhere, Lesbia, is looking
for what he knows will not happen
And then unexpectedly it happens –
The soul is astonished,
As we are now in each other,
an event dearer than gold,
for you have restored yourself, Lesbia, desired
restored yourself, longed for, unlooked for,
brought yourself back
to me. White day in the calendar!
Who happier than I?
What more can life offer
than the longed for unlooked for event when it happens?

Gravel crunching beneath her tires seemed to drown out the surf below, Caroline thought as she slowly moved down Sans Souci's driveway. At the garage alongside the meadow she turned off her headlights, but decided against unbolting the shed's heavy locks. As it was, the click of the car door seemed to reverberate across the fields as she carefully slipped from her seat, left the car parked where it was, and followed the pathway around to the front of the house. Her light, distinctively slow steps resounded like dissonant chords to her as she advanced. Two or three times she stumbled, for the wind had left broken branches on the clay walkway surrounding the porch, and the moon had long since disappeared into the Gulf.

At the staircase she stopped. She listened for signs of Jude stirring within, though she had never known him to be awake at this hour. She heard only fierce tides tumbling onto the dunes down past the wall, and, now and again, another limb snapping somewhere near the path.

Sleeping...yes, undisturbed by the wind, she thought, glancing up at the wide darkened windows on either side of the door, the darkened bay windows above them, the smaller, gabled, equally dark ones under the roof, and then as leaves from the old willow swirled on up onto the porch she felt resurgent foreboding, still somewhat vague but insistent, as though the house had been suddenly emptied, like *Serena II*'s berth in the harbour, all signs of her former days with Jude swept away.

Unavoidable, she concluded. *Inevitable, above all in the beginning.* Her former days *had* changed forever, although she had determined never to reveal this fact to Jude. What had occurred on that boat, the anguished decision that had followed, the far more painful healing to come – all of it would remain forever buried within her. Her choice had been made. Misha was gone, never having learned of that choice. There was no reason for Jude to know of it either.

And yet, more than ever uneasy, she remained rooted to her spot by the stairs, strangely reluctant to proceed, feeling almost revulsion at the sight of the steps and the porch and the heavy doorway beyond. Things would be different, yes – emptied somewhat – that could not be avoided. But the house and the man would be as they'd been in the past. She needed but to advance, walk on up past the porch to the door, the hallway, the staircase, the landing – *why in God's name was the whole house so dark?* Not only dark but in some odd way off-limits. The bedroom windows seemed obscure, impenetrable, as though fortified against assault. The widow's walk on the roof resembled battlements facing the sea.

Madness to go inside like this, Caroline thought, staring up at the house to which she had returned of all things a stranger. *All I need is some time – a few moments. Composure will follow...*

Like a stranger she turned away and followed the long, curving path to the sea. It too was dark, opaque – not a boat or a sail or even a glimmer of dawn to the east, winds out to the west steadily colder. She turned, climbed back up the stairs, looked again at the house and walked into the woods.

Not surprisingly, for she rarely left lamps burning there, her library deep in the maze of fir trees was dark. Never before though – not even in winter – had the secluded, stone structure seemed uninviting, almost hostile, so that again after a while she turned away and moved on.

From the pine grove she walked toward the meadow. From the fields she emerged on the bluff, far to the north of the main house, and found, to her utter astonishment, at the end of those vast silent acres, lamps burning in the place where Jude never worked once it got dark.

She stood by the lighthouse and listened. Only once had Jude worked almost 'til daybreak, not wanting to leave the work later called *Théobald* incomplete. Perhaps again on this night he was working – again unable to leave a painting of compelling significance incomplete.

She strained to hear even one sound. There was only the wind. She saw that the door had been firmly closed and that the large brick Jude had always moved against the screen door was in place, secure, so that the sensations she had experienced outside the main house recurred: impressions of lifelessness, a void, as though the studio too had been emptied of all things – carts, cloths, Jude's easel and all of his works, past, present and those still to come.

And yet, she reminded herself, here there were lights. Somehow here of all places, room where Jude painted, place where she posed and would pose again for him, always, she felt she could enter still.

The brick was easily moved to one side. She opened the door, took a moment to adjust to the brightness and was once more surprised. Absolutely nothing had changed. Jude's cloths were all still neatly folded; his brushes were cleaned and lined up on the cart by his easel; his works in progress – the ones she could recall at least – were where he had left them – some on either side by the entrance, some on the opposite wall behind his large leather chair.

Her footsteps again seemed discordant as she crossed to the easel. Undisturbed, still in its place there, was the painting Jude had been working on for the past week or so – Sans Souci's fruit trees just before harvest. On the floor alongside was another work she remembered, also in progress, a portrait of Père Gabriel. Lying against the cart behind this was a smaller work, draped, which she did not remember, but which must also have been there for a while she assumed, not taking the time to uncover it.

Indeed, everything seemed to be as it had always been, untouched, unmoved, as though Jude had returned late from the long trip to Charlottetown and had gone directly to the main house, bypassing his workroom altogether.

Except for those lamps in the windows. Neither had been lit when she had left Sans Souci that day, long after Jude had gone off.

And two additional things. The first she had noticed just as soon as she'd entered: unmistakable odour of paint – not the pervasive, lingering smell which always filled this large room, but a sharper, more pungent thing – colours that had been recently mixed.

The second was brown paper wrapping, crumpled into a heap behind the front door. Not until she had crossed to close the door had she seen this, finding the carton sent months ago by Dr. Le Brun opened, emptied, leaning against the wall to the rear of the door. And yet *Half Moon*, the painting, was nowhere to be seen. Nor was the picture, whatever it was, which Jude had worked on that evening – painting which must have cost him much effort, to judge from the lamps he'd left burning so far into the night, and, far more important, from the fact that with his assured though never arrogant self-assessment, he had considered it in some way equivalent to his one great masterpiece from the grand years.

She determined to find it. If only to identify, perhaps even put an end to the dread that had steadily deepened since she had left her front porch steps, she would confront the image that had compelled Jude to keep working long into this night, driven, it seemed, to express some forceful perception, heretofore unimagined.

She searched again among the paintings stacked against the back wall, studied the landscape on the easel, the portrait on the floor beneath it, and then abruptly, finally taking note of the carefully draped canvas left near the back of the cart, she stopped.

Just as abruptly, the wind blew the door open behind her. Caroline did not turn this time, did not even hear the sound this time, increasingly drawn as she found herself now by the covered picture she had somehow before, unaccountably, missed. She knelt on the polished wood floor, slowly removed the fine velvet drape from the work and gasped, unprepared for the shock, the sensations that followed, staggered not just by the painting's remarkable beauty but by the story it told, every precise detail achingly rendered, every imprecise, unseen fact even more poignantly offered.

Cap-Egmont Harbour, the work was entitled. Beneath its title there was a date, or rather, again for eyes that could see, an explanation. *Night scene, late autumn.*

Never had Jude painted the sea so bewitchingly – launches and trawlers and houseboat impressionistically sketched – one splendid sloop rendered vividly, pride of place at the end of the dock, larger than all the other boats in the bay, luxuriant beauty reflecting the night's husky allure.

Yes, such a boat was well named, the artist seemed to be saying, carefully reproducing on the sumptuous, smooth, alabaster curve of the stern, in small, precise golden letters, *Serena II. Manhattan.*

Mesmerized, as if in a dream from which she both longed to awaken and felt forever protected, Caroline stared at that painting – scene wholly rendered though much had been merely suggested: impetuous waves breaking offshore, languorous foam submitting to sand, onrushing currents forcing their way through the Narrows, that one, single cabin light dancing as though a song had mixed in with the rain lightly falling, or had perhaps on its own drifted down from the houseboat drowsily moored alongside.

The artist had not missed a thing. He must have remained a long while by that scene to have recalled it so clearly, for the work had not been painted on site – not in such darkness – though not much time had elapsed since the viewing: no doubt around nine Caroline judged from the moon and *Serena II*'s slight windward slant which had been somehow, without effort, portrayed.

Where precisely he'd stood she could not possibly know. Not far from the boardwalk, she guessed, judging again from the painting's perspective – close enough at some point to see the steps leading down to the boat, and her car parked nearby, and those letters, that lamp – light perhaps extinguished while he had remained there – poignancy which would have accounted for the overwhelmingly wistful tone infusing the work.

Yes, even that he had witnessed. He had returned early from Charlottetown, had stopped off in the harbour, had unexpectedly seen Mikhail's boat just as she herself had – and, just like her, had been unable to turn away. Fascinated, horrified – no doubt a combination of both, he had approached. Horrified, he had turned away. In vain from that moment on all reluctance, delay, her preposterous wish to postpone that first encounter with Jude on the farm. The confrontation had already occurred.

Strangely, after the shock of this revelation subsided, the first clear emotion Caroline Devereux felt was rage. Her private, most secret longings – things she had been afraid to confess even to herself before this night, had been observed – if not directly, then for sure at close range, if not entirely, then at least long enough to have had their full import recorded. From henceforth there would be no deliverance, no felicity reconstructed with the man she had chosen, for the man she had chosen had encountered only betrayal, not the struggle which had preceded it in the earlier hours of the evening, nor the far more protracted one in the silent seasons before that, nor, far more decisive conflict, her agonized choice made in the overlook off to the side of the road. That last, lonely battle at the edge of the copse had been a mockery, obsolete exercise, superfluous strife without meaning.

Dried leaves swirling in with the wind scattered about her lap, the cart, the easel, the lamp alongside. An auburn maple leaf, once grand, landed upon Jude's magnificent painting. Carefully, perhaps even protectively – for even there on the floor, in the wind, even in her anger Jude McCallister's work called forth a most powerful, undiminished, transcendentally pure response in her heart – Caroline removed the leaf.

Only then did she realize Jude had not signed this work. She thought at first he had left it unfinished, but as she looked again she realized no, the painting had indeed been completed. It was perfect. Not another touch, stroke, suggestion of colour was needed. It had its title – careful, legible letters in the lower left-hand corner – and, unique to Jude's painting since he had come to Prince Edward, its precise time and locale. Only one other work, she remembered, had been left like this one, unsigned – sketch done in haste overlooking the beach beside Journey's End, subject the same as in his masterpiece – longing – model the same as in that first one, Half Moon at last found.

With a groan on this increasingly sharp, windy night she remembered that day – sand, a warm rock, an even warmer, intense gaze meeting her own. "I knew you would recognize the artist –" she had heard as his shadow had crossed the sheet clutched in her hand then…"Do you recognize the man?"

"Ah, Jude – Jude you are one and the same," she suddenly cried out in response on his floor now, feeling at last immense sorrow surging within her, grief like a tidal wave washing away all resentment, rage, any and all vestige of misplaced recrimination. Sadness only remained. What had begun with a glance and a song and such fierce desperation had ended with just that. For this reason the work was unsigned. It was part of a pair, like the still life and the abstract – companion piece to the sketch made at the start of their Maritime idyll.

Long after the wind had died down Caroline looked away from the work she still held in her hands. A bare streak of grey from over the Labrador Sea presaged a new day. So too did the far distant sound of the coastal supply boat. Just below Dutchman Rock the horn sounded again, then grew fainter and vanished as the boat moved on up the coast. Not until then did Caroline think of the sound she had vaguely heard surrounded by hemlocks off to the side of the road – another horn, not so distant – not a boat but a car descending the coastal road southward, back on down to the bay and beyond, westward toward Summerside, beyond that to

Charlottetown, from there to the mainland with the first outbound flight of the day, from the mainland to Paris, connecting flight whenever he wished…All grimly full circle. How else could it end?

Slowly, as one might move underwater, Caroline re-draped the painting, put it back in its place by the paint cart, turned the last of the lamps out and walked away from the lighthouse back up toward the main house.

The second floor landing creaked slightly. She paused, peered out the window at the black outline of pines flanking the gates and continued on up the stairs. Her light step was unsteady, her mind unfocused as she reached the top floor of the house, for she had eaten little and slept less since she had left Sans Souci on the previous day, and, for the first time since she had come to this place, had lost her way in the woods on her way from the lighthouse.

The windowless corridor was still dark. She moved mechanically toward the last door on her left – slightly ajar, she believed, so that she paused again at the threshold. She could hear nothing. She pushed the door open and stepped uncertainly into the room and saw that the space ahead seem to resemble the fields and the seawall and even the sea itself – a blur, nothing more, shadowed, silent, everything left as it was, she guessed vaguely – although again she could not be sure.

She reached for the wall switch but changed her mind, preferring, for what remained of this night, to remain undisturbed in the stillness which seemed to have settled upon the farm like fine mist. She closed the door softly, closed her eyes slowly, leaned up against the wall, and then, after a moment, opened her eyes again, watchful. Somebody was in the room – not asleep on the bed – that sound would have come from the left – but resting in the wing chair on the opposite side of the room, facing away from the bed, away from the doorway, looking out over the gates, the drive, the pathway that led to the porch steps.

The chair was large, its sides wide, so that even as she approached Caroline could see nothing of the figure resting so calmly there. But there was no mistaking the sound of the breathing she knew as she knew her own life, no misapprehending the presence of Jude in that chair, the force of him, ever restless, creative, even renewing itself at long last in sleep.

Even more carefully than she had approached, she came round to the front of the chair. Disbelieving she looked at him, not daring to move, make a sound, afraid he would vanish should he awaken as the shadows diminished around him, for by then that one earlier streak had become an imperceptible greying of sky, a lightening of the air almost, as though the background of a canvas had been tinted in preparation for a painting of the day soon to arrive.

Sleep had come late to him, she could see that. He was still dressed. There was a trace of paint still on his hands, a bit of sand on his shoes. His silver-grey hair, somewhat dishevelled, seemed to have been rumpled by wind, perhaps his own fingers. His sleeves were rolled up to his elbows, his collar open, shirt halfway unbuttoned, sweater carelessly tossed across the arm of the chair.

Yes, sleep has come late, she thought. *He has been painting, wandering, searching, distraught, and then suddenly peaceful, serene, as though an end to the evening's despair had occurred.*

But what that end was, what Jude had come to see clearly, she could not tell from his face. Not even as the sky continued to lighten and pale rose had replaced grey over the water's reflection, could she discern anything more specific than that most remarkable peace on his face – tranquility superimposed upon the habitual urgency that always marked his expression, compelled as he was, above all since his ordeal, to seek out and somehow render perfection. Even before those days, she thought observing him closely still, a mysterious intensity had always darkened his features. Now though, as if a fine glaze had been applied to that inextinguishable anxiety, as if care had been somehow burnished into a beautiful…

"Caroline?"

The sound of her name, uttered so unexpectedly, startled her.

"Caroline, is that you?"

Softly, after a moment: "Yes, Jude."

He stirred and slowly looked up.

"Yes," she repeated.

"Ah," he replied. "I thought so. I saw the car lights turning in at the gates, heard the tires on the drive, your step on the path. And then I waited…well I had been waiting a while. But for some reason these moments seemed longest. For some reason I – what are you doing? – No, no don't Caroline…*don't*…"

It was too late. She had already knelt by his side, taken his hand and pressed it against her face, then bowed and lowered her head, resting it upon his knees. Though she was silent, he knew she was weeping. She felt his other hand touch her – lightly at first, almost shyly, then with a tender caress that was both instinct and habit, long since one and the same to them both.

"As I said I was waiting," he went on, his voice as hesitant now as his hand had just been, "and then your step seemed to diminish and I assumed you had gone to the beach or your books in the pines or…"

"Jude," she broke in…

"To the orchard of all places – such a late hour – but then again it is a time you have always loved, isn't it, Caroline?" His voice was no longer awkward. "Darkness of night near the sea."

She looked up into his face. As though retouching a painting, he brushed a tear from her cheek.

"At any rate you were home," he continued, matter-of-factness not quite masking the immensity of relief washing over his own restless heart. "Wandering somewhere…but home."

Caroline made no answer. They both knew she had gone to the workroom. They both knew she had seen his night's work, left there perhaps to be discovered, perhaps never to be seen by a woman who never returned. Either way, from out of the night's pain, beauty had been created, which was Jude's way, and somehow restored, which was hers. None of it would be alluded to, that was increasingly clear in the silence that returned, momentarily, as he kept stroking her hair. The imponderables would never be mentioned, for that was indeed what they were – what it had all been and would remain – fathomless, unavoidable, like the force of the tides, which they both vaguely heard had begun falling again – mysterious, enduring attractions never to be altered, never deterred.

"The sea has crested," Jude noted softly, nothing more. And then as he moved to stand he lifted her up against him. "You must be tired, Caroline."

"Yes. Yes, I am."

"As am I…Come. Let us rest. Daylight will not disturb us, I think."

He led her back to their bed and lay down beside her and took her into his arms and said – more like a murmur than words, a coda, signature on a painting at last completed – "There, now," as once more his eyes closed and again such peace on his face, Caroline saw, her own divided heart gladdened.

It would forever remain divided, that too she knew now as the sky turned an imprecise mixture of gold, silver and tourmaline, and Jude was once more at rest and she too closed her eyes and they both slept beneath the portrait that had been carefully placed on the wall over the headboard behind them.

FINALE

Théobald Le Brun paused, inhaled the fragrant night air as though quaffing rare vintage wine, then made his way down the steps toward the hospital's courtyard below. Save for sounds of a few dusty wrens among the dried boxwood leaves, the maze of carefully tended pathways was silent. Most of the day workers had left; the night shift was already on rounds; one person alone remained on a bench under the wide centre archway below, motionless, gazing across the court at the bare, tangled sycamore trees.

Lost in thought, reflected Le Brun, moving across the worn bricks of the walkway. Or perhaps, as he had just done, merely pausing to savour the unexpectedly sweet autumn night.

"Neither," Caroline Devereux smiled, as Le Brun sank down beside her. "It's just that I'd heard you'd begun shortly past dawn today. And that the case was complex..."

"Nothing is ever simple."

"No," she sighed.

"The driver was lost before they arrived. The passengers will survive. It will take time, of course. Still, a highway crash at such speed. They were lucky."

"Far more than luck, Théobald."

"What had to be done has been done," was his modest reply, and then again the courtyard fell silent – profound stillness rare for that space in that time, broken only by the occasional rustle of a dried azalea shrub in the garden, and, now and again, the distinctive swinging of the door to the surgical wing overlooking the court.

Suddenly, as though startled by a pair of blackbirds taking flight from a nearby acacia, Le Brun exclaimed, "I still wonder if in that other instance – I ask myself weekly in fact, *daily*..." He stopped, forced to pause by the sound of a patient's cart rolling across the stones in the upper arcade. By the time the rattle had passed, he was aware of Caroline's eyes on him – of the gentle reproof in her deepening gaze, more than ever remarkable in the twilight.

"What had to be done was done then as well," she said in a tranquil voice, her expression serene. "Precious days with love ransomed."

"Nevertheless –"

"Jude's words, not mine, Théobald."

"But could I have given him more?"

"More than his hands back? His head?"

Caroline shook her head, placed her hand lightly on Le Brun's arm, said mildly,

"No, dearest friend. Not even you could have done that, though what you did do, God only knows how, was a miracle wrought – again Jude's own words...renewal he never ceased to ponder. There in his lighthouse he'd marvel, by his paints and his cloths he would wonder, repeat your name on occasion, reread every letter you sent. Well it's all there in that painting he left – things he could only truly acknowledge on canvas, only with paints and a brush, and of course" – again that soft bittersweet tone – "careful instructions attached. A handwritten note left for me at some point –"

She too stopped abruptly, interrupted by the announcement of visiting hours soon to end for the night. Then she turned toward the lobby, visible through the glass doors at the end of the courtyard.

"Never to be sold, auctioned, or loaned," she reminisced, gazing at a large, stunningly framed abstract – elegant shapes in vivid blue,

gold, cream and cerise tones, entitled *Théobald*, place of composition omitted. *"To be returned to the place I was brought back to one night…* I kept the note, of course."

"The promise too," Le Brun said, gazing as well through the tall doors, "although I still say it should have gone in the new wing."

"Théobald, you are now Chief of Staff."

"Your Trauma Centre saves thousands."

"Ours."

"Your vision created it. Your gift built all those rooms, supplied all those rooms…made an old man's dream come true in the process," he managed.

"You don't look all that old to me in your portrait," she smiled, glancing again at Jude's abstract. "Besides, it didn't belong there. It belongs where it is. The lobby wall was too bare. And I couldn't very well put the only other portrait Jude would not sell out there."

"No – no, I suppose not. At least not with you here in the office each day. No, that would not do," he repeated, more to himself this time, though with a smile too at last. *"Half Moon* looks fine where she is in your house – a little provocative there in your library overlooking Notre-Dame's spires, I'll admit – but then again even here at your desk, starched white coat and all, you still have what I'd call…somewhat unsettling ways."

"Power of suggestion, Théobald. It is what the painter intended."

"The painter suggested far more in that work."

Only the breeze made reply.

"All that he lived for in fact," continued Le Brun. "I'm very glad it now faces those spires, the plaza beyond them, that corner room where he fought so to reclaim you – to reclaim life – one and the same to him until the end, I know. Even if he had not told me so, if every letter up to and including the last had not been all about you, and his work, and the farm which he insisted had been so aptly and beautifully named – I would have known how it was with Jude. It was all there in his work."

Bells began slowly tolling. Puzzled, Caroline looked around, for the sound seemed to be coming from the west, opposite side of the plaza from the cathedral.

"Well," Théobald said, striking his knees with his hands, "I will think no more about what might have been, what else I could have done. We bought him three more years that night, time to paint again, love – a peaceful death when it came, as it had to someday – consolation enough, I suppose, all things considered."

The uncommonly slow chimes continued.

"Yes, it was very peaceful," conceded Caroline Devereux. "And as you say, Théobald, given the blows he'd sustained, a matter of time, I suppose. Still, when that time finally came..." Her voice trailed off, blending with the last of the chimes echoing over the river. Then, as though she were facing not the stone arches across the hospital's garden, but the stone walls by the Gulf around Sans Souci: "...brush in his hand still, September light on the dunes, my name all of a sudden murmured so that I turned, thinking he wanted me to change my pose just a bit, perhaps move in to him slightly, but when I looked up I saw he too had looked up, felt his intense gaze searching mine, and then abruptly he said, 'Yes...yes, that's it.' Nothing more – as though he had found the one thing he needed for the painting in progress – and then he sank down on the grass and red clay he loved so, leaving behind his unfinished picture...I have it still."

"I'm sure someday I'll see it."

"Someday," she echoed, as day's last westerly light faded above the Conciergerie's towers.

"Consolation enough," reprised Théobald, eyes fixed ahead on the lengthening shadows that crept like cats toward their bench. "Meanwhile there are the others, many beautiful ones – although I still say you should have kept more, Caroline."

"There was no need. Whatever he painted for me, of course I kept. The rest was in such demand...Museums. Clinics like this one. Jude's work deserved to be shared."

"Handsome gifts, nevertheless."

"They were not all donations," she reminded him archly. "Auguste and Armand saw to that. Still, I was able to give and that pleased me. I had more than I needed...Raphael's house left to me…Sans Souci, not just the farm but its paintings, far greater treasures – all of Jude's paintings in fact, although I never knew he had planned things that way."

Le Brun had long since known, but said only, "I'm glad you chose to come here."

"It seemed the best thing to do. Carry on with your work, I mean – you whom Jude loved so…your patients here needing so much, as he himself did one night. He continues to help this way, indirectly."

"Not so indirectly."

She reflected a moment. "Let's just say from whatever beckoning landscape he seemed to have glimpsed that last day. In any case, the thought appealed to me. The house on the Île St-Louis steps away…Prince Edward Island a plane ride away."

"You've still no plans to sell that farm?"

She shook her head thoughtfully. "It was my home once, a most remarkable place, not far from the beach where Jude found me. Journey's End by the sea and the abbey remain. There is also a harbour nearby –"

Inexplicably, or so it seemed then to Théobald, Caroline checked herself, smoothed out her skirt, studied the dogwoods as two plum-coloured leaves drifted down to the grass.

"No, I will never sell Sans Souci. Every spring I'll return, like those birds that fly home to Lookout Point after each winter." She stared at the place where the leaves fell, though the ground was too dark to discern them precisely. "Except that Serge and Susannah won't be found there next May. Serge was lost too year before last."

"Yes, so Jude wrote. One of those sudden Gulf storms, he assumed."

"Nobody knows. Serge would sail so far north sometimes. Into the Labrador Sea. Always alone…Hard to say what occurred in those seas except that he vanished."

Discreetly, the last group of visitors moved through the shadowed arcade. In the empty lobby beyond, the main door revolved a few moments as though in farewell after they'd passed.

Soon even that hum faded leaving just the sound of the fountain spilling over its stones in the midst of the courtyard, murmur akin to ebb tide.

"A matter of time for Serge too, Théobald, as I am convinced he understood. Susannah knew too – I have come to believe that as well. How else to explain that strange ending – strange to the outside world, I mean, places beyond Rock of Birds, the Gulf, that house with its cave…certainly not to me."

"Lost at sea too, Jude wrote."

"Not really *lost*," said Caroline softly. "More likely the opposite, I suspected, hearing the boatman's account."

Fingering the fringed edge of her shawl, she pondered. Then, reflectively still: "Come September, when *l'Inattendu* failed to return, Susannah waited only a month, then began preparing things, as though for a journey."

"To where?"

"Again, no one knows. When the last packet arrived in November, Lookout Point was deserted. The little rowboat they always left on the sand – the one where they found me – had vanished. I like to think she found Serge with it."

Le Brun made no answer.

"*I am sure of it*, Théobald. *The Unexpected* was waiting. Serge always insisted on that. Wherever that boat wound up, well – Susannah's there too," she pronounced, and then, barely audible coda before stillness again filled the court: "The Gulf has its secrets. Affinities few understand."

One after the other, shutters were closed across the windows overlooking the garden – mournful sound, thought Le Brun, echoing Caroline's story, although it was resignation not sorrow he heard when she suddenly added, "So you see the circle is closed in its time after all. Everything finished. No. Not so much finished, transformed. Even Todd's Farm, my first home, remains. A town grant was created – a bargain struck you might say, years ago. It has never been challenged. At least I – no, I would have had word," she said in a voice suddenly altered, cryptic almost as the last of the windows above her was fastened. Then, by way of conclusion, as if gently closing the shutters on her own past tumultuous years: "What remains now is this. My life like yours, Théobald, is now here."

For the third and last time on that night, bells from the same indistinct western source began tolling.

"Such an odd, sorrowful sound," Caroline murmured.

"Yes."

"From someplace nearby, but not Notre-Dame," she judged, cocking her head toward the western rooftops ahead, listening carefully.

Théobald also considered. Unwisely perhaps, he had already caused her to relive poignant days come and gone. The rest was perhaps best left unrevealed – for the present at least, solemn event about to begin, evening of which she seemed unaware.

And yet those deep bells rang on, not to be denied. Most likely she too would insist. One way or another – if not from him on this night, then from another soon after – she would be informed. Perhaps she already had some idea – some facts learned on Prince Edward. Unlikely though, he concluded, watching her listen more closely, leaning forward a bit.

"…Not St-Julien," she decided. "That sound would also be from the east –"

"From the Palais de Justice," Le Brun said at last, slowly.

"At this hour?"

"Announcing a concert tonight at the Sainte-Chapelle alongside."

"But concerts are often held there…"

"Never before one like this…well, never before the occasion," Théobald specified. "Mozart. By way of a candlelight service, the *Requiem*."

"A funeral, then –"

"A memorial, yes."

"Fitting," mused Caroline. "All Hallows' Eve, I mean."

"Except that the person remembered wanted no speeches, not even one word of praise. Well such a thing could not be. A formal tribute was called for – if no spoken addresses tonight then music, harmony of higher kind, or so the War Ministry decided. Of course, the church is not large. Only a handful of those arriving will be inside. The rest will listen from the lower church, the steps, even the courtyard beyond. – Ah, here it is still," Le Brun noted, relieved, reaching into his pocket. "I'm to be one of the lucky ones. My wife was also invited, but she's in Algeria still. She was saddened to learn of it all."

"You have lost a friend," Caroline murmured, once again lightly resting her hand on Le Brun's arm. "I am sorry."

Lamps in the archways surrounding the courtyard came on, casting long, diagonal beams onto the garden, although their own bench remained shadowed.

"We have both lost a friend," he replied, "though I'm not certain you know yet." Caroline turned to him, puzzled as he went on, "I assume Jude spoke at length to you about his ordeal here in Paris."

"He spoke of it, yes…I would not say at length, though. And certainly never in depth."

"Did he mention Honfleur?"

"I know he arrived dead of winter, much of his anguish behind him, much to come still before spring. I know too that somehow, *some grace bestowed upon him* were the words he used once, he was given the strength there to move his body again, walk, paint once more – paint more sublimely than he had ever done before then, in fact. Hard to believe, I know…Well not for you. With your own eyes you saw this. But years later hearing it, even now in the retelling, I can scarcely imagine such a place, such a time. The facts astonish me still."

"Go on."

"Little left to be said. There was a driver, I think, who was kind; an ambulance ride to the coast Jude preferred not to describe; a house by the sea, a housekeeper – Marie-Claude, I believe – yes, that was her name…"

"No one else?"

"Well there was you, to be sure; a colleague of yours, Dr. Meurice; neighbours Jude grew to love; fishermen he was fond of; one other helper, much older, though here again, Jude preferred to say nothing. I never pressed him. I haven't even a name, in all those years not one fact, only the feeling, an intuition, that his heart remained too full of love for this person to speak. He might have told me in time – who knows? – a few details perhaps, nothing more – certainly not that profound thing he glimpsed each time he looked back, recollection so powerful that not even on canvas, to the best of my knowledge, did he ever express it. In any case, time ran out. Whatever it was Jude may have wanted to share with me, whoever that nameless soul was he could not bear to remember, remains undisclosed."

Le Brun passed his hand several times over the card he still held. He seemed to be studying its inscription, perhaps the name it bore, dates – she could not tell in the half-light. Distinctly, though – for he had moved slightly into the arc of the lamp by that time – she saw him stare out at the fountain a moment, considering, then slip the card back into his pocket. In low, measured tones, he said, "The person Jude loved so – and you are right, it was profound love surpassing expression which made him unable to speak – was a woman most dear to me too. Many of those who are coming tonight felt the same. It is for her the bells toll, for her the crowds, the candles, Mozart's farewell. Strange how these things come to pass. I was prepared not to speak, thinking to spare you one last sad backward glance. And yet you inquired. I'm very glad now you did. Jude would have told you himself someday – like you I suspect that. At least now, while a moment remains, I can speak in his place."

Steadily then, as the slow distant tolling continued, Théobald recollected. By the time he declared, "Star pupil, top honours," his face, turned to Caroline now, betrayed even more than his words a mixture of pride, love, and suddenly vivid unease – combination strangely familiar to her as she heard, "Barely a child herself when we met and yet within a few years she became my best nurse. Shortly thereafter France fell. Her brother Émil was denounced. Within a year I had burned her valedictorian photo, destroyed all her awards – anything which would have revealed her remarkable abilities, for there was a price on the head of Germaine du Pannier by that time – not on the outwardly tranquil, average nurse in my clinic, but the mysterious medic who performed miracles in some unknown country place after dark They were one and the same, of course, though even among us few knew. Fewer still were the ones who could find that remote farmhouse up in the hills, candlelight only dared, whispers only allowed while bones were mended and burns cured – if there were some hope in the curing, and if not...well let us just say those victims too found salvation. Peace assumed many forms in that house."

Le Brun's thick white hair blew away from his brow as he stared up through the trees at pale, barely emerging stars. "So long ago," he reflected, as though in those secretive lights he could see tapers burning low in the dark. "And yet I found her again, Caroline. In spite of the years come and gone I needed a miracle, nothing less – impossibility, I was advised by colleagues and experts alike – but I refused to believe it. I knew if I asked this last favour, if I begged in person on Christmas four years ago this December, my patient might still have a chance – not to live, I had seen to that, but to work, far more than life in this case.

"My star pupil agreed. How could she not? There remained one last, broken man whom I loved as a brother. There remained her stout hands, her heart – above all Nice, Cannes, Grasse – nights of Resistance we'd shared and both somehow survived. For their sake Germaine helped me."

An ambulance suddenly rumbled out of the ramp onto Pont Notre-Dame just past the emergency doors. Its siren lingered a while, then faded into the maze of steep streets leading up toward Montmartre.

By then, though profound calm had returned to the courtyard, Caroline's hand was no longer a light touch on Le Brun's arm. She said not a word, not even a whisper, made no discernible gesture. There was no need, Théobald knew, as he acknowledged, "Yes...Yes, it was Jude, Caroline. I only restored his bones here in Paris. She gave him his heart back in Honfleur."

And with that, or so Théobald thought, the night's revelations were finished, for all that remained of his tale were the slow-tolling bells, which like the siren soon faded, and the late autumn breeze.

This last steadily quickened, causing the poplars to sway at their posts by the doorway and the spray of the fountain to splash onto the grass as Théobald added, "Caroline, I still have my wife's ticket. You're free to come with me if you like – but only if you like, if you think it will do you good, heal some of the sadness that lingers. I myself have to go. I hate to leave you here – I mean now, like this. I'll pick you up afterward."

She seemed not to hear him, not to see the old caretaker rhythmically sweeping the stones as he neared, not even to feel the increasingly cold, crystalline air as her shawl fell, unnoticed, onto the ground by their bench.

"On second thought, I can stay," he proposed. "The woman remembered tonight would have understood."

Caroline still made no answer, as though present time, like the unusual warmth of October's last radiant day, had unexpectedly vanished.

"*Bonsoir, Madame...Mon Docteur,*" murmured the caretaker, moving along the walkway past their bench on toward the lower arcade. "*C'est étrange cette nuit, non?*" he said in a raspy voice that resembled his rake as he gathered the sycamore leaves into his sack and moved on.

"Yes it is a strange night," Théobald thought, watching the old man stop one more time to remove the last of the dried chrysanthemums from a graceful stone urn by the stairs. Then he too disappeared, leaving behind only the diminishing sound of his boots as he unsteadily climbed the steep steps.

Le Brun turned away. He was about to reach down for Caroline's shawl when he saw that she was already tying it around her shoulders.

"Théobald, I will go with you," he heard her say then, her voice too barely an echo, her manner also unsteady. "You have been very kind."

Tourists and home-going crowds filled Notre-Dame's plaza, the park, the canopied flower stalls near the rue de Lutèce beyond. Leading the way through them all, Théobald felt Caroline's arm leaning on his still, not their habitual closeness – they often walked side by side in this way – but the slight weight of her seeking support of some kind.

That same unexplainable disorientation, he mused, mystified still as to the cause. *One can only hope in the next hours – if not an end to such pain…some relief.*

As it turned out, in the next hours there would be both for Caroline Devereux, although there was no way for her to have known this as they climbed the steep steps toward the Sainte-Chapelle's upper church. Still less could Dr. Le Brun have known what it was that had so unsettled her in the hospital garden. He could never have guessed, retelling the life of Germaine, that his remarkable story was for her, in effect, a twice-told tale, for she had never mentioned her life in Maximilian's d'Olivier's house. It had all remained undisclosed, even to Théobald, above all to Théobald – the morning Max had fallen silent, and she, herself burned, had recorded his trial by fire outside Nice, the afternoon he had recounted his resurrection in a candlelit farmhouse; the elegant night that had followed – Christmas dinner, a concert, presents exchanged, a fateful ride home in the snow with his son.

No, Théobald could not have suspected these facts, these crossings of stars in the constellations of lives he himself in his own richly passionate days had encountered.

Nor could he have imagined the profound impact his revelations would in their turn bring about. He could only observe, perplexed, Caroline's uneven step as she ascended the staircase. Pondering, he could hear only the endless procession behind him, the tuning of instruments high above him, the scraping of chairs, and, vaguely off in the distance, sounds of the city coming to life once again in the dark.

Of the images coming to life inside Caroline's head he could of course discern nothing. Her silent words remained just that – thoughts she alone heard, unspoken reflections which supplanted everything but their own unavoidable implications:

So we are to meet again then, he and I. Not in the flesh, not face-to-face – no, that can never be – who knows where on earth or more likely the seven seas Mikhail finds himself now – but in my mind, in my heart – places refused him in vain every day, only to have the struggle renewed in my sleep every night. Such last bittersweet irony! To have that clear image invoked of all places here…

They reached the door of the church. She took a quickened breath, then a deeper one. Yes it would be little Germaine who would bring the past rushing into her head, much as the thing which had happened out on Susannah's Joubert's lawn, only now there was no choice to make, for she had made her choice, finally, had lived out its terms to the letter. Never, not even once since the night *Serena II* had sailed abruptly from Cap-Egmont harbour, had she heard from or communicated with Mikhail d'Olivier – as they had known it must be. Now, alongside the piercing remembrance of Jude, his will to live, create, love one last time – now of all nights that grand house in Manhattan vividly summoned as well, Todd's Farm with its creatures, Land's End on the Hudson, Antonin, Max – all of it lost to her, all of them gone from her, above all the one who remained still, whereabouts unknown.

She sighed, remembering Serge. Whereabouts also unknown. All that remained was the name of his boat – wise, sad, ironic and beautiful name – sad if apt reference to the Unaccountable: sole paradoxical certainty in her life.

Fitting if bitter refrain, she reflected, pausing one last time at the threshold. It was her destiny to be divided, after all, rootless in heart if no longer in body, confronted forever with the perpetual conflict between what could never exist and what remained keenly perceived.

With her hand still on Théobald's arm, she entered the chapel.

⌐ ❰ ⌐

Magisterial horns, bassoons, timpani, and a grand crescendo of voices repeated the opening supplication, *Requiem, requiem aeternam, eternal rest grant unto them O Lord.* As though in concert, sublime light filled the church. Long rows of chandeliers shone onto the crystalline north and south walls. Moonlight poured through the stained glass window behind the east altar. Westward the rose window glowed with day's perishing tones – transcendence echoed in the music, the text, the combined plea for perpetual light to shine upon the souls of the blessed, forever tranquil.

It was not of Germaine that Caroline thought at this moment, for as the lines were repeated, and the metaphor of light as an image of beatific peace was ever more grandly expressed, she recalled Jude, forever seeking his light, and, along with this image, Maximilian, ever restless, haunted by the allure of what was not only beautiful, but also just. She tried to imagine them both at long last in peace – everlasting tranquility, stasis of contemplation. She tried to picture Jude's hands, restless arc called once *Cathedral*, at long last immobile, content, resigned to be one with ideal form, no longer desperate to paint it. She tried to envision Maximilian's strong hands, unforgiving force wielding his cane at the end, peaceful, stilled, no longer shaping ideal things, at long last unmoving.

Her efforts proved futile. No sooner conceived the images crumbled, as though falsely composed, so overwhelmingly vivid was the recollection of unquenchable thirst that defined both men's lives, so memorable the creativity which like incandescent coal burned within them, never to be extinguished, essential life force defying all challenge.

Unnerved by this inability to place them both, seemingly exiled, among the elect whom the radiant music described, Caroline turned away from the moon's ever-increasing light. Eyes lowered, she willed herself not to hear that last glorious prayer – such disquieting words for her, *et lux perpetua,* so exquisitely sung.

Germaine, she told herself fervently. *I shall try to think of Germaine, picture the girl I never met but whose life I once rendered, see her again decades later, mending a broken man whom it was also my fate to love.* And with that the grand choral fugue of the *Kyrie* – plea for mercy – began.

Yes, she must have been just like that, Caroline thought, feeling herself soothed, uplifted, by the wondrously spirited variations on compassion's theme echoing in the hallowed space.

Yes, she was just like that, recollected Théobald, seeing before him the eager student, the capable healer, the remarkable patriot... the wind-burned serene face of Saint Ann in Honfleur's mariners' church.

And then the image of Jude that same winter came to his mind, for the music had again shifted, and a mournful yet paradoxically thrilling baritone voice – anguish resolving itself against all odds into hope – began. Théobald remembered one solo Christmas bell pealing, Jude's weary eyes in spite of those bells focusing hard on the day that was dawning, hope astir somewhere deep in that gaze, barely discernible, but nonetheless there.

Le Brun let his thoughts drift after that, swept away by the ensuing, radiant *Recordare* – call to remember – four voices blending, merging, drawing apart, rising into eternal spheres like the flames on the tall, slender candles before him, or the Pentecostal aroma of incense suddenly filling the chapel which, while it lasted, conferred something like peace.

Caroline too found herself swept away – impossible to resist the sublimity of the sound and the space – but unlike Dr. Le Brun, she found no peace in the moment. Her mind ranged distractedly from past into present, and then forward again into unknown spheres – for so they remained to her, blurred, despite the increasing conviction of faith conveyed in the text, implied in the notes, expressed in the dazzle of glass walls around her. Tears filled her eyes as they did those of Théobald as she remembered, but consolation escaped her. If she could but picture Max resting! If she could only see Jude bathed in light! *Call them unto thee with the blessed*, one solo angelic voice seemed to pray on her behalf then, invocation reprised by the chorus, as though a heavenly host had just passed.

As though a heavenly host had in passing applauded the wonders of creation, mused a gentleman seated alone toward the back of the chapel, the lofty *Sanctus* began. Such a startling burst of words and music and light, he thought as day's last amber rays poured through the rose window above him! Such a celebration of hope over despair! One could only assent, he reflected, even in the midst of mourning's dark ritual, to such an affirmation of life so unexpectedly grand, for heaven and earth were indeed full of wonders – how well he remembered them all, he who moved best by the light of the stars, who had watched pale mornings break upon mysterious seas, quiescence brood over the tides along undiscovered shores. On only the rarest occasions had the scene before him filled him with pain – darkest of night when a storm overcame his first ship, palest of day heading again out to sea, Gulf of St. Lawrence behind him, woman he loved left behind on its shores.

Now yet again he remembered those shores. Vividly he recalled a walk across Prince Edward Island, a memorial out on its north capes – remembrance not for Caroline Devereux as it turned out, as indeed he had always suspected, but far more fittingly for Maximilian, born by the sea, raised near shores he fought fiercely to save, returned to waters held dear by the woman he too loved.

Fitting as well this memorial, reflected the gentleman, letting his thoughts drift back in time across his father's remarkable life. He was glad he had decided to come to Paris for this service, pleased he could be in attendance among those paying homage, grateful to have received an invitation from Nicholas Ollikainen, throughout the war Maximilian's colleague, afterwards his physician.

Indeed, many if not all who remained from those days seemed to be gathered once more in this church, Misha'd observed as he had glanced around him during the *Recordare*. *Let not such toil be in vain*, had been the quartet's poignant plea then, causing him to think not just of Max, not just of those hands and unique restless heart, but of Jean-Luc Onegin, professor of physics; Didier Franck, attorney; Nicholas Ollikainen, surgeon; Ollikainen's colleague, a Dr. Théobald Le Brun, whom he had never met but of whom he had heard much. Once there'd been hundreds, thousands fighting together in secret...So few remaining.

The service drew to a close. As if from a distance, like an echoing valediction from a disappearing archangel, one last solo voice soared, *Perpetual light be forever vouchsafed unto them, O Lord*, exalted farewell reprised by the chorus, *Eternal rest grant unto them O Lord; In thy compassion, light everlasting.*

Eloquent silence then filled the darkening church. Caroline raised her eyes, staring again at the strangely bright moon passing beyond the windows ahead, hearing not the sublime final lines of the piece, but, like the gentleman far behind her – whom she did not see – recalling that other brief, haunting phrase, her sole prayer at the end. She could only hope for that one thing, all else confounding her still, all other certainties eluding her as she remembered one last time Jude needing light for his work, Max ceaselessly working so as to admit light, Germaine the beacon in darkness. *Let not such toil be in vain*, she entreated silently, unaware of Théobald's touch on her arm, resigned heart aching more keenly than ever that moment, for not 'til that moment had she allowed her thoughts to turn to the one who remained still, wandering somewhere at will in this elegant world the chorus had praised for its glory, golden as well – he would always be that, she mused, seeing his imagined form in her mind with absolute clarity now, his face, that last letter left, her passion from henceforth a deep, silent, enduring thing, like the sea.

The touch on her arm became insistent. "We are almost the last, Caroline, come," Le Brun whispered, forced to disturb the reverie that had cast such a spell upon his companion. They stood, took their places among those exiting still and began making their way down the aisle back to the steep, curving stairway under the western façade.

By then Misha had turned away, unaware of the throng passing by, lost as he was in admiration of the rose window above him. It was not until he heard a man's voice repeat, "Come, Caroline –" for she had turned one last time to gaze at the moon's curious light growing brighter behind the altar – that he looked again at the crowd.

"Take my arm. Remember the steps here are sharp. – No, no," he then heard distinctly, "I had better go first. Follow along close behind me."

He turned toward the voice. The man had moved abruptly down the dark, curving stairs. The woman had paused for a moment and then followed – an instant, two at the most, but it had been enough for Mikhail to have seen Caroline Devereux vanish.

He remained motionless, stunned, disbelieving his senses, mistrusting the moment, the setting, the whole evening spent in each other's presence, lady unseen by his eyes until she had passed him, gentleman unbeknownst to her even then.

It cannot be, he heard himself reason, incredulous, and then…*but why should it not be? She of all people would be here, on this night, to honour the woman who had saved Maximilian. Long ago she left Prince Edward, or so I was told on my last voyage north.*

There in the chapel still, clutching the back of a chair, Misha'd recalled that last trip, when he had heard of Jude's death, of her departure shortly thereafter – when he had made no further inquiries. They had said their farewells after all. Wherever she'd gone to, she had clearly considered them final.

…Wherever she'd gone to. He should have known it was Paris. So many memories. So many ties still to Jude. She herself had had family here. There'd been a house. Perhaps she owned that house now. Perhaps the gentleman with her tonight –

Yes, of course that was it…Brand new life, a new start. She was not a woman to live alone after all. And her companion – even in that brief moment he had seemed somehow like Max – distinguished, established, so concerned for her, such love in the way he had said, "Come, Caroline."

Mikhail sighed. Ever so briefly torn, he remained where he was. He would have stayed longer had not a guard approached to remind him that the church was now closing.

And so he too made his way down the narrow, turned staircase, emerging into the shadows of the now-empty courtyard, passing through the gates out onto the street, all of a sudden regretting he had not spoken – at least a civil hello, a courteous inquiry into her health, introductions made, the new man in her life presented.

And then at the thought of this folly he smiled to himself, bitterly. To what end such a conversation? What earthly purpose could such an exchange have possibly served? He loved her desperately still. As he had said in his last note, to be read in the arc of a lamp not unlike this one outside the gates on the boulevard du Palais, *Wherever I find myself, Mrs. Devereux, it will always be you. There will be no other love.*

⌐☾⌐

The afternoon's warmth was long gone, but the air had remained remarkably clear as Caroline Devereux walked to her house on the Île St-Louis.

"I'll see you home," Le Brun had insisted.

"Théobald, no. It's just a few steps after all, a few streets…the old bridge…"

Crowds from the Sainte-Chapelle had surged past them as her voice trailed off.

"Yes, you will want your own thoughts perhaps," he had acknowledged, while an immensely full, nearly translucent pale moon cleared the Hôtel-Dieu's tower, taking its place among the stars just above the cathedral.

Her arm had rested on his for a moment; her thoughtful gaze had met his kind, deepening eyes; they had kissed on both cheeks, and, finding the gesture inadequate – above all on this night – had shared a brief, fierce embrace alongside the still-opened gates of the Palais de Justice.

"Until tomorrow then," had been her last wistful words as they'd parted. Le Brun had turned north then, striding into the wind and dried leaves swirling around the sinuous Art Deco gates of the Métro. Caroline had turned south, blending among the groups making their way toward the Seine. Suddenly, without exception, the others had continued on hurriedly over the river, so that she had found herself strangely alone on an abruptly deserted Right Bank. For a moment or two she had paused by the bridge; then, turning decisively, she had resumed her steps westward toward Notre-Dame.

Not until she had emerged from under the shadows by the immense Préfecture de Police did Caroline realize, or rather remember, what had called all the others across the river so quickly. Within moments, a rare total eclipse of the moon would occur, seen to best advantage, no doubt, from the steep, higher slopes on the Seine's opposite bank.

And yet even from where she had stopped at the edge of the plaza, the unobstructed, sublime vista directly ahead took her breath away – resplendence perfectly poised between Notre-Dame's massive west towers, light soon to be darkened, never to be extinguished.

Ah, she had reflected gazing up in the silence, *there it is after all. Eternal harmony in the spheres surpassing all understanding. Light so serene it resembles truth. Elegance so enduring one can even imagine the artist content, the soldier becalmed, celestial peace forever stilling their dark, restless hearts.*

For a few moments longer she'd stared. Soon all would be darkness, she knew. *Temporary shadows*, she had reminded herself in what was still an unearthly keen glow. *Lux aeterna beyond them.*

A suddenly brisk gust of wind scattered piles of dried chestnut leaves over the stones. She wrapped her wool shawl around her, hearing her steps resound as she advanced. She passed the long benches, the poplars, Charlemagne's dark, looming statue. And then once more she stopped, transfixed, gazing as the brilliant globe like a light at play's end strategically dimmed. Again she felt the consolation which had escaped her in the chapel. Even stronger though – bittersweet contrast – was the yearning which returned to her heart in that darkness, recollections no longer of Max, nor of Jude, for they belonged to the realm of transcendent light now, but another remembrance, a hunger of body, ache of the heart, things of this earth still, though Misha had moved by the stars.

Only a half moon remained by the time Caroline resumed her walk across the deserted square. By the time she reached the passageway along Notre-Dame's north façade, the sky, the moon, the monumental cathedral towering over the narrow streets were all dark. Save for the sound of her footsteps and, in the distance, a quiet fountain in the gardens beneath the buttressed east side of the church, there was absolute silence.

In contrast the footbridge leading to the Île St-Louis appeared suddenly vibrant ahead, beams from its shimmering lanterns spilling onto the river, sounds of a sensual song echoing over the towpaths.

As she approached, Caroline saw an old man bent over his guitar, music case opened beside him, small crowd gathered around him, faces rapt with attention as tangos from his native Seville drifted up toward the black moon. For a while she too stood among the crowd, hearing not just the song, not just the occasional accompaniment of coins dropped into the worn case, but, like a descant above the unexpected harmonies of this unforeseen night, echoes of a distant *ranchera* strummed in a childhood tribunal. How long ago it all seemed! How far that day of Communion with its transgressions, its retributions, its indelible markings which in their own way, at the end, conferred grace.

She dropped a coin into the case, moved away from the bridge lamp, leaned over the wall to gaze at the river. Beyond the shimmering beams on the water, all was still darkness, for only the barest, pale slice of the moon had managed to force its way back into the sky. Soon there was also renewed stillness around her. The worn case had been closed, the crowds had begun drifting away, bells from the church tolling midnight had ceased.

Caroline turned, about to walk on to the smaller island ahead, when downstream in the distance the low rumble of the last tourist boat suddenly broke the night's silence. Once again there was music – dance band on the upper deck, laughter, sounds of a festive midnight excursion.

Mesmerized, she remained by the railing, so vividly had the vessel's approach brought to mind another wharf, another ship, laughter and song drifting down from a houseboat docked alongside. Then too there was darkness, everything hidden, or so she had thought at the time – but no, here all of a sudden light, blinding light it appeared, as, directly across the water, the poplars and street signs and bookstalls all blazed abruptly.

Astonished, Caroline looked at the sky. The moon was still shadowed. She glanced at the still-darkened tip of the larger island behind her and made out the tourist boat slowly emerging from the shadows of the cathedral. Passing into the wider fork of the river, it had turned its immense spotlights onto the left bank of the Seine, so that not only the doorways and rooftops and quays had been starkly displayed, each in its turn, but also the lovers embracing along the secretive towpaths beneath them.

Oblivious, privileged, the couples remained as they were; their own worlds intact, arms intertwined still, stolen embraces untroubled.

Caroline too stayed as she was, pensive, watching the boat making its slow way upriver. Vaguely, but only vaguely, she noted its slight semicircular detour in her direction, searchlights now trained on the walkways and squares alongside the cathedral, sounds of the Seine lapping against the embankment in the wake of the ship as it approached. Thus she was caught unaware when those same lights, all-seeing, swept away from Notre-Dame's towering spires onto the bridge where she stood. Quickly she faced away, but not before the lights had found her alone on the railing, not before the beams had searched out her features, her neck, her full hair, her slender form on the bridge. An eternity seemed to pass she felt, looking away still, until the boat at last turned away too and began moving eastward again, past the discreet, shuttered homes overlooking the Seine on the Quai de Béthune.

Shaken – for the sudden, unwanted exposure had brought to mind the fall of her drape and all fear on the morning *Half Moon* was created – Caroline stayed in the dark a few moments longer. Then she too moved away from the wall, turned again to the east, and walked on to the Île St-Louis.

Among the few remaining patrons at the café on the tip of the island she paused one last time to glance at the tranquil main street ahead. Its orderly row of lanterns overhanging the shops seemed to her fitting, even comforting – emblematic of the days stretching before her. There remained her work, after all, meaningful days in the steady routine of what she saw clearly as a succession of solitary, uninterrupted years to come. There would be walks such as this, nights such as this, air redolent still of warm chestnuts, mulled wine, late summer roses in the balconied windows along the Quai de Bourbon. As she reflected, resignation if not absolute calm returned to her heart; purpose once more informed her still remarkable, though much deepened expression.

She walked away from the bistro. Passing beneath the verandas on the way to her doorway, she made out what appeared to be one last soft, unexpected beam of light falling upon the stones straight ahead. Its strange, not unwelcome glow seemed to spread upward, brightening the gates, the terraces, the intricate windows above them, so that when she reached her own door – last arched entryway at the curve of the island – she stopped and looked up at the sky once again and saw a newly bronzed moon emerging, as though by dead reckoning, from its overlong exile. With a sigh at the sight – or perhaps it was just a sudden cold chill from the river, she shivered. Reaching into her purse, she took out her key. At that moment the night porter emerged from his post in the archway.

"*Bonsoir, Madame,*" he said in a whisper, unlocking the elegant gates.

"*Bonsoir, Jean-Alain. Merci bien.*"

Caroline walked through the archway, crossed the open court-yard beyond, and disappeared through the heavy oak door in the opposite corner. Echoes of her steps, still distinctively light, still with their sensual sway in spite of the years passed, lingered a moment. Then that sound too vanished into the night.

What remained after that were sounds of the wind and the rustle of leaves in the trees in the tiny park at the curve of the island, and the gentleman seated on the bench beneath them, collar turned up against the breeze, bare hands in his pockets, back to the Seine and the floodlit cathedral on the larger island behind him. Facing him across the curving street were the now silent townhouses, their gates and portals all closed, their windows all darkened, their owners by now no doubt fast asleep.

All but one, Mikhail thought, *all but one*.

Several minutes went by. Sounds of a motorbike heading up toward the Marais disappeared. Beyond the Sorbonne a two-toned police siren also diminished. Somewhere a barge passed; the café on the corner closed; shutters banged in the wind along the rue St-Louis-en-l'Île; and then again silence.

Mikhail looked down the cobblestone Quai de Orleans, tranquil still, up the secretive Quai de Bourbon, street lanterns only aglow, then again at the curving façade straight ahead. Behind the wrought-iron terrace, the second floor windows were dark; those on the third floor were shuttered, as were the small gabled windows under the roof.

Notre-Dame's bells tolled – twelve-thirty exactly. In the ensuing stillness Misha remembered the silence that had fallen like rain on Père Gabriel's abbey. He recalled Caroline's face on that day – so full of purpose, so lovely, though not so fine as he had seen it on this night, purposeful still as she had paused on the footbridge, suddenly bathed in the light of the passing tourist *bateau*, echoes of Argentine songs which resembled her walk still in the air. Had she not been so lost in thought she might have heard him not far behind her, might even have turned to see him standing among the crowds drifting away.

But she had not turned. Nor had she looked back earlier as she had walked in the shadows beside the Préfecture de Police toward the deserted plaza, the church, the darkened alley beyond. All along he had followed, not for a moment since she had left her companion outside the Sainte-Chapelle's gates letting her out of his sight. Absorbed in her thoughts she had not heard his step. Fearing to frighten her he had remained discreetly behind. But he would not lose her, he knew, not on this night of all nights when Max had again brought them together, when alone, it appeared, and yearning still – that too was clear – and more than ever alluring she was making her slow and sensual if reflective way home.

Where precisely that home was he still did not know. The last of the archways on the Quai de Bourbon led to a courtyard beyond, that much he had seen, just as he had seen her pass through the gates to that court. But there were several doors still – several entryways, each with its own awning, each to a separate home, he well knew, as it had been on his father's street. There could be no mistake on this night.

Burnished sycamore leaves glowed in the lamplight beside him. Beyond, in the star-crowded sky, a bronzed and determined full moon slowly resumed pride of place over the shimmering roofs. For a few moments Misha just stared at the sight – clarity all the more wondrous in its unexpected reappearance.

When he looked again at the row of stone houses, he saw the glow of a lamp behind the French doors leading from that second-floor terrace facing the curved street. After a moment a woman passed through the room, sat by the lamp near a desk a while longer, disappeared briefly, then later returned and approached the windows and began to unfasten the drapes.

Mikhail was by then outside the gates of the last archway on the Quai de Bourbon.

"It is very late, Monsieur," protested the porter.

"Yes."

"Almost one."

"If you would just ring the lady though, as I asked."

The old concierge was unsure. His buildings, for so he considered them above all at this hour, loomed silent and grave at the end of the passage behind him. To interrupt a resident now –

A single chime from the church rang out.

"Tomorrow, perhaps, Monsieur…"

"Madame is expecting me now," Misha insisted, tone extremely polite, manner assured, intense and determined fine gaze fixed on the man. "That small message will do." A lone motorboat passed, then disappeared in the mist. "I should be much obliged."

The concierge sighed. Hanging his large ring of keys on the door-knob, he stepped back into his booth, paused one last time, adjusted his hat, then dialled Mme Devereux on the private intercom line.

"*Oui…Oui, Madame*," he confirmed, for the woman was clearly astonished. "*Un homme ici à la porte*…Yes," he repeated emphatically, though still barely a whisper. "Here at the door. He says he has been waiting for you…waiting a long time, Madame, and that you were expecting him, even now."

Mikhail watched the brass keys swaying against the door. He recalled Monsieur Daniel du Lac's rectangular "Closed" sign on Great George Street.

"And your name, please, Monsieur?"

"Mikhail d'Olivier."

Over the sound of the keys Misha made out the night clerk repeating his name, and then he heard something like silence again – interval that seemed to him to last a lifetime – and then the porter's voice once more,

"Madame Devereux asks if you would please go right up, Monsieur."

And then at last Misha heard only the sounds of his own steps crossing the courtyard – path which resembled clay roads in the moonlight, walls which recalled an old orchard in winter, lamp above suddenly lit which like a harbour light beckoned.

⌁ FINIS ⌁

ACKNOWLEDEGMENTS

In Canada, I would like to thank Clyde Rose, President, Breakwater Books; Debbie Hanlon, President, Jesperson Publishing; and most especially Rebecca Rose of Jesperson Publishing, for providing invaluable assistance throughout the preparation of this manuscript. Thanks also to Tamara Reynish, manuscript editor, and, at Jesperson Publishing, Kim O'Keefe, editorial liaison; Rhonda Molloy, production editor; and Michelle Cable-Foote, publicity.

In all things Parisian, for their wise and witty review, I am thankful to Judith S. Armbruster, Ph.D., and Mary Alice Parsons, long-time colleague and mentor.

In New York, for his sensitive and thorough read, I am grateful to George Ellis. Thanks also to T. Eppridge, another irreplaceable colleague, for a most elegant cover.

Finally, as always, for inestimable support which has never wavered over the years, I remain indebted to my family.